BRIM STONE

Callie Hart is the *Sunday Times* and #1 *New York Times* bestselling author of the international phenomenon *Quicksilver*, along with many other bestselling dark romance and dark academia titles. A British expat now living abroad, Callie can most likely be found sequestered away in the corner of a library, fantasising about exciting new realms and the brooding anti-heroes who occupy them.

Books by Callie Hart

Fae and Alchemy series
Quicksilver
Brimstone

Crooked Sinners series
Riot House
Riot Rules
Riot Act

Raleigh Rebels
The Rebel of Raleigh High
Revenge at Raleigh High
Reckless at Raleigh High

Dirty Nasty Freaks series
Dirty
Nasty
Freaks

Roma Royals Duet
Roma King
Roma Queen

Chaos & Ruin series
Violent Things
Savage Things
Wicked Things

Blood and Roses series
Deviant
Fracture
Burn
Fallen
Twisted
Collateral

Dead Man's Ink series
Rebel
Rogue
Ransom

Standalones
Rooke
Between Here and the Horizon
Calico
Vice
Requiem

CALLIE HART

HART

BRIM STONE

HODDERSCAPE

First published in Great Britain in 2025 by Hodderscape
An imprint of Hodder & Stoughton Limited
An Hachette UK company

The authorised representative in the EEA is Hachette Ireland, 8 Castlecourt Centre,
Dublin 15, D15 XTP3, Ireland (email: info@hbgi.ie)

5

A CIP catalogue record for this title is available from the British Library

Hardback ISBN 9781399745475
Trade Paperback ISBN 9781399745482
ebook ISBN 9781399745499

Printed and bound in Great Britain by Clays Ltd, Elcograf S.p.A.

Hodder & Stoughton policy is to use papers that are natural, renewable and
recyclable products and made from wood grown in sustainable forests.
The logging and manufacturing processes are expected to conform
to the environmental regulations of the country of origin.

Hodder & Stoughton Limited
Carmelite House
50 Victoria Embankment
London EC4Y 0DZ

www.hodderscape.co.uk

"Hell is empty and all the devils are here."

—*The Tempest,* William Shakespeare

AJUN SKY

THE MIDNIGHT EYE

WICKER WOOD

THE WINTER PALACE

CAHLISH

YVELIA

OMNAMERRIN

GRAVE'S POINT

IRRÍN

WESTERN DOW

TARAN ROSS ISLAND

AMMONTRÍETH

SANASROTH

THE BREACH

NEVERCROSS

BALQUHIDDER
CLAN LANDS

GILARIA

THE
SHALLOW
MOUNTAINS

THE DARN

GILLETHRYE

BALLARD

INISHTAR

THE SHIELD

LISSIA

PRONUNCIATION GUIDE

PEOPLE

Saeris — Sair-iss

Rusarius — Roo-sar-ee-us

Omnamshacry — Om-nam-sha-cry

Iseabail — Ee-sha-bahl

Belikon — Bell-eh-con

Oshellith — Oh-shay-lith

Taladaius — Tal-ah-day-us

Daianthus — Day-an-thus

Lorreth — Lor-uth

Balquhidder Clan — Bal-kid-er (clan)

Te Léna —Tay Len-ah

Danya — Dan-yah

PLACES

Zilvaren — Zil-var-en

Yvelia — Ee-vel-ee-ah

Cahlish — Call-ish

Sanasroth — San-az-roth

Gilarian — Gil-ah-ree-en

Lìssian — Liss-ee-an

Ammontraíeth — Ah-mon-tray-eth

Omnamerrin — Om-na-mer-in

PROLOGUE

KINGFISHER

A WOLF WAS a versatile creature.

Adaptable.

When part of a pack, it was part of something larger than itself. It had a role to play and a place in the way of things. There was safety to be found in a pack.

But a wolf could survive alone, too.

In the dead of the midnight forest, surrounded by predators on all sides, a wolf could slip like a shadow through the trees. He could take refuge in darkened corners, stalking prey of his own.

He could wait out his enemies, and bite back when they struck...

Especially when he held a god sword in his hands.

I was ready for the vampire when he came. He had been trailing me like a wraith through the echoing halls of Ammontraíeth since I'd left Saeris's chambers. I'd felt him out there, simmering. Waiting.

Reading the living took no great skill. There were those who had spent centuries honing their abilities to control their feelings. It paid to ensure your thoughts and feelings remained private as a member of the Fae. But no matter how practiced a person was at hiding their feelings, their bodies always gave them away in the end. It was unavoidable.

Emotions painted the blood.

Happiness.

Anger.

Sorrow.

Lust.

Each gave off its own energy. A vibration, if you will. In the same vein, each of them had its own scent. The Fae betrayed subtle indicators of their moods, no matter how good they were at masking their emotions.

The scents humans gave off could be overwhelming at times. Humans were *not* good at taming their feelings. They felt everything so rudely, right out in the open, with no awareness of how their reactions might affect those with finer senses.

The dead were a different story. Without a beating heart, their blood was barren black slurry in their veins. The only time a member of the Sanasrothian Court gave off any scent at all was after they had fed, when the spark of life that lingered in their victim's blood still echoed with the emotions *they* had felt as they died. Like the faintest trace of perfume that lingered after a hug.

An hour ago, my head had been full of petrichor as I'd sat next to my mate, listening to the lilt of her voice as she'd bombarded Tal with questions about the Blood Court. Ever since she'd woken, she'd been relentless, trying to understand, to prepare, to ready herself for what was to come. The foundations of our plan were laid, and Saeris understood the part she had to play in carrying them out... but she was nervous. Considering that she had been human only days ago, she was already far more accomplished at tamping down her feelings than she had been, but my nose was sharper than most. I'd sensed her hesitation. It was like the scent of hot stone after rain.

I'd been breathing her in, drowning in her, when I'd detected the *other* smell.

The vampire must have fed on a prodigious amount of blood before it had taken up its hiding place, crouched in the dark outside Saeris's chambers.

I'd excused myself, headed out into the hall, and gone looking for the rot.

Two floors down, heading into the bowels of the Black Palace, I found it with the point of my blade.

The vampire was beautiful. He possessed a face that might have been ordinary in life, the kind of skin that might eventually have turned dull and sagged. But in death, he had been preserved. Perfect. High cheekbones. A regal, aquiline nose. His eyes had probably been blue once, but now they flashed like ghostly opals. His lips peeled back, exposing canines bone-white and vicious. His mouth formed a surprised *O* before he could make a sound. He looked down, stunned to find Nimerelle buried to the hilt in his chest.

"You've...ruined the velvet," he croaked.

It was true; the god sword's blade had rent a three-inch-long hole in his black velvet waistcoat. I gave him an apologetic shrug. "Annoying by-product of killing," I said with a sigh. "Your opponent's clothes often don't survive the process, either. You know all about that, though, don't you?"

A death flower bloomed across the front of his shirt, black as ink. The bastard had the audacity to look affronted as he glanced up at me. "I am...familiar with that problem, yes," he rasped.

"You won't have to worry about it anymore," I told him.

I'd known, even before he'd come streaking out of the shadows, that he hadn't come looking for a fight. With the rest of the Black Palace still sleeping, he shouldn't have even been awake. This vampire, in his finery, with his belly full of innocent blood, had come seeking something he did not deserve. Something only *I* could give him.

He scrambled for balance, trying to hold on to me, but his hands were already turning to ash. When he spoke, his words were dry as a desert wind. "I'm sorry. I just couldn't...face..."

The sun?

Fire?

Fire wasn't such an easy thing to come by in this place. A vampire would go up like a pile of dry kindling if it encountered flame. The hearths burned with evenlight in Ammontraíeth. The torches in the walls, too. This piteous bastard probably wouldn't have even been able to find a match here. And who would have wanted such a final death, anyway? It wasn't an easy way to go. So painful. So dramatic.

The ash was better.

It was a mercy.

"You have saved me from what...I have...become," he wheezed. There was gratitude in his eyes. Relief.

I leaned in as he desiccated, making sure he heard each word as he sank into his final death. "I don't do it for you. I do it for those you have feasted on. Enjoy hell, tick."

Whatever hope of salvation he thought he might find with me faded from his eyes. "They're going to... *destroy* her, you know? It has already...been seen. This court will...fall...with her inside it." His lips twisted, either a grin of relief or a sneer of contempt, I couldn't tell.

"Saeris is safe," I snapped. "I won't let anything happen to her."

But the vampire just laughed. Rasping, hacking barks of laughter. His chin ashed. His cheeks went next. His voice splintered and cracked as his throat went. By the time his canines came loose from his skull and fell from his mouth, he wasn't laughing anymore.

The vampire collapsed, a vampire no more. His teeth hit the floor—*plink, plink!*—and bounced away, down the stairs that led farther into the bowels of Ammontraíeth.

Plink...

Plink...

Plink...

The Black Palace was immense. I'd lost count of how many high bloods I'd dispatched since I'd been here. At first, there had been at least one or two of Malcolm's children lying in wait for me down each dark obsidian corridor, drawn by the heat of my blood. However, the members of the Blood Court had soon realized they were no match for the god sword or the male who was wielding it. They were sleeping now, but soon they would wake. And then, they would *hide* if they knew what was good for them.

"Ahh! There...you are!"

The redheaded figure stood at the bottom of the stairs, panting and out of breath. He glanced down, cocking an eyebrow at the teeth that had come to a stop at his feet, though he didn't mention them. He turned his attention to me. "You need . . . to come. Quickly."

"You shouldn't be outside of your quarters, Carrion."

Sound traveled strangely here. The air was thick. It hummed with an inaudible tone that buzzed against the skin. My words were blunted, but they carried well enough for the smuggler to hear. He let out an exasperated gasp, running up the steps, but I was already walking away, back the way I had come.

"I would . . . *love* to be tucked away in my rooms right now, but . . . dusk's falling. The palace is waking up."

"Exactly."

"Will you *stop* already? Listen. I was just looking out . . . my window, and . . . I saw something—"

"It's called a sunset, Swift. If you want to live to see more of them, I can always escort you back to Cahlish. You can appreciate the sunrise *and* the sunset from there." I could live in hope. I'd offered repeatedly to take the smuggler away from Ammontraíeth—away from Irrín, too— but the male was growing increasingly stubborn.

"An enticing offer, but I'm good, thanks." He had sprinted up the steps to reach me and was now on my heels, keeping pace.

"Dare I ask, once again, *why* you insist on hanging around Ammontraíeth like a bad smell?" I clipped out. "This place is a nightmare."

Carrion answered distractedly, "Oh, y'know. I have my reasons."

And he could *have* his reasons, so long as none of them involved him harboring any sort of hope that Saeris was going to confess her undying love for him. *That* wasn't happening.

"Fisher, gods alive! Just fucking slow down, will you? This is important!"

I huffed out a tortured breath, turning to face him. "Is it *actually* important, or do you just *think* it is?" Carrion thought all kinds of ridiculous things mattered when they did not.

His eyebrows hiked up as he scowled at me. "I don't know. Do you consider your mate's happiness important?"

I glared at him flatly. "Speak. Quickly."

He shook his head. "We need . . . a window."

When sunlight could kill, a window could be a death sentence; they weren't so easy to come across. We found one on the next floor up, just a foot wide and a foot tall, the glass smoked to keep out some of the sun's rays.

The view it afforded could easily have been too narrow to display the source of Swift's anxiety, but mercifully that wasn't the case. I scanned the narrow field of the horizon, searching the scorched land that stretched out between Ammontraíeth and the river, not finding—

Oh, *gods.*

"I thought it was a patch of snow at first," Swift said.

My heart stalled.

"Then I saw that it was moving. Running. Fast," Carrion panted.

I took off at a dead sprint, hurtling past Carrion, flying down the stairs. The smuggler followed suit. "I found you as fast as I could! I didn't know if—I should tell her, or—"

"Just shut up and run!"

"What—what are you doing?" he panted.

"What do you *think* I'm doing?" I snarled. "I'm saving the fucking fox!"

———+———

I'd left him in Cahlish.

Not in Irrín.

In Cahlish. *On the other side of the mountain.*

The Omnamerrin mountain range was one of the most treacherous, lethal ranges in all Yvelia. Its slopes were steep and nigh impossible to climb for a member of the Fae. I only knew of a handful of warriors who'd scaled its jagged peak and survived to tell the tale. Onyx had been born of snow and ice, but even he shouldn't have survived the crossing. There would have been avalanches. They would have buried him, again and again and again. He would have had to dig his way out. He would have had no food. No shelter from the cutting wind.

He'd left the safety of Cahlish. For *her*.

He'd climbed the mountain. For *her*.

He'd snuck through Irrín and crossed the river. For *her*.

And now he was being chased across the dead fields of Sanasroth by a horde of feeders. He must have been tired and ready to give up, but he was still coming. For *her*.

And *I* was not about to let that little fox die.

I sprinted through the palace and down, through the Cogs—the multilevel settlement that had been built over the years around the palace's perimeter. The cobbled streets were empty for now, but they wouldn't be for long.

Bill.

I had to get to *Bill*.

The horses despised Ammontraíeth. They couldn't be kept in the stables. The high bloods kept their deadstock there, and a hungry feeder would pull a wall down with their bare hands to get to warm horse flesh. Bill, Aida, and two other bay mares had been stabled in an outbuilding five hundred feet away from the main yard, just beyond the high wall that enclosed the lowest level of the Cogs. I damn near ripped the outhouse's metal door from its hinges to get to my mount.

I didn't bother with bit or bridle. I vaulted onto Bill's bare back and kicked him out of his stall. My faithful friend didn't need telling twice. Carrion hadn't even made it across the courtyard by the time we came charging through the open doors.

"Get back inside!" I roared.

"No!"

"Gods and fucking sinners." I cursed at him in Old Fae as I galloped past him, reaching down with my right arm. The idiot clasped hold of my forearm and jumped, vaulting up onto Bill's back behind me.

"Aren't you going to ask where I learned how to do that?" the smuggler yelled.

"No," I snapped.

"Lorreth showed me!"

If he wanted congratulating, he was going to have to wait. A mile of ankle-deep ash and loose shale stretched out between us and the fox. Normally, the horses had to pick a path carefully over the loose, dead ground, but there was no time for that now. Bill snorted and blew, charging at the oncoming feeders; he didn't even flinch.

"That's it. Keep going," I whispered under my breath. "Thank you. *Thank you.*"

I should have made Carrion stay behind. There were more feeders sprinting after the fox than I'd first registered. Twenty of them? Thirty? More than I could face down without access to my magic this side of the Darn, and the male was a smuggler, not a blooded warrior. The sun had fallen below the horizon, though. And if the light was dim enough for the feeders, then it wouldn't be long before the high bloods of Sanasroth were awake. Without an escort back through the palace, the moron would have been dead in a matter of seconds...

We were gaining ground.

But so were the feeders.

They were ever hungry, and it had probably been an age since a living creature had dared to cross into Sanasrothian lands. The mindless foot soldiers of Sanasroth wouldn't allow this opportunity to pass them by for anything.

I could see Onyx properly now.

His black-tipped ears were pinned flat to his head as he ran for his life. He launched himself from a rock, soaring through the air, a streak of white against the growing dark, and then his paws were back on solid ground, kicking up a trail of ash as he sprinted.

"Come on," I hissed through my teeth. "Come on. *Run.*"

Less than a mile now. The gap between us was closing... but so was the gap between the feeders and the fox. He was tired, I could tell. His tongue lolled from his mouth, waving like a banner. The whites of his eyes were showing. The little fox was terrified.

I hadn't noticed Carrion was clinging to the back of my armor. With no saddle to grip, he really had no other choice. I bit back an annoyed curse, leaning forward, urging Bill on. Faster he went, faster, never faltering. Not once did he break his stride.

"We're almost there!" Carrion bellowed.

I gritted my teeth so hard my jaw cracked. "Hold on!"

There was no stopping. If we stopped, we died. I grabbed a fistful of Bill's mane and prayed to the gods I hated for the second time in less than a week.

Save the fox.

Save Bill.

Save the fox.

Save Bill.

Please...

White spittle foamed at the feeders' mouths. Their mindless baying filled the air as we drew closer, closer, closer.

Save the fox.

Save Bill.

They were right on top of Onyx now. Only a hair's breadth away. The fastest among them, a male with a filthy, torn shirt, lunged forward, reaching for his prize. Bill pulled back, rearing, whinnying in terror. His hooves slipped on volcanic glass as he desperately tried to turn away from the approaching threat. The feeder's jagged claws grazed the little fox's fur, and the fox *leaped...*

Carrion caught him.

...And then promptly came off Bill, sliding backward over his haunches.

Gods and *fucking* martyrs! *"On your feet, Swift!"* I roared. The copper-haired prince clutched Onyx tight, scrambling to get up. He moved quickly, but it wouldn't be fast enough. I drew Bill around, reining him in a tight circle, facing him toward the feeders, and dropped from his back.

"Steady, friend. Whoa. Wait for me," I whispered to him. Then I drew Nimerelle, and the killing began. The god sword bled black smoke as she scythed through the air. Where I swung her, necrotic flesh and brittle bone parted like wet paper in her wake.

"Draw that weapon, Swift!" I bellowed over my shoulder.

Carrion was on his feet. Simon, his god sword, was in his hand.

Onyx had bolted from his arms and was hiding between Bill's legs now, which wasn't doing much to help calm the horse. Bill stayed close, though, stamping his hooves and blowing, eyes rolling—afraid but wanting to obey. The tide of feeders would be on us any second. "Take their heads," I shouted. "Don't fuck this up, Carrion!"

"I won't!" He took up position next to me, adopting a readying stance, and I was struck with a flicker of surprise. The footwork was there. Almost. And when the ravening feeders fell upon us, he didn't immediately die. *Shocking.*

Silver and Fae steel swept through the air, cutting the bastards down. I caught most of them. The few that avoided me and targeted Carrion dropped to the ground, too. Most of them still had their heads and were still trying to kill the smuggler, but at least he put them down. Behind us, Onyx let out a terrified squeal...

Seven feeders.

Eight...

The three Carrion had downed were joined by a fourth.

Forty feet stood between us and the next wave of feeders. I grabbed Carrion by the scruff of his neck and shoved him back toward Bill. We'd been lucky so far, but we wouldn't stay lucky forever. I scooped up Onyx and vaulted onto Bill's back, pulling Swift up behind me.

Ammontraíeth loomed ahead—a clenched fist with knuckles for spires, punching skyward out of the mist. Not a palace, but a *fortress.*

I gripped Bill's mane, sending one last prayer to the gods, and we rode like the wind.

Hell was awake and grinding its teeth by the time we reached the Cogs. High and low bloods alike peered over the obsidian walls that guarded the small city at the foot of Ammontraíeth, their monstrous eyes full of judgment and hunger as Bill trudged reluctantly back toward the outbuilding. Lorreth was there waiting for us, arms crossed over his chest, a scowl etched deep into his face. "I swear to all the gods. You leave a room and say you'll be right back. Next thing I know, I see you galloping across the dead fields, charging headlong at the undead!"

Carrion groaned as he slid down from Bill.

"And *you*? Are you out of your godscursed mind?" Lorreth hissed. He squinted at the smuggler as if he could actually *see* the stupid on him.

"Don't mind me. I only killed four feeders and saved Fisher's life." He affected his usual devil-may-care tone, but there was a note of true fear beneath it now. Our near brush with death had had the appropriate effect on him, it seemed.

I was going to kill him. "You maimed them at best," I snapped. "And the day you save *me* on a battlefield, I'll put on a dress and dance a fucking jig." He could have gotten us *both* killed by following me down here. He'd fucking fallen. If anything had happened to him, then what? Saeris would have been *pissed* at me.

But...

Onyx whimpered.

He shivered against my chest, tucked into a ball, his glassy black eyes still full of fear. His coat was filthy. Blood matted his fur on his back right leg. He yelped when I ran my hands over the injury, clearly in pain.

There would be time to yell at Carrion Swift later.

"Come on," I said. "Let's just get inside before these fuckers decide to take a bite out of one of us." I looked to my friend. "Any luck finding him?" I asked softly.

Lorreth's nostrils flared, a muscle jumping in his jaw. "No. I've searched high and low. If Foley's here, then I couldn't tell you where."

Unfortunate. We needed Foley. I sighed, shoving down my disappointment. "All right. Well, keep looking. I have a feeling we shouldn't give up just yet."

"Who's Foley?" Carrion asked.

Lorreth opened his mouth, halfway to answering, but then he hesitated, looking to me.

The universe could end and Carrion Swift wouldn't have run out of questions. But in his position, I probably would have felt the same way. I inclined my head, glancing away while Lorreth explained.

"A friend once. Still a friend. One of *us.* We lost him at Ajun."

Saeris said that Lorreth sang a ballad about the Ajun Gate, about the battle that had taken place there, but that the quicksilver had claimed the song in return for allowing Avisiéth, Lorreth's sword, to be forged anew. Carrion had asked about the Ajun Gate since then. While we'd all waited for Saeris to wake after the Midnight Kiss, Lorreth had recounted plenty of our exploits to the smuggler. He'd talked of the friend we'd lost to the dragon. He just hadn't told him the whole story.

"If you lost him in Ajun, then how..." Carrion's brow furrowed, realization dawning on him. "Oh. You *lost* him. But he still lives. Here?" he said, looking up at the razor-sharp walls of the Black Palace that towered above us.

"Yes," Lorreth said. It was remarkable how one word could hold so much tension. The warrior cleared his throat. "I'll tear the place apart if I have to, Fisher. Don't worry. I'll get it done. Go. Get inside. Saeris was putting on a brave face when I left her, but she was panicking. I'll rub Bill down and get him cooled off." Even as he said it, he scrubbed a hand up and down Bill's sweat-slicked neck, clapping him on his shoulder. I got down, careful not to jar Onyx too badly as my boots hit the ground.

I landed softly, but he still yelped. I could feel his bones through his fur. With a sinking heart, I saw that his paws were cracked and bleeding.

"You'll have to hold him," I told Carrion, as we headed back toward the Cogs.

"What? I can't hold him. He does *not* like me."

Quickly, I drew Nimerelle and spun the sword over, holding her up for Carrion to see. "Want to carry this instead?" I asked. "You'll need both god swords if *you* want to carve a path for us back through the Cogs and into the palace."

The smuggler paled as he assessed the sword. At best, you'd wind up with severe burns if you touched another warrior's god sword. At worst, you might lose a hand. Or your life.

"I'll stick to the fox," he said, eyeing Nimerelle warily.

It took longer than I would have liked to make it back up to Saeris's rooms. We left a trail of teeth in our wake, canines skittering and bouncing off the cobbled streets and then off polished floors as we climbed each floor of the palace. By the time we were safely behind closed doors in Saeris's room, I had lost count of the vampires I'd killed, black blood painted Carrion's clothes, and Onyx had passed out from exhaustion.

Saeris was by the door, tears streaking down her pale, beautiful face. She was dressed in a thick black robe with elaborate golden embroidery at the pockets. Her expression was stricken as she took in Onyx. "Gods. Is he okay?" she whispered, as if she were too scared to ask the question for fear of the answer.

"He'll be fine," I told her. Gods, I wanted to sweep her into my arms and hold her. I knew the slope of her shoulders so well. The way the fine wisps of her hair curled at her temples. I knew the hard defiance she wore on her like a shield, but I hadn't met her grief yet. It was an unwelcome stranger I wanted to banish as soon as possible; its presence in the room made my chest ache.

Despite his injuries, the little fox writhed in Carrion's arms, determined to reach his destination at last. Only when he was safe, pressed up against Saeris's chest, did the tension seem to leave his body.

He trembled, panting, as he stared up at Saeris. She had cursed my name and bared her teeth at every threat she'd faced since I'd met her. Even when I'd found her on the steps in the Hall of Mirrors, dying from the injuries Harron had inflicted upon her, she'd been full of defiance. Now, she wept as she cradled the fox in her arms, and I couldn't fucking bear it.

I reached for him. "Here. Give him to me," I said.

Saeris's eyes were the pale blue of a winter dawn breaking over the mountains. Bottom lip quivering, she gave me a questioning look but didn't give it voice. She swallowed hard, took a deep breath, and handed Onyx over to me.

Carrion was gone. For once, the thief had assessed the situation and made himself scarce. Saeris followed me with wide eyes, her heartbeat pounding in her throat as she watched me carry the fox over to the door that led out onto her balcony.

As the first of all the vampires and king of the Blood Court, Malcolm had claimed these rooms once, as was his right, but he hadn't spent much time here. According to Tal, he had slept in the tower above us, his paranoia urging him to lock himself behind a series of two-foot-thick iron doors while he slept. I couldn't imagine him standing out on this balcony, out in the open, with the night sky bristling with stars over his head. He would have been too afraid of his own shadow out here...

Saeris was radiant under the moonlight. Her hair whipped and snapped like a banner on the cold breeze. "Just..." Tears shone in her eyes. "If you have to do it, then at least make sure it's quick."

A band of iron cinched tight around my chest. She thought I was going to put the poor creature out of its misery. She thought that, and she had still handed him over to me. She'd trusted me to do what had needed to be done, to save her companion from pain...

I shook my head, smiling softly. "I told you. He's going to be fine, Osha. I promise." I sank down onto my knees, placing the ball of blood-stained white fluff in my lap. A pair of eyes, black and glassy as jet, stared up at me, wide and trusting.

"Healing is a small magic for me," I whispered to him. "I guess it's lucky for both of us that you're small, too." I waited for the current of magic to warm my palms. I'd used it to heal bruises when I was a Faeling. I'd used it to fix a broken thumb, and that had almost depleted my entire reserve of healing energy. When I was young, I'd complained to my mother that my healing gifts were so negligible, but she had laughed and ruffled my hair.

"Never doubt your powers, sweet one," she'd told me. *"Each one of them is a gift. Each one will prove exactly enough when you have need of it. Have faith in yourself. You will* always *be enough."*

I prayed she was right as I held my hands over the fox's injured hind leg. At first, I felt resistance—a barrier that didn't yield as easily as the one that stood between me and my shadows. It gave eventually, though, allowing a wave of pain to wash over me. I winced—

"What is it?" Saeris asked. "What's happening. What are you doing?"

Onyx whined. His head rested on my leg, his exhaustion seeping through the connection I'd just forged between us. He was weary to his bones, and his leg was pulsing with pain. Not broken, thankfully, but fractured. He'd been running on it for *so* long.

"Fisher!"

"A moment, Osha," I said. "Trust me. This won't take long."

I closed my eyes, and I *pulled*. Some members of the Fae didn't have access to small magics. A small magic wasn't a part of a male or female's birthright, like my shadows were. It was a much smaller well of energy—a faint affinity that a person might have toward a specific line of magic. Unlike birthright magic, small magic was a finite resource.

My hands shook as I dug deep, searching for every scrap of healing magic that still flowed inside of me. Once I'd visualized it there, in the middle of my chest, I poured it all into Onyx.

The fox shuddered, and within seconds, his rapid breathing began to ease. The pain radiating from him ebbed until it was only a dull throb in his leg. His paws were healed. The fractured bone fused...but not fully. I didn't have *quite* enough healing magic to heal him all the way, but it was enough. He could manage the rest on his own.

The little fox yawned, then kicked, wanting to be free of me. His coat was clean again now, the blood that had stained it gone. His limp was barely noticeable as he ran back to his mistress.

Saeris's eyes were full of wonder and relief as she stooped down to pick him up. "What? But...how?" She laughed as the fox nuzzled into her neck and licked her cheek. "I didn't know you could heal!"

I shrugged. "I can't now. Not anymore, anyway. It wasn't much, but I gave him what I had."

Her joy faded a little. "But...if you have healing magic, shouldn't it just replenish? Like it does for Te Léna?"

Ruefully, I shook my head. "Some magics don't work that way, Osha." I would explain it to her some other time. There was still a shocking amount that she didn't know about this realm, its people, and its magic. But that could wait. Onyx was in much better shape, and she had stopped crying. For now, that was all that mattered.

"You sacrificed that magic, then? To help him?" Saeris asked. Gods, she was so fucking beautiful. The moonlight painted her skin silver until she looked like she was glowing.

I nodded.

She didn't seem to know what to say. She buried her face in Onyx's coat for a moment, breathing him in. When she lifted her gaze to meet mine again, she arched an eyebrow at me. "Why?" she asked. "Why make that sacrifice?"

I wouldn't have answered her before. I wouldn't have been able to lie, and so I would have kept my mouth shut. So much had happened now, though. So much had changed between us. The truth slipped out with ease. "Don't you know? There isn't much I wouldn't sacrifice to make you happy, Osha. A little healing magic is the least of it."

Before Gillethrye, we'd been dancing around the tension between us for weeks and weeks. Now, God Bindings marked her hands and her wrists. They were wrapped around my wrists, too. We were *of* one another, bound to one another, in a way that felt strange and thrilling.

There was so much more to be said.

The weight of that hung between us...but the female I had been terrified to fall for simply nodded, trying not to smile. "I see. And here I was thinking that you'd changed your mind about Onyx."

I tried not to smile, too. I couldn't tear my eyes from her. Gods, she was fucking beautiful. "Oh no," I muttered softly. "I still think he'd made a great hat."

1

HELL'S TEETH

SAERIS

THE DRESS WAS made for sinning.

Black.

Strapless.

Sheer.

The slit up the side was cut so high that there was no way I could have worn underwear. The fabric clung to my frame like a second skin, shimmering when it caught the light as if tailored from the night sky itself. Long gloves of the same material covered my arms as if I'd dipped them past the elbows into shimmering ink. This was nothing like any of the ensembles Everlayne had dressed me in when I'd first arrived at the Winter Palace. This was elegant. Stunning. *Painfully* sexy.

I didn't recognize the woman in the full-length mirror of my dressing room . . . and there was a reason for that. The strange creature staring back at me wasn't a woman. Not anymore. Once she might have been, but now she was a Fae-vampire hybrid, touched by the gods.

I was the same as I had ever been, and yet I wasn't. Immortality might have cleaved the meat from the bones of others and made them willowy. It had filled out the parts of *me* that Zilvaren had starved. My cheekbones were rounder now, my lips fuller. Hips, breasts, ass: I'd had all three before, but now I *really* had them.

As it did every time I had caught myself in the mirror over the past forty-eight hours, my attention snagged on my tips of my pointed ears, poking through the dark waves of my hair. Reality seemed to warp and snap back into place whenever I saw them. In the end, I was just as Fisher's mother had drawn me.

This was real.

I was *Fae*.

I was *a vampire*.

The sound of a voice clearing at the back of the room broke the silence. "Well, I suppose if no one else is going to say it, then *I* will. You look downright fuckable, Saeris Fane."

I turned, wearing a chagrined frown, already preparing for the fall-out that would follow on the heels of that comment.

Three males occupied the large dressing room with me, each of them emitting so much testosterone that the air swam with it.

By the large window, the last rays of sunlight burnished Taladaius's silver hair and limned his features in gold. I could sense his emotions now. I was connected to him in a way that I didn't enjoy. Sometimes, as dusk was falling, I would feel him wake on the other side of the palace, and his sadness would steal my breath away. My maker cringed at the male on the other side of the room, sprawled out on a chaise longue like he owned the damned place. "Are you out of your mind?" he asked. "I don't know a single person stupid enough to hit on a newly bonded female, let alone a *God-Bound* female. But to do it right in front of her mate? In front of *him*?" he added, jerking his chin toward the last male leaning against the wall by the door.

I paused before allowing myself to look at *him*.

Paused before I even allowed myself to think his name.

Kingfisher.

My mate.

Fisher's dark, wavy hair tumbled into his face, flicking up around his ears. It had somehow grown longer in the past day or two. He felt bigger, too. Taller, broader, his presence even more imposing. He was armed to the teeth, dressed in leather, his ever-present gorget flashing at his throat. Tendrils of shadow and glittering black sand wound between his fingers, circling his wrists. They twisted down his legs and spilled across the plush carpet like hunting snakes, heading for the chaise.

They had reached the chair and were weaving up its legs toward Carrion when I let out a sigh, folding my arms across my chest. *"Fisher."*

His eyes came alive at the sound of my voice. "Hmm?"

"Stop."

His nostrils flared, his jaw working. *"I* can't help it if he doesn't want to live."

Carrion heaved himself upright, nearly spilling his drink in the process. He was on his fourth whiskey, though he seemed none the worse for wear because of it. It all made sense now—the number of times he'd drunk the other patrons at the House of Kala under the table. The Fae could drink themselves into oblivion if they wanted to; they only had to will it and they were as sober as a judge in their next breath. For as long as I'd known him, Carrion had been hiding his lineage. The glamor Kingfisher's father had wrought on him as a baby had held his whole life, concealing his true appearance. In fairness, he'd always been tall. But his ears had been rounded, his features less chiseled and sharp, his frame not quite so broad. The *reality* of him was taking some getting used to. Thanks to his run-in with Malcolm in the maze, the glamor was gone now, and the male was his natural, true self at last.

"And *I* can't help it if you aren't falling over yourself to compliment your girlfriend," Carrion countered, raising his glass at Kingfisher.

Oh, gods. *This* was going to be bad.

The threads of shadow and sand became ropes. They darted up the chaise longue, lashing around Carrion's wrists and throat, slamming him back down onto the crushed velvet cushion behind him. His whiskey went flying. Fisher did nothing to save the glass as it hit the carpet, bounced, and went tumbling across the floor, spilling its contents everywhere as it rolled.

Not content to assault Carrion with only his magic, Fisher had his fists ready and was moving with purpose across the dressing room with murder in his beautiful green eyes.

My chest squeezed. *"Fisher!"*

Mercifully, Taladaius stepped in, blocking my mate's path before he reached the smuggler. They were of a height, the two males. Just as broad. Just as fearsome. They were similar in many ways. But where my mate was all darkness and quiet brooding, Taladaius was light, his mood often easier than it had any reason to be. There were counter-weights, perhaps. Different sides to the same coin? But also different currencies.

Vampire.

Fae.

Maker.

Mate.

The vampire placed a hand on Kingfisher's shoulder, shooting him a tight smile. "I may be considered enlightened among my kind, Fisher. But the others who have gathered here tonight…" He paused, hiking up an eyebrow for effect. "Are *not*. Spill living blood, even here in Saeris's chamber, and you're asking for a world of hurt. Guaranteeing your safety here is difficult enough as it is."

Fisher's expression was blank. He didn't seem remotely concerned by Taladaius's warning. Slowly, he glanced down at Taladaius's hand resting on his shoulder, as if the point where the two made contact was about to burst into flames. "You aren't *guaranteeing* anything," he said in a low voice. "I'm not here by anyone's good graces. I'm here because my mate is here. Where she goes, I go. And if any more of your brethren feel like taking a swing at me, then believe me, I'm *all* for it. I've waited an age to find myself in the same room as these supercilious pricks."

Taladaius clenched his jaw, exhaling deeply before he spoke again. "You know what those supercilious pricks can scent even more than blood?"

Kingfisher smacked Taladaius's hand away, snarling under his breath. "I'm not *afraid*, Tal."

"Fear *will* be your undoing out there," the vampire gritted out. "If you're worried about her, even for a second, they *will* know, and they'll leap at the opportunity to tear you down because of it. Weaken her claim. Cast her out—"

"Uhhh?" A gurgle came from the chaise behind them, where Fisher's shadows were still strangling Carrion. *"Help?"*

"Gods and martyrs, can you stop posturing, all of you! Fisher, let Carrion go. Taladaius…" I blew out an exasperated breath. "How much time do we have before we need to go out there?"

Straightening the beautifully tailored black jacket he was wearing, Taladaius composed himself, but his glittering eyes remained fixed on my mate. "The sun's set. They're already gathered. If we don't go soon, they'll say you've abandoned your claim."

"They'd do that?"

"They're bureaucrats," he replied.

At last, Kingfisher released Carrion from his magic's hold. "They're *monsters*," he countered.

"They are," Taladaius agreed. "Which is why we have so many rules, and why we stick to them so fiercely. Our court would be carnage without them. Tradition must be honored. The laws of the five must be obeyed. Even by *queens*," he stressed. "Only once she has that circlet on her head will she be in a position to effect change. Change that will benefit *all* of Yvelia."

And there it was. The crux of all of this.

Back in that maze, I hadn't killed Malcolm for his crown. I'd done it to save myself. For vengeance. For my mate. I hadn't asked to become queen of this hateful court. If it were up to me, we'd already be back at Cahlish, celebrating the fact that the king of the vampires was dead. But then where would we be? With another vampire lord rising to power, leaving Yvelia potentially worse off than it already was.

In the past forty-eight hours, I'd had a crash course in vampire court politics. And unlike when I'd found myself being lectured back in the library at the Winter Palace, this time I had paid attention.

Five vampire lords ruled beneath the vampire monarch—the Lords of Midnight—of which Taladaius was one. Regardless of sex, they had always been referred to as Lord, and apparently that wasn't changing anytime soon. I hadn't met the other Lords yet, and truthfully, I had no desire to meet them, either. From what I'd been told, they were savages, cutthroat and power hungry, and any of them would rip my head off for a shot at the crown. They were bound by the Law of Ascension, though. They *had* to acknowledge me first before they could try to steal my throne. And if they acknowledged me, they had to obey me. At least for a time.

That meant there was a window. An opportunity. A chance to stop the war that had been raging for centuries. To put an end to the killing. Claiming the throne was the quickest way to stop the nightmare without a tide of blood staining the land from the mountains to the sea.

I wasn't from here. I wasn't born here. Yvelia was not my home, but I understood suffering, and I was no stranger to the senseless kind of death that nipped at the heels of the weak and the vulnerable. If I could do something to help put an end to the bloodshed here, then I would. I had to *try*, at least. And call it wishful thinking, but I still had *hope* for the members of the Blood Court. Hope that they could be redeemed.

"Can anyone else hear that?" Carrion's voice was raspy from the throttling he'd just earned himself. "Either my blood is still thumping in my ears, or the horde's stampeding this way." Aside from a little redness around his neck, he seemed none the worse for wear. He didn't even flinch as Fisher strode past him toward the door, his boots thudding heavily against the carpet.

"They're calling her out there," he said, his voice distracted.

"Then that's it. We need to go," Taladaius said.

But Fisher came back and stood before me, ignoring my maker. His huge frame filled my vision. Dark hair, strong jaw, and beautiful ink. Not too long ago, I'd dreamed of him standing close to me like this. My fool's heart had craved him more than my lungs had craved air . . . and now that he was mine and I was his, my need for him had only intensified. He had saved Onyx for me. He had risked his life for me, and from the look on his face now, he wouldn't blink if he had to do it again. The tattoos marking his skin shifted as he swallowed, the muscles of his throat working. "You don't need to do this," he whispered. "There are other ways to accomplish our goals."

She's here. Here. Here...

I ignored the whisper that rushed in my ears, refusing to give it my attention. Not here, and not now. This wasn't the first time I'd heard the quicksilver since I'd woken in the palace after my transition. I knew it wouldn't be the last.

I gave my focus to my mate instead, reaching up and cupping his cheek with my gloved hand. What I wouldn't have given to feel the roughness of his stubble against my palm. Gods alive. That I even got to *touch* him like this. That he *was* mine in the first place. "Those other ways involve blood, and death, and fire," I answered softly, my response meant only for him. The others could still hear, of course, but they politely pretended they didn't.

Fisher leaned into my hand, closing his eyes for a moment. "I happen to think making these bastards bleed would be a good thing," he whispered.

"I know. But what about the losses we'll avoid this way? What about our friends? And the people of Cahlish? How can they return to their homes if Sanasroth is still seething away on the other side of the river?"

I had him there. Fisher loved his people. He hated that they had left Cahlish when Malcolm had trapped him inside that godscursed maze. If Fisher wanted his people to come home, then they needed a safe place to come back to. Fisher blew out a tense breath, but he nodded. "Fine. But the moment you don't want to be here—"

"I'll tell you, I promise."

He dipped his head, breaking eye contact with me as he turned and went to the mirror, then collected my sword from the top of the dresser where I had placed it when getting changed. Solace was an ancient blade—one of the few remaining god swords that had once been imbued with magic millennia ago. It had belonged to Fisher's father. The sword that had stilled the quicksilver for an age. The sword I'd drawn from the quicksilver to protect myself, which had accidentally reopened the pathways between worlds.

It was bonded to me now. The god swords were loyal, territorial things. It would have taken Fisher's hands off for touching it had he not used a scrap of silk to pick it up. He held it reverently as he brought it to me.

"You can't be serious. That will *absolutely* ruin her outfit," Carrion said, aghast.

"He's right." Taladaius was standing by the door now, with his hand anxiously resting on the handle. "She can't go out there with Solace strapped to her hip. She needs to appear regal. She can't afford to look worried about her safety."

The look Kingfisher gave the vampire and the smuggler strongly implied that he thought they were both stupid. "I don't care how she *looks*. I care about her ability to defend herself."

"Then give her something else. Something subtler. Something she can hide. And for all the gods' sakes, hurry."

BOOM!

BOOM!

BOOM!

The sound was growing louder, faster, more impatient. Fisher hesitated but then sighed, setting Solace down on the chaise. "All right. Fine." With deft hands, he reached into a small pouch on his belt and drew out a length of fine silver chain. He wrapped it around my waist, looping it at my hip so that its ends hung down almost to my knees.

"She doesn't need a garrote," Taladaius objected.

"It isn't a garrote. It's a belt," Fisher replied amicably. In my head, he said, *It's a garrote.*

I tried not to laugh.

He took one of his own daggers from the sheath at his waist, then dropped down to one knee in front of me. He looked up, his eyes locking with mine again, burning with a myriad of emotions as he slowly... carefully... parted the material of the dress along the slit to expose my bare thigh.

Taladaius threw his hands in the air. "There's no time for this!"

"Oh, I don't know. I think we might be able to spare a *minute*," Carrion said.

I saw Fisher's annoyance spike, but he didn't react. His touch left a trail of burning fire as he ran his hand up my thigh. With his other hand, he pressed his dagger against my flesh. The magic simmering below the surface of my skin registered that, just like the chain he'd wrapped around my waist, the weapon was pure silver, but it didn't burn me the way it would Taladaius or any other vampire. We already discovered I was immune to the effects of both silver *and* iron. Perhaps it was that I wasn't entirely one thing—neither wholly vampire nor Fae. Perhaps it was that I was an Alchemist on top of everything else, and I still had an affinity for metals. Either way, I was grateful for the advantage.

Fisher had no holster or scabbard for the dagger, but he didn't need one. Wisps of black smoke materialized, skating over my skin. They were cold *and* warm, and my skin broke out in goose bumps as I registered the prickle of his power. He was stripped of most of his magic here—he couldn't open a portal, and he certainly couldn't use it to hurt the denizens of the Blood Court on their own ground—but he *could* do this. In a second, an elaborate latticework of shadows and glittering black sand encircled my thigh, holding the dagger flush against my leg. It was beautiful, like lace, delicate as a spiderweb speckled with morning dew. His hands rested there, on my thigh, strong and calloused, and—

He sucked in a sharp breath, shaking his head as he got to his feet. His pupils were blown wide open when he looked down at me. "If any of them even look sideways at you, you stick that straight in their chests."

"I know how a dagger works, Fisher." Most couples flirted by making eyes at each other or complimenting each other's outfits. We did it by discussing how best to murder our enemies. A smile ached at the corners of my mouth, begging to be unleashed...

BOOM!

BOOM, BOOM, BOOM!

Fisher offered me his hand. "Let's go."

"Wait. I—" Gods. There were so many things I wanted to say, but I hadn't had a moment alone with him for nights. He was in danger here. Thanks to the Blood Court's archaic traditions, namely their Rite of Ascension, *I* was safe enough. But Fisher hadn't killed Malcolm. The Blood Court's rule didn't demand that *he* be allowed to rise to power unmolested. He was a mortal enemy of the Blood Court. Thousands of high blood vampires lived within the walls of Ammontraíeth, all of them Malcolm's children, and every one of them hated my mate with an unmatched fury. If he so much as looked sideways at the wrong person here, it would mean trouble. I wanted to remind him of this now, but he already knew, of course, and we were out of time.

"Can you—look, can you just behave yourself out there?" I murmured under my breath.

He looked bemused, the faintest hint of a dimple forming in his right cheek. "I can," he answered. "I can't promise that I *will*."

As we walked past him and out of the chamber, Taladaius advised, "You should leave Nimerelle here. They'll see *you* carrying a weapon as an act of aggression."

"Good." My mate's expression went dark with the promise of violence. "It *is*."

"Holy shit." Carrion whistled softly through his teeth. "The place looks like a prison from the outside. Who would have known they were hiding something *this* ostentatious?"

It was called the Hall of Tears.

Carved faces, grotesque and grimacing, observed us from the obsidian pillars that held up the vaulted cathedral ceilings. Torches burned in sconces, the eerily still evenlight—so different from regular fire—casting a strange white-green glow up the walls. Gold brocade curtains hung from huge windows at the far end of the hall, with scenes of debauchery and all manner of sin stitched into the heavy velvet fabric.

There were more vampires than I could count, gathered in rows on the left and right flanks of the hall. Not feeders. These were males and females, dressed in beautiful gowns and smock shirts. A lean intelligence shone from their eyes as they turned their hungry gazes on me.

At the head of the room, a stately throne made of black stone sat in the center of a raised dais. Before it was an expansive platform of polished obsidian decorated with a pale-stone mosaic depicting a five-pointed star. A Lord of Midnight already waited at the tip of four of the points, each dressed in finery, facing inward. The remaining point stood empty... until Taladaius traversed the long aisle and took his place among his brethren.

My maker had produced a lacquered staff from somewhere. He joined in with the others, smashing its tip down onto the ground at his feet, adding to the cacophonous *BOOM! BOOM! BOOM!* that thundered through the hall. The sound grew louder and louder, hammering in my ears.

And then, without warning, it stopped.

The five figures turned to face me, the expressions of the four strangers turning to granite when they saw I wasn't alone at the foot of the wide staircase that led down to them.

Two of the Lords were males.

Two were female.

One was something else entirely.

There was Taladaius, of course. Next to him stood a rangy-looking dark-haired male with a hooked nose and eyes as black as coal. An even taller, long-limbed creature stood across from him—a pale, strange thing that clearly was not a member of the Fae. It was dressed in a pristine white robe. Its eyes were solid black orbs, its skin translucent. An unnaturally wide slit served for its mouth, bristling with tiny, jagged teeth. Black veins formed a network of spiderwebs across the backs of its too-large, webbed hands.

The females were less disconcerting. The first wore a gown of vivid green. Her hair was bright like hammered gold and wound into braids that fell in ropes down her back. My brother would have fallen in love with her on sight. She was just the type of pretty, fine-boned trouble who would have caught his eye. He wouldn't have stood a chance, though. A hatred burned in her depthless blue eyes that made me want to reach for the dagger that Kingfisher had just strapped to my thigh. I shivered as I turned my gaze upon the last female, glad to have broken eye contact. The final Lord of Midnight was a small thing. A thick mat of gray hair fell into her face, obscuring her features, but I could see from her bare forearms, frail wrists, and gnarled hands that she was old.

"What madness is this?" the blond vampire asked. The second she spoke, the chatter in the hall ceased. The Lord hadn't raised her voice, but her words rang from the walls and rebounded amid the rafters. She lifted her staff and thrust it at me so that I could make out the gleaming golden head of the hissing snake that topped it. "*This* is not the creature who felled my father," she said. "Mighty Malcolm, who reigned over an entire continent and reduced another to ash? Malcolm, who toppled kings, bedded queens, and cheated death so that we might all follow in his footsteps? Laid low by *this?* I think not."

Fisher's warmth was a reassuring hand on my back. On my left, Carrion hovered in my peripheral vision. I looked at neither of them as I tilted my chin back and held my head high, beginning the long descent down the stairs toward the vampires of Sanasroth. "Your father was felled by his own hubris. He was too arrogant. He believed himself invincible, and I had the pleasure of showing him otherwise. A god sword will make worm food out of any of us, no matter who wields it. But, regardless," I called in a clear voice. "I am no child. My name is Saeris Fane, and I *am* your queen."

2

HALL OF TEARS

SAERIS

"SHE ISN'T ONE of us. How can she be our queen when I can hear her heart beating from here?"

The throne was cold as ice. No cushion padded its seat, and the frigid temperature of the hard stone leached into my back and ass. I squirmed uncomfortably as the beautiful vampire with the golden braids called out across the hall for all to hear.

"Ours might be the youngest court in this realm, but Sanasroth has always prided itself on its traditions. For a thousand years, we were ruled over by the *first* vampire. A brilliant male, who carved out a home and a future for his children and earned us all the right to belong. He wasn't just a king. He was a walking god among the living and the dead of this realm, and this . . . this *girl*," she spat, "was human mere days ago. So weak that one of our own had to save her life." She sent a look full of naked malice in Taladaius's direction. "How do we replace the creator of our entire species with *this*?"

She was an excellent actress. Her words overflowed with emotion as she paced around the star, weaving in and out of the other Lords of Midnight. Most would have been fooled by the hitch in her voice when she spoke of losing Malcolm, but I heard the lie.

Her heart was not broken, because she had no heart. I felt her malign energy radiating from her as sure as I used to feel the heat radiating from the suns back in the Third: Whatever soul she might once have possessed had fled the shell of her body long ago. A dark, cruel thing crouched inside of her now, peering out of her wide, pretty eyes, using her voice to speak.

"Do other courts invite the chicken or the calf to sit atop their thrones in fancy dress to preside over *them*?" she bellowed.

A wave of cries went up around the hall in a rising tide of anger. Some of the vampires seated on the benches leaped to their feet, shouting out above the rest.

"*No!*"

"*They would never!*"

"*Perversion!*"

"*Anathema!*"

"Then why do *we* crown a lowly creature that would have been food to us only days ago and give it the power to rule over us? Why do we *embarrass* ourselves like—"

That's Zovena, Kingfisher said. The sound of his deep voice in my mind startled me; I barely kept the surprise from my face. *Though I'm sure you've figured that out by now. Tal gave you all their names.*

Yes, I answered. *She's Keeper of Missives.*

I felt Fisher's approval in the back of my mind. *Yes. See the ring on her hand? The thick band of gold with the purple stone? That marks her as a Lord. All five of them have rings. They're a source of power, gifted to them by Malcolm. Each supposedly contains the same amount of magic, though it's rumored that Tal's is the most powerful. Zovena was Lissian once, like Tal. He loved her. For her part, I think she loved him, too. But that was a long, long time ago.*

I watched the way Zovena glared at my maker now and found no love or warmth of affection for him in her eyes. "You should have left her there to die, Taladaius," the female seethed. "You could have slit the Bane's throat while you were at it, too. But no. We all know how much you care about your precious Kingfisher of the Ajun Gate, don't we? So now you bring them both before us, hand in hand, mates, attempting to install not only a half-blood child as queen but a full-blooded Fae male as king consort along with her! And not just any Fae male. One who has plagued and murdered our people for centuries! Have you forgotten that we are at *war* with him?"

I waited for Kingfisher to say something, but no response came. Glancing over to where he stood on my right, I found that he was yawning.

I spoke into his mind again. *Laying it on a little thick, don't you think?*

His left eye twitched. *No, not really. Zovena and I aren't the best of friends. I've heard it all before.*

The slender male with the hooked nose stepped forward from his point on the star, deep furrows forming in his brow. He looked to be in his thirties, but gods only knew his real age. "That's enough, Zovena. Throwing a temper tantrum won't change anything. Taladaius saved the girl. Now she is of our blood. She killed Malcolm. Therefore, she must ascend. It is our way. We all know it. Hysterics solve nothing."

"This isn't hysterics," Zovena bit out. "This is outrage! On behalf of my brothers and sisters!" She gestured to other members of the Sanasrothian court, seated in their benches, stretching back into darkness. They bayed in response, buying into her rhetoric. "They deserve better. A strong hand. A queen who—"

"Oh, so you still envision a *queen* on the throne, then? A female like yourself, perhaps?" the hook-nosed male asked.

While they bickered back and forth, I spoke again to Fisher. *That's Ereth, I suppose? Keeper of the Evenlight?*

Fisher answered right away. *Yes. He and his followers are religious zealots. They worship one of the demon gods. If he gets his way, every single living being in Yvelia will be drained of their magic and turned into slaves. Every continent will be turned into a wasteland paradise for vampires, where they can hunt and kill anything left alive for sport.*

Sounds delightful, I said.

The other one is the Hazrax. The last of its kind. It is twice as old as anything else that draws breath in Yvelia.

Taladaius had been oddly vague when he'd spoken of the Hazrax. It was not Fae, but it wasn't vampire, either. It had come to Malcolm centuries ago, back when the vampire king was still in the throes of forging his empire, and had offered its services to the king. When Malcolm had asked if it wanted eternity in exchange, the Hazrax had sworn to destroy him if he tried to bite it, and Malcolm had believed every word. When the king had asked it what it *did* want in exchange for its fealty to Sanasroth, the Hazrax had said that it "wanted to watch." From that point onward, the Hazrax had become Keeper of Silence.

Just yesterday, I had asked Taladaius why the vampire king had allowed the creature to remain in his court if he truly did think it capable of destroying him. Taladaius had just shrugged. "The Hazrax's magic is shrouded in mystery. No one here knows what it's capable of... but whatever magic or power it showed to Malcolm scared him enough to allow it to stay."

We knew the Hazrax entered Ammontraieth many years ago, Kingfisher said into my mind. *We haven't heard tell of it leaving since. It's rumored that it doesn't even leave this hall. It doesn't eat or sleep. It just watches.*

The creature's appearance was terrifying enough without wondering how it could just exist here like this, a constant, unsettling presence. As if he could sense my discomfort, Kingfisher moved on. *The old woman is Algat, Keeper of Records. She was a witch once. Cast out by her own clan for meddling in dark magics. She might look like the oldest of the Lords, but she's actually the youngest. I had cause to deal with her once or twice before she transitioned. Pure evil runs through her veins, Little Osha. Do not underestimate her.*

Even as he said it, the old woman's head canted at an unnatural angle, turning toward Kingfisher, as if she could hear the conversation passing between us. I couldn't make out much of her face with all that thick gray hair hanging down, but I could see her hideous grin. Rotten, yellow teeth filled her mouth, long as a rat's. Her canines were so elongated that they pierced her lower lip, streaking her chin red with blood.

Her cloudy eyes locked with mine, and—

I was back in the Third.

I was arguing with Hayden.

I was back in Madra's palace, fighting to free my hands as Harron came to kill me.

I was in Kingfisher's bed in Ballard, safe in his arms.

He was inside me, and my soul was full of fire, and—

"Do you think I can smoke in here?"

I jumped out of my skin at the sound of Carrion's voice.

I'd been staring at the old woman. She had been staring at me. How long had I . . .

An ice-cold sensation flooded my head. It felt as if someone had been rifling through my pockets. I glanced at Fisher out of the corner of my eye, but he was staring at the ceiling, affecting boredom, unaware anything untoward had just happened. When I turned to Carrion, about to ask him to repeat himself, I saw that the idiot had a cigarillo in his mouth and was fishing around in his pocket for his flint box.

"What in all five hells are you *doing*?" I hissed. "Do *not* light that."

Fisher growled, finally noticing what the true heir to the Winter Court was up to. He stepped back behind the throne and ripped the cigarillo out of Carrion's mouth, tossing it to the ground.

"Are we keeping you from something, Your Highness?" The voice rent the air in two like a whip.

Ereth stood at the center of the five-pointed star, his cloak thrown back over one shoulder as if he had spun around in haste. Zovena was as still as a statue, as were the others, but I could tell that she was crowing inside.

Once upon a time, I hadn't been the only apprentice at the Third's most notorious forge. Elroy had caught me whispering to one of his other students and had been furious that I hadn't been paying attention to him waxing poetic about different glass tempering styles. This moment felt a *lot* like that.

I was two seconds away from being scolded like a misbehaving child. That would *not* be good. The Lords needed to be brought to heel, not offered an invitation to chide me. I had to pull the situation back, to take the proceedings in hand. My first instinct was to apologize for the interruption, but a queen did *not* apologize.

I raised my chin and stared Ereth down, filling my veins with ice. "Yes, Ereth. Since you've finally thought to ask, I *do* have better things to do than listen to you all bickering like children. I was told this was supposed to be a coronation, so let's proceed with the business of it, shall we?"

A tense quiet fell over the Hall of Tears. It was only now, with every vampire present stunned to silence, that I realized why this place was called the Hall of Tears: somewhere, out there in the dark, someone was crying. A mournful wail echoed off the columns and then ricocheted around the recessed alcoves—a sound devoid of hope. A shiver ran up my spine as I heard another sob join the first, and then another, and another. Out there, beyond the crowds and the strange white-green glow of the torches, people were suffering.

"My sincere apologies, Your Highness." Ereth had dropped into a deep bow, pale hand pressed to the middle of his chest. He lifted his head, looking up at me from beneath dark brows, and I saw the mockery in his eyes. "You're *absolutely* right. How foolish of me. The night is wasting, and there's much to be done."

"The girl needs to drink before she's crowned." It was Algat who made the declaration. Her cracked voice reminded me of the reckoning wind that used to howl across the dunes and batter the Silver City: dry and angry. "How can she hope to rule if she is not leashed to the blood?"

Taladaius had explained that he would hold his tongue as best he could during the evening's proceedings. He had been Malcolm's favorite—his Keeper of Secrets—which meant that he was *not* a favorite among the five. He hadn't wanted to do or say anything to color the actions of the others, but at Algat's comment, he quickly stepped forward. "She isn't required to drink," he said. "No rule or law prescribes it."

"No law and no rule, maybe, but what of common sense?" the old woman asked, in a sly croak. "Come now, Taladaius. The girl's a virgin—"

"*Excuse* me?" I couldn't stop myself. My indignation erupted from me before I could reel it back. "I assure you, I am *not*."

Algat gave me a pitying look. "Not of the body, child." Her head tipped toward Fisher again, the speed and angle of the motion making my stomach twist. "We smell the sex on both you and your mate perfectly well, I assure you. No, you are a virgin of the blood. You have not fed from the life source of the living—"

"She's still a member of their number," Zovena cut in with obvious disgust. "I said it before and no one cared to comment on the matter, but how can a member of the living *feed* on the living? Again, how can she hope to rule . . ." She trailed off, her eyes growing round in her head as she took me in.

I had risen to my feet.

And my heart had stopped beating.

It hadn't taken long to master the trick. Taladaius had known that his counterparts would take offense over the issue, and so he had taught me how to paralyze the muscle in my chest. It had been simple enough. All I had to do was picture my heart resting, taking a break, and that was precisely what it did.

My blood stopped pumping. Everything inside me stilled. I'd never realized that I could hear the rushing of my blood if I tried to, but I could. And now that it sat dormant in my veins, my inner world felt off kilter. It was like breathing under water; I shouldn't have been able to do it.

"So she can *choose* when to be like us, then," Zovena muttered under her breath. "But that does not make her one of us."

"If she drinks, she will be." Algat pushed, apparently dissatisfied that I hadn't answered to the issue. "This whole court knows that you haven't fed since you awoke from the Midnight Kiss, girl. Drink from someone, and all will be well. We'll place the circlet upon your head and then drown ourselves in wine until sunrise, celebrating you as our new queen if you do."

"And if I don't?"

Taladaius was halfway across the platform, moving toward me. "Saeris."

"Listen to him," Zovena sneered. "*Saeris.* He calls her by her name! And why wouldn't he? He made her. She's beholden to *him.* He pushes her forward as his puppet, for him to control from the shadows. If you accept her, then on your heads be it. But know you are accepting a proxy. Know who you're *truly* bowing and scraping to when you swear fealty."

There were traveling theater companies back in Zilvaren who would have committed murder to secure Zovena as one of their lead players; the female was really beginning to annoy me. Thankfully, Taladaius seemed immune to her dramatics. "You don't have to do any-thing, Saeris. It isn't law."

"It isn't law because it's never needed to be," Zovena hissed. "The ruler of the vampire court should be a *vampire.* Feeding on the blood of the living should be the greatest pleasure imaginable to our regent. They should enact their basest nature without any need for convincing."

For all his preparations over the past couple of days, Taladaius hadn't seen this coming. Maybe he should have. It made sense that these monsters would want reassurances. I was an interloper taking up residence inside their palace. I was half Fae. It was only natural that they were wary of me. Martyrs only knew how they could tell that I hadn't fed, but it was true. I hadn't wanted to. Hadn't *needed* to.

"My sisters are right, Highness," Ereth interjected. "If you'd accept a coronation gift from us, maybe it would set our minds at ease. A beau-tiful young woman to sip from, perhaps?" His pit-black eyes flitted to Kingfisher. "Or... perhaps there is a simpler solution to this quandary?"

"No," I snapped. "If it isn't mandated, then do not seek to make a spectacle of me."

Amid all of this, the Hazrax's head turned from left to right, observ-ing the scene as it unfolded. It said nothing, its odd gills flaring. With its hands clasped together inside the sleeves of its bone-white robe, it took everything in without saying a word. It shifted its body to face me now, though, turning its attention on me... and my mate. Kingfisher had stepped forward and turned his back on the gathering—an unimaginable show of disrespect. But I knew Fisher, and he didn't give a shit about disrespecting the Sanasrothian court. He wanted to look me in the eyes when he spoke to me.

"Just do it, Osha."

"What?"

"Bite me. Drink. Swallow twice and be done with it. They pursue this to undermine you because they're sure you won't do it. But fuck them. This is easy. We take care of this, and we get to leave this room." In my head, he said, *We can go back to Cahlish. Back to Ren, and Lorreth, and Layne.*

"He has a point," Carrion said.

"You shouldn't even be here, Swift," Fisher growled irritably. "Keep your opinions to yourself."

The eyes of a thousand vampires bored into me as I peered around Fisher's side and looked out at the amassed court. What would they do if I still refused? Many of them had died with magic in their veins. It had corrupted and turned black along with their blood. Some of them *were* powerful. The only thing keeping any of them from tearing us apart was the Law of Ascension and Taladaius's edict. But laws were broken all the time, and I did not want to die *here*, of all places.

Gods.

I took a deep breath.

"All right. I'll drink from you," I whispered.

Ereth clapped his hands together, overjoyed. "Wonderful!" He'd heard me, naturally. "Wonderful, wonderful!"

A growl of displeasure issued from the back of Fisher's throat, but his gaze remained fixed on me, never wavering. He began unfastening the leather straps that held his right bracer in place, undoing the armor. "Block them out. Don't pay them any attention. It's just you and me, okay?"

I thanked the gods, the stars, and all four winds because, for once in his life, Carrion Swift kept his mouth shut. If he had made some quip about the fact that *he* was standing there, standing right next to us, he probably would have lost his front teeth.

I focused on my mate, determined not to fumble this. We had one shot. A single chance at turning the tides in this war. If our play had to be this, then so be it. I would keep a steady hand, but gods alive, it would be hard. *This... isn't how I imagined this*, I thought to Fisher.

As he slipped his bracer free, his eyes found mine, burning with intensity. A slow, intrigued smile kicked up the corner of his mouth. *Oh? So you've been imagining this, then, have you, Little Osha?*

My blood lit on fire in my veins. The suggestive tone in his voice in my head would have made even the girls who worked at Kala's blush. *No.* It was too late, though. My cheeks were glowing, and Fisher was chuckling under his breath, rolling back his sleeve.

You can own your fantasies with me, Little Osha. There is nothing in this realm or the next that I won't give to you if you desire it. All you ever need do is ask.

Now was not the time. It sure as hells wasn't the place.

But... Holy gods.

Breathe, Saeris.

"Look at her, just standing there. She's stalling," Zovena muttered down on the platform. I glanced behind Fisher, a wave of nerves cinching tight in my gut, but Fisher gently took hold of my chin and tipped my face so that I was looking back up at him. The ink at his throat was going wild; I could see the black linework morphing and shifting over the top of his gorget. There wasn't much quicksilver left in his eye now, but the small amount that remained was also shifting, forming the geometric shapes and patterns among the vivid green of his iris. "Don't look at her. Look at me. You're okay."

And I was.

When Fisher let go of my chin and turned his hand, offering me his wrist, I didn't think. It was instinctual. The warmth that lived at the back of my throat now became a roaring inferno. I took hold of his arm, a pulse of pleasure already aching in my mouth as I sank my canines into his flesh.

Deep.

So deep.

I hadn't meant to...

I froze, not understanding the overpowering urge I felt to wait...

"Drink, Saeris," Fisher said in a ragged gasp.

No.

No, I needed to wait.

"For the love of the gods, fucking drink," he begged.

In those long, heady moments, I hadn't realized that I wasn't taking anything from him. That I was *giving* something to him instead.

I blinked as black ink shifted beneath Fisher's skin, pouring like water down his arm. It banded his wrist and then disappeared, transferring to me. I felt the cool prickle of it settling right in the center of my chest, just below my collarbone, but I didn't care about the new ink.

I only cared about my mate.

And the *blood*.

When I drew from Fisher for the first time, pulling at his wrist, I felt the reversal of a flow between us. The changing of a tide. As soon as his blood touched my tongue, an explosion of color and sound lit up inside my head like a thousand fireworks. Fire chased through my veins. Need pooled between my legs, sending a rush of pleasure up through my body so powerful that I wanted to scream. I couldn't, though. I'd have to stop drawing from him to do that, and—

"Fuck, Saeris." Breathless. Mindless. Desperate. Fisher's voice was thick with his own desire. His next words went against everything my body was screaming for. "Stop, Osha. Enough."

Suddenly, we were in the Hall of Tears.

I tore my mouth from Fisher's wrist, panting as if I'd been doused with a bucket of cold water.

The Hall of Tears...

A thousand Sanasrothians, on their feet, cheering at my hunger...

My pulse raced away from me, refusing to listen, refusing to be still.

I turned to Kingfisher, lips parted, another wave of heat and pleasure rocking me to the tips of my toes when I saw how flushed his cheeks were beneath his stubble. His pupils had completely swallowed his iris and banished the green *and* the quicksilver. His labored breathing had his chest rising and falling so fast. He glanced at me out of the corner of his eye, and the primal hunger I saw there landed like a physical blow. He was barely in control of himself. If I touched him—

"Don't even think about it, or I'll take you right here," he panted.

Holy.

Fucking.

Gods.

"Well done! Well done!" Ereth stood back in position at his point of the star. His applause echoed above the raucous cheering that flooded the hall. I paid no heed to the Keeper of Evenlight, though. I couldn't tear my gaze from Fisher. He couldn't tear his gaze from me. My mate and I stared at each other, panting, our bodies tensed taut as twin bowstrings. The feeling coursing through me was like nothing I had ever encountered before. It went beyond want. There were no words to describe it.

We hadn't slept together since I'd woken. I'd still been sick from the transition and sore from the injuries I'd sustained in the maze at Gillethrye. But now…

Now.

Fuck, I needed him *now.*

"It's done! She has fed!" Ereth faced the masses with both hands raised in the air like some prophesying messiah. "She is leashed by the blood. Bound to it, as we all are. There can be no question of her commitment to our people now."

What the *hell* was he talking about?

Kingfisher reached out and carefully wiped his thumb over my chin; it came away red. His chest hitched up and down so fast. He hadn't spoken again yet.

"Crown her! *Crown* her!" the crowd roared.

I was drunk. Swimming, sinking, drowning. I needed to lie down.

Suddenly, someone was standing in front of me. I tore my eyes away from Fisher and gasped aloud when I saw the Hall of Tears again. Really looked upon it, as if seeing it for the first time. The figures stitched into the wall hangings writhed and cavorted, glimmering in the torchlight. Flecks of gold and silver danced in the air. The darkness had swept away, revealing sumptuous furnishings, and paintings hanging from the walls, and sprays of night-blooming flowers in tall vases, throughout the hall.

Suddenly, crushingly, the Hall of Tears had become beautiful.

3

DOSE

KINGFISHER

THERE WAS A new tattoo on her chest: a thin black line that marked her skin from one shoulder to the other, right below her collarbone. Just a simple line, but somehow striking. She was breathtaking as she turned and faced the hall, her eyes lit with a galaxy of stars. She was the center of that galaxy. I gravitated toward her anyway, but after what she'd just done—she had no *idea* what she'd done—my cock was the hardest it had ever fucking been, and I could barely think straight.

Gods, that fucking *dress*...

As Ereth climbed the steps of the dais, approaching her, I watched Saeris take in her surroundings, wide-eyed, and I knew what she was feeling. The euphoria was running through my veins, too. I should have been more careful when I'd told her to drink. She couldn't have known what would happen if she stilled with her canines inside me and didn't drink, though. It was my own fucking fault. I should have told her. I should have explained. My cock throbbed relentlessly as I turned around to face the hall.

Ereth reached the top of the steps and bowed reverently, dipping low before my mate. Saeris barely noticed that he was there. My poor Little Osha was reeling from the effects of the bite, but not me. I had years on her. I knew how to shove the high aside. I did so reluctantly;

it would have been nice to float on that sea of pure bliss with her, but Ereth had encouraged her to bite me for a reason. Likely, he'd hoped the experience would put her on her ass. He probably hoped having Saeris feed from me would dull my senses and make me lower my guard, too... but Ereth didn't know me. He'd never faced me on the battlefield. Never visited me when I was trapped inside Malcolm's maze. He had no idea who I was or what I was capable of and, therefore, had no clue what heinous crimes I would commit to ensure my mate's safety.

The beak-nosed bastard raised the golden diadem he carried in his hands, gently placing it atop Saeris's head. Her eyelids fluttered as she came back to herself, and my reality sharpened to a knife's point. She was vulnerable with him standing so close. Too vulnerable. I bristled, my fingers prickling.

Patience, the quicksilver whispered.

Ever since Te Léna had partnered with Iseabail to tease the quicksilver out of me, the whispering in my head had been less frantic. Sharper. Easier to understand. Together, healer and witch had achieved what neither had been able to accomplish alone. The thread of quicksilver that lingered inside of me no longer made me feel like I was hanging on to my sanity by my fingernails. For the first time since it had infected me as a youth, I had begun to think of the quicksilver as more of a blessing than a curse. It urged caution now, as I watched Ereth like a hawk. *Wait. Wait. Be patient...*

Patience had never been my strong suit. The maze had changed that for me. I held my position, giving Ereth the benefit of the doubt. I knew very little of him. It was unlikely that he would move so quickly after—

Nope.

I was right.

I fucking *knew* it.

The blade that appeared in the Lord's hand had a handle wrapped with a leather thong. It must have been causing him serious discomfort this whole time; he'd been keeping it inside his cloak, tucked away against his side. The blade was vicious, needlelike, and flashed bright silver: the perfect weapon for a vampire noble, inexperienced in the art of fighting, to drive through their enemy's eardrum and straight into their brain.

Ereth moved quickly.

I moved quicker.

Saeris reacted, too, the dazed gloss to her eyes fading away. She reached for the dagger I had given her, but I was already there, slamming into the Lord.

Ereth made a guttural *guhhhhh!* sound as he flew back, the air rushing out of him. He crashed down hard on the dais steps. Raising the hand with the blade in it, he went to throw it, but—

I reached over my shoulder.

My hand closed around Nimerelle's hilt.

In a beat, the sword was gone.

I hurled her with all my might.

The honed metal cut through the air, spinning end over end, arcing at the last minute and slicing straight through Ereth's torso on a diagonal, cleaving him in two.

Nimerelle landed point-first, juddering, the blade burying five inches deep into the obsidian dais.

Thunk.

Thunk.

Ereth's body was much less graceful when *he* struck the floor. His insides were black, his organs necrotic, the ichor that oozed out of him thick and stinking of tar. Death had perched on this monster's shoulder for so long that he wasn't going to waste much time claiming his prize now. Nimerelle *was* a god sword, after all—laced with silver and the magic of the gods. I might not have decapitated Ereth, but the bastard was lying in two pieces on the ground. The blow would kill him.

To my left, three high bloods wearing black tabards with bloodred dragons depicted on them writhed on the steps. They'd come to their leader's aid, it seemed, only to be felled by someone *else's* hand. Taladaius stood at the base of the dais, hand outstretched, expression blank as he unleashed his magic upon the vampires. There was a reason the previous king of this court had made Tal his second in command. He never flaunted his magic, but the male was powerful. Even before he'd transitioned, Tal had been able to manipulate most liquids. All liquids, in fact, apart from quicksilver. *Blood* was a liquid...and right now, he was boiling the blood in the high bloods' veins.

Steam poured from their open mouths, their screams silent as they died, and Tal observed their passing with a look of expertly crafted boredom. Scandalized mutters went up throughout the hall—to use such taboo magic against members of his own court was rare indeed, but not unheard of. Rumor had it Malcolm enjoyed watching his subjects smoke whenever they stepped out of line. Saeris hadn't ordered Tal to act, though. He'd acted of his own volition. There would be consequences, to be sure, but that was none of my concern.

Saeris was behind me.

It only took a second to scan her for injuries. She appeared to be unharmed, but I didn't trust my own eyes. I needed to hear her say it. *Are you okay?* I demanded.

Yes. I—I'm fine.

My relief was absolute. *Stay there, then. Wait for me. No one else is getting up these steps.* Amid the screams of horror and panic that erupted throughout the hall, I slowly stepped down from the dais to the platform, toward where the two separate pieces of Ereth's broken body lay.

"I bet you're regretting *that*," I snarled.

Thin black liquid bubbled out of the Lord's mouth, spackling his lips and his chin. "She is...anathema. Cursed," he choked out. "The g-gods denounce...her."

"Really?" I crouched down next to him. "Is that so?" I was still missing my bracer. I raised my right hand to show him what my armor and Saeris's gloves had been hiding from view: the extensive tattoos that marked us—and our union—as divinely bound. Ereth had been Fae once. He knew the stories. He had certainly heard tales of couples who were God-Bound. His eyes went wide when he saw the ink circling my wrists. Ink that had formed in the maze, when Saeris had been pulled through the quicksilver and into the realm of the gods themselves. "They haven't denounced her. They have safeguarded her." And maybe that wasn't true. God-Bound unions often ended in death. But Saeris had already died once, and I'd done way more than my fair share of dying back in the maze. As far as I was concerned, Death had taken his due from us. I *had* to see the marks as a blessing.

Laughter burbled up out of Ereth, the sound a wet rattle. "You f-fool. W-we have *different* gods."

And then he was gone.

Between breaths, the monster's body crumpled to ash.

An enraged scream pierced the air, and there was Zovena, charging not toward me, but toward the sword still embedded in the center of the five-point star mosaic that decorated the platform.

I rose to my feet, baring my teeth. "Touch it, Zovena. Go on, I fuck- ing *dare* you."

The bitch stopped dead in her tracks, but not because common sense had claimed her; a streak of silver rippled across my vision, and Tal was there, tackling the female vampire to the ground.

"*Stop!*"

Saeris's shout crashed through the Hall of Tears, and at her com- mand, the remaining Lords, Tal and Zovena, and the high blood vam- pires rioting in their seats just *stopped*.

"I am ruler of this court, and I *will* be heard!" She stood at the edge of the dais, beautiful and terrible as a storm, the air rippling and distort- ing around her. I wasn't a member of the Sanasrothian Court, but even my ears rang with her authority. It brought a number of the other high born vampires in the front benches to their knees. "From this point forth, whenever you are in my presence, this is how you will greet me: on your *knees*! All subjects of the Blood Court of Sanasroth are forbid- den from harming, hindering, or killing me, my mate, or any of my friends. Additionally, from this moment onward, no feeder enthralled to a high blood of this court may be used for the purposes of war, mal- ice, or mayhem. I have spoken. It is done!"

A shock wave of power blasted through the hall, pulling at people's clothes and causing them to shield their eyes.

Saeris had delivered her own edicts. The first laws of a new monarch, passed with force. The first steps of our plan were in place.

The vampires of Sanasroth had no choice but to obey.

———+———

"She *dosed* you? In front of the whole Sanasrothian Court?"

I trudged through the mud, shaking my head at the amusement in Renfis's voice. He was enjoying this way too much. "I think you're missing the point. I killed a Lord of Midnight. The coronation celebrations were called off. I had to leave Ammontraíeth before a riot broke out."

My friend nodded, rubbing at his jaw. "Yeah. Right. Okay. That wasn't *exactly* how we'd hoped the ceremony would play out. But honestly, who cares about Ereth? They'll have a quorum and replace the bastard. I want to know about you getting dosed. Did you tear her clothes off in front of everyone?"

I clenched my jaw, blowing out a hard exhale. "No, I did not tear her clothes off. She barely even got me. As soon as I realized what she was doing, I told her to drink, and then—" But I was remembering the heat of her venom in my veins and my head was starting to spin out again. "Look, let's focus. I just had to ride out from Ammontraíeth on horseback, and then I had to skate halfway across the fucking Darn before I had access to my magic. How am I supposed to protect her properly if I can't create a godscursed portal?"

Ren had some color in his cheeks. That was good to see. Ever since we'd moved Layne to the East Wing at Cahlish, his mood had been a little more upbeat. My sister had opened her eyes yesterday, which was small progress, yes, but it was progress nonetheless. He'd always been protective of my half sister. Even when we were younger and she used to tease him mercilessly. He seemed to have taken it upon himself to make sure Everlayne made as full a recovery as possible. He ducked his head as he followed me into the war tent.

"Sounds to me like Saeris is one of the most powerful beings this side of the afterlife. They've crowned her. She's spoken her will and made it law."

I grunted unhappily.

"They have to obey her, brother. It's part of the curse of their court. You can thank Malcolm's paranoia for that. Any vampire born of his line *must* obey the Sanasrothian crown. Now that the crown sits on Saeris's head and she's forbidden them from harming her, she's basically untouchable. She doesn't *need* protecting. They have to follow the edicts. They can't hurt her. They can't hurt you. And not only that, but she decommissioned the fucking *horde*, Fisher."

He was right. What he was saying made sense. So why, then, did this niggling, sick feeling persist in my stomach? "They're bound to be trying to figure out a workaround as we speak. Zovena's incandescent with rage—"

"Screw *Zovena*," Ren muttered.

"—and Algat was grinning like an imp when she trotted out of that hall, so the gods only know what *she's* planning."

"Well, well, well. Look who it is. The wanderer returns." The war tent was empty save for a lone figure sitting on a stool by the fire, running a whetstone along the edge of his sword. Avisiéth had once been named Celeandor. It had belonged to another member the Lupo Proelia, but Saeris had reforged it and placed it in Lorreth's hands—the first god sword to channel magic in an age.

"You're going to polish that blade away into nothing if you're not careful," Ren said, taking a seat next to him.

"It gets sulky if I don't clean it every night." Lorreth's tone bore a hint of exasperation. He grinned at us both in greeting. "The damned thing has mood swings worse than a Faeling whose balls are about to drop."

Ren laughed, nodding up at me. "Funny you mention balls. Ask *him* how *his* are."

I groaned, leaning up against the table in the center of the room. "Gods alive, are you going to tell everyone?"

Lorreth frowned. Stooping, he collected a mug of beer from the floor at his feet. "Tell me what? What's wrong with your balls?" He took a swig.

"He gave Saeris a new piece of ink. She had to feed from him before they'd crown her," Renfis said. "And *she* accidentally dosed him."

Lorreth spat his beer everywhere. *"What?"* He grimaced up at me. "In front of the whole court?"

Defeated, I nodded, letting out a sigh. I might as well let them get it over with. "In front of the whole court."

"How did you keep your shit together? Weren't you..." He looked directly at my crotch. "Y'know..."

"Yes, I was harder than that fucking steel in your hands. Is that what you want to hear?"

"Gods, I'm so sorry," Lorreth said. But he was laughing, which made it very clear that he wasn't sorry, and, in fact, the piece of gossip was probably the funniest thing he'd ever heard.

I wasn't laughing. Mainly because I hadn't had a chance to be alone with Saeris since the coronation, but also because of the situation I found myself in now. I was in Irrín. My mate was not. If I'd had my way, we'd have already murdered every single bastard in the Sanasrothian Court and Saeris would be here, by my side. For once, I wanted to be selfish. Wanted to say fuck it and put my own happiness and the happiness of my mate first. But selfishness was not my lot in this life. As if reminding me of my path, the tattoo on my inner left forearm tingled, the ink shivering beneath my skin. *Sacrifice.* It pulsed often, even stung from time to time, as if the ink were still fresh. But it never changed. Never spelled out some other, less painful future.

The plan we had concocted since Saeris's awakening felt pieced together and liable to fall apart at any second. The consequences, should we fail, had kept me from sleep for days.

If Tal didn't keep up his end of the bargain and keep her safe...

If Saeris's royal decree didn't hold, or the Sanasrothian leeches found a way to circumvent it and killed her in her bed...

If she couldn't find the information we so desperately needed in the Sanasrothian libraries...

If Carrion fucking Swift somehow landed himself in shit and dragged the love of my miserable life into it with him...

If.

There were too many ifs to comprehend. They bombarded me, crushing me under a barrage of all-too-real possibilities while I desperately clung to the promise I had made to *have faith*. But having faith was like trying to remember a language I had once known as a child. No, it was worse. It was like trying to run with broken legs. My legs could not carry me right now, and so I was dragging myself along on my hands and knees, the word *faith* a boot on the back of my neck, shoving me down into the dirt.

Ren and Lorreth were still chuckling.

"At least if you're this wound up, you'll be ready for a fight," Lorreth mused, his dark eyes full of mischief.

A part of me wanted to be angry that they could still be so light-hearted in the face of all of this. It was the same part of me that had been trapped in Malcolm's maze for over a century and had gradually lost hope. Always running. Always suffering. Being eaten, and being burned, and being haunted by the burning corpses of an entire city that *I* had put to the torch. The same part of me that was still there, running the passageways of that dark nightmare. The part of me that would *never* be free of that fucking maze.

But the rest of me was relieved that my friends still had laughter in their souls. They had suffered, too. Their losses also piled high. They'd had to watch our people being brutalized, eaten, and turned every day. And if my friends could still find it in themselves to laugh, then I was glad of it. That meant that maybe there was hope for me, too.

I ducked my head, smiling softly as I looked down at my hands. It *was* pretty funny, when you thought about it.

"Honestly, I think I might be partially responsible," Lorreth said, turning his attention back to his sword; the metal cast a sustained bright humming sound as he slid the whetstone along its edge. "She asked me about the blood trade back at the tavern not too long ago. I explained it inasmuch as it felt appropriate. In hindsight, I only gave her half the information she probably needed. But how was *I* supposed to know that she'd find herself turned and in a position to bite *you*? I figured you'd explain it all when the time was right, and you wanted to—"

"Please stop talking." It was entirely unreasonable—the sudden urge I had to wrap my hands around Lorreth's neck and squeeze until he stopped breathing. But a mated Fae didn't like another male talking about his mate at the best of times. And I was newly mated. Hearing that he'd spoken to Saeris about the blood trade at all made me want to turn feral and burn down the fucking war tent.

Lorreth chuckled, unfazed by the way I'd snapped at him. He just shook his head, going about his work. *Shhhhick. Hummmmmm. Shhhhick. Hummmmmm.* Wisely, he changed the subject, though.

"I still haven't found him," he said, a seriousness falling over him.

Ren's smile faded, too. He picked at his nails, staring into the fire as he spoke. "We don't even know he's in there."

I knew who they were talking about, though neither of them said his name. Our friend. Our brother. Foley had been with us when we'd climbed the dragon. Old 'Shacry had shaken him free and sent him hurtling into the dark. The fall had crushed his body, but it was the feeders who had killed him. They'd drunk him dry and left him broken in the snow. It had taken hours to find him. I was free of the dragon's maw and morning had arrived by the time we discovered him, panting and covered in blood, hiding from the dawn in the mouth of a cave.

He should have become a feeder. Malcolm was the only one of his kind capable of creating other vampires with their personalities and minds intact. At least, that was what we'd believed at the time. We'd thought it was a miracle. Years later, I discovered the truth: that Taladaius had been there that night, overseeing the assault on the mountain.

When asked, he'd said that he had done it as a kindness to me. That he had fed Foley his blood and then drained him, if only so that he might have a *choice* in whether he lived or died.

Foley had been angry. Confused. We'd stayed with him. Our friend had screamed for hours as he completed his transition. He'd fed before we'd found him and couldn't stop crying over those he had killed. His horror over what he had become seemed as though it would kill him, though when darkness fell, he left us, fleeing into the night, down the mountain and away.

We heard later that he had fled to Ammontraíeth. There had been many instances over the years when we had reached out to him, but our letters had all gone unanswered.

"He's there," I said softly. "He wouldn't have left. He wouldn't have trusted himself around the living."

None of us spoke again for a time.

Shhhhick. Hummmmmm.

Shhhhick. Hummmmmm.

Even though he sat still, gaze lost in the flames, the tension pulsing from Renfis mounted until it became a fourth presence at the fire, hogging all the warmth. "Will you speak, or will you stew?" I asked eventually.

He inhaled sharply, as if waking from a dream. "I have nothing new to say on the matter."

Lorreth set Avisiéth down at last, leaning back in his chair and resting his cup of ale against the flat of his stomach. "Then say what you've said already, and we'll hear you out again."

It seemed for a moment that Ren was going to hold his tongue, but then he began. "It's been hundreds of years. Close to an age. We knew him once, but Foley's been a vampire longer than he was Fae at this point. Who's to say he is anything like the person we once fought alongside?"

He was right. So much time had passed. But there was that word again. *Faith.* Every once in a while, it let me up from the dirt long enough to take a breath. "He was bound to us by blood, as we were to him. He swore to protect our people, along with all the creatures of Yvelia. If you found yourself in his shoes, would *you* break your oath, Ren?"

Renfis hadn't just stepped in as commander of the Lupo Proelia when I'd been lost to the maze. He'd become general to an army. He had willingly donned a mantle of responsibility that would have crushed most other warriors, as it had almost crushed me. I knew the core of him. He was honest, and true, and good. But still he was foolish enough to shake his fucking head. "I honestly don't know, brother."

"Well, I do. There is no way you'd turn your back on your promise. I choose to believe that Foley hasn't, either."

I'd spent hours looking for him, once I'd known Saeris was going to be okay. So had Lorreth. Taladaius had refused to tell me where he was, which hadn't done much to dull the anger that *I* still harbored toward him. But, in a way, I'd understood.

Foley had needed to carve out a new existence for himself at Ammontraíeth. At some point, he must have needed to accept his new life and move forward with it. He hadn't answered the letters any of us had sent to him, which must have been for a reason. And if Foley didn't want to speak with us, then it stood to reason that he wouldn't want to *see* any of us, either.

A long time ago, he would have died for me and I for him. I would still have laid down my life for him if it would save him in some way. But the damage was done, and of all people, *Tal* seemed to be the only one who could respect that.

"If he is in there somewhere, who's to say he has any interest in helping Saeris?" Lorreth said. "He has no connection to her. No reason to show her any loyalty at all."

"Other than her being my mate?"

Lorreth sipped from his beer. "I mean, honestly, that might make him even *less* inclined to help her."

I shrugged. "We have to hope. We *need* him. His grandfather was one of the last Alchemists. Foley knows more than anyone else about Alchemical magics and practices. Belikon burned all the Alchemists' texts when he seized the crown. The few books that my father collected back at the library in Cahlish don't explain much of anything at all. So that leaves the knowledge that exists in Foley's head. If he won't share that with her…"

"Then Saeris will never be able to realize her full potential. We'll never be able to destroy Ammontraíeth for good. And we'll never be able to put an end to Belikon once and for all and stick Carrion Swift on the throne," Ren admittedly grimly. "I suppose we'd all better hope and pray that Foley changes his mind and wants to be found, then. Because I, for one, would *love* to see peace in my lifetime."

Hah.

Peace.

What would that even look like? Would any of us know what to do with ourselves? I doubted it. Absently, I realized that I hadn't put my bracer back on after I'd let Saeris feed from me. I ran my fingers over the two small puncture wounds at my wrist; they were healing rapidly and would be gone by morning. Sighing, I removed the other bracer and set it down on the table, then unfastened the gorget, too, freeing myself of its weight around my neck. I was rolling up my shirtsleeves when I realized that my brothers were staring at me.

"What?" But I already knew what they were staring at. I had been careful to conceal the rune work that stained the backs of my hands and looped around my wrists ever since Saeris had accepted me as her mate. My hands had always been inked. The runes for *vengeance* and *justice* had been marked into my skin for a very long time...but now there were other runes layered over the top of them. So many runes, in fact, that they were impossible to differentiate from one another. The runes and script that wound their way up my arms—the God Bindings that matched Saeris's own—were beautiful and terrifying, even to me.

I looked down at it all, staining my skin, and smiled ruefully. "Yeah. It's *a lot*."

"I mean, we knew," Ren said breathlessly. "But knowing is one thing. Seeing it in person..."

"Seeing it in person is *wild*," Lorreth agreed. "Does this mean the two of you are going to...y'know." He seemed to be struggling to get the words out. "Will you perform the rites now? Get married?"

A jolt of adrenaline zipped up my spine. I shoved away from the table, quickly rolling down my shirtsleeves, covering the ink. "No. We won't be doing that," I clipped out. "She's not—"

The war tent's flap opened, and Danya burst into the room. "Ren! Oh. You're here." Her eyes landed on me, full of panic. "You need to come outside now. All three of you. Something's wrong."

Ren was already on his feet. "Feeders at the river?" Panic tinged the question; after Saeris's decree earlier, the feeders had been recalled back to Ammontraíeth. They were to be garrisoned a mile from the Black Palace, far from Sanasroth's border with Cahlish.

"No," Danya answered. "Yes. I—I don't know what's happening. I can't explain it. It's best if you come and see for yourself. Hurry."

4

114

KINGFISHER

EIGHT OF THEM stood in a line along the embankment.

They were still as the dead—the *actual* dead, rather than the *undead*. They didn't snarl at the Fae on the other side of the river watching them. They were like decomposing statues, so still that for a second, I wondered if someone had propped them up there.

"What are we looking at?" I asked.

The things Danya had witnessed over the years had made her just as unshakable as the rest of us, but her face was deathly pale as she jerked her chin toward the feeders. "Just watch."

A minute passed.

Another.

And just as I was losing patience and about to demand that Danya explain what was going on, they moved.

Together, they scrambled down the slope toward the river, moving in unnatural unison. Left foot first. Right. All eight of them skidded, losing their footing in the mud. They fell forward, onto all fours, threw back their heads, and screeched.

The sound had every hair on my body at attention.

As one, they came forward, crawling death on hands and knees.

"Do we break the ice?" Danya breathed.

"No. We wait." If they were swept away with the river, we wouldn't be able to inspect them once they were dead. These creatures were different, and we had to know why. As if reading my mind, Ren gathered his magic, forming a blue-white ball of power in his hands. My shadows coiled around my feet, pooling, prowling, ready to be unleashed.

"As soon as they reach halfway..." Ren murmured.

Lorreth already had Avisiéth in his hands. I left Nimerelle strapped to my back. My shadows would be enough for this. The feeders crawled out onto the ice. Further. Their hands and feet met the frozen surface in unison: left hand, right knee, left hand, right foot.

Lorreth twisted the sword in his grip. "I do *not* feel good about this."

I didn't, either. Something foul hung in the air. Toxic. The smell of the campfires and cooking food filled my nose, but there was something else, too. Odorless, but I could feel it snaking up my nostrils and probing down into my lungs. Whatever it was, it was not go—

The feeders sprang.

All eight of them launched into the air like stags. They raced toward the middle of the river, to the point where our magic would take effect, then barreled straight through the invisible boundary without hesitation. The moment it happened, Renfis unleashed his magic, I loosed my shadows, and smoke and light streamed across the Darn. Ren's energy hit first. The orb struck two of the feeders head-on. I diverted my shadows, sending them to the right to take on the remaining feeders, but...

Ren's magic didn't crackle and ebb, leaving bodies in its wake as it normally did. It flared, illuminating the dark, and then it *absorbed* into the two feeders that it had struck. They were male. Shirtless. And where the orb of magic had hit their chests, a network of brilliant white magic fissured outward across their ribs. The two feeders shuddered, and then suddenly all eight of them bore the same white convergence of power.

The light pulsed, glowing, and the feeders juddered again, their spines arching.

"What in all the gods?" Ren whispered.

I urged my shadows out, fanning in all directions, eight narrow tendrils of black, shimmering with my own magic. *Strike hard*, I thought. *End this.* But when they hit home, spearing the feeders through the glowing marks where Ren's magic now appeared to be trapped in their chests, my magic was pulled into them, too. And gods, did I feel it. It was like breathing in ice water. The cold struck hard, ripping my breath away. And the loneliness. The sorrow. It coiled up in my chest and wrapped around my heart so tight that it felt as though it were breaking. In over a hundred years trapped inside Malcolm's maze, I had never felt as bereft as I did in that instant.

I wanted it to stop. The kernel of misery felt like it was taking root of my soul. It was hard to breathe; it was as though I'd forgotten how. I gasped, eventually sucking down a lungful of air, but it tasted all wrong.

I tried to pull my shadows back, but I couldn't. The feeders drank them in and held on tight to them. A metallic black sheen swirled at the center of their chests, roiling amid the white energy they had taken from Renfis.

I looked to Ren and found him pale, his expression full of horror. Was he feeling what I was feeling? It damned well looked like it. "They *fed* on our magic," he whispered.

It was so much worse than being bitten. Worse than them feeding on our blood. Blood was sacred, yes, but our *magic*? I wanted to be sick. In the grand scheme of things, neither of us had expended much of our power, but I could still feel it—that small piece of me that I had sent out into the world and would not be getting back.

The feeders shuddered again, half closing their eyes; they looked as if they were gripped in ecstasy. They groaned, all eight of them, running mangled tongues over their torn lips...and then they snapped back to attention.

"They're still coming!" Danya screamed.

They ran, loping along, their strides unnaturally long, buoyed by their stolen power.

They had almost reached the bank.

Setting his boots in the mud, Lorreth raised Avisíeth in both hands and angled the sword out point-first before his face. "I'll hit them all with Angel's Breath," he growled. "They won't survive that."

"No!" Ren and I cried out at the same time.

"Don't!" I panted. "They're siphoning from us. If they take the Angel's Breath..." It didn't even bear thinking about. Would it make them stronger still? Would...would they be able to wield it back at us? Fuck, my mind was upside down. More of Irrín's warriors were joining us at the bank. "No one use any magic!" I hollered, thick plumes of fog clouding my breath. "Use silver alone. Blades and daggers. Here they come!"

They broke apart as they reached us. Where they had been moving in unison, they now acted independently, their cloudy, bloodred eyes fixing on different members of our party as they attacked.

Had Lorreth heard what I'd said? I fucking hoped so. No rippling forks of Angel's Breath broke apart the night.

One of the feeders—a tall, stocky bastard with shorn hair and arms covered in runes—bared his ruined teeth as he came for me. I reached for the dagger at my waist and my hand closed around nothing. Fuck! I'd given Saeris that blade. There wasn't time to think. I clasped Nimerelle and drew her, sweeping broad as the feeder hit.

No magic. No energy, I pleaded with the sword as I swung. *Just take his fucking head.*

The sword heard and obeyed. When its razor-sharp edge met the feeder's flesh, no plume of smoke or magic erupted from it. The iron drove home, sinking easily through rotten flesh and jellied muscle, skittering along the edge of bone. But where Nimerelle bit through the flesh, a thick black substance crystallized along the blade like frost.

"What the—"

Nimerelle *screamed.*

I heard it in my mind, deafening and full of pain. Nimerelle shook so violently that the vibrations traveled all the way up my arms and rattled my teeth. The feeder didn't even notice that I'd run it through. It came on, teeth snapping, pulling itself along the blade so that it could get to me.

Even without her magic, Nimerelle should have caused the feeder immense pain. She was both silver and iron. *I* could only hold her because of what had transpired at Ajun. The part of the feeder that had once been Fae should have recoiled from the iron, though. The part of it that was vampire should have been affected by the silver. But nothing.

I raised my boot, sliding in the mud, and kicked the feeder in the stomach, shoving it off the blade. The monster staggered back three steps, sliding back down the bank, which gave me enough time to gather myself. I couldn't use the sword again. It had caused her pain. I jammed her back into the scabbard strapped to my back and drew another dagger from my boot, ready when the feeder came flying for me again.

Shouts and screams pierced the night.

There were bodies everywhere now—more of the camp's warriors, rushing to join in the fray. The feeder pounced, springing into the air. It caught a silver-tipped arrow to the throat as it descended, but the weapon had no effect. As the monster landed, I snapped the arrow and drove the splintered shaft into the feeder's eye, but even that didn't slow it. The feeder lunged, swinging its claws at me. Where the male's fingers had once been were now sharp claws curved into hooks, dripping black with ichor. If it so much as scratched me... I wouldn't die, but it would be bad fucking news.

I darted back, out of the fiend's reach. I couldn't use magic or my sword on it, but I was still faster. It snarled, frustrated, as it leaped again—

"The ice!" Someone screamed. "They're breaking it!"

A sinking feeling in my gut told me that the rushing water beneath the frozen surface of the Darn would no longer have any effect on these feeders, though. There were only two similarities between these monsters and the demons we were used to dealing with: They were dead, and they were hungry. Apart from that, these *things* were an entirely different breed.

Sure enough, when the ice shattered below the bank and one of the other feeders toppled into the water, it didn't make a sound. It coiled itself below the waterline, compressing its body in the ink-black water, and then sprang up from the rippling surface, falling on Renfis.

"Ren!" The cry rang out over the sea of warriors. Somewhere, Lorreth sounded like he was fighting for his life, and yet he still called out to our brother.

The feeder snaked forward, its tongue lolling out of its mouth, snagging on its serrated teeth. I spun and whirled to its right, fast as I could, plunging the dagger through the side of its skull.

I needed to take its head, but I wasn't going to be able to do that with it swiping at me with those fucking claws. "Fire!" I shouted. "Light them up!" We were running out of options. If fire didn't work, we were fucked.

My warriors answered the call. In seconds, bright orange flames cast monstrous shadows along the banks of the river. Hundreds of torches appeared, glowing hot and spitting embers. A normal feeder would have balked at the sight of the open flames, but this one just kept coming.

"Stand back, Commander," called a tall warrior with dark hair. He ducked around me, hoisting his torch forward, and I moved out of his way as he hurled the torch at the feeder. Fear whispered in my ear, or maybe it was the remnants of the quicksilver...

It won't work. Won't work, won't work...

But the monster went up like bone-dry kindling as soon as the fire made contact with its moldering flesh.

The feeder didn't make a sound as it was engulfed. Not a peep.

It didn't flail or flee. It just crouched there, burning. Time slowed as the feeder pivoted and turned, sailing through the air and landing on the warrior who had set it alight.

"No!" I moved as quickly as I could, but it turned out I *wasn't* as fast as the cursed creature after all. I was too late. It grabbed the warrior and

CALLIE HART

sank its claws into his skull, crushing bone as it wrenched his head to the side and plunged shattered teeth into his neck.

The fight was over in an instant. The warrior who had come to my aid had his head caved in and blood drained dry in a heartbeat. The feeder was a torch now. It didn't seem to feel the pain or notice that it was slowly incinerating. It hurtled off into the gathered crowd, falling on other warriors, unfazed by the blades and swords they plunged into its chest and at its throat. I watched my men fall as it rampaged.

"Flank it!" someone shouted. Danya. She was there, on the other side of the melee, running fast to meet me. I ran, too, and we both crashed down on the feeder at the same time, grabbing it and forcing it to the ground. We held it, and it burned. The flames licked up our arms and danced as it caught on our clothes. The heat was unimaginable.

"Take it!" I bellowed. *"Take the fucking head!"*

I had no idea whose axe completed the task. As soon as the feeder's head was cleaved from its shoulders, I was dragged back from the flaming corpse by a multitude of hands. The sky overhead swam with streaks of light. The ground ran thick with churned mud and stinking ichor. A thousand knives sank deep into my chest as I was thrown backward into the Darn.

———+———

Being stabbed hurt. Being poisoned by a feeder's toxin, too. But burning alive? That *really* fucking hurt.

I hissed in the war tent as Te Léna administered a cooling salve to my hands. She was doing as much as she could for me, but she had exhausted her supply of magic healing Danya. Healing was her birthright magic, though. Unlike mine, it would replenish soon. She'd tried to help me when I'd been rushed into the tent, but I'd insisted she work on Danya first. I had gone up pretty quickly, but Danya had flared like a living torch. Her injuries had been significant. They would have killed her had the healer not tended to her immediately. Her blistered skin had been transformed to raw meat, her face badly burned. And her hair? Te

Léna had done her best to soothe the angry burns all over Danya's body, but her long pale hair was gone, leaving only singed stubble behind.

"In a couple of hours, I'll be able to take a look at these," Te Léna murmured in a hushed tone, gently applying another layer of the mashed poultice she had created from her store of medicinal healing herbs. I gritted my teeth, giving her a lopsided smile.

"It's all right. I can barely feel a thing."

"Liar," she chided. Her eyes shone bright with unshed tears. "I know how bad that must hurt. You're not doing anyone any favors by hiding it."

"Okay, then. I'll cry about it, shall I?" I winked at her playfully, letting her know that I was just teasing.

She said nothing to that. Just gave me a sorry smile as she went about tending the other open wounds on my hands and my arms. "A few hours," she said again, when she was done. "As soon as I'm about—"

I closed my hand around hers, hissing a little when my skin split. "It's okay, Te Léna. I'll bear it fine." She would never know it—thank the gods—but I had endured far, far worse.

Renfis and Lorreth passed the healer as they entered the war tent. Their faces were both soot stained, their armor plastered with ichor. It had taken them a long time to put down the other feeders. From what I'd been told, they had lashed them with ropes and pinned them in place while they sawed off their heads.

"We have their bodies trussed to a tree," Renfis spat, throwing his gloves onto the chair by the fire. We'd been sitting here, only hours ago, joking about my misfortune and discussing my new inkwork. It felt like an age had passed. "They still won't fucking *die*," Ren seethed.

"We have their heads in a sack down by the river. They're currently trying to chew their way out." Lorreth looked weary to his very bones. He sank into a crouch, leaning his back against the wall; he held his head in his hands for a moment, his breath making rushing sounds as he inhaled and exhaled through his fingers. He struggled to find the right words when he surfaced again. "What in all five hells was that? Centuries, we've been posted here. Only once before have they ever reached this side of the river. That wasn't ideal, but at least we put them down quickly. Half the camp is in ruins right now, thanks to eight feeders. *Eight.* And we still haven't officially managed to kill them."

"I feel sick," Ren said quietly. "In the pit of my stomach. I feel connected to them, like...the magic they took has tied me to them. I can feel them tugging on it, trying to siphon off more. Do you feel that way?" he asked me.

I hadn't wanted to think about it, but yes. That was what it felt like. I nodded. "We need to figure out who was controlling them."

"Do you think *anyone* was?" Lorreth asked. "They seemed feral. Wild." He shivered.

"At the end, maybe. But at the beginning..." The way they'd moved together, in unison, implied that they were under some sort of control. Even Malcolm hadn't been able to work that kind of magic on his feeders, though. It would have required an exorbitant amount of power.

"You know who it was," Ren said. "There's only one person capable of something like this."

I shook my head. "Tal hasn't sired any feeders."

"And you believe that simply because he told you so?" A sharpness rose in Ren's voice.

"Why would he lie, Ren?" Gods, I was tired. My whole body felt like it had been chained to a horse and dragged three miles over rocky ground.

"Because that's who he is. He's a liar. He's never been honest with us about anything. Foley's where he is because of him. And he was there, the other night. With Everlayne. He had her on a fucking *leash*, Fisher."

"Malcolm commanded him to do that—"

"Why do you always defend him!" Ren brought his fist crashing down on the table. His shout echoed off the walls of the war room. His pallor had turned from ash to a furious red. "At every turn, you deny what's staring you right in the face. He abandoned you. He left you over a thousand years ago. He willingly chose to leave us all and go with Malcolm. How do you think he is still walking the realm, hmm? The only way he is still here, proving to be a thorn in all our sides, is because he feeds from the living. He is everything we despise, and yet every time something like this happens, you make excuses for him."

I let him pant away his fury. It wasn't worth trying to speak until he burned through the anger gnawing at him. It struck me, as I watched him, his shoulders hitching up and down as he glared back at me, that the only time I had ever seen Renfis angry was because of Taladaius. In some ways, he was right about him. But in all the ways that really mattered, he was not.

"I'm sorry," I told him. "I know that there can never be anything but bad blood between you and him. But you've never been bound by a curse, brother. You've never been forced to act against your will. And you have never been so in love with someone that you'd sell your soul to the devil to protect them. I pray that when you find your mate and you fall in love, you'll know nothing but an everlasting peace with them. But for others..." I added sadly, "it isn't that simple."

Hours later, when Te Léna had returned to heal me and the sun had broken over the crest of the black horizon beyond Sanasroth, we ventured out to inspect the damage that had occurred in the night. The section of the camp closest to the river had been destroyed. Tents lay in ruin, fabric shredded, supplies strewn all over the churned-up ground. The dead lay along the bank of the river with Widow's Bane blossoms resting over their closed eyes.

I was numb to the core. "How many did we lose?"

"A hundred and fourteen," Lorreth answered.

The number didn't make any sense. We'd never lost that many at Irrín. During open battle, yes, higher losses were to be expected. But not here at our outpost. And not to *eight* feeders. "We'll bury them back at Cahlish," I muttered. "I'll open a portal, and we'll carry them through one at a time."

My brothers said nothing. Frustration still radiated from Ren as we crossed the bank to the large oak tree, but he kept the peace. We would talk again, he and I, when tensions weren't running so high. That was the way it had always been with us when we were at odds.

The oak tree had been there for as long as I could remember, tall and proud despite the cold. Now, its trunk was shriveled, its bark sloughing off in thick slabs. From its roots to the tips of its branches, it festered with slimy mushrooms. The charred, headless bodies of the feeders struggled against their ropes, trying to wrestle free, but thankfully their restraints held true.

"These fell things aren't of Yvelia," Lorreth said in a hushed tone. "Nothing in *our* world could produce this kind of evil."

But we had thought that once about the vampires. And power was an addictive drug. It never surprised me, the terrible things a corrupt soul would do to garner more of it.

5

DEADSTOCK

SAERIS

THE SACK HIT the floor with a thump.

The stench that wafted out of it made me want to gag.

"Smells like your old apartment above the Mirage," Carrion offered in a chipper tone. He carved off a piece of the apple he was holding and ate it straight from the edge of his knife.

I scowled at him, tempted to take the bait. He wanted me to ask him how the hell he thought he knew what the attic space I'd shared with my younger brother above the Mirage had smelled like, but there wasn't time to engage in petty sniping.

Kingfisher and Lorreth had returned, and they'd brought a bag of severed heads with them. It went without saying that the *bag of heads* should have been my primary focus, but apparently I was a terrible person, because the only thing I cared about was him. *Fisher.* My mate was here, and it felt like I could finally breathe again.

He looked as handsome as ever, with his dark hair swept back from his face in waves. The room was full of electricity whenever he was in it. I was drawn to him like a magnet. Like my body was trying to find its way home into his arms. After the *incident* with Ereth, as we were calling it, the coronation celebrations had been canceled, and Fisher had left to check in with Ren and the others. Taladaius had advised that Fisher spend at least a few days away from Ammontraíeth so that the high bloods could cool down a little, but he hadn't seemed at all surprised when my mate had shown up here with Lorreth and the bag as soon as dusk fell.

Fisher sent a withering look in Carrion's direction. "Greetings, Swift. Do you think we might be able to get a little privacy?"

"Are you asking me to leave?"

"Yes."

Carrion pointed his knife at Lorreth. "Does he get to stay?"

"Don't point that at me, boy," the warrior with the dark war braids sighed. "Not if you want to keep it. I'm a collector of pretty daggers."

"Yes, he's staying," Fisher said flatly.

Sheepishly, Carrion lowered the dagger. "Then it stands to reason that I should, too. I'm the heir to the Yvelian throne. If there have been developments that affect Yvelia, I should absolutely be present while they're discussed."

"Do you have any experience with warfare?" Fisher demanded.

"No, not really."

"Any experience whatsoever with necromancy?"

"No."

"The walking dead?"

"No."

"Blood curses?"

"What do *you* think?"

"Then you're no use to us. Leave."

Taladaius entered through the heavy double doors then. Unlike every other member of the Blood Court, he did not kneel before me. I had expressly forbidden him from doing so, though he had suggested that might not be a good idea. He strode across the council chamber with intent, the heels of his boots ringing out against the dove-gray marble. His expression was controlled. Mild, even. But the sadness radiating from him through the connection we shared was stronger than ever today. It left the taste of bitterness and regret on my tongue.

"After the show you put on yesterday, Fisher," he said, "he'll probably be kidnapped and sold into slavery if he leaves this room alone."

"And we *don't* want that to happen?" Fisher said, as if he were getting his facts straight.

"Fisher." This little back-and-forth feud they had going on was becoming borderline infuriating.

My mate just looked at me, innocent as you please. "He's said repeatedly that he has no interest in fighting for his seat at the Winter Palace. And he admitted it himself just now. No tactical training. No knowledge of this." He nudged the bag on the floor with the toe of his boot. "So what good is he?"

I narrowed my eyes at him. *"You're* the one who brought him here. Now you have to tolerate his presence."

"Maybe it's time I took him back to Yvelia?" he countered hopefully.

My maker huffed. Taladaius was dressed in a plain white shirt with loose sleeves, black pants, and black boots. With his silver hair and his pale skin, he was a study in contrasts. He ran a ringed hand through his hair as he dropped down and plucked the sack open, inspecting its contents.

My stomach turned the moment *I* saw what was inside. I'd witnessed plenty of rot in Zilvaren. When you lived in a quarantined sector where people died of starvation or thirst on a daily basis, the dead were not that shocking a sight. But when a head was all that was left of them, and their cheeks were blackened to a crisp and sloughing from the bone…and when they were *blinking* at you with clouded red eyes, that was a slightly different story.

The smell was so much worse now that the bag was open.

Taladaius rocked back on his heels, a look of contemplation on his face.

Lorreth spoke before he did. "Tell us this wasn't you."

My maker's head shot up. He fixed Lorreth with a stunned stare. "Me? I—" He recovered. "No. It wasn't me. I don't have thralls or slaves. And this…" He trailed off, shaking his head. "This is beyond me. Decapitated like this, they shouldn't still be animated."

"Oh, believe me. We know *that*." Lorreth gave a hard laugh. "So how do we kill them?"

Taladaius took a closer look, peering into the bag of heads. He wrinkled his nose. "Honestly, I couldn't say. I've never seen or heard of anything like this before."

You're coming back to Cahlish with me, Little Osha.

Was I ever going to get used to the sound of Fisher speaking into my mind? His voice was so close, as if he were whispering right into my ear. My skin broke out in goose bumps in an instant.

Oh? I thought I needed to stay here? I answered.

A tiny frown formed on Kingfisher's handsome face. *No one will know you're gone. We'll have Tal tell them all you're engaging in blood-fueled orgies all day. That'll convince them to think you're making an effort to fit in.*

I was aware that Lorreth was explaining something to Taladaius about the feeders absorbing Ren's power. *And* Kingfisher's.

I looked to him, startled, but before I could say anything he quieted my worry. *It's okay. We both felt off, but we slept a while and Te Léna worked on us. We're fine now.*

This was hard, loving him. I'd barely slept a wink all day, worrying about him. Some deep, unsettled feeling inside me had told me something was wrong in Irrín. I hadn't pursued romantic connections back in Zilvaren, though I'd had plenty of opportunities to do so. I'd had responsibilities. Keeping Hayden out of trouble had been a full-time job, for one, and then there had always been the problem of keeping food on the table and water in our bellies. Developing a relationship with somebody would have been a fool's errand that would have distracted me from the business of survival.

But this was nothing like that. This . . . was two stars colliding. The end of everything and the beginning at the same time. The idea of forming a relationship with someone back in Zilvaren was trivial in comparison to this. Fisher was *everything*. I was attuned to him. I could feel the shifts in his moods like the ebb and flow of the tides that I had read so much about, and worrying about him while we were apart was enough to drive me mad.

I had to admit, the idea of leaving with him and returning to Cah-lish rather than Irrín, where we would be able to sleep in a warm bed and have some privacy, was appealing. It would halt my thoughts from racing, even if it was only for a night.

Okay. I'll take your word for it. And yes, I'll come back there with you tonight. But on one condition.

Kingfisher arched an eyebrow at me. *Oh? Making demands, are we, Your Highness?*

He was teasing me when he called me that, but I didn't like it. I didn't want there to be any greater a divide between us, and the fact that I was now half vampire was already causing issues. I could stand to be out on the terrace in the early morning daylight, but not for long. Once the sun was high overhead, I found myself exhausted to the point of nausea, and I couldn't bear the direct light on my skin. I could still eat, but my appetite for food was much decreased, which I hated. And I could deny it as much as I liked: I didn't *have* to feed to survive the way Taladaius and the other members of the Sanasrothian Court did...but I *wanted* to. Since I'd awo-ken, a vague curiosity had slumbered within me, and now that I had fed from Fisher, it seemed to have stirred and was stretching its legs. Even now, my throat felt scratchy, as if I was coming down with a cold.

Technically, I represented everything Fisher detested...and I was a queen now, too? My mate's disdain for royalty was understandable. My home was ruled by a tyrant queen. Zilvaren suffered every day because of Madra, but Fisher had also experienced pain at her hands. Madra had closed the quicksilver portals and taken his father from him. Not to mention that the Yvelian throne had been stolen by King Belikon, who had tortured Fisher his entire life, and then Malcolm, ruler of the Blood Court, had come along and thrown him into the maze. It made perfect sense that there would be a sharp edge to his tone when he said the words *Your Highness*. But hearing that edge in his voice when he spoke to me? That hurt more than I cared to admit.

I did my best to cast the niggling sensation in my stomach aside. *I suppose I am*, I told him. *Don't worry. I'm not asking anything too unreason-able. At least, I hope I'm not.*

Go on.

I want to train properly. With you. Our time at the Blood Court isn't for-ever. I am not their real *queen. I have no interest in flouncing around Ammon-traíeth, pretending to lord it over my reluctant subjects. I need to stay fit, and I still need to learn how to wield Solace properly. The sword is so heavy, I can barely hold it.*

Fisher didn't even bat an eyelid. *Done. Though you might want to train with Lorreth, if you* really *want to learn.*

Why not you?

He gave me the faintest look of reproval, as if I should already know the answer to this. *I can run drills with you, Osha. I can raise a sword to you and pull my blows. I can show you footwork and teach you about warcraft. What I* cannot *do is attack you like it's real. And that's what you need, if you truly want to learn how to fight with a sword. The stakes must be genuine for you to learn how to think and react under pressure. And I will never come at you with everything I've got. You are my mate. I'm in love with you. I couldn't do that even if I wanted to. Which...* he added softly, *I do not.*

"Are you two even list—urgh! They're not even listening." Carrion was on his feet, standing over the bag of heads. Lorreth watched him, dark eyes full of amusement, apparently trying not to laugh. Taladaius had rolled one of the heads out of the bag and was inspecting it closely while studiously ignoring Carrion. How he managed it, I would never know. It was as if he could completely tune him out.

I felt a frisson of annoyance rise in Fisher, though he didn't show it outwardly when he addressed the smuggler. "Apologies, Swift. You have our full and rapt attention. What seems to be the issue?"

"I was just going to point out that there is something else worth noting about these feeders," he said tartly. "But if no one's interested in hearing what that is—"

"Just spit it out," Fisher commanded.

"Well, I mean, I haven't spent a great deal of time studying feed-ers, but—" He shoved another slice of apple into his mouth as he bent over the rotting heads, squinting at them. At least he finished chewing before he finished his sentence. "From what I can recall, they normally come from Yvelia, right?"

"Yes, of course," Lorreth answered.

"Well, these ones are from Zilvaren."

"What?" I took an involuntary step forward. "What are you talking about?"

"Are the feeders normally marked here? Tattoos and the like?" Carrion asked.

Taladaius looked up, turning his stoic gaze upon Carrion. "Some slaves are branded when they're turned, yes, but most members of court don't bother. Feeders are bound to the high blood who made them, no matter what. They will only obey their sires. They have no choice in the matter. Runes and tags of ownership are never required since deadstock cannot be stolen."

Feeder. High blood. Deadstock.

There was so much to unpack in that statement and no real time to do so. Taladaius continued, "Why? What have you noticed?"

Carrion shrugged and dropped into a crouch, humming thoughtfully as he studied the head that was half sticking out of the bag. He quickly grew frustrated and took hold of the sack, upending it so that all eight of the heads toppled out and went rolling across the floor.

He went to the female head first—the one that had been sticking out of the bag—and carved himself off another slice of the apple, sliding it into his mouth and crunching loudly. "Two things. The first is right there," he said, nodding down at the head. "On its neck. That looks like a pretty intentional marking to me. Saeris, come and tell me what you make of it."

One of the dismembered heads opened its mouth, thick black ichor running over its chipped teeth and pooling on the floor. Its bloodshot eyes rolled wildly in its head. Nasty. "I can see just fine from here, thanks."

Carrion rolled his eyes. He huffed as he made his way across the council chamber and reached out for my wrist—

Kingfisher was suddenly there, angled in front of me. Surprisingly, his expression was blank. "Do you like having fingernails, Carrion?" he asked politely.

"I—" Carrion gaped. "I do, actually."

"I thought so." My mate said nothing more.

Carrion quirked an eyebrow, pulling a face, widening his eyes as he looked at me out of the corner of his eye. "All right, then. I take it that means that I should *not* attempt to touch your girlfriend?"

"Oh, sinners," Lorreth muttered under his breath.

"She isn't my girlfriend. She's my mate," Fisher said quite amicably. "And if any part of your body, literally *any* part of it, comes into contact with hers, then I will remove it."

Carrion thought about this. "What about if she's hanging off a cliff by one hand and can't hold on much longer? Can I touch her then?"

"Where am I in this *unlikely* scenario?"

"Probably dead."

Fisher just gave him a tight smile. "If *I'm* dead, then—"

"Urgh! You're ridiculous, both of you! I'd rather poke a dismembered head than bear witness to *this*. Just stop already!" I shoved them aside and crossed the chamber to the godscursed heads. Lorreth stooped and picked up the female feeder's head by the hair, holding it out for me to see.

Sure enough, there was a mark on its neck, just as Carrion had said. My stomach bottomed out the second I saw it. Carrion had known *precisely* what it was. "Oh," I whispered.

The mark, an *X* behind the female's earlobe, had once been a simple tattoo, but now it was made of knotted veins, bulging up beneath the skin. They looked necrotic, and they pulsed, echoing with the memory of a heartbeat that no longer fed them.

My hand raised of its own accord, moving to *my* neck and the small black cross hidden behind my hair.

I couldn't say the words. Fisher did it, albeit a little breathlessly. "Your sterilization mark? Is that what..." He nodded to the head that Lorreth still held. *"Does she have it, too?"*

I nodded.

"The *second* clue that these feeders aren't Yvelian is staring you right in the face," Carrion said.

My stomach rolled at the weightless, sick feeling that formed there. "Their ears."

"Gods alive," Taladaius groaned. "How did none of us notice? They're round! Their fucking ears are round. They're *human*."

"They could have been here from before," I said. "Yvelia was full of humans once, back before the blood curse, right?"

But my maker was shaking his head. "Deadstock have a limited shelf life here. The dark magic that causes them to rise from death reanimates them, yes, but it is temporary. Their bodies still decay. Eventually they fall apart and go back to the dirt. Five years. Maybe ten. These feeders have been dead weeks rather than months. They still have their hair. Some of them have their tongues—

"All right. All right. I...get the picture." I was suddenly overcome with the need to sit down. "What does this mean, then? People are jumping into the quicksilver pool in Zilvaren whenever *we* open the gates? They're coming through in Cahlish and...being attacked *there*?"

"No." Fisher's expression was stormy. His leathers creaked as he paced up and down, trying to piece this together. "They can't have come through in Cahlish. They would have been found immediately. And anyway, they would have to *want* to come here specifically for the quicksilver to deliver them here. And forgive me if I'm wrong, but the people in Zilvaren know nothing of this place."

"Right." Carrion nodded.

"It's also impossible for someone to just sneak into Madra's palace and hide in the Hall of Mirrors on the off chance that the quicksilver will wake. No..." Fisher shook his head. "This is intentional. This is *Madra's* doing. This...is how the rot got here in the first place."

"You think *she* infected them with it?" Lorreth asked. "We've seen that kind of warfare before. Fae, sick with one illness or another, sent into the middle of military camps to kill off all the warriors there."

Fisher said nothing, his face a mask of furious concentration. The sound of his footsteps echoed around the chamber as he prowled up and down like a caged beast.

She hears...

The quicksilver laughed in the back of my mind, as if it knew the answer to these questions we were trying to unravel and had no plans of shedding light on the situation. Its whispers had been plaguing me for days now, and they were growing louder. It was perfect timing that it would choose *now* to harass me.

I closed my eyes, hands trembling at my sides. I couldn't think straight. I couldn't *breathe*. A stab of pain relayed up my arm as the whispers grew louder still, the runes on the back of my right hand throbbing...

She hears us. Oh yes, she hears. She will come. Soon. Soon. Soon.

Finally, I'd had enough. My eyes snapped open. "There's a *pool* here, isn't there? It's small, but I can sense it."

Fisher stopped his pacing. He looked at me questioningly, then slowly turned his frown on Taladaius, whose gray eyes seemed reflective as mirrors for a moment. My maker drew a long, displeased breath, and then nodded. "Yes," he said, confirming my suspicions. "Ammontraíeth has *always* had a pool."

6

TITLES

SAERIS

A SEPULCHRE.

The Blood Court kept its quicksilver in *a fucking sepulchre* on one of the lower floors of the palace. I had surveyed the dark necropolis, trying not to stare into the empty eye sockets of the stacked skulls that formed the walls, feeling both vindicated and sick to my stomach. The dull chatter in the back of my head made sense now. I hadn't fabricated it. But the knowledge that the pool—it *was* small; I'd been right about that—was here meant that I would have no peace from it now. It seemed that I wouldn't be able to escape the miserable thrum of pain that beat behind my runes, either.

Fisher hadn't seemed as perturbed as I would have expected him to be. "You know, *this* isn't a bad thing," he'd said.

"It *isn't?*"

"No, Osha. I meant it back in the council chamber. You're coming back to Cahlish with me tonight. This just means our journey will be much easier. No more riding across the dead fields." It took hours to cross the dead fields. Feral feeders lived in burrows dug deep into the ash and char. They hid from the sun below ground during the day, but the moment the sun began to dip, they emerged from their bolt-holes with a mind to feed. They wouldn't attack me, but they posed a threat to the horses. To Kingfisher and Lorreth, too. With Fisher's magic decommissioned on this side of the Darn, we hadn't been able to use his shadow gates, but now we didn't need to.

We had access to a pool.

So I'd made relics out of a chain kindly supplied by Taladaius, a signet ring belonging to Lorreth, and a small charm of one of the gods that Fisher attached to a collar for Onyx, and that had been that. Less than an hour later, we'd made use of the unexpected resource, and now here we were, back at Cahlish, none the worse for wear from the experience.

A stunning dress in hunter-green velvet had been waiting for me, laid out on Fisher's bed, when I'd gone to freshen up. Tiny jewels— emeralds, I suspected—decorated the plunging neckline. The sleeves had been embroidered with green stitching, subtle, barely visible, depicting a pattern that, upon close inspection, turned out to be tiny leaping foxes.

A beautiful dress, undeniably.

I had run my hand over the soft material, something pinching tight behind my solar plexus.

It would fit me perfectly. Evidently, it had been *made* for me. But...

I'd still been wearing my fighting leathers when I'd met Fisher on the stairs. My mate had beamed at me, apparently unfazed that I hadn't chosen to don the dress, but a kernel of guilt had taken root in my chest. I was still feeling a little bad about my decision when we arrived together at the dining room.

"You sure you're ready for this?" Fisher said, holding his hand against the doorknob.

"Yes. I'm sure."

"Really?"

"When did *you* get so anxious?" I grinned at him. "I promise I'm ready. After those feeders crossing the river? And seeing that mark? We all need a moment. This will be good for *all* of us." I said the words. I was supposed to. I smiled because I was supposed to do that, too, but the thoughts churned relentlessly in the back of my head regardless:

Were the infected feeders sent by Madra?

How had they gotten here from Zilvaren?

How the *fuck* were we going to kill them?

Would there be *more*?

I knew the same worries plagued Fisher. He did a beautiful job of hiding it, though. A part of me resented that we were playing this game of pretend, but what I'd just said was true. We *did* need some kind of respite.

"Okay, then. If you're sure—"

"Fisher!" I laughed. "Just open the door!"

He hid a smirk as he turned the handle and swung open the dining room door for me. I seized hold of the image, capturing it quickly; a smile from the Lord of Cahlish was a rare thing. I'd started capturing each moment it happened on an imaginary vellum, filing the memories away in my mind to keep forever. The sight of his upturned mouth and the tentative laughter in his eyes made a nice addition to my collection.

"I told them you were coming," he confessed, the admission shyly made. Had I ever seen him like this before? Nope. It was unbearably sweet. There was no time to savor this new side of Fisher, though, because as soon as the door swung open, a wave of excitement and cheering exploded inside the dining room.

Renfis stood, raising a glass of whiskey in the air.

Te Léna and a handsome male with dark brown skin—her mate, I assumed—grinned, crying out their welcomes.

Joining them were Lorreth and Archer, Danya and Iseabail...

...and over the top of the warm welcome came the excited squeal of a small white fox.

"Onyx!"

As soon as we'd arrived back at Cahlish, the fox had darted off—to go hunting, I'd assumed—but apparently he'd sneaked into the dining room before us and reacquainted himself with our friends. He leaped out of Iseabail's lap and darted across the dining room in a streak of white and black. I barely had time to get my hands out in front of me before he launched himself into my arms and began licking my face and neck. "Oh—Oh my goodness. Hey, buddy. Hi, hi, hi. Yes, I'm happy to see you, too." He chittered, squirming all over the place. Anyone would have thought he hadn't seen me in a year.

Fisher made a show of looking grumpy about it, but there was that shadow of a smile again, hovering at the corners of his mouth as the little fox twisted in my arms and rained affection down on him as well.

"I should probably take him to Ballard," Fisher said. "Wendy could look after him. Just until all of this blows over."

I pretended to scowl at him. "You wouldn't dare."

Fisher winked surreptitiously, letting me know that he was joking. "Far be it from me to come between a female and her fox."

It had only been a couple of days, but Onyx seemed completely recovered from his ordeal, crossing the mountain range and being chased by the feeders. His paws were fine. His coat was pure white, thick and full. The limp that had been troubling him was gone now, too. I buried my face in his fur and inhaled deeply, using the action to hide the fact that I was taking a moment.

This was a lot. I hadn't expected to feel so overwhelmed. I looked up, beaming at my mate. "I didn't realize this was such an official gathering."

"Of course it is!" Ren cried. "The last time most of us saw you, we were shoving you up into a shadow gate in the library. Having you back here at Cahlish in one piece is something to be celebrated!"

Their expressions bore no animosity, but something squeezed unpleasantly in my chest. "In one piece" was a bit of a stretch. I wasn't the same person I had been when Ren and Lorreth had shoved me through that shadow gate. Not even remotely. What was I to them now? Their friend? Their *enemy*?

Fisher still loved me, but our souls had been bound by the gods. No matter what, we were fated to be together. There were no invisible ties binding me to any of the people before me. Lorreth, Ren, and Danya had spent centuries fighting against Malcolm's horde. They'd lost scores of people, people they'd loved, in the pursuit of protecting Yvelia from the evil that inhabited Sanasroth. And now here I was, half vampire, half the thing they hated most in the world, and they were rushing to greet me.

I hadn't had friends in Zilvaren. Friends were expensive. In the end, they always cost you. Your food. Your water. Your money. Your safety. Your *life*. Connections with others taxed your resources in a place like the Third, and I never had enough of anything to begin with. I'd told myself, when I'd woken up in Ammontraíeth and discovered what I'd become, that it didn't matter to me if I lost the people in this room because of it. But now that they were all smiling warmly at me and coming forward to hug me, a part of me cracked and broke inside.

It would have mattered.

It would have mattered *a lot*.

Ren was first to hug me. It was his reaction I'd worried most about. He hadn't come to visit me in Sanasroth like Lorreth had. When I'd asked Fisher if I should expect him, he'd apologized and said he'd left him in charge of Irrín and that he wasn't able to leave the camp, but I'd seen through his reasoning. I'd known it for what it was: an excuse. I hadn't pushed, though. I hadn't wanted to have my suspicions confirmed. But there was no disgust or fear on the general's face as he drew me to him tight. "I can't tell you how good it is to see you," he said into my hair.

"All right, that's enough," Fisher grumbled.

Renfis pulled back, laughing. "I'm not going to say it outright, but you know how you're behaving, right?" he said.

Fisher made a show of scowling, but he shoved his friend playfully. Lorreth threw his arm around my shoulder, which didn't seem to make Fisher any happier, but he bore his brothers showing their affection for me with *some* grace, at least. Lorreth's grin fell when Iseabail, the auburn-haired witch, stepped forward to greet me. He muttered something about treacherous blood, and when she reached out to take my hand in hers, he made a sound of disgust and retracted his arm, stalking away to take his seat at the dining table.

"It's nice to meet again under less stressful circumstances," she said, in her lilting cadence. Now that I came to think about it, her accent was fairly similar to Renfis's. I would have to ask him if they hailed from the same part of Yvelia. The witch was stunning in a loose, dark blue blouse; a leather belt; and a long, flowing black skirt that swirled around her heeled boots. Her thick, wavy hair was unbound and red as a blazing sunset. "I hope you don't mind that I've invaded your welcome-back dinner? Te Léna invited me. I would have returned home a week ago, but I've been put to work here. I'm surprised to find that I'm enjoying some time away from the clan."

She spoke as if she was overstaying her welcome in my home. Cahlish was *Kingfisher's* ancestral seat. It had been in his family for as long as it had stood. It was strange to have anyone act as if it belonged to me. It didn't. Or...sinners, maybe it did now? Just a little bit. It was all so confusing. Fuck, I hadn't had *nearly* enough time to wrap my head around all of this.

"Don't you dare apologize for staying. We would have lost Everlayne without you. And you've been helping Te Léna work the quicksilver out of Kingfisher, too. There isn't a person here who resents your presence."

Iseabail glowed, her eyes dancing as she laughed. Squeezing my hand, she nodded her head back over her shoulder, raising her eyebrows. "I appreciate the sentiment, I really do. But I think there's at least one person who'd prefer it if I were dead in a ditch rather than here, fouling up the halls of Cahlish with my witch's blood."

Lorreth's hearing was just as good as any of the other members of the Fae in the room. He heard every word Iseabail said, and from the thunderous look on his face, he wasn't happy. Iseabail didn't seem to care, though. "Don't worry. *I'm* not one for drama, even when others seem intent on causing it."

There was a loud clatter from the table; Lorreth had knocked over his ale and was furiously trying to mop it up with a napkin.

Iseabail snorted.

"Why does he hate your kind so much?" I knew Lorreth to be funny, kind, and thoughtful. Seeing him like this around a woman who had helped us all so much was genuinely confounding.

Iseabail's smile faded. "Ach. It's probably best if I let him tell you that one."

Te Léna and her mate, Maynir, wore matching outfits of gold and taupe. They overflowed with happiness as they spoke to Fisher and me, telling us all that had happened in the past few days at Cahlish. The light Te Léna cast off only dimmed when I asked after Everlayne's progress, and she had to confess that Kingfisher's sister was still sleeping and couldn't seem to wake. She brightened quickly, though. "I'll take you to see her in the morning, if you like. Hearing your voice might be the final push she needs to wake up."

"I'd love that." I'd spent only a few days with Layne at the Winter Palace before Fisher had swept me away into the night. With the exception of Iseabail and Te Léna, she knew everyone else in the dining room far better than she knew me. It was unlikely that *I* would be the one to break Everlayne's fugue state, but I was willing to give it a shot.

Danya was last to greet me. The last time I'd seen her, her hair had flowed halfway down her back, but it was short now, cropped to her jaw on the left, shorn to the scalp on the right. Dressed in fighting leathers and a patinaed silver breastplate stamped with the head of a howling wolf, she was stiff as a board when she came to stand in front of me.

"Alchemist," she said curtly.

"Danya," I answered.

"Where's the redhead?"

"Who?"

"The annoying male with witty comebacks."

"You think *Carrion* is funny?"

Danya rolled her eyes. "Never mind."

"He'll be here soon," I said quickly. "He went to the bath house. He was taking longer than expected, so we came on ahead."

"Okay. I'll go find him," she said, shrugging.

"No! No, uh...don't do that." He hadn't said as much, but I had a sneaking suspicion that Carrion had gone in search of more than a bath. The water sprites he had *befriended* recently apparently spent most of their time down in the baths, and I didn't want Danya walking in on him in a compromising situation with any—or all—of them. Why, I didn't know. Carrion and Danya together would be the kind of living hell that I had no desire to experience firsthand—but he *was* my friend, and friends watched each other's backs. "He'll be here any moment, and I...I wanted to ask you about your new hairstyle. What prompted the dramatic cut?"

She stared at me blankly. "A burning corpse set me on fire."

Gods a-fucking-live. Perfect. "Oh. Okay. I thought it was some new, edgy form of self-expression."

"The length of a warrior's hair is directly related to their skill in battle. Mine was longer than Ren's and Lorreth's put together. I would never have cut it to look... *edgy*."

Whew. I was not getting *anywhere* here. "I heard that you were injured during the fight. Couldn't Te Léna have restored your hair when she healed you?"

The female looked at me like she did not understand me one bit. "There are no shortcuts to glory, Alchemist. For my brother's sake, I'm glad you didn't die in Gillethrye. He already lost enough people to that accursed city. For my own part, I'm glad you didn't die because an Alchemist is a rare thing." She quickly cast her eyes to the floor, dipping her head in a perfunctory display of deference. "If you'll excuse me."

She took up a place at the table opposite Lorreth. She didn't seem particularly impressed by his presence, either. Since I'd splintered her sword into hundreds of shards, reforged it, and inadvertently gifted it to Lorreth, she'd been far from civil toward the other member of the Lupo Proelia. Not that I'd seen her have a kind word for anybody, ever, mind you.

Across the dining room, I felt the weight of Fisher's eyes on me. He stood with Ren, head bowed as he listened to his friend, but his focus was all for me. He had come to Ammontraíeth kitted out for war, but here, in his home, with his family close, he wore only a loose black shirt and black pants. The fire behind the two males painted their faces with an orange glow and lightened the waves of his thick hair to a warm, dark brown.

Gods, but he was perfect.

His cheeks were flushed from the heat of the fire, his jaw marked with dark stubble, full lips parted. He nodded, sparing Ren the shortest of sidelong glances, then looked back at me. His burning gaze landed with the force of a blow that would have taken me to my knees if we weren't among friends.

I can hear you from here, y'know. Fisher's deep growl brushed against my mind like velvet.

What? I didn't say a word. I didn't even think *anything.*

The left side of his mouth kicked up a touch. *You didn't need to. Your eyes are saying plenty.*

Fuck.

You okay, Little Osha? You've gone red.

I'm fine. I'm over here, minding my own business. Are you *fine? You're supposed to be listening to your friend, not accusing* me *of things.*

Oh, I'm listening to him. He lowered his eyes to his feet. A weightlessness pulled at my stomach when he looked back up at me from under ink-black lashes. *It's hard to concentrate on camp logistics when I can smell you across the room, though, Osha.*

I was going to die of embarrassment. *You cannot.*

Across the room, I caught the flash of wickedly sharp canine as a suggestive smile parted Fisher's lips. *Be under no illusion, Little Osha. You are* all *I can smell.*

He was exaggerating. But could he exaggerate? Did the Fae consider emphasizing the truth to be the same as lying? I made a mental note to look that up. For now, I found myself growing more convinced that he was telling the truth. Because I could smell *him*, too.

Bruised herbs.

Citrus.

Smoke.

Leather.

Pine, and cold mountain air.

And underneath it all, the maddening scent of him—the scent that made him unique and made *me* want to climb the fucking walls. A trace of pheromones that sent electricity zipping up the length of my spine and—

"Dinner is about to be served, mistress."

Oh.

Archer was standing right in front of me. The top of the fire sprite's head barely reached my stomach. He had no hair to speak of. His skin was made of blackened coal, and thin fissures snaked across his fore- head and his cheeks, threads of what looked like embers burning within the depths of them. I'd never seen him wear clothes before, but tonight he had donned a thick hunter-green vest with gold buttons down the front that covered most of his rotund little belly.

"Wow. You're looking very handsome tonight, Archer!" I stepped back, making a show of taking him in.

Archer beamed with pride. "Thank you, mistress. We normally have no need for clothes, but sometimes we dress nicely for special occasions." He tugged at the bottom of the vest—or jerkin—proudly puffing out his chest. "We all consider your return to Cahlish a very special occasion indeed!"

"Well, thank you, Archer. That's very sweet."

The fire sprite held out his hands, gesturing for me to follow him as he crossed the dining room. When I'd first dined in this hall, Archer had damn near had a heart attack when he'd discovered me sitting in the seat on Fisher's left—but that was precisely where he led me now, as he guided me to the table.

"Come, come. You must sit. It is custom, mistress. The lady of the house should be seated before the food is brought in."

"Oh. Oh, I don't think—you don't need to call me mistress, Archer. I'm not the lady of the house."

"Yes, you are."

The words sent a bolt of panic through me. Fisher was behind me, and he'd heard every word.

"No other will ever claim this seat." He said it matter-of-factly, drawing out the chair in question, gesturing for me to sit down. "From now on, you *are* Lady of Cahlish."

Archer made a little squeak of excitement, covering his mouth with his hand, the flames flickering within his otherwise black eyes flaring brightly.

Well, shit. I sat down. What choice did I have? If I didn't, my legs were going to give out and dump me in the chair regardless. *Don't you think I have enough new titles for the time being?*

Whatever do you mean? Fisher took his seat at the head of the table next to me, his expression carefully controlled as he took in those gathered around him in their respective seats.

Mate. Queen of Sanasroth. King Killer—

A tightness formed between Fisher's brows. *They're calling you that?*

They are. And now you want to add Lady of Cahlish to the mix? It wasn't that I didn't want to be his partner in all things. I did. But the past few weeks had been surreal. I had been bound to him, forced to obey if he issued a command, fed and clothed only by the good graces of others. And now I was a queen with unknown resources at my fingertips. Even though tensions ran high back in Ammontraíeth, I was still regent, and as such I needn't want for anything. It boggled the mind to consider it: me, a street rat from the Third, with handmaids to help dress me and bathe me, and seamstresses falling over themselves to be the first to make me a dress. But all those things felt like they were pulling me away from myself. I didn't need rich foods and rare wines. I didn't want fine dresses and people fussing over me.

I was still a plague rat from the Third. Clean water and simple fare were all I needed. A second set of sturdy clothes and a comfortable place to sleep were still a luxury beyond measure, and Fisher understood that. I knew he did. He had suffered far longer than I had and in far worse conditions. The Third had been bad at the best of times, but the maze had been infinitely worse. Yet... he was no stranger to aristocracy. Born into a noble house, he'd *come* from this, which made it easy to return to. I was still figuring things out.

Kingfisher placed a hand on my leg under the table. He didn't say anything else on the matter and didn't need to. A soothing calm washed over me, easing the tension in my bones. He didn't want me to worry or feel uncomfortable, especially in front of everyone else. There would be time to discuss the matter of my title later.

Food started streaming in on platters. Roasted pork and dressed fowl. A variety of cheeses and colorful fruits. Vegetables and hearty pies with steam rising from their crusts. Sweet and savory smells hung thick in the air, complementing each other and causing several stomachs around the table to growl. The army of fire sprites who carried in our dinner weren't surprised when Kingfisher conjured a low, long stone table that ran parallel to our own, complete with small stone stools, and told the sprites to join us and eat; this was obviously something that had happened before. Archer sat at the head of the sprites' table, kicking his short legs, looking pleased as punch as he and his friends fell upon their food.

Sprites were messy eaters. A good deal of food dropped to the floor before ever making it to their mouths, which made their table far more popular with Onyx than ours. The fox slipped between the stools and table legs, scarfing down morsels of chicken and pastry like he worried he'd never be fed again.

An easy peace existed as we ate, one that I had never known before. Lorreth and Ren traded playful insults back and forth. Danya made stilted but polite conversation with Maynir. Te Léna and Iseabail chatted with Fisher and me, and though there were plenty of serious things to be discussed, the conversation was kept as light as possible.

An evening of kinship and calm.

There was still so much to be uncertain about, but tonight we were all taking a collective breath, and it felt good.

Just as the main course was winding down, the dining room doors swung open and Carrion entered, wearing a loose white shirt unbuttoned halfway down his chest and a pair of black pants. His hair was swept back from his face, clumped together in wet strands, still damp from the baths, the usual gold and copper highlights temporarily cast in bronze. His skin had a healthy glow to it, either from the heat of the baths or from some other deviant activity that I didn't want to think about. He grinned rakishly at the entire table as he crossed the room and took up the empty seat next to me that Iseabail had saved for him.

"Evening all. Apologies for the late entrance. I had to work up an appetite before I came to eat." Before anyone had a chance to answer, he leaned close to me and whispered, "I heard from Lorreth that you got yourself a new sex tattoo at your coronation. Can I see it?"

Merciful saints and sinners. He'd been in the room three seconds, and I already wanted to kill him. It was bad enough that I'd had to drink from Fisher in front of the entire Blood Court. I liked the new tattoo I'd earned in the process, but acquiring it that way, in front of everyone, had been mortifying. "I will pay you twenty chits to fuck off right now," I growled back at him.

Carrion laughed off the offer, and his scent hit the back of my nose—not necessarily offensive, but very, *very* obvious. It was pungent as wine and rich as perfume. I knew the others smelled it, too, from the way they all started politely breathing though their mouths.

This is what they'd all been smelling on me whenever Fisher and I were together? Gods alive, that was mortifying.

"Smells like you worked hard for that appetite," Danya drawled, spearing a piece of fish onto her fork. Now that I looked at her, she wasn't breathing through her mouth. Strangely enough, she seemed to be the only one who was inhaling deeply through her nose. Gross. She leaned across the table, angling her torso in Carrion's direction. "From the smell of you, you must be ravenous."

Oh no. No, no, no. This wasn't happening. Was she *flirting* with him? Knowing that he'd just come from having sex with *at least* one other person? That was just…right up Carrion's street. Urgh. Kingfisher groaned quietly next to me, as disturbed by what was happening as I was.

"If they procreate, I'm banishing them from Cahlish. A combination of the two of *them* would probably tear open some sort of hell gate and suck the entire estate through it."

"I heard that," Carrion said, cheerfully shoving a piece of roasted carrot into his mouth.

"You were supposed to. Don't get any ideas," Fisher grumbled. "You're not allowed to fuck a member of the Lupo Proelia."

Danya lounged back into her seat, eyeing Carrion with a predatory glint in her eye that made me a little afraid for him. "And what about me? Can a member of the Lupo Proelia fuck a newly anointed member of the Fae?"

Fisher was a member of the Lupo Proelia, and he was fucking a newly anointed member of the Fae. Or at least I hoped he would soon. Since he couldn't say no to Danya, he tactfully chose to say nothing at all.

Carrion waggled his eyebrows at me suggestively. "Don't worry, sunshine. I'm sure she doesn't want to marry me."

Danya snorted, inspecting her nails. "Definitely not."

"See." The smuggler looked delighted. "There's nothing wrong with blowing off a little steam here and there, as *you* well know." He started loading up his plate with a thick slab of pie. "It's not like I'll be planning a wedding anytime soon. I won't be overshadowing *yours*."

I choked on my wine. "What the *hell?*"

Archer halted his conversation with his friends and let out a gasp. In a split second he had jumped up on his stool and was standing on it, shaking with excitement. Flames broke out on his right shoulder, but he was so distracted that he didn't even try to put it out. "Oh, yes. *Yes!* I've been waiting to start making the wedding arrangements. Is it time?"

Te Léna and Iseabail laughed at the sprite's enthusiasm. But Ren and Lorreth both looked uncomfortably down at their plates.

A wedding? No one had said anything about a *wedding*. Fisher had never specifically asked me if I would marry him. Did the Fae even do the whole dropping-down-on-one-knee-proposal thing?

Maybe agreeing to the mating bond was tantamount to agreeing to marry someone. I was so woefully uneducated when it came to Fae traditions. I was covered in a cold sweat when I turned to Fisher...

And found his face devoid of emotion. "There isn't going to be a wedding," he said.

Te Léna's broad smile evaporated. She sagged back into her chair. "Don't be silly. Of course there will." She blinked as she tried to process what she was hearing. "You can't tell me that you don't *want* to get married?"

"We don't need a ceremony to join us together, Te Léna." He laughed, but the sound felt clipped. Off, somehow. "We're God-Bound. I'd say that trumps getting married, don't you?"

"Well, yes. The way you two are bound is remarkable." Her warm brown eyes traveled up and down our inked arms even as she said it. "But... the ceremony is... it's beautiful, and..." She looked like she was about to cry.

"I don't need a ceremony," Fisher said, softening his tone a little. His jade eyes speared me through when they landed on me. "Do you, Osha? A hall full of people you don't know, poking and prodding at you. Everybody looking at us? Everybody watching?"

Relief coursed through me. Gods, I would have married him, of course I would have, but it wasn't something I *needed* in any way, either. And after the coronation ceremony in Ammontraíeth, the last thing I wanted right now was to be made a spectacle of all over again. "No. No, I don't." I answered quickly. Definitively. And it was the answer Fisher was looking for, which was why the look of relief on his face made sense... but not the flicker of disappointment that came after it.

Archer looked like *he* was about to cry.

Slowly, the little fire sprite sank back down onto his stool.

7

HOME

SAERIS

IT WAS LATE by the time dinner was done. Everyone was yawning and complaining that they had overeaten. Everyone, that was, except me.

I was wide awake, and I'd barely touched the food on my plate. My stomach was a quarter of the size it had been, and it had already been small to begin with, thanks to growing up in the Third.

Kingfisher walked me through the halls of Cahlish back to his rooms with his hand resting easily in the small of my back.

We had barely been alone since I'd transitioned, and this... well, it felt a little strange. There had always been tension between us, but this felt different. I knew him better now. It was strange, but it was as if I knew *myself* better. I had undergone a major transformation, there was no denying that. But I kept searching for the things that were different about myself, and all I kept finding were things that were the same. The things that really mattered hadn't changed, and that was reassuring.

I was independent. My temper was still quick to rise. My sense of humor was still dry. I still loved the smell of coffee, and the thick flaky pastries I had first eaten in Ballard.

And I still loved the male walking beside me.

I'd fought my feelings for him for so long that giving them space to breathe now felt a little frightening.

As I could now feel Fisher's emotions bleeding into mine, my own must have bled into his, too. When we reached his bedroom, he didn't immediately go inside. Instead, he spun me around, hands at my waist, and pressed me back against the carved oak door, leaning into me so his chest was flush against mine. His huge frame dwarfed mine. A wall of muscle met my palms when I laid them against his chest.

"You know I would marry you," he rushed out. "You must know that I *want* to."

Blood rushed to my cheeks. "Oh. Uh…" I didn't have the first clue what to say. "It's okay. Really. If you're not the marrying type—"

"I'm not." His eyes were *burning*. "The marrying type. I never have been. Before, the very idea would have sent me running for the hills. I just… I could never imagine the kind of love I would need to feel to choose that path for myself. But now I don't need to imagine. Now I can't think of anything I want to do more. Marrying you would be…" He shook his head, his eyes searching my face.

"Then *why?*" I whispered. "Back at dinner, you said…" I frowned, trying to remember his exact words.

"I didn't lie. I still can't do that," he said, tucking a wave of my hair gently back behind my ear. "I said there wouldn't be a wedding. Because there *can't* be, Saeris."

"I… I'm sorry, I… don't understand."

He blew out a long, sad breath. "A Fae wedding ceremony is extremely sacred. It is the greatest commitment two lovers can undertake in Yvelia. Not because they swear to love and honor each other for all their days. Not because they give each other their hearts, either. It's sacred because they give each other their names. Their *true* names. And I can give you everything else, Osha. But I can't give you that."

He'd explained this to me once. A person's true name held power. With it, a person could control the other. They could command them to do whatever they pleased.

"It's okay, Fisher. You don't need to give me that. I…" I shrugged, not knowing what to say. "I understand. If telling me your true name is impossible, then—"

"I don't know it," he whispered. "I've never known it. We usually receive our true names on our fourteenth birthdays, and my mother—" He blinked. "Well, she died before I turned fourteen. And my father was already gone. So..."

He had never looked so uncomfortable. He ducked his head, not meeting my gaze. "No one knows. If they did, it wouldn't be good. I've hunted through her papers. Her books. I used to hope that she might have written it down in a private journal, perhaps, but I never found one. Her notebooks were full of drawings. Of me, mostly. And of little birds with flashing blue wings. But she drew you a lot, as well." He laughed softly under his breath. "She really did like drawing you. But you see, that's why I wasn't forthright about it before. We can't get married because I don't have a true name to trade."

I stared at him, waiting. When he didn't lift his head to look me in the eyes, a blast of laughter ripped out of me, startling him. "What? What's funny?" he asked.

"I don't have a true name to trade, either, Fisher. I'm just Saeris. You can be just Kingfisher, too."

I expected him to laugh as well. To realize that he was sad for no reason, but gently, he reached for my hand and slowly raised it to his lips. He kissed me, his warm breath fanning out over my skin. "It doesn't work that way, Osha. It doesn't matter that you weren't given a true name. I was, and unless I share it with you, the ceremony can't take root. There's nothing to be done about it. So...I do understand. If marriage is important to you, then—"

"Please stop talking," I breathed. "I think you're about to say something stupid, and I already told you at dinner. I don't need to get married. You were right. We're God-Bound. That's far more significant than a wedding ceremony. We'll live our lives together and be happy, no matter what."

I couldn't read him. His expression was so guarded. It felt as though he were trying to peer into my soul. Clenching his jaw, he exhaled down his nose, then said, "You're sure?"

"Yes, I'm sure!" I laughed, but then sobered quickly, knowing what

I was about to say. "I love you, Fisher." It was the first time I'd said it. "I love you, and nothing else matters beyond that. Wherever *you* are, I'll beg the gods and all the fates to let me be there, too," I whispered.

A slender tendril of shadow trailed along the line of my cheekbone, caressing my skin, soft as a butterfly's wing, as Kingfisher's eyes flashed. "Good," he growled. And then my feet were off the floor, and his hands were below my thighs, lifting me. I reacted, wrapping my legs around his waist, looping my arms around his neck, as he kicked his bedroom door open at last and carried me inside.

"Say it again," he growled.

My cheeks were burning. "Say what?"

"Don't play with me."

"But I—"

"Please."

I leaned back so that I could look at him properly, and the open, raw emotion on his face stole my smile. The hope in his eyes destroyed me.

Like there was a possibility that it wasn't true. Like there was any realm or reality in which I didn't love him, but he was praying that I might. He was out of his godscursed mind. "I love you, Fisher. Of *course* I do. Always. Forever."

His mouth slammed down onto mine. The kiss was pure fire, and relief, and a culmination of all the unanswered tension that had been mounting between us for the past few days. He tasted me, his tongue exploring my mouth, his heart racing against my chest as he wound his fingers into my hair.

When he drew back, the quicksilver in his eye had formed a fine corona around his iris. "There are too many pricked ears in this god-scursed manor," he groaned. "They aren't going to like what they hear over the next few hours."

A shiver sank into my bones at that. He planned on being inside of me for *hours.* He was planning on making me scream. Gods...

When he kissed me again, cradling the back of my head in his hand, something within me shifted. A pin falling into place inside the tumbler of a lock. I could suddenly *feel* the air inside the room. The way it eddied around the furniture and rose up to bloom against the roof rafters. I didn't understand how I knew to do it, but I felt the air thickening. The molecules swaying with the tide of the room stopped, stilling, and my ears suddenly felt as if they were full of cotton wool.

The instant it happened, Fisher noticed, too. He stopped carrying me toward the bed. His spine stiffened, his demeanor changing in an instant. "What just happened?" he asked breathily. "Something…"

"I don't know. I just…I didn't want anyone to hear us. I reached out, and I did it."

He turned his attention back to me, his dark waves falling into his eyes as he ran the bridge of his nose along my jawline. "That's a neat trick, Little Osha. An affinity to a small magic, perhaps. I wonder how many others you have up your sleeve." His voice was a deep rumble that started somewhere down in his boots. "I can't wait for you to show me."

He had a level of faith in me that I had struggled to have in myself over the past few days. The marks on my hands didn't move underneath my skin the way his did sometimes. They were locked in place, the lines beautiful and intricate. I had no idea what they meant, or what I might be capable of because of them.

Fisher's hands skated over my bare arms, fingertips tracing the script that wound around my wrists as if he were contemplating the same thing—but he said nothing further about the binding. A wave of euphoria rocked me as he ducked, running the bridge of his nose along the line of my jaw a second time.

Things had been hard after my mother had died. Hayden was even more of a handful then than he was now. For a few months, after I'd made sure my brother was out cold and dead to the world at night, I'd go and lay on the cracked roof tiles and smoke myself into oblivion. Getting high wasn't the answer. I knew that even as I did it. But, for a brief period of time, it was a crutch that helped get me through the day. I'd stopped when I started feeling like I needed it instead of wanted it.

The high that came whenever Fisher looked at me was way better than any bliss I'd found on the rooftops overlooking the Third. There was no stopping this. And why would I want to stop it? He was more than an addiction. He was life itself. We were separate beating chambers of the same heart now.

My head swam as he buried his face into the crook of my neck and inhaled deeply. He did that so often now, especially when he thought no one else would notice. Goose bumps broke out all over my body as he drew the air into his nose, over my skin. I was boneless. Limp. I couldn't even hold my head up with him standing so close to me. "Do I smell the same?" I whispered.

Fisher cradled the back of my head in his hand, supporting its weight as he pulled back and looked down at me. "Yes," he said roughly. And then, in the same breath, "No. Before, you smelled like fresh crushed leaves and the mountain air before a cold snap. A subtle hint of spices and citrus, and fire smoke."

I stared at his mouth, watching him speak, mesmerized. "And... now?"

"Now, those scents are amplified a thousandfold. You smell like excitement. You smell like laughter. And peace. And love."

"Those things have scents, do they?" I said, teasing him softly.

He sucked his bottom lip into his mouth, nodding. "Mm-hmm. Memories and scents have always been heavily interlinked for me. I smell something, and I immediately experience the association."

"I'm surprised you didn't liken me to the smell of melting sugar, then. Or the warmth of the sun. Or..." It was so hard to breathe properly when he was staring at me like this.

"You forget that I'm a winter creature, Saeris," Fisher murmured. "I don't crave the attention of the sun. The snowcapped mountains, the forest, the frozen river... those places are my home. *You* are home."

He held my face in his hands, lightly stroking my cheeks with his thumbs. He studied my features as if seeing something only he could see—and he couldn't bring himself to look away. It was thrilling to be witnessed so thoroughly. A little frightening, too. I always found myself waiting for the moment, the slight twitch of his mouth, the shadow falling across his eyes, where he took in my flaws and realized that I wasn't perfect. It was like waiting for an ax to fall...only the moment never came.

"Beautiful," he whispered.

"Fisher—"

His eyes had been fixed on my chin; they snapped up to my eyes. "No." He shook his head. "Let me enjoy it. I can already feel what you're thinking, and I want none of it."

"But—"

"I despise the gods, Saeris. I'm Oath Bound by this land and the blood of kings. I swore I would never offer up a word of gratitude to them again, but you *have* made a liar of me. You're a gift that cannot be ignored. My heart..." He swallowed, giving a tiny shake of his head. "I've killed more people than I can count. I lost the parts of myself that knew how to feel anything other than pain and sorrow centuries ago. But for better or worse, you have brought me back to life."

His mouth came crashing down onto mine. I had stilled the air in the bedroom, but Fisher stilled my soul. This was what peace felt like. My chest burned. My throat. My ears. Beneath my palms, Fisher's pulse pounded as he plunged his tongue past my teeth and claimed my mouth.

Pressing a hand into my back, he pulled me into him, huffing a strained breath down his nose. He was hard. Everywhere. All of him. His chest was all packed muscle. His arms, wound tight around me, were bands of steel. And his cock? I could feel just how hard *that* was, straining against his pants; the head of his erection dug into my stomach as he curved himself over me and rocked his hips forward, groaning.

"Three nights. That's how long I've paced this room, fantasizing about fucking you raw, Saeris Fane."

I gasped when he dipped to lave his tongue against my neck. The noises he teased out of me were borderline embarrassing, but I didn't have it in me to care right now. "Only...the past...three?"

"I was praying you'd live all of the others."

I didn't want reminding of the fact that I'd nearly died. Not now, with his strong hands on my body and the sound of the blood in his veins roaring in my ears. "I want you," I whispered. "Please…"

Take me.

Claim me.

Fuck me.

Own me.

The thoughts hammered like a war drum in my head. They were all I could think…and I knew that my mate could hear them, too.

"Careful, Osha," he said roughly, kissing along my jawline. He stopped when he reached my ear, tugging on my earlobe with his teeth. "You might just get what you wish for."

Grabbing mindlessly at his shirt, I arched my back, melting into him. "Please. Please…" I made a strangled sound when I felt his teeth again, this time at my neck. The blissful prick of his canines at the hollow of my throat made me go *very* still. "Oh, fuck," I panted. "Fuck. Fisher…" He didn't bite me. The sharp points of his teeth had broken my skin—I could smell the blood already—but he didn't press further. He hovered there, his heat making my head swim, the smell of him wreaking havoc on my insides, the shape of the sinful smile at his mouth brushing teasingly against me.

He flicked the tip of his tongue over the two points where his teeth had punctured my neck, slowly licking away the blood.

"You taste like the end of the fucking world," he purred. "Just kill me and be done with it. Nothing will ever be better than this."

Fuck!

My body had a mind of its own. I reached up, winding my fingers into Fisher's thick waves, desperately trying to pull him down onto my neck, but he just chuckled, the sound of his rich, deep laughter eliciting an explosion of need right behind my solar plexus.

"You're much stronger than you used to be," he mused. "But I'm still stronger, Little Osha."

In a second, he'd picked me up, thrown me down onto his bed, and pinned my hands over my head. With one leg on either side of my hips, he straddled me, his massive frame looming over me. Dark waves hung into his face, throwing his features into shadow as he smirked suggestively. "Are you particularly attached to those clothes, Osha?"

"Yes!" I laughed, trying to pull my hands free. He was right, I was stronger now, but he was always going to be stronger. And he had gravity on his side, too.

"Then I apologize," he answered with false contrition. Tendrils of smoke and shadow spiraled out of him from his hands and his chest, slipping up from the open neck of his loose shirt like serpents. They snaked around my arms, sliding over my body, leaving a trail of heat in their wake. Particles of magic flashed and caught the light, made manifest as Fisher's power collected and pooled at the center of my heaving chest, slipping beneath my shirt. They diverged, splitting into a hundred even finer threads of power, and then went about its work. My shirt didn't stand a chance.

Where Fisher's shadows touched, the cotton disintegrated and vanished, leaving no trace of its existence behind. My skin was exposed, little by little, until I was naked beneath him. A fire crackled happily in the grate; I was far from cold, but I broke out in goose bumps all the same. My nipples stood proud, my chest rising and falling rapidly as Kingfisher took a long moment to look over my body.

"You are the single most stunning thing I have ever seen, Saeris."

"This...is hardly...fair," I panted. "You're fully clothed and I'm naked as the day I was born."

His smile turned a little lopsided. "You possess the kind of magic that could undress *me*, I'm sure of it. Care to give it a shot?"

"No! Gods, no. What if—what if I set you on fire or something? Or—or, I don't know, accidentally dismember you?"

He laughed wickedly. His eyes didn't leave mine as he lowered himself and slowly took my right nipple into his mouth. *You won't.*

He sucked, pulling gently on the bud of flesh, and my back arched away from the bed. *Gods*, that felt good. He was driving me fucking crazy. I was going to scream if he kept that up...

"Magic is all about intention, Little Osha. You would have to want me dead to set me ablaze. Likewise, you would need to hate me pretty badly to conjure the kind of energy that would sever flesh and bone."

There had been a time when I'd hated him that badly. But now...

The tips of his canines were visible. I stared at them, transfixed. His lips brushed my nipple as he spoke, and shivers cascaded up and down my body.

Now there wasn't a single thing I wouldn't do for this male; he slowly began to move down my body, peppering light kisses over my skin as he went. The underside of my breast. Rib cage. Stomach. Hip bone...

"Where do you think you're going?" I sounded so breathless.

Kingfisher huffed, smiling as he ran the tip of his nose along the skin that led south of my belly button. "Come now, Osha. Where else would an acolyte kneel to worship but at the altar of his god?"

Sinners. The heat of his tongue parted my flesh, and I lost the ability to think. It... it turned out that Fisher's altar was the sensitive flesh between my thighs, and I was... *I* was his god. "Holy shit. That... that feels incredible!"

For over a hundred years, Fisher hadn't eaten a single thing inside that maze. Malcolm had suspended him in a perpetual state of hunger, never dying of that hunger but also never satisfied. He'd always seemed half-starved whenever he'd eaten back at the Winter Palace, and I could never understand why. The way he ate *me* now was just like that—like he was still starving and could not be sated.

He growled into my pussy. "Fuck! You taste incredible."

His hair was so thick; I wound my fingers through it, pulling his head down onto me. Groaning low and deep, Fisher laved the flat of his tongue between my wet folds, and I started to unravel.

It was a disconcerting feeling, coming apart for someone. I could count on one hand the number of people I'd lowered my walls around during sex, but I didn't have a choice with Fisher. He demanded all of me. No half measure would do.

His pace quickened. Sucking gently against my clit, he slowly slid a finger inside me, and I gave in. It was too much. A wave of pleasure rolled lazily up my body. By the time the wave reached my chest, I was arching away from the bed and gasping out loud. "Fuck! Oh my gods!"

"Mm. I like that..." Fisher purred. "No, don't stop. You can grind yourself against my mouth all you want."

Fuuuuuuuck, I was going to *scream.* Fisher hooked an arm around my leg, leveraging his shoulder to pin me down by the hip. He continued to slide his fingers inside me with his other hand, moving faster as he licked and sucked at my core. I rocked against him, feeling my release hovering just out of reach. It was right there. Any second now, I was going to hurtle face-first over the edge—

—and then he did the unthinkable: He stopped.

"Fisher! Wha—*why?*"

He chuckled darkly, the edge of his laughter rough as sin. "Hold on, Little Osha. I'm afraid it's time for a little payback."

"What? What does that m—OhhhhholyfffUCK!" I bounded up from the bed so fast that my spine cracked.

White light filled my head.

A high-pitched hum roared in my ears.

The bright stab of pain at the inside of my thigh electrified my nerve endings. In an instant, the pain became something else.

In Zilvaren, the desert winds blew so hard sometimes that they had been known to strip flesh from bone. This felt a lot like that—ripping apart, one fragment at a time—but in the most addicting, breathtaking way.

Fisher had bitten me and had started to drink. The gods only knew how much of his venom he'd injected into me at once, but I came. On. The. *Spot.*

No sound.

No breath.

No thoughts.

Just a mindless, body-wide orgasm that felt like it was about to break bone.

I barely heard Fisher's satisfied drawl over the explosions going off in my head. "Thaaat's it. Good girl. Ride it out."

I needed to breathe.

Hah!

No chance.

Tiny black spots danced in my vision.

My pulse throbbed slow and hard at my temples.

Dum.

Dum.

Dum!

I dragged down a breath of air, the room coming back into focus.

My pulse was trapped thunder in my veins. "Oh, shit! Oh, shit! What—what the fuck?"

"Easy," Fisher whispered. He prowled up my body, his pupils blown wide open. That narrow silver thread of quicksilver still completely banded his right iris. "Easy. That's it. Breathe." My head swam all over again as he hovered over me, keeping his weight off me, and began slowly kissing my neck.

I swallowed, forcing myself to speak around the spikes of ecstasy that were still rippling through me. "What...the hell just...*happened*?"

"You passed out," Fisher murmured into my neck.

"Passed *out*?"

"Just a little." He made it sound like it was no big deal. That he made females pass out all the time. "Only for a second."

"Fisher!"

He pulled back, fixing me in his gaze from the top of his pushup. "I told you once that I was disappointed by how breakable humans were. Remember?"

Oh, I remembered.

"You're not human anymore, Saeris. Think you can keep up with me now?"

Martyrs. That cocky grin. The taunting glint in his eyes, oscillating between mischief and mayhem. He was so fucking sure of himself... and it was *such* a turn-on.

I wasn't recovered from the bite he'd administered to the inside of my thigh. I felt high, actually, and the delicious buzz floating around inside me was making me feel reckless. I wanted him so fucking badly.

"I can take it," I answered. "Are *you* sure you can handle *me?*"

Laughter erupted out of him, and the sound of it caressed my skin, making me shiver all over again. I had to fight to stop my eyes from rolling back into my head. "Honestly, I'm not sure, Osha," he mused. "I guess there's only one way to find out."

I stripped him out of his clothes, tugging frantically at his shirt and his pants, desperate to be rid of them. He refused to help, insisting that I try to undress him with my magic, but I wouldn't. I couldn't tell him the truth—that I *wanted* to try my new powers, but I was too afraid. I felt the magic spiraling out of control below my solar plexus. In my palms, dancing at my fingertips, too. A storm raged beneath my skin, and I had no idea how to tame it. I had no business being the caretaker of so much magic when I had no comprehension of what it was, how it worked, or how to control it. And I wasn't about to unleash it on my mate under these circumstances, when I wasn't even in control of my *own* body.

I growled, shoving Fisher back onto the bed and yanking his boots from his feet. I *had* to have him, and he was not helping. Nope, he was laughing.

"Feeling a little feral there, Osha?"

I hurled one of his boots across the room; it sailed through the ward I'd created, a ripple distorting the air, the sound of it thumping to the floor on the other side blocked out by my unintentional magic. "It's almost as if you *don't* want to fuck me," I snarled.

More laughter. This time lower. Rougher. "Oh, believe me. I want to fuck you. Need proof?"

I knelt at the end of the bed and watched as he finally relented and helped with his disrobing, easing his pants slowly down over his hips. I stared, my mouth suddenly drier than the fucking dunes, as that cut muscular *V* that dipped down into his groin was exposed...and then his cock sprang free.

He was hard all right. Harder than I'd ever seen him. He was so godscursed *big*. Fisher kicked out of his pants and tossed them onto the floor, then stacked his hands one on top of the other and wrapped them both around his straining length.

He stared at me, shuttling his hands up, and when he squeezed himself, a bead of pre-cum pearled from his swollen head. "This little bubble you've created is trapping your scent, you know," he said. "The scent of you is driving me fucking crazy."

I ran my hand between my legs, dipping my fingers past my folds, hissing when I realized how hard he'd made me come when he bit me.

Fisher watched me with hazy eyes, still pumping his hands up and down his cock. "Come. Here. *Now*," he ground out.

I obeyed. Not because he didn't give me a choice. The oath he had bound me with had been broken when I'd died back in Gillethrye. No, I did it because I wanted to.

"Give me those fingers," he commanded.

I knew perfectly well what he meant by that; I wasn't even remotely self-conscious as I reached out to his mouth and painted myself all over his lips. He groaned, eyes flashing with need, when I pushed my index and middle finger into his mouth.

"Suck," I told him.

His eyes rolled back into his head, and Kingfisher of the Ajun Gate, slayer of the last dragon and Lord of Cahlish, obeyed *me*.

Hot air rushed over the back of my hand as Fisher exhaled hard down his nose.

You're trying to kill me, he rasped in my mind.

I bent over him, withdrawing my fingers and replacing them, flicking his lips with the tip of my tongue before plunging it into his mouth.

Not kill you, I answered. *But maybe I* will *torture you a little in light of that stunt you just pulled.*

Quickly, I straddled him, grabbing him by the wrists and pulling his hands up over his head. He could have fought me. Refused to let me manhandle him. But he didn't. His cock butted up against my core, but I didn't slide myself down onto him. Not yet. Positioning myself so the head of his length was pressing right at my entrance, I lowered down a hair's breadth... and then I rocked my hips back an inch, relishing the sight of him squirming.

"Osha," he said in a warning tone.

I ignored him, lowering my chest, making it *very* clear that he needed to be quiet and pay more attention to my breasts, which were now *right* in his face.

He didn't hold back. My right nipple was trapped between his teeth in the next breath. I let out a hiss of pain as he bit down—not enough to cause real pain, but enough to send a shock wave chasing along my nerve endings. As quickly as he had clamped down, he released, swirling his tongue over the pink bud reverently, as if to make up for the discomfort he'd caused.

When I sink all the way down onto your cock, you're not allowed to touch me, I informed him.

I'm just a male, he answered in an agonized tone. *I've never worked a miracle in my life. What gives you... the impression I'd be able to start... working them now?*

Your stubborn nature. I lowered one more inch. *If you touch me, I win.*

Fuck, Saeris, he snarled. I was rocking now, rolling my hips the smallest amount, working the head of his cock in and out of my pussy. "You have any idea how fucking incredible you look right now?" He spoke these words out loud, and his voice was so raw. Full of need. The sound of it lit a fire in me that promised to burn forever.

"Cruel, *cruel* female," he chided.

Oh, if he thought this was cruel, then he was probably going to brand me pure evil for what I was *about* to do. I undulated against him, lowering yet another inch, and when he hissed through his teeth, cursing in Old Fae, I swept down and plunged my canines into his neck.

That was when I sank down onto him... *all the way to the hilt.*

I didn't draw on him. Didn't fucking move. I paused there, pulsing around him from the inside, listening to his breath stutter as I let my venom pour into his veins.

He went rigid beneath me. "Saeris." The warning was calm, but there was heat in that word. *Careful.*

I whimpered a little as I arched and my nipples grazed his tattooed chest. *I'm so tired of being careful,* I said into his mind. And then I drank. I laced my fingers with his, digging my fingernails into the backs of his hands, and I ground against him, angling my hips, fucking him as I swallowed him down.

It had been bewildering, tasting him up there on the dais at my coronation. I hadn't been ready for it. Fisher's blood was an eternal song. It cleaved my soul from my body. The taste of him was more exquisite than fresh, clean water. His blood was holy, and I drank like I needed to be saved.

His hands closed tight around mine. The veins in his arms stood proud, his muscles tensed. This was killing him, not being able to touch me properly. But the fact that he was allowing this was monumental.

There was something very empowering about a male like King-fisher relinquishing control and offering free rein over his body. It was an act of trust. Submission, even. And a lethal creature baring his neck to you was a heady thing indeed.

I could feel the effect my venom was having on him, floating from his mind to mine. Strange. I could tell that this was his high now, but it still made me feel as though I were being buoyed up on a cloud into the ether. No words or direct thoughts passed between us for a while. I felt the deep well of love between us, though. The sensation was so immense that I thought I might die from the sheer magnitude of it. Was it my love for him? His love for me? The lines were so blurred I couldn't tell where his feelings ended and mine started. It didn't really matter in the end.

I stopped drinking, my body alive with foreign, unusual energy that didn't belong to me. Fisher's cock strained as he thrust up into me, and the walls of his bedroom began to sway.

Gods, he was so deep. So fucking perfect. I couldn't stop staring at him as I sank down on his cock again, again, again...

"Look at you," Fisher rumbled. "Fucking magnificent, aren't you."

I released his hands, leaning back to give him a better view. I was hardly shy in bed as a rule. But with Fisher, my confidence felt electric. How could I not feel that way, when I could still feel his emotions in his blood. He meant what he said. He *did* think that I was magnificent.

"I'm done holding you back," I said. "You can use your ha—" I didn't even get to finish the sentence.

"Thank the fucking gods," he snarled. Sitting upright, his hands went to my hips. I braced for the shift in gravity, to be thrown onto my back, but Fisher just held me there, fingers gouging into my ass cheeks and my thighs, and he slammed himself up inside me.

"My turn," he rumbled. I didn't even react when I felt the sharp sting of pain this time. I knew what was coming the second his canines sank into the swell of my breast, and I braced myself for that instead. He was more cautious this time. He didn't dose me anywhere near as hard. A spike of dizzying pleasure crashed down on top of me, but I didn't come, and I didn't pass out. His hands slid up my back, hooking over my shoulders, pulling me down onto him, and the delicious friction between our sweat-slicked bodies began to push me closer toward an inevitable cliff.

"You feel so fucking good," I moaned. "I want—I want to feel how hard you get. I want to feel you inside me when you come."

Hell's fucking teeth, he growled inside my head. *I'll give you what you want, Little Osha, don't you worry.*

I rocked against him harder, threading my fingers through his hair, pulling him down onto my breast. He drank deeper, following my cue, and the feeling of him growing hard as tempered steel inside me stole my godscursed breath.

Yes. Good. Come for me. Come. His encouragement was all I needed. I came apart with his arms wrapped around me and his tongue working over my nipple.

His bedroom went black as midnight, my vision failing. But...it hadn't failed. Fisher's shadows exploded out of him as he reached his climax, too. They fanned around him, broad and wide, forming the shape of gossamer wings, and then they swallowed me whole.

His magic cocooned us, cradling our bodies as we shook and trembled. There was no need to speak. We clung to each other for a long while, blood-high and love-drunk.

Eventually, our growling stomachs made us move, though; it turned out that sharing blood and spending an extended amount of time in a Fae warrior's bed meant that you'd be ravenous after a while.

Fisher watched me get dressed, a small smile playing over the corners of his mouth.

I threw one of his socks at him, pulling a face. "Why do you look so pleased with yourself?" I teased.

And Kingfisher laughed. "Because I *am* pleased with myself. Because I'm the luckiest bastard alive. And because *you* look like you've just been thoroughly fucked."

8

MAKE YOUR PEACE

KINGFISHER

ANOTHER DRESS LAY over the back of the chair, untouched. I'd chosen it yesterday, pulling it from the garment bags safely tucked away at the back of my mother's dressing chamber. They hadn't belonged to my mother; I found the dresses there shortly after bringing Saeris to Cahlish for the first time. They weren't my mother's style or her colors at all. She had simply foreseen a day when Saeris would come and had left an entire wardrobe for her—a gift for the beloved female that she would never call daughter.

Ivory white, the rich satin dress flashed like lucent faerie wings. The skirts were simple. Understated. No tulle or frills. There were no over-the-top adornments to it at all, really. The subtle pink-blue undertone that shone through when the fabric caught the light was enough.

Saeris's scent hung thick in the air around the chair. She had stood there and studied the dress, I fancied. Run her hand over the corset. Once again, she'd chosen to pull on her fighting leathers and her boots before disappearing to take on the day.

I grinned, shaking my head as I turned and took in the dented pillow next to me.

She was already gone.

Hah! Well, *that* was a turn up for the books. How many times had I disappeared from a female's bed before she'd woken? Honestly, not that many. Not as many times as Lorreth, that was for sure. The women I'd taken to bed had always known that fucking me was not a pathway toward anything meaningful. They'd known that it would be a one-off, and most of the time they were happy to proceed with that knowledge in mind. That's what they said, anyway. There had been plenty of females who had been surprised when I had taken my leave of them the next morning, shocked that *they* hadn't been the one to change me.

And they had been sweet.

Beautiful.

Breathtaking, even.

But they hadn't been *her*. And when armed or cursed with the knowledge that one day your mate would show up and change everything, no one else could ever come close. So mostly I hadn't bothered with the distraction of sex. Mostly I'd busied myself with the business of killing. And now she was here, my Little Osha, and she was more than I could have hoped for.

And her side of the bed was empty.

I couldn't blame her for it. Vampires slept, it was true. When the sun was high in the sky, it was virtually impossible for the newly turned to remain conscious. Most of them had to rest at that point, but not Saeris. She'd tried to hide it from me, but from what I could tell, she hadn't slept *at all* since she'd awoken in this strange new form she occupied. The past three nights, she had paced her rooms at Ammontraíeth, waiting for the court she ruled over to come back to life, waiting for me to return to her, but she hadn't slept.

She didn't want me to worry. I knew that. The God Binding was still so new between us. She hadn't learned yet that she could tell me anything and I would be there for her, no matter what. It wasn't my job to fix all her problems or shield her from this new existence, though. There was plenty she had to figure out by herself. And when the time came, I would be ready and waiting if she needed help.

In the meantime, she could explore the estate where I had spent the early years of my life and explore what this new life of hers had to offer at the same time. I wouldn't stop her. I stretched, enjoying the bright scent of her that still clung to the pillows and the sheets for a second, and then I got out of bed and went to hunt down some food.

———+———

"What kind of grown male bypasses *bacon* and goes straight for the pastries? You're not right in the head."

I found Renfis perusing the breakfast feast that Archer had laid out in the dining room. His sandy brown hair was loose for once, unbound from his war braids. It hung down his back, still wet from his morning dip in the lake by the orchard, the strands soaking through his shirt. We pocketed two or three items from the steaming platters, and then I opened a shadow gate to transport us back to camp.

We were halfway back to his tent—and I was halfway through a custard tart—when he started in with the teasing. "I've never met another warrior with such a sweet tooth. It's a miracle you even have any teeth left in that head of yours."

I grinned, flashing every single one of the teeth in question at him. "Blame Everlayne. She was the one who fed me her sweet treats when she was little."

As always, the mention of my half sister made my friend's back straighten a little. As always, I didn't mention his reaction.

Renfis rubbed the back of his neck, his eyes skipping over the steep hill that still stood between us and camp. "Ah yes. Speaking of your sister, I checked in on her briefly this morning. As I was leaving, I ran into Saeris. She was looking a little... *disheveled.*"

I understood his meaning perfectly well, but I feigned ignorance. "Oh, really? She must have had a restless night."

Renfis snorted. "A *very* restless night."

He would never bring up the fact that she must have smelled like a brothel. He hadn't mentioned that I did, either. It wasn't polite.

"How are things going between you two, then? Well, I take it."

I shrugged, playing coy. "Ah, y'know. I like her well enough."

"Well enough?" A hint of frustration colored his tone. "What do you mean, well enough? You're God-Bound to her. Doesn't that mean that—Well, aren't you—Gods and martyrs, are you *laughing?"*

He hit me squarely in the arm, so hard that I dropped the last of my custard tart in the mud. I considered it morosely for a second before I carried on walking. "Yes, Renfis," I said, finally giving in. "Things are going very well. More than well. They're amazing."

"And you're in love with her?"

I scowled darkly at him out of the corner of my eye, pulling a face. "Yes," I admitted. It wasn't that I begrudged the feelings I had for my mate. I just hated admitting it out loud to someone to whom I had repeatedly sworn I would never fall in love. It was more than a little embarrassing.

Renfis beamed, his smile monopolizing most of his face. "I knew it!"

"Don't breathe another word," I growled. "I'm not going to gossip about my romantic life with you like some sort of sheep herder."

He frowned. "Are sheep herders gossipmongers?"

"Yes. You'd be surprised by the scandalous things bored sheep herders are privy to. Especially the ones in the foothills of the Shallow Mountains."

"Huh. Who knew. You learn something new every day. So, you and Saeris. In love. That's exciting."

"Fuck off, Ren," I grumbled. "Why don't we talk about your little outburst over Tal instead, huh?"

That shut him up. I *almost* wished I hadn't mentioned it. But there was a tension hanging between us still, despite his playful teasing over Saeris, and one of us had to bring it up eventually. The sooner we cleared the air, the better.

My brother hung his head, thinking hard as we trudged up the slope. It had snowed in the night, and a fresh blanket of powder hid the frozen mud and the black scorch marks that scarred the ground below.

"I know I have a blind spot when it comes to him," he said after a while. "I know it's not as easy for you to hate him as it is for me."

"Nothing is ever easy here," I muttered. "And no matter how badly we might want things to be black and white, most situations never are. *You* taught me that."

"I know, I know." His breath plumed around him as he kicked a pathway through the loose snow. "The atrocities he committed at Malcolm's behest, though..." He shook his head, unable to make his peace with it.

"You know what I'm going to say."

"I do," he agreed quietly. "And I *do* understand. He didn't have a choice. If Malcolm commanded him to do something, he had to obey. But he should never have found himself in that position in the first place, should he?"

And this was what it all boiled down to: the night when Taladaius should have joined our brotherhood and foolishly chose death instead. I chewed on the pain of that memory, uncomfortable to find myself thrown back into the past.

"You've never made a mistake, then?" I asked softly. "I know I have. Too many to count."

My brother made an unhappy sound, clearing his throat. He held his tongue, but I already knew the answer to the question. There were scores of decisions that he would have changed if he could have. Plenty of harsh words he would have taken back. A thousand instances where he would have altered the course of his actions, knowing the consequences they would have after the fact. But it was useless, glancing over a shoulder and wishing to change the past. That was the pastime of fools and politicians. A warrior couldn't afford such luxuries.

"Let me ask you this," I said. "Aside from the decision he made to join Malcolm, what would you have done in his shoes? That night outside the gates of Ajun. Foley was his friend, too, once. If you'd found me there, lying in the snow, my neck broken, dying... what would you have done?"

He stewed for a moment, but not long enough to convince me that he'd really thought about it. "I would have let you go. We are Proelia, Fisher. Our sole mission is to fight the horde, not join its fucking ranks."

I let him fume as we summited the hill. Then, quietly I asked, "Are you *sure* about that?"

A sharp wind cut through my leathers, tossing my hair. I looked to Ren, expecting to find him annoyed by my probing, but I found that his mouth was parted in surprise instead. He was looking down the other side of the slope, at the camp...

...and the utter destruction that lay before us.

Irrín wasn't a city. It was a living organism. Moveable. It grew and shifted. Where there were no tents one day, a whole new section of the camp was liable to have sprung up by the next. But now there were no tents at all. The encampment was in ruins. Where Irrín had once stood, buttressed against the banks of the Darn, a scorched black crater now stretched for as far as the eye could see. Smoke rose from smoldering patches of ground where the embers of a fire still glowed red hot amid the debris.

Charred wood.

Scraps of cloth.

Swords abandoned and blackened in the dirt.

We hadn't smelled the smoke. It was too cold to smell anything at all, and we hadn't been paying attention besides.

We hadn't noticed the quiet.

The camp was destroyed. The tavern was gone. The armory. Everything. Only black ash and bones remained.

"What in all the holy gods' fucking names?" Ren whispered.

I opened my mouth, but no sound came out.

Eleven thousand warriors had been camped here. More, probably. And now there was no sign of them. There were dead, yes. But not enough bones to account for all who had called Irrín home. It wasn't *possible*.

The sparse vegetation that had grown along the riverside was all cinder now. Only the huge oak remained—the very same tree we had tied the feeders to yesterday, before I'd gone to Ammontraíeth to show Saeris and Tal the heads of the feeders we'd fought to put down.

Their bodies were still strapped to the tree, but something had changed. The feeders' limbs were fused with the rough trunk, flesh melting into bark. Their skin was gray and sallow, covered in a thin network of black vines that wrapped around the oak, strangling it. From the base of the tree, blackened roots as thick as a warrior's arm burst out of the ground, snaking over the exposed dirt for thirty feet before plunging back below. The roots bore deep gashes, as if someone had taken an ax to them but hadn't managed to cleave them through.

"What *is* that?" I asked, squinting down at the destruction. My stomach clenched like a fist around my breakfast. "Down there? Coming out of those roots?"

My brother peered down at the nightmare scene, his face drained of color. "It looks like blood," he answered. "Black blood, pouring from the gashes as if they're wounds. Look." He pointed down at an area of ground by the river that hadn't been touched by fire. "It's contaminating the ground."

And sure enough, it was.

Where the black ooze spread, rot and decay followed after it.

9

HIDDEN

SAERIS

SHE WAS AS beautiful as ever.

Her thick blond hair fanned across the pillow beneath her head. Cheeks as pale as porcelain, lips a blush pink, Everlayne didn't look as though she was still battling the remnants of Malcolm's venom. But I knew better. Along her jawline, fine black tendrils of poison marred her perfect skin. Her hands had been stacked one on top of the other over her stomach—a restful pose—but her fingernails were too long. Tinged black.

Onyx lay sleeping at her feet by the bottom of the bed. I'd assumed he was darting off to hunt last night when Fisher carried me into his room, but it was nice to know that he'd ended up here with Everlayne. She didn't deserve to be alone…though it seemed Onyx hadn't been the only one keeping watch over my mate's sister.

The seat Ren had been occupying when I'd entered Layne's room earlier still sat pushed back from the bed, abandoned. The general probably had a room of his own here at Cahlish. I sincerely doubted that he'd slept in it at all since Everlayne had fallen through that shadow gate and come crashing down onto the table in the library, though. I had a feeling that he'd spent quite a few long nights dozing uncomfortably in that chair, waiting for the female in the bed to wake up.

The white fox had fallen asleep right after I'd settled in to keep Layne company. Now, the soft sounds of his snoring filled the bedroom. He kicked his legs fitfully, running in his dreams.

The room that had been prepared for Everlayne's recovery was beautiful. The windows overlooked a sweeping snowy field that dipped down a shallow hill to meet the tree line of a sprawling evergreen forest. The trees were dressed in white, their boughs bent under the weight of fresh snow. Beyond, the mountain ridge scraped the sky. The sleeping giant, Omnamerrin, with his sheer face turned toward Cahlish, glittered as the first light of dawn crept over the crest of his peak.

A thrill of mild discomfort hit me as those very same pale rays washed the walls of Everlayne's bedroom, painting them orange. The light held no warmth this early in the morning, but a rising heat grew in my hands as I watched it dapple my skin. I would need to retreat from it soon. But not yet.

"I owe you an apology," I said softly, lifting Layne's topmost hand from her stomach and taking it in my own. Her skin felt cool to the touch—a little too cool. "I didn't mean to leave without saying goodbye, y'know. But there were extenuating circumstances," I said dryly. "Your brother wasn't exactly the easiest to deal with. I wound up having the choice taken from me, I'm afraid. We've moved on from that now, but...still. It didn't feel good, going without thanking you, at least. You took care of me, Layne. You watched out for me. If it hadn't been for you then, the gods only know who would have been charged with watching over me at the palace. I'm sure it would have been a much scarier experie—"

She hears you. She feels you. Open the gate. The gate...The gate...The gate. Open it. Open the gate.

I jerked back into my seat, tipping my head to one side.

The susurrus of sound was very familiar. It was the quicksilver. I knew the cadence of its voice. Was used to being bossed around by it now. It had spoken to me...but there was no one here with me. I didn't have Solace with me. Ren didn't even *have* a god sword, and he hadn't left anything behind, anyway. It was just me and Everlayne, and Layne didn't have a weapon on her. Nothing that could possibly contain any quicksilver. Not that I—

My mind stilled.

Oh.

By the gods, but she *did* have quicksilver on her body. I hadn't noticed it before, but her tiny earrings flashed in the pre-dawn light, didn't they? Simple. Plain. The metal was cast into flowers, their petals pointed upward like tiny daggers.

"*You* aren't supposed to be here." I leaned closer to inspect the earrings.

We are, we are, we are, came the quicksilver's indignant response. *Always have been.*

"And how am I supposed to open a gate when there's so little of you?" I asked.

I reached for the metal in Layne's earlobe, but as soon as my fingers touched it, the earring liquified and dripped into my palm.

"*Fuck.*" I hadn't willed it to change. I wasn't wearing a relic, and it was touching me. Panic rose up, ready to come crashing down on me, but before that could happen, a droplet of the quicksilver landed on Layne's shoulder. As soon as the liquid metal touched her skin, her eyelids flew open, and Fisher's sister drew in a wheezing breath.

It is done, then. Done, done, done, the quicksilver chanted excitedly. Only this time, the layered voices of the quicksilver came out of Everlayne's mouth. Her eyes were green. Unfocused. She blinked, and when she opened them again, they were a perfect white. Her head snapped to the left, facing me, her jaw working from side to side.

"At last," she sighed. "You're here." The voice was a lot like Everlayne's, but it didn't belong to her. It was deeper than it should have been. Richer. A tremulous smile spread across her face as she stared at me with those white eyes. "I've been waiting a long, long time to speak with you, Saeris Fane."

Her hand snapped out and closed around my wrist, her grip unnaturally strong.

"Everlayne?" Her name was a question on my lips, but I already knew that this wasn't Fisher's sister. The thing that was occupying Layne's body blinked at me slowly, as if it had forgotten *how* to blink, shaking its head.

"No. Everlayne isn't here, I'm afraid. I don't—I don't know if she will be strong enough to return." I tried to pull my hand back, fear climbing my spine, but the thing inside Layne's body held on tight. "Now, now, now..." Layne's teeth chattered.

"Let me go!" I didn't want to have to break Everlayne's fingers, but I would if I had to.

The thing puppeting Layne released me. "At last," it sighed. "I've... waited so...long. Waited for cen-cen-centuries."

I leaped up. The chair fell. It crashed to the floor, but Onyx, still lying in a huddle of blankets by Everlayne's feet, didn't even stir. Whatever fell magic this was, I didn't fucking like it. "What are you talking about?" I hissed. "What are you? Why are you here?"

"Ed-Edina," the thing stuttered. "Edina. Edina. I am Edina."

The name was so familiar to me. I'd heard someone speak it recently, hadn't I? Seen it written down somewhere. "What are you doing to Layne?" I demanded. "Release her body. Let her wake up."

The thing—Edina—slowly closed her eyes, and tears chased down Everlayne's cheeks. "Sh-she is...beyond my reach. I am...not keeping her from this...body."

"Then where is she?"

Edina's answer caught in Everlayne's throat. She could hardly speak as it was, but these words seemed especially difficult for her to say. "She is in sha-sha-shadow. I cannot see."

"You're scaring me."

"Fear is not...real, Saeris Fane," she croaked.

I took a giant step back from the bed. "How the fuck do you know my name?"

"You must g-g-go."

"Yeah, no shit."

"The library. Go to the library," she said, her teeth chattering even harder. "There, you will fi-find a b-b-book."

"Libraries are full of books," I whispered. This wasn't right. It was unnatural. Honestly, it was freaking me the hell out. A voice in the back of my head urged me not to run, though. It was the same voice that had told me to steal that guardian's gauntlet. The same one that had made me fight and kill two of Madra's men outside the Mirage. It couldn't be trusted, but I was nothing if not a creature of habit. "What kind of book?" I demanded. "And why do I need it?"

"Sm-small," she wheezed. "But thick. Blue. There is a butterfly..."

"A butterfly? On the cover?"

Edina couldn't manipulate Layne's facial features too much, it seemed. Her pale eyes were full of pain. I could feel it, feel her confusion, all underpinned by a sorrow that made me want to weep. "It's hidden," she rasped, "among the stars."

"What does that mean?"

"The *stars*..." Edina's eyes rolled back into her head.

"Hey!"

"Hundreds and...hundreds of...stars."

"Edina!" Why was I suddenly choking on panic? It suffocated me, shoving me back to the bed. I picked up Layne's hand and clasped it tight, fighting for air. "Edina, what's in the book? Why is it so important? Tell me!"

An eerie calm settled over the visitor in Layne's body. Her sightless gaze found mine, and for a second, her confusion slipped away. "They told you. About the rot," she said in a clear voice. "They told you it would come. It's here, now. You must find the book in order to stop it. Without it, the decay will spread until it swallows this realm and millions more with it. I have seen it, Saeris. Find the book. Stop the spread. It's the only way."

"Edina—"

She squeezed my hand tighter than tight. "Find it. But do *not* tell him about it. I mean it. It's important. He can't know about the book. Only you. Do you understand?"

I didn't. Not even a little bit, but I heard the desperation in her tone and the lie came easily. "Yes. I understand."

"Thank you. Make sure he knows how much I loved him, Saeris," she said. "At the end, make sure he knows that I'd do it all again."

What did *that* mean? The question was there, ready to be asked, but it wouldn't come out. Layne's—*Edina's*—grip on my hand had tightened, and it was beginning to hurt. Not my hand. But...the ink that marked it. The runes on my fingers, the backs of my hands, chaining my wrists and spiraling up my forearms—suddenly it felt as though the runes were on fire. Were they glowing? No. Oh, gods, they were burning. A wisp of smoke curled away from my skin, and Edina's milk-white eyes went wide. "You haven't *sealed* them?" she gasped.

"Sealed them? What does that mean? I don't understand."

"An Alchemist must seal her runes," she rasped. "You are a well that runs deep. When you were marked with your runes, their magic began pouring into you. It flows and it flows. It will not...stop..."

"Edina!" She was drifting. Her eyes were still clouded, but I sensed that they'd lost focus. The pain around my wrists and up my arms had intensified, almost unbearable. I tried to pull my hand back, ready to claw away my own skin if it meant escaping the burn, but Edina suddenly seemed to return. Her grip held little strength, but I could *not* let go of her hand. "Seal them, Saeris. If you do not..."

"What? What'll happen if I don't?" The pain was too much now. Acrid smoke rose from the runes on the back of my right hand; my flesh was burning. I watched in horror as the marks glowed like a brand, sinking deeper and deeper into my skin. Blisters rose, angry, spreading up my arm. This was worse than a sword in the stomach. It was agony. Tears welled in my eyes, streaming down my cheeks. "Edina! What are you *doing*?"

"Not me, not me. I did what I could." She sighed regretfully. "Now the rest...is up to you."

"Edina, *help* me!"

"Find the book. The book..." The white of her eyes started to clear, like silt settling to the bottom of a canister, leaving behind clear water. She was fading.

"Edina? *Edina!*"

The bedroom door crashed open.

The pain vanished. My hand...it was fine. The runes no longer formed raw burns. The blisters were gone. My God Bindings looked normal.

"Osha?"

I dropped Layne's lifeless hand, spinning to face my mate. Fisher stood by the door, his face white as a sheet, his leathers spattered with mud.

His voice was rough when he said, "Why were you calling my mother's name?"

10

ROT

SAERIS

"YOU'RE SURE YOU'RE fine? You're so pale."

Fisher had been fussing like a mother hen for the past hour. He'd heard me shouting Edina's name. His *mother's* name. I'd considered making an excuse, some other reason to explain why I had been calling out to her—it seemed cruel to tell him what had happened without properly understanding what *had* happened—but that thought hadn't fully taken shape before I'd dismissed it. Fisher deserved to know.

Edina had only told me not to tell him about the book, anyway. I honored her request and kept that to myself. I didn't care about a mystery book. I was far more concerned about what she'd said regarding my runes. The pain I'd experienced in Everlayne's bedroom hadn't been normal. It had felt like it was burning my *soul* as well as my body. As if the river of magic flowing through me had caught fire and was unmaking me. It had been terrifying...and I did *not* want it to happen again.

"Yes, I'm sure. I'm fine," I told him. "Just a little shaken, that's all."

We were gathered in Cahlish's library. Ren was still at Irrín, waiting for the remainder of the Yvelian forces who had fled the encroaching rot to meet at a rally point downriver. Lorreth had gone to help him figure out shelter for the warriors whose homes had been lost during the attack.

Te Léna, Maynir, and Iseabail had been poking and prodding at me since Fisher had sent for them. Carrion had already been in the library, lounging on a plush sofa by the fire and reading a book when we'd arrived. He hadn't moved an inch. The token concern he'd shown over my well-being had presented itself as a crooked eyebrow, a quick glance up and down, and two questions that were neither tactful nor kind: "Is she contagious?" and "She'll be fine after she eats something. What time's dinner?"

He'd been buried in his book ever since.

"I wish I knew more about all of this," Te Léna said, pinching the bridge of her nose. "It's been a long time since I was this woefully uneducated on a subject. Even dealing with the quicksilver inside Fisher was easier than this. There are plenty of documented cases that speak of quicksilver contamination and how to try to remedy it, but Belikon's men were thorough when they scourged the realm of information regarding the Alchemists and their power. There's nothing in the library here about it. There's nothing in the archives at the Winter Palace on the subject, either. Maynir spent years trawling through the stacks there before we met. He had a personal interest in the Alchemists and their abilities. He's always been fascinated by the lost arts. He said that entire chapters were missing out of books that probably only mentioned the word *Alchemy*."

"What about you, Iseabail? Do you know anything about sealing Alchemical runes?" Fisher asked. His voice was tight. He seemed distracted. "Belikon didn't raid your lands when he purged Yvelia of all the Alchemists' texts. Do you think there might still be anything useful in Nevercross?"

I hated being so out of the loop sometimes. "What's Nevercross?"

Iseabail herself answered the question. "It's our political seat," she said, in her soft, lilting accent. "A city unlike any other. Our buildings have stood for millennia, protected from the outside world. We school our children there. We heal the sick there."

"And your histories are kept there," Fisher added. "In the catacombs below the city."

The redheaded witch scowled, implying Kingfisher wasn't supposed to know this. "Our histories are exactly that. *Ours.* There are no records of the Alchemists or their practices below Nevercross. And even if there were," she said, holding up a finger and cutting Fisher off before he could interrupt her. "Only Guild witches are allowed down into the catacombs. I couldn't get you access to those death chambers even if I wanted to. And I don't. There are secrets down there that should never be experienced by outsiders."

"Experienced?" That was a strange way of wording it.

Iseabail nodded. "The catacombs are unearthly. I wouldn't even go down there unless I had no other choice. And we do have other choices. Until we've exhausted all of them, it would be foolish to even think about petitioning for access."

Fisher drummed his fingertips absently against the table. Late morning light spilled through the window gilding his hair. A few short hours ago, we'd been tangled up in each other, embraced by his glittering magic. It had been blissful inside that silent velvet sanctuary. Now he was troubled. Deeply troubled. It was almost as though I could feel his pain. His chair creaked as he shoved back in it, balancing it on two legs. Covering his mouth with a heavily inked hand, he sighed.

"All right. I can respect that. The witches deserve their peace, too," he said. "We'll avoid traveling to Nevercross for as long as we can. But this rot can survive ice and snow, Iseabail. The mountains won't stop it. Before too long, this corruption will make its way to your home, and it *will* become the Guild's problem."

Iseabail inclined her head, the ends of her auburn braids coiling on the table as she accepted this truth. "Unfortunately, my mother and her sisters will probably wait to act until that day arrives. I'll tell them of what I've seen here. But I wouldn't count on any expedient support from the north, I'm afraid."

Silence reigned over the library for a time, all of us lost in our thoughts, doing our best to figure out how best to proceed. The quiet was disturbed by the door to the library bursting open and the arrival of Ren and Lorreth in a whirlwind of leather, soot, and war braids.

Fisher rose quickly. "You found them?"

Ren's face was grave, but he nodded. "The vast majority of them were waiting for us at the rally point. We lost a thousand more warriors, though."

"More feeders?"

Lorreth shook his head. "The rot. It infected them somehow. The same way it must have infected the feeders. It took them in an hour. Two at most. The other fighters had to put them down. Their friends. Family. It wasn't good. There's a trail of bodies from the war camp all the way into the foothills."

"And where those bodies lay, the rot spreads and multiplies," Ren said. "It claims any vegetation. Any creature, living or dead. It travels over snow and scorched ground without issue. We've yet to figure out a way to stop it."

The color drained from Fisher's face. His gaze met mine, clouded with worry, the thin strand of quicksilver banding his right eye flashing bright. *We need to tell them*, he said into my mind. *Do I have your permission?*

I gave him a small nod. I had described to him in great detail what had happened when I'd been pulled into the quicksilver back at Gillethrye. I hadn't left anything out. But Fisher had wanted to keep the full account to ourselves for a little while so as not to alarm the others unnecessarily. But now it seemed as though alarm was warranted. He took a deep breath and began. "Back in Gillethrye, Saeris wasn't just pulled into the quicksilver. She was called by the gods."

Five baffled faces turned toward me. Over the back of the sofa, Carrion's head popped up out of nowhere, his auburn strands disheveled as if he'd just woken up. "What does that mean, *called by the gods*? Like, you found religion?"

"No. It means that I was summoned by them. Zareth was the one who yanked me through the—"

"Excuse me. *Zareth?*" Te Léna squeaked. "*The* Zareth. God of chaos Zareth?"

"God of chaos *and* change," I said wearily. "He was very adamant about the 'and change' part."

"You met with *a god?*"

"Yes. Three of them, actually." I shrugged. "Bal and Mithin were there, too. Kind of."

Te Léna looked like she might pass out. She pressed her index finger and middle finger to her brow with reverence. "What did Zareth say?"

"He said he was severing us from the tapestry of the universe. That the gods wouldn't be able to see us anymore."

"Wait," Maynir interjected. "So you and Fisher... you're *not* God-Bound anymore?"

Fisher shifted, absently rubbing the tattoos across the back of his hand that now matched my own. "We are. If anything, the connection between us is even stronger. The gods are just blind to us now. Zareth felt that it would protect us. Some of the other gods aren't too optimistic about what's happening. They'd rather birth a new universe than wait to see what happens with this one, so..."

"No. No, no, no." Iseabail shook her head. "Impossible. The Yvelian gods aren't real. They're metaphors."

Lorreth's eyes narrowed imperceptibly. "But the Balquhidder gods are real, though, right? Those elemental spirits who whisper in your ears? The ones who tell you whether you should prevent or commit atrocities for 'the greater good'?" He heaped sarcasm onto those last three words.

"Our deities aren't myths, Lorreth. They've always been here, and their will cannot be questioned. If we don't obey them, the consequences—"

"*Enough.*" Fisher didn't raise his voice, but the command echoed around the library. Frown lines etched deep grooves between his brows. "The gods are real. They're bastards, but they're real. I've met with them myself. We aren't telling you this now to spark a debate about theology. I'm bringing this up because of what they told Saeris."

Everyone looked expectantly at me, which was just *great*. Being stared at was my favorite. "Zareth showed me this tree," I explained. "There were thousands of leaves on its branches. He said that each leaf represented a realm occupied by countless living beings. Some of the leaves withered and fell as we spoke. He said that those realms were infected by a rot spreading throughout the universe. Whole branches of the tree were blackened and dying. Zareth said that it meant the end. Of everything. Of all realms. That the other gods wanted to wipe the slate clean and start over again, rebuilding the universe from scratch. But he had refused."

"And so," Iseabail said, "this male who claimed to be a God said that you and Fisher were the only ones who could prevent the end of everything, then? Is that what you're telling us?" The witch didn't sound upset, per se. Her tone was measured, but there was a whirlwind of emotion in her blue eyes.

"No. He said that Fisher and I are an axis of some kind. A convergence in the threads of fate. He told me that none of the gods could see around us. He said that we *had* to find a way to fix this, otherwise everything was lost. I'm not saying we're special, Iseabail. I'm just saying that..." I fumbled for the right words. "A god rolled the dice on an unlikely outcome, just to see if it would pay off. That's it. That's what we are currently working with."

No one looked happy to hear this.

I was met with tight, grim expressions as I glanced around the room. That is, until my gaze fell on Carrion. With his arms draped over the back of the couch and his chin resting on the cushion, he shot me a roguish wink. "You'll come up with something, Fane. You always do. You're very smart for a twenty-five-year-old."

I choked out a laugh, and the tension sucking up all the air in the room suddenly broke. "If you're going to mock me for my youth, Swift, you might as well get my age right. I'm twenty-four."

He angled his head, waggling his eyebrows. "Are you, though?"

"I—" Oh. Huh. I trailed off, frowning as I tried to do the math. How long had I been in Yvelia now? It felt like a long, long time, but... gods, I had no clue. I'd been here long enough, though. I'd missed my own birthday. I *was* twenty-five now.

Carrion turned his attention back to his book. "Don't worry, Fane. We'll have a big birthday party just as soon as people stop dying all over the place."

"I don't want a party."

"Why not? You always used to come to *my* birthday parties."

"I used to go to *Kala's*," I corrected. "You and your drunk friends just so happened to be there too sometimes."

Lorreth shot Carrion a smirk. "Only Faelings have birthday parties, y'know. We stop celebrating that kind of stuff when we turn fourteen. What are you now, seventeen hundred years old?"

"Watch your tongue, old man. I'm not ancient like the rest of you," Carrion snorted, turning a page. "I'm only one thousand and ninety-*six*, thank you very much."

"Impossible. The Daianthus heir went missing when we were Fael-ings. I was..." Lorreth frowned, searching his memory. "I was thir-teen when it happened. I was preparing for my oath. What about you, Fisher?"

Unlike Lorreth, my mate was neither perturbed nor confused by the revelation the warrior had stumbled upon. "Nearly ten," he said.

"Right. So that means you *are* nearly our age." Lorreth raised dark brows at Carrion.

"He isn't," Fisher said softly. "It's as he says. He's probably only eleven hundred or so."

Carrion pointed at Fisher. "Thank you. I *do* know how to count, Lorreth of the Broken Spire."

"So he's *not* the heir, then?" Te Léna sounded just as confused as the rest of us.

"Wait. I'm not?" Carrion was sitting up very straight all of a sudden. "I'm off the hook?"

"He *is* the heir. I've thought about it a lot since the maze, and there's a plausible explanation for Carrion's age," Kingfisher explained. "When my father took him through the quicksilver, something must have happened. My money's on the gods, interfering again."

"You think there's a chance they wanted to speak to him?" I asked. "The way Zareth spoke to me?"

Slowly, my mate nodded. "Time is strange in their realm. When they took me at Ajun, I stood with Bal and Mithin in the middle of a field of swaying tall grass. I saw two figures up on a hill in the distance. The first was Zareth. The second... was *you*, Osha."

Whatever I'd been expecting him to say, it wasn't *that*. Fisher had fought and nearly died at the Ajun Gate over a thousand years ago. I had been pulled through the quicksilver and into the gods' realm only a few short weeks ago. "But... how? And how do you know it was me?"

I didn't know your name. I didn't see your face. But I knew, Osha. My soul recognized a flicker of itself burning inside someone else and it knew. The explanation was for me alone. Fisher's eyes burned with intensity as he conveyed the message. To the rest of the room, he said, "When my father fled with the Daianthus heir, one or more of the gods must have delayed their escape. At least at their destination, anyway. Time continued here in Yvelia, but in Zilvaren, I believe it stood still."

It was certainly within their power. And the gods did love to interfere in the matters of the living. I wouldn't have put it past them. But the question was wh—

"Why?" Carrion asked the question before I'd had the chance to finish thinking it. "To what end? I don't remember going there. I remember nothing. I don't even remember your father, Fisher. Did he have some kind of plan for me? Do the *gods*?"

My mate chewed the inside of his cheek, staring down at his hand where it rested on the table in front of him. It took him a long time to speak. "I barely remember my father, either. And I don't pretend to know anything of plans made by gods. All we can do is make our own and hope for the best."

"Agreed." Until now, Renfis had been notably silent throughout this exchange. He rubbed his jaw, looking around the room. "The agendas of the gods will have to be tackled later. For now, nothing is more important than the task at hand. We're woefully low on silver, but that doesn't even seem to be an issue anymore. The horde is at bay. Saeris has forbidden them from leaving the dead fields. We don't have to worry about them showing up at the river anymore. It's true that we don't have the relics yet, but we can do without them for now."

"Oh, we still need them," I said.

Everyone looked at me again.

"We need them even more than we did before. The feeders at the river yesterday shouldn't have been able to disobey my edict, and yet they did."

"Because they were infected by the rot," Ren said, slowly. His shoulders slumped, his face falling. "And the rot is spreading. If the horde at Ammontraíeth becomes infected..."

"We're screwed," Fisher finished. "Fuck." He frowned, his eyes a million miles away as he processed that.

"The relics still won't help us if we need to face an infected army," Lorreth muttered.

I kept my mouth shut this time. *I* wasn't going to be the one to say it. As usual, Fisher took on the burden of the difficult task, bearing the weight of it for the rest of us. "If it comes to that, *nothing* will help us," he said. "We'll have to leave Yvelia. And for a mass evacuation on that level, we'll need far more than fifteen thousand relics."

There were other realms. Places where we might be able to outrun the decay for a while. But it would be a temporary fix. From what Zareth had said, the rot that was fast spreading toward the mountain range separating Irrín from Cahlish was already finding ways to hop from one realm to another.

Renfis inclined his head, nodding. "Okay. I stand corrected. We *will* need more silver. More than we could hope to access here in Yvelia."

"Agreed." Fisher pressed his fingertips into his temples. After thinking for a moment, he looked up at me. "There's a forge at Ammontraíeth. There has to be."

"I'll find it. And as soon as I do, I'll get to work."

"Thank you. While you're there, Carrion can hunt for information about sealing your runes. And mastering your abilities in general, for that matter."

Carrion let out a pained sigh and heaved himself up from the sofa. He slapped his hands at his clothes, straightening himself out. "No," he said. "Carrion can*not*."

"Why? Got something better to do?" Fisher asked.

"Well, I wouldn't say better, but..." He rolled his eyes. "I know where you're heading, and unfortunately for the both of us, I'm better off accompanying *you*."

"What are you talking about?" I asked.

"Where can we easily lay our hands on a bunch of silver outside of this realm?" the smuggler asked.

Oh.

Oh, no.

I flinched when I realized where this was going.

"We also need to figure out if the infected feeders are coming from Zilvaren. And I'm just guessing here, but I'm sure that now that you're mated and all starry eyed, you're going to want to go and fetch Saeris's brother and finally honor the deal you made with her—"

"*Careful*, Swift," Fisher grumbled.

"And who knows *exactly* what the notorious Hayden Fane looks like, hmm?"

"You've made your point."

"If that task's left up to you again, you'll probably bring back some random...hey, what was that guy called?" Carrion snapped his fingers at me, frowning. "Y'know, that blond guy who kissed you at Kala's that time? You chipped his front tooth when you punched him in the mouth."

I was going to punch *him* in the mouth very soon. "Carrion, stop."

He held up his hands in surrender. "All right. All *right*. I'm just saying. While you keep shit in check with the Blood Court and figure out some new magic tricks, Fisher and I will head back to the Silver City and take care of business there, too. It only makes sense."

A thick silence filled the library as everyone processed this. I waited for Fisher to refuse the suggestion, but when I saw his dark scowl, I realized that he wasn't going to shoot down Carrion's plan after all. He looked like he wanted to murder him. Instead, he said, "Fine. But I swear to the gods, if you talk the entire time, I *will* kill you and leave your carcass for the crows, Carrion Swift."

11

FOOL'S PARADISE

SAERIS

GOODBYES WEREN'T EASY.

We made it quick.

If Madra *was* responsible for sending the infected feeders to Yvelia, then every second the quicksilver was awake was yet another opportunity for her to deploy more of them.

When Kingfisher and Carrion stepped into the silver, my emotions were so high that I'd cracked the lintel that ran around Cahlish's pool. I'd nearly begged Fisher not to go. Instead, I'd given Carrion the relic I'd made for him, and I'd given Fisher the relic I'd made for Hayden. I'd kissed my mate long and deep, promising to reopen the gate for them in three days.

In return, Fisher had left a shadow gate open for us at Cahlish. Using a warding sigil painted below the gate in his blood, he had essentially propped the door open, so that we could move between the estate and a safe, uninfected point on the banks of the Darn, where we could cross the river and ride back and forth to Ammontraíeth.

I'd been thinking about my mate as we'd saddled the horses. I hadn't been able to stop thinking about him during the two-hour ride across the dead fields. Not when I'd swept through the echoing halls of the palace, high bloods dropping to their knees and bowing their heads as

I blew past them. Not while I'd read in my rooms to pass some time. Not while I'd picked halfheartedly at the meal a low blood—the lowest ranking of all the vampires in Ammontraíeth—brought to my chamber. I couldn't stop thinking about him *now*, either.

"Hold it up. You're dropping your guard."

The sword came crashing down, its edge slicing through the air dangerously close to my face. A thrill of adrenaline buzzed right below the surface of my skin, making me break out in a cold sweat.

Lorreth probably didn't want to be here. How selfish of me not to have considered it before: The warrior had come close to being drained by three rogue feeders once and had nearly died as a result. Fisher had needed to bind a piece of his soul with Lorreth's in order to drag the male back from the brink of death. That had been centuries ago now, but you didn't just get over something like that without it leaving a mark.

Ammontraíeth was a place of shadows—an element I had grown trusting of lately. But the dark that welled in the corners of the Blood Court's palace was not made to caress or seduce as Fisher's shadows were, at least when he used them on *me*, anyway. Ammontraíeth's shadows hid danger and watchful eyes. I wasn't the only one who noticed that when we'd arrived earlier, shortly after dusk.

Lorreth was on high alert, his gaze everywhere but on me as we sparred. The training facility was lit by evenlight, the strange, lazy flames swaying like tall grass in a light breeze as the warrior and I wheeled around one another.

There were no windows here. The walls and the floor were made of slick, polished obsidian, which blunted the air somehow. My quickened breath and the sound of our bare feet slapping against the cool black surface seemed too loud. Too close.

Lorreth launched himself forward, grunting as he brought Avisiéth swinging down. The sound echoed once and didn't come again. I spun away from the blow, light on my feet, careful not to take my eyes from the warrior lest he bring the god sword's pommel down on my head in a backhand.

"I should have gone," I said, bringing Solace's guard up. "I should be with *them*."

Lorreth easily sidestepped the thrust I aimed at his shoulder, batting Solace away. He *tsk*ed through his teeth, shaking his head. "Sloppy. Higher. Like this." He demonstrated how I should hold my sword, making a point of raising his elbows so that they were in line with his jaw. He nodded when I had mimicked the posture to his satisfaction, then attacked. "You couldn't go with them," he said, rushing forward. "In case you've forgotten, your old home has two suns and no night."

"I could have worn a cloak." I ducked a slashing strike he aimed at my stomach. "Kept my skin covered."

"Sure. That wouldn't have made you stick out like a sore thumb. And what about the exhaustion? You're weaker at midday here—"

I straightened, lowering Solace. "Hey!"

"I said weak*er*. Not weak. Guard!" The flat of his blade landed on my upper arm—a punishment for dropping out of my stance. Pain jarred my shoulder and shot straight up into my head. My teeth cracked together so hard that I bit my tongue and tasted blood.

"That wasn't very polite," I grumbled.

"Oh, damn. I didn't realize we were doing this to be polite. Sorry. Let me fix that." He snapped his bare heels together, adopting a stiff-backed stance. With his chin lifted, he peered down his nose at me and fixed me with an imperious stare. "I challenge you to a duel, Saeris Fane. Would you please stab me with that shiny sword of yours? It would be *such* an honor."

"Fuck you, Lorreth."

He made a face. "You kiss my commander with that mouth?"

"I've done far worse than *kiss* him with it."

His mouth pulled down at the corners, his eyes going wide. "Okay. I don't need to hear about *that*, thank you very much."

"I wasn't going...to tell you." I gasped for breath as I spun around again, twisting at the ankles, then the knees, then the hips as I brought Solace arcing through the air. Sword fighting was much harder than fighting with daggers. A dagger was an extension of my hand. I was quick with a set of daggers. Nimble. The sheer size and weight of Solace made moving hard.

Lorreth tracked me as I spun; he took a step back, raised his boot, and kicked me in the side.

I went down hard, the air rushing out of me as I slammed against the floor. *"Ooof!"*

"Form was good. Shame about the lack of speed," the warrior mused, pacing in a circle around me.

"I was just...thinking...that...myself." Shit, my ribs hurt.

Lorreth crouched down by my head, laying Avisiéth flat across the tops of his knees and then resting his elbows on the god sword's blade. The bastard wasn't even out of breath. "You're right where you need to be, Saeris," he said. "Well. Not on the floor. You definitely shouldn't be on the floor. But here, I mean. If you stayed away from Ammontraíeth any longer, one of the other Lords would have declared the throne abandoned and claimed it for themselves. They'd call it a dereliction of duty or something. People think the Blood Court's all debauchery and blood-soaked orgies, but it's mostly bureaucracy and political back-biting, from my experience."

"You sound disappointed."

He shrugged, offering me a hand as I got back to my feet. "I mean, who doesn't love a blood-soaked orgy?"

"Can't say I've ever participated in one."

He shrugged. "Not missing much, honestly. They get...sticky."

"Can we pause this super interesting conversation for just a moment? I think my shoulder's dislocated."

Lorreth barely even looked at it before thumping me in the shoulder. The resulting pop and twist of my arm slipping back into place made bile rise up the back of my throat. I glowered at him through watering eyes. "Thank you?"

"You're welcome. Now, come on. Guard."

"I can't lift this damn sword again. Not for at least ten minutes. I think I'm gonna puke."

Mouth open, he was going to try bullying me to my feet again, but his eyes met mine and something in him softened. He took pity on me. "All right. You get five minutes. Take a breath. And..." Suddenly, he sounded awkward. "I know you feel bad, okay? Useless, even, stuck here in this shitty fucking palace while everyone else is out there without us. Ren's warning the Gilarians. Danya's orchestrating efforts to keep the infected at bay. Fisher and Carrion are scoping out whatever they can in Zilvaren while they hunt down the silver and your brother—"

"Oh, *gods!*" I cried, an awful realization striking me out of nowhere.

Lorreth's eyes grew round. "What? What is it?"

"He made you promise to stay here and watch over me, didn't he?"

Immediately, Lorreth's expression went blank.

"He made you promise to stay and protect me!" Gods, I was *so* blind. "That's the only reason you're trapped here in this training room with me, isn't it? Otherwise, you'd be out there with everyone else, doing something useful, too!"

After hashing out the finer points of our plan, we had each set off about our individual tasks. Te Léna and Maynir had gone to tend to the wounded among the warriors who fled Irrín. Iseabail had returned to her people to ask *politely* if any of the witch elders knew how to seal Alchemical runes. Ren had ridden out to the small settlements east of Cahlish and along the coast to warn them of the rot. With what was left of the war camp at her disposal, Danya was sending out hunting parties to keep the infected at bay or at least keep them from progressing inland any farther.

The plan was to all meet back in Cahlish in three days' time, come what may.

But *Lorreth* had claimed he wanted to stay here and help me train.

He was incapable of lying; he probably *did* want to help me train. But I would have bet my left eye that he'd rather have been out there with Danya, tackling the infected instead. The warrior shrugged off my accusation, trying to feign ignorance.

"Don't you worry about any of that. All you need to focus on is keeping these vampires distracted and figuring out your runes."

"Lorreth!"

"All right, all right! I'm not going to confirm or deny your suspicions either way. But if you don't kick up a stink right now and you finish training with me, I *will* tell you the story of Ajun Gate. All of it, every single gruesome detail."

"I know the story—"

"Hah!" Lorreth grunted. "No, you don't. Do you know about Merelle?" he demanded.

Merelle. The name was familiar, somehow? Maybe? I shook my head. "No. I don't."

The tension in Lorreth's shoulders fell away; he knew he'd already won. "Merelle was Ren's sister. She died on the side of that frozen mountain, and none of us have been the same since."

"Tell me." Now that he'd mentioned her, I *had* to know. "Ren had a sister?"

"Not just a sister. A *twin...*"

I was already back on my feet, the pain in my shoulder forgotten. I raised Solace, but Lorreth let out an annoyed groan and batted the sword away before I could adopt a defensive stance.

"Y'know what? On second thought, if we're talking about Merelle, we shouldn't be fighting at the same time. We should be doing the next best thing."

I had a feeling I already knew what Lorreth was going to suggest next, but I still had to ask. "What's that?"

"Drinking, of course. Come on. These blood suckers are too fancy for beer, I'm afraid, but they *really* know their wine."

What had I expected? An armed escort through the palace? A crowd lining the streets, cheering me as I passed? No, of course not. That would have been ridiculous. But I hadn't expected Lorreth to toss a cloak around my shoulders, yank my hood up, and bully me out of Ammontraíeth without anyone stopping us or saying a word. That just seemed too *easy*. Though I hated it, I was getting used to residents of the Blood Court kneeling whenever I passed them in a hallway or entered a room. With my hood drawn up tonight, my reluctant subjects didn't recognize me for who I was, and so I slipped out of Ammontraíeth unmolested.

I knew there were buildings outside the palace. Lots of them. I could see them from the balcony outside my bedroom. I hadn't paid much attention to them, though. When I stood out on the balcony at night, my attention turned northward, across the barren plains that stood between me and my mate, and not down at the hub of activity that bustled around Ammontraíeth's feet. The Cogs—that's what Lorreth called the circular, interlocking neighborhoods, each connected by a steep downward staircase until they reached street level.

Rain hammered on the rooftops of the narrow buildings, sluicing over slate and pouring from cracked clay gutters onto the cobbled streets. We cut through the second tier of the Cogs—an area frequented by blood mages, the lich-born, and outcast paladins looking to trade questionable goods, according to Lorreth. Shadowy courtyards waited down narrow covered walkways that branched off the main thoroughfare. Brick-built shops with crooked roofs and windows fogged with condensation advertised tinctures, tarot readings, and familiars for sale.

As we walked, Lorreth held true to his promise and told the tale of the Ajun Gate. I was the only one who remembered the song he'd once sung about that terrible night on the mountain, but even *that* hadn't covered all of it. Renfis's poor sister Merelle had burned to death in the most horrific way, and Ren had been there when it had happened. She lived on in a small way, part of her spirit bound to Fisher's sword, but…it was hard to imagine how her loss had affected the band of warriors.

Hard.

An appropriate thought. Everything about this place was hard, and the Cogs was no exception.

There were plenty of people out and about their business as we walked—mostly high bloods, with the exception of a feeder every once in a while, collared and being used in lieu of a packhorse. I tried not to stare from underneath the hood of my oilskin cloak. The feeders were gaunt and thin, little more than rotting skin stretched over bone. Their eyes bore a hunger that could never be sated. Their masters dragged them along on chains, taunting them with vials of pungent blood and laughing at their desperation as they strained for their prize.

Everywhere I looked, some new form of cruelty unfolded before my eyes. A female, stripped to the waist and lashed to a post, the pale skin of her back parting like wet paper as she was whipped.

A child wailing, crimson tears rolling down his cheeks, shoved this way and that, ignored by the other high bloods as they hurried about their errands. A spindly-legged creature crouched on the top of a low stone wall, tearing the limbs off a rat before ripping its head off and drinking from its body like a cup.

But...there was beauty to be found here, too. It felt wrong to acknowledge that anything in Sanasroth could be beautiful, but I found myself awed as I followed Lorreth through the winding, narrow pathways that cut between the buildings.

From window boxes, night-blooming flowers cast fragrant spores up into the cool air. They crept in vines up the fascias of the buildings, carpeting the stonework with tiny white flowers that smelled like jasmine.

Some of the shop windows had stained glass that caught and refracted the glow from evenlight candles that shimmered within. The designs were stunning, a myriad of colors cleverly soldered together to depict some of the most intricate, expertly crafted scenes I had ever seen. And then there were the high bloods themselves. They wore cruel smiles, and their eyes flashed like knives in the dark, but their features were delicate, their skin flawless, their shirts exquisitely tailored, their dresses sheer in silk and satin.

Lorreth led the way, eyes pinned straight ahead as he confidently cut through the crowds. He didn't see the writhing bodies down each darkened side street—the painted females, perfect as dolls, with their heads thrown back in ecstasy as well-dressed, raven-haired princes of the night dipped fingers between their bare thighs and drank deep from the hollows of their necks. He didn't seem to notice the hissing, either.

Wherever Lorreth passed, high bloods recoiled, baring their fangs at him. Hatred burned bright as fire in their eyes, but not one of them made to touch him.

"You're popular," I mused from beneath my hood. "Must be nice."

"They have no idea who I am," Lorreth answered. "They sense the silver strapped to my back. That's all that matters to them."

"Mm. I'm sure the fact that you're the only Fae male in Ammontraíeth hasn't escaped their notice, either."

Lorreth bared his teeth at one brave high blood female who dared block his path. She spat curses at him in an unfamiliar, guttural language until he was within arm's reach, then she spun around and vaulted away up the side of a building. "You'd be surprised," Lorreth said airily, ignoring the angry female. "There are more Fae here than you'd think."

"What? No way. No member of the Fae would come here willingly."

The warrior placed a hand on the door of the dilapidated building in front of him, raising his eyebrows as he faced me. "No one said anything about willingly. Most of them are thralls." He raised his voice so that the high bloods staring at us in the street could hear him. "After all, who do you think these fuckers *eat*?"

He made a good point. Truthfully, I'd spent a good deal of time trying *not* to think about how such a large court sustained itself when its sole food source was blood.

Lorreth gave me a wry smile as he pushed open the door and gestured me inside. "Welcome to the Fool's Paradise, Saeris Fane."

———+———

There were Fae everywhere. Males. Females. *Children.* It made no sense. The tavern was *full* of them. They sat in booths, laughing with high bloods. They picked at meals, listening with intense fascination as they were talked at by one high blood while another casually fed from their wrist.

A row of booths ran along the back wall with thick brocade curtains drawn across them for privacy, but a couple of the curtains *hadn't* been drawn, and all I could make out was a tangle of writhing naked flesh. Mouths on breasts, and wrapped around cocks, and—okay, yeah, that was enough of that. I looked away, my cheeks coloring hotly.

"What do you call a fully dressed Sanasrothian?" Lorreth asked, his tone droll as he made a beeline for the bar.

"I don't know," I replied.

"Me, either. I've never fucking seen one."

"I remember *you*, Faeling." The sneering voice came from behind the bar. It belonged to a tall high blood with pinched, narrow features; quick, dark eyes; and a deep-set scowl. "You were in here a while ago."

Even with my hood down now, the male behind the bar didn't remember *me*. The denizens of the Cogs had no clue what their new queen looked like. Therefore none of them knelt, which was *perfectly* fine by me.

"If, by a while ago you mean six hundred years and some change, then yes, you're probably right," Lorreth said, dumping a leather pouch full of coins on the bar and sitting down heavily on a stool. "What of it?"

"You got into a fight and broke one of my tables. You also left without paying your tab."

"Gods and martyrs. Six hundred years go by, and you're still bent out of shape over a rickety table and a glass of wine?"

The high blood—presumably the owner of the Fool's Paradise—narrowed his eyes to slits. "All debts are paid." He pointed an index finger with a disturbingly long fingernail up at a sign above the bar that, indeed, said, ALL DEBTS ARE PAID. "You'll have to settle your tab if you expect service from me."

"I don't want any kind of *service* from you. My sister and I came for a glass or two. Let's not make this any more uncomfortable than it already is."

The high blood turned to me for the first time, the icy cold weight of his attention pressing down on me. I was too taken aback by what Lorreth had called me to care much about the male's distasteful sneer, though.

Sister.

He had called me his *sister*.

"I don't even waive the rules for my own kind," the male seethed. "What makes you think I'd waive them for the likes of *you*?"

"My handsome face?"

The high blood gave Lorreth a look that could have stripped the flocked wallpaper from the walls.

"No? All right then. What about this?" The warrior reached back over his shoulder and drew Avisiéth, setting the engraved sword down onto the bar with a clunk.

The high blood's eyes shuttered momentarily, but I had to give it to him. He had balls. He didn't balk for long at the sight of all that sharpened silver. "We accept coin or blood." He paused, assessing Lorreth, and then said, "Blood is preferred."

"Go fuck yourself, tick. The only way you're getting at my blood is if you drain it from me yourself."

The high blood perked up. "That could be arranged."

"You'll have to kill me first," Lorreth added, baring his teeth.

The high blood folded his arms across his chest, pursing his lips. "It's high treason to draw silver in Sanasroth, you realize. What is your name, Faeling? Who is your master?"

A harsh bark of laughter burst out of Lorreth. "My name is Lorreth of the Broken Spires. And I have no master."

At last, the high blood's imperious scowl faded away. There was something oddly satisfying about watching him slowly begin to panic. "Only thralls are permitted here. Ungoverned Fae aren't welcome." He took a step back from the bar top.

"Don't worry. We'll leave once we've enjoyed a carafe of your finest Lìssian red."

Two more high bloods had risen from the nearest table and had come to stand behind us. They were both male and significantly bigger than the vampire behind the bar. One laid a hand on Lorreth's shoulder. "You seem to have forgotten where your kind stand on the food chain around here, warm blood," the one on the right said. A thick, silvered scar ran down his right cheek. "Errigan told you to leave. Get up, right now, and we might give you a head start before—"

I knew it was coming.

Watching it happen was still shocking, though.

Lorreth left Avisiéth where she sat on the bar. Didn't even touch her. He became a black blur as he spun and launched out of his seat. One moment, the scarred high blood had been trying to pull the warrior back, off the stool, and the next, his hand was no longer attached to his wrist. Lorreth had it in *his* hand. Ichor spurted and sprayed from the high blood's wrist (now a meaty stump). The high blood looked down, opened his mouth to scream, and Lorreth jammed the male's hand down his own throat, fingers first.

I staggered back into a stool, nearly losing my footing. "Holy fuck! *Lorreth!*"

"What in all five hells is going *on* here?"

The music that had been playing when we'd entered stopped. Leaden silence blanketed the tavern as everyone turned to look at the newcomer. Taladaius stood by the tavern's entrance. A dark figure in a cloak stood beside him, angled toward the exit, their hood drawn up to conceal their features.

Lorreth stiffened, a dark look forming on his face. He took a step toward Taladaius, but the Lord of Midnight held up a hand, closing his eyes in frustration. "Wait there, Lore. You're covered in blood and not fit for polite company." Taladaius spoke quickly to the stranger in the cloak. Even with my vastly improved hearing, I couldn't make out a word. If I wasn't mistaken, a soundproof shield had temporarily gone up around the two of them.

The cloaked stranger nodded and left without a backward glance, leaving Taladaius standing in the tavern doorway. As always, his clothes were immaculate, his silver hair was swept back, not a strand out of place, but his eyes were wild, his nostrils flared, and his usual composure was compromised. "When I heard you'd left the palace, I knew trouble would find the two of you. But I didn't think you'd be reckless enough to go *looking* for it."

"Lord." Errigan—the other high blood had called the vampire behind the bar by that name—lowered his head, averting his eyes from Taladaius. "I didn't expect you yet. We haven't tallied the night's tithing. Apologies. If you give me a moment—"

"I don't care about the tithe, Errigan. I care about the pool of rapidly growing blood on my tavern floor, and the fact that one of my regulars is currently choking on his own hand. Care to explain what's going on here?"

My tavern floor? This place belonged to Taladaius?

My sire looked fit to burst a blood vessel as he stepped over the pool of blood and planted his hands against the bar top. "Well?"

"The male was causing trouble," Errigan muttered.

Taladaius squinted sidelong at Lorreth. "Is that true?"

"Yes."

"God—" He let out a frustrated huff. "Can't you even *pretend* to lie, for pity's sake?"

"That's not how being Oath Bound works, Tal. You must have forgotten."

For a split second, the echo of sorrow coming from Taladaius faltered, a spike of something that felt a lot like hurt assuming its place. It was gone just as quickly as it had come.

"We only came to get a drink," Lorreth continued. "But this one wouldn't let up about a six-hundred-year-old debt."

"What?" Tal looked like he was at his wit's end.

"I know. Ridiculous," said Lorreth, completely missing the fact that Taladaius was frustrated with *him*.

"All right. Errigan, bring me the ledger. And once you've done that, bring them the wine they wanted. Sinners have mercy."

"But, Lord—"

"Do it, Errigan."

The high blood grew even paler. With his eyes glued to the floor, he disappeared through a doorway into the back of the tavern. Taladaius turned to the two high bloods who had attempted to intervene on Errigan's behalf, sighing as the one with the scar held up the dismembered hand that he had managed to dislodge from his mouth.

"This demands reparation, Lord. Like for like. A hand for a hand!" He spat flecks of his own black blood when he spoke.

"Come now, Anterrin. A hand for a hand is hardly like for like. *Yours* will grow back," Taladaius argued.

"In a month or more! How am I supposed to do anything like this?" He waved his dismembered hand in the air.

Against all good judgment that I *knew* he possessed, Lorreth laughed. "When it grows back all tiny like, at least it'll be in better proportion when you wrap it around your cock."

"Enough!" Taladaius hadn't shouted before. Not even when Ereth attacked me on the dais and Fisher had cut him down. His hands were clenched into fists when Errigan returned with a large, dusty ledger, slamming it down onto the bar. "How much coin will you lose while the hand regrows?" Taladaius asked.

The high blood, Anterrin, considered. "A hundred cröna a day."

The Lord let out an exasperated sound. "You're a gatekeeper, Anterrin. At best, you make ten cröna a day. I'll give you that, though I should halve it for the lie. Come back for the money tomorrow. Errigan will have it ready for you. Khol, get your brother out of here now before he says something stupid and winds up losing his other hand as well."

The two high bloods left, casting venomous glances back over their shoulders as they exited the tavern. As soon as they were gone, Taladaius turned and cracked open the dusty ledger. "Show me the record of this debt," he ordered.

Errigan leafed through the pages from the other side of the bar, craning his neck around until he found it. "There, Lord." He tapped the middle of the page with that creepily long fingernail.

Taladaius looked down at the ledger entry, then looked back up at the high blood. "Eight *thousand* cröna, Errigan? For a bottle of wine and a repair to a table?"

"Compounding interest, Lord! The Faeling left the debt unpaid for centuries!"

Wearily, Taladaius picked up the quill Errigan had brought along with the ledger and drew an impressively straight line through the entry.

"Lord!" Errigan looked set to faint. "I owned this place for eight hundred years and I never *once* forgave a debt!"

My sire snapped the ledger closed and shoved it across the bar toward the other vampire. "And you sold the place to me fifty years ago, along with all its debt, and now I *have* forgiven one of them. That's the end of it. Get him the wine," he commanded. "On the house. And you?" he said, taking me by the arm. "You're coming with me. I need to talk with *you.*"

12

TAL

SARIS

"WHO WAS YOUR friend?"

Taladaius slammed the door to his office closed behind us, growling with frustration. "None of your business."

I hadn't expected him to tell me, but I'd still figured it was worth asking. "I didn't have you pegged as a tavern owner, Taladaius. There's an awful lot of fucking and feeding going on out there, y'know."

I went to pick up the obsidian crow's head paperweight from the vampire's extraordinarily tidy desk, but he slapped my hand away from it, growling irritably. "Oh really? I hadn't noticed. *Where is your mate?*"

I did a three-sixty, taking in the artwork on the walls and his shelves and shelves of books. He had quite the collection. It smelled good in here—like dry paper and earth, warm vanilla and chocolate. Comforting. "Oh, I don't know," I said in a singsong voice. "Nowhere in this realm that I could really pinpoint right now."

Taladaius stared at me blankly.

"Do you not need to blink? *I* need to, but maybe that's my half-Fae side."

Very slowly, he closed his eyes and left them that way. "*Tell* me he hasn't gone through the quicksilver again."

I sat down in the chair on the other side of his desk, studying him quietly for a moment. Again, I went to pick up the crow's head, but when I reached for it, a rope of fire lashed up my arm. I was wearing my gloves—the God Bindings were still best hidden from prying eyes for the time being—but light spilled out of the bottom of the leather cuff, washing up my arm.

Ow.

My hand shook violently. I shoved it into my armpit, pinning it against my side, screwing my eyes shut as I waited for the pain to pass.

"Saeris? What's wrong?"

I dropped my hand into my lap. The light seeping out of my glove was no longer visible, but the pain was still breathtaking. "Nothing. I'm fine." Wow, I needed to find a Sanasrothian actors' troupe and start auditioning for parts; I really sounded like I was telling the truth.

Despite my plausible performance, I could tell that Taladaius wasn't convinced. Not that he contradicted me. "If Kingfisher isn't in Yvelia right now, I need to know."

I slumped back into the chair. "You do?"

"Yes! The entire Blood Court knows what Fisher is capable of. He reminded them when he scythed Ereth down like he was a stalk of brittle wheat in the Hall of Tears. Which, by the way, is causing all kinds of headaches for me. There can't be *four* Lords of Midnight, Saeris. There *have* to be five, which means that a vote now has to be organized..." He stopped himself, huffing. "Never mind that. Look, people are too scared to act against you while Fisher's around. They'll be willing to try their luck if they think you're weak or unprotected. We need to post extra guards at your rooms."

"Do *not* post extra guards." Pain shot up my arm like liquid lightning, pooling in my shoulder. I tried not to flinch. "If you don't want me to look weak, you should remove the guard detail that's already assigned to my rooms. My edict prevents them from stepping out of line, anyway."

Boom.

Boom.

Boom.

I wanted to scream.

My runes were burning through my skin again, all the way down to the bone.

"Mm," Taladaius said, drumming his fingers along the edge of his desk. "Maybe you're right. Let's think about it a moment. In the meantime, why are you hiding your hand down there?"

"I'm not hiding my hand." But I was. I had it tucked between my knees under his desk, and I was pressing it between my thighs in the vain hope that that might make the pain go away.

"Saeris. I'm going to let you off because you're new to all of this, but a vampire can't lie to its maker. A blue aura comes off you when you try. The stronger the aura, the bigger the lie, and right now, you're lighting up my office like a torch. But even if you weren't, I can feel that you're in pain. A *lot* of pain. Tell me what's going on."

Every now and then, I had gotten sick in the Third. After my mother was killed, there had been no one to tend to me while I was ill. Hayden was too young and irresponsible to rely on, and anyway, it was my job to look after him, not the other way around. It hadn't felt right, asking Elroy for help. He had already given me work and offered what protection he could from Madra's guardians, so asking for anything else had felt like too much. So I had been alone. I had shivered my way through fevers without an arm around my shoulder or any words to comfort me. I had told myself I didn't need the help, because I couldn't have it, and what was the point of craving something that would never come? I had convinced myself so thoroughly of this—that I was strong, that I was all I needed, that I didn't *want* anyone else's concern—that now it made me feel like crawling out of my own skin when anyone showed the slightest bit of care for me.

But apparently it was impossible to lie to Taladaius, so I didn't have much choice but to tell him the truth.

"My marks," I said. "They keep flaring." It was the only way to describe it. "I can feel this pressure building inside of me. All the time. And sometimes, it...it swells. It feels like it wants to burst out of my skin. And then it just...goes away."

My maker looked down at my hands. "Take off the gloves. Show me."

Absolutely no part of me wanted to do that. But I did it. I was too tired. Tired of putting up the front. Tired of telling myself I had to deal with everything by myself, when, for the first time since my mother died, I had people again. I wasn't *alone* anymore.

I showed him my hands. Taladaius didn't react when he saw the blackened skin around my runes. Nor did he comment about the fact that they were still glowing, or that they had nearly corroded their way through my skin and hit bone. He twisted his ring of office around his index finger, spinning it so that the warm citrine-colored stone at its center caught the light while he inspected my runes, and his calm confidence and lack of panic eased my own.

I told him about the visit with Everlayne that had unexpectedly turned into a visit with Edina. I described what had happened with my runes then and told him what Edina had said about my Alchemist's runes being unsealed. I even told him about Edina's warning that I needed to find her book in the libraries at Cahlish. After all, she'd told me not to breathe a word of it to Fisher, but she hadn't said anything about enlisting the help of a vampire lord. When I was done, Taladaius mulled the information I had given him over, his storm-gray eyes distant. Eventually, he said, "And she spoke to you? Edina? She had an actual *conversation* with you?"

I nodded. "I mean, it was stilted. She seemed like she was struggling to speak, but yes."

"She wasn't repeating phrases? It didn't seem like she was talking to someone who wasn't there?"

"No. It wasn't like that. She was definitely talking to me. She called me by name."

Taladaius rocked back, balancing his chair on two legs. He whistled. "Well, that's troubling."

"The whole thing was troubling, Taladaius."

"Yes. Yes, of course. But I mean...there are plenty of shades in this realm. They're echoes. Trapped memories a person leaves behind when they die. It often signifies a horrific death, but at least the person's soul moves on. Shades aren't capable of thought, though. They can't have conversations with people."

"Okay?"

"So that means that the entity that puppeted Everlayne's body wasn't an echo of Fisher's mother. It *was* Fisher's mother."

"No, that can't be the case. That would mean that her soul has been here ever since she died. Trapped."

"Right. But not trapped. As far as I know, Edina never gave away a piece of her soul like Fisher did when he saved that idiot out there," he said, jerking his chin back toward the bar. "She wouldn't have been tethered to anyone on this side of the veil, which means that she stayed by sheer force of will alone. And that..." He slowly shook his head. "I don't know what that would have done to a person's soul, but it wouldn't have been good. It would have been torture."

Fisher had been very careful not to let his emotions show when I'd told him that I'd spoken to Edina. His face had remained blank, but he'd known all of this. He'd chosen not to say anything about it, and I knew why. I'd been so worried about my unsealed runes...

Which, once again, were completely fine now. The pain had started to diminish while I was explaining everything to Taladaius. My hands didn't hurt at all, and my skin wasn't peeling or burnt anymore, either. My maker noted as much when he looked down and saw them. "That's a neat trick, Alchemist."

"You think so? I'm a little less impressed by it than you are, I think."

"Perhaps you're just looking at it the wrong way."

"Enlighten me. How *should* I be looking at burning runes and excruciating pain?" From where I was sitting, I had yet to find a silver lining to the situation.

"Well. The way your runes smoldered would indicate that you have access to elemental fire magic. Once harnessed, that will be incredibly useful, no? And the fact that your hands are healed now, after the damage I just witnessed, implies that you also have regenerative magic. Physical magic. Power over the body. At some point, you might be able to heal *others* with your abilities. Yet another thread that connects you to your Alchemist heritage. These things that are happening to your body can all be seen as signs of positive things to come."

"Signs won't do me much good if I can't access the magic, Taladaius. They won't do much good if these powers keep pouring into me and I explode and kill everybody in a forty-mile radius."

My maker snorted. "If that did happen, the blast zone would be more than forty miles. You'd probably destroy half of Yvelia. In fact, that much magic being unmade by itself would probably trigger a chain reaction that would unmake all magic. Everywhere. The whole realm would probably be—"

"You're. Not. Helping."

He had the decency to look contrite. "You're right. I'm sorry. I do want to help. I think I might be able to as well. But first, there *was* something I wanted to talk to you about, Saeris. Something important."

I let my head thump against the back of my chair. "Let's hear it."

He didn't seem overly pleased by my lack of enthusiasm. "I'm not sure if you're aware of this, but you're only the second person I've sired." He waited, watching me. Expecting me to react somehow?

"Okay."

"I saved the life of another, a very long time ago. I'm glad I saved him, and I'm glad I saved you, too. But..."

"But you never wanted children," I offered. "Is that even an appropriate term for what I am to you?" The term felt weird.

Taladaius smiled. "Hmm. Yes and no. The relationship between maker and made could be compared to that of parent and offspring, I suppose. So, yes," he said, observing me with steady eyes. "To use your analogy, I've never wanted children. It isn't my path. So, while I am happy to have prevented your true death, I find myself conflicted. I made you. Most high bloods don't care about the ramifications of that act, but to me, it is a *grave* responsibility..." He trailed off, smiling softly. "Pardon the pun. You are in this position, in part, because of me. It's my duty to make sure that you understand what it is to be a member of this court. It's incumbent on me to make sure you're equipped to survive this place, too.

"For most people, the adjustment from their old existence to the new is more than they can handle. Without guidance, it's easy to make poor choices here. There are many roads to take in Ammontraíeth, and nearly all of them lead to hell. But things are different for you, Saeris. You aren't a full-blooded vampire. Your thirst doesn't rage the way it does with the newly turned. You don't *need* blood. And while you might not know the rules and restrictions of our court, you find yourself in the unique position of not being bound by any of them." He shrugged a shoulder. "Perks of being queen. With all that said, I wanted to speak with you about... well, about Fisher. Your bond with him is unique. My own relationship with him is..."

"Complicated?"

He nodded. "I've found myself in a position where I've held power over him of late. In Gillethrye..." His eyes took on a distant, glazed look. "Let's just say, Gillethrye was no fun for me, either. I would never have stepped foot into that maze if I'd had my way, but... I suppose it was better that Malcolm did send me there in some ways." Taladaius stared down at his hands for a moment, still lost in his thoughts. "Anyway. You're God-Bound with Fisher. And right now, you're bound to me, too. I don't want to hurt Fisher by having any sort of power over his mate. And I definitely don't want your rule over this court undermined by continual accusations from the other Lords of Midnight, claiming that you're my puppet. So, my question to you, Saeris, is this: Would it offend you very badly"—he winced—"if I publicly disavowed you and severed our bond?"

I let out the breath I'd been holding. "Gods alive, Taladaius!"

His eyes went wide. "What?"

"I thought you were trying to break some horrific news to me. I thought someone was *dead*."

"So, you *don't* mind, then? About being disavowed?"

"No, of course I don't mind. I agree with you on all fronts. And I've got to be honest, being able to sense you sometimes is pretty confusing. It doesn't seem right that I have a front row seat to your emotions. But!"

I cut him off before he could speak. "If you want this thing of me, I'm afraid I'm going to have to ask for something in return."

A wary tightness formed at the corners of his storm-gray eyes. "Which is?"

"Presiding over this place is beyond me. I have no experience of ruling over a court and no desire to learn, either. I need someone to cover for me and act on my behalf when I'm in Cahlish. In general, really. I need that to be you."

Taladaius was already shaking his head. "The optics—"

"I don't give a fuck about optics. You were Malcolm's second in command. *He* trusted you with the position, so the court can hardly criticize *me* for doing the same."

He couldn't really argue with that. No one could, which was specifically why I'd made the decision. Taladaius groped for something to say but then gave up, shaking his head. "Are you sure that's what you want?"

"Yes."

"All right, then. So be it. I'll go ahead and make the arrangements on both counts, then. As far as the disavowment goes, it's a simple rite, but we should make a spectacle out of it. I'm sorry," he said. "I know you're not one for grand scenes. Believe me, I'm not, either. But we have to sell it to make the high bloods believe it, and that will unfortunately require some... *theatrics.*"

Great. Just what I needed. Even so, I said, "If you think it's important, then I trust you." And I realized that I did. There were long years of history between the vampire sitting opposite me and the members of the Lupo Proelia. The air was thick with tension whenever anyone even mentioned his name back at Cahlish. There was so much I didn't know when it came to their relationship with Taladaius, but at the end of the day, I could only go by my own experiences with him.

I knew that he had saved my life.

I knew that he was sad.

I knew that I believed him when he said this disavowment was for the best, and honestly, I had hated the idea of sharing such an intimate connection with anyone other than my mate since the second I had woken up. What Taladaius was offering me was a kindness.

I stood up and held out my hand to him. "All right, then. Disavowed it is. No more maker and made bullshit for us."

The tide of Taladaius's sadness broke for a moment, and I felt his relief rushing in. He accepted my hand and shook it. "No more maker and made bullshit," he agreed. "But how about...friends?"

I grinned, because the vampire who had saved me, who was at least fifteen hundred years older than me and had half of Ammontraíeth pissing in their pants whenever he walked lest he turn their blood to smoke, actually seemed nervous. "I think I'd like that."

At that, he returned my grin. "In that case, you'd better call me Tal."

13

SILVER CITY

KINGFISHER

I WAS READY for the bloodshed.

Carrion Swift was not.

Scores of iron-tipped arrows *ting*ed off the heavy shield I held in front of us as we emerged from the quicksilver. The sliver of metal that still clung to the rim of my iris cackled with delight as Swift let out a panicked yelp and grabbed hold of my leather backplate, almost unbalancing both of us and sending us back into the pool.

The Smart Mouth is not so smart now, it purred. *The Smart Mouth sounds stupid.*

"Shit. Shit, shit, shit! We are *definitely* going to die."

"You're choking me, Carrion. Let *go* so I can move!"

The smuggler relinquished his hold on my armor. He staggered to the left, taking up position where I'd told him I would need him to stand earlier. We hadn't had much time to make plans, so I'd made it very simple: *"Stand right there, behind me, on my left. Follow me no matter what."*

This had been much, much easier the last time. Madra's guardians hadn't expected anyone to come bursting out of the quicksilver then. There had been only eight or so archers, and while that had been annoying, I'd overcome them quickly. Now, there was a whole *unit* of archers firing on us. And just to round things out so *very* nicely, I was also babysitting a jackass who was struggling not to trip over his own fucking feet.

The heat in the air hit me like a physical blow.

I ground my teeth together, throwing my shoulder into the shield, and I pushed forward. The second we'd made it out of the pool and the soles of my boots had hit the sandstone floor, I threw the world into darkness.

"My eyes!"

"I can't see!"

"Where are they? Keep firing!"

Cries went up throughout the Hall of Mirrors. My shadows filled the huge hall from floor to ceiling; the air hummed with my magic, blotting out the light, and suddenly, it didn't matter that Madra had assigned an entire unit to guard the quicksilver pool. Her men were human, and humans couldn't see in the dark. One of their *many* flaws.

In fairness, the Fae couldn't see when my shadows flooded their vision, either. I'd warned Carrion of this before we'd entered the pool and had told him what to expect.

There would be shouting. There would be large-scale panic. There would be a lot of scrambling... and then the dying would start.

To my eyes, the room was in monochrome, the chaos unfolding before me in different tones of gray. Guardians fumbled around in their cumbersome armor, crashing into one another. Those who fell to the ground were taken out by their inability to find their own feet again. Archers shot at each other in the dark. Arrows cut through the air, aimed high, aimed at pillars, aimed at anywhere but us. I made sure of that.

It didn't take much. A gentle nudge here. A little tap there. Bow-strings snapped. Guardians went down screaming, shot by their own friends. I led the way through the melee, deflecting any stray arrows that chanced to sail in our direction, and all the while, Carrion yammered away in my ear.

"What's happening? What can you see?"

"Be quiet."

"What's that smell?"

"How the fuck should *I* know?"

"Ow! Oh, oh shit, I'm standing on something soft."

"Pick up your fucking feet!"

"Fisher? Fisher. Are we nearly at the door? Ow, what the hell was *that*? Something hit my arm really hard."

"It was *my fist*. Now shut. The fuck. Up."

We reached the door in one piece, which I was less than thrilled about. If Carrion had taken an iron-tipped arrow to the ass cheek, that would have definitely shut him up. Trouble was, it would have shut him up for good, and Saeris would *not* have been happy about that.

For whatever reason, my mate didn't seem to want the smuggler dead, and I had no choice but to let him live as a result. Worse, I had to *protect* him now, and holy gods, wasn't that just a kicker? I shoved him ahead of me as soon as we were through the door that led out of the Hall of Mirrors and into Madra's palace. We didn't need those gold-clad idiots busting down the door as soon as they realized we weren't inside the hall with them anymore, so I urged a wisp of shadows into the lock and ordered them to stay. The keyhole would no longer accept its key. For a time, at least. The door itself was already triple reinforced, from what I remembered of it from my first visit, and there was no way they'd be able to kick it down. Not until we were long gone.

It was the middle of the night, but the long hallway ahead was washed in brilliant sunlight. *Sunslight*, I thought, correcting myself. I would never get over the fact that Zilvaren had two su—

What in all the gods' names...

The smuggler was standing frozen in the middle of the hall with his hands outstretched, knees bent, ass sticking out like he'd shit himself.

"Why the fuck are your eyes closed?" I demanded.

Carrion cracked one eye open, looking up at me. As soon as he realized we were on the other side of the door, he exhaled, standing up straight, brushing himself off. "I don't know! It was weird, not being able to see anything. Closing them helped."

He was the strangest male. "Okay. Sure. That makes perfect sense," I said.

"All right. No need for that tone. I'd probably have felt a little braver if I'd had *Simon* with me."

Lorreth had called his god sword Avisiéth. A fine, strong name for a sword. Carrion had called his Simon. Maybe that name meant something impressive in Zilvaren, but as far as I had been able to glean thus far, it did not. "For the last time, we could *not* bring two fucking god swords back into this realm. If Madra got a hold of one of them—"

"I know, I know." He waved me off, pulling a face. "She could have used one of them to still the quicksilver again."

"I don't like being here without my sword any more than you do. *Trust* me. But I am *not* getting trapped in this hellhole. Now come on. We need to move." I didn't give him the opportunity to say anything else. I set off running down the hall, and to his credit, the smuggler kept up.

We passed door after door. Sweat trickled between my shoulder blades as I pumped my arms, pushing harder.

Ten.

Nine.

"Wait," Carrion panted.

Eight.

"The plan. Why didn't you tell me what came after the hall?"

Seven.

"Because I knew... you wouldn't *like* it," I grunted.

Six.

Five.

"Fisher?"

Four.

"Fisher, why are we sprinting straight for that window?"

Three.

He started to slow, but I grabbed him by the back of the armor Renfis had lent him, and I held on tight.

Two.

"Pick up your fucking *feet*, Your Highness," I snarled.

One.

I threw him out of the window.

Howling, dry wind ripped at my clothes as I launched out of the damned thing after him.

"Fuck you, Fisher!" Even hurtling toward the ground at a rate of knots, the smuggler still didn't shut up.

I reached for Carrion and a rope made of smoke and flashing black sand erupted from my hand, zipping through the air and lashing around the male's ankles.

Below, the tops of faded red tents rushed up to greet us. Grains of sand stung my eyes, but I kept them open so I could judge when to act.

The fall was easy.

Quick.

Sixty feet from the ground, I reached for my secondary magic and prayed that it answered. It was fickle and often off wandering when I called. Luck was on my side today, though. I pictured a vast net stretching across the wide street below, and the crosshatched rope began to lash and twine across the gap.

It anchored to the roof of the building on the left. One corner of it anchored to the building on the right—

Shit.

Carrion hit the net. The rope sagged in the middle, cushioning his weight. By the time I landed after him, the anchor point on the roof of the right building was hanging on by a thread.

It snapped.

I fell straight through the netting, through the canopy of the bleached red tent beneath it, and landed with a hard *"Ooof!"* on something *very* uncomfortable.

The sound of rotten, creaking wood reached my ears, and a second later I was deposited unceremoniously onto blistering hot sand. Stale bread rolls thumped down on top of me.

Swift appeared in my field of view, his auburn hair backlit and glowing like a sunset on fire. "That was *not* okay," he said in a flat tone.

I blinked sand out of my eyes. "Ahh, quiet. I broke *your* fall, didn't I?"

"My cart! Bastards! You've destroyed my—" The shout cut off when the old woman took in the two miscreants who had destroyed her property. Carrion had lived in Zilvaren for lifetimes, but he had done so as one of them. Glamored. He'd been tall and broad for a human, but now he was hovering near seven feet and possessed the pointed ears of the Fae. As for me? I was a sight taller than Swift. Significantly better-looking, too, but that was beside the point. I flashed my canines at the sunburnt woman, giving her a broad smile.

"Apologies, madam. We had a little argument with gravity. Looks like gravity won."

I acted fast. It would have been smarter to glamor us as soon as we'd left the Hall of Mirrors, but there hadn't been time. I dove deep into my magic and cast it over myself and the smuggler, the change taking effect in the blink of an eye. I didn't feel any different, per se, but the layer of illusion clung close to my body like a second skin—an itchy one that I immediately wanted to shed. When I looked at Carrion, he was shorter again. Rounded ears. Shoulders narrower. Stubby, ineffective teeth. He looked human. I tried not to think about what I looked like, masquerading as one of them...

The stall owner righted her lopsided hat, rubbing her forehead. Was she about to pass out? She *had* just seen us morph from Fae to human, which accounted for the confusion on her face.

"Hah. Looks like gravity won. That was *almost* funny," Carrion groused. He thrust out his hand, offering to help me up. Loath as I was, I accepted; my ribs were on fire, and I was so caught up in the debris I'd made of the woman's bread cart that I kind of needed the help. The smuggler looked far too pleased with himself as he hauled me to my feet. "Where to now?" he asked.

"You tell me. The whole point of you coming back to Zilvaren was because you know this city. Better than anyone, you said."

"And that's true," Carrion snapped back. "But I need to know what you want to take care of first. The silver, the infected feeders, or the brother?"

"There! Down in the square!"

Through the gigantic hole we'd ripped in the tent's canopy, we could see three guardians leaning out of the window high above, peering down onto the street. They'd already spotted us. It wouldn't be long before they were on top of us.

"The silver," I answered. "We'll take care of the silver first. Now let's move."

———+———

"You're too pale," Carrion hissed. He charged headfirst through a network of winding side streets, keeping his eyes firmly fixed on the tops of his boots. I followed, hand resting on the hilt of the dagger at my hip.

"What do you mean, *too* pale?"

"I mean, even the dead in Zilvaren have more color in their cheeks than you do. The suns are pretty intense here. Everyone's burned or tanned, or both. You look like you've lived underground all your life. It's making people stare."

I glanced around and saw that he was right. People were staring. "And?"

"And it would be better if we went unnoticed right now. We don't fit in here as it is."

"I've already glamored us. I can't do any more than that. My magic needs time to replenish."

Carrion's pace slowed a fraction. "Replenish? What does *that* mean?"

"It means to refill, refuel, re—"

"Saints and martyrs, do you have to be so literal? I know what the *word* means. I want to know why your *magic* needs to replenish."

I bit back a sigh, eyeing the crowd from deep inside my drawn-up hood. "I'm not Zilvaren-born, Carrion. My magic isn't of this place. I can't draw from it as freely as I would back in Yvelia. We're lucky I can draw from it at all. There are realms and worlds amid the void of this universe that are entirely barren of magic. If a seed of magic didn't still cling for purchase somewhere within the bowels of this miserable place, I'd be completely cut off from my gifts. I just exhausted a good portion of the magic available to me back in the hall. It'll be a while before I have full access to my magic again. Glamoring us might not demand much of my resources, but that doesn't mean I'm going to sacrifice precious energy by giving myself a fucking tan."

Carrion didn't say anything for a beat. But then a thought occurred to him. "If you exhaust all of your magic, you'll be as powerless as me, then?"

I scoffed at that. "Of course not. Don't be ridiculous. I'll still know how to hold a fucking *sword*."

"All right. There's no need to be rude about it. Can you—look, can you just stop scowling at people? This is the Hub. Zilvaren's elite live here. Everybody knows everybody, and we do *not* look like we belong to the city's rich and well-to-do. If you keep glowering like that, they're definitely going to notice us."

"This is the *nice* part of the city?"

"Believe it or not, yes. Quickly, we're going this way." Carrion squinted up and down the street before darting down a side alley. I grumbled, following, not liking any of this one bit.

We had three days until Saeris awoke the quicksilver again, though. There was a lot to be accomplished in that time, and Carrion's knowledge of Zilvaren was already paying off. He *seemed* to know where he was going. Or...wait a minute. "We're heading away from the palace, Swift. Do you know of some secret way into the treasury?"

Rats skittered out of narrow gaps between the buildings, screeching as they bolted away from us. There was nothing back here but a few ancient-looking sandstone houses that looked like they would crumble with the smallest shove.

"We're not going to the treasury," Carrion said, forging ahead toward the end of the alley.

He was joking. Had to be. "Say that again?"

"Madra stripped this whole city of all metal, precious and otherwise, a long time ago. She's paranoid as hell about people having access to it. So what do you think her treasury is going to be like, Kingfisher? Is she likely to store all of her metals in the kind of place that would be easy to break into? Or is she going to put them someplace not even the gods themselves would be able to access?"

We had reached the end of the alleyway. "Your point?"

"No one has ever broken into Madra's treasury. No one even knows where it is. And believe me, I spent a good part of the last thousand years trying to figure that out myself. We don't have time to solve that mystery right now, so I'm taking you to the next best source of silver I can think of." He cut me a roguish grin. "The Brigand's Bank."

"Why am I not surprised that you have an account at a place called the Brigand's Bank?"

"Oh, I don't have an account, Lord Cahlish." He winked at me. "I *own* it."

He arced his boot over the ground between us, sweeping back waves of sand to reveal a worn wooden hatch with no handle beneath. The bastard was unbearably smug as he squatted down and pressed his palm against the splintered wood. I heard the inner workings of a lock being opened from the other side, and then the small hatch popped up just enough for Carrion to wedge his fingers into the gap and lift it open.

An act of small magic.

I shouldn't have been surprised that he was capable of such things. Even uneducated and untrained in his powers, Carrion must have noticed he could do things that other people couldn't. The Daianthus line possessed more magic than many of the other houses in Yvelia.

"That smells like a sewer," I observed, peering into the dark hole.

Swift laughed. "It does. But you'll be relieved to know that this is actually how the Hub's supply of clean water is delivered. Delightful, right?"

Zilvaren was an ancient city. It had existed long before Madra ascended to the throne. A feat of engineering, it had once been the seat of a council of magic users. Laws had been passed here. There had been hanging gardens, and beautiful water fountains large enough for the city's children to play in. The history of this place was well documented in Yvelia. It had always been circular, shaped like a wheel, yes, but it was Madra who had segregated it into wards. The huge walls that divided Zilvaren—and its *people*—sank deep underground. When you wanted to build high on an unstable foundation, you had no choice but to dig deep for purchase. The dank tunnels Carrion guided us through were tall enough for a man to stand at his full height, but not a Fae male. I habitually ducked my head along most of the route, forgetting I was shorter than normal. Whenever we hit one of the walls' buttresses— Carrion using magic I hadn't known he possessed to open heavy wooden doors in the meter-thick stonework—we *did* have to double over to make it through the gap.

Carrion had found a torch that he'd apparently left at the tunnel entrance for this exact purpose. Its orange glow threw a halo of light up the walls and gave off just enough light for us to see by as we sloshed through the ankle-deep water.

The smell had gone from unpleasant to downright foul as we'd passed beneath one ward, then another, then another. I had smelled fields of corpses after a battle that were less offensive than these tunnels. I started breathing through my mouth after the fourth door we passed through... and then quickly reverted back to inhaling through my nose. Breathing through my mouth meant I could *taste* it.

"I admit, this was a whole lot less disgusting when I was glamored before," Carrion groaned. "You might have changed the way I looked, but I think I retained my Fae sense of smell this time around."

I kept my mouth shut and glowered at the back of his head.

Eventually, he announced that we had come far enough and gestured to yet another wooden hatch overhead. "I can't reach it. There's nothing for me to stand on," he said. "You're gonna have to let me boost up on your shoulder."

"No."

"All right, then, you boost yourself up on *my* shoulder. Either way, one of us has to get up there, and unless you can grow your arms or something..."

"For fuck's sake." I made a cradle for his boot out of my hands. "Just get it over with already."

The next few minutes were very annoying. I had Swift's ass in my face for at least thirty seconds, which were thirty seconds I would have to remember to blot from my memory once all of this was done. Then I had to help push him out of the fucking hole. And then I had to jump up and grab the sides of the hatch and pull myself up anyway because he couldn't find anything long enough to lower down and pull me up.

Useless.

The light from the twin suns had somehow gotten stronger while we'd been navigating the tunnels. My eyes took a moment to adjust to the brightness as I stretched my back and brushed off my leathers.

Carrion sat on top of a low, crumbling wall, watching me with that telltale glimmer in his eyes that meant he was about to say something that would make my blood boil. And sure enough...

"Y'know, I've just realized something."

"What?"

"You are completely at my disposal right now, aren't you. This next step in our plan relies entirely on me taking us somewhere and securing us an inordinate amount of silver. Which I think is probably worth something, no?"

"*No.*"

"And that got me to thinking that I could probably leverage the deep gratitude you must be feeling toward me right now by suggesting that we go and visit an old haunt of mine along the way."

"We don't have time, Carrion."

"I beg to differ. It should take us no more than a couple of hours to load up with the silver. Once we've done that, we'll have to wait until tomorrow to go and fetch Hayden, anyway."

"You could just point me in the direction of Saeris's brother and go about your business, Swift."

Carrion looked off down the side street we had stepped into, the corners of his mouth tugging down as he thought about this. The sight of his face like that, in profile, stirred a long-dead memory from the archives of my mind. A memory that was faded and moth-eaten at its corners.

The courtyard in front of the apartment back in Ballard.

My mother had been speaking with someone, and I had been tugging on her skirts, pestering her for Bettell biscuits. In that gentle way of hers, she had urged me to go and buy the biscuits for myself since I wasn't a Faeling anymore and had pressed a coin made of brass into my hands. A whole cröna. An old one, worth twice as much as the new ones among the right circles. The piece of brass had been the most money I had ever held in my hands back then. I had marveled at it, stroking its surface reverently as I'd walked barefoot down the pathways of Ballard, on my way to Wendy's to spend my fortune.

The face stamped into the coin had been regal and proud.

The face of Rurik Daianthus.

It took me by surprise, in that moment, that Carrion Swift bore a striking resemblance to his father.

He turned away from the street and looked back at me, his eyes clear and sharp. "I know I'm not very useful to anyone in Yvelia, Fisher. But I want to be. And I can be useful in this. I told Saeris I'd help. I told her I'd come back. So, no. I can't just leave you."

A pang of *something* spasmed in my chest, but I pushed it away, for once annoyed with myself for letting the past work its way under my skin. There was no denying it: Yes, Saeris had slept with the smuggler. But she wasn't sleeping with him now. And she was entitled to her past, as I was entitled to mine. There was no sense regretting events that had helped form us as beings. And she was my mate now. My *mate*. She was beautiful, fierce, clever, independent, and strong. It made sense that even Carrion Swift—a seasoned thief and well versed in the art of duplicity, by all accounts—wanted to keep his word when he gave it to her. He was her friend, much as it irked me. And I would accept that.

"All right." I set my jaw, huffing unhappily. "Fine. Where is this old haunt of yours?"

Swift leaped up from the wall, kicking up a cloud of powder-fine sand when he landed on the ground. He clapped, crowing. "You are going to *love* this place. They have this ale that, well, yes, it *is* distilled from rat urine, but—"

"Carrion!"

"I'm joking, I'm joking!" He held up his hands. Still grinning, he turned and started walking up the alley. "Seriously. Can't you *tell* when someone's joking, Fisher?"

The beer tasted so bad that I feared Carrion had not been joking. He was putting it back so enthusiastically that I figured it wouldn't kill me, though. I sipped on the contents of my tankard, watching the humans as they came in and out of the tavern. The woman behind the bar had recognized Carrion immediately. She obviously knew him well, too, given that she warned him to behave himself or else she would toss him out on his ass.

A line of questionable-looking individuals stopped by our table. They all greeted the smuggler and asked him where he'd been, and Carrion came up with a new—and even more unbelievable—excuse for his absence every time. I hid my face in my beer, ignoring the stares from Swift's compatriots. Their curiosity had them loitering at the table for longer than felt polite as they waited for Carrion to introduce his new friend, but Carrion was only *loosely* acquainted with the universal rules of etiquette and tolerated the awkward silence while he waited for them to leave without breaking a sweat.

I, on the other hand, *was* sweating. My shirt was plastered to my back. My hair was damp. It was hotter than the fifth level of hell in the tavern, and the temperature showed no signs of abating anytime soon.

CALLIE HART

"I fucking hate it here," I murmured into my cup.

Carrion huffed out a breath of laughter. "Ahh, the Third grows on you after a while."

I shot him an incredulous look. "Which part? The children starving in the streets? Or is it the hot beer?"

"Isn't beer supposed to be hot?"

"No. No, it is not."

"Huh. I didn't know that." He shrugged, downing another huge mouthful of his drink.

The magnanimous mood that had struck me earlier had fled a while back, and now I was getting restless. I threw back what was left in my tankard, wincing as I swallowed, and then slammed it down onto the table. "We're done here, Carrion. Time to go."

"No, we're not. We're nowhere near done!" He looked like a Faeling who'd been told he had to go home early from winter fair.

"I get that you're popular. I'm sure it must be nice to see your very interesting friends, Carrion, but we have things to take care of. I want to leave this godscursed place and get back to my mate, and there is literally nothing you can say that will change my mind on this. So let's go."

"Fisher, Fisher, whoa, whoa, whoa." He grabbed my arm and yanked me back down into my seat. "Okay, all right. So I might not have been one hundred percent honest earlier back in the alley. I didn't just feel like stopping by here for a drink. I kind of *had* to come by Kala's."

Gods alive, this male. He was something else. *"Explain."*

"Well, as I said before, I *am* the owner of the Brigand's Bank. But I'm the joint owner. I have a business partner. We have a vault where we store our items—"

"Contraband."

"All right, yes. Our contraband." He pulled a sour face at me. "The door to that vault requires two keys to open it. I have one. Eric has the other. But since I disappeared some time ago and he probably spent a long time scouring the city for me and came up blank, I'm betting Eric employed the services of a vault breaker and has subsequently gone to ground with our goods."

This was precisely the kind of nonsense I'd been expecting. I shoved the table back so I could stand up.

"Wait, where are you going?"

I hoped my expression communicated my feelings effectively, because I didn't have the words. "I'm going back to the palace. I'm going to find Madra's treasury, even if I have to tear the palace down brick by brick. And then I am going to find somewhere hopefully a little less hot to wait until Saeris reopens the quicksilver. And then I am going home."

"You don't need to *do* that," Carrion whispered loudly. "We just need to wait for the vault breaker. Once he gets here, we'll have him tell us where Eric has taken our stuff and we'll be in the clear. We'll go and pick out what we need, nice and quietlike. I keep the silver. Eric can keep the gold and all the jewels. I get to help Yvelia. We find Hayden. We go home, and everyone's happy."

I was going to have no teeth left by the end of this excursion; I would have ground them all to dust. "So your plan is entirely contingent on this vault breaker showing up here?"

"Yes. But he *is* going to show."

"And how the hell can you know that?"

"Because he *always* comes here once his dealings are done for the night."

"How can you even tell what time it is?"

"There are clocks everywhere, Fisher. Look." He pointed at a metal prong jutting out of the wall over by the door. It was bathed in light and casting a thin finger of shadow perpendicularly across the stonework.

"That isn't a clock—"

Carrion jumped to his feet, nearly upending his beer in the process. "Vorath! Vorath Shah!"

A man stood in the tavern doorway, half in, half out. His black hair was wild, tinged with gray at his temples, sticking up in all directions.

His dark brown eyes rounded with surprise when he looked in our direction.

"Where d'you—no," Carrion sputtered. "Don't you do it. Don't you run!"

The man ran.

Carrion hurdled over the table, knocking both our beers over.

"Carrion *fucking* Swift! If that's another of my tables broken because of you!" hollered the woman behind the bar, but Carrion didn't waste any time checking the furniture. He was sprinting after the man in the sun-stained shirt and dusty pants who had just fled the tavern without a backward glance.

I had no business chasing vault breakers through the streets of Zilvaren. And clearly that was who this Vorath Shah was. But I followed Carrion all the same, because the vault breaker Vorath Shah hadn't been looking at Carrion when he'd bolted.

The stranger had been looking right at *me*.

14

BLOOD IN THE MILK

SAERIS

Total known dead: 1,373
Total known infected: 1,665
Estimated infected landmass: 2,039 hectares

TAL DIDN'T BLINK as he led the way through the chaotic halls of Ammontraíeth.

The high bloods knelt for me, but it was *him* they shied away from, averting their eyes—only natural, really, considering the male could boil the blood in their veins with only a flick of his wrist. I'd watched it happen during my coronation, when Ereth's followers had tried to climb the steps to the dais, and the horrific sight lingered with me even now. It made sense that the members of the Blood Court feared the male.

The pale ghost of his reflection kept pace beside him in the obsidian walls, the image of him so near perfect in the glassy black stonework that I almost had trouble telling them apart. My doppelgänger strode beside me, too, gait confident, head held high. When my hands moved to the silver-tipped daggers at my hips, her hands moved, too. When I turned to stare at her, she stared coolly back at me, her face a mask of indifference, but I recognized the weariness in her. There were shadows beneath her blue eyes.

We'd had *news* this evening. The kind of troubling news that caused panic. Lorreth had procured a swift-winged hawk from somewhere and was using it to trade messages with the temporary camp on the other side of the mountain range. Every evening, they would update us with our losses and an estimation of total land lost to the rot ... and so far, the numbers were not good.

Over thirteen hundred dead.

More infected.

Huge swaths of land blackened and dead.

Teams of warriors were riding out each morning, Danya among them. They were cornering and dismembering as many of the infected feeders as they could, but it wasn't enough.

A tide of destruction was creeping across the land, and I was stuck here at the Black Palace, shackled by a crown I didn't want and a court of high bloods who didn't want *me*. It was a sacrifice that had to be made, though. If I refused to lead the Blood Court, then another high blood would assume the role, and that would be far, *far* worse ...

The sound of our heels striking the polished floor echoed loudly as we made our way deeper into the bowels of the palace. Lorreth was with Carrion in the training hall, attempting to whip him into shape, and without the warrior at my side to remind them of their manners, it seemed as though the members of the Blood Court had taken to staring. Groups of high bloods halted their hushed conversations, their eyes carving chunks out of me before resentfully dropping to their knees as we passed.

"Ignore them," Taladaius said, as we rounded a corner and found ourselves alone. We stood at the foot of a long, steep flight of stairs that rose into darkness. "The Blood Court is an archaic place. Its members are like insects trapped in amber. Nothing changes here. We are predictable in our cruelty. Predictable in our violence. It's change that is feared most in a place like this. They aren't worried about you, per se. More ... what you represent."

I hummed thoughtfully, glancing back in the direction of the well-dressed vipers who had been sizing me up so openly. "I know I've given you discretionary rule here, Tal. But I still have ultimate power over this entire court. Have you thought that maybe they *should* be worried about me?"

My maker—my *new friend*—hovered in place, foot placed on the first step of the staircase, something dark and intrigued glittering in his pale gray eyes. "I have found myself wondering that question, actually," he mused.

"And?" A lot hinged on this moment. There was so much unspoken between us. He had saved me and brought me here. He had placed the crown on my head and given me this power...and he had never once asked me what I intended to do with it. I was mated to an enemy of Sanasroth. I had already decommissioned their army, as it were. At any moment, it was within my purview to defang the entire court and bring the black spires of Ammontraíeth crashing down on all their heads.

Tal was more aware of this than anyone.

And yet he shrugged.

"I know you hope to save the high bloods who live here, Saeris. To instill in them some kind of belated moral compass. I know you hope to eradicate the horde and put them in the ground eventually, after you've given the court some time to get used to the idea. Apart from that...I try not to bother myself with the politics of regents, Your Highness." His voice held no emotion, but the slight bow he offered me gave the impression that he was being *very* sarcastic. "I'm but a lowly Lord of Midnight. It would be impertinent of me to second-guess the motives of our esteemed queen."

I was puffing and clutching a stitch in my side by the time we reached the top of the stairs. Five hundred and seventy-three steps. That's how far I'd gotten before I'd given up counting and focused on my breathing; apparently, even half-vampires didn't possess a bottomless well of energy.

"Why the hell...do you guys always insist on...making your libraries so fucking...hard to get to?"

Tal wasn't nearly as out of breath as me, but it was satisfying to see he wasn't totally unaffected by the climb. "It's a Fae tradition, actually. Malcolm rejected most of the old conventions when he realized what he had become, but this was one he held to. Our elders considered knowledge a sublime resource. They decided that the closer to the heavens a court's gathered knowledge could be housed, the better. There was also some consideration for the idea that the harder you had to work for the knowledge you were seeking, the more you had earned the right to benefit from it. Hence..." He gestured to the fifteen-foot-tall lacquered doors in front of us. They were black with panels brushed in gold leaf; twin hissing snakes cast in gleaming gold made for door handles, fangs bared, tongues forking from their open mouths.

Tal wrapped a hand around the snake closest to him, using it to pull the door open. "This was once one of Malcolm's favorite places in the palace. He began to hate it after a while, though. He stopped coming, which made it one of *my* favorite places."

"Close that damned door! Do *not* let the cat out!" The croaky command came from far away. Female? I wasn't sure. The voice was too rough to tell. Tal winced, ushering me into the library; he scanned the floor, presumably watching for a cat that may or may not be trying to escape.

Once we were inside and the door was closed, the vampire visibly relaxed.

The Ammontraíeth library was beautiful. It wasn't as large as the one at the Winter Palace, and there was no glass dome overhead to display the night sky, but that didn't matter. All libraries contained magic. Even libraries that didn't specialize in such things. Because what was a book, if not a portal into another realm, another time, another life even. But magic hung thick in the air in this library. It was no one thing I could pinpoint. Not the way the evenlight bathed the spines of the books that sat in the stacks. Not the way the strange pale green fire that burned in the grate by the windows seemed to flicker backward, or down, or... *in* on itself. And certainly not the little birds that flitted and swooped through the air, buzzing the top of Tal's head as he approached the long table that ran the length of the room.

"Oh. Oh, wow. Is that bird made of..." I squinted, trying to make sure I wasn't seeing things.

Tal snatched the tiny bird that was dive-bombing his head from out of the air. He held it out for me to see. "Paper," he said. "Folded to represent one of Yvelia's rare breeds. They're called stargazers."

The paper bird's wings rustled as it tried to escape Tal's grasp. It opened and closed its beak, pecking at the vampire's hand, clearly annoyed at having been caught.

"It looks so real," I whispered.

"It is real. It lives here, in the library, among the books. It lays its eggs. It rears its young. It will die here one day." The bird seemed to object to that statement; it pecked the back of Tal's hand even harder. The vampire tutted, smiling softly as he raised the little stargazer up and opened his hand, releasing it. It was gone in a flash of white, pinwheeling off into the stacks.

"There are hundreds and hundreds of them up there, nesting in the rafters. They've been here for as long as anyone can remember. Over a thousand years, probably. Someone folded mating pairs a long time ago and gave them a spark of magic. They kept hold of that magic, and passed it on, and passed it on again."

"But...how?" It didn't seem possible. "They're just *paper*."

Tal was solemn, letting his head hang as he pulled out a chair at the end of the long reading table and slowly sat down. He stacked his hands on his stomach, storm-gray gaze finding me at last. "Aren't we just the same? Made from the same material as the sea and the dirt and the sky? Folded from the scraps of the gods and entrusted with a spark of magic that makes *us* real?"

The statement rocked me a little. It undid me at the same time. "You believe that we were made by the gods? Put here by them, as part of some grand design?"

Taladaius snorted. "No, I don't. I think that one day a magician folded some paper and created these birds." He let his head drop back, a small smile twitching at the corners of his mouth as he watched the silent birds swooping and wheeling high above our heads. "I think it took a curious mind to combine the ingredients it took to make us, too. But that's all. Where any kind of life exists, *magic* proliferates, Saeris. We create all the wonders of this realm just by being present to witness them, and it's always magic that lights the way. That is what *I* believe."

"He speaks like he knows what he's talking about," a dry voice observed from the shadows. It was the same voice that had demanded we close the door.

Tal's smile became rueful as he turned to face the female who hobbled out of the stacks. She was stooped double, her back hunched, shoulders hiked up around her ears. Deep wrinkles lined her face. The puff of hair floating around her head was as white as the fresh snow that capped Omnamerrin. I had only seen her once before, at my coronation.

Algat's eyes were shrunken into her head, black and glassy as the obsidian walls of the palace. They skipped over Taladaius as if she found nothing of import where he was sitting and homed in on me with startling intensity. Hobbling, she descended the stairs and crossed the library, then gripped the back of a chair as, slowly and grumbling openly, she sank to her knees in front of me. "What an *honor* this is, my queen," she rasped. "A visit from our new regent. And so finely dressed, too."

She didn't hide her sarcasm; it was an artless jab. My fighting leathers were in poor taste, apparently. My boots were mud-spattered and worn. But this was the Lord of Midnight who had made me feed from Fisher in front of the entire court. She was also the one my mate had told me to be most wary of. I didn't give a flying fuck what she thought about my clothes or the state of my boots. She was lucky I didn't make her clean them while she was down there.

She grinned up at me, displaying yellowed, blunt canines. "I knew you'd find your way up here eventually. I've been waiting for you."

"Is that so?" Ice hardened my words. I liked very little about the old female. I especially didn't like the way she eyed me as she scratched the back of her hand.

"Indeed, indeed. Might I get up now, child? These old bones of mine don't like the draft down here."

It would have been petty to say no. Reluctantly, I gave her a stiff nod. "You may rise."

"Thank you, Your Majesty. You have my *deepest* gratitude." The crone didn't even flinch as she popped up from the floor and sprang away, suddenly as nimble as a newborn lamb. "As I was saying, I have been waiting for your arrival. After all, you *are* hungry."

The accusation made the hairs on the back of my neck rise. "No, I'm not."

"Oh, yes. Yes, you are. I feel your hunger beating like a pulse all the time."

"I don't need to feed," I told her in a clipped tone, but she shook her head, her jowls wobbling.

"Not for blood, King Killer. For information. For home. For *release*." She cackled as she spoke that last word, like it was something lewd, to be ashamed of. "I feel you hungering at all hours," she continued. "Insatiable, you are. Always *wanting*."

I rounded on Tal. "This is what you brought me here for? *This* is how you thought you were going to help me?"

The vampire splayed his hands wide, sighing. "Sometimes the medicine tastes bad, Saeris."

"How is *she* the medicine?"

"I am the Keeper of Records, child," Algat sniffed. "I know them all better than they know themselves. There are books within this room that you would like to meet. It's within *my* power to facilitate an introduction."

My spine stiffened. "This library doesn't have any books on Alchemy," I said.

Algat's eyebrows had ceased to exist a long time ago, it seemed, but the patch of skin where they had once been rose high up her forehead. "Is that so?"

"Yes. Belikon wiped the whole realm clean of any information pertaining to the Alchemists and their power."

The ancient female aimed a very serious expression at me, nodding her head sagely, but she couldn't keep it up; she burst out laughing before I was finished speaking. "Oh, child. You *are* wet behind the ears. Did you finish suckling at your mother's teat yesterday?"

"Algat," Tal said in a warning tone. "Remember who you're speaking to."

The female scowled at the silver-haired Lord. "My memory is as sharp as yours and then some, wraith. I know exactly to whom I speak. King Killer. Day's End. The Last Tide. Namebreaker—"

"Enough!" Tal brought his fist crashing down onto the table. The ancient female cut off her tirade, a rope of spittle dangling from her top lip. She stared at Tal for a second, her face expressionless, but the air was suddenly still, thick with a prickling tension.

Tal kept her locked in his sights. He did *not* look away.

"All right, then!" Algat clapped her hands together, suddenly standing on the other side of the table. Where the hell had she *come* from? I hadn't seen her move. As she swung around, her body moved in a jerky, unnatural way that made my skin crawl. "Belikon De Barra! Belikon De Barra!" she chanted in a childish, high-pitched voice that was nothing like her earlier croak. "The king of the Yvelian Fae has never stepped foot across the threshold of your domain, *my queen*," she said mockingly. "My father forbade it. That poisonous old toad has never sought an audience with *my* books. They are intact."

I didn't want her to know what kind of an effect this news was having on me, but I wasn't quick enough. The stooped female heard my pulse quicken, and a rotten smile slowly crept across her face.

"My father was a patron of the Alchemists. He supported their crafts. Nurtured them. Where others saw only danger, Malcolm of Sanasroth saw power."

"What do you mean, danger?"

"Oh, yes. An Alchemist is a *dangerous* thing. Has no one ever told you what you are? No one's told you why Belikon and your precious Queen Madra both hunted down and murdered all your kind?"

"Algat." Tal didn't raise his voice this time, but he didn't need to. The single word resonated around the library with the force of a thunderclap. Algat jumped, the wild light in her eyes sputtering out as she cowed, lowering her head away from the vampire. I felt it, too: a crushing force against the back of my neck that wanted me to bow, kneel, crawl for the male sitting at the end of the table. It was by sheer force of will alone that I didn't drop to my knees. "Enough of the games," Tal said. "She wants to understand who she is and what she's capable of. She doesn't need to be scared out of her mind along the way. You will help her find facts and nothing more—"

A wisp of shadow coalesced in the air before me, taking shape. The blur darkened, falling, and by the time it hit the surface of the reading table, it had become a cat. A black cat, to be precise, with glowing red eyes.

It fixed me with a leonine stare that reminded me of other, far larger cats I had encountered out in the dunes back home, and a thrill of panic chased up my spine.

"Where the fuck did that come from?" I breathed.

"That is Guru," Algat said, disgruntled. The hold that Tal had exerted over her was broken now; she shot the other vampire a filthy glance as she shuffled down to the other end of the table and started aggressively petting the cat with a gnarled hand.

The cat *was* there. She was *stroking* it.

"He keeps the rats and *other* pests at bay," she said meaningfully, again serving up another baleful glare for Taladaius. "I hear you have a white fox living in your chambers, King Killer. I wouldn't let it out roaming, if I were you. Guru doesn't like canines of *any* persuasion."

I had made the decision to keep Onyx in my rooms for this very reason. I had no idea what kind of trouble he might find himself in at the Black Palace, and I didn't intend on finding out, either. Guru seemed pleasant enough, but still. The cat threw back his head and squinted, enjoying the attention as Algat petted him, his tail flicking left and right.

Taladaius shuddered. "I have some other matters to attend to, Saeris," he said, rising stiffly. "Algat will behave and make herself available to you for as long as you want to stay here and conduct your research. Right, Algat?"

The female just sniffed.

My maker—he *was* still my maker, at least for now—made his exit, leaving me with the old female and the cat.

Algat had produced a saucer from her ratty skirts and was pouring a thin stream of milk from a ewer into it when I faced her again. "Do not think," she said, "that just because that wraith commanded me to assist you, there will not be a cost associated with the labor, Your Highness."

I huffed. "Wouldn't dream of it. I *am* your queen, though. Doesn't that count for anything?" There was something unsettling about the way the female moved, like a spider that scuttled too quickly. I didn't like it.

Tucking a mat of unruly hair behind a flopping ear, the female tutted under her breath. "Even a queen must pay her debts, Your Highness. *Especially* a queen."

Guru ducked his head and delicately sniffed the saucer of milk. He yowled, sounding displeased, turning away from it and raising his hackles.

"And what will your help cost me tonight?" My tone was sharp, but I was tired of the old female. There wasn't time for her to be *purposefully* difficult.

She grinned, as if she was plucking the thoughts right out of my head and didn't care a jot about my impatience. "Come now. You haven't ruled over this court for very long, it's true. But you should know by now that the cost for most things is *always* blood."

The crimson marbled the white, blood swirling amid the milk.

Just five drops.

That's all it had been. I'd watched each ruby teardrop tremble and fall from the pad of my index finger only half as intently as Guru, who had seemed poised to pounce and start lapping my blood straight from the puncture wound on my finger at any moment.

Now his pink tongue rasped at the contents of the saucer with fervor, a rattling, low-pitched purr working out of his throat while he drank.

"He likes the taste of you," Algat observed, hands on her hips.

"That's *really* disturbing." We had cats back in Zilvaren. People kept them for the same reason Algat kept Guru in the library: They made excellent rat catchers. But cats did not make good pets, as far as I was concerned. They couldn't be trusted. At least a dog was loyal enough to die in solidarity if its owner dropped down dead in their own home. I'd heard too many tales of cats eating their owners' faces under those circumstances.

"Guru's very discerning," Algat observed, watching proudly as the feline cleared the saucer. "He won't drink from just anyone."

"I'm honored," I said dryly.

Algat *harrumph*ed. "You should be. Now. Books. I'm feeling very generous tonight. Five drops of blood equate to one whole book."

"Wow. You're right. *So* generous."

"Consider yourself lucky. Normally, I'd only relinquish a few pages. And they would have been in Alchimeran. I'm assuming you don't read, write, or speak the language of your people?"

Gods, I wanted to punch her. "No."

"Hm." She flared her nostrils, looking unimpressed. "Like I said. *Lucky.*"

Algat disappeared into the stacks, and I stayed put, declining to follow her into the shadows. Guru remained, perched on the edge of the table like some red-eyed gargoyle, staring at me like he was trying to *will* more blood out of me. Gods only knew why I did it, but I squeezed my fingertip over his empty saucer, pressing two more droplets out onto the plate for him. The cat fell upon the gifted blood like he was starving, making a weird gurgling sound as it licked the saucer clean for a second time.

"Here we a—" Algat looked at me. "Tell me you didn't give him undiluted blood?"

"I did."

"Great." She slapped her hands against her sides, and a puff of dust exploded from her skirts. "He'll be up chasing the birds and howling for hours now."

Good. I hope he keeps it up all fucking day, I thought.

Algat huffed. "Well, aren't you the rudest thing?"

Fuck. She'd heard me? How the hell had she heard me?

"Because hearing things is my special skill, child. And you might as well be screaming your thoughts at the top of your lungs, the way you project them."

Wonderful. So it wasn't just Fisher I had to be careful around now. I had to watch out for this old witch, too. "Is there a way I can prevent you from digging through my mind?" I laced the question with as much authority as I could muster.

I had no idea if the female responded because she had to or because she felt like it. "You can command me not to," she said. "But I would strongly advise against it. You never know when you might need me to hear your thoughts."

Yeah. I was never going to *need* her to hear my thoughts. "I command you to never listen to my thoughts or invade the privacy of my mind again, Lord of Midnight. I command you to never read or invade the minds of my friends or my mate ever again, either, too."

The vampire hissed, baring her fangs, and the air suddenly felt very cold. Guru arched his back, his fur standing on end. He mirrored his master, hissing, and then launched off the end of the table, turning into a puddle of shadow that fell across the floor and merged with the large shadow cast by a grand writing desk.

"You come with your hand out, asking for help from Algat, and then you bind *her* hands behind her back?"

"I'll bind more than just your hands if you prove to be a problem for me." It wasn't a threat. Threats weren't going to make this female bend to my will. It was a fact and nothing more. "I'd like to see that book now. I don't have all night to waste on this."

"Seems to me that this should be the only thing you're focusing on right now," the female observed. Her eyes had roved down my body and were fixed on my gloves—and the glowing runes that were burning right through the leather.

Quickly, I hid my hands behind my back, alarm prickling across my shoulder blades. "The book, Algat. Please." Was it unqueenly to say please? It was probably un-Sanasrothian in general, but I was surprised when the female's hard glower softened a touch.

"Give me a moment," she said stiffly. "If Guru comes back, sniffing around for more blood while I'm gone, don't give him any. He's had more than enough, thank you."

She had nothing to worry about on that front. I wasn't opening my finger for the cat again. Algat disappeared in the stacks, and I spent the next little while inspecting the library's ceiling.

The stars were a myth in Zilvaren. We were told of strange lights in the sky, brilliant as diamonds in their millions, but without any frame of reference I had never been able to conjure an image of what they would look like. What I had cobbled together in my mind's eye had fallen woefully short of the truth. Zilvaren's sky was a void, punctuated by two burning hot, unrelenting balls of light. But the night sky in Yvelia was spectacular. The glittering expanse was both far away and right there at the same time, as if I could reach out my fingers and touch the whole universe. What had always seemed empty bristled with light and promise. And there were worlds out there. An incomprehensible number of realms.

Whoever had painted the night sky on the roof of Ammontraíeth's library was a master of their craft. It was remarkable, what they'd accomplished with some paint and some gold leaf. It was so real. If I just reached up—

I didn't make a sound as I hurtled sideways.

I didn't have time.

The projectile hit me in the ribs, impacting with breathtaking force.

I slammed down onto the floor, not understanding what was happening for a split second. And then I was moving.

My daggers were in my hands.

I was twisting under the thrashing weight that was trying to pin me to the ground.

Black and gray and streaks of gold filled my vision.

"Get... *off* me!"

But the feral creature—the dark-haired male with the furious blue eyes—did not get off me. He bared his teeth, flashing gold-plated, engraved fangs as he snapped at me, trying to use them to rip out my throat.

"You're done," he snarled. So confident. So godscursed sure of himself. He grappled with me, trying to lock a massive hand around my wrists so he could pin my hands above my head...but he had made a grave mistake. He'd assumed that I wasn't going to put up a fight.

He was on top of me—a very heavy problem. I rectified the situation the best way I knew how. It was a dirty move, but so was tackling someone from the shadows and catching them off guard. I brought my knee up hard and smashed it into his balls.

The vampire locked up, wheezing, but he didn't release me. Not fully. The brief lapse in his grip gave me room to yank a hand free, though. Took me all of two seconds to find the dagger I'd dropped when he'd pinned me. I didn't flinch as I drove the point of the blade into his side, up, between his ribs.

The vampire shuddered, pulling back. "What...?" He looked down in confusion. "I..."

"I stabbed you," I spat. "Now I'm gonna pull out the blade and watch you bleed."

His eyes shuttered when I did it. Blood didn't spurt out of vampires the way it did from the living. It ebbed, escaping under a loss of pressure. I felt it, finding its way through the gaps in my leathers, saturating my shirt beneath and slicking my skin. It was unnaturally cool, but at least it didn't reek the way a feeder's did. It smelled stale. Strange. Unappealing.

"Sil...ver," the vampire wheezed. "That blade was never...silver." He sagged sideways, hitting the ground with a thump and rolling onto his back.

I was free.

I rocketed to my feet, ready to stab the fucker again if he so much as lifted a finger in my direction. He was still staring at the blade in my hand—the one Fisher had given me to wear at my coronation. I studied it, then held it up for my attacker to see. "Silver tipped. It won't kill you, but you are not going to enjoy the next few hours. Appropriate," I panted, "since you just tried to *tear out my throat*. Now who the fuck are you? And why did you just try to kill me?"

But the vampire didn't get to answer. Before he could, the interlocking runes on the back of my right hand lit up like a signal flare, and an ungodly pain blazed up my arm.

Oh, gods, no...

Light filled the library.

I had no control over the wave of power that rose up, up, up....and then *out* of my hand in a white-blue shock wave.

The writing desk in front of me *disappeared*. It was there, and then it was gone. Then the bookcase behind it, and all its leather-bound tomes. Gone. The leather couch by the window, gone. The wall, with its portrait of Malcolm smirking knowingly out of its frame... *gone*.

Wind whistled into the library, a cloud of dust and pulverized stone swirling in the air like fine snow. The cold crept in and wrapped around my boots, climbing up my legs, into my bones, making me shiver as I stared at what I had done.

There was a twenty-foot hole in the side of Ammontraíeth.

And *I* had put it there.

15

VORATH

KINGFISHER

"I SWEAR ON all four winds, I didn't want to help him. He *made* me do it!"

Carrion had caught up with the vault breaker quickly. The other man wasn't in peak physical condition, it turned out, and Swift was light on his feet.

"*You* know Eric," Vorath Shah said, holding his hands aloft. "He can be pretty persuasive when he wants to be."

If Carrion didn't ease off, he was either going to snap the human's neck or cut off his airway until he passed out. I placed a hand on Swift's shoulder, raising my eyebrows when he looked at me.

"You can tell him what a bad man he is later. Find out where the silver is."

We were inside the human's shop. It turned out he wasn't just a vault breaker. He was a merchant, too. A purveyor of all kinds of bizarre and interesting goods. There were tiny heads in jars on his shelves. A vast array of powders and crushed herbs in small glass containers. Bones strung onto rope and knotted in strange shapes that looked *almost* like runes. Everything was covered in a fine layer of sand.

The air was thick with the smell of unfamiliar—but not unpleasant—spices. I paid little attention to the details of our surroundings. Beyond knowing how many entrances the shop had and where they were, the rest was unimportant. The silver was all that mattered.

For the fifth time in as many minutes, Shah's dark eyes darted to find me. He was wary of me, that much was clear. The reason for his interest was less clear.

"I don't know where Eric took it all," Shah rushed out. "He's paranoid. You know he'd never let anyone else know where he was planning on housing that much capital."

"Ugh." Carrion huffed. "I'm so bored of this conversation already. Eric is the laziest, most arrogant person in the Third. He would never have transported those trunks by himself. That kind of grunt work is beneath him. And he wouldn't have brought anyone else in to deal with it, because you're right, he *is* paranoid. Which means he got *you* to shift it all. That also means that this," he said, waving a hand at the human, pinned against the counter of his own store, "is pointless, and you are wasting my time. Where's my money, Vorath?"

Again, Shah glanced at me and flinched.

I was wearing armor, but he couldn't see that. I was glamored. He was looking at me strangely for some *other* reason, and that had piqued my interest.

"If I tell you where he is, I'm siding with *you*," Shah gasped. "If I don't tell you where he is, I'm siding with *him*. You're both out of your godscursed minds. How am I supposed to decide which one of you to piss off?"

"Oh, you should definitely piss off the one who isn't here," Carrion suggested. "Or the one who *is* here will rip out your fingernails."

"I—Yes, I can see the wisdom in that," the human said. He squeezed his eyes shut when Carrion strengthened the grip he had on his throat. "I don't mean to complain, Carrion, but your elbow is digging into my rib cage."

Shah wasn't as afraid as he needed to be. He knew there might be some pain along the path that stretched before him, but he wasn't concerned about any real consequences. Not from Carrion. But *I* was an unknown entity. "Just kill him and have done with it," I said, affecting an air of boredom.

The vault breaker began thrashing his arms and legs. "No! No, you don't need to do that. I-I'll tell you. It's fine. You just have to understand, the Third isn't the kind of place you can just double-cross someone and walk away."

Shah had double-crossed plenty of people in his time. My gut instincts were rarely wrong. There was something untrustworthy about the human. He was cleverer than he was making out to be. His mind was working a mile a minute.

"I can't tell you where Eric's taken your money, but I *can* show you," he said.

"And why the hell would I want you tagging along on this adventure? It's already zero percent fun," Carrion said, shooting a none-too-subtle look in my direction.

"Because I'm useful. Because I want to make it up—" He coughed, struggling to swallow around the forearm Carrion was pressing into his windpipe. "Up to you for running just now. You know how it is. I panicked. I'm sorry, Carrion. Come on. We're *friends*."

This man had no friends.

If I was right about him, then he had a barrow where he dumped the bodies of his victims, but I kept my thoughts to myself.

Carrion pulled back, easing the pressure from Shah's throat a little. His pale blue eyes went to me. "Well? Are we letting him escort us to the goods or what?"

"I say we torture the location out of him and then dispose of him."

Thum.

Thum.

Thum.

Shah's pulse was as lazy as could be. It didn't spike at all, as he pretended to panic again. "No! Eric's laid out traps. You'll need me if you want to get past them!"

Why did he want to come with us so badly? I supposed there was only one way to find out. "All right. Fine. He can come. But he's *your* pet, Swift. Make sure you keep him on a short leash."

It was morning now. At least I *thought* it was. It was impossible to tell. I "borrowed" an oversized gray scarf from the human and used it to shield my head from the suns and the Third's prying eyes as we made our way through the ward, silently hating the sensation of the sweat running down my back.

Carrion kept his head down, moving with the flow of the crowded streets. His shoulders were relaxed, his gait unhurried and easy, but his eyes skipped over the faces of the humans who passed us. His hand rested casually at his side, but his fingers brushed his hip, where I knew a dagger was strapped to his side, concealed beneath his shirt.

He was ready.

If we had to run, he wouldn't need telling twice. If we had to fight, that steel would be in his hand in a heartbeat, and he wouldn't be afraid to use it.

A little ruefully, I squirreled away the observation to process later.

Shah was twitchy as a ferret. Ten feet ahead of us, he wove through the press of bodies like a minnow swimming upstream. I kept an eye on the back of his head, determined not to let him give us the slip among the crowds.

"What are all these people *doing* out here?" I muttered. "Don't they have homes? Work?"

Next to me, Carrion laughed bitterly down his nose. "They're on their way to the ward gate to claim their water ration for the day. If they don't get there early, there'll be none left, and they'll have to wait until tomorrow."

It was one thing, knowing that Madra kept her people under the heel of her boot by keeping them thirsty. Seeing it in action was another thing entirely. The humans who shuffled toward the ward's entrance were dirty, their clothes worn. Many of them were rail thin, eyes sunken in their sockets. But...there were smiles on their faces. They laughed and catcalled at one another as they made their way to collect *just* enough water to keep them going until tomorrow. Their homes were little more than crumbling shells. They were beaten and oppressed at every turn. They barely had enough food to feed their children, and it had become *normal*. They had accepted it. Found a way to cope with it. In the face of abject misery, they had built lives for themselves, and community. They weren't yet broken.

As we approached the wall that separated the Third from its neighboring wards, Vorath Shah hooked a hard left and ducked between a short, squat building and a tall tower of some kind. The gap between the two buildings was barely enough to accommodate the width of my shoulders. As I entered the narrow corridor, following after him, I was sure I would see him sprinting away, but no. Shah was right there, waiting for us, just a couple of feet into the alleyway.

"There's a door up ahead, in the wall. You'll need to open it, Carrion."

Swift squeezed past me, not even remotely concerned about stepping on my feet. "You can crack a vault, Vorath. Why do you need *me* to open a simple door?"

"Because it's not a simple door. You'll see for yourself. You'll see."

Moments later, we were standing in front of said door, and Shah's issue became apparent. There was no door handle. There was no keyhole. There was no lock. In fact, the wall was so smooth and free of defining features that it was almost impossible to tell there was a door there at all. If it weren't for the thin, oblong seam in the sandstone, even I would have missed it. Shah held out his hands in a universal *See what I mean?* kind of gesture.

Carrion frowned, running a hand along the seam. "How did you get in here when you were with Eric?"

"He has a special key. He holds it against the wall and sweeps it to the left. It opens without a sound." The awe in Shah's tone was there for anybody to hear. "I don't know how he has access to charmed objects. All I know is that he didn't get it from me."

Did Carrion know that this magic trick of Eric's wasn't magic at all? From the way he snorted, reaching for the dagger beneath his shirt, it seemed that he did.

"Give me some space," he murmured. The blade flashed as he drew it and held it against the wall. He angled his body, blocking his movements from Shah.

"What are you doing?" The vault breaker stood on his tiptoes, trying to peer over Carrion's shoulder.

Carrion's eyes met mine. There was a question there: *Should I tell him?* I shrugged, not caring either way.

"It isn't magic, Shah. It's just a really big magnet." Carrion swept his dagger along the middle of the door, grinning with satisfaction when the metal *caught* the metal on the other side, and he began dragging it to the left. Surprising, really. The dagger was made of Fae steel. The iron had been refined out of it, and it had been tempered with other alloys to make it strong. Turned out that Fae steel *was* highly magnetic, though.

"What's a magnet?" Shah asked.

"I'll tell you later. No time for that now. We have silver to collect."

As Carrion spoke, the huge sandstone block popped out and swung open, revealing a darkened passageway beyond.

"The bell tower is the highest point in the Third. There's a ladder bolted to the outside of it but no door," Shah prattled. "My whole life, I always assumed it was a solid structure, but no. Look at all this. Rooms and rooms. All empty, but still. I asked Eric how he found out about all of this, but he wouldn't say."

He led us up the internal spiral staircase that wound up the center of the bell tower. Without any windows, the interior of the building was pitch-black, but Shah had come prepared. He had handed out small vials filled with a glowing green substance that looked an awful lot like liquified concentrated evenlight. All three of us held the vials aloft as we climbed, using them to light the way. I could see perfectly well in the dark. I suspected Carrion could, too, since this darkness wasn't caused by my shadows—I would have to remember to ask him about that later—but we still carried the vials for appearances' sake.

The light painted the walls a sickly color, illuminating thick cobwebs and the bones of small rodents that littered the stairs.

When we were what I assumed to be halfway up the stairs, Vorath advised, "Watch your step here." A skeleton lay sprawled out on the steps, the bones pitted with age. At first glance, I assumed it was the remains of a human, but then I realized my mistake. The corpse's canines were far too long to have belonged to a human.

Carrion saw the dead Fae's teeth, too. He glanced back over his shoulder at me, raising an eyebrow, his profile washed in pale green.

An unsettled feeling solidified in my stomach. As we rose higher up the bell tower, that feeling grew heavier, weightier, settling like a stone inside me. There once had been a time when I might have chalked up a feeling like this to paranoia or being overly cautious, but I'd learned my lesson in the maze. My weapons were sharp, but my intuition was sharper. It had never led me astray. My nerves were screaming by the time I made out the open archway at the top of the stairs.

I stopped dead, reaching for my daggers and a handful of shadow. "Carrion."

Up ahead, the smuggler was only a couple of steps behind Shah. The shorter human waited at the dark archway, dramatic shadows from the vial of green light twisting his features into a hideous mask as he turned back to face us. "It's just through here," he said.

"*Carrion,*" I growled.

The smuggler stopped on the second to last step, twisting to look back at me. "What is it?"

"We're done here," I told him.

"Uhh, no, we're not?" He sounded incredulous. "We haven't got what we came for."

"We'll find the silver another way."

"What are you talking about? This is *my* money. These are *my* goods. I have a right to claim them. Why would we make things harder for ourselves?"

"If you walk into that room, Swift," I said calmly, "you won't be walking out again."

"What do you me—"

But the vault breaker didn't give him the opportunity to change his mind; he grabbed Carrion by the arm and pulled him up the last step. "Sorry, Carrion," he said. "I am your friend ... but *he's* still hungry."

"Who's hungry?" Swift tripped on the top step, falling forward, past Shah, who moved out of Carrion's way, pressing his back against the archway. Carrion's hands slapped down onto the ground, his torso crossing the boundary into the room beyond . . .

. . . and nothing happened.

Swift cursed roundly, glowering up at Shah. "The hell is *wrong* with you, Vorath?"

The sound came softly at first.

Then it became a *hum.*

"What is that?" Carrion asked, his eyes roving upward into the dark.

Then it became a *roar.*

"He said it was the only way," Shah inched away from Carrion. "I wouldn't have done it otherwise."

"Vorath?" Carrion went to get up, but as he tried to stand, he realized that he couldn't. "Why are my hands glued to the floor?"

Gods a-fucking-live. Sighing, I trudged up the last few steps, already regretting the fact that I hadn't just turned and left. "It's a demon's trap," I said, peering down at the ground in front of Carrion. I couldn't see anything marking the floor of the empty room beyond. Not until I kicked away the glowing vial Carrion had dropped when he'd fallen and tossed the one Vorath had given me over my shoulder, too. As soon as the green glow was gone, the marks flared to life, brilliant and white. They were everywhere: runes, scrawled messily into a layer of centuries-old dust, interlocking, hundreds of them. Thousands. The walls of the room at the top of the stairs were covered in them. The ceiling. The floor, too. And Carrion had just slapped his hands down right in the middle of them.

"What the hell is a demon trap?" Carrion asked in an oddly calm voice.

I crouched down beside him, squinting at the runes. They were

Gilarian maybe. Ancient Gilarian? Or...Ahh. Shit. No. It wasn't Gilarian.

"Why is your face doing that?" Carrion tugged hard, trying to free his hands from the floor without any success. "And why's that rushing sound getting louder?"

"You might as well stop," I grumbled, getting to my feet. "You could cut your hands off and you'd still be fucked. A demon trap is old magic. Alchimeran magic. And it's exactly what it sounds like. A trap that catches demons."

"Then why the hell has it trapped *me*?" he demanded.

"Because magic this old is powerful, yes, but it does deteriorate over time. Not enough to be broken altogether. But it can be manipulated. The beast that was imprisoned here is using the trap like a spider's web now, isn't it, Shah? The beast is using it so that it can *eat*."

The vault breaker's eyes sparkled with an unhinged delight. *This* was who he was—the version of himself that he had been hiding. "My master does have a *prodigious* appetite," he said.

"What is it?" I demanded. "Arrangoth? Noltick? Bresheth?" It couldn't have been Morthil; Morthil had been trapped in the maze with me for the past century. I couldn't remember the names of any of the other lost demons.

From the mad excitement on Vorath Shah's face, I knew that whatever he was about to say was going to be bad. "His holy name is Joshin. Lord of the Desert. King of the Dark Dream."

Aaaaand I was right. It was bad. Really, really, *really* bad. "Fuck."

"Will someone *please* tell me what that sound is!" Carrion bellowed.

Drawing my hands together, I called on my primary and my secondary magic, gritting my teeth as the sword—a replica of Nimerelle, cast in silver—formed in my hands.

"Scorpions, Carrion. That is the sound of a million fucking *scorpions*."

16

THE BLOOD

SAERIS

"HOW MANY MORE times do I have to tell you?" I protested. "I didn't do it on purpose!"

When I was a child, I accidentally melted my mother's only cooking pot. I'd told her I'd left it hanging over the fire, unattended, and had forgotten about it. That hadn't been true, of course. I'd touched it, and the metal had liquified unexpectedly, splashing to the floor like water. It had solidified there like that—a puddle of metal that had once been one of my mother's most prized possessions. When she'd returned home and found the remains of her pot lying on the kitchen table, her anger had been the stuff of legends. I hadn't been able to sit down for a week.

But this? This was far worse.

The whole palace was in chaos, and Algat was baying for blood. Guru had escaped.

Not for the first time in the past hour, I thought the old female was about to try to put me over her knee to spank my hide like my mother had. "He is an *indoor* cat, *Your Highness*," she spat viciously. "He's never stepped foot outside of this library."

I almost laughed. Guru was a shadow, and a shadow would go wherever it pleased, regardless of a closed door or a rule that couldn't be enforced. Guru had probably explored the entire palace from top to bottom, and if Algat didn't know that, then she was an idiot.

She jabbed a book at me across the reading table. "There are far worse things out there than Guru. Far bigger predators that would inhale him without a second thought."

"He's going to be fine, Algat. He's probably just sitting up on the roof, watching everyone freaking out in the courtyard."

"He doesn't like the wind," the crone said sourly. "It scatters him when he's transitioning from one form to the other."

"Mmmfffmf mmmhhhnnn."

Algat's eyes widened, overflowing with annoyance. She jabbed the book at the vampire asshole with the gold-plated teeth. "And what the hell have you done to *him?*" she demanded.

"Nothing he didn't deserve. He attacked me. Ergo, he gets tied up in chains and lashed to a chair." I had used the length of silver that Fisher had given to me before my coronation—the one he had tied around my waist to act as a belt.

Algat let out a stiff laugh. "Well, I can't wait for you to explain that one to your sire, child, I really can't. He's going to get a kick out of *this.*"

My hand throbbed like crazy. Before, when the runes had blazed through my skin, my hands had healed themselves instantly once the episode was over. This time, I hadn't been so lucky. My fingertips were split open, the skin charred and black from where the magic had discharged from my hand. Blood dripped from deep slices on my palms, and my runes were still raw and blistered, as if someone had just pressed a burning brand to my skin. It was healing, I could feel that it was, but it was taking way longer than I would have liked. It fucking *hurt.*

"Tal won't have anything to say about me defending myself, Algat. I'm the queen of this court. By rights, this crazy bastard should be dead already."

A calculating look flashed in Algat's eyes. "Oh, *I* agree. Assaulting the monarch of the Blood Court is high treason, after all. So why *isn't* he dead?"

Shit. I kind of walked myself into that one. I could have ended the stranger. I'd had the window and the opportunity. I could have fired the overflow of my power at *him* instead of the wall and left nothing behind but a black scorch mark on the rug. But killing someone was always a last resort. It *had* to be. Even if they were technically already dead. "I'm not just going to kill him without questioning him first," I said in a bored tone. "How will I know who sent him otherwise?"

Disappointment flickered briefly in Algat's cloudy eyes. "Then you'd better take that fabric out of his mouth, hadn't you? What did you stuff in there? Wait. *Are those my velvet gloves?*"

The gloves were the first thing I found when I'd been searching for something to quiet the angry vampire. He'd been yelling at me in Old Fae; I hadn't understood what he was saying, but I could tell from the sneer on his face and the acid in his tone that he hadn't been paying me any compliments.

Algat scurried around the reading table and ripped the balled-up gloves out of the vampire's mouth. She held them up in the air, scowling at me. "These were expensive!"

"My apologies. I'll buy you some new ones."

"Be sure that you do!"

"I will."

"Swear it." The old female set her jaw.

"I swear it! Gods!"

"You should be careful, making flippant promises like that," a male voice said. The vampire on the chair wasn't pulling against his silver restraints anymore. He was sweating, his head resting against the back of his chair, as if he'd given up and had resigned himself to his fate.

"*Quiet*, you," Algat snapped.

The vampire laughed breathlessly, rolling his head along the wood to smirk arrogantly at the female. "What, you don't like it when people interfere with your groundwork, hag?"

Her shoulders hunched up around her ears. She looked ready to climb onto the table and claw at his face. "I should cut out your tongue—"

"Go on, then. Why not. You've done it before." The vampire closed his eyes, swallowing hard. "It only grows back again," he added wearily.

I stood before the stranger, folding my arms over my chest. He looked like he was in his early thirties, perhaps. He was considerably older, of course. It was going to take some time for me to shift the way I thought about how people aged here.

His hair was dark and shorn close to his scalp. The strands were unevenly cut and messy. His eyes were pale blue with a bright golden starburst around his pupil, which…oh. Wow. His pupil was vertical, like a snake's.

I hadn't registered that he had turned back to me. I hadn't registered the hatred on his face, either. Not until he bared his teeth, flashing those sharp, golden canines at me again. "Please. Feel free to stare," he snarled. "You might as well kill me now, unless you want to be looking over your shoulder for the rest of your life. I won't stop coming for you. Not until I've cleaved that pretty head from your shoulders."

I huffed, rocking on my heels. "Am I supposed to be grateful that you think I'm pretty?"

He ignored the question. "What did you do to him?" he spat.

The change in direction sent my eyebrows skyrocketing upward. "Him? I didn't do anything to him. Taladaius is fine. I'm guessing you've been lurking in the shadows since I got here. You must have watched him lea—"

"Not Tal. What did you do to *Kingfisher?*"

I jerked, taking a step back. I hadn't been expecting my mate's name to come out of the vampire's mouth. It would have been better to keep the surprise from my face, but it was too late for that now. The vampire had definitely registered my reaction. He narrowed his strange eyes at me, anger flaring in them as he strained forward against the silver chain that tied him to the chair.

"That's right. I *know*," he said. "You killed him, didn't you." An accusation, not a question.

I sized the vampire up. "Why the hell would you think *that*?"

"That dagger you stabbed me with. I know it well. I know its owner even better, and he wouldn't have been parted from it without a fight.

So, either you killed him and took it, or someone else killed him, and *they* gave it to you. Which is it?"

"First, I *am* queen of this court. I am not obliged to explain myself or my weaponry to the likes of *you*." I spoke slowly, my words laced with sarcasm. "But aside from that fact, there's obviously no possibility in your mind that the blade was *given* to me, of course. Because I'm unworthy, or because I'm female, or—"

"You're a *vampire*," he hissed. "I can smell it on you. *The blood.*"

I cleared my throat, staring down at my boots as I considered how to word this next part. "I'm half vampire, yes. But the only blood I have tasted was given freely. *By my mate.* Maybe it's the scent of *his* blood that you can smell on me."

"I don't care who you drank from, or if they—" He stopped speaking, his mouth open, still forming the shape of whatever word he had been about to speak. I saw the shock ripple over his features. "No. No, you're not . . . That's not *possible*," he whispered.

"Isn't it?" My gloves were already ruined, the leather hanging in tatters. I took them off gingerly, trying to avoid the burns on my palms. Once the gloves were gone, I slowly pushed up my sleeves, revealing the black scrolling inkwork that spread across the backs of my hands and up my forearms.

"What in the name of sin and salt is *that*?" Algat had been watching our exchange with obvious amusement, but now her mirth fled her. She pointed a shaking finger at my hands. "Stupid female. It's sacrilege to ink your skin with those kinds of marks."

I didn't have the energy to explain this to her. And she didn't deserve my truth, anyway. I focused on the male with the cat eyes who seemed to care so much about Fisher's well-being. "You broke a royal edict," I said. "I made it law that no member of this court would be able to attack me or any of my friends, and yet you still did it. How?"

The male stared at me, dumbfounded, his eyes bouncing between my hands and my face. He couldn't seem to believe what he was seeing.

"He broke your edict because he isn't bound by it," a voice said from the library's entrance. It was Lorreth. He was out of breath and disheveled, his hair falling loose from his braids, his cheeks bright pink. He gave me a meaningful look as he entered the library—the kind of look that said Kingfisher would be hearing about this. His attention flitted to the yawning hole in the side of the library tower's curved wall, and then to the restrained vampire, who was staring at Lorreth like he was hallucinating.

"That's right, isn't it? You aren't obliged to follow the rules of this court, because you never swore fealty to it, did you?"

The vampire slowly shook his head. "No." The word barely made a sound as it left his lips. Were those *tears* in his eyes?

"Because, no matter what. . . ." Lorreth said under his breath.

"A wolf never becomes a leech," the vampire finished.

Lorreth stood in front of him, an array of emotions fighting for control of his features. "Hello, Foley. It's been too long. I can't tell you how good it is to see you, brother."

17

THE DARK DOOR

KINGFISHER

THEY ROLLED IN on a skittering black tide.

Up the steps. Over the walls. Crawling out of the stonework.

Hundreds of them. Thousands.

Vorath Shah threw back his head and laughed as they came. He knew they wouldn't hurt him ... but the same couldn't be said for us.

The first prick came at the back of my neck. A trail of fire blazed up into my head, fireworks going off right between my eyes.

"Ahh! Shit!" Carrion hissed, his body jolting as he, too, was stung. His hands were still glued to the ground in the entrance of the octagonal room, though, so he couldn't brush the scorpions away as they crawled up his arms and into his hair. "Kingfisher!" he called, a note of panic rising in his voice. "A little help?"

But I couldn't help him. The scorpions were under my armor, crawling up my back, stinging me as they went. Each individual sting was like a hot bolt of lightning, racing along my nerve endings, stealing my breath.

The scorpions were many, but they were also one. The demons of old weren't spoken of very often anymore, but *I* still knew of them. I'd spent countless afternoons in my mother's library while the rain hammered at the windows of Cahlish, reading the books my mother set out for me. Old legends. Tomes on old magics, written in Old Fae. Tales of grand heroism and good prevailing over evil. And then stories about the old demons who had once plagued the lands of Yvelia. She had read them to me over and over again, giggling with me as she'd tucked me into bed, pretending to be one demon or another as she "attacked" me.

When she had been Joshin, demon of the desert, fractured into his multitude of stinging scorpions, she had pinched me lightly, tickling me, all the while demanding as she always did, "And how will you stop me, sweetheart? What will you do to send me scattering into the dark?"

I hadn't been able to breathe then from the tickling.

I couldn't breathe now from the pain.

As a boy, I had panted, "The—the li-li—"

Now, I did the same. "We need to let—let in the li-light!"

Joshin, Lord of the Desert, King of the Dark Dream, couldn't bear the light. That's why he had chosen to hide inside this black, windowless tower. Why the demon trap had been laid for him here on the floor as well. Whoever had etched the Alchimeran runes into the floor of the room up ahead had known this would be the only place a beast like Joshin could seek refuge.

"Light," I gasped. Gods, even being eaten by Morthil in the maze hadn't been this painful. "We need... *light.*"

Shah cackled. "This place is a tomb. No cracks in the walls. No holes in the floorboards. Joshin will come! Joshin will feed!"

Ahh, fuck this. I wasn't being eaten by another demon. Not this time, when the magic of Malcolm's cursed maze wouldn't bring me back from the dead.

Carrion sprawled out on the floor and started screaming. The pain was total. No breath. No thought. No way out. The smuggler wasn't used to it.

A carpet of glistening, oily black carapaces and vicious pincers swept over him, swallowing him from view. And then he was gone.

Fuck.

We didn't have much time.

I wasn't trapped by the snare that had been etched into the floor. Not yet. Two paths stood before me: I could turn, and I could run. *Or* I could enter the demon trap and commit to the dark nightmare that was already unfolding in my blood.

If I left, I could find the silver on my own. I could find Hayden Fane and drag his ass back to Yvelia. But if I left, the smuggler would die a horrific death—one I knew all too well—and I would have to explain to Saeris that I had abandoned her friend.

"Orillith ken mas cree, Carrion Swift," I spat under my breath. I hadn't cursed in Old Fae in centuries, but sinners, did the situation warrant it.

I stepped over Swift's prone body and into the demon trap.

The ground seethed, lit up by the glowing runes. With every step, I felt the crack and the give of the scorpions beneath the soles of my boots.

Now that I'd entered the demon trap, I saw the trunks stacked high on the other side of the room. Ten of them. More. Jewels, coins, and beaten golden cups spilled out from the closest trunk, reflecting the light cast off by the shining marks etched into the walls. The body of a man lay curled in the fetal position close by. His clothing was torn to shreds. Flesh still clung to his bones. Joshin had obviously been savoring his last meal.

"Fisher!" Carrion's cry was panicked.

Darts of agony struck all over my body. The scorpions stung through my pants. They were in my boots. In my hair. I crossed the room, slowing with each step, bile rising hot up the back of my throat.

"Hate to be...a bother," Carrion wheezed. "But if you're not in a position to...save me right...now, then...could you possibly kill me instead? This...really *sucks.*"

Gods, how was he *still* talking? I couldn't even think.

"Oh no, he can't kill you. No, no, no," Shah chattered. "Joshin wants his prey alive. Joshin *prefers* it that way."

I was going to flay Vorath Shah. Just as soon as I tore a hole in the side of this bell tower. See if I didn't.

The very fibers of my being were alight and burning by the time I made it to the wall. Tears streamed down my face, but even so, I could see Vorath had been right. There were no cracks in the stonework. No seams between the blocks of sandstone. The room *had* been sealed by magic. The only thing that could counter this kind of magic was magic itself—the kind of magic that would hurt.

I drew back my fist and took a deep breath.

"It won't work," Shah said in a sing-song tone. "Joshin couldn't break the wall. That was before he knew, though. Two suns. I told him, I did. Two suns and no night. No safety from the light. A thousand years, he tried. I heard him pounding from the tunnels. That's how I found him. *Boom. Boom. Boom.*"

I had thought he was just evil, but there was more to it. Vorath Shah was mad. He crowed with delight as I brought my fist forward and sent it crashing into the wall.

"Joshin didn't have…my magic," I grunted. My shadows could only do so much. They could either protect my fist from the impact, or they could shock the magic that was spelled into the walls.

I sent all my power into the wall.

"Oh gods. Fisher?" Suddenly, Carrion wasn't screaming anymore. He sounded very concerned.

I brought my fist back and smashed it into the wall again. A ripple of shadows fanned out over the stone, and an answering ripple of black energy chased after it. I frowned at the sight, not trusting what I was seeing. Why was my magic pulsing twice?

"Kingfisher. The scorpions," Carrion rasped. "They aren't stinging me anymore. They're…they're leaving."

Again, I drove my fist into the wall.

Again, a shock wave of my magic shot across the surface of the wall, and again, a secondary wave of shadows chased after it. I gritted my teeth against the rope of pain that shot up my arm, into my shoulder, my jaw. "They're not leaving, Swift," I said grimly. "They're *coalescing.*"

"What the hell does *that* mean?"

I reached deep and commanded my shadows to gather. I gave the strike everything I had. My knuckles split open this time, leaving my blood smeared on the sandstone when I drew back. I was going to break bone at this rate. From head to toe, I was raw. The throbbing behind my eyes intensified, making my vision swim.

"They can be many," I said through gritted teeth. "Or they can be one. Right now...they're becoming one."

"I do not like the sound of that. Should I be worried?"

I pulled back and hurled my fist at the wall. "Most definitely."

"He is magnificent. You should both be *honored* by his presence," Vorath said in an awed tone.

I knew what it would look like—the mass of writhing flesh and bone in the darkened corner of the room. I shouldn't have looked. But I did.

If my mother's books had contained illustrations of the demon, she hadn't shown them to me. It was a horrible vision, all forming teeth and twisted, wet, glistening meat, pulsing and fibrous. The scorpions scuttled up the growing mass and split open along their backs, fusing with the gathering, bleeding shape. Arms were forming. Legs. A bulbous body, rising into a vaguely humanoid-shaped torso.

"Ugh. I think I'm going to throw up," Carrion groaned.

He would definitely be throwing up soon. He had just been hit with a monumental amount of venom. It was a wonder he wasn't hallucinating already. The edges of my vision were dancing with a shimmering green light that did not bode well for the next few hours, and Carrion had been stung *way* more than me.

I gathered my shadows faster, whispering to them, urging them to help me break the magic that protected the wall. I struck the stone again, again, again, and finally felt the bones in my hand give way.

"Wendalith cohmerin tas." The rumbling sound shook the entire tower—many rushing, whispering, shouting voices, intertwining and layering on top of each other. It didn't resemble the voice of any Fae or human. This voice belonged to something far, far older. A creature not born but constructed from the base elements of hell itself.

The demon's head was not yet formed. Its lower and upper jaw were there, as were two narrow slits where a nose might have been...but the rest of its face was nowhere to be seen. Tiny stingers probed and struck at the air, rising up from the demon's half-formed head. Its left arm terminated in a hand—normal, for all intents and purposes—but its right ended in a huge, glossy hard-shelled pincer that snapped open and closed reflexively. Its lower half was all scorpion, but nightmarishly large. Eight legs. A long carapace. A curved stinger dripping with venom.

Great.

"Wendalith cohmerin tas," the demon repeated, spittle flying from its mouth as it spoke.

I turned from it and gave my attention to the wall. We were officially out of time. If I didn't break this thing open soon, we were *so* fucked.

"What the hell is it saying?" Carrion called.

"He's singing to you," Shah cooed. "Listen to him sing."

I snorted. "It's asking who stands before it. Who walks its path. Something like that. It's speaking Old Fae, *which it should not know,*" I said pointedly, throwing those last words over my shoulder at the ancient monster.

Click, click, click.

It scuttled forward.

"I know many languages I should not know," it rasped. "I hearrrrr them through the walls."

"Great. It speaks Common Fae, too. Perfect," I muttered to myself as I drove my fist into the wall again, staining the stone even redder with my blood.

"Two souls, I sense. Two strong bodies, too. A feast for a weak prince such as myself."

"You're no prince," I growled. "You're an abomination. One I'll gladly be sending back to hell momentarily."

"Don't antagonize it," Carrion hissed. "Its teeth are really fucking sharp. I do *not* want to get eaten!"

"Be quiet, Swift. It can't eat you if it can't *find* you."

It was true that most demons didn't have eyes. There were tales of how this had come to pass, but many agreed demons resided in darkness and didn't need to see to torment their victims. That had certainly been the case with Morthil. But according to lore, Joshin was different. It didn't share the same abilities its siblings had been gifted with. It was dangerous, yes, but it possessed no heightened spatial awareness.

Boom! Boom!

The bones in my hand splintered, but still I pounded against the magic that held the wall together. I watched my shadows roil across the stone, shivering as a second wave came again and again, rolling after my magic and merging with it. It made no sense. My shadows should be having some effect. The old magic that formed the demon trap should have weakened a little, but it wasn't even reacting. At least not how it *should* have been. It was almost as though—

Click, click, click, click, CLACK.

"Fisher! Holy gods, fuck me, Fisher. *Do* something!"

I fell forward against the wall, exhausted. Turning, I found that the demon was steady on its eight legs now and venturing forward in search of its prey.

"Here, Master. This way," Vorath coaxed. "Follow the sound of my voice."

Gods curse it all. I'd had enough of this human. I shoved away from the wall and staggered forward.

And suddenly, there she was. My mother, standing next to me.

She wore her favorite dress. Blue, with birds embroidered onto the skirt. I realized with a start that they were kingfishers. Their wings flashed metallic blue; their proud chests were painted umber. She looked as she had always looked: beautiful and sad. Her long black hair fell in waves to her waist, blowing on an invisible wind.

"Where are you going, sweet boy? Have you lost your way?"

The soft lilt of her voice. Gods, how I had missed the sound of it. I shook my head. "I'm not lost. I'm going to kill that fucking human."

A deep sorrow filled her eyes. "Who is he to trouble *you*? Great and mighty Kingfisher. Leave him be, my love."

"This is his fault." I was sweating again, even worse than before. My skin was prickling all over. "If he hadn't brought us here—"

"Excuses," my mother said sharply. "You always *were* one for excuses."

I felt it then—the sick twist in the pit of my stomach. The nausea had taken a back seat to the pain, but my limbs were turning numb now. My hand barely even ached, even though it was badly broken. Fuck, I was going to throw up.

I doubled over, the room seesawing as I emptied my stomach onto the ground.

"And so it begins," Joshin said.

Click. Click. Click.

He wasn't heading for Carrion anymore. He was coming for me.

"Even as a child, you were a nuisance. Always following me like a pathetic little puppy. I never had a moment's peace. You were the reason your father went away, you know. *You* were the reason he died."

I straightened and found my mother's face twisted with disgust.

"Look at the mess you've made. Always making such a mess. And now you want to hurt that man? Why? Because *you* were stupid enough to follow him into this tower? Because *you* weren't paying attention, hmm? Because you were lazy and too distracted by thoughts of the half-breed you left back in Yvelia to pay attention to the task at hand?" The words spewed out of her in a torrent, dripping with disdain. "What sort of male have you become? I don't even recognize you. I've never been more ashamed."

And at that, the room and the situation snapped into focus.

The figure standing beside me looked real. I bet that if I reached out and touched her, she'd feel real, too. But my mother was nothing like the cold-hearted illusion that stalked after me as I turned away from

Vorath Shah and went back to the wall. My mother was too kind and too sweet for such harsh words.

The dark dream had begun.

"Where are you going? What are you doing?" She hurried after me, her skirts swishing over the glowing runes at her feet. "So now you *aren't* going to kill the human? Weak. Weak in your convictions. Weak-willed. That's all you will ever be, Fisher. *Weak.*"

Her words flowed over me and fell away, having no effect.

My mother knew I wasn't weak. She'd made sure of that herself. And I'd had way too much practice closing my mind off to the madness of the quicksilver to be affected by any vision that Joshin's venom could show me.

I went back to work.

The section of the wall that I had struck just now was glowing softly. I hadn't noticed before, but now that my eyes were clearing, the room sharpening, I was picking up things I hadn't seen before. It was...it was glowing because of the blood.

"Not content with leaving your dinner on the floor? You need to smear your blood all over the walls as well?" the female who was not my mother said. "Just give in already. Haven't you had enough of all this? The constant challenges, and the pain, and the sacrifices. Always you. No matter what. *You* are the one who must give up his freedom. *You* are the one who must tolerate the pain. *You* are always the one who must sacrifice, when there are other people in the world who could be called upon every once in a while. Aren't you *tired?*" She sounded incredulous.

"Oh, yes. I'm tired," I admitted. "But I doubt that's going to change. And what's the alternative? Death?"

"*Rest,*" the female wearing my mother's face countered. "*Peace.* Isn't that what you crave? No more pain. No more worry. No more—"

The gods only knew what other weak reasoning she came up with. I had stopped listening. I was dragging my finger through the blood I'd left on the wall, tracing out the lines of a very specific rune.

The rune meaning *break.*

As soon as the final line was drawn, the hallucination shook her head. "Well, there you are. You've done it now. I hope you're happy."

I stepped back, observing my handiwork. "I am actually." The rune lit up, blazing and white. It sank into the wall, its lines forming deep grooves in the stone. The magic that shielded the wall stretched thin. A veil of shadows shivered over the stonework—strange, since I hadn't even reached for my magic—and I watched (and *felt*) the ward that protected the demon's trap splinter and come apart.

"Gottith man soh frayah!" Joshin crowed.

The dark door is undone!

Its cry was elated. It felt the thin blanket of power removed at last from its tomb. The lifting of the ward meant its escape, its freedom after how many centuries, squatting and waiting in the dark. But *I* wasn't about to let that happen. I didn't love this realm, but it had produced someone I loved with a fierceness that took my breath away, and I was not going to leave this place worse off than when I had found it. For Saeris's sake, I would protect it.

The demon trembled, individual scorpions jittering free of its mass and dropping to the floor. They skittered away in droves toward the stairs.

"Where do you think you're going?" I asked.

"A city lies beyond these walls. A million beating hearts. A million humans to visit while they sleep. I will invite them all to the dream. I will...invite them all to *sing*!"

To dream meant to wander, trapped inside their nightmares.

To sing meant to scream out their fear so long and so loud that Joshin would feed from their pain for years before the city died.

The tunnels below Zilvaren were the perfect means of transport for Joshin's scorpions. They could move in darkness. Discover ways to slip into people's houses. They would sting them in their sleep, and the resulting symphony of fear it conducted would encompass the entire Silver City and sustain it for years.

But *only* if more than half of his scorpions managed to leave this room.

I turned and I hurled my fist at the wall. *This* time, it shuddered. *This* time, it cracked. Dust rained down from the ceiling, hissing in waterfalls down the walls. The second time I struck the wall, it crumbled, a large section of the sandstone exploded outward.

Light burst into the tomb, cutting through the dark, and Joshin roared. The demon flailed, pitching sideways, half of its lower body already disassembled and running away from the light. It looked half melted, its form caught at the midpoint between scorpion and demon, its raw flesh exposed to the powerful light of the twin suns.

For the first time ever, I found myself happy to see Balea and Min.

"Ashelgrin Fas!" the demon roared. *Make it stop.* Smoke rose from its jellied form. It gnashed its teeth, scrambling to retreat out of the path of the light, but it had nowhere to go.

I had no qualms smashing another hole into the tower wall. My hand was already broken, and the pain paled in comparison to the burn of Joshin's venom.

"Stop! You must stop!" Joshin wailed.

"Fisher? I—" Carrion was on his knees. His eyes rolled, wild and terrified. Shah had him in a headlock, a crude blade held against his throat.

"Leave my master be, or I spill his blood," he snarled, cracked, yellowed teeth on show.

Gods alive, I was teaching Carrion to take care of himself. I was teaching him to fight. I—

Carrion rammed his elbow back into Shah's stomach. He kicked out his leg to the side and twisted, sweeping Shah's feet out from underneath him. A second later, the traitorous human had dropped his weapon onto the sand-covered stone, and Swift was wrestling him to the ground. Scorpions clambered over their thrashing forms, stinging them both as they scurried over their bodies and scuttled away down the stairs.

I assessed the situation quickly. This obviously wasn't the first time Shah had fought for his life. He was quick, spinning in Carrion's grip, slippery as an eel...but every time he almost pulled free and wriggled away, Carrion pulled him back. Swift was ghost-white, his face and his forearms dotted with bleeding puncture wounds from where he'd been stung. He wore a look of grim determination that I had seen many times before. The face of a male who knew he was about to kill and was set upon the task.

He put a knee into Shah's chest, pinning him to the ground. The black-market trader spat, his hands scrabbling in the sand, trying to find the blade he'd dropped. He found it and quick as a snake slashed at Carrion's leg, cutting his thigh open. I stepped forward, ready to intervene, but Carrion took Shah's head in his hands and twisted sharply, breaking the bastard's neck.

Fire lashed around my knee and up my leg, exploding into my hip.

"Fuck!" I looked down, and there was Joshin's dagger-sized stinger, embedded in the side of my leg. I had been distracted. I'd let it get too close. Clouds of steam rose from the demon as it twitched, burning in the light.

"Is your mind...a dark place, warrior?" Joshin's lips trembled around the words. It was down on its side. I watched, horrified, as bloody, fibrous strands of its heavy pincer fell away and pulsed on the ground, transforming into scorpions the length of my thumb.

I hissed as its oversized stinger drew back, pulling out of my thigh. My legs went weak, threatening to give out, but I steadied myself as blood spurted from the wound the barb left behind.

"You are a creature of shadows. Yes, I know your kind well," the demon said, in a wheedling voice. "A mind full of shadows is a dangerous thing. When you already live in the darkness, hell is right there at your fingertips. So thin, the veil. Are you re-ready for the dream, shadow weaver? Will you have...the strength to wake?"

The demon's tomb pitched. I could already feel the dream—the *nightmare*—closing in around me, fighting to take shape before my eyes.

"We need to go. The guardians will be here any second. We need to kill it." Carrion swayed, dragging his right leg behind him as he crossed the tomb. With the sun hitting him square in the face, his hair shone brilliant copper and gold. There was blood on his hands. Blood on the blade he carried. Blood staining his clothes and running down his forearms. His cheeks had a sickly greenish cast to them, the blue of his eyes too pale. He raised his dagger, about to bring it down on Joshin's weakened form himself, but I caught a hold of his wrist.

"No. Wait."

"This piece of shit *is* dying. Fisher. Now. Do *not* tell me you're experiencing an uncharacteristic bout of mercy."

"Not in the slightest."

Crackling laughter filled the tomb, dry as the desert wind. "He will not kill me," Joshin said. Its many-layered voice was weak but still sent shivers chasing through my body.

"Believe me, he will." Carrion kicked away a scorpion that was trying to scale the toe of his boot, stomping on it. "And if he doesn't, *I* sure as shit will."

"I am older than this city. Older than the wheels of fate that turn your tides, princeling. The secrets I know are more valuable to him than revenge. And I *must* live if you hope to do the same. At least for now."

A wave of nausea rolled over me, gathering in the pit of my stomach like a spiked ball. More than anything, I wanted to be sick, to rid myself of the poison in my gut, but I swallowed down the urge. "It's right," I admitted. "We need it alive."

"Bullshit we do!"

"Are you feeling tired yet?" I asked wearily. "I am. Soon, you won't be able to fight it. You'll have to sleep, and when you do, you'll be walking straight into the kind of hellscape that will make you want to curl up and die. The demon's venom is systemic. It'll stay in our bodies for the rest of our lives if we don't get rid of it. We'll wake from our sleep, yes. But from this point onward, every time we pass out, we'll be thrust back into that hellscape. The nightmares will get longer. Eventually, either we *won't* wake up, or we'll go mad and kill ourselves. Is *that* what you want?"

"Sure. Sounds like a vacation in paradise." Sarcasm dripped from Carrion's words, but there was fear there, too.

"We need to make an anti-venom." Gods, it would be so easy. To sit down. To fall asleep right here. Right now. I breathed deep, blinking hard. "And to do that, we need a dose of venom from the demon."

Joshin laughed, ropes of saliva dangling from its sharp, needle-sharp teeth. Out of nowhere, the walls and the floor shook as a deafening *DONNNNNNGGGG!* reverberated overhead.

Loud. *So* loud.

The thunder of it resonated in my bones. Rattled my teeth.

Carrion clapped his hands over his ears, shielding them from the head-splitting sound. "Reckoning!" he shouted. "It's midday!"

The Twins didn't go down in Zilvaren, but they *did* peak in the sky. At midday, they drew close to each other, close enough for the sisters to hold hands, and the temperatures spiked to unbearable degrees. My mother's books had told me so.

The bell above our heads must have been massive. It only tolled once, thank the gods, but the thunder of it echoed in my blood and rocked the ground for a full minute afterward.

I was first to speak. "Does the trader have some of your venom?" I demanded.

The demon laughed—the sound of rock scraping on rock. "And I would tell you this? Just give the information to you freely? I think *not*, warrior."

"If Vorath had its venom, it'll be back in his shop," Carrion said. "We should just kill the monster and go there. It isn't going to tell us anything."

"Are you willing to risk it?" *I* wasn't.

Carrion looked conflicted. He wanted to disregard my advice and destroy the hideous thing that had attacked us...but the prospect of an unending cycle of nightmares rightfully gave him pause. "So, we don't kill it yet. We make the anti-venom, and *then* we kill it." It sounded as if this idea was the only thing keeping him going.

"You must have my...permission," the demon wheezed. "The venom to create its cure must be given...freely."

"Well, of course *you'd* say that." Carrion made a face at the demon. "What if we just cut off its stinger and take it back to Vorath's shop? The guy has everything we need to create a cure there. I'd put money on it."

"You're sure? Sure enough to risk it?" I let him stew on that for half a second. Thankfully, he lowered his dagger and sighed; I really didn't feel like wrestling it away from him right now, with my gut churning and traces of light streaking across my vision.

"I am not dragging that melted carcass through the tunnels," Swift said.

"Stop talking, Carrion," I rumbled. "The grown-ups are about to strike a bargain."

"Why the fuck are we *bargaining* with it?"

Giving the demon a hard stare, I worked my jaw, flaring my nostrils; the tomb smelled rank, like sulfur and death. "Because the Fae and demon kind have one thing and one thing alone in common. We are both bound by our oaths, aren't we, fiend?"

Again, Joshin laughed, and it seemed as if all of Zilvaren trembled at the unholy sound. "Go ahead and...make your opening offer, shadow weaver. It...will not...be enough."

"There's no opening offer." I shook my head. "There's *the* offer. We will spare you and allow you to live if you provide two droplets of your venom to heal us."

The demon shuddered with fury. "An uneven bargain. Two lives for one!"

"Are you equal to me, demon?" I snarled. "Are you not more powerful? More important? More valuable in the eyes of your kind?"

"Infinitelyyyyy," Joshin rumbled in a disturbing, guttural tone.

"Then the deal is unevenly weighted on *your* end, wouldn't you say? In that case, you owe us one of your precious secrets, too."

The demon snapped its teeth, caught out by its own pride. "What *kind* of secret?"

"One valuable enough to balance the scales of our bargain," I answered, knowing what I was demanding.

The demon's own vanity would require it to give us an impressive secret. Something monumental. It peeled back its bloody lips and barked in derision. "You ask for too much. A bargain has *not* been struck."

"All right, then. So be it. Carrion, get ready to light this asshole up."

The smuggler whipped around to look at me. "What?"

"*Fire*, Carrion. You're about to get your way. We're going to set this thing on fire and watch it burn."

"But I can't—"

"And once we've made ash of it," I said, cutting him off, "we'll gather the demon's leavings and sell it in little glass bottles to the humans. We'll tell them it's seasoning for their gruel."

"Sacrilege!" Joshin roared. "I am a god! You cannot—"

I dropped into a crouch and stared the thing in its twisted, hideous face. Its flesh fluttered and rippled, distorting thanks to the poison in my veins, but I took a deep breath and focused. "Nightmares or no, you are whatever I say you are once you're dead, demon. Maybe I'll say you're bonfire ash. Or the remains of a goat."

"No! All right. One secret and my venom in exchange for my life. But you must agree to release me. I will not be imprisoned in another one of these traps for the rest of time."

I thought about this. Scoured the deal for holes. It didn't take long for me to find numerous ways to manipulate the bargain to my own advantage. "All right," I said. "Bleed for it and be done."

A piece of the demon's shoulder came away, strands of flesh that morphed and took shape, solidifying into a small scorpion. It tapped toward me, light on its eight feet...and I crushed it under the heel of my boot.

The demon hissed its displeasure at the rough treatment. "Now you, warrior," it said. "*Bleed.*"

I wasn't going to cut myself and seal our pact the polite way. No chance. I pierced my bottom lip with my canines, sucked the blood into my mouth, and spat it at him. "Your life for ours. A secret, and a promise that you will be released and not caught in another demon trap," I said.

"Yes. Your lives for mine. The secret. The promise," the demon chanted back. And it was done.

Carrion wrinkled his nose. He somehow managed to look sicker than he had a moment ago. "Like I said. You're carrying it."

"No, I'm not." The floor felt like sand beneath my boots as I crossed the rune-etched stone, toward the trunks on the far side of the room. I had to step over the half-eaten body to reach my goal. Thankfully, I found what I was looking for quicker than I'd hoped. Inside the first trunk, nestled among a pile of coins and golden rings, I found a small wooden box. It contained gems. Rubies, sapphires, diamonds. I dumped them on the floor and returned to Joshin. I didn't ask for the demon's permission; I stooped and picked up a scorpion from the ground, pinching it by its stinger.

Into the box it went.

I snapped the lid closed on it, and the demon cocked its head. "What are you doing, shadow weaver?"

"The secret, Joshin."

The demon inched back, pressing its back against the wall. "I will give you the secret once I am free."

Grimly, I shook my head. "Now, Joshin. While you can still speak."

"You can't kill me!" it shrieked.

"And I won't. As long as I have your little friend in this box here, you won't be dead, will you?"

"Cheat! Liar!" Joshin spat. "You *swore*!"

"I am Oath Bound, Demon. I cannot lie. I cannot break my oath. Now tell me your secret, before you break *yours*."

"If you destroy this body, it will take me lifetimes to regenerate," he snarled.

"Sounds like a *you* problem to me." I had no control over fire; it wasn't my element to command. A part of me suspected that it *might* be Carrion's, but he was in no fit state to try conjuring unknown magic. There would be time for that later. For now, I took out my tinderbox and struck the piece of flint against the wall, using the spark to light the dried moss inside. In seconds I had one of the old torches lit, and the hungry flames were throwing shadows up the walls.

"You wouldn't dare," the demon said.

I crouched down in front of it, closer than I would have liked, clenching my jaw as its half-formed head whipped around to face me. "You can smell me, yes?" I asked.

The demon snapped its jaws.

"Then tell me, Joshin. You filled me with enough venom to take down three horses . . . but do you scent *any* fear on me? Do you think I am afraid to face my demons? I've faced them before. I know them all by name. I've conquered them and bent them to my will more times than the sun has risen over Yvelia in my lifetime. I'll face your nightmares if I have to, and I will *still* be the most frightening thing prowling around in the dark."

The slits in Joshin's face flared, quivering as the demon tentatively sniffed—and then snarled, pulling away.

"The secret, Joshin," I repeated. "It's now or never."

The demon let out a cry of frustration, but then it said, "Where there is light, there is *always* darkness, shadow weaver. To kill a queen, you will need to visit the darkest of *all* places. You will need to strike a deal far more costly than this one if you hope to succeed. And the beast who lies in wait for you there will not be so easy to trick as me. She will eat you whole, shadow weaver!" Joshin roared as I held the flickering torch to its body. "She will tear away your soul and feed on it for decades!"

The demon lit up like a beacon. With a *woompf*, the flames swallowed what was left of its mangled torso.

Joshin screamed, and all around us the scattered scorpions that had shivered free from the demon's body also burst into flames. Down in the tunnels, those that had escaped would be burning, too. Save for the invertebrate I shielded inside the wooden box, they all went up in flames. Their screams echoed through the tower, agonized and furious.

"Ahh, I get it now," Carrion groaned, observing the horror of it all. "I'm already *in* the nightmare, aren't I?"

I surprised myself by letting out a harsh bark of laughter. "No. Unfortunately, *that* part is only just beginning."

18

BROTHER

SAERIS

LORRETH'S LEATHERS CREAKED as he shifted, staring at the vampire. "I never thought I'd see you again."

I watched the two males, waiting for the first fist to fly. The way they were looking at each other certainly promised violence. Leaning back against a pillar, Lorreth folded his arms casually in front of his chest. He'd unwound the silver chain that I'd used to restrain the other male, and I hadn't done anything to stop him. If Lorreth deemed it safe to release him, who was I to say otherwise?

Foley—this stranger with blue-black hair; pale soulful cat eyes; and gold that flashed in his mouth every time he spoke—glowered up at my friend from under drawn brows. "I didn't think I'd ever see you *here*, Lorreth. Walking around in the open like you're on a godscursed vacation." He spoke the words without emotion, but there was an anger behind them that ran deep. It charged the air, making the hairs on the back of my neck prickle.

Lorreth huffed down his nose, looking down at his boots. "It's not like I *want* to be here, brother," he said.

"If you two aren't going to draw blood, then I have a cat to find," Algat sniped. The look she sent me could have killed a dead man twice.

"Here. The book that was promised." She held up the tome with the faded black cloth cover that she had stabbed at me earlier. "I can't guarantee you'll find what you're looking for inside it, but then again, what do I care? I'm here from an hour after dusk until an hour before sunrise. Do *not* return during those hours. You may peruse the shelves, but do not remove any other books from the library without written consent."

She held out the book across the reading table. I went to take it, but she snatched it back at the last second. "Do you understand?" She squinted at me through narrowed eyes.

"Do I understand that I'm only permitted to enter the library for an hour in the evening and an hour before dawn? In my own court? Yes, I understand perfectly."

"Good." Algat shoved the book at me and left.

As soon as the stooped Lord of Midnight was gone, Foley rose from his seat. "She's a vampire, Lorreth. She's wearing Fisher's dagger like she didn't have to pry it from his cold, dead hands. And the way you're angling your body right now tells me you'd stand against me if I went for her throat again."

Lorreth looked over his shoulder at me, raising both eyebrows in query. "He went for your throat?" he asked.

I shrugged, nodding.

"And you don't have a mark on you? Impressive."

Foley made a sound of annoyance. "That really isn't the point."

"You must be getting rusty in your old age, Foley. Or perhaps you're just out of practice because you've hidden yourself away in a fucking *library* of all places."

The vampire's hands curled into fists, tension drawing his shoulders up around his ears. "No one comes here," he said. "No one apart from that old witch. This is the only place I can be without causing friction."

I held up a hand, laughing quietly. "Uh, I'd say you just caused plenty of friction."

Foley rounded on me, features drawn into a sneer. "I wasn't talking to *you*."

It happened fast. The chair behind Foley flew into the air and then crashed down onto the reading table. The vampire was lifted off his feet and flung backward. A banner of black streamed across the library, and then Lorreth was holding the vampire out of the hole I had created in the library wall by the front of his shirt.

"You'd be wise to adjust that attitude," he said.

In a flash, I was at his side. "Lorreth, it's okay. Pull him back in."

But Lorreth didn't obey. "She is a vampire. *Half* vampire. But she's also half Fae. And she did not pry that blade from Fisher's cold dead hand." He laughed, shaking his head, as if he couldn't even believe what he was saying himself. "He *gave* it to her."

"Bullshit. He would *never* do that." The male was angry, yes, but otherwise appeared unconcerned that he was being dangled precariously over the side of the building. "The only reason he would do that was if she was..."

Lorreth dipped his head, eyebrows up again. He made a '*go on. You're almost there. Finish the thought,*' kind of motion with his free hand.

Foley's eyes darted to me, going wide. "No." He shook his head. "That's not true."

"Isn't it?" Lorreth scoffed. "Are you telling me you can't smell him on her from here? It's been two days since he was here last, and I can still—"

"Excuse me, but I'd prefer it if you didn't finish that thought. While I'm fairly immune to the judgment of others, I don't think I can handle my friend gossiping about the fact that I reek of sex right in front of me."

"So, she's tricked him, then," Foley said uncertainly. "She's found a way to control him. But that doesn't explain why you're protecting her like this. She's the enemy, Lorreth."

The dark-haired warrior glanced back at me again, a crooked smile taking over his handsome face. "She's my *drinking* partner. And since you're the one who left that spot wide open, you don't get to complain about someone else filling the role."

"She's their queen," he hissed.

"And apparently, you're a vampire now, too. But you don't see me trying to kill *you*."

"Really? You're holding me over a hundred-foot drop!" he cried.

"Ahh. Right." The warrior snorted sheepishly, pulling in the other male and setting him back down onto his feet. "I'll rectify that. But don't think for a second that I won't launch you back out of that hole if you try to pull anything," he said.

Foley gave me a wary sidelong glance as he stepped back onto the library's rug. Clearly, I still wasn't to be trusted.

Well, the feeling was fucking mutual.

If Lorreth called this male brother, then he was closer than close. Somehow, he was family. But nothing about him made sense. For starters, he was a vampire who hated vampires. I had too many questions to count, and I wanted answers. "You look at me like I'm a monster, but I smell blood on you too, Foley. You're just like me."

His eyes glittered with malice as he stalked around the table. "Not so," he whispered.

"No? Explain yourself, then. How do you know my mate? How is it that you live within this court and yet are not a part of it and not bound by its rules?"

Foley looked to Lorreth, a question on his face. "You're telling me she is Fisher's mate, and she doesn't even know who I am?"

Apparently, Lorreth had decided that the danger had passed and his friend no longer posed a threat. He sat down heavily in a seat at the head of the reading table, holding out a hand and gesturing to me to hand over the book Algat had given to me. I gave it to him. "A lot's been going on lately," he said, cracking it open. Frowning down at the pages, he scanned the text on the front page and then began leafing through the book's subsequent pages. "And I hate to break it to you, brother, but you've been gone a long time. We've written to you. Sent messengers. Tried to visit. And our attempts to make contact have been rebuffed at every turn. So, no. You haven't been at the forefront of conversation lately."

Foley stood at the end of the table, resting his splayed fingertips against its surface. He pondered his words for a long time before he spoke. Not to Lorreth, but to me. The ice had vanished from his tone, but it hadn't been replaced by anything that resembled warmth. "I didn't volunteer to become this. My death was taken from me. I've since tried to return the 'gift' that was given to me a number of times, though I have yet to be successful. I came to Ammontraíeth when I transitioned because there are no living creatures here for me to endanger. Or rather, far fewer warm-blooded folk who might tempt me to give in to my lesser instincts. In answer to your first question, I know your *mate*"—he heaped emphasis onto the word, as if he still didn't quite trust that the information Lorreth had given him was true—"because I once considered him family. He trained me to fight. He saved my life more times than I can count."

"You saved his life once, too. Remember?" Lorreth interjected.

Foley bowed his head, waving the memory away as if it didn't matter. "In answer to your second question, I'm not bound by the rules of this court because, as Lorreth said, I'm not a part of it. I'm permitted to exist here at Taladaius's discretion, but I do not align myself with Sanasroth. If I had my way, I'd kill each and every one of the monsters housed in this black city and watch them turn to ash."

"I'm honestly surprised that you *haven't* done that," Lorreth mused. He was still buried in the book, his eyes skipping over the text within. "But I'm also surprised that you still feel that way." Gently, he closed the book and set it down, looking up at his friend. "You've been living among them—"

"I've been living here, among these books," he said. "Not among *them*. I made a promise when I joined the Lupo Proelia. I swore to defend the living against these wretches. I might not have been able to uphold that oath of late...." His cat eyes glowed unnaturally. "But I certainly haven't *broken* it."

Lorreth's face was unreadable. He met Foley's gaze, and a lot seemed to pass in the silence between them. It felt like a personal moment. The two males hadn't seen each other in an age. They had plenty to catch up on, and I wasn't particularly enjoying the way the vampire's quick, odd eyes kept flitting to me, as if he were making sure to track my movements.

"I'm going to find somewhere else to be," I told Lorreth. "I'm gonna be honest. This is pretty awkward. And I don't feel like being here when they realize where all that debris came from and come to check on the tower."

Lorreth chuckled, but he held up his hand. "Wait a minute, Saeris. Here. Take this." He held out the book, its dusty, frayed cover displaying a foiled silver title that I hadn't noticed before.

Elemental Runes and Their Purposes.

A Comprehensive Guide to Alchemy.

I took it—

"You heard Algat. She forbade you from removing that from the library," Foley snapped.

I glanced down at the book, then back at the male, smiling coldly. "Just as you aren't mine to command, *I* am not *hers*. She is Keeper of Records. *I* am queen of all Sanasroth. I'll take this book and any other I see fit. If she has a problem with that, let her come and tell me so to my face."

The arrogance didn't come naturally. It was like new muscle, stubbornly refusing to bear weight, but I wouldn't be chided by the likes of him. The male snorted, as if he pitied my naivety. He went to speak, but his eyes caught on the title of the book in my hand and flared.

"What do you need with *that* book?" he demanded.

His eyes simmered with intensity when I met them. Why I needed the book was none of his fucking business. The male had tried to kill me, and I was ninety-nine percent sure he'd still try again, even knowing what he knew about me now. Regardless, Lorreth looked at me like he hoped I would respond in a civil way, and I didn't want to disappoint him.

I sighed heavily and explained. "I'm an Alchemist. I'm also God-Bound to Fisher. My hands are covered in runes, and I don't know what they mean or how to control the magic they channel. My power is erratic, hence the giant hole that Lorreth just dangled you out of. So, yes. My life's pretty complicated right now. And I've also been thrust into this world where everyone wants me dead, and—" I frowned, trying to analyze the vampire's expression. "What? What is it? Why are you looking at me like that?"

"You're an Alchemist."

"I am."

"The runes are real."

"They are."

"They're not just tattoos?"

"No. Look, is this going somewhere? Because I have a forge to get to."

"When was the last time you slept?"

I blinked at the unexpected change in questioning. "I'm sorry?"

"Alchemists required a lot of sleep to regulate their power. Their bodies needed rest in order to tap into their magic effectively. You look like you haven't rested in weeks."

"Wow. *Thanks.*" The vampire sure had a way with words. My skin was porcelain these days, pale and flawless. There were no bags under my eyes. My eyes were bright. Personally, I thought I looked pretty good for someone who had just been through hell and back, but according to Foley, I looked like shit. He must have been able to read my annoyance on my face, because he averted his eyes, dipping his chin—the closest I was going to get to an apology, I presumed.

"When I first transitioned, I didn't sleep, either," he admitted. I got the feeling this wasn't something he enjoyed talking about a great deal. "My body didn't feel tired. I was . . . restless. That's how it goes for some people. But rest is important even for vampires. I learned the hard way that the consequences can be dire if you don't rest the body and the mind."

Restless. That was precisely how I felt. I couldn't seem to sit still. "And how am I supposed to make myself sleep if my body simply won't let me?" I asked.

"I don't know what will work for you," he replied. "I found I had to enter a trance state to trick my body into it at first. That helped."

"A trance state? How did you manage *that*?" My mind was so loud.

There were five trains of thought careening through my head at all times. The very idea of trying to quiet them enough to enter a trance was laughable.

"Find a focal point and fix your gaze to it," Foley said. "Try to hear nothing but what is happening in the room around you. Let your eyes lose focus. Drift." He spread his fingers, palm up. "It isn't easy to accomplish. But mastery of the mind is a pursuit worthy of queens and peasants alike. And an especially worthy pastime for an Alchemist. Some magics are reflexive. They come to a person automatically, like breathing. But an Alchemist's magic can only be harnessed."

A brightness had come to him. A spark of interest in his eyes that hadn't been there before. It opened his features. Made him look younger. Less angry.

I was going to ask the question, but Lorreth got there first. Leaning across the table toward his friend, he said, "We hoped you might remember information about the Alchemists. From your grandfather."

The vampire smiled for the first time since he had tackled me to the ground. When I was human, I probably wouldn't have been able to see the engraved swirls on the gold that plated his canines, but my senses had improved significantly of late. The pattern was intricate and beautiful. It was hard not to stare at them. "I learned from him, yes. But as I told you a moment ago, I've spent the past thousand years with only these books and the stars for company. I know them all like the backs of my hands."

"Will you help us, then?" Lorreth was a measured male. He kept his emotions in check at the best of times, but now he seemed to be guarding them extra closely. It was almost as if he didn't want Foley to know how badly we needed guidance. "Can you help us figure out how to seal her runes?"

I resented having to ask the male for anything at all, given the stunt he'd just pulled, but Foley was the first person we had come across in all of Yvelia who knew anything about the Alchemists and their magic. And if I didn't get help soon, something bad was going to happen. I could feel it in my bones.

"If you do know how to seal these things," I said, holding up my hands, "providing a little guidance would go a long way toward making up for the fact that you just tried to snap my neck."

The vampire's expression implied he didn't really feel bad about what had transpired and didn't care about making it up to me, either. But he inclined his head, wearing a stiff smile. "Anything for King-fisher's mate."

"Great. Let's get to work, then. The sooner I can close off the magic pouring into these—"

"Sleep first," he said. "Without rest, you won't be able to accomplish anything at all. And besides, I need time to collate the knowledge I've acquired over the years. I must track down numerous titles and cross-check information—"

"But you saw what I just did to the wall! What if I destroy an entire *wing* of the palace next?"

"You won't destroy anything. *You'll be asleep.*"

He was firm in his answer, but I tried one last time, just in case. "Foley—"

"You are *not* my queen." There was no hate in this now. Only resolve. "I will help you, but not now. Your body might not feel it, but your control is clearly weak," he said, gesturing to the gaping hole in the stonework on the other side of the library. "I'm only half sure of the steps we need to take, and I don't know about you, but any situation I have entered into tired and uninformed has never gone well. So you should sleep, and I should read. Those are the only conditions under which I will help you in this."

"Still stubborn as a mule, then," Lorreth said. He grunted, getting to his feet. "Glad to see *that* hasn't changed, at least. He *is* right, though, Saeris. If resting will give you a better chance of controlling your magic come evening tomorrow, then I can't see the hurt in it. It's just one more day."

This was worse than when Elroy had refused to teach me how to make weapons until I'd mastered the art of making glass. The old man's words damn near rang in my ears even now.

"Until you learn how to be gentle, I will not teach you how to be violent."

There had been sense in his approach; I'd been too eager to construct the method of my revenge against Madra and her guardians. I had been reckless and foolish back then and liable to get myself killed doing something stupid. But learning how to blow and manipulate the glass Elroy was known for had taught me patience. Ish.

"All right. Fine. First thing tomorrow evening, then. I'll be back here just as dusk is settling," I conceded.

Foley nodded. "Make sure you get that sleep . . . *Saeris*," he said, trying out my name for the first time. "I'll know you're lying if you don't."

19

I'LL LIVE

KINGFISHER

VORATH SHAH'S SHOP was a disaster. Or...there was a strong chance that maybe I was hallucinating. Had it been like this before? I couldn't remember. Either way, glass bulbs and shattered wooden crates cluttered the floor. The shelves were hanging off the walls, lopsided, the contents spilled onto the ground. A strange, musky scent filled the shop, too, pungent and sour. Carrion and I had both wrinkled our noses when we'd entered, and we were now breathing through our noses as we combed through the debris, searching for an alembic still that hadn't been smashed to pieces.

"I swear I know that smell." Carrion swayed, pressing his hand against the wall for support. "It's *so* familiar." He wasn't far from passing out. It was a miracle, really, that he hadn't toppled like a fallen tree with all the demon venom chugging through his veins. He'd thrown up multiple times on our way back through the tunnels across the Third, but then again so had I. Now, we were both running on empty, and much as I didn't want to admit it, it wouldn't be long before consciousness slipped away from both of us.

"Worry less about the smell and more about that still," I told him.

My arms were tired. My thigh was screaming with pain. The

puncture wound from Joshin's stinger was deep and burned like someone had poured acid into it. Putting weight on the leg was excruciating, but I could baby the wound later. For now, the anti-venom was...was our only priority.

"Don't we need...Oh, gods..." Carrion stiffened, his face turning gray. He closed his eyes, and I knew what he was experiencing: the rolling nausea, the spinning vision. I regretted thinking about it immediately as the same sensations passed over me. "Don't we need a healer to make this for us?" he gritted out. "This anti-venom?"

I kicked a plank of rotting wood out of my way, scattering shards of glass and a pile of fine blueish powder, frustration building as my eyes didn't alight upon a still. "No. All warriors know how to make anti-venom. We learn basic healing skills before we even learn how to wield a sword. There are plenty of things that want to poison a person in your kingdom, *Your Highness.* A warrior needs to know how to reverse a toxin when they find themselves in the frozen woods of Yvelia. They won't get very far if they don't."

"I don't like that," the smuggler groused.

"Really? I'd say it's really fucking handy that I'm trained in plant medicines."

"No, not...that." He had to take a breath between words. "*Your Highness.* I don't like it when you call me...Your Highness."

I snorted. "You *are* the true heir to the Winter Throne, are you not?"

"All right. I'll start calling you Lord Cahlish, then, shall I?"

"Not if you want to keep your fucking tongue," I growled.

Carrion straightened, looking up at the ceiling as he thought about this. "Umm. Yeah, I kinda need my tongue." He took a deep breath and then sighed it back out. "People *do* seem to like it."

I almost laughed. *Almost.* Gods, I was losing my mind. The male was ridiculous. "Just keep searching for the still, Swift."

For the first time since we'd arrived in Zilvaren, luck decided to favor us. We didn't find a still, but we did find a shallow crucible in the back of Shah's store that would suffice. The black-market trader had a full distiller constructed back there, out of sight from prying eyes, where he had clearly been up to no good. I broke down most of his setup, lit a taper beneath the burner, and got to work.

"You're too late. Why even bother?" My mother was back. She sat on the end of Vorath Shah's bench, swinging her legs beneath her long skirts, eating an apple. Her long black hair swirled around her head like she was underwater. "You're just like your father, aren't you, darling. Always too late." She took a huge bite of the apple, offering it out to me.

"No." I shook my head. "I don't want it."

"Is a dead person talking to you right now?" Carrion asked. He was bent over by the door with his hands on his knees again; it was probably the only position that helped with his nausea.

"Yes," I told him.

"Oh, good," he said in a high-pitched voice. "I thought that was just me."

Whatever phantoms were haunting Carrion, he chose not to share, and I chose not to pry. A male's ghosts were his own business, and I was having enough problems with my own.

"Well, look at you. Putting people in the line of danger. *Again.*"

I cut the palm of my broken hand—two inches long, at least half an inch deep—and clenched my hand into a fist as best I could, grunting through the pain. Blood welled in the crucible's bowl, gathering quickly.

I didn't look at the other, sandy-haired female who had joined us and was leaning against the bench next to me. I couldn't bear to see her face. Not now. Not here. Not after so many years of mourning her. I hadn't heard her voice in centuries. The sound of it now, familiar, knocked the wind out of me. It hurt more than everything else I'd endured today combined.

"It's not that you're evil. You're not unkind, either. You're just *careless,*" she said. "You promise to look out for people, and they put their trust in you. And then you let them down, don't you? Too concerned about covering yourself in glory to pay attention to what's happening to those around you."

I took a pinch of salt from an open bowl on Shah's bench and dropped it into the crucible. My chest felt like it was being cleaved wide open.

"See. You're so worried about saving the day right now that you can't even be bothered to look at me, can you?"

On the other side of the room, Carrion yelped and jumped away from the wall, batting away an invisible assailant.

I took out the little wooden box and set it down on the bench. My good hand shook as I tried to slide back the lid.

"Always the same. Always a coward. Always too afraid to acknowledge the consequences of his actions," the female snapped.

The little scorpion inside the box was furious. It was the last remnant of Joshin's form. The demon had been right—it would take lifetimes to replicate itself and return to full size. It stabbed at me, trying to sting my fingers, but I was done being stung by this motherfucker. I grabbed it by the tail and took it out of the box.

"Look at me, Fisher," the female said.

I held the scorpion up, trying and failing to focus on it. "Hold up your end of the deal, Joshin. If you don't, I'll smear you across the fucking wall."

"Fisher, *look* at me."

The scorpion squirmed, trying to escape, but I wasn't letting it out of my sight. It was growing harder to open my eyes every time I blinked. I held the scorpion against the side of the crucible, pressing its stinger against the lip of the metal. At first nothing happened.

Understandably, the demon was livid. We'd burned it to a crisp back in the bell tower. Its true form had died screaming, and this little piece of the demon had felt it all. It didn't want to oblige me by producing some of its venom . . . but it would die for good if it didn't.

Petulantly, the scorpion struck the side of the crucible at last, and a thin stream of clear liquid beaded and rolled down into the blood and salt.

As soon as the task was done, I shoved the scorpion back into the box, careful not to let it escape. Back into my pocket it went.

"Kingfisher, look *at what you did to me!"*

I spun without thinking. Renfis's sister stood there, the ends of her lovely long hair frazzled and black. Her once beautiful face was blistered and raw, skin slick like melted candle wax. Her left eye was missing. Her lips were fused together on the left side of her face. She was mostly naked, but there were scraps of scorched leather stuck to the exposed bones of her rib cage. Tears ran from her right eye, coursing down her ruined cheek.

"The wages of your pride, Fisher," she said out of the corner of her mouth. "What do you think? Am I still beautiful?"

"Always," I whispered.

"Do you know what it feels like to be burned alive?" she seethed.

Sadly, I nodded. "I do, Merelle. And I'm sorry."

I knew Merelle didn't blame me for her death. She would have had every right to, but she hadn't. She had chosen to bind her soul with my blade, to remain a part of the Lupo Proelia and stay close to those she loved. It hadn't been my choice. I would have preferred her to move on to the shores of the afterlife, to find her peace, but Merelle had always been a strong-willed female, even in death. This horror show was a manifestation of my own guilt and nothing more... but it shattered my heart into pieces.

I stepped around the charred corpse of my friend and placed my hands over the crucible, closing my eyes.

Venom laced with magic required an anti-venom laced with the same. Like for like. An exchange of power greater than the original to cancel it out. I threaded my shadows into the metal cup, sending them into the blood, salt, and venom, infusing the concoction with my power.

I felt it take hold.

"It's pointless, trying to wring a drop of remorse out of him, child," my mother said, looking back over her shoulder at Merelle. "He's incapable of real emotion. Aren't you?"

This wasn't going to be pleasant, but it *would* work. I collected the crucible and tipped its contents into two dusty cups.

"That's what you're afraid of, isn't it?" my mother spat. "That you'll have to truly feel the weight of everything you've done if you really want to love *her*. The hate. The shame. The horror."

She didn't say Saeris's name. Didn't need to. The female eating the apple on the bench was me. I knew exactly who she was talking about.

I faltered, suddenly unable to lift my own feet. "I *know* I'll have to do that," I muttered. "But I'm not afraid. She's worth it."

I walked through the image of my mother, leaving her behind as I crossed the room.

"Stop! No! Don't! She's sick! Please! Please, please, please, don't take it. I can't help her without it. I'll do anything, please, I promise—" Carrion's eyes went wide when I put my hand on his shoulder. His pupils refocused, whatever he had been seeing vanishing as he realized I was standing in front of him.

"You've done it?" he panted.

"I have."

He took the cup I handed to him, peering suspiciously at the liquid inside. "I've never considered drinking your blood before now, Fisher, but…I've got to say, I'm pretty fucking excited about this."

I clinked my cup against his. "You're welcome, Swift."

We both downed the concoction and immediately began seizing.

My bones were broken. All of them. They had been badly set, their edges scraping against my flesh. My stomach churned with acid, my eyes burning so badly that I almost wished I was blind.

But I *was* alive.

"Do you ever wake up sometimes…and think…'Gods, wouldn't it be nice if I *hadn't* just gone toe-to-toe with a scorpion demon from hell?'" Carrion croaked.

"Hah!" I pressed my good hand against my solar plexus, curious to see if the pressure might ease the stabbing pain there. It did not. "More often than I'd like."

We were sprawled on the floor, lying among the broken glass and destroyed furniture. We'd been here for at least an hour, twitching, and spasming, and foaming at the mouth. The fates must have been feeling particularly vicious today, because we'd been conscious the entire time as the anti-venom had wrought its work.

Slowly, I closed my eyes. "How do you feel?"

"Shitty," Carrion answered. His voice was stronger now, though. His breathing didn't sound as labored as it had twenty minutes ago. "You?" he asked.

"Shitty," I agreed.

"Are you still seeing dead people?"

I took a moment to answer. Then: "No."

"Me, either."

"Congratulations."

"Thanks. Appreciate that." He shifted, the sound of broken glass crunching underneath him. "If I lie here for much longer, I'm going to pass out. And I do *not* want to pass out here."

"Me, either."

Carrion made a pained sound as slowly he dragged himself up into a sitting position and then miraculously up onto his feet. "Come on, then. Let's go."

I opened my eyes, and there he was, holding his hand out to me again. For the second time in less than twenty-four hours, I let the smuggler help me to my feet. But this time, I was too tired to scowl at him all that much.

"Careful. Last time I was home, there was a bartender in my bed. There's a good chance she might still be here." Carrion ducked his head, scooting through the window he'd just jimmied open, disappearing into the darkened room beyond.

I was drenched in sweat. According to Swift, reckoning wasn't as hot as usual today, but the heat was hellish. Moving through the Third's deserted streets *had* been easier, though. The people of Saeris's ward knew to find shade during the hottest part of the day, when life slowed and those who were smart found a place to rest for a few hours.

I followed Carrion, vaulting through the window and immediately wishing I'd taken it slower, cradling my broken hand to my chest. The rooms were quiet. Still. There wasn't much by way of furniture within. A chair. A desk. A bed. The kitchen was small, but there were pots stacked, neat and clean on the counter. In the living area, Carrion found a note waiting for him on the rickety table. He plucked it up and read it, then screwed it up into a ball and tossed it into a bucket in the corner of the room.

"The bartender?" I asked.

He huffed a breath of laughter down his nose. "The bartender. I am now officially banned from the Dusty Crab."

"Shame."

"I'll live." The smuggler grunted. "They do have the best whiskey in the ward, though. Speaking of which..." He headed into the kitchen. Cupboard doors squeaked open and *thunk*ed closed. When he came back, he was carrying two cut-glass tumblers half full of pale amber liquid. He didn't ask if I wanted the drink. Even a priest chained tight to his morals would need one after what we'd just gone through. I accepted the glass and threw back the liquor inside, and Swift did the same.

The alcohol burned much like Joshin's venom, but this time the sensation was self-inflicted, so it didn't count. I considered the glass, processing the past few hours. We had our silver—bags of it, courtesy of the trunks stowed in the bell tower—but gods above, it had cost us.

"She made that, y'know."

I looked up.

Carrion was propped up against the side of his small dining table, leaning his hip against it. He gestured tiredly toward the glass. "You had her hammering out quicksilver, but she made other things before. The man who gave her work after her mother died? Elroy? He makes incredible etched glassware. Delicate. Sells them to the people in the Hub. The stuff Saeris made was never fine enough for the likes of them, but they were more than good enough for the people of the Third."

Suddenly, the glass in my hand became brand new.

It was a lovely thing. Small. The rim was embellished with a wound glass rope. A pattern was engraved into the sides of the glass, depicting a tower that looked an awful lot like Madra's palace being engulfed in flames. Dogs with curled tongues chased each other around the glass's base.

She had made this.

When I'd found her, I'd been full of panic. How was this woman, this *human*, the person I was supposed to fall in love with? How was I going to protect her from the kind of life I lived? She had surprised me. Where I had thought her weak, she was strong. Her heart was bigger than the horizon half the time—too big for her own good. I'd misjudged her. She was incredible. For twenty-five years, she had survived this harsh place and still had fire enough in her soul to create the kind of art that would undoubtedly have cost her life were it to end up in the wrong hands.

As if reading my mind, Carrion said, "She had a penchant for incendiary designs. Elroy couldn't sell them. I'd take them off his hands sometimes, when I could convince him to part with them." Carrion disappeared into the kitchen and came back with an earthen stoneware jug. Again, he didn't ask. I watched him pour the whiskey into the glass in my hands, chewing on the inside of my cheek.

A nest of vipers writhed behind my rib cage. They wanted me to punch Carrion in the face. *Hard.* But it was exhausting, this blind anger I harbored toward the male. It served no purpose. I was tired down to the marrow of my bones, and I didn't have the energy to maintain it. I knocked back the shot and set the glass down carefully, still staring at it.

Her hands had touched it. Her hands had made it.

That made me feel...

Fuck, I just *ached* for her. I wanted her here, next to me. I wanted to hold her; the fact that she wasn't in my arms right now felt like the greatest injustice that had ever been inflicted upon me. There was no breathing my way past it.

When I looked up, Carrion was watching me. "Go on," he said. "Ask."

It was beneath me to pretend that I didn't know what he was talking about. So I asked. "Are you in love with her?"

He let his head drop, laughing quietly as he pulled out a chair at the table and sank down heavily in it. Stretching his legs out in front of himself, he rested his hands on his stomach, one on top of the other, and looked up to meet my gaze. "No," he said simply. And then, immediately, "Yes?"

Heat flared up inside me, making my throat close.

"It's not a simple thing, Fisher. She's...well..."

"Spectacular," I whispered.

The smile that spread across his face was sad. "Right. Exactly. She always has been. When other people are full of the kind of fire that burns inside her, it eats them alive. It hollows them out until there's nothing left inside them *but* the fire. They burn everyone around them with it, until all that remains is scorched earth. But not Saeris. Her fire keeps others warm in the cold dark. It is her strength, not her weakness. Being around her reminds you that you're alive."

It made me want to vomit, hearing him talk about her like this. But he wasn't saying anything that was untrue. If I could see how incredible she was after knowing her for such a short time, then how the hell could I expect him to be blind to it when he had known her for years?

No, I couldn't blame the male for seeing what was obvious. I could only pity him that she wasn't his and be fucking thankful that she *was* mine.

"I could have loved her. Truly," Carrion said softly. "But this place broke me *centuries* before Saeris was born. I made the mistake of letting myself fall for a human once, and believe me when I say that once was enough. A long time ago, someone told me that the pain of loss was a temporary thing. That it would soften as the years went by, until the ache became an old friend that felt comfortable to be around. But the person who told me that was human." He sighed the kind of sigh that had been held in for a thousand years. "I didn't have much to go on when it came to my kind, but it always seemed to me that the Fae must experience grief differently from humans. Humans live for such a short time. It made sense that their pain visited them and left soon enough after. It would be cruel. Would swallow up their entire lives otherwise. But for me..." He shook his head, looking down at his hands. "Every year that I live, it seems the magnitude of my loss eclipses the last. So yes. I love Saeris Fane, because she's electric, and fierce, and loyal, and being around her brings the world back into focus. But I'm not *in* love with her, Fisher. I tried. But my heart was just too full of sorrow to make room for her."

The fire in my chest had gone out as the smuggler was speaking. Renfis would have had something profound or comforting to say in this situation. But I knew the eternal well of grief, how deep it ran, on and on forever, so I just nodded. It was all I had to give him—my understanding, and my presence. I dragged myself over to the chair in the corner of the room and sat, my broken hand singing with pain as I tried to hold the glass that Saeris had made in it.

"You barely even flinched today," the smuggler noted. "The pain of that venom. The pain of your dead." He didn't say anything for a moment, but then he asked, "Will you show me?"

"*Show* you?"

"How to close it off. To shut it all down, so I don't have to feel it anymore?"

Sinners. I puffed out my cheeks, unable to look at him for a moment. "No, Carrion. I won't."

"Why not?" He sounded like I'd just kicked him.

"There's only one way to learn how to endure pain the way I have. You have to suffer through it. Again, and again, and again. It galvanizes you. Tempers you like steel. But I wouldn't wish the kind of pain I've lived through on anyone. I've borne it because I had to and for no other reason. Feel the pain you've been given, Carrion. Don't be fool enough to ask for more. It's a curse I would spare you from, believe me."

20

HUNTSMAN

SAERIS

THERE WAS A crack in the wall.

A tiny one, only an inch long or so.

I stared at it until my eyes played tricks on me and the marbling in the obsidian walls began to melt. Five feet away, in front of the fire, Onyx was curled into a little ball, snoring loudly.

He didn't have any trouble passing out, of course. Life was simple for him. His brain didn't have countless questions and concerns bouncing around inside it.

An hour passed.

Another.

I was ready to sob when at last my restless exhaustion finally pulled me under.

Falling asleep didn't feel the same as it used to, though. This was more like...consciously stepping from one room into another. One moment, I was sitting on the floor of my rooms, resting against a mountain of cushions, and the next, I was somewhere else.

It was snowing.

The light was waning—the same kind of half-muted dusk that washed the walls of Cahlish a pale gray right before evening fell. The air was thick with pine and smoke, so cold that it stung the inside of my nostrils. I found myself overlooking a narrow valley blanketed with snow. A shallow stream cut through it, only a couple of feet wide, the water burbling and flowing swiftly.

On the hillside, halfway up the valley side in a clearing, stood a small cottage with white-painted walls and smoke trickling from its chimney.

Thwack.

Thwack.

Thwack.

To the left of the house: a figure moving in a repetitive, jerking way.

Thwack.

It was Fisher. I knew it was him the moment I saw him.

I set off running without a second thought. The cold pierced my lungs and bit at my cheeks. I skidded in the snow, losing my footing again and again, but I scrambled up and kept running. I couldn't breathe by the time I reached the pathway to the cottage.

Thwack.

Thwack.

He was there, up ahead. It was freezing, but my mate apparently wasn't affected by the cold. His black pants were slung low on his hips, his feet bare. He was shirtless, too, black ink swirling across his sweat-slicked shoulder blades as he swung an ax around, one-handed, bringing it over his head and down onto a block of wood, splitting it into two.

Thwack!

His hair was damp—wavy and thick, brushing the tops of his broad shoulders as he kicked aside the split wood and collected another large piece from a stack next to the cottage. Setting it down, I watched the muscles in his back shift and move as he brought the ax up and swung it around and down again, splitting that piece, too.

Thwack!

I spoke his name softly, inside my head rather than out loud. *Fisher?*

My mate stilled. His shoulders tensed, head angled slightly, tipped to one side, as if he were listening. *Saeris?*

I couldn't help myself; I started to run again. When he turned—tattooed chest heaving from his exertion, cheeks flushed, eyes bright—a glorious smile spread across his face. But just as soon as it had appeared, it fell away again. In a heartbeat, his cheeks lost their color. He took a staggering step backward, the ax falling from his hand and thudding to the ground.

I stopped running. "Fisher? What...what is it?"

He seemed to draw himself upright, standing as tall as he could manage, and then he asked out loud, "Are you dead?"

"Why would you *ask* that?"

His hands closed into fists at his sides. "You look...so real," he said. "I know I'm dreaming. I..."

"*I'm* dreaming, Fisher. I just fell asleep, and here you were."

"I've been here over an hour," he said. "I cleared a fallen tree down by the river. I dragged it up here. I've been breaking it down for firewood ever since."

"Well, we can't both be dreaming. Not the same dream," I said.

"We'll figure that out in a moment, Osha," he said quietly. "First, answer the question for me? Please?"

"What? Oh, no. No, I'm not dead. Not...officially," I added awkwardly. "The whole beating heart thing—"

Fisher strode toward me and swept me into his arms. He crushed me to him so tight that I thought my ribs were about to crack. I could hear him breathing, the sound ragged, as if he were struggling to keep his composure.

"Thank the gods. I thought something must have happened to you. I've been waiting to see if this becomes a nightmare. I thought... Fuck!"

He squeezed me even harder. I tapped frantically on his shoulder. "Fisher? Fisher, I can't breathe."

He pulled away, cupping my face in his hands, the beautiful green of his eyes almost glowing in the waning light as he took me in. "I'm sorry. Today's just been..." He shook his head, sucking on his bottom lip. "I fucking *hate* your city, Osha. I really can't overstate how much I really, *really* hate it. Gods, it's good to see you."

This didn't feel like a dream. I was too conscious. The world around me was too crisp. Too sharp. And this didn't feel like a sub-conscious rendering of my mate. His skin was warm to the touch. I could smell him. The details of him were too in focus. He swallowed, and I watched the muscles in his throat move, and there they were: the twin marks that were slowly fading at the hollow of his neck where I had bitten him.

"This is real, isn't it?" I whispered.

Fisher stepped back, releasing me. He turned sideways, eyes picking me apart as he paced around me, taking every bit of me in. The snow came down harder, fat flakes dusting the dark waves of his hair and melting as they hit his shoulders and his chest. I never felt more seen than when he looked at me. And like this, with his eyes devouring me, I could feel myself coming undone.

He stalked behind me and drew close. His body heat warmed my back, his breath skating over the back of my neck as he swept my hair over my shoulder, leaned into the crook of my neck, and smelled me.

"It's as real as anything else I've ever felt," he murmured. "You smell like you. You look like you." Suddenly his hands were at my waist, his fingers digging lightly into my hips. "You... *feel* like you."

We'd been apart for a little over a day, yet it felt like years had gone by. It was more than just missing him. I'd missed people before. I knew what that felt like. But the distance between us was a tangible tugging on my soul that made me panic.

"Witchcraft, perhaps?" he mused. His lips brushed the shell of my ear as he spoke, and a shiver ran up my body. He let out a suggestive rumble of laughter at that. "So responsive. I love how your body reacts to me, Little Osha. It lets me know that you're mine."

"Was there ever any doubt?"

He ran his nose up, behind my ear, into my hair, breathing deep again as he inhaled me. "Oh, I don't know. I had an interesting conversation with Carrion Swift before I passed out in his living room a little while ago. I thought for a moment I was going to have to fight him for you."

I snorted at the mere thought of that. "Don't hurt him, Fisher. You don't have anything to worry about where Carrion is concerned."

He hummed thoughtfully. "Mm. It's okay. I think I know that now."

I placed my hands lightly on top of his, enjoying the proximity of him, knowing that he was right behind me, but Fisher hissed, pulling back his right hand.

I turned in the circle of his arms, looking up at him, then down at his hand. It was horribly bruised, his knuckles crusted with dried blood. "Gods, what the hell happened?"

There was discomfort on his face, plain as day, but he still tried to downplay his injuries. "It's nothing. My hand's just a little broken. I had to punch a hole in a tower wall."

"You had to do *what?*"

I shivered as he explained what had transpired since I had seen him last. He and Carrion had secured the silver we needed, but they'd come face-to-face with some kind of scorpion demon while they were at it. They *hadn't* seen Hayden yet, but they were going to find him in the morning. By the time Fisher finished talking, the sweat had cooled on his body and my teeth were chattering. "I want to know what's been going on with you," he said. "But it looks like you're about to freeze to death. Let's get you inside."

He tucked me into his side and led me toward the cottage. Kicking open the door, he guided me inside, and the savory smell of spiced meat hit the back of my nose. Apparently, Kingfisher had been cooking before I had shown up and infiltrated his dream. "What *is* this place?" I asked.

"The huntsman's cottage at the boundaries of Cahlish. My father brought me here a few times when I was young. I haven't thought about this place in..." He looked up at the ceiling. "Years?"

The cottage was small. The kitchen was a sink in the corner and a small counter, stacked with glass jars full of what looked like pickled items. Bundles of drying herbs hung from the thick beamed rafters. The roof was low and stained with soot above the fireplace. Wingback armchairs sat in front of the hearth, sagging from years of use. A small white dog was stretched out in front of the crackling—

Hah! It wasn't a dog.

It was Onyx.

He jumped to his feet when he saw me, letting out a squeal. I dropped to my knees just as he leaped into my arms, squiggling and squirming, licking my face.

"Oh, hi. Hi, hi, hi!" I'd been with him just minutes ago, and he was reacting like he'd been waiting for me to show up for years. "How—" His tongue went into my ear. I pulled back, trying to block him with my shoulder, but he quickly skirted around it and did it again. "Ahh! How is *he* here, too?" I laughed. Onyx bolted across the room and snatched something from the armchair by the window. He shook his prize as if it were a squirrel he'd just caught, then deposited it into my lap: a length of green silk ribbon. A present, it seemed.

Still hovering in the doorway, still unbelievably shirtless, my mate sighed, folding his arms across his chest. "I don't know. The damned thing's been following me around in my dreams for a couple of weeks now. Even when he was back in Cahlish."

I looked back at Fisher, raising an eyebrow. "You know, the fake annoyance isn't necessary anymore. I know you love him, and so does he."

Onyx went to town, licking my wrist. His pink tongue rasped against my skin. Fisher watched him at work, shaking his head. "I'd say we *tolerate* each other at best," he argued.

"I've seen you with him when you think I'm not looking. And why would he already be here with you, in this, what, this dream space, if he didn't love you?"

Kingfisher spent another drawn out moment studying the ceiling again. "I don't know. Maybe he's just been waiting here for *you*."

"Fisher." Onyx jumped up, putting his paws up onto my shoulders, and started rubbing the top of his head against my jaw. "Just accept it. My fox is your fox, too."

He didn't say anything, just growled, making a face as he kicked the cottage door closed.

The simple act of him crossing the room to stand by the fire had me holding my breath. How could you fall in love with someone because of something so simple as crossing a room? Was it because of the way his skin was dotted with goose bumps now? Was it the way the muscles clenched in his jaw as he stooped down to tend to the pot that was bubbling over the fire? Or the small lines that formed between his brow when he was concentrating? Or the way he caught me watching him and gazed at me over the top of his shoulder, smirking?

Holy shit. I was so fucked. Every single thing this male did made me want him. Made me want to scream. Made me want to—

"Haven't you learned your lesson yet, Osha?" Fisher rose from the fireplace and slowly paced across the threadbare rug toward me. He stood before me, his powerful thighs at my eye level. I looked up at him, trying not to get caught up in the fact that I had to bypass the wall of muscle that made up his stomach and his chest before I could reach his eyes. It was a miracle that I found them at all. His smirk had gone from slightly amused to deeply interested. "Your heart's racing, Saeris Fane. Why might *that* be?"

It was, too. Now that I couldn't control whether my heart even had to beat or not, the fact that it got away from me so often when I was around him seemed to entertain my mate even more than it already had.

"You look so pleased with yourself," I said. But I was blushing. *Hard.*

"Oh, really? Let…me…see." His eyes were full of sin. Moving very slowly, he reached up and dipped his thumb into his mouth, sucking on it. I couldn't take my eyes off him as he lowered his hand and brought his thumb to *my* mouth, rubbing it across my bottom lip, wetting it with his own saliva. "The most unique, most beautiful creature in the entire realm, on her knees in front of me, looking up at me like she's feeling feral and might just like to fuck me? Yes," he said, "I'd say I'm feeling pretty pleased with myself."

My nerve endings buzzed with electricity.

This male.

This. Fucking. Male.

Was this what life was going to be like now? Falling more and more in love with him? Just wanting him, and needing him more than anything else I had ever needed? I hoped with every fiber of my being that it would be, because this felt... whew. I didn't even know how to describe *what* it felt like to have this male looking down at me, like he was feeling everything I was feeling. Like he was feeling feral and wanted me, too.

Onyx saw a moth and darted from my lap, pouncing after it, forgetting me for the moment. I reached out for Fisher, wrapping my hand around his ankle, just needing to feel his skin against mine. His pant legs were wet. The tops of his feet were cold. He studied the point where I held him, smiling softly as a tendril of black ink swirled down my fingers and pooled on his skin, twisting and turning as it chased around his ankle and then disappeared underneath the cuff of his wet pants.

I looked up at my mate in amazement. "What the hell was *that*? Did *I* just give you a tattoo?"

He smiled, arching a dark brow at me. "Looked like it."

"I thought... wait, so that doesn't *only* happen when we're having sex?"

Fisher chuckled as he tugged the bottom of his pants up as high as they would go over his muscled calf, revealing half of what appeared to be ornate inkwork of a dagger. He nodded approvingly, shooting me a wink. *"Nice."*

"Fisher! Is this going to happen every time we touch each other?"

The bastard was trying not to grin. There was really no need for him to be so godsdamned smug right now. He stroked his fingers along my jaw, curling his index finger and using it to lift my chin higher, so that my gaze met his. "No, it won't happen every time, Osha." His smile grew in size, despite his visible efforts to leash it. "It'll only happen when you're thinking"—he ran his tongue over his bottom lip—"very *bad* thoughts."

After everything we'd done with and to each other, how was it that he could still make me blush like a little girl? Why did I want to hide from the suggestive, raw lust on his face? "I wasn't thinking anything!" I protested. "I just touched your *ankle!*"

"Hey, it's okay. Some people have a thing for feet. And mine aren't as hairy as most people's."

The wicked glint in his eyes let me know that he was teasing me and loving it, but I couldn't let it stand. "I do not have a thing for feet!"

"It's okay, Saeris. Really. I can understand how touching *any* part of me would drive you to distraction."

"Gods!" I tried to slap his leg, but he darted out of my reach, flashing sharp canines as he laughed. "You can stop being so *arrogant,* too!"

I was both vampire and Fae. I had excellent vision now, but all I saw was a blur of shadow and light as Fisher sped forward and took me by the throat again. His fingers pressed into the side of my neck *ever* so slightly as he rubbed his thumb back and forth over my jawline.

He was all seriousness now, his smile gone. "I'm not arrogant. I'm fucking proud. I hear how your pulse quickens when you touch my body, and it makes me feel fucking invincible. You can hear my pulse do the same when I touch you, can't you?"

Holy *fuck.*

He was trying to kill me, I swore it. "I—"

His grip around my throat tightened a fraction. "Stop protesting. Own it."

"All right. Yes. I can. I do." Fuck. He had me breathless and back to front for him, and he knew it. His eyes simmered with desire as he crouched barefoot in front of me and cupped my face again with his uninjured hand. "I don't know what *this* is right now," he said, gesturing to the cottage around us, "but it feels like a gift. We're alone. It feels safe. It's snowing out there. We have the fire, and food is cooking, and the fox is chasing insects. This is all I need, Saeris. Something simple. And *you*. I'm claiming you, Osha. Come on. You're coming with me."

———————

The bedroom was nowhere near as luxurious as his room at Cahlish. The bed barely looked wide enough to fit the both of us, but that didn't matter. There were plenty of sacrifices I would willingly make to spend time naked with this male, and a decent-sized bed was the least of them. He was already half naked from his wood chopping adventure earlier, which meant that most of the undressing needed to happen on my end.

Kingfisher took care of that.

He'd used his shadows to divest me of my clothes in the past, but not now. He used his hands, and he damned well savored the task. He flinched every once in a while, his broken hand causing issues, but he wouldn't abandon his mission, no matter how hard I objected.

When he pulled my shirt over my head and then leaned into me, he wrapped my braided hair around his good fist and pulled my head back so that my mouth tipped up to meet his. "If you think a broken hand is going to stop me from fucking you properly, Osha, then please..." He spoke against my mouth, his lips brushing mine, his breath fanning over my face. "Let me disabuse you of that notion."

He fell on me with a snarl that made the air rush out of my lungs. He lifted me off my feet and slammed me up against the cottage's wall. A portrait of a very dour-looking Fae female wearing a black high-necked dress fell to the ground, its frame splintering at Fisher's feet as he pushed his way between my legs and settled himself between my thighs.

"I could spend the rest of eternity right here and die happy," he rumbled. "I could fuck you and feast on you until the ages turned and the suns all died and burned out in the skies, and I still wouldn't have had enough of you."

He hiked me higher up the wall, bowing himself over me so that he could kiss the hollow of my throat. I hissed through my teeth when the heat of his tongue met my skin, trailing upward toward my ear. When he caught my earlobe between his teeth and tugged, my back arched away from the wall and I was suddenly very, *very* aware of how hard he was between my legs.

Could this kind of thing happen in a dreamscape? Was it even possible? It certainly felt like it. If Fisher could chop wood, and he could hold me and kiss me here, then it stood to reason that he could fuck me here, too.

Thank the gods, I chanted in my head. *Thank the fucking gods.*

Don't thank them, came Fisher's low, resonant reply. *Thank* me. *I'm the one who's about to make you scream.*

His hands were in my hair. He bared his teeth, flashing elongated canines as he knocked his injured hand again, but when I tried to take it in *my* hands, to look at it properly, he breathlessly shook his head. "Not yet. I need to feel it a little longer."

It didn't make sense to me, but I shrugged, letting him have his pain.

Fisher cradled my lower jaw, gripping my face between his thumb on one side and his index and middle finger on the other. "You're so fucking beautiful," he whispered. "You've existed in my mother's drawings for most of my life, but you were never real to me before. I didn't believe..." His eyes were wide and full of awe. "I had no idea what you would mean to me. I had no idea what I would do to keep you safe. When I close my eyes, you are all I fucking see, Saeris Fane. I could be dead in the ground five thousand years and the frosts could have taken my bones, and still no other male will ever have loved another female the way that I love you."

My heart tripped in my chest. Hearing him speak this way? To me? Having him love me like this? It *healed* me. I wouldn't have been able to let anyone else do it. The intensity of the emotions I experienced whenever I was with him would have terrified the hell out of me. I would have run.

But it was different with him.

He was larger than life. Stronger. More powerful. He was bigger than the swell I felt in my chest whenever I heard him say those three words.

I.

Love.

You.

He could *handle* all the bullshit and the complications that came with loving me. He knew me. Saw me. Was capable of holding the both of us together if it all became too much. It was safe to love him back because, no matter what, he was never going to let me fall.

"Please..." It hit me out of nowhere: the sudden, awful realization that we didn't know how long we had together like this. He could disappear at any moment. *I* could. Maybe I'd lost my mind, and I was imagining all of this and none of it was real... but I didn't want it to end without feeling him inside me first. "I need you," I said.

I laid my hands flat against his chest, my fingers splayed wide, as if I could reach inside of him and take hold of his very soul. If I could have, I would never have let go.

Fisher's hand moved from my jaw, traveling down, closing around my throat. His grip wasn't tight—it was a suggestion of something that could happen, that *might* happen, if I wanted it to.

"Sinners and martyrs, Little Osha. The *things* I think about," he growled. "If only you knew..." I wanted to know. I wanted to hear all the filthy things he imagined when he thought about me. I would have asked him to elaborate, but my mate grinned wickedly, swooping down to claim my mouth with his before I could speak.

*I want you on all fours for me, Saeris. Crawling...*he drawled inside my head. Tongue dipping past my lips, past my teeth, he claimed my mouth.

I threw my arms around his neck and kissed him back, whimpering.

I want to stand behind you and watch you on your hands and knees. I wanna see your slickness running down the inside of your thighs, your pretty pink little pussy on show for me, aching for my cock.

I pulled back, gasping for air, searching his features and screaming inside at the look of pure need on his face. "You do *not* get to say things like that and not already be inside me."

"You're ready for me?" His expression was one hundred percent serious, but there was a teasing note in his voice.

"Yes."

"Are you aching for me, Osha?"

"Yes!"

He grinned, then, his whole face lighting up; it was like the sun breaking through the clouds. "Good girl. Don't worry. You won't have to wait much longer." Heat filled his eyes, the tiny sliver of quicksilver rimming his eye shifting frantically as he ripped down the front of my shirt, exposing my right breast, then the left.

He cupped the swell of me in his uninjured hand, kneading my flesh, pinching my nipple. Taking my other nipple into his mouth, he sucked, licked, bit, sending me hurtling toward the gates of insanity.

I threw back my head and cracked my skull against the wall.

It didn't matter.

My blood pounded in my ears.

It roared.

I need you.

I want you.

I need you.

I want you.

The tides of our desire crashed together, consuming us both.

Quickly, he set me down and dropped to his knees, ripping off my boots. My socks went next, and then my pants. The second he had them past my hips, he buried his face between the apex of my thighs, groaning as he drove his nose and his mouth into my folds, biting at me softly and breathing me in through the thin fabric of my panties.

"Sweet fucking mercy," he panted. "Kill me. Sit on my face and ride my tongue until I fucking die. I can't take it anymore."

"Fisher!" I threaded my fingers into his hair, pulling him down onto me. I was vaguely aware that he had dragged my pants the rest of the way down my legs and was yanking the material off my feet, but I didn't care about that. I cared about the soaking wet material that he was sucking into his mouth. His heart rate spiked, thumping loud enough for me to hear it.

"Fuck, Saeris! The way you taste. I can't get enough of you."

His hands found the backs of my calves, the backs of my knees, the backs of my thighs. I was hyperventilating by the time they reached my hips. Not many males could have lifted me from this position, but Fisher picked me up and shrugged my legs over his shoulders without a second thought.

Holy... *gods.*

I wrapped my legs around his head, and Fisher leaned in, tearing my panties with his teeth. When the heat of his mouth met my slick core, I cried out so loud that my long-dead ancestors now knew my mate's name. "Fisher! Fuck! Gods... I... want you inside me. Please. *Please!*"

"Breathe, love. I've got you."

But when he went to slide his fingers into me, he let out another sharp hiss, his pain catching up with him, and I had finally had enough. "Bite me," I commanded. "Heal yourself, for the love of the gods. Just do it!"

Fisher growled unhappily into my inner thigh. He drove his tongue between my folds one more time, flicking my clit—so damned cruel. "All right. Fine. I'll drink from you, Saeris. But not out of any love I have for the gods. I'll do it to make you come on my tongue and my fingers. I'll do it to make you *scream.*"

The bright zip of pain fired from my inner thigh straight up into my brain. It was staggering, so sharp that I couldn't breathe... but then it became bliss. Fisher didn't drink right away. He locked his arm around my leg, holding me in place. Vivid, bright green eyes met mine as I looked down my body, over the rise of my breasts, to find him watching me. His mouth kicked up at the corner—a ruinous smile that would be the end of me—as he took his other hand, the uninjured one, and he began slowly rubbing circles over my clit with the pad of his thumb.

The pleasure was almost too much already, but it was the anticipation that was about to kill me. His canines were plunged deep into my skin, depositing a flow of his venom into my blood that was making my head spin.

"Drink," I said.

But the wicked gleam in Fisher's eyes only intensified.

"Fisher..." I could barely keep my eyes from rolling back into my head. My blood charged up and down my body, delivering his venom to every organ and every nerve ending. He saturated me with it until it felt like I was lifting away from him, floating toward the ceiling. "Fi-Fisher..."

Are you ready? His voice was a velvet soft caress at the back of my mind.

I couldn't speak. I could barely shake my head no.

Fisher chuckled darkly into my thigh...and then he drank.

Again, it was instantaneous.

The orgasm came up through me, a rippling wave of pleasure that rocked me to my bones, but it wasn't as powerful as the last time he had drunk from me. It was manageable. It was...

"Oh..."

It was only just the beginning.

"Oh, fffffuuuuu..." I ran out of air. My teeth clenched together so hard, it felt like they would crack. I lost all control of my body...and *then* the explosion hit.

Fisher drank, his thumb still working tight, tiny circles over my clit, his breath sawing out of him as he fed, and I came.

I didn't make a sound.

Couldn't.

My muscles locked up, and my vision went white, and mindlessly I rode out the most incredible climax I had ever experienced. I was still coming, shuddering uncontrollably, when Fisher pulled back from my thigh, withdrawing his canines, and picked me up, carrying me over to the hearth.

I couldn't stand. My ears were ringing. He held me close, pressing me against his chest as he set me down on...on something soft? Something that hadn't been there a moment ago. I didn't give a fuck what he'd set me down on. I just didn't want him to leave me. Not for a second.

"Hush, love. I'm not going anywhere. I'm right here."

I hadn't realized I was speaking to him in my head. I hadn't even known the words had taken shape. My desperation to be close to him was an animal *need*.

I felt wrung out as I watched him taking off his pants. He was magnificent to behold, the lines of him so perfect that he looked as though he had been carved from marble. His ink rushed across his pecs, down the tops of his muscled arms...but not the God Bindings that marked his forearms, chained his wrists, and stained the backs of his hands. The mirror of my own God Bindings, those runes and scripts stayed firmly in place, ever-present. Steady. Immutable. Undeniable.

His cock stood proud, so hard that the head of his erection almost brushed against his belly button. I reached for him, but he was already coming for me, already planting himself between my legs, his mouth seeking mine.

"Watching you come is a fucking *gift*." His hands locked around my wrists, swiftly pinning them above my head. "I could watch you fall apart for me forever."

His venom was still burning through me like a wildfire. I was powerless to it. The ecstasy was blinding.

"Let me bite you," I whispered.

"No, Nissarhin." His voice was so rough. He shook his head.

"I won't drink. I just...I want you to feel..."

"I'm feeling everything I need to right now." A teasing smile took over his features as he rocked his hips forward, letting me know that he was *right* there, the head of his cock *right* at my entrance. "Believe me. This is perfect."

"Please..."

But he shook his head more firmly this time. "I have no idea if any of this is real. But if it is, we don't have any idea where we are, Osha. I don't understand any of this, but I'm gonna damn well make sure my head's on straight if I need to react quickly. I'm not about to let anything happen to you here."

I would have kneed a guy in the balls for saying that back in Zilvaren. The idea that any man considered me incapable of taking care of myself at *any* point would have had me seeing red. With Fisher, it just wasn't that simple.

"It's very rude of you to make me feel so good and...deny me the opportunity to...return the favor." Whew. *So* many words.

Fisher leaned his weight on one elbow, lifting his injured hand for me to see it now. "I *do* feel good. Much better than I did." He flexed his hand, demonstrating that he had full range of movement again. The scuffs at his knuckles were gone. His hand was completely healed. "And this?" His lips parted, his eyes shuttering as he slowly...slowly ...*slowly* slid himself inside me. "This feels fucking incredible, Saeris. I don't need to be bitten to enjoy *this*."

The embers of pleasure that had been smoldering in my stomach rekindled, roaring back to life. I was so *full* of him. Fisher shook as he held himself over me, his teeth scraping over his bottom lip. I lived for the moment when his eyes lost focus and his eyelids closed. He had existed for entire lifetimes before I'd even been born. He had won battles and defeated enemy forces that far outnumbered his own, the odds ever stacked against him. He had seen the rise and fall of monarchs, bargained for his life with monsters, fought off countless demons, and never backed down.

It was here in the quiet and the dark with *me* that he surrendered.

Blood beaded on his bottom lip when he released it from his mouth. A thin crimson trail chased down his chin.

"You're bleeding," I whispered.

He hung his head, laughing a little as he nodded. "Sometimes, a male needs a little pain to push back the pleasure, Saeris Fane." He ran his tongue over his bottom lip. It came away red. *"Especially* when his mate is this fucking incredible."

He fell on me, then. Rocking his hips back, he slammed himself home, burying himself all the way to the hilt inside me. The flames dancing atop the candles on the table flared, growing taller, the air buzzing with power as he drew back and did it again.

"Kiss me. Please. Hold me down and fuck me."

A dangerous growl rolled at the back of his throat. He didn't speak out loud or into my mind. He did as I bid him and fucked me. This time, I clung to him, fingernails digging into his back, and he rode out his climax right along with me. The walls of the cottage trembled as we both came, and for one timeless second, reality—or nonreality—sank away, and we floated on a sea of nothingness.

We held each other for a long time, listening to the wood snap in the hearth as the fire died. Out of the window, the world was all darkness and quiet.

"There's no one out there," Fisher said eventually. His voice got so deep when he was tired; the bass tenor of it resonated in my bones. His eyes were closed, which gave me leave to study his features in detail. His eyelashes were long and black, like strokes of ink against his pale skin. The frown that often marred his brow was nowhere to be seen. He was always so intense when we were around others. On edge. Ready for a fight. History had proven to him that he had to be ready—but now, here, he was languid and relaxed.

I traced the outline of his wolf's head tattoo lightly with my fingertips, drinking him in like this. He was so fucking beautiful.

I pressed my lips to his chest, kissing him just above his nipple, and Fisher made a contented humming sound. "How can you tell?" I asked him. "That we're alone."

He shifted, rolling onto his back, taking me with him so that I wound up lying on top of his chest. He wrapped his arms around me, resting his chin on the top of my head. "I don't know. It's an ability most warriors develop over the years. A sensitivity. If you close down everything else in your mind and reach out, you can feel if there are other creatures close by. It's like listening very hard. Or straining to see something in the distance. I'm sure you can do it, too."

I couldn't say that I'd ever noticed that sensation, but it sounded easy enough.

Fisher stroked his hand absently up and down my side, breathing softly into my hair. His heart beat out a slow, reassuring rhythm beneath my ear. This was the most relaxed I had been in my entire life. I knew that with a certainty. Even in Ballard, the outside world had intruded upon our time together in the little apartment above the square. The smell of roasting coffee and buttery pastries had been divine, but it had also signaled that there were others out there, in the bakery below, roasting the coffee and baking the bread. For now, I couldn't scan the valley the way Fisher could, but I knew that he was right. The world was ours, here in this place. And I did *not* want that to end.

"Strange how we can be tired here, while we already sleep," Fisher said drowsily. "To fall asleep within a dream is to commune with the gods."

"Is that true?"

He laughed quietly, his breath stirring my hair. "Yvelia is full of strangeness. Who knows. Maybe it was once the way of things. But now? I don't intend on finding out. I've had enough run-ins with those bastards. I don't need to spend a single second more with them, thank you very much." He took a deep breath, his rib cage lifting me as it expanded. "Are you hungry, Little Osha?"

I groaned in protest as he rolled onto his side, setting me back down again onto the welter of blankets. "Mm. Yes. I suppose so." I hadn't drunk from him tonight, but he had drunk deeply from me. The loss of blood made me hungrier than I had felt since I'd woken up in Ammontraíeth. But... "But I'd rather just stay here, curled up with you," I mumbled.

"Ahh. Come, Osha." He peppered the side of my face with light kisses. "What kind of mate would I be if I didn't tend to *all* of your appetites?"

"You could feel my stomach growling, couldn't you?" I groaned.

"Mm-hm." Gently, he swept my messy hair out of my face, tucking it behind my ear. "I still need to hear what's been happening back in Ammontraíeth," he reminded me. "You can tell me all about it over a bowl of stew."

"So, right about the time I was punching a hole in the Third's bell tower, you were blasting a hole in the side of the library in the Blood Court?" Kingfisher nodded, smiling at this, as if he found this symmetry between our days pleasing. I had told him about my meeting at the Fool's Paradise with Taladaius, and while Fisher hadn't said much about the fact that Tal wanted to publicly denounce me in front of the whole court, I could tell that he was both a little surprised and confused at the same time. His emotions over the news that Foley had been located at last were more difficult to read.

Fisher swirled his spoon in his bowl of stew, studying it hard. He sat cross-legged on the floor in front of the newly built fire, Onyx curled up into the triangle of space made by his legs. He hadn't tried to stop the little fox from hopping into his lap. I'd caught him feeding him some of his stew earlier as well.

Fisher frowned, wearing a curious expression when he looked up at me. "How did he look? Foley? Is he well?"

"I didn't know what he looked like before, I guess. He's pale, but then he *is* a vampire. His hair is cropped short. His canines are plated with gold."

A tightness formed at the corners of Fisher's eyes upon hearing that. He ran a hand over Onyx's head, absently scratching him behind his ears.

"The sign of a shunned vampire," he explained. "The court rips out their fangs if they won't swear allegiance to the crown. It's a dark judgment, being consigned to a slow and miserable death. Without fangs, a high blood can't feed. At first, they starve. And then they go mad.

Then, they wither away to husks. Malcolm told me he'd ripped Foley's fangs out personally. He liked to find me in the maze and tell me how he was keeping him alive just to torture him. I hadn't believed him but..." He sighed. "Most shunned vampires end up out on the dead fields, trapped between the Ammontraíeth and the Darn. If a high blood comes across a vampire with missing teeth, they're encouraged to execute them on sight."

It must have been excruciating, having his teeth ripped out like that. And not to be able to feed? That really would be a slow death. But Foley had been at Ammontraíeth for centuries. There was no way he was still starving to death. He looked fit. Healthy enough. Which begged the question, "If they shunned him and Malcolm removed his teeth, then how is he still alive?"

Fisher set aside his stew, his appetite gone. "I'm assuming Tal has kept him fed. He wouldn't have let them banish him to the dead fields."

"So, Malcolm let Tal save him?"

"Malcolm let Tal *keep* him as a pet, more like. Foley disrespected the crown when he wouldn't kneel, but Taladaius was always Malcolm's primary project. He probably let Tal keep Foley as a way to mess with him. Or to use as a bargaining chip in exchange for Tal's obedience. There are a million ways he could have used Foley's presence at Ammontraíeth to his own purposes."

Malcolm had forced Tal to do unspeakable things. He had held him close, his cruel eye fixed upon him, but for more than a thousand years, the vampire hadn't broken. He'd found subtle ways of rebelling against his master. He'd been a force for good wherever he could. He had saved Foley's life, and mine. And yet... "Why does Ren hate him so much? Tal?" I asked. "Anytime anyone mentions his name, Ren gets up and leaves the room." I'd seen it happen more than once.

Fisher sighed. "It's complicated. But the short version of it is this: Everlayne was in love with Taladaius once. They were betrothed. And the night before they were due to be married, Tal fled the Winter Palace, against his father's wishes and his king's command, and he knelt at the feet of Sanasroth's throne."

"Willingly?"

Kingfisher nodded.

"But why? If he hated Malcolm and all he stood for, then *why* would he have done such a thing?"

"Why does any male act recklessly, Saeris? He did it because he was in love with someone else. He did it for Zovena."

21

DAIANTHUS

KINGFISHER

ONCE, THERE HAD been a pirate named Jackin Pröst.

The male had resembled a wind-blown tree. His gnarled hands had been made of knots, the veins snaking up and down his arms proud and twisted like thick roots in search of good soil. I had punched him once, when I'd caught him cheating at a game of cards. This was before Gillethrye, of course. Before many things, back when I still knew what laughter was, and all my friends were still alive. But that was beside the point. The point *was* that I had punched him and shattered my hand in the process. The broken bones had taken a full week to heal, and even then, a dull ache had persisted in my tendons for almost a month thanks to that cheating bastard's thick skull.

When I awoke from my sleep, I braced myself, waiting for the familiar starburst of pain to flare through my right hand. But no pain came.

It was...raining?

The soft, rushing noise I could hear outside sounded like rain, but...no. I was in Zilvaren. The sound wasn't rain at all; it was sand *ting*ing against the window and making *shushhhh*ing sounds as it slid off the slate roof overhead.

I listened to the sand, slowly remembering what had happened in my dreams.

The valley at the edge of Cahlish's borders.

The huntsman's cottage.

I had just been there with Saeris.

I'd stripped her out of her clothes and fucked her raw, and she'd fed me so that I would heal.

When I pulled up my pant leg, there was the tip of the dagger tattoo she'd given me. And my hand? I held it up in front of my face, turning it this way and that. Light spilled in through the window, washing my skin gold as I searched for some sign of injury.

There was no way...

"No. Fucking. Way!" Carrion did *not* sound impressed.

I splayed my fingers and peered through them to find him standing in the doorway, shirtless, rubbing a dry cloth at the raised welts that dotted his chest and his sides. "You look like you have the pox," I told him.

"What? What *kind* of pox?"

"The kind you get from doing dumb stuff with your dick."

He looked horror-stricken.

"Don't worry. They'll fade in a couple of days. In the meantime, don't scratch at them."

"They weren't even itching until you said that! Why the hell aren't *you* covered in hives? And, yes, while we're at it, how the hell *is* your hand fixed? Your knuckles were the size of Gollish nuts when we got back here earlier."

I didn't know what a Gollish nut was or how big they usually were, but my knuckles *had* been grotesquely swollen before I'd fallen asleep. A bouquet of black and purple bruises had flowered beneath my skin, and now the bruises were gone. My hand was healed.

Hmm. How was I supposed to explain this, when I had no real clue what had happened myself? "I think Saeris might have healed me. In my sleep."

Carrion arched an eyebrow, angling himself in the doorway, as if that might help him see me better. "Is that why you reek of sex?" he asked flatly.

I rolled my eyes, hauling myself up and out of the chair. "And with that, this conversation is officially over."

Carrion threw the cloth he was holding onto the table beside him. "The injustice! You dream of your girlfriend, you're healed by her, get *laid*, and wake up brand-spanking-new. Meanwhile, I dream that I'd been turned into a goat, and I wake up with a mouth drier than the glass flats, covered in suspect pox marks!"

"She isn't my *girlfriend*, Carrion."

He gave me a pointed, very unimpressed look. "Your relationship status with Saeris Fane was the *least* important thing I just said, Kingfisher."

I rocked my head from side to side, trying not to crack a smile. "Was it, though? I beg to differ."

He stomped from the room, muttering under his breath. When he came back, he had a pile of folded clothes in his hands. "We may be glamored, but we have to move aboveground today, and you're covered in blood. Here. You should change into these."

I eyed the stack of clothes Carrion held out to me with healthy suspicion. They were an off-white, gray color. Loose-fitting, by the looks of things. I couldn't remember the last time I'd worn anything other than black or maybe dark green. "I could just magic the blood away," I said dubiously. "Or conjure up a new set of clothes."

Swift gave me a look that suggested I was stupid. "We might have to deal with a bunch of guardians today, and you're willing to deplete your magic for a fresh outfit? Wow." He tapped his chin annoyingly with his index finger. "I didn't know you were so *vain*. And after you refused to give yourself a tan yesterday, too."

My top lip twitched, but I refrained from showing my teeth. He was infuriating... but he was right. I took the clothes from him reluctantly. "Fine."

"Use the room through there to change. I don't need to see you half naked after you apparently went on a sexcapade last night, thanks oh so much. God knows what kind of teeth mar—" Carrion saw my face. Carrion stopped talking. He smirked, as if he knew how close he'd come to losing his life. "Never mind," he said. "Just go and get changed. I'll wait for you out here."

I passed him and entered what turned out to be his bedroom. The space was small in the grand scheme of things, but it was comfortable. There was a bed large enough to fit at least three humans in it shoved up against the wall by the window. A chipped dresser was placed on the adjacent wall, with a few knickknacks lined up neatly on top of it. A small mirror hung on the opposite wall, surrounded by sheets of paper, tacked to the stonework. I got changed quickly, pleased to note that Saeris's blood had also healed the gaping wound in my leg and the other, smaller sting sites that had covered my body, too. I spent a full second feeling sorry for Carrion, knowing how uncomfortable he must be, but then I remembered how annoying he was, and my pity went away.

I was on my way to the door, leathers folded in my hands, when one of the sheets of paper on the wall caught my attention. It was a drawing, the style similar to the way my mother had loved to sketch when I was a child. A woman stared out of the yellowed piece of paper, eyes intense and bright. She had high cheekbones and full lips, and a heart-shaped face that stirred a flurry of memories in the back of my mind.

Amelia Daianthus.

The former queen of the Yvelian Fae.

Belikon had found her in the bathhouses in the lower levels of the Winter Palace. He'd been carrying her husband Rurik's god sword, Bitterbane, in his hands. The blade had dripped with blood. The queen had taken one look at the sword and the blood and known her husband was dead.

I had seen her fleeing through the palace, robes billowing around her as she ran. I hadn't witnessed her handing the child over to my father, whispering for him to take him, to hide him, to keep him safe. My mother had told me about that later, after we'd fled the palace in the night and escaped south to Cahlish.

Carrion had drawn his mother with surprising precision. The image of his father, pinned next to Amelia, was less exact. Only half of Rurik Daianthus's face had been captured on the paper, only one of his eyes sketched out. But the old king's kindness was there, a familiar warmth radiating from that one eye.

There were other people trapped on the sheets of paper. Members of the Fae I didn't recognize. Females wearing renegade armor with bows slung across their backs. Males wearing fierce expressions, long hair tied back into war braids, mighty swords held aloft over their heads. Faelings, fire sprites, dragons, and all manner of other creatures, drawn in exacting detail everywhere I looked.

Over by the window, landscapes covered the wall—scenes with snowcapped mountains, raging rivers, and ships out at sea, sailing along a tropical coast that bore a startling resemblance to the Shield— the chain of islands that guarded the beaches of Lissia. It was all here. Pieces of Yvelia, caught on paper like insects trapped in amber. There were so many drawings, layered one on top of the other on top of the other. It must have taken Carrion a long time to create all of this. *Years.* There were more illustrations of his mother, though those pictures were less faithful renderings. Her eyes were slightly too wide apart, perhaps. The end of her nose was a little too upturned. She—

"I know what you're thinking."

I let out the breath I'd been holding, still staring at the wall. I didn't look at Carrion, though I could feel him hovering there in the doorway behind me. "And what's that?" I asked.

"You think I'm pathetic. Obsessive. You think I was stupid, sitting here every night, copying all this out of a book like some kind of heart-sick moron. It's okay. You can say it. I have very thick skin these days. It doesn't bother me. Not anymore."

Slowly, I shook my head. Scanning the images, my eyes landed on a surprisingly accurate illustration of the Winter Palace, its soaring towers scraping a clear night sky, and I couldn't help it: I reached out and I plucked it from the wall. "That's not what I'm thinking at all," I said quietly.

There was a defensive light in Carrion's eyes when I faced him. He was always so easy. So unfazed by the chaos that surrounded him. Had there been a time when I'd caught him looking like this? Caught out? On the back foot? If there had been, I couldn't remember. "Go on, then," he said coldly, gesturing to the wall. "Tell me what you see when you look at all of this."

I thought for a moment, long and hard, staring down at his drawing of the Winter Palace. At the top of the turrets, he had drawn banners unfurled and waving on the wind. Not De Barra banners. *Daianthus* banners.

"I see a male longing for a place and a people he has never known," I said simply. "That's all." I gave him the drawing as I passed him, leaving his room. "You should keep hold of that, Carrion," I told him. "Bring it home with you."

22

STARGAZER

SAERIS

THERE THEY WERE.

Two puncture wounds on the inside of my left thigh.

The cottage had been real.

I didn't remember leaving the dream. I recalled eating the stew, talking some more with Fisher, and curling up in the blankets by the fire with Onyx. Things grew hazy after that. Fisher had said he was going to step outside to get some more wood for the fire. He had opened the cottage door, and stepped out into the night, and...

Ahh.

That's when it had happened. He'd walked through the cottage door, and everything had gone black. I had woken up on the floor, lying on a stack of pillows with a blanket draped over me that hadn't been there when I'd set my mind to go to sleep. My body had ached deliciously from the night's adventures, and I had found the two small marks on the inside of my thigh, already half-healed but definitely still *there*.

It was still early, or late in the day, depending on how you looked at it. The shutters were drawn to keep out the fading afternoon light as I hurried through the halls of Ammontraíeth, still wrestling on my clothes.

I was approaching the foot of the stairs that led up to the library when my name echoed down the hallway after me. "Saeris Fane! Where in all five hells do you think you're going?"

Lorreth's shirt was damp with sweat across his chest, his dark hair fully bound back for once as he jogged after me. "I think you're forgetting something," he said, when he reached my side.

"I'm sorry, but I think training might have to be postponed today, don't you? My wildly dangerous magic might just need to take priority. Unless you don't think anyone will mind if I blow up Ammontraíeth."

"*I* personally wouldn't mind." Lorreth slapped his hands down on top of my shoulders and bodily turned me around. He gave me a shove, pushing me back in the direction I had just come from, away from the library. "The rest of this court is still sleeping, Saeris. No one else is awake, and that includes Foley. He won't be able to help you for at least a couple of hours, which means—" He sniffed, and immediately took a step back.

I'd been waiting for him to notice. I had my explanation ready. "Something strange happened last night. I went to sleep like Foley told me to, and Fisher was there."

"Okay." He looked dubious. "We've all had *those* kinds of dreams before, Saeris. But—" He cleared his throat uncomfortably. "I don't think I've ever heard of anyone waking up covered in their partner's scent from a *dream*."

"It wasn't a dream. Well, it *was* a dream. But it was more than that."

"How can you tell? Besides the way you, uh…" He waved a hand around me, gesturing in my vague direction. "*Smell*."

"There's other… *physical* evidence," I said, staring straight ahead. Gods, this was fucking awkward.

"Okay, okay. I'm gonna take your word for it. I think I have enough information." He cocked his head to one side. "Are you sure it was him?"

"What do you mean, *am I sure it was him?* Yes, it was him. I think I know what my mate looks like, Lorreth."

A sneaky little smile hovered over his lips. "Wanna hit me yet?" he asked.

"Yes. I do, actually. You know what? *Fine.* Let's go train."

———————

The training room was cold. All of Ammontraíeth was cold, for that matter. When the people of a court were immune to temperature and an open fire might have them going up in flames, it was no great shock most rooms didn't have fireplaces. It had been enough of a problem in my own personal chambers that I'd had a fireplace constructed—I was the queen, after all—but the vast, windowless obsidian box where Lorreth brought me to train was freezing. There was nothing on the walls. Nothing on the floor. A soft white light glowed from a recessed gap that ran around the perimeter of the ceiling, but other than that, there were no torches of evenlight flickering in the sconces. The room was featureless, the air oddly still, as if it had stagnated here for many years.

Lorreth tossed me a staff, and the sound of the wood hitting my palm made a dead, unnaturally flat sound that quieted as soon as I curled my fingers around the weapon. I considered the length of wood briefly. "No swords today?"

Lorreth shook his head. "A staff has its uses. You may find yourself without your sword one day. In a bar, for instance," he said, waggling his eyebrows. "Your asshole friend might be having a bad day, and he might start a fight with two knucklehead leeches for no good reason. A tavern will always have a broom, Saeris. A mop. Something with a long handle. It's smart to know how to utilize the items you have around you, lest you need to come to a grumpy friend's rescue."

The context of his comments was loud and clear: He was feeling a *mite* foolish over what he had done at the Fool's Paradise, and this was his roundabout way of letting me know he wasn't feeling so great about it. Who was I to judge, though? I'd caused plenty of scenes at Kala's whenever I'd had a shitty day, which was *most* days in the Third.

I spun the staff, rolling it over the back of my hand, giving Lorreth a sideways grin. "There was never enough metal to forge weapons out of back home. In the desert, wood is a scarce commodity, too ... but it's easy enough to lay your hands on some if you know who to ask."

I moved fast, light on my feet, taking the warrior by surprise. He still had hundreds of years' worth of experience on me, though. I wasn't too shocked when he swung his staff around his head and brought it around his shoulder, blocking my blow before it could land.

"Faster this morning," he noted, his dark eyes gleaming. "Great. If this is what a good night's sleep can do for you, then I'd say you're going to be in good shape with a staff."

"Oh, I won't be in good shape with a staff. I'm going to be in *excellent* shape."

The next hour whipped by in a blur. My reactions were stunningly fast. I knew where Lorreth was going to be three seconds before he got there. Not only did my blows land, but they landed hard. I felt stronger than I ever had. The training space filled with the hollow slap of our feet against the obsidian and our muted grunts of exertion, and by the time Lorreth held up a hand and announced that we were done for the day, I wasn't the only one who was sweating and sore from the blows I had taken. Lorreth was, too.

He pointed the end of his staff at me, eyebrows raised as we headed for the exit. "If you can do what you just did wielding Solace, then your enemies don't know what's in store for them. Tomorrow, we'll go back to the swords."

"About the sword," I said, wiping sweat from my brow. "How attached is Fisher to Solace?"

Lorreth pulled up short. "Well, pretty attached, I'd say. It was his father's weapon. But..." He shrugged. "Solace is *yours* now, Saeris. You can do whatever you want with it. Fisher isn't going to mind."

I believed that. I had just wanted confirmation. I'd struggled with the blade and knew how to wield it well enough to take off a feeder's head, but it was just so *big*. It had been forged for a full-blooded Fae warrior, and even though I wasn't human anymore, I hadn't gotten any taller. My arms were still the same length they'd always been, and carrying a sword around that was two-thirds of my body long was tricky sometimes.

"In that case, I'm going to consider my options. I have relics to make today. After we're done with Foley, I'll head to the forge. While I'm there, I might just have a little chat with my sword."

A flurry of paper stargazers greeted me when I entered the library. Their wings rustled as they flitted around my head, darting this way and that, inspecting the newcomer who had entered their sanctuary. One of them hovered in front of my face, its tiny paper head tilting left and right as it took me in, waiting to see if I posed a threat.

"Good evening," I told the paper bird. "Are you friendly?" I held out my hand, extending a finger to see if it would land for moment, but an emotionless voice spoke from above, startling the little thing away.

"I wouldn't do that if I were you." Foley stood at the top of a small set of stairs over by the window—a window that had not been there yesterday. It was circular, around the same diameter as the hole I'd blasted in the wall, as coincidence would have it. Whoever had come to fix the damage I'd caused had been quick about it and had done an excellent job of the repair.

"The stargazers might seem harmless, but interacting with them can be quite hazardous." Foley descended the stairs slowly, his pale hand resting lightly on the banister rail. I hadn't paid too much attention to his attire yesterday. Today, he wore a plain, tailored black shirt and plain black pants, with black boots that laced high over his ankles. He carried no weapons that I could see, but that didn't mean he didn't have a thin blade secreted away on his person somewhere.

"They like to steal strands of people's hair for their nests," he explained, as he reached the bottom step. "But a piece of hair can be used for many nefarious purposes. In the wrong hands, a single strand of hair can be a male's—or a female's—undoing."

"Bargains?" I asked.

Foley shook his head. "Witchcraft. A fell witch would do terrible things to lay their hands on a strand of your hair. There's no saying what they would be able to accomplish with it. These birds," Foley said, gesturing to the swarm of stargazers overhead. "They're pure. Trusting. They have no concept of right or wrong. If a wayward witch were to compel one of them to bring her a strand of your hair, they wouldn't know to refuse."

The paper birds wheeled high above, zipping from one end of the library to the other. They were graceful. Beautiful. Silent, apart from the quiet rustle of their wings.

Still staring up at them, I said, "Lorreth is on his way. He just went to get changed."

"He's coming here again? Why?"

"Because Lorreth's supposed be your *friend*," I answered tartly. "He wants to make sure we don't get into another fight and I don't kill you. Plus I want him here to make sure you're not lying about whatever you've found in these books."

There were a lot of books. A *lot*. The sight of them was cheering. If Foley hadn't found anything to help me with my conundrum, then surely he wouldn't have bothered to gather so many of them. I tossed a net over my emotions, caught them on a line, trapping them tight. The vampire had been a member of the Lupo Proelia once. He'd also been Fisher's friend. There was no denying either of those facts, but *I* had no reason to trust him.

Plenty had changed during the years Foley had been sequestered away in his high tower. He was a shunned member of the Blood Court, yet he had remained here, reading books for hundreds of years, with no one for company but a Lord of Midnight he resented, a Lord of Midnight who ignored him, and a salty cat made of shadows. Who knew what kind of person he was now, after so much time and torment?

"The chances of you killing me are nil, *Your Majesty*. And Lorreth won't be able to tell if I'm lying. He isn't my maker. Even Tal can't read me like that anymore." I had used that same sour tone whenever I'd kowtowed to a guardian back home in Zilvaren. My disdain had been a blunt instrument that had lacked finesse, but Foley's was a subtle knife. It cut. "He denounced me and rescinded his claim on me. I'm sure he's proposed the same to *you* as well by now."

I ran my fingers lightly over the spines of the first stack of books. "He has," I confirmed.

"Hm." Foley processed this. "So Tal doesn't want you, either. He must see you as the rest of us do. Weak. Vulnerable. Naive..."

"Are you trying to hurt my feelings, Foley?" I ran my tongue over my top row of teeth, slowing down my heart; letting it thunder accomplished nothing. "I wouldn't waste your time if I were you."

"Oh, but you *aren't* me," he snapped out of nowhere, his control slipping for a second—just one *tiny* split second—showing me the truth of what lay beneath.

He was afraid.

"You think you've known hardship, stealing water and fending off bullies for a quarter of a century? Try *eight hundred years*, fighting for your right to exist. This place is worse than hell, because no matter how bad things get, there's always a light at the end of the tunnel. A hope that you *might* escape—"

"Then why haven't you?"

Foley's jaw snapped closed.

"If you hate it here, then why haven't you left? Why didn't you just go back to your friends, where you belonged? You've been up here throwing yourself a fucking pity party for the better part of a millennium, complaining about how terrible it all is, when you could have left at any time."

"How?" he whispered. "How could I have gone back to them, when I had become one of the monsters they swore to kill? They would *never* have accepted me."

"Lorreth said they wrote to you! They wanted you to leave Sanasroth. Fisher *commanded* you to come home!" I didn't need to shout at him, but gods, he was exhausting to be around. Tal might have felt bad about giving Foley this new life. He had let him skulk around up here, feeling sorry for himself, but *I* had no tolerance for this kind of defeatism. Zilvaren wrung that out of a person pretty quickly. Either that, or it killed you.

Foley turned to look at the pale green evenlight fluttering in the huge hearth by the stairs. I watched the muscles feather in his jaw, his nostrils flaring. "You're misinformed. There were no letters. They left me to my fate here, and I can't condemn them for it."

"Fool. Are you seriously that stupid?"

I was getting better at sensing Lorreth. Over time, my awareness was sharpening, blossoming in the back of my mind. I hadn't felt him sneaking up on me earlier at dusk, but I *had* registered him climbing the stairs up to the library this time. Foley had felt his approach, too. Would he look at Lorreth, though? Like hell he would. "There's no need to pretend, bard. I *know* how it is," he said.

Lorreth strode across the room and set Avisiéth down on the reading table with a loud clunk. The vampire flinched, his lips peeling back to reveal those plated golden teeth. He had his fear well under wraps again now, but his discomfort was harder to conceal. Avisiéth had plenty of silver folded into its blade. But it wasn't just that; Avisiéth was a god sword. The magic of the gods ran through it—magic made to undo the likes of Foley and the other members of the Blood Court.

It seemed unkind of Lorreth to have tossed the blade down so carelessly, considering the effect he knew it would have on his old friend, but then I saw the hard light in his eyes and knew there was more to the action.

"I'm not pretending, and you *know* I can't lie. Look at me, Foley," he said.

Reluctantly, the vampire looked at him.

"We wrote to you. Many times. I did. Ren did. I know for a fact that Fisher sent you many missives during those first five years after that night at Ajun. After that he cut down to one letter a year. Even *Danya* wrote to you. Her letters were mostly curse words, calling you every name under the sun for ignoring the rest of us for so long, but I know she asked you to come home. All of us have asked. And all of us have told you the same thing: It might be tricky, sure, but we would find a way to make it work. For you to have a place in Cahlish, with your family."

Foley had set his jaw defiantly as Lorreth had been speaking. "So many letters," he mused. "And yet *none* of them reached me."

"For the love of the gods," I snapped. "Look, neither of you can lie. So you're both telling the truth. There are plenty of ways that can be true. The letters could have been intercepted and stolen, for one. In fact, that seems like a reasonable assumption, given that the vampires of this court are nosy as all hell and spiteful to boot. Now, can we please put this—"

"Saeris?"

"—aside and move on, because—"

"Saeris," Lorreth said more firmly, speaking over me for a second time. "Your *hands*."

They were glowing again.

Fuck.

I'd worn a new pair of leather gloves today. I still didn't want my runes becoming a major talking point in the halls of Ammontraíeth—it was bad enough that I kept catching my friends staring at my hands—and besides, the gloves made me feel powerful. Capable. They were a part of the costume I had donned when I'd walked down those stairs into the Coronation Hall and declared myself queen of this court. And right now, they were smoldering.

"Gods fucking *damn* it." I bit out the words, my canines lengthening with frustration. I ripped off the gloves. The pain wasn't so bad right now, but it was getting worse. The backs of my hands blackened as the runes throbbed with power, embers of fire flaring just below the surface of my skin.

"Does it hurt?" Foley asked curiously.

I gave him a look. "What do *you* think?"

He snorted, peering over to study the smoke curling away from my burning skin. The tendons in my hand looked like they were lit up from the inside. "Yes, that does *look* painful," he conceded. He picked up a quill from an ink pot in the middle of the reading table, using its sleek black feather to point out the lines of one of the runic shapes in particular. "This one seems especially inflamed," he observed. "This—"

He cast a wary glance at Avisiéth; he'd had to come closer to Lorreth's sword to reach me. "You see this rune here? The one that looks like an arrow bisecting a circle? This is one of the most important Alchemical symbols."

I saw the rune he was talking about, all right. The shape had already burned through my skin and was weeping plasma; the clear liquid ran over my hand and dripped from my wrist. "What does it mean?" I asked.

Foley's eyes snapped to mine. "I think you can probably guess that one," he said. "That rune is so predominant because you've already been utilizing its magic for some time."

"It's the rune for quicksilver?"

Foley nodded. "The quicksilver's sentient. It pulls power to it. It makes sense that this rune is hurting you the most. In the records I've found, the quicksilver rune has always been the hungriest. The first to awaken."

Oh, I knew how greedy the quicksilver was. Always wanting something. Always making demands. I had plenty of firsthand experience with *that*.

The vampire's curiosity rose as he angled his head, inspecting the back of my right hand. "Remarkable. Truly. I've never seen an Alchimeran shield this intricate before."

"Alchimeran shield?"

"Yes. This," he said impatiently, tapping the back of my hand. "*This* is your shield. All Alchemists had them."

"You don't need to talk to me like I'm stupid. Magic hasn't existed in Zilvaren for a very, very long time. How am *I* supposed to know any of this?"

From his expression, Foley wasn't about to accept my upbringing or my background as an excuse for my ignorance. "You cannot eradicate magic from a city. Once it takes root within a community, it never leaves. It will find a way to thrive, one way or another. You just didn't care to look for it. Like within yourself, for example."

"I kind of had some other things going on at the time. Y'know, trying to make sure my brother and I didn't die of dysentery."

Foley disregarded the comment, refusing to give it weight. "Your power didn't just show up overnight. It's been with you since birth. You must have been using it haphazardly for many years without any attempt to control it. You've been utilizing your affinity with quicksilver even more of late. That's how you find yourself in *this* position."

"All right, Foley. Leave her be. She had no clue what she was dealing with back in Zilvaren. You judging her for it won't help us now, will it?"

Foley cracked his knuckles as he skirted around the table toward the tallest stack of books he had compiled. Casually, Lorreth picked up Avisiéth and moved the sword, placing it down close to the vampire again. Foley saw what he did; he shot the warrior a look full of recrimination, then took up a book and flicked through it for a moment, his dark eyes scanning the pages until he found what he was looking for.

He handed the book to me, open toward the front, the aged pages marked with small, hand-drawn symbols. "Can you read this?" he demanded.

My eyes skipped over the page, taking in the spidery black handwriting that filled it from top to bottom.

...unorthodox Tria Prima, the basis of which is always the same: Salt. Quicksilver. Brimstone. The uses for all three are varied and wide. Combined, they...

I looked up from the page. "I can."

"Good. Turn the page. Read the exercise at the top of the page there, on the left."

I did as he bid, reading out loud. "A Faeling may be fearful at first. Opening themselves to the energetic flow of the quicksilver can be an overwhelming sensation. The Faeling should learn to embody the quicksilver's energy, aligning themselves with it in body and mind, before they try to transmute the substance from a metal to a solid. Every day, the Faeling should be encouraged to alter the quicksilver repeatedly between its natural states until this skill comes easily and they have built a rapport with the quicksilver itself. Once the Faeling has mastered this skill, they will be ready to set their affinity for the quicksilver's magic and seal their first Alchemical rune."

I sought out Lorreth, relief building inside me. "You heard that, right? I'm ready to seal the quicksilver's rune at least."

Foley jumped in before Lorreth could. "You're *far* from ready, Saeris."

"But I can already transmute the quicksilver from one state to another. According to this, I *am* ready to seal the rune."

"Is that so? Is it as simple as turning a handle and stepping through the door? Or do you kick the door down and fall ass over tit through it as a result?"

Slowly but surely, I was beginning to hate this vampire. "I don't see that it matters how I get the job done, so long as it gets done."

"If you have to force your magic to obey your will, then you haven't mastered it. You've learned how to violate it. You can either develop a partnership with your magic, with give-and-take and understanding, or you can cow it into submission. Which do you think would prove to be the more beneficial relationship? No, tell me, since you seem to be such an expert on the matter, what happens when something or someone is oppressed for long enough that it finally rises up and says enough? Hm?"

The gods and martyrs damn him all the way to the bottom circle of hell. He had a point. "I want to treat the quicksilver fairly. I want to partner with it in the right way, believe me. I'm just very worried that I don't have time to master *children's* exercises, or ... or these simple, non-sense pictures!"

"Simple, nonsense ...?" His expression indicated that my comment had left a foul taste in his mouth. "Show me this simple, nonsense picture you're referring to."

I looked down at the book and huffed. "There. How about this one. A circle. How is a circle supposed to be important?"

Foley looked down at the plain black band of ink that formed a circle on the page I held out to him, then gave me a bone-dry look. He spoke slowly as if he were dealing with someone too simple to understand basic constructs. "That is not *just* a circle. *That* is the foundation of *all* powerful sigils and runes. The strongest magic is circular, like a wheel. It is the symbol of forever, the beginning and the end of everything. It carries magic on a loop, amplifying it, giving it strength. That is the most important magical symbol there *is*."

Ahh.

Shit.

My cheeks flushed hotly.

"Additionally, those exercises *aren't* for children. They're for Faelings. Faelings are far smarter than human young. But that's academic. The skills this book teaches are designed for an individual starting out on a journey to become a proficient Alchemist, no matter their age. They form the foundation upon which all other skills and abilities rely. Would you build a house on top of shifting sand, Saeris Fane? Willingly? Knowing that it *will* come crashing down around your ears?"

If he had used any other analogy, literally *any* other, I wouldn't have had any qualms about ignoring him. But he *had* used that one, and it tore at a buried hurt deep inside me that still woke me, sweating, from my dreams sometimes.

Did he know somehow? About my father? No, he couldn't have.

I closed the book and pinned it under my arm. "All right. I'll take it to the forge. I'll practice for an hour if you think that'll make a difference—"

"I think practicing for *two* hours would make an even bigger difference," Foley said. "That way, you won't pose such a threat to the whole court, will you?"

I turned away from Foley, fixing a mutinous glare at the male who I'd assumed would have my back. "You're terrible, you know that?"

Lorreth gave me an apologetic shrug. "Sorry, Saeris. But he's right."

Whether Foley was right or wrong had no bearing on the situation. I set my jaw and made for the stairs that led back down into Ammontraíeth, fuming under my breath. I had almost reached the stairs when the bright kiss of pain stung the back of my neck. Hissing, I rubbed the point just below my hairline, which still hurt, and my fingers came away stained red.

Something had bitten me.

No, something had *cut* me.

The source of the injury became apparent as the sound of rustling paper filled my ears. A stargazer flapped its paper wings a couple of feet away, hovering in place. My first instinct was to check its beak to see if there were any strands of long black hair hanging from its mouth, but there were none. Foley had gotten into my head, the bastard. I hated that I'd let it happen—but the paper bird *had* attacked me, hadn't it?

It was small, its body the length of my thumb. Its wings flapped so hard that they were a blur as the tiny thing drifted toward me and stilled again. It had no eyes. No features at all, really. It was a creature made of plain white paper, animated by magic, but I got the feeling it was trying to get my attention. I took another step backward toward the stairs, and the little stargazer followed again, rising so it hovered at eye level.

"What? You want something?" I asked it.

Over on the other side of the library, Lorreth and Foley were locked in a tense conversation. Neither noticed that I was still loitering at the top of the stairs. The bird zipped forward and plucked at the front of my shirt with its tiny beak. It wasn't very strong. It barely had the strength to lift the fabric.

"You cut me," I told it. "That wasn't very polite."

The bird rose above my head, executing a tight roll in the air before it descended back to eye level. Was that supposed to be an apology? I couldn't tell. I didn't have time to hang around and find out, either.

"Next time," I told it. "I'll come back and see you tomorrow." If I didn't get to the forge soon, half the night would have passed and I still wouldn't have made any of the relics I'd promised Fisher. I backed away, stepping out of the library, down the first step—

The stargazer flew right at me. Its wing grazed my cheek, and a second later, a sting of pain lashed across my cheek. "Ow! What the *fuck*?" The bird's momentum carried it forward, through the library's door— where it fell out of the air, dead.

It landed on the fourth step of the stairs, stark white against the black stone. I picked it up, turning it over in my hands, marveling at the transformation that had taken place. As soon as it had left the boundaries of the library, it had been severed from its magic. I cradled it in my hands, suddenly feeling terrible. It had wanted something from me. Wanted that something bad enough that it had left its sanctuary to get it, and it had lost its little spark in the process.

Quickly, I stepped back into the library, holding out my hand, holding in my breath, waiting for the creature's little paper wings to stir back to life in my palm.

But the stargazer didn't move.

The little bird was gone.

With a pang of sadness, I slipped it into my pocket and left.

23

YOUR MISTAKE

KINGFISHER

HE WAS TALLER than her.

His hair was blond and was curly—not an uncommon trait in Zilvaren, it seemed.

As we stalked the boy's movements through the streets of the Second Ward, I studied the slope of his shoulders, his gait, the way he left his hands in his pockets, like he had no idea they should be out and free, ready to hold a knife, and I couldn't do it. I could *not* find a scrap of his sister in him.

If I'd passed Hayden Fane in the halls of the Winter Palace, I would never have known he was related to my mate. Not on a surface level.

But then, there *was* the matter of his blood.

I'd failed to sense it the last time I'd come here at Saeris's behest. I'd forgotten how weak the familial scent smelled between humans, or maybe I'd never even known. I'd met so few humans when I was young, and the chances of any of them having been related to each other were slim. Among so many millions of people, it was no great surprise that I hadn't been able to find him before. But now, twenty feet behind him, I could smell it, trailing like a ribbon behind him as he wove through the bustling crowds: something like sunlight, a little like home. But different. The boy up ahead, with the red scarf protecting his face, was Saeris's brother, and we were *this* close to bringing him back to Yvelia.

"He might not be happy to see me," Carrion muttered into his own scarf next to me.

I tried not to laugh. "Really? I'm *shocked.*"

"Y'know, sarcasm *is* a form of humor. The lowest, basest form, yes, but it still counts. If you're not careful, I'll start to think I'm rubbing off on you."

"Don't use the word *rub* and then refer to me in the same sentence, please," I volleyed back at him. But there was no sharpness to the retort. Like the fine sand that constantly battered the city's walls, Carrion Swift *was* slowly wearing me down.

"Oh, *please,*" the smuggler drawled. "You are *not* my—" He craned his neck, scanning the crowd over the tops of their heads. "Ahhh, fuck. He's gone. I think we lost him."

I grabbed him by the arm and shoved him to the left, out of the flow of bodies all shuffling to go and get their morning allotment of water. "You might have," I said. "*I* don't lose people. He ducked down here just now, right before you were about to lie and say I'm not your type." I gestured to the side street next to us, my senses on high alert. Saeris's brother was nowhere to be seen now, but he had come this way. Crumbling buildings stood to the left and the right. Faded clothing hung limp from the windowsills, the air too still and heavy to stir them.

"I wasn't lying. I prefer my women *and* my men a whole lot prettier than you." Carrion stepped into the alley, but I grabbed him by the scruff of his neck, dragging him back. The blade came a split second later; it wouldn't have hit the smuggler anywhere vital, but it *would* have hit him. It would have hurt.

The dagger embedded into the pale stone next to Carrion's chest, its handle shuddering from the force it had slammed into the wall.

"Gods and fucking martyrs!" Carrion wheeled on the disheveled human who had stepped out from the gap between the buildings to our right.

His eyes were brown, not blue. Saeris's chin was elfin and almost sharp, but Hayden's was cleft. There was a similarity in the shape of their eyes, though. The overall structure of the rest of his face was much like hers. And the way he tipped his head to one side and scowled at me was suspiciously familiar.

"Sorry, Swift. I saw *him* first and reacted." He looked young, but his voice had some gravel to it. Hayden's eyes hadn't left mine; his whole body was angled toward me.

"Sorry? You nearly cut my *nipples* off." My hand was still resting on Carrion's shoulder; he shrugged me off, grumbling under his breath as he stalked toward the human. "You go around hurling knives at strangers in the open now?" He pointed at the knife. "Where the hell did you even *get* that?"

"Saeris left them hidden all over the city. She said you never knew when you might need to arm yourself—and it looks like she was right. What are you doing with that traitor?" His attention flitted to Carrion, but it didn't roam far before it returned to me. Plenty of people had looked at me the way Hayden Fane was looking at me now—disgusted, angry, furious—but they'd had reason to. I hadn't been able to save their fathers or their husbands. They'd heard the stories of cruelty Belikon had spread about me. But Hayden Fane had lived his whole life here in Zilvaren, and he had no right to look so offended by my presence.

"It's customary to get to know a male before you judge him, boy," I rumbled.

"Oh, I know you," Hayden spat. "You're *him*, aren't you? Kingfisher of the Ajun Gate, whatever *that* is. Look, there! I can see it on your face. I'm right, aren't I?" Hayden barked. There was hysteria in his eyes. His cheeks had flushed the same color as the scarf that hung around his neck.

Carrion jerked. "How do you know his name?"

Hayden snorted derisively. "Where the hell have you *been*, Carrion? Last I saw of you, you promised you'd come back the next day with some supplies and word about Saeris, then you disappear for weeks on end. I can't move through the city like you can. Things have been crazy here. The guardians have everything locked down so tight, you can't breathe without one of them clubbing you over the back of the head for taking more than your fair share of air. Everyone heard about the explosion in the Third yesterday. Half the fucking bell tower's missing. The guardians have been passing these out all morning." I tensed when he reached into his pocket, ready for whatever ill-advised nonsense he was about to embark upon, but he pulled paper from his pocket, not metal. He passed the crumpled sheets to Carrion, who unfolded them and began to read. His eyes skipped over the printed text, sifting through the papers with the shadow of disbelief growing on his face.

"That fucking *asshole*," he muttered.

"Which one?" We'd been dealing with a lot of assholes lately.

Carrion gathered the papers back into a pile and turned them around for me to see the image that was printed on the top one: my face, crudely sketched, my eyes a little too small, my nose a little too sharp, my lips drawn back, teeth dripping blood. It was clever, really— the caricature was clearly me, but the artist had exaggerated my features. I looked sinister, bestial, but familiar enough that I would be recognized in the street if someone saw me.

Below the drawing were the words THE BUTCHER OF ZILVAREN.

They *had* to get a little more creative when coining villainous names for me. There were only so many places I could butcher.

"Madra's telling people that you used magic to break into the palace. She's saying that you murdered a bunch of people who were about to be pardoned and released from the cells. She says you're a political zealot from the south."

"Let me see that." I took the papers from Carrion. It was just as he'd said. There were more fantastical lies on Madra's flyers, each more unbelievable than the last. But the thing about a city full of starving, oppressed people was that there were plenty of people looking for someone to blame for their suffering. And who better for Madra to paint the villain than a male who had promised to step out of the shadows and murder her in her sleep? It made perfect sense.

"This bastard killed Saeris," Hayden snarled. "She was being pardoned, and he slit her throat, Carrion."

"I haven't harmed your sister."

"They dragged her body through the Third. They *showed* everyone what you did!"

Swift shook his head at the lunatic. "Sinners. He's telling the truth, all right. He hasn't harmed a hair on her head, Hayden. Saeris is fine, I promise."

"Then whose body was it? Hm? There were chi—" Hayden choked on the word. "*Children*. They were cut to ribbons. Their—their faces were—" I couldn't tell if he was horrified or furious. Hayden couldn't decide either, apparently. His eyes darted to the knife he'd thrown at Carrion. Clearly, he was wishing the weapon were back in his hand so he could take another run at cutting my throat.

He lunged, trying to skirt around us, heading for the blade or the alley's exit, I didn't know. I stepped in front of him, slowly shaking my head. I didn't lay a finger on him, just stared down at him, and the boy wilted like a cut flower.

"Saeris is *fine*," Carrion repeated. "At least she was okay when we *left* her," he amended. "Whoever you saw being dragged through the city was not your sister."

"Well, I didn't actually see her myself," Hayden sniffed. "But there were drawings. Drawings like that one." His gaze drifted down to the papers I was still holding.

I stepped back, searching his face, not sure whether to laugh or cry. "Wait. So your queen, the same queen who's been depriving you of water and starving you and murdering the people of your ward for generations, draws some pictures and tells you your sister's dead, and you *believed* her? Great fucking gods, this is fucking perfect." I turned away from the boy; he was too fucking stupid to deal with directly. "Fix this, Carrion. I'm out of patience."

Prowling back and forth in the mouth of the alleyway, I waited for the smuggler to wrangle the human. He started out strong...

"Saeris isn't in Yvelia anymore, Hayden. She accidentally opened a Fae portal, and Fisher here came through, in Zilvaren."

But then immediately took a wrong turn...

"He took her back to his realm and tricked her into a bargain. Then he came and kidnapped *me* because he thought I was *you*—"

"Fuck me, Carrion." I shoved him out of the way and grabbed the boy by the shirt. The sour tang of his fear flooded my nose. "Do you want to see your sister?" I growled.

"Y-yes!" he stammered.

"All right, then. Let's fucking go."

"Wait! Wait—We *can't* go!" He dug his boot heels into the sand, almost losing his balance when I pulled him forward.

I was *this* close to knocking the fucker out and throwing him over my shoulder. "Why not?"

Hayden's eyes darted to Carrion—wide, afraid, sad. His shoulders sagged, the fight suddenly leaving him. "We need to go back to the Third first," he whispered. "You need...to say goodbye, Carrion. I'm sorry. I..."

I watched Carrion's jaw set. He backed away, hands balled into fists, knuckles white.

"What is it?" I asked.

Hayden didn't have the heart to answer, it seemed. But somehow Carrion already knew.

"Gracia," he said softly. "Gracia is dead."

—+—

A lonely parade of mourners trudged single file up the dunes. Their scarves whipped in the wind, streaming westward like prayer flags. Sand stung my cheeks and brought tears to my eyes as I fought my way up the steep incline behind Hayden. Carrion led the way, his gait the resigned lumber of a male headed toward the gallows. He didn't say anything. No one did.

The occupants of the Third were quarantined. They were forbidden from leaving their ward under any circumstances—apart from one. The poorest residents of the Silver City *were* permitted to leave their ward to bury their dead.

It was not a kindness.

There were no graveyards in the Third. No mausoleums or crypts. The corpses of the downtrodden and oppressed had to go somewhere, and Madra made sure that the friends and the family of the newly deceased disposed of their remains in a timely fashion. There would be consequences otherwise.

We had left by the south gate. No guardian had stood watch. None was required. Madra knew all too well that those who made the pilgrimage across the blistering dunes would make their way back soon enough.

The gateway into the desert might as well have been the gateway into hell. There was nowhere to go. No reprieve to be found out here among the endless, haunted dunes. Only death. The people who left to say goodbye to their dead always came back. What other choice did they have?

I was soaked with sweat and beginning to feel the first signs of dehydration by the time we reached the pyre site—impressive, considering it normally took a week or two for a member of the Fae to *need* water.

Thirty or more men and women stood in a silent circle around the burning stack of wood. The shrouded figure laid out atop the pyre was already engulfed in flames. A pillar of flames leaped up at the pale sky, making the air shiver with heat.

In a city of stone and sand, there wasn't much to burn. Everyone had brought something to feed Gracia Swift's farewell fire. A shawl. A blanket. Armloads of straw. The woman from the bar yesterday, the one who had screamed at Carrion for causing a scene, tossed pieces of a broken chair onto the fire, crying softly. When she saw Carrion, she shook her head, tears cutting tracks over her dust marked cheeks. "I'm sorry, Carrion. I would have told you. I didn't know."

Carrion didn't see her. He only saw the fire. The woman placed a hand on his shoulder, squeezed it, and left, heading down the dunes, back toward the city.

We stood there, watched the pyre turn white-hot. Eventually, he stepped forward and tossed a book onto the fire. I had seen him pack it into his bag when we'd left his apartment, had noted its title then. *Fae Creatures of the Gilarian Mountains.* The book had been his only link to his people. His heritage. His entire realm. Gracia's family had safeguarded the book—and Carrion—his entire life.

The ancient tome went up like kindling.

"I should have been here," he whispered. "I should have sat with her." He frowned, confusion tugging at his features. "I don't...even know why we do it. Seventy-two hours. That's how long we sit with them when they die. The people that we love."

I tucked my chin, exhaling. "Zilvarens do it for the same reason we do it. You sit with your loved ones to make sure they don't rise. After three days, the chance of them transitioning ends. The dead stay dead. For us, it's a practical safeguard. It must have become tradition here."

Hayden hadn't said much until now. He stared at us both, eyes wide. "What are you talking about, transitioning?"

Carrion didn't reply. He was lost in the fire again.

"Later," I told him. "There'll be plenty of time for explanations once we get back to Yvelia." The answer didn't assuage his concern, by the looks of things. But Hayden nodded, his throat working as he swallowed.

Somewhere, deep in the desert, a haunting, mournful cry went up. Crying? No, it was...*singing.* Beautiful. Sad. Eerie. The woman's sorrow echoed across the dunes, the melody so haunting and lonely that I knew I would never forget it.

We watched the pyre for an hour, until the heat became unmanageable and Carrion's knees buckled. I caught him by the back of his shirt and held him up. The poor bastard's face and neck were still marked from Joshin's stingers. He looked exhausted. Ready to give up. He nodded, breathing deep, indicating that he could stand on his own, but rather than letting him go, I pulled him into a hug.

Saeris wasn't here. But if she was, this is what she would have done for him.

Carrion immediately tried to pull away, but I hugged him tighter—too tight, maybe—refusing to let him go. He sagged, burying a single, choked cry into my chest, and that was all I heard out of him. His body rocked with silent sobs for a minute, and I held him. And then he stopped, and it was over.

When he pulled away again, I let him go. His face was bright red, his eyes hollow. He nodded, his voice cracked with emotion. "Come on. Let's get the fuck out of here."

This way. Thisss way. This is the way.

The quicksilver was restless today. It whispered in the back of my mind, directing me as we traveled through the tunnels beneath the city, back toward the Third. So little of it remained in me now that its voice was singular. Almost childlike. Easily ignored. It felt different today, though. More insistent. It was happy when we were heading in the direction it *wanted* us to travel in, but the moment we changed course, it wreaked havoc on my insides.

The sensation would have been less infuriating had Hayden Fane shut up once since we'd entered the tunnels.

"It stinks down here," he mumbled.

I bit my tongue.

"I can barely see."

I stared ahead, jaw clenched.

"There are *rats* down here."

I spun around and pinned the fucker to the wall.

"Are you done?" I seethed. He couldn't exactly reply—not with my hand wrapped around his fucking throat. His eyes rolled in his head like a spooked horse. "I really think you *should* be. Because you're starting to sound like a petulant, spoiled little shit who hasn't had to deal with hardship a day in his fucking life."

Hayden's eyes rolled back into his head. He passed out.

"Perfect." Carrion sounded unfazed by the turn of events. "You scared him unconscious. That's just . . . *perfect*."

"At least he'll be quiet for a moment."

The moment didn't last long. Hayden was awake and looking like he'd shit his britches less than a minute later. I crouched down and shoved a finger in his face. "Do not say a fucking *word*. Come on. On your feet. Move."

The rest of the journey back to the tunnels was relatively peaceful. We collected the bags of silver from the abandoned maintenance room where we had stowed them earlier. I was desperate for daylight by the time Carrion launched himself up and out of an access hatch he claimed was close to *another* apartment that he used—apparently, he had more than one.

The smuggler lifted himself up through the hole and then reached back down again for Hayden. I barely had to help the human up; Carrion had already pulled him through. I followed after, irritation hot at the back of my throat. "How is it that I had to deal with your ass in my face the last time you tried to climb out of a tunnel, and yet now you're perfectly capable of climbing out by yourself?"

The look Carrion gave me spoke volumes. "It's very simple, Fisher. If you treat me like I'm the court jester, I'll be the court jester. If I'm the laughingstock, or the drunk, or the idiot, then you're not thinking about who I *really* am, are you. I survived here for over a thousand years. Do you really think I'd have been able to do that if I couldn't pull myself out of a fucking *hole*? If at any point, you underestimate me . . ." He smirked, arching a dark copper eyebrow. "Then I'd say that was *your* mistake rather than mine. Wouldn't you?"

There were posters on the walls, now, as we slipped through the Third. Thick, blocky text screamed:

DANGER! ENEMIES OF THE CROWN!

<u>Wanted for:</u>
Unauthorized Magic Use
Murder
Theft
Intent to Incite Violence

Harboring these criminals is an offense punishable by death.
Remember: Magic is a disease.
Keep Zilvaren Safe!

My face wasn't drawn in caricature this time. The rendering was faithful enough. Carrion's face was plastered up there with mine now. Images of our faces stared out of scores of posters as we made our way through the ward.

With our hoods drawn up and our scarves concealing our features, we were safe from the prying eyes of those we passed. Men and women gathered around the posters, arguing among themselves on every street corner.

"Unauthorized *magic* use?"

"Magic isn't real."

"Of course it is.

"That's the Swift boy. I always knew there was something *wrong* about him."

"It's a joke. She rants and raves about make-believe every Evenlight. The Fae this. Magic that. She's finally convinced herself it's all real, though. She's lost touch with reality."

"What are we supposed to do, then? Lie? Tackle one of our own in the street?"

"Look, there's a reward..."

"A reward..."

"A reward..."

Reward.

A year's supply of water for your household: That's what Madra was promising to the person who came forward with information that led to our capture. It was worth more than money. In a lot of cases, it meant the difference between life and death. It was the kind of reward that turned friends into enemies in the blink of an eye.

We didn't linger in the street. We were only minutes from safety when we saw the first guardians.

They were waiting for us. Concealed deep inside the alleyway opposite Carrion's apartment, I wouldn't have seen them until it was too late. But the Twins always shone in Zilvaren, and the Madra insisted that her guardians look resplendent in their glorious golden armor, didn't she? Patches of shimmering gold danced on the shop front below Carrion's bedroom window, betraying the soldiers before they'd even come into view.

Swift noticed the mirrored gold on the stonework only a split second after I did. We both grabbed Hayden, pulling him back. The three of us backtracked the way we had come... but it was already too late.

"Here! They're here! We've got them!"

The guardians spilled out of the alleyway like hornets swarming from a hive.

"Fuck!" I hissed. The men weren't anywhere near as fast as Carrion and me, but we had a human in tow now—a human who couldn't run very fast. We took off, sprinting, urging Hayden along as we barreled through the streets.

Thisss way, the quicksilver hissed.

"Shut. Up."

This way, this way, this way! The tugging on my insides grew stronger, but the quicksilver was trying to pull me in the wrong direction, back toward the fucking guardians.

"What are we going to do?" Carrion panted.

People shouted, leaping out of the way as we hurtled by them.

We had no choice. Nowhere to go. The only option open to us was—

Ting!

"FUCK!"

An iron-tipped arrow ricocheted off the wall next to my head; they were fucking *shooting* at us.

"We have to fight!" I shouted. "It's our only option. But we need somewhere open. Somewhere they can't pen us in!"

If we kept running through this rabbit warren of streets, we were doomed. Fish in a barrel. It wouldn't be long before one or all of us wound up shot.

Carrion nodded, quickly assessing our options up ahead. "All right. The square, then. This way. Follow me."

Ting!

Ting!

Arrows struck the walls.

A woman to my left screamed, a spurt of bright red blood arcing in the air as an arrow intended for my back clipped her throat.

Carrion wheeled to the left. I took up position behind Hayden, using my body as a shield, covering him as best I could. "Faster, Fane. Hurry," I growled.

"I'm going...as fast...as I...can!"

This way! Come! Find me! This way!

For such a tiny fragment of quicksilver, it certainly had some strength. I found myself veering to the right, my feet carrying me off in a direction I didn't want to go.

Left.

Right.

Then right again.

My pulse thundered behind my breastbone, my heart beating like a fucking war drum. "If I die in Zilvaren, I am *not* going to be happy," I snarled.

The square was large. At its center, a huge wooden platform had been erected. It was covered in sprays of flowers. Pinks, reds, and purples. I saw immediately that they weren't real. At the center of the podium was a long table, on top of which a line of bodies had been laid out in the baking reckoning suns. Flies choked the air above them, their drone loud enough to hear above the shouting guardians.

"Stop! Stop those men!"

A large group of girls stood on the far side of the square. They were young. Only teenagers. Their eyes were full of fear. Two guardians already stood with them, and one of them had a girl pinned up against the wall. She screamed as a male in a black shirt and pants approached and plunged something into her neck.

The square might not have been a good idea. The buildings were taller here. If any of the guardians made it up there, they would rain holy hellfire down on us. On the other side of the courtyard, the human in black directed the guardian to lay the girl—who was now limp in his arms—on the back of a horse-drawn cart.

Three seconds. That's all the time we had before the guardians were on top of us and this went to shit. I drew my hands together and pulled them apart, conjuring a sword identical to Nimerelle in every way but the one that fucking mattered. It was *not* a god sword.

"What are they doing here, Carrion?" I called, jerking my chin toward the group of girls.

"It must be cleansing day," he answered. "Once a month, they come and round up the marked girls who've turned fourteen. Seven out of every ten. They'll sedate them and take them up to the palace."

My blood ran cold.

Cleansing day.

At least twelve girls stood with their backs to the wall. Most of them were crying. The one at the front of the line wasn't crying, though. She glowered defiantly at the man dressed in black, as he lifted the cylindrical silver object to her neck. She spat in his face.

"Here they come," Carrion called. "I hope you have a fucking plan."

I'd had one: Put the bastards down as quickly and quietly as possible. Try not to cause a scene. But I wasn't liking that plan very much anymore.

No. That plan was no longer viable.

Because boy oh fucking boy, was I going to cause a *fucking* scene.

I didn't need a god sword for this. I only needed my rage.

The second the guardians ran into the square, I leashed my magic and called on it. Every last drop. It roiled below the surface of my skin, angry as a rabid dog.

There were fifteen of them. That's how many trained soldiers they'd thought they'd need to bring us down. They were going to regret that choice. It wouldn't have mattered, though. They could have brought ten times as many men with them and it still wouldn't be enough.

The men hesitated a second, taking in the scene, realizing that we were just standing there waiting for them—

"I don't like this," Hayden whispered.

"Get him out of harm's way, Carrion. *Now.*"

—and then they charged.

Swift took my mate's brother. They ran. I didn't see where. Didn't care.

These fuckers had rounded up Saeris and brought her here, too, once. I knew her. She would have stared them down and spat in their faces, just like that girl had a moment ago. She would have cursed them as they stole her choices from her. She would have raged.

When I drew on my power and set it free, I didn't make shadows.

I made *knives.*

The blades weren't made of metal. They were magic itself. Corporeal, shimmering magic. Like my shadows, they were black. Their edges were sharp, and when they hurtled through the air and found their targets, they pierced armor, flesh, and bone alike.

The guardians dropped like flies.

My vision sharpened, the square coming into focus. More guardians were arriving from the square's south entrance. The two who were dealing with the girls had noticed what was happening now and were running straight for me. They were dead before their bodies hit the ground.

Blood soaked the sand.

The world was all crimson and death. More guardians thundered into the square, their armor clanking over angry shouts and the frightened screams of the young girls. I was deaf to it all.

Madra's men appeared in droves, and as quickly as they came, they died. My senses weren't my own. Arrows rained down from the rooftops—my instincts had been right. They'd sought higher ground in the hopes of making a kill box out of the square. But *I* was the one who'd made the kill box, and it was piling up with *their* fucking dead.

I brought them down with ropes of shadow. I lashed them around their arms, ankles, torsos, and dragged them to their ends.

They had brought Saeris here.

My mate.

They'd hurt her. They'd taken something sacred from her here, in this awful place. Not her right to have children. But her right to make such an important decision for herself.

I made them pay, and I did not stop. Not when the new guardians who arrived turned and tried to flee. Not when they scrambled on their hands and knees and begged for mercy.

The men of this ward treated their women like chattel. Like possessions, without minds, dreams, or hopes of their own. They used them for sex, or else violated their bodies and stole their rights. They had murdered Saeris's mother. They didn't deserve to *breathe*...

"Kingfisher! Stop!" The voice was near. Distant. It echoed around the square. The haze fogging my mind cleared, and I found Carrion twenty feet away, holding up his hands in a placating gesture. "We're good! It's okay. They're gone. They're all gone. We have to *leave*, Fisher."

There were bodies piled high all over the square. Too many bodies to count and still not enough. This was just a small percentage of Madra's troops. The fire burning in my soul demanded I claim all of them for their cruelty, but Carrion was right. We needed to get the fuck out of here. The ground shook, the sand vibrating as the sound of an approaching *army* filled the air.

"We *have* to go," Carrion urged.

I was numb down into the basement of my soul. "Okay. Yes." I nodded. "You're right."

"Carrion? *Carrion!*" The hiss came from the other side of the square. It was Hayden, stooped down and hiding behind the horse-drawn cart. The boy's hair was wild, sticking up in every direction like he'd been struck by lightning. His face was spattered with blood. There was a knife in his hand. "Carrion, this way. I know where we should go."

The smuggler didn't even ask. He grabbed my arm and pulled me along after him, following Saeris's brother. Houses whipped past in a blur. I ran hard, keeping up, and with every step I came back to myself a little more. I had just killed forty guardians. Fifty of them. And I didn't feel remotely bad about doing it.

Yessss, this is the way, the quicksilver purred in my head. *This is the way!*

The ground was quaking beneath our feet now. As we sped through the Third, toward our unknown end, Madra's men drew closer, and a stillness settled inside me.

The guardians wouldn't pose a problem to us if they couldn't *find* us.

My magic should have been gone. The source of my power felt *so* far away, and yet there it was, ready to answer my call. I had just used a prodigious amount of magic back in the square, and yet, when I ran my fingertips along the surface of it, I found a mind-bending well of energy waiting for me.

I stopped running and brought it forth.

It slammed out of me in a tide of glittering black sand and shadow so overwhelming that it swallowed the street we were standing in. And then the ward. And then the entire city.

My magic encompassed all Zilvaren.

For the first time in history, the shining banner in the north fell into darkness.

24

TRIA PRIMA

SAERIS

At the first stages of ascension, equilibrium must be found. Every acolyte has an affinity toward a certain path. Without the appropriate guidance and training, the path will claim the acolyte. They must marry the Tria Prima into one within themselves if they are to truly master their power.

The enlightened Alchemist walks all three paths.

—Elemental Runes and Their Purposes:
A Comprehensive Guide to Alchemy.

THE FORGE WAS unlike any other I'd ever found myself in. For starters, there was no fire. The Blood Court, it seemed, was firm in its view that fire had no place within the walls of Ammontraíeth and hadn't made an exception even here.

Evenlight flickered in the hearth where hungry flames should have been. Not long ago, on the side of the mountain above Irrín, I had handed a sword over to Lorreth, and the sky had exploded with dancing light. The aurora, Fisher had called it. The evenlight bore more than a passing resemblance to that aurora as it writhed and danced in the grate. Vivid green and tinged with pink, it was hypnotizing to watch. It gave off no heat. I could run my fingers through it, even, and I didn't feel a thing. Yet I knew, deep down, that this was more than just light. That when I thrust the crucible I had prepared into the flow of it, a *change* would come about.

There was a token amount of quicksilver inside the crucible. Very little was required for this purpose. I felt the moment that it entered the evenlight, as if a chord had been struck, a note plucked, and the sustained hum of a note was ringing all around me.

I reached out with my mind, searching for the quicksilver, and found it almost instantly. According to the book, I should have been able to "connect" with it at this point. I was still trying to figure out what that meant when the quicksilver spoke.

She sees us. She hears us. She sees us…

I clenched my jaw, angling my head, trying to focus.

She doesn't speak to us. Why does she not speak?

I filled my lungs until I could inhale no more. It was right there, an intangible buzzing source of energy, at the periphery of my mind. It felt as though I should have been able to close a hand around it, but whenever I tried, it evaded my grasp, slippery, like a piece of soap.

"Gods *damn* it," I spat, opening my eyes.

Filthy mouth. The quicksilver chuckled. *So ill-tempered. Bad, bad, bad.*

"Oh, shut up, you." I *willed* the quicksilver to change. It did so without complaint, but I couldn't escape the wrongness of the sensation that shivered down my back as the flat, matte bead of quicksilver became molten and rolled around the bottom of the crucible. Much as I disliked admitting it, Foley's words had stuck with me. Willing the quicksilver to do anything was not forming a partnership with it. There was another way. A better way…

Quickly, I plucked a ring from the tray I had set out on the bench when I'd arrived and dropped it into the crucible. The ring was made of silver, but it was impure enough that I needed to add a little more to help the process along. The quicksilver formed a snake-like thread, winding around the ring's band, mimicking the tiny vines that were engraved into the piece of jewelry.

Pretty, it hissed. *A pretty one. Yes.*

"Will you bind with it? Will you make it a relic?" I half expected it to say no, but I felt the quicksilver's attention prick up at the request.

A memory, it purred. *We will become a relic in exchange for a memory.*

"*Any* memory?" I asked.

The tiny thread of quicksilver thought about this for a second. *Any memory will do*, it concluded.

Any memory. Without thinking, I reached for the most painful one.

My mother, on her knees.

The blade, slicing her throat open.

Her blood spilling into the sand…

The quicksilver probed around it, encircling that awful moment in my mind. I felt it tighten around it. Felt the memory work loose…

"Stop!" the cry bounced around the windowless forge. "Wait." I panted, my heart suddenly beating too fast. Swallowing, I shook my head. "Not that one." I used to wake in the night, covered in sweat, that scene playing out on repeat in my head. It haunted me. It had been the very last time I'd seen my mother alive. Horrific as it was, I *needed* that memory. Without it, I didn't know who I would be.

The quicksilver laughed softly, relinquishing its hold on the memory. The vision of my mother dying in the sand became all too real once more.

"Take this one," I whispered, drawing forth a different memory. A morning, one much like any other, sitting in the loft of the Mirage. I had been counting money. I had been telling Hayden…

Been telling Hayden…

I gasped, a sudden, sharp, shooting pain at my temple. It was there and then gone again.

Wait.

What had I just been thinking about?

A relic, the quicksilver purred at the bottom of the crucible. *A pretty one. We are made. Seal us now. Give us the blood.*

It was a disconcerting thing, staring down at the ring. The quicksilver was gone, bound into it. The tiny scrap of normal silver, too. I had traded a memory, but for the life of me I had no idea what kernel of my past I had given up to facilitate the exchange.

The blood, the quicksilver chanted. *The blood. The blood.*

I pricked myself with the end of the dagger Fisher gave me and let the crimson bead at the end of my finger, still reeling from the void that the deal had left behind in my mind. It was a strange feeling, like probing at the space in your mouth where a tooth used to be, knowing what it should feel like but finding an empty space instead.

My blood hissed when it hit the bottom of the crucible.

That was new.

The quicksilver hummed, singing quietly to itself as it absorbed the blood.

I held my breath. Waited.

It's done. Done. Done.

I exhaled, relief washing over me as—

"You are surprised."

I spun around, dropping the crucible and the set of tongs I was holding it in. The metal clanged heavily when it struck the ground. "Fucking saints! What the f-f-f-f..."

It was the Hazrax.

I'd only seen it once and from a distance. The coronation had only been a few days ago, and yet it felt like a lifetime had passed since then. The creature was bigger than I remembered. Taller. It had to bow its head to fit through the doorframe as it slowly entered the forge.

Its skin was a sickly pale color, translucent in places. A network of black veins pulsed below the surface of its skin. Its eyes were solid black and featureless. Its mouth...gods, it had so many *teeth*.

I took a step back, fumbling to steady myself against the bench.

The Hazrax's features remained expressionless as it took another floating step into the forge, though I got the creeping sense that it was *smiling*.

Oh, gods.

It was getting closer.

"You do not need to be afraid, child queen."

I gripped the edge of the bench until it began to hurt. "I'm not afraid. I'm...surprised."

The creature tilted its head to an unnatural angle, and I caught a flash of its gills. "Surprised that the quicksilver still accepted your blood?" it said, its tone quizzical. I would have expected its voice to be strange. Alien, even. But the Hazrax's voice was normal. It could have belonged to any member of the Fae—except for the fact that I couldn't quite tell if it sounded male or female.

"Yes," I answered. "That surprised me."

"Because you are no longer human. This is the first deal you have struck with the quicksilver in your new form?"

My heart was in my throat. "No. I made relics for my friend. For my brother. This one just felt...reluctant."

The Hazrax seemed to think about this. It stooped down where I had dropped the crucible and the tongs, its long fingers carefully plucking up the ring that had also fallen to the floor. It held it up, its jet-black eyes studying the piece of jewelry. While it did so, I noticed the thick-banded golden ring that *it* wore on its left hand—a bulky thing with large, blood-red ruby at its center. The ring of office that marked the Hazrax as a Lord of Midnight. Slowly, a stream of smoke began to rise from the creator's bony fingers. The relic I'd just created was *burning* it. The Hazrax almost seemed chagrined as it placed the relic down on the table.

"Mm. You're also surprised by my presence here," it said, turning to me. "You've heard that I do not leave the Hall of Tears."

"Yes."

Its eyelids closed vertically, snapping closed and open again, the action startling me. "You're surprised by the fact that I'm speaking to you like this, as well. You're surprised by my appearance. You are surprised by *many* things."

"Yes." The word was out of my mouth before I could stop it. "Are you inside my head?" I had felt Algat when she'd rifled through my thoughts. If this creature was doing the same now, it had a far lighter touch.

But the Hazrax shook its head. "One as old as I does not need to steal information. The power of deduction proves sufficient."

"Why are you here?" It seemed pointless to beat around the bush.

The Hazrax splayed its fingers, displaying the diaphanous webbing between each of its digits. "In some cultures, it is considered rude to talk business without first observing the rules of etiquette. Some small and meaningless exchange between strangers that... helps them know each other better."

"What meaningless exchange should *we* have then?" The forge was small. A box. There were no windows. No way out, bar the door that stood behind the Hazrax, twenty feet away. Every second the creature was here, breathing the same air as me, the more my skin prickled and goose bumped. It wasn't the physical threat the thing posed, though I was sure it could have hurt me if it wanted to. It was the power it exuded. Raw, ancient, dangerous power. It radiated from the creature like heat thrown off by a sun.

It turned its strange, smooth face to me and blinked again. "Let us talk of the book on the table, shall we? A noble tome. There were once many of these books... but now there is just one."

A fraction of my caution gave ground to curiosity. "You've read it?"

"I am an observer. A collector of information. It is my duty to read books," the Hazrax replied. "I have read *that* book many times."

Tentatively, I stepped away from the bench. "And you understand it. You understand who I am? *What* I am?"

The Hazrax skirted around the bench, its long white robes swishing around its legs as it moved. It veered away from the evenlight burning in the hearth. "I'm not gifted with the Sight, as some beings of this realm appear to be. I see avenues. Pathways. Light. I see... *possibilities*." It spun around to face me. "Blood magic is a crude thing, Saeris Fane."

I rocked back onto my heels. Where had *that* come from? "I don't... know anything about blood magic."

"Of course you do." The strange creature drew itself up, tucking its hands into its billowing sleeves. "The quicksilver is greedy. You give it whatever it desires. Songs. Jokes. *Memories*," it said. "Your mate wishes you to create many thousands of these relics, and yet you bargain for each one that you make. You shave off a piece of yourself for each one. Tell me, how will you know exactly what it is that you've forgotten, what you've *lost*, when your mind is riddled full of holes?"

It could hear the quicksilver. That was the only explanation. It couldn't have known that I'd traded a memory just now otherwise. "I'm doing what needs to be done," I said.

"Mm. What needs to be done." A statement. And then, "What needs to be done?" A question. "Do those runes on your hands need to be sealed? Does your mate need to be wary of new faces? Do you need to create thousands of relics, so that you can whisk the weak and the small away from this place? Does the black rot spreading throughout this land need to be stopped? Tell me, I saw the low blood carrying the message to your chamber earlier this evening. How many have fallen to the infected now? How much land has been lost?"

Today's numbers sent over from the war camp were branded into my mind:

Total known dead: 1,976
Total known infected: 2,409
Estimated infected landmass: 8,162 hectares

We were losing ground at an alarming rate, and there was no hope of the rot's rate of expansion slowing anytime soon. Every time I unraveled a new tally, my hope took another hit. But I wasn't going to let the Hazrax know that. It was toying with me. By peppering me with these questions, hoping for a spark of fear, maybe. A reaction. Inside, I did exactly that—*reacted*—but I trained my face into a blank mask. Whatever this creature was, whatever its motives were, I refused to play into them. "For someone who proclaims they don't have the Sight, you sure seem to *see* a lot."

The Hazrax blinked again, its membranous eyelids flicking closed, open, closed, open. Unreadable as its facial features were, I thought I could still feel a flash of annoyance emanating from it as it moved serenely around the forge. It left its comments hanging there between us, the most worrying of which—*"Does your mate need to be wary of new faces?"*—causing all kinds of chaos to unfold inside me, but I did not give in to panic.

Fisher was an exceptional warrior. He'd led armies into battle. He knew how to take care of himself. He didn't need me worrying over vague comments like this. He needed me focused, so I could contend with the task at hand.

"These pleasantries are nice, Hazrax, but as I'm sure *you* already know, I have a monumental task ahead of me and not much time to accomplish it in. These relics aren't going to make themselves, so—"

"Let us return to the blood, then. Blood magic is artless. It requires no true skill. Do you intend on trading every last drop of blood you have to make your precious relics, Saeris? Or do you have another plan that will *not* require you to exsanguinate?"

"Yes, it's taking me too long to make a single relic. I can't keep making trades. I can't keep bartering away my blood. Believe me. *I get it.*"

"Then what else is there, Saeris Fane?"

"I thought this was supposed to be a *meaningless* exchange." I wanted it to leave. I couldn't help but notice that no matter where it moved, the Hazrax was always in a position to block the forge's exit in a couple of steps.

The creature spread its webbed fingers. "In the grand scheme of things, yes. This conversation *is* meaningless."

"It seems pretty important to me."

"I can imagine." It smiled at last. Thin, translucent lips peeled back to reveal rows and rows of needle-sharp teeth. A shudder of revulsion started at my fingertips and prickled all the way to the crown of my head. I wasn't going to be able to unsee the sight. "If *you* consider the topic to be of import, then perhaps you should consider my question, no?"

The Hazrax was supposed to be the Keeper of Silence. Seemed to me the creepy bastard didn't know when to shut up. I tamped down my rising frustration and analyzed what it had said. If I couldn't rely on bargains or blood to create the relics, then what did I have? The answer was so obvious, I felt like kicking myself.

The godscursed *fucking* magic. "I need to figure out how to activate the quicksilver rune." I held up my right hand, studying the intricate inkwork there.

"An impressive shield," the Hazrax noted. "Perhaps the most complex shield this realm has ever seen. It will be a formidable weapon...if it doesn't kill you before you can seal it."

Foley had called my runes a shield. Now the Hazrax had, too. I stared at the linework, feeling the steady, quick drumming of an ancient pulse, separate from my own heartbeat, beneath the interlocking runes.

"That's what the book is for," I said. "It's supposed to teach me how to make a compact with the quicksilver. But the book only teaches me how to hear it. How to communicate with it. And I can already do that."

The Hazrax made a strange, ticking sound somewhere deep in its throat as it thought. "I hear the wind. Am I *one* with the wind because I listen to it blow?"

"Enough! Please, just... *enough*." I was so fucking *tired* of this. "If you know something, then please just spit it out."

The disturbing ticking sound grew louder. "I do not know something. I know *everything*, Saeris Fane. But it is not my part to reveal truths that must be discovered."

How had I *known* it wasn't going to put me out of my misery? "All right. Then in that case, I think it's time for you to leave."

The Keeper of Silence made a sound that resembled laughter. "I fear I must disclose the real reason for my visit before I can do that, child."

Heat spiked in my belly, pooling like molten lava. "You call me child where others here call me *Your Highness*."

"Indeed. I do. And I mean no disrespect by the title. But much like the friend you have found in the library, I am not a servant of this court. I am a *private* individual, with *private* interests."

"I was led to believe you swore fealty to the Blood Court."

Slowly, the Hazrax shook its head. "A deal was struck between myself and the vampire king. I was allowed to observe him, and in return, he was permitted one favor for each year that I remained here."

"What kind of favor?" I asked.

The Hazrax flashed its teeth again. "That was up to the king, of course. If it was within my power to grant it, it was done."

"And what exactly *is* the nature of your power? What *are* you?"

The Hazrax stepped toward me, its feet silent against the stone floor. "Mine is the power to put out a sun, perhaps? The power to... untether gravity?"

I watched, stunned speechless, as the relic on the counter slowly rose into the air. The tongs. The crucible. Up they floated, lifted by invisible strings. The loose strands of my hair that had escaped my braid began to float around my face.

"As for what I am..." The creature trailed off. "Who knows anymore? This body is just a vessel. My mind is very old. It can be in many places at once. I see through the eyes of others from time to time. These are very useful skills to have."

I wasn't listening. A weightless sensation was pulling at my stomach, causing it to roll. The soles of my boots began to lift off the ground, and a bark of panic burst out of my mouth. "Stop! Enough. That's enough!"

The crucible crashed back down to the ground, cracking the stone where it landed. The tongs caught on the side of the bench and then hit the ground, spinning. The relic I'd just made remained suspended in the air, though. It rotated slowly, the light catching on the tiny vines and leaves that wound around its band.

"I am capable of many things. You just need to know how to ask," the Hazrax said.

"And, so, what?" It was a miracle that my voice didn't shake. "You want to strike a bargain with me now that Malcolm is dead?"

There was no mistaking the sound now—the Hazrax was definitely laughing. "I would make the same deal with you that I made with Malcolm, yes," it said.

"And if I refuse?"

Its lips spread wider, the dark, hollow void of its jet eyes boring into me as it flicked its finger, and the floating relic began to spin faster, faster, faster...

"I must remain, Saeris," it said evenly. "There *must* be a deal." The threat was veiled, but it was there. I had no idea what the Hazrax would do if I denied its request, but I knew with every bone in my body that it wouldn't be good.

If this thing had been human—or *Fae* even—I would have come up with some very colorful language to describe what it should go do to itself. But this was no member of the Fae. Despite the position it held, it was no member of the Blood Court, either. There was something deeply sinister about the creature, and I sensed that pissing it off *might* not be the smartest idea.

"Okay," I said. "Fine. One favor a year, in exchange for permission to stay and observe. But I want the opportunity to renew the bargain each year. I don't want to be locked into an agreement with you until the day I die."

"I see no issue with that arrangement." The creature inclined its head. "You will quickly realize how valuable my favors are and will not mind honoring my simple request in return. I agree to your stipulation."

I wouldn't be queen of this wretched court for much longer. I had no idea what possessed me to make the demand, but some part of me urged caution when dealing with this creature. My gut instinct had proven right many times in the past; I wasn't about to start ignoring it now.

The Hazrax had turned and was walking away. It appeared our business was at an end, then. "Wait! Don't we need to seal the agreement in blood?"

The strange creature did not turn around. "I've already told you, Saeris Fane. Blood magic is crude. We have no need for it, you and I."

The forge seemed to double in size once the Hazrax had gone. It was suddenly easier to breathe. The relic still hung suspended in the air, spinning fast—a blur of silver and black. I went to reach for it, and it abruptly stopped spinning and dropped like a stone into my hand.

The second the cool metal hit my palm, the world pitched on its side. Blinding white light flared behind my eyes.

Pain...

The gods knew I was familiar with pain, but this was the kind of pain that tore a soul apart.

It was everywhere. My hands—my eyes. I couldn't see. Couldn't breathe.

Ever since I'd woken up in the Black Palace, I'd fought to partition my magic behind a thick, high wall. It escaped often, activating my quicksilver rune. It had spilled over too much in the library, yes, but this? This wasn't an overflow of power. The wall inside my head was gone. It was as though it had never even existed, and now there was *nothing* holding my power back. It blazed through me, all of it at once, lighting me up like a torch and searching for an avenue of escape.

Fuck! The silent curse scraped the back of my throat.

I was going to destroy Ammontraíeth. Worse, I was going to fucking *die*, and I wouldn't even get to say goodbye to my own mate.

Panic merged my scattered thoughts into one urgent command:

Run.

25

FOUNDATIONS

KINGFISHER

SCREAMS RANG OUT in the darkness.

Like a contagion, chaos was spreading throughout the city.

"Quickly! This way!"

Carrion led the charge. It had been the work of a second to give him the Sight so that he could guide us through my shadows. He was now one of only four people in existence who boasted that capability—a number I hadn't *planned* on increasing today, but necessity had required it.

Around us, crowds of people swarmed out of buildings, their panicked shouts filling the air as they stumbled around, searching for familiarity. Next to me, Hayden tripped on a lip in the cobbled street. I barely had time to catch him before he hit the ground face-first. Grabbing a fistful of his shirt, I wrenched him to the left. "Just keep running, Hayden. I've got you."

"This way!" Carrion was a head and a half taller than anyone else on the street now. At some point during the assault in the square, I'd relinquished my hold on the glamor that had been hiding our true Fae nature. My canines were sharp in my mouth again. It felt good to be back in my own skin.

Like wraiths, we darted through the streets, careening around people as they stumbled blindly, calling out for their loved ones.

"Take this right," Carrion hissed. "Here!"

Up ahead, a phalanx of guardians was proceeding down the tight street, keeping close formation. The pale green glow of the evenlight torches they carried barely cut through the shadows. They shouldn't have even *had* evenlight here. The burning heat rose up within me again—the same heat that had all but suffocated me back in the square, until I couldn't fucking breathe around it. I wanted to kill the bastards for what they'd done to my mate. For what they'd done to her mother. For what they were *still* doing to this ward. My vengeance was incomplete. A heavy debt was still owed by the men who carried out Madra's orders. It wouldn't be settled until the streets of this city were piled high with their corpses and a mountain of golden armor blotted out the suns. But vengeance was going to have to wait.

We swung right, turning mere seconds before the guardians reached us.

"There. Up ahead. That wide building with the heavy wooden door! Go, go, go!" Carrion whispered.

I shoved Hayden toward the door first. He found the handle and turned it—but the door didn't open.

"Gods alive. Move out of the way." I would kick the fucking thing down if I had to.

"No, no. Wait!" Hayden held out a hand behind him, urging me back. "It sticks is all." Leaning his shoulder against the wood, Saeris's brother gave the door a firm nudge. "You just need to . . . finesse . . ." The door swung open.

He couldn't see, but he knew where he was? There wasn't time to process *that* piece of information. Exhaustion sank its claws into me. My shadows were dissipating. As I looked back over my shoulder, I saw that the air was clearing, swaths of black silk disintegrating right before my eyes.

Inside. Inside! the quicksilver urged. It was louder than it had been since Gillethrye.

Carrion's eyes met mine, his worry matching my own. "After you." He gestured for me to head inside. Hayden had already crossed the threshold and disappeared. Cursing under my breath, I slipped through the doorway. My shadows had already vanished here. The room was sweltering, a fire raging in a—

"*Fuck!*" Pain exploded between my shoulder blades. My head spun, my vision seesawing. I'd been struck with something hard. Something *really* fucking heavy. The air rushed out of my lungs, but I kept my feet beneath me. Just. "What in the fifth circle of hell?" I wheeled to face my attacker, ready to tear them limb from limb, but there was Carrion, blocking my path, standing in front of a grizzled old man brandishing a fire iron.

"Whoa, whoa, whoa!" Carrion held his hands up. "Don't do anything rash. It was only a pat on the back."

"I was aiming for his head," the old man seethed. "I wasn't expecting the bastard to be so *tall*."

A pat on the back? A pat on the back didn't leave a fucking bruise. I stepped forward, ready to forcibly remove Carrion if I had to, but the smuggler grabbed me by the shoulders. "Don't hurt him, Fisher. For the love of the gods—"

"He tried to cave my *skull* in, Carrion."

The human shoved Swift aside himself, pushing him out of the way. His hair had once been dark brown but most of it was salt-and-pepper now. Lines marked the man's face. He was strong and broad, like a bull. Massive by human standards. A fire burned in his eyes as he squared up to me and snapped, "And what else should I have done, then? *You're* the one who broke into *my* forge!"

———†———

Saeris had made Elroy sound pleasant to be around. She'd spoken of him fondly, but my first impressions of him were not particularly favorable.

My back was throbbing, and I was developing a tension headache—an ailment that *wasn't* being eased by the glassmaker's whisper-shouting.

"He *cannot* be here!" The old man hadn't moved away from the door since we'd arrived. He really wanted us gone. "You can stay. Hayden can stay. But *he* has to go."

Carrion wasn't proving to be a great negotiator. "Calm down, Elroy. It's going to be fine. We just need a place to lay low for a couple of hours until it all calms down out there."

"I won't say it again. I know who he is. I know what kind of trouble he has chasing on his heels."

Hayden had been lurking by an array of heavy, well-used tools hanging on the wall. He stepped forward and spoke, reminding us all that he was in the room. "He says Saeris is alive, Elroy."

"I don't doubt it." The old man narrowed his eyes at me accusingly. "She's *Saeris*. Of course she's alive. But it looks like she's jumped out of the frying pan and straight into the fire with this one, doesn't it?"

Carrion slipped behind me, pressing his back to the door so that Elroy couldn't open it. "He isn't a *rebel*, El."

"I can see that plain as day. He's a Fae warrior, and he's about as subtle as a sledgehammer." He shoved the end of the poker he was holding into my face. "Those shadows you just cast across the whole city? That could have gotten us all killed. How would that have helped your cause?"

Gotten them all killed? Gods alive, the *dramatics*. "It would have helped immensely actually. If everyone in Zilvaren was dead, I'd be able to just *go home*," I growled.

"He doesn't mean that! He doesn't mean that. Okay, whew, everybody just take a deep breath." Carrion dragged his hands through his hair as he paced in front of the door. "You're going to have to forgive my friend here. He hails from cooler climes. The heat makes him irritable."

"Don't apologize for *me!*" I was going to open-palm slap him. "If he wanted cordiality, he shouldn't have struck me, should he?"

Shouting from the street cut off whatever angry retort Elroy had been about to fire back at me. The ground rumbled with the thunder of many boots. The forge boasted one small, shuttered window; Hayden had cracked the wooden shutters open an inch and stared morosely out of the gap like he was watching the end of the world unfold. "We can't go back out there," he said. "Not yet."

"*You* aren't going anywhere," Elroy stated. "Saeris would string me up if she knew I let you leave with him."

I bared my teeth. "Who do you think sent me here to *fetch* him, old man?"

"All right. We're done with this!" Carrion had found a hammer. Not a difficult thing to do, considering where we were. He held it up like a gavel, a very serious look on his face. "Normally, I'm all for a solid argument in the name of fun, but over the past few days I've been stung by a million scorpions, been chased repeatedly, and had to kill a ravening lunatic, and I just watched a woman who cared for me and protected me go up in flames. So now…we are fucking *done*." His voice cracked. He shrugged, laughing that roguish, devil-may-care laugh of his, but I'd heard the break in his voice. Elroy had, too. I watched, amazed, as the fight visibly drained out of the old man.

"I was heartsore to hear about Gracia, Carrion. I really was."

Carrion lowered the hammer. "She was old." He said this with no emotion at all. As if he'd said this to himself a million times over the past few hours, and the words were the only things holding him together. "I just wish I'd been here to say goodbye. She was…the last of her line. There won't be any more Swifts."

I felt the gravity of that in my bones. The Swift women had cared for Carrion and explained away his existence over the course of centuries. As far as the outside world had known, they had been his sisters. His mothers. His aunts. His grandmothers. But they had been his friends. His protectors. And now they were all gone. Carrion had lived in Zilvaren a long, long time, but he had *never* been without a Swift.

For the hurt the smuggler was enduring right now, I set aside my

irritation and took a calming breath. "Tell me, Elroy. How many promises have you made to Saeris and then broken?"

The human's eyelids shuttered. "None."

"Me either. And I plan on keeping it that way. Make no mistake. I
will burn worlds to keep my word to her, old man. There isn't a single
person in this realm or any other that I wouldn't sacrifice to make sure
I don't let her down. I promised her that I'd bring her brother home.
Will you test my resolve in this?"

A loud crash shook the air outside, followed by a piercing scream.
Elroy stared at me, the lines around his eyes tightening a fraction. I met
his scrutiny, unflinching. The old man looked away. "No. I don't suppose I will." Resignation colored his words. "But the boy should have a
say in the matter, don't you think? You say that you've made a promise
to bring him home . . . but *this* is the only home he's ever known."

Murder. Starvation. Oppression. Hate.

These were the foundations Zilvaren was built upon. It was no
wonder the footings of this city were incapable of holding itself up.
This place was no *home*. It was a cage. A death sentence. But the old
man was right. It *should* be the boy's choice.

Reluctantly, I dipped my head.

Three pairs of eyes turned to Hayden Fane.

Gods, he was nothing like her. Nothing like her at all. But when he
met our gazes and I saw the resolution in his eyes, the way his jaw set, I
saw the fleeting shadow of her there. A part of her I recognized. Something I could get behind. "It's okay, Elroy," he said. "I want to go."

Carrion explained everything.

I sat at the window, watching the people of Zilvaren slowly
disperse back to their homes. Hours passed, and I listened to Carrion's story take shape. Every once in a while, a unit of guardians
marched past the forge, armor clanking loudly, feet striking the sand

with purpose. It was rare that the guardians patrolled the Third in these numbers. Saeris had explained that many of them believed the lie Madra perpetuated—that the Third was a plague ward. Infected. It helped her cause if her own soldiers were afraid of the people here. An army wasn't as effective if it didn't hate its enemy.

Elroy paced the forge as he listened to Carrion speak. Occasionally, he worked the bellows, feeding oxygen to the fire that burned in the hearth. I saw Saeris's movements in him. The way he held his tools. The way he simply moved around the space. But they were *his* movements, I knew. He had been the one to teach Saeris how to work a forge, after all. He said nothing to interrupt Carrion. Not when he explained about the Fae. His transformation. The portals that enabled transport between this world and Yvelia. Hayden interrupted plenty, rapt, eyes the size of saucers. But not the old man. He took it all in stride.

When Carrion was finished, Elroy sat down heavily on a rickety stool that looked older than he was. The weight of the entire realm seemed to be pressing down on his shoulders. I left the window and faced him, arms folded across my chest.

"How do you know all about this?" I demanded.

The clues were all there.

He'd called me a Fae warrior.

He'd known they were *my* shadows, blotting out the suns.

He hadn't even blinked when Carrion had stormed into his forge, much taller than he'd been before, sporting pointed ears and the kind of teeth that could do some serious damage.

He had *known*.

Elroy looked up at me, the truth right there in his eyes. I was right. "Plenty of people still tell stories about before. When your kind still visited Zilvaren," he said.

I shot him a disappointed look. "No. That's not it. Try again."

Wearily, he shrugged, shaking his head. "Fine. You're right. I've known about the Fae my whole life." He nodded at Carrion. "I've always known about him, too."

"I'm sorry, *what?*" Carrion's voice was three octaves higher than normal. "You've always *known* about me? Always known about—" He threw his hands in the air, staring up at the ceiling. "Don't you think you should have mentioned that? Y'know, during any of the *hundreds* of interactions we've had over the years?"

"Why?" Elroy looked genuinely confused. "It wouldn't have changed anything. You would have still been an annoying, loud-mouthed smuggler with a penchant for stealing my glassware."

"Oh, I don't know. Maybe it would have been nice for me to talk to someone who knew who I really was? Maybe it would have been nice to—to—Oh, never mind. Forget it. You're right. It *wouldn't* have changed anything. *You'd* still have been a miserable git with no sense of humor!"

Elroy leaned his elbows on his thighs, hands clasped together. "You had *Gracia.*" He sounded exhausted.

"I did." Carrion nodded. "And she was enough. But one person out of millions? It would have been nice if that number had been two."

"Look, I'm sorry, okay. But I wasn't supposed to tell you I knew, anyway. There were rules I was supposed to keep, and—"

"What rules?" My body felt strange. Too hot. It could have been the fact that I was standing in a forge, in a realm that was already *unreasonably* fucking hot, but this felt different. I could feel my heart beating all over my body.

Elroy huffed, annoyance carved into the lines of his face, but he answered. "Don't tell anyone about the Fae. Don't talk to Carrion about the Fae. Don't tell anyone about any magic users I came across. Things like that."

"And who made you promise to observe these rules?"

"My father," he said. "And *his* father made *him* promise. I'm a forge master, warrior. The son of forge masters. The Swift family wasn't the *only* bloodline that was charged with a task they handed down through the generations. Gracia and her lot watched over the boy. Me and mine were given a different job to do."

I could hear it now, pounding in my ears.

Thrum.

Thrum.

Thrum.

I swallowed hard and spoke, my voice just a whisper. "Tell me."

Elroy grimaced, running his tongue over his teeth. Slapping his palms against his thighs, he got to his feet. "I think it's probably better if I just show you."

"I'm not offended, per se. Just a little ... *outraged.*"

Carrion hadn't stopped grousing since the glassmaker had yanked back the rug that covered the wall and revealed a secret door. The tiniest scrap of magic, cleverly woven, was all that hid the door. When Elroy had pricked his finger and daubed a small amount of his blood against the wall, the heavy blocks of sandstone had moved back, filling the forge with a grinding sound that had set my teeth on edge.

Elroy had grabbed a torch and descended the stairs first, followed by Hayden. Carrion had followed behind me, which meant that I was the one who had to listen to his string of complaints.

"Centuries. *Centuries!* There were Fae plans underway here for years, taking place right beneath my nose, and no one thought to tell *me*, the only member of the Fae in Zilvaren?"

"Your friend says they had their reasons," I muttered over my shoulder. "So they must have had their reasons." I didn't know if that was true—humans lied all the time, sometimes for no good reason whatsoever. Elroy could have been making all of this up for all we knew, but he had no discernible reason to lie. None that *I* could see, anyway.

The stairs went on forever. Down, down, down ...

The walls weren't made of sandstone here. They were granite. Smooth, cool, and hard. The kind of stone that could withstand the test of time *and* a shifting sea of sand. Wherever Elroy was leading us, he did so in silence, the back of his head and his shaggy shoulder-length gray hair the only part of him I could see over Hayden's shoulder. I could feel the tension pouring off him, though—felt it strongly enough that I confused it with my own.

"How much farther?" Hayden asked softly. He'd intended the question for Elroy's ears alone, but the boy didn't know anything of Fae hearing yet. He sounded nervous.

"Another two hundred steps or so," Elroy answered.

"How many *are* there?"

"Twelve hundred and twenty-three." Elroy's whisper echoed off the walls.

Eventually, we reached the bottom of the stairs. The space ahead was vast and cloaked in darkness. When I saw what lay before us, I felt like I'd been kicked square in the chest by a horse.

"Gods and sinners..." I gaped at the sight.

"What? What is it?" Hayden hissed.

"Our way out of this mess," Carrion answered breathlessly. His mouth hung open, his eyes roving over the pillars that held up the arched ceiling, and the stacks of discarded pieces of armor, and the coins, and the chalices, and trunks overflowing with all manner of metal goods. Finally, his eyes went to the huge, recessed pool at the center of the cavern...

A spark of light bloomed on the other side of the cavern. The flicker was just a small orange-golden glow at first. Soon, there were two sparks of light, then three. Elroy skirted the perimeter of the space, lighting torches as he went. I'd been so distracted by the contents of his secret trove that I hadn't even noticed him leaving us. By the time he had lit half the torches in their sconces and returned to us, the cavern was suffused with a dim light strong enough to see by.

Hayden was wild-eyed as he stepped toward the giant pool.

It was the first of its kind I had seen: recessed so that its steps led down to the still, solid surface of the pool below.

You came, you came. Came. You came... The sound flooded my ears.

It was loud again. Many voices. Scores of them, all speaking at once. I hadn't heard the voices this loud since Iseabail and Te Léna had begun working together to heal me.

Join us. Come, come, come...

Hayden cocked his head, squinting at the surface of the mirrored metal that slept at the bottom of the pool. "What *is* that?" he asked.

Elroy grunted, gruffly clearing his throat. "That, my boy, is a *dangerous* amount of quicksilver."

26

IN THE END

SAERIS

YOU CAME, YOU came. Came. You came…

The words slammed around inside my skull.

Came. Came. You came…

Ammontraíeth stopped and fell to its knees as I'd sprinted through its halls, making my way down into the bowels of the palace, to the tomb that housed the Blood Court's quicksilver. The sharp, cold eyes of scores of high bloods had followed me as I'd run.

The crypt was just as Kingfisher, Carrion, Lorreth, and I had left it. Our footprints still marked the thick layer of dust on the ground. The lintel around the pool was still damaged, the stone shattered around the lip. A long, jagged crack shaped like a lightning bolt in the obsidian forked off toward the door. I'd said goodbye to Fisher here. He'd kissed me and held me, and I'd felt safe.

I didn't feel safe anymore. I felt like I was about to explode. My nerve endings screamed as I ran to the pool and—and—

Fuck! What was I supposed to *do*?

You came. You came. Came…

The words boomed around the tomb. Hollow. Singular. They sank into my bones, reverberating, calling to me.

Join us. Come to us. Join us. We will help…

I'd dropped the relic back in the forge. The last time I'd gone into the quicksilver, I hadn't had a relic. The gods had pulled me through. It had been instantaneous: One second, Fisher had been carrying me in his arms. The next, I'd woken up in that field of tall grass with two gods giggling over me. Fisher thought my Alchemist's blood prevented the quicksilver from affecting me the way it had affected him once, but was it true? If I stepped into this quicksilver now, would it drive me crazy? Would it just *kill* me?

Come. Come to us. Join us…

Or was entering this pool now the only thing that would save me? Was this the key to my magic? Was this something I *had* to do to bond with the quicksilver? To show it that I *trusted* it?

No time to decide.

I had to *do* something. The light from my runes lit the tomb so brightly that the glow hurt my eyes. It was building, straining, probing, mounting—more power than I could comprehend. It wanted out, to be free, and *I* didn't want to fucking die.

I had no choice.

Yes. Yes, come to us. The quicksilver's voice was hypnotic.

The room spun as I closed my eyes and let my power in.

The void that fell over me ate me whole.

No light.

No up.

No down.

This was immortality; looking it in the eye felt like staring into a black hole.

Fear ran ice-cold fingers through my mind, paralyzing me.

Breathe, Saeris. Do not *give in to it.*

Fear would be my undoing. I would cede no ground to it.

I retreated into myself, searching for that which was already a part of me. This tide of magic scared me. Whenever I'd sensed it before, raging just below the surface of my consciousness, I'd shied away, afraid of its immenseness. I had worried that I wouldn't be able to find my way back to the surface again if I allowed the power to swallow me—and I was *still* afraid of that. But the storm wasn't going to abate this time. It was growing by the second.

I dove into the stream of my power and was immediately swept away. Oh gods, it was too much. It was—

Pulling.

Pushing.

Tugging.

Screaming.

Spinning.

Swimming.

Sinking…

Drowning…

Breathe, Saeris. Breathe, *or it's all* over.

I gasped for a deep breath, forcing the air into my lungs.

This isn't something to be afraid of.

This is a part of you.

A part of yourself that you hadn't gotten to know yet.

You can *do this.*

When you had no one else to lean on, you relied on yourself. When no one rode to the rescue and saved you and Hayden from dying of thirst, you saved yourself.

Save yourself now, Saeris.

You've got this.

I stopped fighting it. Magic zipped along my nerve endings, and there it was, like a tangible, pliable thing at the ends of my fingertips: raw, divine energy. Opening my eyes, I expected to see it there, visible to the naked eye, but my fingers looked normal. My shield flared with blue-white energy as I reached for the quicksilver and summoned it.

It was as easy as breathing.

I decided that the portal was open, and suddenly it was. The difference was astonishing. It felt *right*. But I couldn't afford to celebrate just yet. I was only halfway through the process.

Gods, I was going to look pretty stupid if I didn't make it through this. My mate had suffered horribly because of the quicksilver. It had come damned close to destroying his mind on countless occasions, and I'd been on hand to witness that. But Kingfisher wasn't an Alchemist.

I stepped into the pool before I could second-guess myself.

The molten metal felt like ice around my ankles. Cold cut through my boots, through my pants, pain racing up my legs. The pool churned violently, sloshing and bubbling like water boiling over in a pot. It happened quickly. Unexpectedly. Every part of me screamed that I should get out. That I should run. That this was the biggest fucking mistake I had ever made. The quicksilver formed rivulets, like the tributaries of a river, and began to rise. The sight of it climbing my body transported me back to the Hall of Mirrors. Captain Harron had just run me through with his sword. I had melted his dagger. It had snaked up his body like this, probing, seeking, looking for a way in.

"Saeris? Saeris! Call it off! You don't—you don't understand—"

He'd begged me for his life. He had been terrified of what the quicksilver would do to him, and rightly so; it had driven him mad.

I can do this.

It had reached my waist now. The cold leached through my shirt as it climbed higher. Clenching my hands into fists, I closed my eyes and braced.

I can *do this.*

Half-breed. Who are you to be blessed by us?

The quicksilver was on my skin now. My arms. My neck. It was inside my *head.* It was everywhere—an alien, agile presence. It didn't sound as fractured as it usually did. This was a primeval power, older than the universe itself, and all its attention was focused on me.

I am an Alchemist. I didn't dare speak out loud. I was too worried that the words would turn into a scream, so I spoke them internally instead.

You are a pretender, the voice accused.

My name is Saeris Fane—

Your name is ruination, the voice snorted. *Blight. Curse worker. You do not deserve to live.*

I do!

There are others more worthy.

None of them *stand before you now!* It roiled in my chest: the anger of a lifetime, condensing into one white-hot point. I had been told every single day in Zilvaren that I was worthless, that my life meant nothing, that I didn't deserve to live. Madra's disdain for my people ran so deep that even the residents of the Third had started to believe that they didn't matter.

Well, I wouldn't believe that. Not. Any. More. "*I* stand before you." I spoke out loud this time, no longer afraid. "I *am* worthy."

Only the unworthy seek power.

"I don't seek power! I didn't *ask* for this. I seek peace! For my friends and my people to be safe."

And you would employ your power to achieve that end? There was something sly in the speaker's tone. I couldn't think of it as the quicksilver. It was something *more* than sentient portal magic...and it was trying to trick me.

My mind raced. "I wouldn't employ it for anything. It...isn't a weapon. It's just a part of me."

Foolish child. Power is always a weapon. Wield it, or it wields you.

Pain exploded behind my eyes. The quicksilver was in my mouth, pouring down my throat. It was slipping into my ears. *I don't know what you want from me! I don't know what you need—*

Wield it! the speaker snapped. *A dark horizon looms. What will you do to prevent it?*

Anything!

You would die?

Yes!

You would kill?

Yes!

You would give up that which is most dear to you?

I opened my mouth...and nothing came out. I tried to form the word, but I couldn't. "No. I can't," I said. "I won't sacrifice *him*."

The tomb stilled. The quicksilver fell silent, and a fresh wave of alarm rushed over me. It was over, then. This was a test, and I had failed. I could feel the quicksilver's claws invading my mind, sinking deep, sharp and cruel.

Good, the speaker purred.

Good. Wait, *good?* Had it really just said that? "I don't…understand…"

Every Alchemist must have something they are afraid to lose.

The cold coating my bones with ice began to retreat. Slowly, the pain piercing my mind faded, the tomb coming back into focus. I was crying. When I brushed my tears away, my fingers came away coated in silver.

This pathway is clear, the speaker declared. *Receive this gift all in fear and trembling. In the end, it will be your end.*

I flew backward, out of the pool.

My back hit the wall with a bone-crunching crack…

…and everything went black.

27

WHAT'S DONE IS DONE

KINGFISHER

"WE'RE METALWORKERS. WHO else was going to do it?"

I prowled around the quicksilver pool, not fully understanding what I was seeing. It didn't make sense. "This is the largest quicksilver pool I've ever seen. This amount of quicksilver in one place is *unheard* of."

This information didn't seem to impress Elroy. "Really? Huh. We've been adding to it for years. Every time a piece of metal laced with quicksilver came across the threshold of our forge, we refined it. Pulled it out of the weapon or piece of jewelry and set it aside. Until recently, this was all just individual pieces of metal. Separate. But when Saeris was taken, the metal turned to liquid. That's when it fused together and became this." He gestured to the massive body of quicksilver. "I knew Saeris had something to do with it. The girl never could resist touching weapons that didn't belong to her. I figured she'd pulled the sword, and—"

"You *knew* about the sword?"

"Well, naturally." He seemed baffled by the question. "Solace. The sword that kept the doorways closed. The Fae sword. I've never seen it in person, of course. But there were drawings, when I was a boy."

"Where are they, these drawings? I need to see them."

"Gone," Elroy said. "Burned up in a fire when I was about fifteen. My father was fond of an afternoon whiskey or five. It was the only thing that helped with the voices. He fell asleep one afternoon and the hearth raged out of control. Gutted the ground floor of the forge. The smoke nearly killed him."

"So there's nothing? No documents? No...no *books*?"

The glassmaker shook his head. "Nothing. What few papers did remain after the fire, I burned myself five years ago."

"What? *Why?*" The question was poised on my lips, but it exploded out of Carrion's mouth. "What possible reason could have driven you to do *that*?"

"I did it for *Saeris*," Elroy said, his tone hard and cold. "Her power was greater than she knew, and she was terrible at hiding it. The air in the forge would prickle the moment she walked in the door. Even when she was a child, the fucking tools would rattle on the walls when she walked by." He scowled at Carrion. "You were blind not to have noticed it."

"Hey, *I* had no experience with magic. I felt something, I guess, but I just thought she was hot." He winced in my direction, making a face. "Sorry."

An angry rumble filled the cavern, but it didn't come from me. Hayden looked like he was about to start pummeling Swift's face with his fists.

"All right. Okay, everyone, let's just forget I said that, shall we?"

Elroy huffed, continuing. "I took her as my apprentice so I could keep an eye on her. But when her mother died—" He dropped his head, swallowing, eyes on his dusty boots. "When her mother died, she and the boy had no one. The energy that followed her around was getting stronger, and I couldn't have her here all the time. It killed me to force her out on the street, but she was safer there. If one of the guardians had walked into the forge and felt how strange it was in there when she was around, they would have taken her away.

"I couldn't risk having those papers here anymore. Not when they could damn her and the rest of us along with her, too. So yes, I tossed them into the fire. That's when I stopped refining the quicksilver, too. Working that demon metal leads to madness and death. I saw what it did to my father. I didn't see what it did to my grandfather, but my old man did, and from what he told me, it wasn't pretty. I accepted my fate a long time ago. I didn't mind protecting this secret when it was just me, even if it did kill me. But Saeris needed *someone*, and I wasn't going to abandon her."

What had been in those papers that they could have damned Saeris? I was beginning to suspect I knew the answer to that question, but I didn't know how to approach it in my mind. I sat on the edge of the pool, working through it, trying to decide how I felt.

"What's done is done," Carrion said behind me. "At least this means we don't need to go back to the palace now."

I splayed my fingers wide, holding my hand palm-down an inch above the surface of the quicksilver. Gods, I hated it. But I loved it, too. I had to. It had given me Saeris. Without the quicksilver, we would have lived out our lives in separate realms, never having known each other. Sometimes, it was as though it connected us. The remaining quicksilver in my eye was far more active when she was around. When she wasn't, it echoed her mood somehow. It was hard to explain. Even now, it was as if I could feel her, just inches away...

"What do you mean?" I asked, in response to Carrion's statement.

"Hm?"

"Why wouldn't we need to go back to the palace?"

Carrion laughed. "I think that's fairly obvious, don't you? When Saeris awakens the quicksilver, all the pools will awaken, not just the one in the palace. *This* pool will awaken. We won't have to try to sneak back into the palace, past the guardians. I, for one, am deeply grateful that we won't need to fight our way back into the Hall of Mirrors. That was an absolute..."

There were many parts of the plan I had neglected to share with Carrion. He chattered away, the relief thick in his voice, unaware that he still wasn't in possession of the whole picture. It *would* have been tricky to get all three of us back into the palace. I would have figured it out, though. Now, he and Hayden could travel through this pool back to Yvelia. I would use the pool at the palace. *After* I'd figured out if—and *how*—Madra was sending the infected feeders from Zilvaren. After I had killed the immortal queen and balanced the scales of justice. I started to explain. "I can't go with you. When you head through, tell—"

The pool *exploded.*

Quicksilver erupted, instantly liquid. It splattered up my arm, hitting me in the chest.

I leaped up, vaulting away, immediately drawing a replica of Nimerelle from the well of my magic.

"What the *fuck!*" Hayden fell on his ass in his haste to retreat. "What's happening?"

"Nothing good," Elroy gritted out. "Stand back. Don't let it touch your skin."

"Wasn't planning on it."

"Here. Catch." I hadn't given Hayden the ring Saeris had made for him. I hadn't thought I'd needed to yet. I tossed it to him, and the boy caught it out of the air. "Put that on and do *not* take it off.

The quicksilver churned, bubbling in a way I hadn't seen it behave before.

"Careful. Look," Carrion said, gesturing to my chest. Quicksilver ran down my chest plate and dripped from my fingers. It was inert. Harmless, thanks to the relic that hung around my neck protecting me. But I couldn't hear it. I could *always* hear it. Even the fragment that remained within me was silent, as the quicksilver that had landed on me pooled and left me, venturing across the stone floor, heading back to the pool.

"Did I lose track of time? The pool wasn't supposed to be open for another twelve hours at least. Right?" Carrion said.

"Right."

"Then what's *this* about?"

"I don't know. But Saeris must have opened it. She's the only Alchemist that we know of."

"That we know of," Carrion repeated, stressing each word. "What if there are others? What if—"

"Quiet a second. I'm thinking." Carrion was right. There was a chance there was another Alchemist out there. Highly unlikely, but it *was* possible. More likely was the probability that Saeris had woken the quicksilver for a reason...and I could think of no *good* reason she would do that. It would be a last resort...which meant that there was a chance she was in danger.

The pool was still open. *For now.* It could close at any second.

"I'm going in." There was no two ways about it. I was already striding back toward the pool.

"Wait a second. Shouldn't we think this through? I mean, that could lead anywhere," Carrion said.

"It goes where you want to go, remember. No matter *who* opened it, it'll take me to Saeris. I'll come back for you if it's safe."

"No! Fisher, if you're going, I'm coming, too. I'm not waiting here, not knowing what the hell's going on."

"Me, too." Hayden didn't sound as confident as Carrion, but he approached the pool along with him. "If there's a chance Saeris is in danger, I'm not waiting here. I let her down last time I saw her. I won't do it again."

Gods, they were infuriating. I didn't have time to argue with them, though. "So be it. Looks like this is where we leave you, forge master," I said.

Elroy scratched his beard. "Oh, I'm sure I'll be hearing from you soon enough."

He was right about that. I would be back. I still had a queen to kill.

"Think of Saeris," I told the smuggler and the human, and then I stepped into the quicksilver.

28

SENESCHAL

SAERIS

MY EARS WERE ringing.

The air was full of dust.

I opened my mouth wide, working it side to side, unsure of why it was hurting so badly. My throat was raw. Fuck, the back of my head was hurting, too. Why was I on the ground? And where—

The quicksilver was awake.

Holy *fucking* gods.

I jumped up, my back screaming, hip thrumming with pain. Broken chunks of stone cut into my bare feet, but I hobbled forward, reaching for my power, unthinking. I *had* to get it closed. Worry sang through me—a plucked string, vibrating in my chest. How long had it been open? It felt like only moments. I had been in the pool, and then I'd hit the wall.

I—

Oh, gods. Something was coming through. The quicksilver reacted quickly when I called it now, quietly, but I was asking it to do something that it could not do. The gate couldn't close while someone was traveling through it. No one had ever told me that. I just *knew* it now.

I had to wait.

The crown of a dark head of hair appeared first.

Black waves.

Pale skin.

My panic began to subside.

But then...

I knew the face.

I had seen it only once before, but it had stayed with me. The male had barely spoken to me, but I recalled his words all too well. *"Do you not bow before a king, creature?"*

I couldn't remember his name. He had sat next to Belikon up on the dais, outraged that I had not shown the proper deference to his master. What had Belikon called him? Orith? Arriash?

The male was tall and rail thin, his nose crooked, his chin square and jutting. With his skin crinkled like old, thin paper and lank black strands of hair falling into his face, he didn't project a sense of health. In fact, he looked pretty damned unwell.

"Ah. Saeris Fane." He clicked blackened teeth together. "Thank you for so graciously leaving the door open for us. We've been waiting for an invitation into Ammontraíeth for a very long time. You may remember me. My name is Orious. I am seneschal to the king."

A thick chain hung around his neck, a golden orb dangling from it. The male clutched it tightly, his bony fingers clamped around it as if worried someone would try to steal it from him.

"What the hell is a seneschal?" I asked.

The male, Orious, shuttled the orb along his chain thoughtfully. "I am an advisor. My remit is broad. I attend to matters on behalf of the king that are... *beneath* him."

The implication was clear: Whatever had brought this anemic-looking fucker through the quicksilver today wasn't important enough to bring Belikon here himself. *I* wasn't important enough. I nodded to myself. "Ahhh, right. Where I come from, we call those *bootlickers*."

"Watch your tongue, girl. You'll wish you'd made a friend of me soon enough."

"I prefer my friends a little less creepy. You're not welcome here, Orious," I said. "Go back the way you came."

The male tittered softly, sweeping a greasy lock of hair behind one ear as he stepped out of the pool and onto the cracked marble floor. "I don't think that's on the agenda, I'm afraid. You see, *my* friends and I have always wanted to travel." His voice took on a tight, sinister edge. "And my master bid me come *treat* with you."

He sprang from the edge of the pool, arms spread wide, like some kind of pouncing would-be predator. Behind him, rising from the quicksilver, came two more figures, then three more: Fae guards dressed in green velvet, with arrows nocked in their bows. Their eyes were sharp, pupils dilated wide, leaving no room for their irises.

"This is Blood Court land. Belikon has no sovereignty here. I reign over this—"

"Stop." Orious gave a bored flick of his wrist. "Don't bore me with such ridiculousness. You're naught but an inexperienced little girl, trapped in a prison of her own making. You don't want to be here. The high bloods don't want you here. It would benefit you to listen and take heed when I speak. My liege has sent me here with an offer for you."

He spoke with confidence but didn't come any closer. The guards behind him stood in a line, their arrows pointed at my head.

"I'm not interested in offers from Belikon De Barra."

"*King* Belikon," Orious barked, "has graciously sent me here with terms. Personally, it makes no difference to me if you hear them. It's no skin off *my* nose. But you may regret not listening to the generous offer he bid me present to you very soon."

"What could I *possibly* need from him?"

"Sanasroth is a barren wasteland. This court you have declared your own is comprised of genteel high bloods who like to throw parties and sip blood out of jeweled chalices. But watch how quickly their manners fail them when their food supply is cut off, *Your Highness*. See how fast they devolve into the monsters the second the blood runs out. Are you prepared to deal with the aftermath of that scenario? Hm?"

Had Belikon kept Malcolm's court fed under his reign? Fisher hadn't said anything about that before. Neither had Renfis. It didn't seem likely, but the cruel light in this male's eyes said otherwise. "I'm sure you've noticed by now," he said, "but a strange canker spreads across the South Lands. Black rot swallows the vegetation. It affects the wild-life here in the most shocking way. Deer, wolves, bears. It infects them quickly. Death is unavoidable, it seems. It's too late for these lands...but my master would provide shelter and protection from the spread of this vile disease. He offers safe harbor at the Winter Palace for you, in exchange for a *small* number of concessions on your end."

"Let me guess. He has a vacancy for an Alchemist and thinks I'd make a fine addition to his court?" The words, my tone: Everything about what I'd just said left a sour taste in my mouth.

Orious smirked, his lips thinning. "Fine. Yes, a fine addition indeed. Your services would be a small part of the payment required to ensure your safety. And you *would* be the jewel in his crown, so to speak. You would be showered with fine clothes. Fine food. Fine wines—"

"What else?" I demanded, cutting him off. "What else does he seek in exchange for a safety he *cannot* provide?"

Behind the intruder, a bowstring creaked, and one of the Winter Palace guards swallowed thickly. In his loose black robes, Orious smiled. "My king wishes his beloved daughter returned to him. He misses her dearly. It wounds his heart to know she is unwell and far from his loving care."

"And?"

"Kingfisher. In shackles. A public execu—"

I drew Solace. The air hummed with crackling power as I unleashed her naked steel. The stranger stopped talking, tapping his index finger impatiently against his thumb pad.

"There are other things, of course. Smaller, inconsequential acts, each of them a show of good faith. In light of your recent transition, you are now half Fae, and would be required to swear an oath before the Firinn Stone—"

"I will not be a tool for that bastard to use whenever he sees fit," I seethed. It was laughable—the fact that he had come here with such an outrageous list of demands. Had Belikon really thought I would agree to *any* of this? "I will not be swearing any oaths. And no one will be harming a single fucking *hair* on my mate's head. My friends and I—"

"Your friends? Oh, yes, that's right." The bastard laughed, stepping closer. "Your friends. Let's see, shall we? Renfis of the Orrithian? An oath-sworn general in King Belikon's army. Lorreth of the Broken Spire? Also an oath-sworn soldier in my master's army. Your darling mate..." The smirk twisted his features, turning him into something evil. *"Oath sworn,"* he whispered. "My master will have them all. They are his to do with as he wishes. But you..." He extended a long, crooked finger toward me. "Reject my master's generous offer, and *you* will die here in this room."

Oath sworn.

The fucking Firinn Stone. Lorreth had told me all about it once—how they knelt before it when they came of age and pledged to be bound by their word on pain of death for the rest of their lives. For *honor's* sake. This bastard was right: Every single member of the Fae who fought and defended the banks of the Darn at Irrín had pledged to serve the Winter Palace—to serve *Belikon*—my friends and my mate included.

We were so fucked.

But an oath was like a bargain. There were loopholes. Language to be manipulated. There *had* to be a way out of the pledge of fealty they had made. For now, I raised Solace, feeling the air grow heavy around the blade as I held it aloft.

"The king also requires the return of that sword," Orious added. "Your obsidian palace is full of rats, Saeris. They whisper in the dark. They tell tales of how the new queen of the Blood Court cannot wield her weapon. Of how Saeris Fane cannot contain her power. Runes unsealed and—"

I twisted the sword and showed the fucker the flat of the blade. Coincidentally, the movement also showed him the back of my hand. Which was still covered in a mass of runes, yes... but now, at the center of my shield, a single, bold, circular rune bisected with an arrow-like shape glowed brilliant blue.

The smug smile died on Orious's lips. "Fuck," he whispered.

"Yeah. *Fuck.*"

I'd planned to reforge Solace into something more manageable, but I hadn't yet had the time. That no longer mattered. I didn't need a forge anymore. Would never need one again. A door had unlocked within me. Behind it, a vast knowledge waited there for me. It belonged to me, as I now belonged to the quicksilver. I only had to think now, and the fabric of reality shifted.

Placing both hands around Solace's hilt, I imagined the sword becoming two. When I drew my hands apart, I knew that the god sword would be reformed, brand new, brilliant and shining. And so it was.

The short swords were beautiful. Old Fae ran along the edges of both honed blades, engraved in winding script. I still couldn't read the language. A message from the gods, maybe. I would decipher them later . . . *if* I lived through the next twenty minutes.

"Come now, child. An affiliation with the Winter Palace *could* be beneficial to you." Orious's eyes were twice the size they'd been moments ago. "My king is benevolent."

"Tell me something, Orious. Did *you* swear an oath before the Firinn Stone?"

The truth flickered the seneschal's eyes before the lie could reach his lips. "Naturally," he said. "You can trust *me* to honor my word."

I just laughed.

The earnest look on his face faltered. "All right, then. Have it your way. *Kill her.*"

The soldiers streamed past Orious toward me, bows raised. They loosed their arrows, but an Alchemist couldn't *only* manipulate quicksilver. I was an element worker. *All* metals were at my command. The pointed iron came for me, and I pushed with my mind, gently, as if nudging a leaf floating on top of flowing water. The arrows weren't even halfway across the room before they changed direction, all five snapping upward and embedding into the ceiling. Their shafts juddered from their impact, their fletching quivering.

The soldiers hesitated. They looked up at the ceiling, and then back down at me. All at once, they reached for new arrows.

"I wouldn't bother," I told them. "The next ones will be coming back at you."

"For the love of the gods, use your knives!" Orious snarled. "Hold on to them tight."

The archers discarded their bows, drawing steel from scabbards. Their knives were made from alloys, I sensed. There was a strangeness to them. I could close my will around them, but only just. They barely moved when I tried to shove them with my mind.

"The Winter Palace remembers," Orious said, shaking his head. "That's right. Your kind were dangerous. No power that vast should have ever been gifted to one group of people. My king discovered how to limit your magic a long time ago. Our traditions have lasted far longer than your kind did. Every soldier in the king's army is equipped with a null blade on the day they complete their training. Good luck fending off five of *those*, Alchemist."

Null blade. The term was unknown to me. Fisher hadn't ever used that term. Nor had Renfis or Lorreth.

As Belikon's men approached, each armed with a dagger, that sense of strangeness hit me again. Unnatural. Their weapons bore simple handles, their blades straight and unembellished. They were unremarkable in every way. And yet...

I saw them in a new manner. A second sight that seemed to overlap reality. The air shivered and distorted around the blades, as if it were being pulled *into* them. The closer the guards came, the more my skin crawled.

The short swords blazed in my hands, humming with energy. Solace's magic had returned to it back in Gillethrye. It had flared to life when Malcolm had attacked me, but it had lain dormant ever since. I hadn't called on it. There had been no need. And in truth, I'd been too scared to try. The quicksilver had granted Avisiéth magic because it had judged Lorreth's blood and found him worthy. I wasn't the girl I had been back in the maze. I was different now. Changed. The idea that Solace would recoil from the person I was now had been enough to keep me from trying. But as I drew the newly formed short swords, Solace's magic surged down the lengths of metal, buzzing up my arms like lightning.

Not Solace's power, halved to accommodate the new split weapons. This was *twice* the power, and it was electrifying.

The first male came for me. He was light on his feet. Limber. He swung at me with his dagger, and I blocked upward, easily deflecting the blow. The shock of his weapon, clashing with my short sword, rocked me, though—a wave of nausea that made me suck in a sharp breath.

Unpleasant.

Very fucking unpleasant. But not enough to distract me from the task at hand. He was already twisting, finding new footing, coming at me from a different approach. Two more of the males came, lunging for me, their metal gleaming. With a monumental force of will, I shoved the first male's dagger away with my mind, managing only to avert it at the last second. The male stumbled forward, balance lost as his weapon suddenly jerked to the side—and I met his friends in a flurry of steel and gritted teeth.

The forms Lorreth had drilled with me flowed, making sense at last, second nature... but they weren't enough. A fourth male joined in the fight, the fifth hot on his heels.

The sounds of scraping metal thundered in the air.

Fire lashed around the top of my right arm. One of them landed a hit on me, their blade slashing through my shirt. Heat spilled down my arm, the copper-bright smell of blood exploding in the back of my nose.

Footwork, Saeris. Footwork. Concentrate. Lorreth's voice was stern in the back of my mind.

I had been training only with him, though. One male. I was trying to fend off five now.

I could almost hear him laughing as I spun and dropped low, striking up and sinking my right short sword into one of the male's chests. *Come on, Fane. You're selling both of us short. You don't think I'm worth five of these fuckers?*

The guard gasped. I yanked my weapon back without assessing the damage and immediately blocked up, parrying another null blade.

A thud to my left.

I slashed at another of the male's ankle tendons.

Spun away.

Blocked.

Mentally shoved another blade away with everything I had.

Blocked.

Blocked.

Retreated.

One of them—the one I'd stabbed in the chest—was on the floor, dead.

Only four of them now.

Ha! *Only* four of them.

I danced back on the balls of my feet—that's what this was now, a dance—letting them come for me. They prowled forward, eyes blank, faces emotionless.

Don't panic. You've got this. Preempt them. You know *where they're going to be, Saeris.*

"Last chance," Orious called. "There's still time to change your mind. The *king* won't extend another opportunity."

My canines felt long in my mouth. I was bleeding from my leg somewhere; I could smell it. Setting my jaw, I ran the edges of the short swords together, and burning blue-white sparks leaped from the metal. "I *gave* you my answer," I snarled. "Let's get this over with."

The guards didn't wait for Orious's command. They charged.

Sharpened steel rained down on me.

I gulped down air, forcing myself to breathe. One at a time, faster than fast, I rebuffed the males, pushing their weapons away with my mind as best I could, or else meeting them with my own.

One of them broke through my guard. Fire tore up my side, pain igniting fury in me as I went after the bastard who had cut me. I scythed my right god sword at him, the weapon trailing blue-white light behind it, and slit the male's throat wide open. Blood spurted from the clean slash I left behind, and down the male went.

Three left now.

My breath sawed out of me. I'd never moved this fast in my entire fucking life.

One of them kicked, aiming to blow my knee out, but I darted closer to him, hooking my elbow and smashing it into his face. He staggered back—

—and the other two were in my face.

"Fuck!"

I ducked and spun through them, scissoring my swords, spinning them in my hands. One found its mark, biting through the guard on the right's arm. The other guard lunged sideways. I followed him, blocking his downward blow, driving upward into his gut—

"Saeris!"

My heart stilled.

I didn't dare look for him.

I could feel him, though.

Suddenly, the tomb was wreathed in bands of glittering black sand.

Kingfisher.

Kingfisher.

Kingfisher.

His name had replaced my heartbeat.

A black rope lashed around the closest male's throat, and suddenly his head was no longer attached to his body. Blood sprayed everywhere as his body lifted into the air and was hurled away as if it weighed nothing.

And there he was.

My mate's hair was wild. His eyes locked onto mine, simmering with rage.

Say something, he said into my mind.

"I'm okay," I panted.

Do you need me?

I dodged a blow from the male on the right—I'd broken his nose with that elbow—and pivoted, kicking out at the other male hard. The sole of my boot slammed into his rib cage. Staggering sideways, he righted himself and came again, but I was ready.

My short swords blazed light, power singing like lightning through my veins.

No. I was firm. *I've got this.*

"Don't! Don't you dare!" Orious was screaming somewhere.

The tomb walls blurred as I moved, ducking, lunging, spinning on the balls of my feet.

Another shout echoed around the small space—a yell of anger—but I stayed focused on what was in front of me. My power was building, flowing, rising inside me. My runes didn't burn this time. They pulsed hard, my magic begging to be set free.

Without thinking, I slammed my short swords together, and suddenly they were one again, Solace humming with energy in my left hand. I thrust my right hand up, out in front of me, and—

"Holy *fuck*!" Carrion's shout bounced around the tomb.

He was there, on the other side of the tomb. His face was bathed in blue as a giant icon formed in the air in front of me, projecting from my hand. It was my shield! The interlocking runes were an *exact* copy of the sigil on the back of my hand. Most of the icons' lines were dull, apart from one rune: a circle bisecting a cross with a line cutting through it at the top. It *blazed* with magic, hovering there...waiting.

I spread my fingers and twisted my hand, noting how the veins at my wrist were strangely silvered beneath my skin, and the quicksilver rune turned in the air like a key turning into a lock. It snapped into place, and a wall of energy detonated out from it, hurling the two remaining guards across the tomb.

They hit the ceiling, their necks snapping instantly. A second later, they dropped to the floor again, lifeless.

Deafening silence blanketed the tomb. I held my breath, frozen in place, eyes wide. I didn't dare move. Energy crackled from the shield, tiny filaments snapping from it as it held its position six feet off the floor.

I finally let out a shaky breath that fogged in the air, and clenched my hand closed. And just like that, the glowing shield blinked out of existence, as if it had never been there at all.

"Well, fuck *me*," Carrion said. "Looks like a lot's changed *here* in the past few days."

Look at me, Osha.

Fisher was at the base of the pool. He stood over Orious's prone figure, his shadows pinning Belikon's seneschal to the ground. *You're okay,* he said softly, the words shared with me alone. *You're safe. Shake it off.*

I was still in a defensive stance. Every muscle in my body was rigid, ready for another attack. "You're here? You're really here?" Gods, my voice sounded so small. Slowly, Fisher nodded, and the tension rushed from my body. He was real. He was here. Everything was okay.

I'm going to get you out of here in two minutes, he told me. *But I need you to be here a little longer first. Is that okay? Can you do that?*

I nodded.

Good girl. Come here, then. Stand with me.

I went to him.

Orious had no magic of his own. I felt the hungry void in him, pulsing with jealousy. Fisher's shadows cinched tighter, closing around the male's throat, chest, hips, ankles, wrists. He squirmed fruitlessly, hissing up at us. "You'll die...for what you've...just done," he wheezed.

"Really?" I was too hot. I felt strange. "'Cause you said I was about to die just now, and..." I swallowed breathlessly. "*That* didn't seem to go the way you thought it would."

"Stupid bitch! You have no idea—" He gurgled, his airway shutting off.

Fisher dropped down, crouching next to the male. "Torture isn't in my nature normally." Oh so calm. Oh so dangerous. Gods alive, he was going to kill him. "But for *you*, Orious? For what you've done here today? I think I'll make the exception."

"Fisher, no."

My mate looked up at me, his dark hair wavy and wild. The quicksilver in his eye was *rioting*. His expression was blank, but I knew him now: He was going out of his mind with anger and worry. The bridge of his nose was red. There were grains of sand buried into the seams of his leathers. He smelled of mint and pine as he always did, but also of the desert, and of the reckoning heat, and of a place I never thought for one moment I could ever miss.

He was so fucking beautiful, it destroyed me. I cupped his cheek with my hand, his stubble rough against my palm.

"We need to send him back," I whispered. "Belikon needs to know what I'm now capable of. That he will never bend us to his will. All of this and more."

Fisher didn't blink. "Does he need his *fingers* to impart that message?"

I laughed shakily, rubbing my thumb along his jawline. "Send him back. We aren't like them."

He looked like he wanted to argue, but then his shoulders sagged. Reluctantly, he got to his feet. "You are the *only* thing that keeps my moral compass pointing north, Little Osha," he rumbled.

His fingers brushed mine, the tip of his index finger hooking around my own, as he walked around Orious's pinned body. "You should be grateful. I wouldn't have shown such strength of character," he said to the seneschal. "But Saeris—"

"She is weak!" Orious's eyes rolled to find me. He would have spat, I think, but Fisher's shadows still had him by the throat. "You are all weak," he wheezed. "That is why you won't win this fight. You will crawl on your hands and knees, begging for mercy before my king, and I shall watch and revel in the indignity you suffer before you die."

I could prevent Fisher from severing the bastard's fingers, but I couldn't stem his anger in the shadow of this proclamation. He grabbed Orious by the front of his loose-fitting robe and yanked him up, spinning him around and throwing him back down again so that he landed on his front. "You are the only one who'll be crawling, worm. Drag yourself. On your stomach. Go on. Go back to Belikon and tell him what happened here. And tell him what will happen if he dares try to come here again uninvited, won't you."

"You might as well...kill me. I won't—"

"There are tens of thousands of vampires on the other side of the door to this tomb. I wouldn't even have to ask nicely to convince one of them to drain you. Do you want to be a feeder, Orious? A mindless, ravening monster, incapable of thought or self-control?" A slow, cruel smile spread across Fisher's face. "You already know a fair bit about that, though, don't you? You don't have two brain cells of your own to rub together. Regardless, you have two choices, and one of them is a lot less painful than the other. You crawl, or I toss you into a pit of hungry leeches."

"Fine! Fine." Orious's eyes flickered with hate as, grumbling, he got to his knees. He crawled up the steps to the pool, his shoulders hunched up around his ears. There was something rodent-like about him. The way he moved across the cold stone made me think of a rat. Casting a look over his shoulder at me, he said, "Remember what I said, child. Oath bou—"

Fisher lifted his foot and booted the seneschal in the ass, shoving him forward. Orious let out a yelp and tumbled face-first into the quicksilver.

"Close it quickly, before any more unwelcome visitors decide to come through," he said under his breath. The quicksilver moved differently when I reached out with my magic and closed it now. It solidified from the center outward, easily, smooth as you like. It didn't whisper a single curse word as it stilled. Fisher watched the molten metal return to its solid state with one eyebrow arched, clearly amused by what he was seeing.

The moment the gate was closed, I threw myself at him. "Don't leave without me again." I spoke into his hair, inhaling him in as I clung to him. He folded me into his arms, locking me against his chest and pressing a kiss against my temple as he did so.

"Don't worry," he whispered. "Rabid mountain trolls couldn't drag me away from you now."

"Ahem. Hello? Could you...just, uh, save this part for..."

I waited. Any second now, Fisher was going to round on Carrion and threaten to skin him or something. But the threat never came. My mate didn't even grumble as he loosened his hold on me and turned to face him.

"Come on, then," he said. "Show her what we did."

Carrion's hair seemed redder than it had been when he'd left somehow. There were angry welts all over his neck, and a couple on his cheeks, too. It was impossible to miss the unconscious body he was carrying over his shoulder.

"Hey, Saeris." He shot me a roguish wink. "I think this belongs to you."

29

FORTUNES OF THE UNIVERSE

SAERIS

HAYDEN WAS HERE.

Really here, in Yvelia.

He lay in the bed, crisp white sheets drawn up underneath his chin, his bright blond curls messy against the feather pillow underneath his head. Beneath his eyelids, I watched his eyes shuttle left, right, left, right, imagining what he could be dreaming about.

Onyx sniffed my brother's face and whined, giving his cheek a cursory lick. He hadn't even met Hayden properly, and yet he seemed anxious for him to wake up.

I was anxious for that, too. The last time I'd seen Hayden had not been pleasant.

"I didn't realize I was such a burden," he'd said.

"Well, you are, Hayden. Your entire fucking life, that's all you've been. Now leave me alone. Don't follow. Do not come looking for me. GO!"

I'd screamed at him. It had been out of fear. I'd wanted to hurt him, to make him run, so that he wouldn't follow me into the horror that I knew awaited me up at the palace, but it was hard to *unspeak* words sometimes. Especially when there was a grain of truth in them.

"Carrion slept for less than a day when he came through the quicksilver for the first time. But he was Fae beneath that glamor of his. It could be a while before your brother wakes up, Saeris." Te Léna pressed the back of her hand to Hayden's forehead, pursing her lips together. No doubt her magic was flowing into Hayden, checking his body for injury or malady.

We couldn't keep Hayden at Ammontraíeth. He wouldn't have been safe, and there were no healers there who knew anything about human physiology. The decision had been made, risky as it was, to use the gate to hop from the Blood Court back to Cahlish, and so it had been done—the work of moments.

It had been only days since I'd been here, but everything felt different suddenly. *I* felt different.

"Where's Kingfisher?" Te Léna asked. Her soft, warm voice broke apart my thoughts.

"He and Carrion managed to secure the silver we need. Two big bags of it. They went to take it to the armory. Fisher said he'd find me in his rooms as soon as he was done."

The healer smiled gently, rubbing the top of my arm in a comforting up and down motion. "You should go, then. Physically, Hayden is fine. It's just a big shift, moving from one plane of existence into another. He won't wake for a while yet."

I was already arguing. "I should be here—"

"You should be in bed. You look exhausted." Te Léna's hairstyle was new. It was tightly braided to her scalp, the ends, which were halfway down her back, decorated with bright orange beads. As always, she looked beautiful. "I'll stay with him. If he wakes up, I'll come and get you, I promise."

Gods and martyrs, Hayden was going to be almost as disappointed as Carrion had been over the fact that Te Léna was mated and married. I sighed, knowing how pointless it was to push back against her once she'd decided something.

"The *moment* he wakes up?" I asked.

She nodded. "I'll make sure he's comfortable first, and then I'll find you."

"All right. I'll go. But only because I *am* tired." More tired than I had ever been in my life. I could barely keep my eyes open. Channeling the amount of power I'd used back in the tomb was a massive drain on my energy supplies, both magical and physiological. I probably wasn't going to struggle to sleep ever again.

My hand was on the doorknob when Te Léna called after me. She sat at Hayden's bedside, holding his hand, with the morning light gilding her bronze skin. "I'm sorry I couldn't help you. I can't quite explain it. I . . ." She puffed out her cheeks and then let them deflate. "It isn't an issue that I've ever encountered before."

She had tried to heal me when we'd first arrived at Cahlish, but her magic had felt like water, beading and rolling off my skin. It hadn't felt wrong per se. Just . . . strange. I still had a gash on my arm, as well as a cut on my thigh, but both were already knitting closed on their own.

"It's okay, I promise. They were just scratches." I shot her a tired smile.

Upstairs in Fisher's rooms, Archer was busy organizing a bath. Three other fire sprites lugged smooth, round stones from a metal bin by the fireplace and held them in their hands, heating them before lowering them into a tub by the window that was full of water. Steam rose from the water, the stones hissing as they drew them back out of the bathwater and reheated them again. Another fire sprite was busy cleaning off the nightstands and the desk, sorting through the scraps of paper and other bits and pieces I had been dumping there after emptying out my pockets.

Fisher's friend squawked when he saw me. "No, no, no! Oh no. Apologies, my lady. We've been too slow. The room was supposed to be clean by the time you got here. Your bath was supposed to be poured!"

"It's okay, Archer. Please don't worry—"

"No." He shook his head vehemently, and a tiny ember flew off him and began to smolder on the rug. I stepped on it before he noticed and got even more upset. "There's a way things are supposed to be done, my lady. You aren't even supposed to see us unless we're serving dinner."

"I *want* to see you, Archer. I want to be your friend. All of you. Yes, I want to be friends with you three, too..." I trailed off, the words dying on my lips when fire broke out atop one of the other fire sprite's heads. The little sprite stared at me, mouth hanging open, fiery eyes wide.

"There's a way things are supposed to be done." Archer repeated this slowly, in an exasperated tone, as if I just wasn't understanding what he was saying.

"I hear you. I do. But the realm outside the walls of this estate changes all the time, doesn't it?"

I'd never seen a fire sprite pout before. I had now. "Not really."

"Archer, come on. One day, maybe I'll live here, and it would be nice if we didn't have to stand on ceremony all the time. You should be able to relax around me. You shouldn't call me my lady, either."

"What are we *supposed* to call you, then?"

"You should call me Saeris. It's my name."

Archer wobbled like he might fall over. The sprite who had been cleaning the nightstands was standing over by the bookshelf now and had a little knickknack in his hands. A ceramic bird, by the looks of things. Archer squawked when he noticed what the other sprite was doing. "Put that down! That was Lady Edina's favorite!"

"It's okay, I'm sure he's just looking at it."

The offending sprite pulled a sheepish face, put the bird back on the shelf, then scurried away. "No, mistress. You don't understand. That ornament is how Kingfisher got his name! Lady Edina saw it in a market in Ballard when she was pregnant with the master. She wasn't usually taken by things like that. She didn't own many knickknacks, but she said she had to have it. She was so taken by it that on his first birthday, she announced people should call her son Kingfisher. She set that ornament there herself, on that shelf, when the master was just a Faeling. She didn't like anyone to touch it."

"Okay, Archer. It's okay," I said, laughing a little at his anxious rambling. "The ornament's fine. It's back on the shelf. We all know now not to touch it."

But Archer wouldn't be consoled. One of the sprites helping to heat the bath dropped the stone he was holding into the bathtub with a *splosh*, and that was it. "Out! Get out, all of you! Go! I'll leave you out in the snow," Archer cried. "I'll turn you into doorstops. Go!"

The one who'd been investigating the Kingfisher ornament ran out of the room first. He was smaller than the others, which made me think he might be the youngest, but I honestly knew nothing of how fire sprites grew or aged. The others, who had been warming my bath-water, scuttled out with their eyes glued to the ground. Archer was last to go. He backed out of the room, his voice warbling with stress as he went.

"There's some food on the tray for you, my lady. A clean robe on the bed."

"Archer, come on."

"If you need anything, just pull on that tassel there by the bed. Yes, you know the one."

"Things are going to have to change!" I called after him as he drew the door closed. "We can't go on like this!"

The tub was heavenly. The rocks—still sitting at the bottom of the bath—radiated heat for a long time, keeping the water nice and hot. I let my head fall against the back of the tub, and before I knew it, I was dozing.

I didn't want to fall asleep yet, though. Not until I'd seen Fisher. Once my fingers had pruned and my muscles felt loose, I climbed out of the bath and dried myself off, dressed in one of Fisher's loose shirts, and prepared to settle in the with the book on Alchemy that I'd removed from Ammontraíeth's library against Algat's wishes.

But then the door opened.

He stood in the rectangular square of light for a moment, watching me, then slowly stepped into the room and swung the door closed behind him.

CALLIE HART

I didn't say anything, and neither did he. We just savored the sight of each other. Relished the fact that we were both in the same room, breathing the same air, and nothing had succeeded in killing us while we'd been apart.

Fisher took a couple of steps toward me, eyes pensive. He bent and drew off one of his boots, his mouth forming a disapproving line as he upended it and a stream of sand poured out of it onto the floor. It kept coming and coming...

I covered my mouth, trying not to laugh.

He repeated the motion with his other boot, turning it upside down, gaze locked stoically on me while he waited for the sand to be done pouring out of his footwear.

When he was finished, he dropped both boots to the floor with a *thump, thump* and took another small step forward. "Do you know how incredible you were back there?" he asked.

"When I was fighting for my life?"

He shook his head. "When you single-handedly took down five guards with those pretty new short swords of yours. That was really..." He trailed off, eyes burning.

"Stupid?"

"Hot," he corrected, the tips of his canines glinting between his lips as he emphasized the word.

I tried even harder not to smile. Compliments from this male were still new. My insides behaved ridiculously whenever he even *looked* at me. "You like the swords?" I asked, my gaze going to where they sat on top of the dresser to his right. Fisher arched an eyebrow, slowly heading over to take a look at the naked Fae steel.

"They're beautiful," he said softly. "Incredible. They were made for you, Osha."

"I still don't know what the writing means. The engraving is in Old Fae. The one on the right with the abalone inlay in the hilt says Erromar. The one on the left with the ivory inlay says Selanir."

Fisher angled his head, frowning as he read the inscriptions on both swords. He nodded, smiling softly. "Erromar means *mercy*," he said, in a reverent voice. "Selanir means *honor*."

"Huh. Mercy and Honor. The gods named my swords *for* me, then."

"Maybe," Fisher agreed. He stepped away from the dresser, facing me again. "Or maybe those are traits they decided to bless *you* with. Either way, they're appropriate names for your new weapons. Now enough about swords. Come here. If you can bear the fact that our bodies aren't touching for one more second, then you're a better person than me, Saeris Fane," he whispered.

Those words lit a fire in me. I ran, crossing the room and launching myself at him. He caught me, his arms like steel bands around me as he held me tight.

Life was so unsafe right now. A million hurdles lay between us and peace. I couldn't remotely begin to comprehend how we were going to overcome it all, and yet the world fell away. Nothing could touch me here, in his arms like this. I pressed my face into the crook of his neck so hard that his leathers muffled my words when I spoke. "What took you so long?"

He stroked my wet hair, laughing quietly.

"I went to get Lorreth," he said. We hadn't been able to find our friend before we'd left Ammontraíeth. Fisher had left a note for him in my rooms, telling him to head back across the dead fields as soon as he discovered we were gone. "I asked him to bring Bill and Aida back across the river for me. They were miserable in that dank barn. He had to find a safe place to cross, though. The narrowest part of the river, where the camp was..." He shook his head. "The rot has destroyed everything there now. The snow is black. I...I've never seen anything like it."

"But he's back here now? Safe?"

Fisher nodded.

Now that I knew that, I had to ask the question burning a hole in the back of my throat. "How does an oath-sworn Fae break their oath, Fisher?"

He drew back immediately, searching my eyes. "They don't," he said. "Why?"

There were freckles on the bridge of his nose. Just a few small dots of brown against the paleness of his skin. I focused on them, too afraid to repeat what Orious had said back in the tomb. "You're sworn to Belikon. So are Lorreth, Ren, Danya, and everyone else who fought at Irrín. Orious said that he can command you—"

"Orious was trying to scare you. Belikon can command us until he's blue in the face, but he can't touch us here. The wards that prevent him from coming here also prevent his compulsion from reaching us. As long as we stay here in Cahlish or in Ammontraíeth, we're all fine. And even if we do leave these lands, we would have to be in his physical presence for him to command us. There is no way he's leaving the Winter Palace—"

I kissed him, my heart rising in my chest. I couldn't bear to hear any more. I needed *him* more than I needed words of reasoning right now. His surprise was fleeting. His mouth answered mine, his tongue sweeping into my mouth, and the room faded to black. The heavy curtains were drawn, shutting out the cold morning light. His shadows were nowhere to be seen, though. He didn't even call upon them when his hands roved south, tugging at the bottom of my shirt.

Don't tell me you're going to undress me the normal way this time, I said teasingly into his head.

He flicked his tongue over my lips, a low rumble sounding at the back of his throat. *Does this feel normal to you?* He took my left hand and placed it in the center of his chest, mirroring what he'd done the very first time he'd shown me how fast I had made his heart race back in his tent.

I could hardly feel his pulse hammering beneath his thick leathers... but I *could* hear it now. "No," I whispered.

And this? He took hold of my other hand, guiding it low until it rested on top of his hard cock. He wasn't just hard. He was rock solid, his erection straining at the front of his pants like it needed to be free.

No. That doesn't feel normal at all, I said. *That feels... extraordinary.*

When Fisher lifted my hand again, he paused, turning it over so that my palm faced up. The quicksilver in his eye flared a little as he gently ran his fingers over the inside of my wrist. I'd noticed it, of course: the veins that had once been green-blue there now shone metallic silver through my skin.

Does it hurt? he asked.

I shook my head. *No.*

Do you feel... He narrowed his eyes a fraction. *Unwell?*

Unwell was a tactful way of asking if I was being plagued by a million voices that were gradually driving me insane. Again, I shook my head. *No. It isn't like that. It feels... like magic. Like power, right there under my skin.*

Lightly, he kissed the inside of my wrist. *All right, then. We'll unpack that later. Because right now...* He spoke the question out loud. "Do you have any idea how good you look in that shirt, Osha? Two days was too long."

"Technically, we *did* have sex in the cottage."

He walked me backward, cradling my cheeks in his hands, raining kisses down onto my face. "It doesn't matter. My soul is on fire. Tell me yours isn't."

He bent over me, pressing his lips to my jaw, up to my ear, over the sensitive skin of my neck. My eyes rolled back into my head, my breath faltering. "My soul is on the winds," I panted. "You're carrying it away."

He was so strong beneath my hands. Packed muscle and power. In his arms, the dangers of this place couldn't touch me. I was sheltered. Safe. He held me tight to him—as tight as he could without crushing me—and didn't let me go. Did he know this was what I needed? Could he sense that in me? He held me as if he would use his body as a shield against the dangers of this world. I could think of occasions when he already had, and my throat hurt from the memory of it. His shoulders tensed as he lowered me to the bed, but still he didn't let me go.

"Never again," he murmured. "Wherever we go, we go together."

"Yes. Promise me."

His mouth was hot on my skin, his hands possessive. A promise was the same as an oath in Fae, but Fisher made this one without a second's hesitation. "I promise. I swear it. You're mine."

"And you are mine.

The words weren't enough. I needed him inside me. Needed to be as close to him as I could get. I was raw with emotion as I unfastened his chest plate; my fingers were too numb to feed the leather straps through the buckles. Fisher placed a hand over mine, stilling them, and I saw the ink on the back of his hand had changed, too. The quicksilver rune was solid now, marked in metallic blue-black. Fisher saw where I was looking and began working free of his armor with one hand, using the other to lift my chin so that my eyes met his. "Don't think about that right now. Don't worry about any of it. Just be here with me."

My prince of shadows.

I had been born into the light, but my salvation had been waiting for me in the dark. It was a miracle that we'd found each other. I'd learned the hard way that anyone could have come through the quicksilver that day in the Hall of Mirrors. But it hadn't been just anyone. It had been him, the tides of fate turning, or the machinations of the universe at play. Whatever it had been, I was grateful for it. I wouldn't have changed it for the world.

I watched him undress. He watched me while I did the same. Naked, he lay back down beside me and turned to face me, examining each of my facial features in turn. So many people were afraid of this male. Yvelia was full of Fae who would gladly have seen him strung up and put to death. He'd destroyed an entire city. He had gone to war. He had slain a dragon and faced the Iron Death at the Ajun Gate. Earlier, he'd ripped a male's head off with his magic and hadn't batted an eyelid. He *was* a creature of violence—it was his creed. But he was also *this*, too. When he loved, it was with everything he had.

He blinked at me owlishly, his expression very serious as he stroked his hand over my hair. Pulling his bottom lip into his mouth, he frowned slightly, as if he were still learning how to be gentle with his hands. "When I look at you, I feel as though I'm peering into a mirror," he said quietly. "I can speak into your mind, but it's still a mystery to me. I feel as if I should already know your every thought."

Laughing silently, I curled a lock of his ink-black hair around my index finger. "You wouldn't like it if you could."

"I already know what I'd find," he replied, his eyes dancing.

"Oh, really? Please enlighten me."

Fisher rolled onto his back, throwing an arm up over his head. There was a dimple in his cheek—only his true friends knew it existed, since they were the only ones who'd ever seen him smile broadly enough for it to be coaxed out. I could see it there, an inch from the right corner of his mouth, fighting to make an appearance. "Oh, y'know. 'I am *so* in love with Kingfisher. Kingfisher is *so* handsome. Look at his ass in those pants—'"

"Hey!" I prodded him in the ribs, hard. "I do have other things to think about besides *you!*"

Pulling both his lips into his mouth now, forcefully preventing himself from smiling, he rolled his head to face me. He couldn't keep it from his eyes, though. "It's okay, Osha. Many women have appreciated my posterior in a pair of leathers. I don't let it go to my head."

I flicked the top of his pointed ear, and the Bane of Gillethrye yelped like a startled dog. In a blur of movement, he was straddling me and had my hands pinned above my head. "You think I'm above tickling you?" he asked in a deadly serious tone.

I looked him dead in the eye. "Go on. Do it. I'm not ticklish."

Squinting, he looked me over, trying to see if I was telling the truth. "Well, *that's* no fun," he said at last.

"What about you? Are *you* ticklish?"

Fisher sniffed, his hair tumbling into his eyes. He lowered himself so that his face was only a couple of inches from mine and butted the end of my nose gently with his own. "I'm afraid I'm not going to answer that question."

"Because you can't *lie!*" I squealed, laughing, trying to wrestle free from his grip so I could test my theory, but Fisher held on tight.

"A warrior never reveals his weaknesses." He spoke the words breathlessly against my mouth, and I could feel his smile there now. He was loving this.

"That really isn't fair. You know all my flaws," I complained.

Martyrs, he was so godsdamned hot. He looked like he had been carved out of marble by the hands of the gods themselves, all muscle, the lines of him sheer perfection. And he was naked, lying on top of me, and he was *mine*. He sobered a little, pulling back so that he could take a look at me. "You have no flaws, Saeris Fane. You are perfect in my eyes, imperfections and all. I'm in love with every part of you. Your stubbornness. Your wicked tongue. Your foul temper when you're tired. Your inability to close *any* door quietly—"

"All right, all right, I think that's enough of *that*, thank you."

"Every part. I love *all* of you." He blew a dark curl out of his eyes. "I'd spend the fortunes of the universe to protect you. I'd drain the seas dry. Fell every tree. I would sacrifice the sun from the fucking sky and surrender the stars, too, if I could. But those things aren't mine to give. All I have is my life. It isn't much, but I'd spend it and consider the price small if it meant keeping you safe."

He spoke so easily, but I would never be able to describe what his words meant to me. There was nothing in any dictionary, in any language, that could possibly come close to explaining what I was feeling right now. "There it is," I whispered.

"What?"

"The way that you love me. Some would say *that* is your weakness."

The lines of his face softened. "Some would say that," he agreed. "But they would be wrong. It's my *strength*."

We slept for a while. Fisher knew how badly I wanted him, but he could also tell how tired I was. We sank into nothingness, curved tight around one another, skin on skin. I woke hours later with his hard cock butting up against my ass and his fingers trailing over my hip bone.

He moved slowly, waiting to make sure I was awake, to make sure that I was aware of what he was doing. My breath hitched in my throat when his hand moved down, between my thighs, and he slowly began working tight circles with his fingertips against my clit.

The action was lazy at first. Languid and teasing. I shifted my top leg down a little, giving him better access as I arched back against him, letting out a stifled sigh.

"Fuck me, Osha." His voice was rough from sleep. "That sound haunts my fucking dreams. I want to make you moan for hours."

I trembled, my heart stuttering, as he worked his right arm underneath me and wrapped it around my waist so he could change hands. With his left, he began stroking my breast, toying gently with my nipple. "We have lifetimes of this ahead of us. Lifetimes to explore each other."

Shit, that felt *so* good. "Lifetimes? We'll... lose our minds..."

I felt Fisher laugh rather than heard it. "There are worse ways to go mad, Osha. If I get to fuck my way to insanity with you, then I'd call that a win." He rocked his hips forward, grinding against my ass, and my skin broke out in goose bumps. A fire burned in the grate. It hadn't been lit when we'd fallen asleep, which meant that someone, probably Archer, had come in and lit it for us while we'd been lying here, naked on top of Fisher's bed.

I couldn't make myself care in the moment. My body had come alive, responding to his touch, his breath, his pulse. His fingers worked the small, slick bundle of nerves between my thighs, moving in circles, coaxing heat to build in the pit of my stomach.

"Relax," he murmured. "I've got you. You can let go." He kissed my neck, my cheek, my jaw, and the anxiety of the past few days slipped away.

Only he could do this for me. Only him. This thing between us, it was love, yes. But it was obsession, too. He was the making of me and my ruin. I thought about him relentlessly. And when he slid his fingers through my wet heat and thrust them up inside me, his name was a prayer on my lips.

"Fisher! Fuck!"

"Shhh, shhh, shhh." He soothed me, murmuring softly to me in Old Fae. "Irrellieth ka tintar shey an mé correshan dow."

I let out another wordless cry, unable to stop myself. Reaching back for him, I buried my fingers in his hair. "What are you saying?" I gasped.

"Only whispering secrets," he rumbled in response.

"Tell me."

He rubbed his thumb against my core, driving his fingers into me and then stroking from the inside in a *come here* motion. I hissed when I registered the sharp nip of his teeth at my earlobe. "I said, 'I'm going to drown myself between your thighs.' Or something close to that. There's no word for what I'm trying to say in High Fae. *Correshan* means lethal bliss. Death by pleasure, perhaps. Old Fae was a far more descriptive language."

"Ahh! Oh my fucking gods," I panted. "That...that feels..." I cried out when he roughly rolled my nipple between his thumb and forefinger, squeezing it.

"The good comes with the bad. The pleasure comes with the pain. I'm going to make this hurt so good for you, Osha. Are you ready?"

"I—" I didn't know what to say, so I nodded. I didn't want him to caress me, or hold me, or make love to me. I wanted raw emotion. I wanted electricity. I wanted to fucking *scream*. When Fisher sank himself into me from behind, his fingers gouged into my hip bones, biting deep, and a feral snarl worked free from his throat. It was the sound the hellcats made as they prowled the dunes outside of the walls of the Third at night. It was a claiming.

His arm banded around my ribs like a vise, and he fucked me hard until I came apart.

Our bodies formed a bridge to heaven, and both of us ascended.

The whole of Cahlish heard my screams.

When Fisher came moments after me, I watched, amazed, as a swirl of ink rippled away from the God Bindings that wound around my wrist and arm, transferring from my hand to his. It didn't stop there. I turned in the circle of his arms, watching as it rose over his biceps until it settled on his skin, just below his collarbone.

Fisher bent down and kissed me deeply, his heart racing from the workout he'd just undertaken. "Why are you smirking like that?" he asked, curving a dark brow.

He hadn't seen what had happened.

I would let him discover his new ink the same way he had let me discover *mine*.

30

LEASH

SAERIS

"SIRE! SIRE, COME quick. Te Léna needs your help!"

Archer's call outside the bedroom door woke us. Fisher was on his feet and moving before I'd fully opened my eyes. He kicked his way into a pair of pants and hurtled out of the door, barefoot and shirtless. It took me ten seconds longer to dress. I followed behind, a million anxious questions streaking through my mind like meteors across the night sky.

I nearly crashed into Archer, who was still standing in the hallway outside the room.

"Mistress! Wait, mistress! You're—"

I ran.

What's happened? Hayden was fine when we left him last night. Did traveling through the quicksilver do something to him?

Did his relic not work? Oh—oh, gods, did I fuck up his relic somehow?

Is he awake?

Is he sick?

Is...

I stumbled to a halt in the open doorway. Evening light spilled through the window of the bedroom, falling in rectangles across the rumpled duvet that was still drawn up to my brother's chin. His head was tipped back, his mouth open, and he was snoring loudly.

Besides my brother, the room was empty.

"Mistress! Miss...tress!" Archer thudded into the room, fighting for breath and struggling to speak. "You went...the wrong...way. It isn't your...brother. It's...the master's *sister*."

Everlayne.

I took off again, sidling past the fire sprite and bolting for the stairs. I could smell him now—my mate had come this way and had left a trail of his scent thick in the air behind him. I raced down the hallway and turned right, vaulting up the stairs four at a time. There was a commotion up ahead; Everlayne's room was fit to bursting, too many people packed inside the small space.

Te Léna. Her husband, Maynir. Danya. Fisher. Carrion—gods, everyone was here.

"Hold her still!" Te Léna cried. "She's going to bite through her tongue!"

On the bed, Everlayne was in the grips of a seizure. Her body was bowed so badly that the only part of her touching the sweat-soaked sheets was the crown of her head and the heels of her feet. She shook, eyes rolled back into her head, jaw wrenched to one side, her fingers bent at odd angles and spasming. Fisher had his sister by the head. He was trying to work a piece of leather between her teeth. "I'm going to break her fucking jaw if I pull any harder," he hissed.

"Everlayne? Layne, can you hear me?" Te Léna called. The healer's eyes were wild with worry.

I took in the scene—the noise, and scents, the panic. "What the hell's going *on*?"

Carrion was trying to hold Layne's hand, but the female was thrashing so hard that maintaining his grip looked to be proving difficult. "I was up in the bedroom across the way, *absolutely* minding my own business, and I heard screaming. I had to kick the door down to get in. She was strangling Te Léna."

"*Who* was?"

"Who do you think? *Layne*," Danya barked. "It took both of us to pry her fingers from Te Léna's throat."

"Why were you up here?" Fisher had climbed down from the bed; he had managed to slip the leather between his sister's teeth and was now trying to gather her hair out of her face.

Danya didn't look at him. "I was *also* minding my own business," she snapped.

"Gods a-fucking-live." Fisher shook his head. "Go find Lorreth, Danya. Tell him he's needed up here."

The warrior wiped her nose with the back of her hand, smearing blood across her cheek—she must have caught a stray fist from Layne. Her eyes flitted to Carrion and lingered there. "I'm on it."

"Stay.... *back!*" Layne yelled. She had already spat out the leather. "Just leave me! Leave me *alone!*" Fear echoed off the walls. It hung thick in the air. This was nothing like what had happened when I'd been alone with Layne. It wasn't Edina's voice that rushed past Layne's lips. It was Layne's herself. "Please! Please, please nooooo!" she begged.

"What the fuck is wrong with her?" Fisher demanded, eyes sharp on Te Léna.

The healer rubbed her neck, but she was still there beside the bed, peering down at Layne, holding her other hand over the female's chest. "I don't know. I can feel...." She shook her head. "Something. It doesn't feel right. Like there's a weight pressing down on her. Her soul is dressed in shadows."

"What the hell does *that* mean?"

"Easy." Maynir stepped forward, placing a hand on his mate's shoulder. "She's doing her best. The girl nearly snapped her neck just now." His tone was testimony to how much he cared for Te Léna. In the face of how terrifying Fisher looked right now, most males would have quailed in his presence rather than dared to reprimand him. The air thrummed with Fisher's mounting power. He was clearly drawing his magic to him, though the act was futile; there was nowhere for him to direct it. No enemy for him to strike down.

"Noooo, no, no, no, no. Please!" Layne suddenly dropped back down onto the bed, her head bouncing off the mattress. Her eyes snapped wide open. "Don't! Please, don't. Don't…don't…" A figure lurked in her pale green eyes—the dark outline of a looming figure. It seemed to grow, getting closer…

"Please…" Layne sobbed. Her voice had lost all power. It was a whisper now, desperate and resigned.

Fisher was pale as a ghost. It was freezing in the bedroom despite the fire that roared on the other side of the room. The ink on Fisher's chest writhed, scattered to jagged lines. "Is she awake?" Fisher asked. "Who is she talking to?"

Te Léna shook her head. "No. Yes, I—She isn't *here*. I—I can feel her mind, as if she is awake, but her consciousness feels like it's behind a wall or something."

"Can you break through it?"

"No." Te Léna's eyes had adopted a strange, vacant look. "It's so thick. So high. There's no way to bring it down."

"Try! Please! Just try!"

"Oh, gods, no. Stop! *Plea*—" Layne's shriek cut off dead. Her back arched again, her heels hammering like pistons against the bed as she convulsed.

"Something's *hurting* her!" Fisher stepped back from the bedside, dragging his hands through his hair, pulling on fists of it. His eyes found mine, and all was hopelessness and panic there. Fisher could wield a sword. Could cut down his foes. He could form shadow gates and fly to his friends' sides when they needed him. But there was no enemy to face here. No destination he could fathom.

He could do nothing to help, and that knowledge was killing him.

I was in no better position. My throat was burning so badly that it felt scorched. I reached out with the strange magic that roiled beneath my skin and found only the quicksilver, whispering softly, calm as a slow-flowing river.

Run. Run. Run. Run…

Dread crept along my bones like hoarfrost. I went to Layne, placing my hand on the top of her head. Her blond hair was tangled, wet with sweat. Her breathing faltered for a second, but then resumed its rapid pace, sawing in and out of her, her shaking growing even faster.

I felt what Te Léna had felt: a dark hand hovering over my friend, pressing her down into the wet soils of hell. And she was *not* alone in that place.

Layne's eyelids flew open again, her pupils the size of pinpricks. Her tongue protruded awkwardly from her mouth, wet with saliva. Her teeth were stained red. *The gate is open*, a dread voice said, speaking from her mouth. *It cannot be closed. The gate is open. The gate is open. The gate is—*

I snatched back my hand like her skin had burned me.

The voice stopped.

Layne gave a terrible shudder, her eyes rolling back into her head, and then she fell motionless, the tension fleeing her body.

The air in the room was oppressively still, thick with a horror-laden silence.

No one moved.

No one said a word.

Fisher let go of his sister's hand. His eyes were hollow as he padded stiffly, barefoot, from the room.

"Could it be connected to the rot?" Lorreth paced up and down, the thud of his boots pounding like a second pulse in my temples. We had all migrated to the dining room, one by one, not sure where else to go. Before the fireplace, Fisher's hands were planted high over his head against the stone lintel of the hearth, the muscles in his back bunched into knots. He was lost in the flames.

"It's possible," Maynir said. His hand rested on top of Te Léna's, his fingers intertwined with hers. "I've never read of anything like this happening in Yvelia before. But my research has revolved mostly around court politics. My own personal interest in varying magics has given me some insight into elemental magics, shadow magics, blood magics and the like...but this?" He puffed out his cheeks. "This infection stems from no vein of magic that *I've* heard of before. It is either very old or very new. Either way, we currently have no way of stopping it, and we have no clue how it might be affecting the realm. The presence of some magics have been known to cause seizures in the very young. It could be that, as this rot approached Cahlish, it affects Everlayne somehow?"

Conjecture. That's all this was.

Maynir was grasping at straws, but he couldn't be faulted for it. No one else had any idea what was going on.

Lorreth scratched at his stubble. "We need to find Ren—"

"No." Fisher took a deep breath, speaking for the first time since we'd relocated. "Not yet. He needs to warn as many of the villages and the small holdings along the coast and into the forests as he can. There's nothing he can do for Layne here, and the people need to know what's happening."

Uncertainty flickered in Lorreth's eyes, but he nodded. "You're right. There's nothing he can do. So what are *we* going to do?"

"We'll go back to the river and see how far the rot has spread since yesterday." Fisher turned away from the hearth, wearing a look of weary determination. Back in Zilvaren, there had been days when the odds had felt stacked against us and then some. No water. No food. No way out of the ward for one reason or another. Every time I'd managed to solve one problem, another seemed to stand between me and a moment's rest. I'd had no other choice but to figure out a solution to the obstacle that blocked my path in the knowledge that more would only follow after it. But the alternative would have been to give up and die, and I wasn't the give-up-and-die type.

Neither was my mate.

He drew in a deep breath. When he exhaled, smoke rippled from his shoulders downward, leaving a full set of leathers in its wake. At his throat: a silver, shining gorget stamped with the wolf's head of the Lupo Proelia. Nimerelle's hilt was visible over his shoulder, her black hilt snapping with energy and drawing in the light. A moment ago, Fisher had looked like he had come undone. The Fisher standing before me was ready to go to war.

"Saeris and I will go back to Ammontraíeth. There are more books we should retrieve from the library. Algat can complain all she wants, but we need them. Danya, you go back to the temporary rally point and check in with the warriors there. Tell them to pack up and make ready. I'll be coming to bring them back to Cahlish tomorrow."

The female's stoic expression wavered. "We're *abandoning* the border?"

Fisher nodded once. "We're abandoning it."

"But—"

"Stop."

Danya worked her jaw, but she held her tongue.

"The border doesn't matter anymore. Infected feeders will cross no matter what. The land on the other side of the Darn is dead. There's nothing there to defend. Our new line will be formed here. Lorreth, I need you to get Iseabail. We don't need access to the catacombs at Nevercross anymore. Not now that we have the books at the Blood Court. We do need a witch with us to help with Everlayne, though. Maybe there's something we're overlooking. A way Te Léna and Iseabail can help bring her out of this fugue state."

Lorreth's response to the command was visceral; he spun around and marched toward Fisher, mouth open and ready to start hollering, but he saw the stony look on Fisher's face, the way the rest of us did, and he threw up his hands and turned right back around again. "You're right," he said. "You're right. I'm sorry. I'll go. Never mind."

Fisher's expression softened a little. "Te Léna, you stay with Layne and Hayden. The boy will be waking soon, I'm sure, and he's going to have questions. Answer them as best you can, and do not let him out of your sight. He has a tendency to wander."

I almost laughed. Fisher had spent only a few hours with my brother, but he was already speaking as if he knew him and had claimed reluctant ownership of him.

"And what about me?" Carrion asked. He was sitting in Fisher's seat, picking at his nails. He affected an air of boredom, but he was sitting a little straighter than usual. He hadn't even kicked his feet up onto the table. "I should stay here and make sure no birds land on the trees outside, right? Or should I melt the snow from the front lawn instead? I'm sure there's something sufficiently inane you can busy me with while everyone else is off doing their important tasks."

Let him come to Ammontraieth.

That was the thought I was *going* to send to Fisher... but I didn't get the chance.

"Shut up, Carrion," Fisher said. "You're coming with us."

The heavy door to the tomb was barred from the outside. No order had been left to lock it once we had traveled through the quicksilver back to Cahlish, which meant that the high bloods had taken matters into their own hands. They must have known that a barred door wouldn't keep us at bay for long, but the message was clear all the same: You aren't welcome here. We don't *want* you.

The door exploded outward, reduced to splinters by the heel of Fisher's boot. Two high bloods stood in the hallway, by the window, armed with iron rapiers. I didn't recognize them immediately, but then I saw the ridiculously small right hand that belonged to the vampire who hovered closest and I remembered them from the Fool's Paradise. I'd assumed Lorreth had been joking when he'd made that quip about the high blood's hand growing back small at first, but it seemed that he had *not*.

Both males—Anterrin? Khol? Gods only knew why I remembered their names—dropped their rapiers and retreated across the hall until their backs hit the wall behind them. "Don't! Wait!" Khol gasped. The bastard's eyes flashed, his expression quickly morphing into hunger when they landed on the cargo in my arms. I always carried Onyx through the quicksilver. Even with my edicts in place, it seemed like the best policy. I didn't like how the high bloods eyed him, as if they were dead set on finding a loophole and making a meal out of him.

Onyx rumbled in my arms, sensing danger, and bared his teeth.

"You have one second to look away from that fox," Fisher said flatly.

Khol did exactly that, his attention snapping to my mate. Fisher had Nimerelle in his hand, and the blade was issuing sinister black smoke. "We're sorry, okay! We didn't do it to keep *you* out. He told us to watch for Belikon's men." Khol closed his eyes as Fisher held the tip of the sword beneath the vampire's chin. "He—he—he—"

"He?" Fisher parroted.

"He told us to let you out the moment you came through! We would have! We—"

"Go." The word resonated in the air, a single command that threatened violence if it was not obeyed. Anterrin, who hadn't said a word, took off first, running down the hall. His brother didn't waste time chasing after him.

Carrion squinted at Fisher, hand in the air. "Is it weird, knowing that people's balls retract up into their bodies whenever you're around?" He made a cupping motion of something being sucked upward.

Fisher crooked an eyebrow at him, but only for a moment. He sheathed Nimerelle, turning to me as he did so. "I'm going to find Foley. I'll take Onyx back to your chambers first, though. Perhaps you should go check in with the male who posted those idiots outside the tomb. See what *he* has to report?"

"Sounds like a good idea." I surrendered Onyx reluctantly, kissing the fox on his head before handing him off to my mate.

"Don't worry. I'll keep this one safe," Carrion said, giving my mate a wink. The comment was probably supposed to rankle Fisher, but the dig only earned him an amused snort.

"Please. Saeris could have half of the Blood Court in their eternal graves before you even drew your blade. Even the fox would stand a better chance of seeing off a threat." Something seemed to occur to him out of nowhere. "Wait. Speaking of your blade, where *is* Simon, by the way?"

Over the years, I'd seen Carrion successfully hide an array of emotions. He was too slow to hide the color that leaped to his cheeks today. "Don't you concern yourself with Simon," he said. "I know exactly where my god sword is, thank you very much."

Ammontraíeth was a hive of activity as we moved through its halls. High bloods hurried about, carrying stunning bolts of damask, stacks of gold-leafed plates, and all manner of serving tureens. They smelled Carrion before they saw me. A few of them hissed at the scent of fresh, living blood in such close proximity, but the moment they saw Carrion's auburn hair, they drew back, my edict hobbling their hunger. When they saw *me*, they sank down in supplication, bowing their heads, only rising after I'd passed and was out of view. Carrion watched them drop to their knees, shaking his head. "You've spent your whole life hiding, hoping no one recognizes you, and now whenever anyone sees you, they *kneel*. You must be fucking hating this."

My hard-edged laughter echoed around the corridor as we walked. "Oh no. I don't hate it, Carrion. I *loathe* it."

"Then why make them do it? You didn't need to make that demand when you passed those edicts."

I had a feeling that he already knew the answer to that question. He wanted to hear me say it out loud, maybe. To remind myself of the necessity. "They have to fear me. Or at least be reminded that I have power over them."

"I wonder if they have any idea how close they came to being wiped out?" Swift said a little *too* loudly, as a female in a purple gossamer gown scowled up at us. "You could have ended their lives with a simple command once that crown was placed on your head."

Indeed, that avenue had been discussed at length before my coronation. Lorreth had voted for Ammontraíeth to be destroyed. Renfis had too, casting his vote from Irrín. Danya had voted for public dismemberment and the kind of torture that smacked of revenge, not justice. Only I had begged for the opportunity to see if the members of the Blood Court could be redeemed. Fisher had hesitantly agreed to wait and see how things turned out, aaaand yeah. So far, things weren't looking too great.

"We're going to see Tal, then?" Carrion said, abruptly changing the subject. He spun around, walking backward to keep pace as he returned the beautiful female high blood's scowl.

"Yes. We're going to see Tal," I confirmed.

"How the hell are we supposed to find him in this hellscape of a palace?"

I cleared my throat, not meeting his gaze. "I know exactly where he is."

Carrion's eyes burned into my cheek, but still, I refused to look at him. "And *how* do you know that exactly?"

"Because he's my sire. I can sense him, the way he can sense me. I *always* know where he is. Come on, keep up."

"Wow. That must get confusing when the three of you are all in the same place. Half of you is on alert, sensing Tal, and the other half is being drawn toward Fisher."

"My connection with Fisher doesn't work like that."

"*What?*" Carrion came to a theatrical dead stop. "You can sense Tal, but you can't sense Fisher?"

I kept walking.

"Hey! Hey, *wait!*" He ran to catch up. "Sorry if I'm a little confused, but aren't you two supposed to share a love that puts all other love to shame?"

I took a left and jogged down a set of stairs. "I do have a connection with Fisher, yes. And yes, I can sense where he is. It...just isn't the same. The connection I share with him feels like a deep well. Calm and peaceful."

"And what does the connection with Tal feel like?"

I gritted my teeth, reaching the bottom of the stairs. I turned right. "A *leash*."

I'd never been to Tal's rooms before. There had never been any need for me to go there. As Carrion and I drew up outside the arched doorway with the golden scrolled door handles, I was struck with a wave of déjà vu. I knew the shape of the doorknob in my hand. I knew that the door would squeak a little as I pushed it open. I knew what the air would smell like when I entered the chambers beyond.

Borrowed memories.

Echoes in the blood.

I knew these things because they were so familiar to Tal, and I was a product of *his* line. I raised my hand to knock on the door and hesitated. A strange sensation tickled at the back of my mind. There were people with Tal on the other side of this door. Lots of people. There was a tension in the rooms beyond that made the air bristle with electricity.

An argument, maybe? But who would he be arguing with?

"I wouldn't do that if I were you."

I wheeled around, fist still poised to knock. Zovena strolled along the hallway toward us, her bright blond hair scraped back into a severe braid that looked so tight it must have been giving her a head- ache. The rope of hair fell over her shoulder and dangled almost to her waist. Her black, high-collared dress clung to her curves, accen- tuating her hips and cleavage, which was almost spilling over the lace cups. I hadn't seen her since the coronation; I could have lived with *never* seeing her again and been perfectly happy, but no. Ammon- traíeth was vast—a person could get lost in the windowless, dark corridors of this place—but it was still just one building. It had only been a matter of time before I crossed paths with her again.

She smiled smugly as she knelt and sat back on her heels, making herself comfortable.

I lowered my hand, looking down at the female, crossing my arms over my chest. I didn't know precisely what had gone on between her and Tal, but I knew enough. She was the reason he had come here and given himself over to Malcolm. He had loved her, and she had aban- doned him somehow. Now it seemed as though she wanted nothing more than to see the Keeper of Secrets dead and buried in the ground.

"Your Majesty." The greeting was sweet as rotten fruit. When she spoke, a gust of something sensual and exotic rose from her and hit the back of my nose. The scent was intoxicating. It made my head spin a little.

"I have a bone to pick with you," I said.

"Me?" Zovena laughed prettily, tossing her braid back over her shoulder. "What have *I* done to offend the queen of the Blood Court? Tell me, and I'll be sure to make reparations immediately." I'd met women like her back in Zilvaren. Women who would have traded their own family members to the guardians in exchange for the smallest of luxuries. The kind of woman who would sell her soul to the devil if it guaranteed her power, temporary or otherwise. Zovena was far more dangerous than those women had been, though. She was Fae turned vampire. If she played her cards right, she'd live to see this empire crumble to dust—and a part of me knew she would have something to do with its fall.

"You're a Lord of Midnight," I said.

Malice shone from her eyes. "Oh! My, my. I really thought you'd forgotten that." The sound of her laughter made my skin crawl. "I am a Lord of Midnight, yes. My beloved maker bestowed the title upon me seven hundred and eighty-three years ago. May I rise?"

"Your beloved maker." I nodded, huffing down my nose. "Malcolm?"

The metallic tang of anger marred the air, and yet Zovena's face showed nothing of it. "You would have *crawled* to speak his name in another life, King Killer," she said.

Oh ho ho, boy. She wanted to play. "I suppose I have *you* to thank for that honorific, Zovena. Is the name supposed to upset me? Because, personally, I'm rather proud of that accomplishment. Tell me," I said, before she could reply. "In Ammontraíeth, is it considered incest if you sleep with your maker? 'Cause it sounds to me like someone was fuck-ing *Daddy*."

"Bitch!" Zovena's serene façade disintegrated, revealing the depths of her hatred at last. Her features warped, her mouth suddenly too large, pulling up at the corners. She lunged, but her body immediately recoiled, held in place by the fact that she was prohibited from hurting me *and* I hadn't given her leave to stand.

Carrion grabbed hold of the doorframe, clutching hold of it as he pretended to stagger sideways. "Gods and martyrs! What's wrong with your *face?*"

Zovena hissed like a hellcat. "Be mindful of that tongue, sheascah. I'm no fool. I know who you are. There are those who would pay handsomely for delivery of your head on a pike."

I stepped in front of her, blocking her view of the smuggler. "You won't touch him. You won't look sideways at him again. You won't tell anyone anything about Carrion, do you understand me? You'll rip your own tongue out trying."

The Lord flinched under the weight of the command. She saw me as a little girl, wandering blind and scared in a dark forest. She had forgotten who she was talking to—impressive, given *she* was the one on her knees.

"Say it. Tell me that you understand." I could have spoken with anger or a hatred that would easily have matched hers, but I served the order up in a bland, disinterested tone instead.

"I...understand." Zovena tried to trap the words behind her teeth, but even she had to obey a direct command from the queen. "Anterrian goaneth tiel ran lir—"

"Stop." The air vibrated, and Zovena rocked back as if I'd struck her across the face. I tilted my head to one side, frowning down at her. "You are the Keeper of Missives, are you not?"

"Yes."

"What exactly does the Keeper of Missives *do?* Tell me."

"It's an important role," Zovena blurted out. "The Keeper of Missives is in charge of all communication in and out of Ammontraíeth. Battle orders, news, secrets. All must go through me."

"Sounds like a glorified message runner. We have those back in Zilvaren, y'know. But the job is considered pretty *lowly* there."

The female had almost regained her composure; her facial features had returned to normal, but her eyes flashed like knives at this. "May... I...rise?" she gritted out.

"*No.*"

"You have no idea how difficult it is to deliver messages to the spies we have sequestered abroad—"

"How hard is it to deliver a letter to a high blood, right here in this court?"

She blinked, taken aback. "A letter? Here?"

"Mm-hmm. A piece of paper, in an envelope. Sealed, I assume." I looked at Carrion. "Letters are usually sealed, aren't they?"

"Usually," he agreed.

I faced the female again. "A letter like that would be relatively easy to deliver here, in the palace, no?"

"Obviously. Of *course*." She considered this line of questioning not worthy of her time, it seemed.

"So, explain something to me, then. My mate and my friends have written a number of letters to someone here at the Blood Court over the years. Did those letters not reach Ammontraíeth?"

Zovena bared her fangs, brow creasing with unnaturally deep furrows. "That male is *not* a member of this court. He is shunned. The shunned do not receive missives. And the enemies of my home do not get to address their allies here!"

"So they *did* arrive."

Zovena said nothing.

"I could *make* you tell me."

"Yes, they arrived. But—"

"Do you still have them in your *lair*, wherever that might be?" It wasn't wise to provoke her. I wasn't stupid enough to believe that this dynamic would exist between us for long. The high bloods of Sanasroth would find a way to oust me sooner or later, and then I wouldn't be able to bend Zovena to my will with words alone. It would take violence, but I was okay with that. If it was violence these monsters understood, then I would give it to them. I could be violent if I had to be. I could be cruel.

I let Zovena see the promise of that when she met my steady gaze. "Yes," she said tartly. "I do still have them."

"Then you'll give them to their intended recipient. Today."

The female set her jaw. "He can come down to my chambers and fetch them like the dog that he—"

"You will deliver them to the library. Personally." I spoke slowly, enunciating every single word. "Or I will come and find you. And when I'm done with you, there will be nothing left of you but your fucking *teeth*. Are we clear?"

She looked like she wanted to spit in my face; it was killing her not to. "As a winter's morn," she said.

My desires back in the Third had never been grand or grasping. Clean water. A decent meal. Clothes that wouldn't fall apart on me. I hadn't dreamed of much. I certainly hadn't dreamed of power. I wasn't enjoying any of this, but it had to be done. It was as I'd told Carrion just now: Zovena needed to know that, no matter how badly she wished otherwise, I *was* her better and I was *not* to be fucked with. I was about to dismiss her from my presence like a scolded child when the door to Tal's chambers swung open, and my maker appeared in the open doorway.

He was naked and spattered with blood...and his cock jutted *outrageously* hard from between his thighs. "If you're not coming in to join the fun, then *please* move this along. You're making me look like a bad host."

31

VAPOR AND SMOKE

KINGFISHER

THE FOX SMELLED like wild winter and frost-bitten mornings. I held him tightly under one arm, humming a lullaby that my mother had sung to me as an infant quietly under my breath.

Not to the fox.

I wasn't humming *to* the fox.

That would have been weird.

I just liked the song, and I had a feeling he did, too. There was nothing wrong with *that*.

Ana drowan, doyath drowan, teyra drowan cal su marn. Massurith, massurith, kalminan tu dan shay…

One fish, two fish, three fish in the tub. Around they go, around they go, swimming off to sea…

Onyx didn't so much as wriggle as I transported him through the palace. He didn't growl at the high bloods we passed. He didn't study the cold, unwelcoming surroundings he found himself in. He fixed his eyes on me, nose twitching, and he listened to me sing.

My magic was useless here—a source of unending frustration. *I* should have been able to ward Saeris's chambers against unwelcome visitors, but even that was beyond me here. Tal had been the one to take care of that task. He'd made sure I would have access to her rooms whenever I wanted, but the knowledge that it was *his* magic that provided an extra layer of security to her rooms and not mine chafed horribly as I made my way through the double doors to her bedroom.

The fox sat patiently in my arms as I carried him over to her bed.

Hris drowan mayth tair, hris drowan brin gilterrith, ayen hris drowan farh miniethh loss...

The first fish drowned, the second fish froze, and the third fish swallowed them all...

I ended the song with a flourish, setting the fox down onto the bed. He blinked up at me, eyes glassy and black as jet, not really sure what to make of my performance, it seemed.

"I'm sorry, little one. Now that I think about it, that isn't a very happy song, is it? Do you like fish? I bet you do, huh?"

The fox blinked.

"I bet you'd like some now, huh? Some tasty trout?"

His ears pricked up. I would have sworn to all the gods that he was smiling hopefully.

"Okay, okay. Let me see." My illusions were real as long as they were observed. A bath could be real. Clothes. But not food. It just didn't work like that. I had to pull that kind of magic from somewhere else, and that took concentration. I reached...reached...and grunted with the effort as I reached into my small magic, into a different place entirely, and I drew a silver bowl containing half a smoked piece of trout. Right about now, a barmaid at the Shag's Nest in Western Dow was wondering where in all five hells the order of smoked trout she'd just been carrying had disappeared to. It was no matter, though. I'd make sure to go there and pay them for the meal soon enough.

I set the little bowl down and then watched with straight-faced satisfaction as the fox hopped down from Saeris's bed and promptly scarfed the lot. The fish was gone in moments.

"All right, little one. I have to go now. Don't be causing any trouble while you wait for your mistress, okay?"

Onyx looked up at me, pink tongue licking his lips as he savored the taste of the meal I'd stolen for him.

"Go on. Go take a nap or something."

The fox yawned and then turned and darted under Saeris's bed.

I was at the door, hand on the knob, when I heard his soft whine. "What is it, hm?" Glancing back over my shoulder, I watched as the little white fox popped his head out from under the bed and then came trotting over to me with purpose. When he reached me, he ducked his head, and something small and brown hit the rug.

It was a pine cone.

One of the smallest—and most perfectly formed—I had ever seen.

Onyx nudged it with his nose, huffing, then looked up at me expectantly.

I stared down at the fox and the pine cone, hand still on the doorknob, not sure what to do. "Is that...for *me?*"

Onyx nudged the little spiked pine cone, butting it with his nose again, until it rolled and hit the toe of my boot. It *was* for me.

A gift.

I bent and collected it, tucking the memento into the inside pocket of my leathers. Before I turned and left, I scratched the little fox between his black-tipped ears, trying and failing to pretend that I was unmoved by the gesture. "*Thank* you, little one."

The library was deserted.

Lamps dotted the length of the clerk's table, their pale green glow forming small pools of light. Books were gathered in five neat stacks, ten tomes high each, at the far end of the table. The place was as silent as the grave.

As I crossed the entryway of the library, headed for the steps that led up to the stacks, a small black cat made of shadow appeared out of *my* shadow, taking me by surprise. Plenty of shadows had come from me before—that went without saying. But they'd done so at my behest, and none of them had ever solidified into something *living* afterward.

The cat dug its claws into the rug as it stretched, peering up at me with bloodred eyes.

"Where did *you* come from?" I asked it.

The shadow cat sniffed my leg curiously, tiny nostrils flaring.

"What can you smell?" I asked. "A fox? I don't know if the two of you would get along." As if it knew what I was saying, the shadow cat butted its head against my shins and began purring loud enough to wake the dead.

I stooped down to pet it, and the damned thing darted away, making for the stairs. On the bottom step, it paused, glancing over its shoulder as if to say, *Well, then. Are you coming?*

Saeris's scent hung in the air, faint but detectable, as I crossed the library and headed up the stairs. I lost her as I entered the stacks, following the feline, who trotted on ahead, occasionally looking back to make sure I was still there. I had always made it a rule to follow a cat. Particularly a *black* cat. This one was the darkest shade of midnight there was—an absence of light I knew all too well. My senses were on high alert as we wound through the high stacks, left, then right, then straight ahead for two rows. Magic hung thick in the air here, as the rows grew closer together and the light grew dim, veiling the titles of the hundreds of books that we passed.

The cat's feet barely seemed to touch the ground as it padded softly ahead. It rubbed its side against the corner of a shelf as it waited for me to catch up, its long, dexterous tail swaying side to side like a blade of tall grass on a breeze. Once I was close enough for its liking, it took a left, disappearing into a walkway (or more of a tunnel, perhaps), constructed entirely from dusty old books.

Golden light flickered at the end of the tunnel.

When I exited the tunnel, I found myself in a high-ceilinged section of the library that felt very different from the rest of it. A table. A chair. In the far corner: a bed, half-concealed behind a maroon velvet curtain edged with a golden tassel fringe. The walls were made of the stacks themselves, which had been arranged to form a sort of internal sanctuary, separate from everything else.

The rug underfoot was threadbare at the entrance to the snug. Threadbare also along the section before the large hearth on the far wall, in which a fire crackled merrily in the grate; the bald spots in there indicated many hours during which someone had paced, lost in their thoughts.

In the center of the cloistered space was a large table, on top of which sat a contraption made of cogs and long, spindled arms with shining brass balls attached at their ends. The arms were still, but over time, they would move. It was an orrery. A beautiful one, too. Once, there had been one in my father's study. As a Faeling, I'd been fascinated by the complex workings of it. My parents had sat at the device, studying it at length. They'd shown me the planets as they were represented by the globes of inlaid silver and copper—how they danced around one another, all spinning around the much larger golden sun at its center.

This orrery was very different from the one in my father's study. The alignment and the *number* of the planets were different. It was beautiful to be sure.

If there were time, I would have stayed and appreciated the crafts-manship of the device a little longer—orreries were notoriously diffi-cult to make—but I had come in search of its owner, and I had a feeling I would find him among the *real* stars.

A rolling ladder had been bolted to the wall to the right. Twenty feet up, a small window stood open, the heavy curtain that was par-tially drawn across it billowing on a cold breeze. The cat sat at the bot-tom of the ladder and looked up at the open window, its meaning clear: Your friend is waiting for you up there.

So be it.

At the foot of the ladder, the cat meowed, blinking slowly at me. It did a turn, the way cats do when they're about to lie down and nap, but when this one stretched its front paws out, it became a thing of ink and darkness again and disappeared into the long shadow I cast across the moth-eaten rug.

"All right, then," I muttered to myself.

I felt no different. Aside from having just seen it happen with my own two eyes, I had no evidence that the cat had just *merged* with me somehow. I shrugged and climbed the ladder. The window was three feet tall and only two feet wide. I had to fold myself considerably and angle my shoulders to slide through and out onto the narrow walkway beyond. A low parapet ran around the domed roof, providing minimal protection from the three-hundred-foot drop that fell away on the other side of it.

Above, the stars rioted, blistering and brilliant.

I had walked halfway around the dome before I came across the recessed flat section of roof where a male sat at a small, weather-beaten desk, perched high above the world, scrawling away in a book with a feather quill. Though he didn't look at me, he knew that I had come: the brief pause... and then resumption of his scribbling confirmed it.

Once, Foley had been a lord's son. His father, Warrick Briarstone, had been advisor to King Rurik. Their family line had been second only to the Daianthuses in power and pride. If the true king had not been slain by Belikon, Foley would have eventually risen in rank to become the second most powerful male in all Yvelia. It was the duty of a king's advisor to act in his stead in emergencies, and as such, a lot of responsibility was placed on his shoulders. Foley had been born to be respected and to work diligently in service of his realm, and instead he had learned how to fight and had joined the Lupo Proelia. And now he hid here in his tower on top of the world, among an ocean of books, a shunned vampire who was too afraid to look up and face an old friend.

The scratching of his quill stopped at last. He set it down. "I see Guru hitched a ride with you," he said quietly. "He does that sometimes."

When I looked down, I found that the cat was already there, looking back up at me. Whole. Alive. Purring.

"He likes to chase the birds. They used to roost here at night, a long... time ago." He seemed to get lost along the way as he spoke, as if he were, in truth, too weary to complete the thought out loud and had to force himself to finish it.

"Foley." I said his name, and the male flinched at the sound of it. "Foley, *look* at me."

He stared down at his book, frozen solid.

"All right. Fine." There was no second chair on the roof, only the one Foley currently sat in, but there was a wooden crate full of odds and ends that he'd obviously used to carry items up here in. I upended the crate, dumping the leather tubes, ink bottles, and other bits and pieces onto the roof, flipped the crate upside down, and sat down across from him.

Where was I supposed to start? Foley and I had never laughed together all that much. He'd always been far more serious than the others. More serious than Renfis, even. But there had been an easy camaraderie between this male and me. An understanding, it could be said, of a life that should have been, now lost. We had both been subject to Belikon's ire—heirs to a future that he had gone to great pains to destroy—and had suffered his close attention until it had become too much to bear. We'd become brothers out of necessity, more than anything. Inseparable. But so much time had passed. Lifetimes during which we'd both endured the kind of misery that would have ended most other males.

I didn't know where to begin, but the last thing I would do was rush him. I sat silently, leaning down to pet the cat when he approached and started begging for affection. Guru was an appropriate name for him; he seemed wise. The wind teased at our hair and plucked at our shirts. It scattered Guru's solid edges, smudging him as if he were a charcoal drawing being swept from a page.

Foley looked up from his book, glancing off to the right, at the rise of the tower's domed slate roof. He covered his mouth with his hand. "You don't need to do this," he said, his fingers muffling his words.

I smiled slowly, sadly, arching a brow at him. "And when have you ever known *me* to do something I don't want to do?"

He huffed, as if acknowledging the truth in that, but didn't say anything else.

I let the silence sit a moment longer, then I said, "You have a fire burning down there. Real flames, not evenlight."

He nodded. "I like the warmth of it," he said. "It... *reminds* me."

Of what it was like to live. The words went unsaid, but I gathered his meaning perfectly well. "I noticed the titles on some of those books down there, too. You made your home in the philosophy and morality section?" I allowed myself a small smile.

Foley did the same, but *his* smile was tight around his eyes. "Hm," he said. "The creatures here have very little interest in either. Seemed like the safest place for me." He laughed bitterly, finally turning his gaze to me. "You look the same," he said. "Tal used to tell me what you were going through. I..." Both of his eyebrows rose. "I thought you'd never be free of it. I wanted to help. I..."

Slowly, I shook my head. "It's gone. Done. Passed. I'm okay."

"Are you just saying that to make me feel better?" he asked.

I shook my head. "I mean it." And I *did*. My dreams were often nightmares, but they were nothing I couldn't handle. Carefully, I said, "*She* has a tendency to make things feel better." I laughed, a little chagrined by the admission. "Even when they're *not*."

Foley's chair creaked as he sat back in it. His eyes narrowed at me, and for the first time, I saw that he *didn't* look the same anymore. Not quite. His pupils were vertical now, rather than round. There was a flighty, hunted shadow behind his eyes that made my chest hurt.

His hair was cut short.

It should have been longer.

"She?" he said. "The female? Saeris?"

I chuckled at his apparent surprise. "That's the one."

He seemed to struggle for his next words. "It's real, then? The God Bindings? All of it?"

I pursed my lips, taking a beat to stare down at the table. "God, I hope so. If it isn't, then I've officially lost my mind. It feels more real than anything else I've ever experienced. She's..." Gods. How in all five hells did you describe Saeris Fane?

"Remarkable," Foley said. The way he said it didn't sound wholly like it was meant to be a compliment. The word was at least half of a condemnation.

Again, I laughed. "She's changed everything," I admitted.

"And the fact that she's half vampire? That she's the ruler of this place?"

"Means nothing," I said. "She isn't a half of anything. She's all *Saeris*. I love her."

My old friend watched me, his quick eyes scouring my face. After a long moment, he said, "Okay," as if that settled the matter and it would never be spoken of again. "What else?" he said.

"You're coming back to Cahlish," I told him.

Foley shook his head. "I'm not. I'm staying here."

"Foley, you don't belong here. You're—"

"I'm not going anywhere. I can't leave Ammontraíeth—"

"Your place is with us. Your friends. We miss you. You need you. We—"

"GODSDAMNIT, FISHER! YOU DON'T UNDERSTAND WHAT IT'S LIKE!" He smashed his fist onto the table. His feather quill jumped and rolled onto the roof with a clatter. "There are people I love out there in the world. You. Lorreth. Vash. Mayen. I would sell my soul to keep all of you safe, but the demon crouching on my shoulder's already fucking taken it. I have no soul left. The hunger eats *me*, Fisher." Tears welled in his eyes, ruby red and confronting—a truth that could not be denied. He spoke it out loud, though, so there could be no misunderstanding. "I am a vampire. I feed on the blood of the living." He bared his teeth, showing them to me. Gold, engraved, and vicious. "They ripped my canines out when I wouldn't kneel and shoved these in my mouth so I couldn't feed. But I still drink, Fisher. Ask me how."

"It doesn't matter.

"From rats. Birds. Anything I can hunt, catch, and kill. Because it's a part of me now. The hunting. The killing. I pull them apart and I drain them dry, and then I do it again, and again, and again—"

"It doesn't matter."

A trail of blood streaked down his cheek. "There is no dignity left in this body, Fisher. I'm not your brother anymore. I am something so low and reviled that I cannot even settle on a name for myself. Monster. Devil. Murderer. None comes close enough to explain the evil that crawls in my veins. I—"

"You are my brother. And it doesn't matter."

Foley drew in a shaking breath. "I cannot leave this place," he whispered.

"When was the last time you took a life?"

He closed his eyes. "I..."

"When was the last time you attacked a member of the Fae and drank them dry?"

He shook his head, swallowing. "Not since... Ajun."

"You haven't fed on Fae blood since *Ajun*?" I wanted to bury my face in my hands and scream. "Whe—" I stopped. Sighed heavily. "When was the last time you were around a living, breathing member of the Fae?"

"Your mate..." he said, trailing off.

"Did you think about eating her?"

"No, I... I was more focused on *killing* her, I'm afraid."

"But you saw Lorreth, too, didn't you? Did you try to kill *him*?"

A deep crease formed between Foley's brows, as if he hadn't even considered this. "No, I... didn't. I remember thinking his scent was enticing, but... I didn't think about *feeding* from him."

"And before then, when was the last time? When were you around someone and the hunger felt too strong to control?"

He thought long and hard. "Seven hundred years ago."

"And did you eat *that* person?"

"No."

"Gods alive, Foley. You're so fucking... urgh!" Frustration transformed my words into a snarl. Quickly, before he could stop me, I sank my teeth into my wrist and made a small incision. He was up and out of his seat and clinging to the parapet rail before the first drop of my blood hit the table.

"Mercy! Gods!" he panted. "What are you *doing*?" His eyes were full of fear.

"You aren't new to this life anymore, Foley." I didn't get up. Between us, Guru sat quite comfortably, batting the feather quill that had fallen to the roof with his paw. *Tap. Tap, tap.* He jumped up and came running when he noticed the bead of blood that had dropped to the ground at my feet. Yowling, he looked up at me, as if asking for my permission; *of course* the strange little thing drank blood. "Go ahead, little prince," I told him.

Foley's tormented eyes nearly rolled back into his head as the cat began to lap.

"Seven hundred years ago, you were young. The thirst still had hold of you. You didn't know how to control it. I hate to break it to you, but there are members of the Fae down there, in the town. I can scent them from here, which means you *certainly* can. You haven't torn down there and laid waste to any of them, have you?"

"No," he said breathlessly. "I haven't."

"There you are, then."

He seemed to shatter out of nowhere, his fear getting the better of him. More tears fell, staining his pale skin with tributaries of blood. "How am I supposed to know? How am I supposed to *trust* myself?"

"You'll know that when you can walk across this roof and come sit back at this table with me."

He eyed my blood, pooling on the table in front of me. I had created only a small wound, nothing that would pose me any real problems. The bleeding was already slowing. Soon it would stop altogether.

"I *can't*, Fisher! I—"

"Don't look at it. Here. Look at this." I reached into my pocket and took out the small wooden box I had been carrying.

Foley's attention bounced from my blood to the box, my blood, the box, my blood... It settled on the box. "What is it?"

"It's a box."

"I can *see* that," he shot back. "But... what's *inside* it?"

I tapped the box's lid. "A *real* demon," I told him.

Foley spun around, facing out into the night. He interlaced his fingers behind his head, hissing in Old Fae. "Otariallan dyer mé."

"No," I said. "I'm *not* kidding. Believe me, I wish I was, but I'm not."

Slowly, Foley turned to look at the box over his shoulder. "Which one?" he asked.

"Joshin."

"Which one is that? I can't remember."

"The scorpion demon," I said dryly. "King of the Dark Dream."

"Gods and sinners have mercy." Foley lowered his arms, turning, his golden teeth glinting in the muted light. "And what are you doing, carrying it around *in a box*?"

"I made a deal with it."

"You did *what*?"

"I didn't have a choice. It stung me. Carrion, too. We needed its venom."

"Who's Carrion?"

I almost laughed. In another life, gods almighty, they would have relied upon each other, those two males. Ruefully, I admitted, "He's a friend. You'll meet him soon enough, I'm sure."

Foley chewed the inside of his cheek, processing that. His eyes darted to the small puddle of cooling blood on the table but quickly flitted away again. "All right. So . . . what kind of deal?"

I recounted it for him, word for word. "One secret and its venom in exchange for our lives. But I had to agree to release it once we were okay. I swore that I wouldn't place it into a demon trap."

"Fuck. So it's in there, then? All of it?"

"What's *left* of it."

"And you're okay now? Why haven't you released it?"

Ahh, the beauty of the fine print. Even in a rush and dancing on death's doorstep, there was always a way to swing a bargain in your favor if you paid close attention to the details. "Because I didn't say *when* I'd release it," I explained. "Nor did I say *where*. And the box isn't a demon trap. It's just a box." I tapped my finger against the lid again, and the furious scorpion inside threw itself at the walls of its new prison. "Don't worry, Joshin. I'll uphold my end of the bargain soon enough. I'm a male of my word, after all." The box rattled again. Slowly, Foley crept toward the table to get a better look.

"Why have you brought it here?" he asked.

"Because I won't risk leaving it at Cahlish. I just can't. And I can't keep carrying it around with me. I can hear it whispering all the time, and well, it doesn't exactly have anything *nice* to say to me." I gave him a lopsided smile. "Are you still a member of the Lupo Proelia, Foley? In there?" I pointed at his chest.

The vampire looked down at his solar plexus, his right hand closing around the hilt of a sword that he hadn't been able to hold for nearly a thousand years. His eyes shone bright when he looked back up at me. "Yes. Sometimes. When I dare to dream of a reality in which I still might be *good*."

"Dreams are just vapor and smoke," I said. "They mean nothing unless you're willing to live them. You *are* good. You *are* my brother. *You are a wolf.* Nothing will ever change that." I slid the box toward him across the table, holding my breath. Would he do it? Would he sit?

Gingerly, Foley took the chair he had kicked away when he'd leaped up and placed it back at the table. He moved painfully slowly as he sat down, but still he sat. A long moment passed, in which he looked at the glossy, near-black pool of blood on the surface of the table and shivered. Eventually, he reached out a shaking hand and picked up the small wooden box. "I'll keep it here for you for now. I'll watch over it until you ask for it back. But in the meantime...tell me about the demon's secret."

32

THE THING ABOUT LEANING

SAERIS

IT HADN'T BEEN angry tension I'd sensed behind Tal's door.

It had been *sexual*.

For fuck's sake.

I stared dutifully up at the ceiling as we followed the Keeper of Secrets into his chambers, determined not to witness any more of Tal's naked form than I already had. My cheeks were on fire. "Where were you back there?" I hissed, clouting Carrion's arm. "What happened to 'I'll make sure no one messes with her'?"

"*Ow!* You're so fucking violent! You had that entire situation under control. And far be it from *me* to break up the beginnings of a cat fight. She's gone now, anyway. She scurried off real quick the moment your *man* showed up here." There was a tone to his voice, something that sounded decidedly nefarious. When I glimpsed him out of the corner of my eye, I saw that *his* eyes were not on the ceiling. They were fixed ahead and moving down, down...

I hit him even harder this time. "*What* are you *doing*?"

"If he didn't want anyone admiring his bare ass, then he would have thrown on a robe before he came to the door, Saeris."

"Can you just *stop*—"

Tal turned around. My eyes shot back up to the ceiling.

"It's commendable that you're trying to protect my modesty, Saeris, but Carrion's right. I have none. I really don't care if he's checking out my ass. Unfortunately for you, Swift, my sexuality doesn't lean in your direction."

"That's okay. The thing about leaning is that it's *very* unstable. The ground could shift, and you find yourself leaning in a completely different direction at any moment. I, myself, have experienced all *kinds* of leanings."

Tal smiled a little dubiously at him. "You'll be the first to know if the ground shifts beneath my feet."

Carrion sighed, walking past my maker. "It's all right. It would have happened by now if it was going to. That kind of thing usually occurs *on sight* where I'm concerned." Clearly, now that the possibility of sex was off the table, he'd lost interest in my maker. He pointed at the open doorway in front of us. "What the hell's going on in there, then?"

"Some friends and I were enjoying a glass of wine," Tal said in a vague, noncommittal kind of way.

Seven naked Fae females sprawled out on an unbelievably big bed in the room beyond. They were in various stages of undress; I'd spent enough time at Kala's to be very accustomed to seeing women wandering around in their bare skin, but this was different.

The women at Kala's used sex to their benefit. It paid their bills and kept them safe, and there was nothing wrong with that. But there was a hunger in the room up ahead that I'd never witnessed at Kala's. The Fae females on that bed were watching Taladaius like they had been starving all their lives, and he was their first chance at a real meal. Their desire clouded the air until the room was thick with it. It felt as though the whole place would combust if someone mistakenly lit a match.

One of the females in the center of the bed started kissing the female next to her, touching herself between her legs as she did so, and Carrion dragged his bottom lip through his teeth. "What does a person have to do to secure an invitation to one of your wine soirees, Taladaius?"

Tal's silver hair fell into his face as he bent to collect a shirt from the floor. When he straightened again, slipping his arms in the shirt, he was smirking wickedly. "Oh, you're welcome anytime, Carrion Swift. You can join us for a glass now, if you like. But these females have been *friends* of mine for a while now. They're used to a certain level of... *conversation*. D'you think you can..." His eyebrows hiked halfway up his forehead, his eyes drifting down to Carrion's crotch. "*Keep up?*"

I'd seen Carrion charm the most beautiful women in the Third out of their clothes. He'd managed to talk *me* into his bed, and I had put up a valiant fight, too. I'd never seen him back down from a challenge, but Tal's implication—that the women on that bed were used to a certain level of pleasure that apparently Tal was more than capable of proving to all seven of them, all by himself? Yeah, that made the smuggler blink.

"Hm. I'm pretty good at conversation, but... maybe not so versed in talking to *that* many females at once."

Tal tried not to let his smirk get away from him, I could tell. He clapped Carrion on the shoulder. "Don't worry, Daianthus. Practice makes perfect." He kicked his way into a pair of pants that looked like they had been discarded on the floor in a hurry, biting the tip of his tongue as he carefully fastened himself into them.

Gods almighty, this was terrible. "Maybe we should come back later," I said. The females on the bed had all started touching and caressing each other, their soft moans urging Tal to return to them. He held up a finger as he walked backward toward the open doorway. "Just one minute." He closed the door behind himself, and the room erupted into giggles and even louder moaning.

Carrion and I looked at each other awkwardly.

"Did you hear that?" he asked.

"I'm trying not to hear *anything* right now."

"He called me Daianthus."

"Oh. Right. Yeah, well, I mean... you *are* a Daianthus." Poor Carrion. Ever since we'd discovered who he really was, we'd kept calling him Swift. No one had thought to ask him if he wanted to be referred to as his proper name: Carrion Daianthus. It was a Fae custom, I'd learned not too long ago, that parents didn't name their newborns for a full year after their birth. It had started as a practical matter—a long time ago, a high percentage of Faelings didn't survive their first year of life, and naming them felt like an invitation for ill luck to visit them. If Death didn't know the name of a child, then how could he possibly find it and carry it away? Many thousands of years had passed since then. Faelings almost never died during infancy now, but the practice of the nameless child remained out of long-standing tradition.

Rurik and Amelia Daianthus never got the chance to name their firstborn son. He had been called Carrion by the woman who had saved him from the quicksilver pool back in Zilvaren. Carrion, because she hadn't known what that word had meant, and some guards had called him that as she'd snuck him out of the palace. And Swift, because *she* was a Swift, and the moment she had laid eyes on him, squalling and naked, he had become hers.

"Do you want to be called Daianthus now? I can tell the others. It *is* your right. And it's not as though we're keeping your identity a secret or anything. You did announce it to everyone back in the maze. That cat is *definitely* out of the bag."

Carrion rubbed the back of his neck awkwardly. "No, it's fine. Swift's only one syllable. Daianthus is three. It'd be a mouthful for you guys to spit out when you're yelling at me. I wouldn't want to inconvenience anyone."

"*Carrion.*"

"Swift's fine, Saeris. That's as much my name as any other. I'm happy being who I've always been."

"I get that. I understand. Listen, Carrion. I haven't had a chance to talk to you properly since you got back, but, well, Fisher told me about Gracia, and, well…" Gods alive, I was bad at this. The second I said Gracia's name, Carrion shut down. I saw it happen.

"It's fine. You don't need to say anything, Saeris. She was an old lady. A *grumpy* one. She was bound to die eventually. I'm used to it. I've *had* to be. We don't need to—"

The door to Tal's bedroom flew open, and the pale-haired male strode through it with purpose. He wiped his mouth with the back of his hand, discreetly cleaning away a thin trail of blood from his chin. "All right, then. I presume you need to discuss something with me? I doubt you would have been lurking outside my chambers otherwise. What is it?"

What with the tricky conversation I'd just utterly botched and the sight of all those naked females in Tal's room, I'd temporarily misplaced our reason for coming here. "*Fae* females, Tal?"

The vampire met my eye, unabashed. "Absolutely. I prefer my bedmates warm," he said. "They're here willingly. They'd never go home and I wouldn't know a moment's peace if I didn't force them to leave. I assure you, the exchange is voluntary and mutually beneficial. But I think you know all about *that*."

The blood trade.

The females got high from Tal's venom and had the most intense orgasms imaginable, and Tal got to feed. Just a little sip from each of them was probably enough to sate his hunger, and they had the time of their lives. I supposed that *did* sound mutually beneficial.

"One of these days, I'm going to stop feeling like I'm on the back foot, here," Carrion grumbled. "Why are you blushing, Saeris? *You do not blush.*"

"Never mind that. Just...I can blush if I want to, okay?" I exhaled, slow and steady. "Tal, the door to the tomb was barred, and those two idiots from your tavern were there waiting for us."

"You have a *tavern*?" Tal had just risen even higher in Carrion's estimation.

My maker ignored the remark. "Yes. I told them to do it. I heard from Lorreth that Belikon's advisor and a handful of his guards slipped through the silver while you were in the tomb last. I can't have Belikon's guards—or *anyone*, for that matter—just showing up in Ammontraíeth. It made sense to lock the door and post Anterrin and Khol there. I had to find something for them to do, didn't I, since Lorreth *maimed* one of them."

"And that was supposed to keep magic users out? A locked door?"

"No, obviously not. It was supposed to give Anterrin and Khol enough time to alert me as to what was happening, so I could deal with the situation in a manner I saw fit."

"Shouldn't *I* be dealing with any issues that come through the quicksilver?"

"Yes, Saeris, you should. But since you keep disappearing off with your mate and not telling me where you're going, I have to be ready to take matters into my own hands, don't I?" There was no malice to his words. No ire. He flashed me a beatific smile and started walking toward the door to his chambers. "I found *this* when I went to inspect the tomb for structural damage first thing this evening." He reached the side table by the entrance to his chambers and used a black silk scarf to pick up the weapon sitting on the polished wood.

It was one of the blades Belikon's men had been carrying the other day. I had barely been able to affect them. They possessed unnatural properties—it had made my temples pound to even *try* to read the metals with my power. Everything about the weapons had felt wrong. Even now, this one pulled at the light and leached the air from the room.

"I do not like this dagger. Touching it nearly put me in the ground for good. It made me..." He pondered the ceiling, frowning. "It made me want to peel out of my skin and throw myself into a burning lake of fire. It's evil, and I do not want it in my chambers any longer."

He thrust it out at me, gesturing for me to take it. I hadn't felt the way he'd described when I'd fought Belikon's guards, but then again, I hadn't touched any of their daggers with my bare hands. It probably wasn't wise to do so now, either, just in case. Maybe it was like a god sword. Maybe only its owner was supposed to touch it like that. I accepted the dagger from Tal, using the silk scarf to protect my hand the same way he had.

"What *is* it?" he asked.

"I don't know what it is. Orious called it a null blade."

"Never heard the term," Tal said. "It doesn't really matter what it is, I suppose, just so long as it isn't *here* anymore. You need to throw it into a very deep pit or something."

"And where might I find one of *those*?"

"Beyond the western ridge. Ride for thirty minutes in that direction and you'll find plenty of holes in the ground."

There was a knock at the door. Tal opened it, and a bone-thin female with razor-sharp cheekbones and eyes as black as coal stood on the other side of it. She wasn't Fae. Wasn't a high blood, either. There were strange, frilled gills at her elongated neck; however, it looked as though they had been sewn shut. Her straight black hair hung like a sheet of silk to her shoulders, hiding her mutilated gills for the most part. She bowed her head, surprise flashing over her face when she registered my presence. She was halfway to the ground when I reached out and caught her by the elbow.

"Please don't do that," I told her. "Not right now." I'd well and truly had enough of all the kneeling for one day.

The female's eyes widened, but she didn't protest. "My apologies, Your Highness. Lord, I'm sorry to disturb you. I came to tell you that I had as yet been unsuccessful in tracking down the venerable queen for her fitting, but it appears that the fates smile upon me tonight. I've found her here with you." The female placed her hand on her chest and bowed slightly, and the light caught on her metallic, talon-like fingernails. Her fingers were twice as long as mine and half as thin. There was something unnervingly spiderlike about them.

"My *fitting*?" I asked.

"Yes. For the ball tomorrow night. Come in, Yanica. You can take her measurements while she's here. She's bound to slip away otherwise. You should measure *him* up, too." He gestured to Carrion.

I smiled distractedly at the female as she floated into the room. Once she was inside and had begun unraveling a black roll full of sewing implements, I turned on Tal. "I'm sorry, what *ball*?"

"The Evenlight Ball, of course. Don't you celebrate that in Zilvaren?"

I was about to say no, of course we don't, but I wasn't able to. "We do, actually. But it's a festival, not a ball," I admitted.

"Madra stands on a dais and addresses the whole city for an hour," Carrion added. "Ranting and raving about the dangers of magic and how mythical Fae monsters are trying to infiltrate the city to corrupt us and steal our children." He grinned, waggling his fingers.

I rolled my eyes at him. "After that, she gives everyone a double ration of water and a bowl of greasy stew, and then there's music. It's the only day of the year when people don't have to work."

"Sounds *delightful*," Tal said dryly. "It's a little more fun here. Food. Wine. Dancing. Sex. Historically, there have been no grand speeches. You could change that if you're feeling homesick, but I wouldn't recommend it. You're already pretty unpopular."

"I can't attend a ball right now, Tal. I don't have *time*."

"You're mistaken. You don't have a *choice*. The Evenlight Ball is non-negotiable. The ruler of the Blood Court presides over the evening and must officially open the celebrations. The party cannot begin without their official say-so. If you don't attend, you will be openly shirking your position as queen here and letting everyone know exactly what you think of Sanasroth and the Blood Court. It wouldn't be a good look. And even if all of that wasn't the case, it is even more vital that you attend this year's festivities, since the Evenlight Ball is now doubling as a selection evening."

"Selection evening?"

"Yes. We've held only one before. Until fairly recently, there was another Lord of Midnight, Xarris. He was killed by his own brother after some pointless disagreement. A selection was held, and that's when Malcolm named Algat as a Lord and Keeper of Records. We must have another selection, so that candidates who wish to present themselves to become the new Lord of Midnight might be considered."

"I'm not overseeing that. *I* can't be in charge of making that decision."

"Well, then, your mate should have considered that before he killed Ereth. Not that I'm complaining, of course. Ereth was a repugnant zealot with really bad breath. But now there are only four Lords of Midnight, and there have to be five, which means that, yes, *you* have to hear people's petitions, and *you* have to select a new one. My advice?

Do it quickly. The high bloods will get antsy if they have to wait too long to indulge their appetites."

My mouth fell open. "Tal!"

"And then there's also that small matter we discussed at the Fool's Paradise not too long ago," he said, leaning in close. "The ball is the perfect opportunity to take care of that as well. I would consider it a personal favor to me if you could see your way to sticking around long enough so that can be taken care of, too. And I *did* save your life, so..."

I was fucked.

Royally so, it would seem.

I gave up. "All right. A ball." I threw my hands up, exasperated. "I'm going to a ball. *Great.*"

"If you could just lift your arms again for me, Your Highness?" Yanica, with her silky hair and metallic fingernails, made me jump. She hadn't made a sound as she'd crept up behind me. Her scent hadn't given her away, either. She didn't smell of anything at all.

"I'm sorry, Yanica. I don't have time for a fitting right now. There are other matters I need to attend to. I'm sure you're an excellent dressmaker, though. Can't you just eyeball it?"

The female stepped back, nearly dropping the measuring tape she was holding. "Eyeball? I'm sorry, Your Highness. Far be it from me to correct the illustrious queen, but I am not a *dressmaker.* I am the royal master tailor. I have served this court faithfully for the past two hundred years. It is my privilege and right to dress the Blood Court's nobility. The gown you wear tomorrow evening is a showcase of my talents. It must fit you like a glove. I'm sorry, I—I cannot just *guess* your measurements. An ill-fitting garment will bring shame to my household and my name."

Tal said nothing. Carrion slid his hands into his pockets, giving me a shrug. "Sorry, sunshine. I don't think you can really argue with that."

Grudgingly, I let the woman take my measurements.

The null blade thrummed in the scabbard on my thigh as I climbed. By the time I reached the library, my leg was numb from my hip to my knee, and I wanted to cry. My runes ached, pain shuttling up and down my arm in waves. I wanted to be rid of the weapon just as badly as Tal had, but without knowing exactly what it was or what it was capable of, hurling it off a cliff felt like a missed opportunity. Orious had said that all Belikon's guards were equipped with these things, and after what had transpired in the tomb, it was pretty obvious we were going to have to face them again. There would be more guards. More null blades.

This was an opportunity, and, as uncomfortable as carrying the blade was, I didn't really have a choice. It *needed* to be studied.

Carrion had stayed back at Tal's chambers to be measured. He'd said something about going to fetch his sword, too, but had promised to catch up with me as soon as he was done. On the stairs, the sound of my footsteps was my only company.

When I arrived at last, the library rang with a deafening silence. Fisher's scent hung thick in the air, telling me exactly which direction he had gone when he'd come up here earlier. But before I headed into the stacks, I needed to take precautions.

"Algat?" My cry bounced around the vaulted space.

Nothing.

"Algat!" The Keeper of Records had been very clear when she'd told me I should only visit the library during the hour right after dusk and the hour directly before dawn. She was in no position to tell me what to do, but even so, if I was about to go toe-to-toe with the old crone, I'd prefer to know about it beforehand, especially since she was probably furious that I'd taken a book from the library.

The female didn't come.

I took off and headed for the stacks. I hummed as I went, trying to ease the disquiet in the back of my mind—the urgency to rip the null blade from the scabbard and hurl it as far as possible. It was an awful sensation, one that couldn't be described, but the knife was full of hate. It *wanted* to cause harm.

Fisher's scent grew stronger as I wound through the rows and rows of books. Every step I took drew me closer to him, and with it, the tension between my shoulder blades eased. It was like this now: a rope pulled taut between us, and the farther apart we were, the tighter it pulled. It was only when we were together that I felt like I could breathe properly. He was clo—

"Oh!" I pressed my hand to my chest. "Hello." I'd jolted back, surprised, but the sudden movement up ahead was only one of the library's stargazers. The paper bird hovered in the air about two feet from my face, flitting from side to side as it watched me. I took a step forward, and it hovered backward in concert with my movement. Its tiny head seemed to cock to one side, its wings flapping a mile a minute.

"Inquisitive little creature, aren't you?" I extended my hand, curious to see if the bird would alight on the end of my finger, but it darted back and away. "Oops. Sorry. It's okay. I'm not gonna hurt you."

It flew off.

"Okay. Bye, then." It was a wonder. I was sad to see it go. But when I went left, turning down another row of books, there were *three* stargazers there, hovering, waiting for me.

"Huh. Are we playing a game?" There was a note of suspicion in my voice now. Foley's warning hadn't wandered far from the forefront of my mind. He'd said the birds were guileless things. Easily coerced. I wasn't concerned about the birds themselves. Foley had also mentioned malcontent witches, tricking them into stealing my hair, and it was *that* idea that gave me pause.

I shifted my weight into my left foot, resting my hands on top of Erromar and Selanir, where they hung at my hips. "Are you going to let me by?"

As if they understood what I had said, two of the stargazers moved to the left, the other to the right, making room for me to pass.

"Thank you." Slightly bemused, I kept walking, turning down another stack—where another five stargazers were waiting. Over my shoulder, the three I had just passed were following close behind. "Okay, this is getting a little creepy, folks." More of them darted around the corner. More, suddenly swooping over the top of the stacks and diving down. Tens of them. Hundreds. They gathered overhead, flocking in a circle, the rustle of paper wings growing louder until it was all that I could hear.

"*Fuck,*" I whispered.

And then I ran.

Bone-white missiles zipped past my ears as I careened through the library. Left. Right. Right again. Left. The stargazers buzzed my head, swooping, snagging in my hair, teasing it loose from my braid. They crashed into me, pinwheeling to the floor and sliding, only to take off again, whirling around my head.

I swatted them away, batting them out of the air, but they only rose again. I spun left and collided with a pile of books that had been stacked haphazardly on the floor. They crashed to the ground, skidding in every direction, nearly bringing me down with them, but I kept my feet. I charged forward, emerging into a small clearing amid the stacks, and my frustration finally won out over my alarm.

They were birds.

Paper *birds.*

I stopped running and shielded my eyes with my hands, peering through my fingers to assess the situation. There were so many stargazers now, hundreds of them; they flew around me, faster, faster, faster—a vortex of them, whipping around and up toward the library's rafters like one of the dust devils that tore across the dunes back in Zilvaren, only much, much bigger.

It...it was *beautiful.*

Cautiously, I lowered my hands and took it all in. The stargazers formed a tunnel, and I was at its center. The birds stirred the air, creating a breeze that blew my loose strands of hair around my head.

I'd never seen anything quite so lovely—or *magical*—in all my life.

If crows had their murders and vultures had their wakes, then the spectacle of these stargazers, moving harmony, could only be one thing: a constellation.

"Impressive..." The thought was whispered out loud, and the birds reacted. A single stargazer broke away from the wheeling mass and dropped from the air like a stone. A split second before it hit the floor, it pulled up and hair-pinned in the air, coming right at me.

It happened too quickly; I didn't get my hand up in time. The edge of the stargazer's wing sliced my cheekbone, leaving a bright sting of pain in its wake.

"*Ahhh!* What—" This was the *second* time one of them had cut me. "That *really* isn't *nice*," I hissed. I prepared for what would come next— the raining hail of angry stargazers all set on drawing blood. Death by a thousand cuts—but none of the other birds fell from the cyclone of flapping wings. The air seemed to thicken with tension. The birds flew faster. Faster still. They flew so fast that it became impossible to discern one bird from another, and the entire mass became a fluttering, rushing mass of white.

Craning my neck, I looked up and shook my head. "What . . . the hell . . . is *happening?*"

At once, the cyclone stopped dead. The birds began to fall out of the air, spinning or else nosediving, just like the first bird who had cut me and fallen, lifeless, to the steps outside the library. I watched, speechless, as the first birds to hit the floor began to unfold, their wings snapping open, their bodies, their beaks, until they were crumpled sheets of paper. Others unfolded midair and floated down much slower, like fat flakes of snow. The world became fluttering, creased sheets of paper.

I plucked one out of the air as it drifted past my face, and there, on the paper, were lines and lines of elegant, slanted handwriting.

In most cases, the power is too great. The Alchemist will need to surrender . . .
My heart pounded.

I plucked another sheet of paper from the air.

. . . often painful. Historically, it was recommended that a counterbalance be used as a kind of Alchemical overflow mechanism . . .

The writing spoke of Alchemical magic. All of the pages—*so many pages!*—were *full* of text about Alchemy. My mind would not comprehend it. I'd picked the library at Cahlish clean. Both Algat and Foley *had* confirmed that there were books on Alchemy in this library here, but neither of them had considered the stargazers.

The birds had been here for centuries. Longer than anyone could remember...

And all along, they had been the pages of a book.

Fast as I could, I started to collect them from the floor. Sheaves and sheaves of paper. They were wrinkled and yellowed by time around the edges, but the writing had been on the *inside* of the pages; the words there, written in black ink, had been protected by the stargazer's folds. I'd collected half of the pages from the floor when they started to rattle in my hands. I clamped the pile between my fingers, determined to keep hold of them, but then they were ripped free by some invisible force.

"No!" My shout echoed around the library. *"Please!"*

The pages didn't listen. They flew through the air and tumbled one over the other, gathering into a ball. Before my eyes, they organized themselves into a single, ordered pile... and then they *were* a book.

Navy blue cloth cover.

Thick.

A tiny silver butterfly was stamped in foil on the front cover.

Other than that, there were no gilded edges. No fancy woven tassel.

It was a plain bound book with no extraordinary embellishments... and it landed on the floor at my feet with a *thump*.

Holy gods.

I held my breath as I picked it up. The spine creaked as I drew back the hardcover, as if it were any old book that simply hadn't been opened in a long time.

For you, gods blessed.
Thank you for loving my boy.

–E

A single droplet of blood marked the page below the writing. Bright red, it was still fresh. *Mine.* The stargazer had cut me because it had

wanted to test my blood. To make sure I was who it thought I was—
who it had been waiting over a millennium for.

That first stargazer had nicked me, too. But I had backed out of the
library, and...the stargazers could not exist outside of their sanctuary.
It had lost its magic before it could confirm who I was...

Holy.

Fucking.

Gods.

Edina's book. It had been here, all along, waiting to find me...

"Saeris?"

I spun around, pulse flying. Kingfisher stepped out of the shadows,
and without thinking, I quickly tucked the book behind my back.

His cheeks were red, his hair ruffled, as if he'd been outside in the
cold. A small smile played over his lips as he saw me and stopped, leaning against the wooden bay of shelves next to him, tucking his thumbs
into the belt at his waist. "Everything okay? I heard you cursing like a
pirate back here."

"Yes, everything's fine. I—"

*Find it. But do not tell him about it. I mean it. It's important. He can't
know about the book. Only you. Do you understand?*

Edina's voice echoed through my mind. Memories of her, cloudy-
eyed and desperate as she'd spoken through Everlayne back in the bedroom back in Cahlish. She hadn't just asked me not to tell Fisher about
the book. She had *commanded* me not to.

I looked upon my mate's face now and saw the tired shadows
beneath his eyes. He had just gone through hell and back for me. Yes,
we badly needed the silver he and Carrion had brought back from Zilvaren, but that hadn't been the *only* reason he'd gone back to my city.
He had gone for *me*, so that he could bring Hayden here. He would go
back there again, even though he hated it—I wouldn't even have to ask.

And that was as far as I got.

I produced the book from behind my back and held it out to him.
"Your mother told me about a book," I said. "Back in Cahlish, when she
told me I had to seal my runes. She told me I needed to find it, and that

once I did, I shouldn't tell you about it, but . . ." I shook my head, holding it out to him. "That doesn't feel right. Here. I found it. This is the book."

Fisher's smile slowly faded, but it didn't disappear altogether. It took on a sad edge as he pushed away from the bookshelves and slowly came toward me. Pensively, he took the book and opened it. Turning past the first page with the note to me and my droplet of blood, his eyes skipped quickly over the text there, before he set his jaw, letting go of a long, deep breath. His eyes shone bright as mirrors when he closed the book and handed it back to me. The next thing I knew, he was cradling the back of my head in his hand and pressing a kiss against my forehead.

"The book is for *you*, Saeris," he whispered. "But thank you for sharing it with me." He drew back, not even bothering to hide that his eyes were filling with tears.

I looked down at the book, brushing my fingers over the foiled silver butterfly stamped onto the front cover. "But . . . don't you want to read it?" It made no sense. If there was a whole book full of my mother's handwriting, I didn't know what kind of crimes I would commit if it meant I got to read it. This was a message from the grave. A hand, reaching out from the dark. And Fisher didn't want to take it?

That heavy, sad smile reappeared again. "No," he said softly. "This is what she wanted. I trust her. And I trust *you*, Little Osha. Whatever revelations might be in that book, they're for you and you alone. You'll know what you need to do with them."

33

NO REGRETS

KINGFISHER

My son,

I close my eyes and dream of the universe, and there are such events that stretch out before my mind like way markers upon a road. They are firm and undeniable in their existence. But there are pathways that veer from that road along the way. Side streets that might lead a player on the grand stage of fate off in another direction. There are many of these such diversions on the road that lies before you, and many that lie before your mate, as well.

Today, she stands at a fork in the road. I see the way before you both, and I see you tread the path together. But the bond that binds you both will be strongest if she places this book into your hands.

I wish I could explain more. I wish I had lived to see you grow into the man I know you will become, but do not worry. I have witnessed it in death, and I wouldn't have changed that for anything. Your soul is shattered by the knowledge that I remained here for so long after I passed, but please know that it was necessary. And know that I

CALLIE HART

have cherished every second that I have gotten to watch you
from this side of the veil.
   I have no regrets.
   I love you.
   I am proud of you.
   Now give her back the book.

Your mother,
Edina

34

VERY WRONG INDEED

SAERIS

EDINA OF THE fucking *Seven Towers.*

I would have felt like a complete asshole if I hadn't made the decision to give Fisher the book. I would have read the note she'd left for him and known immediately I had failed some kind of test in her eyes. And sure, the female was dead, but I still wanted her to *like* me. I was in love with her son, after all. Stupid though it might seem, I wanted to be *worthy* of him in her eyes.

I was itching to read the book from cover to cover now, but Ammontraíeth was abuzz with preparations for tomorrow night's ball, and even my own chambers provided no privacy. Every five seconds, someone new knocked at the door with an urgent question.

Which flowers ought to be placed on the dais?

Should the wine be laced with newborns' blood or adolescent virgins' blood? (I had answered definitively that the wine should not be laced with any blood, and that anyone found bleeding newborns would be chained to a post and left outside to greet the dawn.)

Did I wish for the Lords of Midnight to be seated at my table for dinner, in a place of honor?

Did I wish for music before the petitions? If so, what *kind* of music?

Did I have a specific dance set in mind?

It went on and on and on, and all the while, the book felt like a ten-ton weight tucked into the front of my shirt.

The book held answers, *important* answers, and all the Evenlight Ball nonsense was getting in the way.

Fisher had gone back to spend more time with Foley after he'd found me in the library. Carrion had eventually shown up at my chambers, Simon at his hip and a cocksure smile plastered on his face. The second Fisher returned at last, I grabbed the book and my blades and made the announcement: "Come on. We're leaving."

"Leaving?" Fisher smirked. "We only just got here. Don't you have royal decrees to sign? Important decisions to make about the big party—"

"I need quiet. I can't think here. I'm leaving a note about the ball. I'm delegating all decisions about the party to Tal. *He* can deal with it. I just need a moment's peace, and I'm not going to get it here."

"I definitely want to be back for the party. I want to see who you appoint as Lord," Carrion said, looking up from the book he was reading. "The new outfit that Yanice promised sounded amazing, too. I desperately need to expand my wardrobe."

Trust Carrion to be thinking of his appearance while the rest of us were trying to prevent the end of the world.

"All right, then," Fisher said. "You don't have to twist my arm. Let's get you back to Cahlish for the rest of the night. I have plenty to take care of there, myself. As soon as we're back, I'll open a shadow gate and find Lorreth. I wasn't going to fetch him until morning, but I'm sure he'll be happy to come home early. I'll open one for Renfis, too. He's bound to have reached Ballard by now."

"That thing is making me feel *weird*." Carrion squinted at the null blade, eyes full of suspicion. It sat on the edge of the bench in the forge, its graphite-colored blade unmarked, despite the fact that I'd spent the past hour trying to shave off a little of its metal to test its composition.

I could precisely sense what kind of metals and alloys other objects were comprised of now. The doorknobs. The window latches. The snuffers the fire sprites used to put out the candles. The various weapons dotted throughout the estate. I knew what all of them were made of without even having to think about it. But trying to get a read on the null blade made me feel like I was falling headfirst down a dark hole every time I turned my mind toward it. The sensation was unsettling, to say the least, and left me feeling unbalanced and nauseous.

"I know. I don't like it either," I said.

"We should bury it."

"Unfortunately, that isn't really an option. We need to know what it is so that we can figure out how to render it useless. Right now, I'm barely able to affect it with my magic. Fisher can't affect it at all." *That* had been a troubling realization. He'd tried to push it from one side of the bench to another when we first got back to Cahlish, and nothing had happened. "We're going to have to face Belikon's forces at some point, and if all of his guards have these blades, we'll be screwed."

Fisher had left to open the shadow gates for Lorreth and Renfis— he'd done a commendable job of hiding his concern over his inability to move the blade, but I'd seen it lurking behind his brittle smile. He hadn't experienced anything like the null blade before, either. The fact that they couldn't be shattered with a god sword was extra concerning to everyone, as well. In the recorded histories of Yvelia, no weapon had ever withstood a direct strike from an Alchimeran blade.

"Mm. I say we bury it and figure that out if and when we need to." Carrion scowled at the dagger even harder, trying to balance on the back legs of his chair. "If the problem isn't causing immediate issues, it's always been my policy to let sleeping dogs lie."

"Bury your head in the sand, you mean?" Edina's book sat on the shelf along the back wall. What I wouldn't have given to already be halfway through the damned thing. I wanted to be alone when I cracked it open, though, and the very worst thing you could do with Carrion is let him suspect even for a second that you didn't want him around. You would never be rid of him if you did that.

"No. All I mean to say is that there's really no point in worrying about an issue if you can worry about it later. Or y'know. Just put it off."

"Mm. Like how you're doing with your birthright?"

Carrion wobbled, nearly losing his balance and toppling backward. He grabbed the edge of the bench and saved himself in the nick of time. "*Excuse* me? My birthright? What the hell are you talking about?"

I gave him a long, pointed look. "Your *throne*, Carrion. At some point, you're going to have to think seriously about the fact that you are the rightful heir to the Yvelian throne. You—"

"*I* have already said that I have no interest in pursuing that job, Saeris."

"And that would all be well and good if there were a kind, benevolent king ruling the realm. One who cared for his people and wasn't sacrificing their lives left, right, and center for his own ends. But that doesn't seem to be the case now, *does* it?"

The forge was still open to the elements along one wall—for ventilation, Fisher had said, back when he'd first brought me here—and the light breeze had been steadily blowing gusts of snow into the workshop for the past hour. Fat snowflakes settled on Carrion's shoulders, the white a stark contrast against the black of his shirt and the vivid auburn of his hair. He splayed his fingers, giving me a helpless look. "A couple of weeks ago, I was a thief and a black-market trader."

"No, you weren't."

Carrion ignored me. "My entire living memory was of Zilvaren, and all of the people I had known there—"

"You were *always* the Daianthus heir, Carrion. You were trapped in a realm you didn't belong in."

"And now, all of a sudden, I'm dragged here, to a place I had no real notion of, and I'm expected to fight for a crown I've never seen, and a royal seat I know very little about, and a people who do not know me or care one bit about me?"

"You're wrong about that last part, sire. Very wrong indeed."

Archer.

He had entered the forge while Carrion had been rambling. He was carrying bowls of stew on a tray toward the small table on the other side of the hearth, but he had stopped now and was regarding Carrion very seriously. "The Fae and folk of Yvelia might not know you, Master Swift, but they care about you a great deal. In many houses, prayers are offered up for you daily, and have been ever since your parents, well..." He grimaced. "Since your parents were taken from us. Rurik and Amelia Daianthus were kind and just monarchs. They cared about the small folk. From Ajun to Western Dow, people dream that one day the Daianthus heir will return, and the cruelty they suffer at present will come to an end."

It was the most I had ever heard Archer speak in one go without him stammering nervously. His voice was pitchy and squeaked in places, but it did not waver.

Carrion stared at the fire sprite. A muscle in his jaw ticked, but for once, the male was silent, no quick comeback at the tip of his tongue. When he didn't say anything, Archer gave him a small, polite bow, and then took the bowls of stew over to the table, where he set them down and waited, with his back to us. He was so small—only three feet high or so. His diminutive stature often reminded me of a child, though he was older than me by considerable years. Maybe, actually, it was how innocent he seemed. Of all the Yvelian creatures I'd encountered since coming through the quicksilver, the fire sprites seemed to be the sweetest.

When he turned around and smiled at us, the sadness in his flame-filled eyes showed his age, at last. "You have come home during troubled times, master," he said. "You have seen so little of your kingdom. You do not know it, but it *does* know you. It knows your blood. Your family has ruled over Yvelia for generations. The Daianthuses weren't always perfect. Your ancestors made their fair share of mistakes, but they always fought to correct themselves when they veered from the path. And they *always* put their people first. I know, in my heart, that you will do the same, Master Swift. After all, it's in your blood."

Carrion had turned a ghastly shade of gray. He looked like he was about to throw up at any moment. His eyes followed Archer as he carried a bowl of stew and a spoon over to him, but he wasn't seeing the sprite. He was a million miles away, back in Zilvaren perhaps, or drawn elsewhere, to the corners of this realm he hadn't even seen yet.

"For you, my lady." I had followed Carrion's lead and allowed my mind to drift; I hadn't noticed Archer bringing me my stew, either.

"Thank you, Archer." I took the bowl, smiling distractedly, when a thought occurred to me. "Archer, you've been here at Cahlish a long time, haven't you?"

The sprite looked startled. "Oh, I, uh—yes, my lady. Since before Master Fisher was born. But I assure you . . . I love my position, my lady. I don't . . . I wouldn't want to *leave*."

"Archer, I don't want you to leave. Why would you think such a thing?"

The sprite shuffled nervously from one foot to the other. "Well, it is known among creatures such as myself that when there is a new lady of a house, she often likes to replace the staff with members of her own household and such. It is known among creatures such as myself that a new lady of the house might mean having to find a new position."

"Oh gods, no, Archer. You don't have to worry about that, I promise. I don't have any staff from my house. I didn't even *have* a house back in Zilvaren—"

"It's true," Carrion said. "She was as feral as a hellcat. She would slink through any open window and take a nap when she could."

I gave him a look. "Yes, *thank* you, Carrion. The point is, I wasn't asking because I wanted to fire you. I only wanted to know if you'd been here before, when Edina was still here. But I suppose you would have been if you took your place at Cahlish before Fisher's birth."

"Oh, yes. Yes, absolutely. I knew Lady Edina very well. She was quiet. Very considerate. Always thinking of others. A very graceful female, too, my lady. When she moved, it was as though her feet never even touched the ground." His tone had turned wistful, his eyes glassier than normal. The fire within them seemed to glow a little hotter. "I didn't know that she was an Oracle. Not for a long time. Some Seers become distant as their gifts grow. They know too much. They see too much. But not Lady Edina. She remained exactly who she had always been. Even when that monster sent for her, and she had to go..." He shook his head. "She was sweet about it. Didn't put up a fight. She was scared, though. I could tell. You know, *she* used to love coming to this forge, too!" He brightened as if he had just remembered this fact. "She knew nothing about metalwork or the workings of a forge, but she would come and sit in that chair, yes, that one, the one next to yours, and she would say that she was visiting with a friend. I never understood what she meant, but...but!" He held a stubby index finger in the air, and I noticed for the very first time that Archer only had *three* fingers, plus his thumb.

"Her favorite flowers always grew here, out in the courtyard, along the far wall. I used to pick them for her. She loved the smell. Wait right here! I'll fetch you some."

"Archer! Archer, it's okay. It's cold out there, away from the fire!"

He paid me no heed, bolting out of the forge. In less than a second, he was up to his knees in snow, and then little more than a glowing spark of light smoldering in the dark.

"The fire sprites are dying out. Did you know that?" Carrion spooned some stew into his mouth, eating with far less fervor than usual. He barely seemed interested in his food at all, in fact, which meant the situation must have been dire indeed.

"I didn't know that," I confessed. "How do *you* know?"

He jerked his left shoulder in an approximation of a shrug. "A water sprite told me."

"Oh? What *else* did this water sprite tell you?"

"That it was rude to pry into other people's personal conversations."

"I see *that* lesson didn't stick."

"What's that supposed to—"

A ball of fire ignited in the courtyard outside, a pillar of flaring orange in the dark. I dropped the spoon I was holding. It landed with a clatter in my stew, splashing food all over the bench. A weapon. I needed a weapon. I grabbed the first thing I could lay my hands on and charged outside, arms pumping as I sprinted.

"Help!" Archer's terrified cry rang loud in my ears. *"Help!"*

The fire sprite was past the large live oak that sat in the middle of the clearing; his body was wreathed in flames... and there was a *feeder* lunging at him.

"Archer!"

My blood sang a hymn in my ears. Magic tore up my right arm, my runes flaring bright blue in the dark. Copper coated my tongue. My canines. Gods, my canines had grown so long in my mouth that they sank straight into my bottom lip.

It took but a second to cross the clearing, but it was a second too long. The feeder had Archer by the arm, and it was trying to drag him back over the wall.

In life, it had been a male. A tall one, with long, warm brown hair that reminded me of Ren's. Now that I was closer, I could see that there *were* war braids in his hair—and he was wearing worn, brown leather renegade's armor as well. My heart skipped a beat at the possibility— was it him? Had something awful happened to him while he'd been gone? But the feeder twisted unnaturally at the waist, turning a full one hundred and eighty degrees to look back over its shoulder as it attempted to scale the wall, and I saw its features.

A broad, flat face, with a wide, square jaw. Crooked nose. Lips that were too thin, and torn to shreds besides. The male had been dead for days before it had risen. And the rot...

Oh, gods.

"Infected! It's *infected*!" I skidded to a stop five feet away from it, alarm rattling my nerve endings like a jailer rattling a set of keys.

Thick black veins spiderwebbed beneath the feeder's sallow skin. Its eyes were completely black. A strange white light pulsed through its waxy throat and glowed within its chest. Its arm was on fire now, but for some reason, the rest of it remained unaffected by Archer's flames.

"My Lady!" Archer wailed. *"Please!"*

The fire sprite was a ball of fire, his black, rock-like body kicking and scrambling at its center. Try as he might, though, he couldn't get free. The feeder bared its teeth, snarling, and then it *sprang* up the wall, holding on to the thick vines of ivy that covered the face of the stone-work with its free hand.

I reacted without thinking.

I threw the blade I was holding—not Erromar or Selanir. The *null* blade. I must have grabbed it from the bench. Fuck! I sent it sailing through the air, praying as it flew... and then rocked with relief when it speared the feeder through the shoulder and pinned it to the wall. My relief was short lived. The second the dagger struck the feeder, it sank *into* its body, as if it were being absorbed. The monster threw back its head and unleashed an unholy shriek that sounded more like ecstasy than pain. Muscles bulged along its back, multiplying, its biceps doubling in size. It was responding to the blade somehow. Growing. Becoming stronger.

Horror warred with amazement inside me. "What the *fuck?*"

Archer whimpered, hanging limp in the feeder's grip. The sprite was made of solid rock and was as heavy as one of the small boulders that lined the banks of the Darn, but the feeder lifted him as if he weighed nothing.

"It's taking him! It's going over the wall!" Carrion shouted behind me.

If it managed to vault over the top of the stone wall, it'd be over. Archer would never be seen again.

This time, I took Erromar in hand. I leaped up the wall after the feeder, determined to take its head, but as I lashed out with the sword, metal singing through the air in search of its mark, the feeder let out an ungodly roar and shoved backward, the vines it was clinging to ripping free from the wall. Both the feeder and Archer came toppling backward... onto *me*.

I hit the ground first.

My head lit up with pain, thoughts fracturing and then shattering completely as the feeder slammed into my chest.

"Saeris!" Carrion wasn't far, only a few feet away. He had Simon in his hands and was charging—

"Carrion, be *careful*!"

I wasn't fully Fae. A bite from a normal feeder probably wouldn't do much to me—not that I was a hundred percent *sure* on that—but it could definitely kill Carrion. And this was no ordinary feeder. I hadn't been there on the banks of the river at Irrín when those infected feeders had attacked. I hadn't seen the devastation they had wrought, either, but I knew how quickly the rot spread. I knew how *easily* it passed to the living and the dead alike.

"Don't touch it!" I yelled.

I needn't have worried. The second Carrion got close to the feeder and tried to pull it off me, it snarled, batting him away.

It happened so fast.

Carrion hit the corner wall of the courtyard, a winded *"Guh!"* coming out of him as he tried to right himself. Behind him, the vines choking the crumbling brickwork suddenly bloomed, a thousand tiny white flowers exploding open and wilting right before my eyes. Dried petals rained down on the smuggler, landing in his hair as he shoved away from the wall.

"My lady!" On his back, Archer kicked his feet, trying to stand. The feeder had rolled off me and was on all fours, prowling forward across the dirtied snow again, hoping to secure a better angle of attack. Black ichor dripped from its awful, shattered teeth as it came.

My right hand ached, my magic pulsing, begging to be released, but

Fisher's voice was still clear in my head. He had unleashed his magic upon the infected feeders he had faced along the banks of the Darn. Renfis had, too, and neither male's power had injured the infected. On the contrary, the feeders had absorbed their magic and taken it *into* themselves, and the very last thing I intended was to give this mother-fucker free magic. I'd already given it the fucking null blade.

"It's going to spring, Saeris!" Carrion called. "Watch out. I'll clip it—"

"Carrion, no! Stay back!"

As he said it would, the feeder sprang. It wasn't the smuggler that I watched leap forward to tackle the maddened monster back to the ground, though. It was Archer.

"Run, my lady!" he cried.

Flames filled my vision as a harrowing, pained scream tore through the night.

"Archer! No!"

The feeder sank its teeth into Archer's neck and tore it wide open. I wouldn't have known a fire sprite's body could be penetrated by tooth or blade, but I watched as it happened, horror scaling my spine like a ladder.

Jets of glowing orange-yellow magma spewed from Archer's throat. It glowed so bright that it burned my eyes as it sprayed all over the feeder, landing on its chest, face, and arms. The feeder didn't react at all to the—

Wait.

No. It *was* reacting.

The monster convulsed, its ink-black eyes widening as an aware-ness that hadn't been there before returned to it. Its jaw hinged, too wide, opening and closing, its mangled, black stump of a tongue pro-truding from its mouth as the feeder let out a silent scream. Its waxy skin started to melt from its body. Wherever the glowing hot magma touched the fell creature's body, the black, knotted veins beneath the surface of its skin bulged to the surface and split open, disgorging the foul-smelling decay within.

Ichor hit the snow in viscous ropes. It behaved similarly to the quicksilver at first—gathering, probing, seeking—but then it began to smoke. To bubble. To *boil*.

Language was a foreign concept to the putrefied mind of a feeder, and yet it sounded as if it were trying to scream for help as the rot blistered and burned inside it. It spasmed, fingers twisted into hooks, falling back into the snow...

"Archer!" The fire sprite's flames had gone out. He lay on his side, his legs twitching, only a few small fissures in his craggy skin still lit from within on his arms and his chest.

"Fuck me," Carrion whispered. He was on his knees next to the sprite in a heartbeat. "Is he dying?"

"I don't know! I—" I reached out, not knowing what to do, not sure if I should, or *could* touch him. In the end, I didn't have a choice. Archer *needed* our help. My palms hissed, skin singeing, as I took hold of him and turned him onto his back. The sprite's eyes were open, though the flames that normally danced within them had almost all gone out.

Archer opened his mouth, gasping, but only a gravelly rasping sound passed his lips. His throat was a mess. Embers burned there, around the edge of his wound. A kind of molten rock ebbed sluggishly from the rent left behind by the feeder's fangs—it smelled terrible, like the very vapors of hell itself. The sprite's hand opened and closed in the air, groping for something, anything, his cooling eyes full of fear when his gaze met mine.

"We need to get him inside," I bit out. "Is it dead?" I couldn't even bring myself to look at the feeder.

"Yes," Carrion answered. "It looks like that stew. That null blade is all that's left of it."

"Okay. Good. Can you run and—We need something to lift him with. He's too heavy." Tears burned my eyes. My throat was aching horribly; forcing myself to speak felt like regurgitating razor blades.

"Fuck that," Carrion growled. He crouched down at the other end of Archer's body and looked me square in the eye. "You get his hands. I'll get his feet."

The sprite tried to pull away as we lifted him from the bitter ground; even this close to death, he didn't want to injure us with his heat. But we were single-minded, and the forge was only fifty feet away. The burns would hurt, the scars would be ugly, but we weren't going to leave our friend to die out in the snow.

35

BRIMSTONE

KINGFISHER

"IT'S CALLED BRIMSTONE. It isn't like our blood, exactly. It *is* what keeps a fire sprite alive, though," Lorreth said.

Archer lay on the mossy plinth, his eyes closed. He looked like a small pile of rocks. Sweat ran over my temple and down my cheek, dripping from my chin as I stared down at him, my fury building by the second.

Of course it was brimstone.

Of *course* it fucking would be.

Lorreth had just come through the shadow gate when I'd heard the cries coming from the courtyard outside. Iseabail had come through moments before him. I'd bolted from the dining room without speaking to either of them properly. Now, we were all in the bowels of the estate, deep underground, where the fire sprites were quartered. There was an entire fire sprite *village* down here in the bedrock, much deeper than the foundations of the estate. The sprites tended thousands of fires, ensuring the temperatures ran to unbearable degrees. The air was so hot that it burned the eyes and drained the moisture from a person like they were a cloth being wrung dry. We wouldn't be able to stay down here for long. We would die otherwise, cooked alive, and that wouldn't serve anybody, least of all Archer.

Saeris and Carrion had saved him.

The two looked like they were drowning in their own sweat as they stood at the end of what passed as Archer's bed. Their hands were swollen and covered in brutal blisters, but neither of them made a peep of complaint. They stared at Archer's chest, waiting for the tiny rise and fall that signified he was still breathing, while Lorreth explained what I had found I could not.

"It's an element, really. Brimstone. A kind of magic all on its own. It gives the fire sprites life."

"*And* it kills the rot," Carrion said.

"Yes. It looks that way." Lorreth's eyes darted to me, troubled. "The feeder up there was destroyed. It seems to have partially melted and then burned away to ash. The rot had started to spread to the vines along the wall, but we used some of the brimstone that Archer lost up there to burn the affected plants, and yes, it killed the spread there, too."

"Okay. This is good news, then," Saeris said. "Brimstone stops the rot. Great! So why do you two look like you're about to start punching holes in the walls?"

She looked at me, beautiful even with strands of her dark hair plastered to her cheeks, and spoke into my mind so that only I could hear. *What are we missing here? Shouldn't we be celebrating?*

We can't use the brimstone, Osha.

Iseabail, who had been notably quiet since she'd arrived, moved to Archer's bedside. She wore the traditional leather gauntlets of her clan on her forearms, each embossed with the swirling lines that represented the frozen waters to the east of Balquhidder lands. Her red hair was braided and neatly bound. She had been a novice in the eyes of her people when she had come to Cahlish a few weeks ago. Her loose hair and flowing skirts had denoted her as such. She returned to us now a prioress, dressed in accordance with her family's arcane line. In the span of the few days she had been away, she had undergone the most intense trial she was ever likely to face in her lifetime. She was probably exhausted and wounded, and yet she had still returned here to Cahlish to help.

"As Lorreth mentioned, the fire sprite's brimstone *is* like our blood, and yet it is not," she said. "The brimstone keeps them alive. Like blood, it flows throughout their bodies, keeping their core temperatures high. *Unlike* blood, they cannot lose a significant amount of it. A few drops at most. It does not regenerate as our blood does. There is a finite amount of brimstone in Yvelia, and every last drop of it is spoken for by the sprites. When they want to procreate, the whole community agrees to donate a small part of themselves. Archer will only live because other members of his pyre have given some of their own brimstone to bring his core temperature back up again."

"The *pyre?*" Carrion asked.

Iseabail nodded. "The name for an individual fire sprite community. His family."

"So they don't have sex?"

Under normal circumstances, I would have snarled at the smuggler for being such a shallow halfwit during such a worrying time, but for once the question wasn't laced with innuendo. Carrion seemed genuinely confused. He peppered Iseabail with questions about the fire sprites, meanwhile my mate chewed on her bottom lip, staring at Archer's still form. Though she kept her own counsel, I knew what she was thinking. I waited for her to say it.

After a long moment, she spoke into my head again. *We can't use the brimstone. To secure enough of it to eradicate the rot and kill the infected feeders, every fire sprite in Yvelia would have to die.*

Yes.

So we're still fucked.

Yes.

Gods, I need a drink.

I sighed heavily, another bead of sweat dripping from my chin. *Yes.*

"In Zilvaren, I always thought the city should have looked bigger from the rooftops." Saeris took a swig from my hip flask and passed it back to me. She stared out over the lightening forest that bounded the estate, squinting toward the horizon. "It never did. I could see the walls of every ward from the rooftops. Could see the walls hemming us in. Bars on a window." She scowled at the memory, making a chopping motion with the blade of her bandaged hand in the air. Te Léna had healed her as best she could, but the burns had been deep. It would take a little while for her palms to fully recover. "There are no walls up here. No bars on this prison window. The world feels as though it might go on and on forever."

It would be dawn soon. She was exhausted and maybe in a little pain, too, but when she had asked to be brought up to the roof, I hadn't had the heart to deny the request. I'd needed to breathe in the fresh night air after the penetrating heat of Archer's home, anyway.

The land surrounding Cahlish was crowded with trees that had known the names of my ancestors. My mother and father had met out in those forests. Had courted each other out there, below their snow-clad boughs. The stories I had heard about them in their youth—two very serious people made utter fools by love.

"My father lost a toe out there." I gestured to the small, dark patch of wood, just beyond the rise of the closest hill. "You see that shadowy spot? The one where no snow has settled?"

Saeris looked in the direction I pointed, nodding.

"A graven lives there."

She looked to me, eyes wide. "What's a graven?"

"Mm. A kind of..." I considered how to describe it. "Half satyr, half troll? With a little bit of basilisk thrown in for good measure."

"What's a basilisk?"

I laughed softly at the distaste in her tone. I took a swig of the whiskey I'd brought up for us and handed the flask back to her again. "A snake. Kind of. Bigger. Angrier."

"So, part troll, part satyr, part snake." She sniffed, brushing her face with the back of her hand; there were snowflakes on her eyelashes. "I can't even begin to picture what that looks like, but okay. What about this graven, then?"

"It lives in a little wooden cottage out there." I pointed at the shady, snow-free patch of the forest again. "It makes tinctures and salves and the like. A long time ago, people used to trade with the graven for potions and spells they believed would end hexes, heal ailments, or make people fall in love with them. My father had his own magic, but he was like me. He commanded shadows and not much of anything else. When he met my mother, he was relying on charm alone to woo her, and he didn't have much faith in his own capabilities in that department, so one day, he decided to visit the graven."

"For a love potion?" Saeris rolled her eyes at the ridiculousness of it.

I did the same. "For a love potion, yes. And the graven said to him, 'I'll make you a deal. I will give you my strongest, most effective love potion. A potion so potent that the object of your heart's desire will be powerless against your advances. She will be yours for all of time if she drinks this potion that I will make for you.'"

"And? What was the catch? What bargain did he have to strike?"

My mate was clever. She was *learning.*

I smiled a little as I took the flask from her and drank again. The whiskey warmed me all the way down to the seat of my diaphragm. "The graven said to my father, 'I will give you this potion, and you will live out your days with a wife and a family, and you will be blissfully happy. You will be able to create powerful wards, and you will be a role model to your people and all who follow you and support you.' And my father was wowed by this prospect, and he said, as you so astutely guessed, 'Wonderful. This is all I've ever dreamed of and more. *What do you want in return for these gifts?*' And the Graven replied, "Your right foot. I want your whole right foot."

"*What?*"

"Mm-hm. His foot. It wanted his foot. And my father said..."

I pointed at Saeris, who wrinkled her nose, confused, and said, "*Why?*"

"And the graven said, 'Well, I'm sick of these cloven things. I've always wanted two proper *Fae* feet to walk around on. I bargained with someone for their left foot a while back, and I've been trying to complete the set ever since.' And the graven showed my father a severed left foot, sitting on a flocked red pillow by the fireplace, and that was all it would say on the matter."

"But your father wouldn't trade his foot for the potion," Saeris said.

"He would not. So the graven said, 'Fine. You won't be parted with your foot, so how about this. When I stand in the sun, I cast no shadow, and it makes others around me nervous. They sense that I'm different, and they run from me. Give me your shadows, and I will give you my very best love potion.'"

"He said no again," Saeris guessed.

"My father's shadows were his greatest strength. Of course he said no. So the graven was very frustrated by this point and growing rather tired of the negotiations, so he said, 'Okay. This is my final offer. You give me just *one* of your shadows, one that you deem fitting to someone like me, and we'll call it even.' So my father thought about this, and having decided that one single shadow was a seed of magic he was willing and able to part with, he agreed. The graven mixed up some stinking concoction and passed it off to my father, and in return my father handed over the graven's new shadow. The deal was done. The graven walked my father to the door of his cottage and stepped outside to admire his new shadow, but it was midday, and the sun was high overhead."

"So the graven cast no shadow," Saeris groaned.

I nodded. "It took up a scythe and went after my father. It called him a liar and a cheat, and didn't notice, as it chased him through the forest, that the angle of the sun had changed, and the shadow of a majestic ox was now stitched to its satyr's hooves. It swung its scythe back and forth, trying to claim my father's right foot. It came damn close to taking it, too, but in the end, it only managed to sever his little toe."

Saeris frowned as she looked back toward the darkened area of the forest. I let her have her thoughts for a while. Eventually, she said, "And the love potion? It worked?"

CALLIE HART

I laughed softly. "No, Osha. My father was young and foolish at the time, and didn't know any better, but there's no such thing as love potions. A person cannot be coerced into truly loving another. It would rob them of their free will. My mother loved my father because of who he was. It turned out his charm *was* enough in the end."

Saeris pondered this for a long while. "Did your mother tell you that story?"

I swallowed down a mouthful of whiskey, wincing at the burn, then placed the cap back onto the hip flask and twisted it closed. "No. *Archer* did. Nearly all the stories I know of my father have come from him. Come on. It's growing early. There's something I want to show you, Little Osha."

The huntsman's cottage was washed blue by the dawn. The river below burbled away, singing the same song it carried all the way from high in the mountains down to where it met the sea. Saeris turned her face toward the dawn and basked in the first rays of sunlight that summited Omnamerrin and speared down into the valley below.

"I didn't realize how much I missed this," she whispered. "Things have just been so crazy."

Saeris wasn't one for unnecessary tears. She cried when she was angry, not when she was sad. But I knew that she was sad this morning, as she opened her eyes to watch the sun peek over the mountains, and a lone tear chased down her cheek.

"You can come here and enjoy it any time you like." I stood behind her, winding one arm around her waist, pulling her close so that her back was flush with my chest. "A dream is just a fabrication. A manifestation of what *could* be. In-between places, and whispers of other realms. I had a feeling the sun wouldn't affect you here."

Smoke poured merrily from the cottage's chimney, but we hadn't gone inside yet. The air was brisk and fresh, and the wide-open clear sky overhead felt like freedom. Saeris was far too short for me to rest my chin on her shoulder, so I rested it lightly on the top of her head instead, humming quietly under my breath.

"What are we going to do abou—" She began to speak, but I cut her off.

"Peace, Osha," I whispered into her hair. "The rot. Ammontraíeth. Everlayne. Our problems aren't going anywhere. They'll be right where we left them, waiting for us when we wake up. For now, let's just take a moment to breathe. We deserve it."

I knew it was true. Unequivocally so. It was easy to say it to someone else, to look at all we had been through lately and see that a person who had dealt with even half of the issues we had would deserve a second to catch their breath. But I was just as guilty as Saeris in this regard. My own mind wouldn't stop caroming out of control, hundreds of thoughts vying for attention, questions demanding to be answered. It took a monumental effort to convince my worries to settle.

Saeris turned away from the valley and wrapped her arms around my shoulders, looking up at me. Her cheeks were rosy from the cold, her eyes paler than the sky and twice as bright. The tips of her ears were red, too. I touched my fingertip to the point of her left ear, smiling softly to myself. "I got so used to them being round," I said. "I was appalled by the sight of them at first."

"Wow, *thanks*."

I laughed. "Sorry. I don't mean to offend." I tapped the tip of her sloped ear again. "I was just very...*very* worried. Humans are difficult to keep alive in a place like this. I..." Even now, confessing this made my voice catch. "I didn't want to lose you."

Other females had looked at me adoringly in the past. I'd let them, feeling only further and further away as they tried to draw closer. When Saeris turned her blue eyes on me, I didn't have a choice. I was laid bare before her. I was brought to my godscursed knees. "You had a funny way of showing it," she said, smiling crookedly. "And you still let me train with a sword, even as a human."

I raised my eyebrows at her. "You mean I could have *stopped* you?"

"Technically, yes," she said. "You could have compelled me not to touch a weapon here in Yvelia, and I wouldn't have been able to."

"Mm. Yes, well..." I kissed her lightly, barely grazing her temple with my lips. "You would never have spoken to me again. And anyway...I know you, Saeris Fane. Even as a fragile human, you were strong. Independent. It would have crushed your spirit if I had sheltered you from this world. Your choices had to be your own. I saw that in the end. I see it now, too. Every day. You have a *right* to walk the road that stretches out before you. I will not rob you of your path by insisting I carry you."

She was quiet for a while, mulling this over. The wind kicked up, toying with her hair, blowing it around her face. A bank of clouds passed in front of the sun, leaching the valley of color, and at last, Saeris drew in a breath and sighed. "Thank you," she said simply. "For not trying to control me."

An odd thing to be thanked for, that. I had no idea what the men back in Zilvaren were like, but I had never been under the illusion that I needed to *control* a lover. I kept all of this to myself, though. She didn't need to hear it. Instead, I ducked down and whispered into her ear. "You're a wildfire, Saeris Fane. There's no controlling *you*."

She laughed, leaning her head back so it rested on my chest. "I'll take that as a compliment, then."

"You should."

"And what if there comes a day when all of this becomes too much, and I *want* to be carried? At least for a little while?"

"Then it would be my honor and a privilege to do so, Saeris. *Never* doubt that. Whenever you need me to catch you, I am here, ready and willing. I'll face the Blood Court for you, if you want me to. I'll face Belikon, and Madra, and anyone or anything that wishes to do you harm."

At that moment, the bank of thick snow clouds broke, and Saeris flinched reflexively, her vampire blood telling her that she should hide from the sun's rays. She huffed down her nose, relaxing when she remembered that the light wouldn't hurt her here. "You'll have to face the sun for me, too, in that case," she mused.

"Gladly."

"And I will become *your* shadow."

I held on to her a little tighter, needing to feel her close. "You should know, Saeris...I am my father's son. My strength has *always* been my shadows."

36

WOULD THAT I COULD

SAERIS

"SAERIS! SAERIS! HE'S *awake*!"

I jolted from sleep, too startled to comprehend where I was or what was going on. For a foggy moment, I thought I was still in Zilvaren, delirious from trying to sleep through reckoning. Reality came back piece by piece...and then there was Archer standing at the bottom of the bed, peering over the footboard with eyes as big as saucers.

Wait, *what*?

I sat up too fast, my vision pitching. "Archer! You're here! You're awake!"

The fire sprite had no eyebrows, but I could still tell that he was frowning. "Not *me*, my lady. Your brother. *Master Hayden* has woken up!"

Next to me, Fisher was sprawled on his front, his inked arms splayed out, both hands tucked beneath the pillow. When he pushed himself up, propping himself up groggily on his elbows, his hair was sticking up in five different directions. The second he registered who was hovering at the foot of the bed, he sat up brushing his waves back out of his face. "Archer. What in all five hells are you doing here?"

The fire sprite stepped back, a small flame kindling on his shoulder. "Me, Master? I, well, I came to let the mistress know that her brother—"

"No, why are you up here, in the house? Why are you *working*?"

"I—I am sorry, Master. I did *try* to stop that feeder—"

"It's okay, Archer. You did more than you should have. I only mean to say that you should be down with the pyre, healing from your injuries."

"Oh." The fire sprite relaxed. "That's all right, Master Fisher. Fire sprites don't need recovery time after we're injured. We're either alive or we're dead." He let out a squeaky laugh. "The brimstone my brothers donated to me took all night to cool. Once my wounds were solid again, I woke up right as rain."

He turned, hands in the air, wiggling his hips side to side in a little dance that seemed far braver than normal. When he had completed his dance, he cleared his throat and said rather seriously, "I am one inch taller than I used to be."

"Oh. Uh . . . congratulations? Well done," I told him.

He bowed his head, accepting the compliment. "Your brother is in the sitting room, my lady. He's quite anxious to see you."

Hayden.

After everything, he was here, and he was awake. Inside, I was brimming with excitement, but made myself stay calm as I got up and got ready to go see him. Long before she died, I'd promised my mother I would watch out for him. Keep him out of trouble and make sure he didn't wind up in Madra's cells. Honoring that promise had been a full-time job. I'd bailed him out of countless situations where he'd gambled away water or money he didn't have. I'd protected him from Carrion more than once. The things I had sacrificed, sold, or traded to guarantee my brother didn't die of dehydration . . . and I'd brought him here. There was an abundance of water in Yvelia. Plenty of food, too. But after everything I had done to keep Hayden alive and safe in Zilvaren, would bringing him *here* be the thing that finally did him in?

With the rot and everything else going on in Yvelia, the truth was that Hayden might have actually been safer staying in the desert.

The irony of that was far too bitter to swallow.

What had I brought him here to face?

What was he going to do?

Fisher had said it himself while we were resting: Humans were difficult to keep alive in a place like this, and there was still so much about Fae and Yvelian politics that I didn't know. I had barely scratched the surface of what it meant to be a part of this realm, and now I had brought my brother here. When I'd arrived, I had been the only human in Yvelia. Now the mantle of that title fell to Hayden... and I had no idea how he was going to handle it.

I moved slowly, getting dressed, watching Fisher out of the corner of my eye as he did the same. The muscles in his back shifted as he shrugged on a shirt and turned to face me, tattooed fingers deftly fastening the buttons. "I can feel you worrying," he said quietly.

I ducked my head, pulling on my boots. "There's no point telling me not to worry," I replied. "He's my brother."

"I wasn't going to." Fisher lifted his leathers over his head, settling his chest protector in place. He had the straps fastened over his ribs in no time. "There's every reason to be worried. The future's very uncertain for your brother. It's uncertain for *all* of us." The floorboards creaked as he crossed the bedroom and came to stand before me. "But we're going to figure it out together, Osha. We'll get through all of this and have a far better idea of what the lay of the land looks like in time, too."

I smiled up at him sadly. "I actually *did* want you to tell me not to worry," I admitted. "Can you rephrase all of that for me, please?"

Kingfisher's eyes danced with amusement as he bent down to kiss me. "Would that I could, Osha. Would that I could."

———†———

Cahlish was a huge place, full of hidden, secret corners. I'd spent days exploring when Fisher had left me here after I'd been attacked by the feeder in the dining room, but there were still entire wings of the estate I hadn't investigated. Rooms I hadn't set foot inside.

This was one such room.

The south drawing room, Archer called it. A bank of tall windows overlooked a rose garden shrouded in white. The buds on the thorny bushes were all open despite the cold, and a sea of velveteen blooms swayed on the other side of the glass, their petals dark as blood and dusted with snow.

A tufted armchair sat before a crackling fire. Gilt-framed portraits hung on the walls. A writing desk had been positioned in the window, as if whoever had penned their correspondence there had liked to look out over the garden while they contemplated their words. That was where Hayden stood, on the other side of the writing desk, looking out the window with his hands in his pockets.

The door creaked as I entered the room, startling him. He turned, his blond curls just as crazy as ever, his face deeply tanned, lips cracked. His eyes widened when he saw me. He didn't speak. I'd imagined this scene in my head so many times since I'd come to Yvelia, but now that Hayden was here and it was happening, none of the scenarios I had anticipated was coming to fruition. My brother didn't look pleased to be here with me. He looked *scared*.

"It's true, then. He didn't kill you—that gigantic asshole with the pointed ears."

I lowered my head, unsure whether to smile at that or not. "No. He did not."

"Where is he, then?"

"His name is Kingfisher. And he's gone to fetch one of our friends. He was supposed to bring him back to Cahlish yesterday, but...something came up."

Archer, in the courtyard, leaping to my defense.

Archer, nearly dying to save me.

I blinked away the memories of his brimstone jetting from his throat.

Hayden huffed. Stepping away from the window, he crossed the room and stood in front of me, looking me up and down. The bridge of his nose was dotted with freckles.

Pacing around me in a slow circle, he performed a full inspection of me; his shoulders tensed when he caught sight of my ears poking through my loose hair, but he made no comment on them. At last, he came to a stop, facing me with his hands still shoved into his pockets.

"You look well," he said stiffly. "Healthy. Carrion told me you'd changed." He frowned, his eyes growing distant. "He said you'd become something different. Like him," he said in a small voice. "I understand now."

"*Do* you?"

He nodded. "Madra, she's been telling everyone that you're dead. Murdered by Fae rebels. She gave a very convincing speech."

"I'll bet she did."

"She's painting you as a martyr to her cause. Using your name and your story. Twisting everything, making you sound like some kind of Zilvaren patriot who loved her city. She said you were working for her, a loyal subject, violently killed by strangers wielding outlawed magic."

"And people are *believing* her?"

Hayden shrugged. "I don't know. It's hard to tell. Madra's always said strange things about the Fae. Especially around this time of year, with the Evenlight Festival right on top of us."

"I don't mean about the *Fae*, Hayden. I mean about *me*. That I was working for her. That I was a loyal Zilvaren subject!" The very idea of it was preposterous. Madra had told some lies in her time, but this one was the most galling. My whole life, I'd railed against her rule. I'd done whatever I could to cause dissent and mayhem for her house without getting myself killed, and now she was spreading rumors that I had been *working* for her all along? Working for her meant spying on my neighbors. It meant whispering secrets in her ear that weren't meant to be shared. It meant that I was a traitor and a liar, and I had betrayed my friends.

Hayden wouldn't meet my eyes. "She gave the whole city extra food rations and a triple water supply to honor you. For your service to the crown."

"*What?*"

"The people of the Third wouldn't accept it. They poured their canteens out in the street. They gave their bread to the crows. They cursed you as they did it."

That fucking *bitch*.

I didn't want to be a hero to my people. I didn't care if they never knew my name. Anything I had done to aid Zilvaren's rebels had been in secret and in silence. I'd never needed to draw attention to myself. I sure as hell didn't need a clap on the back from anyone in recognition of my "good deeds." But the idea that the people of the Third, *my* people, were cursing my name and refusing extra water in *protest* of me? Fuck me. I was going to throw up.

"I need to go back. I need to set them straight. All my contacts across the city—"

"Don't bother, Saeris." Hayden looked at me now, and the cold hard truth I found on his face was a blow I could never have expected. "They don't want you."

"But surely, Elroy—"

"Elroy believes you're innocent. He defends you whenever he hears anyone speak ill of you."

Well, *that* was a relief. Of course the old man knew the truth. Him better than anyone. But the others? Many of them had trusted me. Many of them had traded with me, counted on me, and now they thought that I had been informing on them to the guardians?

It was a clever play. Discredit someone the people of the Third thought they could trust. Make them question *anyone* who claimed to stand against Madra. Make them cease their incendiary activities, for fear of who might whisper *their* names into the queen's ear.

"He's black and blue." Hayden's harsh tone cut through my racing thoughts. "Elroy. Every time he stands up for you, someone throws a punch at him. He's had a lifetime's worth of split lips and black eyes lately, and he's not as tough as he thinks he is anymore."

My head snapped up, something troubling suddenly clicking into place in my head. *Elroy believes you're innocent.* That's what Hayden had said. *Elroy* believes and not *we know.*

445

There wasn't a single mark on my brother. No cuts, no scrapes, no bruises.

No one had thrown a punch at *him* lately.

It occurred to me all at once that since I'd entered the room, he hadn't smiled at me. He hadn't fucking hugged me. Hadn't even seemed all that relieved to see me.

Numb to my core, I took a wobbly step back from him, angling my head to one side in the vain hope that I might be able to get a better read on what it was that he was thinking. "You think I did it, don't you?" I whispered.

Hayden clenched his jaw, looking away.

"You think I betrayed my friends. *You* think I actually worked for her!"

"I didn't *say* that," he snapped.

"But you're not denying it! Gods and sinners, you actually think I worked for her, *don't* you?"

"I don't know!" he exploded. "How the hell am I supposed to know? You never included me in any of the things you were working on. You never let me go anywhere with you after reckoning. You were always off to one secret meeting or another. You'd never breathe a word of where you were going, would you?"

"So that must mean I was in league with the guardians, then? Is *that* it?"

"Maybe." He set his jaw, looking imperiously down his nose at me. "You shut me out. Kept me a million miles away from anything that was important. I don't know anything, Saeris, and that's because of *you*. And we always *did* seem to have more water and more food than everyone el—"

He didn't finish that thought. He couldn't, with my fist slamming into his jaw. Hayden's head whipped around so fast that I worried for a moment I'd hit him too hard and broken something, but then the rage his comment had elicited flared full force, and I hoped that I *had* broken something. I grabbed him by the front of his shirt and shoved him away.

"*Fuck* you, Hayden. More food?" I shoved him again. "More water?"

Again. Harder. Tears blurred my vision. I stabbed my finger in his face, trying to speak, but only a sound of pure fury came out of me. I had to start again. "If we had *anything*, if you didn't starve and die in the fucking sand, it was because I *bled* to keep you alive. I had to crawl on my stomach through sewer lines to reach the royal reserves. Once a week, I had to do that for you. Do you have any idea how *disgusting* that was? And did you *ever* hear me complain?" I shoved him hard enough that he fell down this time, but just like always, Hayden Fane was given a soft fucking landing. The tufted chair caught him, saving him from the indignity of landing ass-first on the rug.

My mouth was all bile and copper. Heat rose up my throat from somewhere deep within the basement of my soul. "I didn't tell you what I was doing every day because I had to go into tense situations, in fucking horrible places, and do unpleasant things," I spat. "I didn't bring you with me to those places, because I didn't want life to be hard for you like it was for me. But I see now that I've done you a disservice. You have this...this fucking *illusion* that life should be easy, that it *owes* you something, and that's on me." I thumped my own chest, clenching my jaw to the point of pain. "I broke myself to look after you. I slipped into every other ward in Zilvaren, and I robbed, and I stole, and I bartered and traded, just to make sure that you were comfortable and your belly was full. And then you have the *audacity* to turn around and accuse me of the most heinous thing I can possibly think of, because I made life too fucking easy for you while everyone around us had to suffer."

"Saeris—"

"Shut up, Hayden. Just shut the *fuck* up."

"No. Your hand," he whispered. "There's something wrong with your *hand*."

Another rune on fire.

This time, the rune for brimstone.

It swept artfully around the solid quicksilver rune, intertwined with it, connected and yet separate. If possible, it hurt twice as much as the quicksilver rune had, and the lines of fire trailing up my arm reached all the way to my elbow. For an hour, I just held my arm, breathing, trying to meditate my way through the pain. The gods only knew whether the breathing and meditating worked, but eventually the smoldering embers the rune cut into my flesh went out and the symbol glowed a soft red instead.

It was then that I had run to Fisher's bedroom; the place that had been a prison to me once was now the place I felt safest in all Cahlish. Surrounded by my mate's scent, I sat on the rug, back resting against the side of the bed, and I took out the book at last.

Not the tome Algat had given me.

Edina's book.

Dear child, I know you might not be feeling very trusting of me right now. I misled you with my request to keep this book secret from my son, and I apologize for any ill feelings that may have caused. I am not a woman given to participating in cruel games, and it brings me no pleasure to trick you. I can only hope that you will forgive me for the subterfuge and one day understand why it had to be done.

I am afraid, with that trickery still fresh in your memory, that I must ask you for a solemn promise. I am breaking all the laws of the universe with this gambit, but for it to work, you cannot skip ahead in this book. You will read things that will prevent you from facing the challenges in front of you for fear of the ones ahead, to the ruin of us all.

I implore you, please. Do not do it.

Each entry in this book had been written in service of a specific moment to come. For any of this to bear fruit, the dominoes must fall in order.

With that said, I must acknowledge that there are many ways to approach what comes next, and nearly all of them will kill you.

Your second rune has awoken. By now, you must know that brimstone is not a plentiful resource in Yvelia, as it once was. Historically, Alchemists shied away from the second bough of the Tria Prima, not only because it was too powerful and difficult to wield, but because its only purpose seemed to be linked with death and destruction. Even knowing you must conquer this rune, it pains me to advise that you must do so, as sealing this magic to your soul will come at great cost.

You will have to unlock a door within yourself that will be hard to close thereafter. I will not—cannot—lie to you. You will change if you choose to walk down this path. But with the brimstone rune sealed to you, there is a chance you will be able to use it to help save Yvelia from the veil I see descending upon it. If you decide to reject this rune, there are still other courses of action that can be taken to fend off the darkness, but the odds of those plans working are slight in comparison.

In fairness to you, I will first explain how you can reject your brimstone rune . . .

I read on, skimming over Edina's elegant handwriting, devouring her words. She had known everything, then. Seen everything. It was all here: a map to surviving the chaos and the pain that lay ahead. It was almost impossible not to flick through the book and go to the end, to see what might tip the scales of victory to our favor . . . but Edina's warning rang voiceless in my head.

You will read things that will prevent you from facing the challenges in front of you for fear of the ones ahead, to the ruin of us all.

The warning did not inspire confidence in me. The book was *long*, after all. But as I read past Edina's instructions for rejecting my brimstone rune—I would need to submerge my hand in quicksilver and instruct it to *strip* the magic from me—she went on to explain that the first half of the book was a guidebook to my powers. It was the *latter* half of the book that contained instructions with regard to the rot.

The beginning of her prophecies read thus:

Concerning the Evenlight Ball: turn this page before leaving your chambers.
An appointment awaits.

Hours later, my head was still buried in Edina's book. I had learned more from her in the span of an evening than I could have gleaned in a lifetime scouring the libraries of Yvelia for scraps. And, honestly, I was scared. The Alchemists were often corrupted by their powers. Their fates were ruled by their strength of will, but also by the heritage of their blood. If I was born an Alchemist, then I definitely had a Fae relative somewhere in my ancestry. Knowing nothing about them meant I had no idea whether I had a predisposition to succumb to my magic or not, and that was frightening in and of itself. But there was more.

The Alchemists hadn't just channeled quicksilver. In some cases, they had become so intertwined with it that they merged with it altogether to become silver-eyed heralds of the gods. These were the Alchemists who had spurred Belikon and his ilk to murder the Alchimeran line and eradicate them from this realm and all others—because they had become powerful beyond all measure and threatened the grasp of the Triumvirate's power.

As I read, the pain in my hand slowly ebbed, until the new rune on the back of my hand was healed. It was only an outline, not filled in like the quicksilver rune that had preceded it. Incomplete. A door that went to nowhere. There was no magic to it yet. I could sense that. But maybe soon there *would* be.

Fisher found me staring into space, attempting to process all that I had read, just as dusk was bruising the sky and ushering in the night. He carried Onyx in his arms; my mate had taken him along when he'd left Cahlish earlier, and now the little fox was excited to see me.

Chittering loudly, he yelped, slipping out of Fisher's arms, then collided with my chest, tumbling over himself, hind legs sticking up, tufts of white fluff floating into the air.

"Good gods. You're ridiculous." I sniffed as I ruffled his fur, scratching his sides and the base of his skull, behind his ears—his favorite spot.

Fisher smelled like fresh snow, smoke, and the *faintest* hint of powdered sugar, which told me that he'd stayed at Wendy's long enough to share a cup of tea and a Bettell biscuit with the female before returning home from Ballard. I reached for his hand, and he brushed my fingertips with his own as he stepped over me and sank down on the floor next to me, sagging back against the bed. It was then that I saw how drawn he looked.

Onyx was busy licking my ear. I petted him distractedly, frowning at my mate. "What is it? What's wrong?"

He rolled his head to the right so that he was looking at me. "Ren," he said. "He was supposed to ride along the Darn and then up into the Shallow Mountains to treat with the Gilarian Fae, then down through the forests to Ballard, then on to Inishtar, where I would collect him. I went to Inishtar first, but the satyrs haven't seen him. They knew nothing of the rot. I had to tell them of it myself. I went on to Ballard to see if Ren had stayed there to wait for me, but Wendy hasn't seen him, either. I checked in with Royan, king of the Gilarian Fae, next. Ren did warn them. They've already started taking steps to quarantine their cities in the mountains. Royan said Ren left their stronghold a day and a half ago and hasn't been seen in the Shallow Mountains since."

"*What?*"

"I visited every small town between Gilaria and Ballard to see if he'd been waylaid, but no one's seen hide nor hair of him."

A lead weight, ice-cold, formed in the pit of my stomach. "You don't think...Belikon..."

Fisher shook his head, dark waves brushing the tops of his shoulders. "No. Ren's smarter than every single one of Belikon's guards put together. He moves like a ghost along those forest roads. There's no way anyone stumbled across him and knew to command him to return to the Winter Palace on behalf of the king. No, this is something else. I just can't put my finger on it."

"Do you think he's in danger?"

Fisher gave me a sidelong look that answered that question in no uncertain terms. "We're all in danger, Osha. But yes, I think Ren might be in some kind of hot water. And I have no idea how to find him so we can get him out of it."

37

THREE MINUTES

KINGFISHER

THE BLUE BOOK sat on Saeris's nightstand in her rooms at Ammontraíeth. I avoided looking at it as best I could, but it was no easy thing, leashing my curiosity this way. I wouldn't open the book. I wouldn't even touch it. But the knowledge that my mother had written the entire thing made a hole burn right through my chest where my heart should have been.

Before Malcolm's maze, there had been days when I had felt her presence so keenly that I'd known she was there, standing by the window, or sitting by a fireplace, reading a book. I had felt her there with me, walking the halls of the estate for years, and I had chastised myself for allowing myself such childish fantasies.

I think a part of me had known somehow that she was still there with me. I'd spoken to her often, whenever I was alone and didn't think anyone would overhear. I would have paid anything, given anything to hear her speak back. And now there was an entire book written by her sitting not fifteen feet away—a chance to hear her voice again, in a way—and I would never be able to read what she had written in those pages, because they had not been written for me.

It was okay. I still had a childhood full of memories of my mother. They were enough to temper the sting of her loss. And it was only right that Saeris have her own private connection with Edina of the Seven Towers. My mother would have wanted it that way.

But the book. Was there something in there about Ren's whereabouts? Maybe. Maybe I was worrying over nothing, and Ren was perfectly safe and riding back to Cahlish even now. Saeris had explained my mother's request that she not read ahead in the book, so we couldn't use it to discover where he was. When we'd left the estate an hour ago, I had charged Iseabail with scrying for the general to see if we could locate him that way. Scrying was a notoriously unreliable means of tracking a person, though, and we wouldn't have any answers on that front until we could speak with the witch. So that meant suffering through this ball while trying not to worry ourselves sick.

"Well, this...this is *ridiculous*." Saeris looked deeply uncomfortable as she ran her hands down the front of her dress. The selkie seamstress who had made the dress for her had stitched her *into* it only moments ago. She had left, glowing with pride over the masterpiece she had created, and the second Saeris's chamber door had closed behind her, my mate had begun trying to claw her way out of the garment.

I sat on the chaise, legs stretched out in front of me, arms extended and resting on the back of the chair, appreciating the sight of my mate looking decidedly queenly. "You're beautiful," I told her. Even I was aware that the register of my voice dipped whenever we were alone. The dark, predatory part of me pulled at its fetters, wishing to be free and held unaccountable for the acts of depravity it would commit without the steady hand of restraint holding it by the collar.

Mine.

She was *mine*. And sometimes, the urge to throw her over a table and fuck her raw in front of everyone so that *they* would know that was too much to fucking bear. My cock stirred in my pants just thinking about it.

Saeris cast a questioning glance over her shoulder, a knowing smile teasing the corners of her mouth. "And what's *that* I smell?" she asked, in a playfully innocent tone.

"The same scent I used to catch rolling off *you* every second we were alone together in the Winter Palace," I rumbled. I took my time rising from the chaise and moving toward her. I wanted to take her in. Wanted to savor that moment when her eyes dilated, her arousal tinged with a little panic.

Her face was tilted toward me, her lips slightly parted in anticipation of a kiss... but I positioned myself behind her and placed my hands on her hips, angling them forward.

"Face the mirror," I commanded.

Saeris huffed, disappointed, I thought, but she did as I had instructed.

We stood together there, reflected in the glass: two pale creatures, both raven-haired, one with eyes of blue, the other green. Saeris's arms were already covered by long silk gloves, made from the same material as her gown. Black as murder, and sin, and ink, and the void of the heavens on a midwinter night. It was the kind of dress I hadn't seen since I was a Faeling, rustling around my mother's skirts at one of the many balls my parents had held when I was young. I had always marveled at the finery of the folk in attendance—their long-tailed coats; the bustles; the corsets; the square-toed, buckled shoes; the scent of perfume heavy in the air.

"Look at yourself," I told my mate. The tailor had wanted to apply makeup to her face, and Saeris had balked at that. They'd gone to war over the matter, but eventually, Saeris had allowed a touch of pink blush for her cheeks and a little mascara for her eyelashes. You could barely tell she was wearing anything at all. Her skin was flawless, cheekbones high, eyes bright and clear. And the dress...

Her waist was already narrow, but the corset top cinched her in tight. The décolletage was devastatingly low, cupping her breasts so that her cleavage swelled every time she breathed. The skirts were fuller than was fashionable in other Fae courts, more traditional, but they made Saeris look regal.

Over her shoulder, the black evening attire I wore complimented her dress, embellished with the same velvet trim as her dress at cuff and collar.

Black on black on black.

My shadows spilled over her shoulder and up the column of her neck, caressing her, and Saeris's breath stuttered, her skin forming goose bumps in reaction to my magic. I knew *exactly* what I was doing when I bent down and held her eye contact in the mirror, whispering softly into her ear.

"A lesser male would sink his teeth into you right here and now and fuck you until you screamed."

Her tongue darted out, wetting her lips. I could see her pulse thrumming in the hollow of her throat. "A lesser female would *beg* you to," she answered.

Oh, my Little Osha. She knew how to walk a dangerous line. "It wouldn't be wise to provoke me to action, Osha. Not with you looking like this. I do love to mar a pretty thing."

"Is that so?"

I replaced my shadows with my hand, curling my fingers lightly around her throat. "Mm-hmm."

"And how would you mar *me?*" she whispered.

I had a feeling she would ask. Running my tongue over my canines, I fisted a handful of her skirts and lifted them, hitching them up to her waist. I had to repeat the action twice more before I'd wrangled all the layers of tulle below and pinned it in my left hand. It was a shame to release her neck—I loved the sensation of her pulse flying against my palm—but I was in grave need of my other hand. Saeris watched me slide it down her body in the mirror, her pupils swallowing her irises as I stroked her exposed thighs, growling in approval when I found that she had my dagger strapped to her thigh again.

"Good girl, Saeris."

"If you only mean...to see if I'm armed, then...I could have saved you the time and told y—Oh, gods!" Her mouth fell open. I hadn't wasted any time. Her black silk panties were pulled aside, and I was sliding my fingers through her slick folds. She let out another breathless curse as I stroked her clit, her legs already starting to shake.

Good.

I was going to do more than make her shake.

I was going to make her fucking tremble.

I was going to make her *weak* for me.

The shoes she wore were beautiful, sparkling black, the heels staggering, a black silk ribbon tying at the front of each ankle. I shoved my right foot between hers and lifted her a fraction, knocking her feet out so that her stance was a little wider. I needed better access for this.

Saeris closed her eyes, turning her head, resting her cheek against my chest. "What are you doing?" she whispered.

Fuck. I needed another hand...

Magic would do. I was limited with what I could accomplish here. My small magics were available to me, such as they were. Minor illusions. Other trifles. But attempting to summon my shadows only led to frustration. My hands were bound, the vastness of my magic beyond reach. When I called, only diaphanous tendrils of shadow answered— tendrils that, for now, at least, would perfectly suffice.

The gods had gifted my father with his shadows so that he might do good with them. My father had passed them down to me for the same purpose. Over the course of my life, I had used them to help and protect many people... but right now I used them to pin Saeris's gathered skirts to her hip so that I could take her by the chin and turn her gaze back to the mirror. Would the gods punish me for such a flagrant misuse of power? Fuck it. Let them. I would use my gifts for far more scandalous things over the course of the life I shared with Saeris, and if that meant languishing in the fires of damnation when I died, then that was a price I would just have to pay.

"A queen should never enter into a political setting feeling stressed, Osha," I purred. "I'm helping, I promise."

She was slick against my fingers. Hot. Wet. I stared at her in the mirror, smiling open-mouthed at her need. Before I could remark upon it, Saeris let out a groan. "Don't tease me," she pleaded. "I can't help it. I..."

"Because you want me?" My voice was rough.

"Yes." Her voice was a plea.

I withdrew my fingers from between her legs and held up my index and middle finger for her to see: wet, shining, coated in her arousal. "I'll never tease you for this, Osha. *This* is the hottest thing in the world to me. It drives me to madness like nothing else. And I want you just as badly as you want me. *Always*. I walk around this hellhole with the head of my cock tucked into my waistband so that these leeches don't get the wrong idea."

"Fisher—"

"I would *bottle* this if I could," I said. "Now stop worrying and watch."

"*Saeris?*" Taladaius was at the door. I had sensed him there some moments ago, but he'd had the decency to keep his mouth shut. It appeared that he couldn't do that any longer.

I held Saeris's chin in place, making sure she looked straight ahead. "Don't answer."

"But—"

"Your body is mine for the next three minutes. *Surrender.*" She didn't want to. The command in my voice made her want to fight it, fight me, but she needed this. "Do you love me?"

"What! That...isn't fair."

"*Do* you?"

"Yes! Of course I love you."

I grinned wolfishly at her reflection. "A part of loving me is yielding sometimes."

"You want my obedience?"

I slipped my hand back between her thighs, my fingers teasing circles over the bud of sensitive nerve endings I found there. "No, Osha. I want your *trust*."

"*Ah!* And do I have...yours?"

I kissed her neck, still maintaining eye contact with her in the mirror. "Anything I ask of you, I give freely and willingly in return. Always. I promise." Grazing my canines over the skin just below her earlobe rendered her immobile for a split second. She sagged back against me, losing control of her muscles, her eyes rolling back into her head.

"Saeris! It's time!"

Her eyes snapped open again. "I need *three minutes*, Tal!"

I chuckled darkly under my breath. "Good girl, Osha."

Tal hissed on the other side of the door. "You know I can hear you in there. Sinners, I'll be waiting at the end of the hall."

Saeris whimpered, pushing back against me, rubbing her ass against my increasingly painful erection. I let her do it, ignoring the way my own desire burned brighter, and the way my cock was begging for attention. This was about *her*, not me. There would be plenty of other opportunities where the roles might be reversed, but for now...

Saeris was starting to shake.

I plunged my fingers up inside her, snarling with satisfaction at the low moan she let out. "I'm going to make you come now. And for the rest of the night, anyone who comes within five feet of you will scent the orgasm I'm about to give to you."

Yes, it was primal.

Yes, it was petty.

No, it was *not* very progressive of me to want to mark her in this way.

I didn't fucking care.

This female, who shone brighter than the suns of her home and mine combined, was *my* mate, and every single member of this court would be reminded of that fact.

"Oh my gods," Saeris panted.

"Good?"

She nodded.

I turned into her, pressing my mouth right up against the shell of her ear. "Watch my hand," I breathed. "Watch me fucking you with my fingers. See how pretty your pussy looks like this, cupped in my palm. Do you see?"

My hand shielded most of her, but there it was, every few seconds: a glimpse of delicate coral pink.

Saeris moaned, her fingers digging into the rustling fabric of her skirts. "Yes," she gasped. "Yes!"

Trembling became shaking. Shaking became full-body convulsions. She was close.

"Now look at me," I demanded. "Don't close your eyes. Listen. I want to feel you clenching around my fingers, Saeris Fane. I want to feel that burst of sweet, wet heat in my hand when you come apart. Do it for me. That's it. Do it now."

She clenched, her jaw locking, nostrils flaring . . . and she came.

As she did so, threads of black swirled down my arm and spread from my skin to hers. Not magic, but ink. Another tattoo. Beautiful roses bloomed across the tops of her thighs as she moaned—an entire bouquet's worth, shaded with delicate dot work yet still stark against the pale, creamy perfection of her thighs.

The untamed beast inside me roared as she released a wordless, desperate cry, clinging to my arm, grinding herself into my hand, and rolling her hips.

"That's it. Breathe. Breathe. Breathe."

She let go of another cry. The sound was unrestrained and beautiful, fucking music to my ears, so guttural and free, and then she was done.

"Holy fucking hell . . . I . . . I . . ." She tried to support her own weight, leaning forward, but she tottered on her heels, nearly losing her balance.

"Steady, Osha." I caged her loosely in my arms, supporting her as if she was drunk.

"Whoa." She blinked quickly, as if she was having trouble seeing properly. "Those are . . . huge," she gasped, eyeing the inkwork over the tops of her legs. "But . . . *beautiful.*"

Grinning wickedly over her shoulder, I slowly slid my fingers into my mouth. I sucked them clean, winking at her in the mirror. "Don't say I never give you flowers, Osha."

"Gods alive . . ." She shook her head, trembling a little. "How am I supposed to go out there now? I can't even *stand.*"

So hyperbolic. "You're fine," I chided her playfully, laughing a little as I helped her find her feet. Once it didn't look like her legs were going to quit on her anymore, I dropped to my knees in front of her and carefully undid the magic I had used to keep her skirts lifted while I teased her. Moving slowly, I fixed her underskirts layer by layer, making sure that none of the tulle was rucked up or sticking out anywhere. Once that was done, I settled the heavier fabric of her skirt back down, smoothing it out until she looked just as put together as she had when the tailor had left.

Her eyes still looked a little unfocused when I looked up at her and winked. "Feeling less stressed?" I inquired.

My mate blew out her cheeks, shaking her head slowly from side to side. "My ears are ringing so hard, I'm not going to be able to hear any of these petitions, Fisher."

I got to my feet and placed a quick, chaste kiss against her lips. "You're welcome. Come on. If we keep Tal waiting another minute, his head might actually implode."

"Okay. Yeah, let's—oh, wait, no! I need to..." Saeris hurried across her chambers and picked up the book that was still sitting on his nightstand. "I nearly forgot. I need to read the next page in your mother's journal."

She flipped through the front half of the book and paused, her eyes sliding from one side of the page to the other, fast, like a metronome. The post-orgasm haze left her face as she took in whatever secret lay before her and tried to wrap her head around it. When she looked up from the page, she gave a small nod and set the book down on the end of the bed, a strange look of determination on her face.

"All right, then. *Now* I'm ready. Let's go."

38

SCION OF NO ONE

KINGFISHER

THE HALL OF Tears was transformed.

The benches were gone. Long tables lined the vast space on the left and the right, the center of the hall reserved for dancing. Tall pillars of evenlight swayed and danced along the perimeter of the hall, the haunting, heatless flames almost soaring all the way up to the vaulted ceiling high overhead. Glassy-eyed Fae thralls dressed in the crimson red of the Blood Court carried pitchers of wine to the hundreds of high bloods gathered in their finery, beautiful despite the too-pale quality of their skin and the flinty, cold judgment in their eyes.

Many of the female high bloods whispered behind lace fans or their hands, venomous gazes darting furtively toward Saeris. I sat sprawled in the chair next to her, playing the game. I wanted to rip out their snake tongues for even uttering Saeris's name. I did *not* do that, because that would cause a scene—the kind of scene that would end the ball early—and after what had happened at Saeris's coronation, I doubted I would get away with ruining two ceremonies, back to back. Tal would skin me alive for complicating matters further than I already had. So here I would sit, on my very best behavior, not ruining anything for anyone.

For only the second time since we'd arrived at Ammontraíeth,

Saeris presided over the court on her throne, a golden diadem studded with diamonds glittering atop her head. Now that all of the kneeling was out of the way, her shoulders were relaxed, her eyes soft as they passed over the gathered high bloods, but her hands gripped the arms of her chair a little too tightly. Her knuckles were white.

There's blood in the air, she said into my mind. *So many different people, bleeding freely. I can smell it.*

With a casual roll of my shoulders, I nodded in the direction of a Fae male at the foot of the dais, pouring wine for a high blood noble. As soon as he was done filling the glass, he set his pitcher down and prickled the inside of his wrist with a metallic spiked ring that he wore around the tip of his thumb, drawing blood. Holding his wrist over the nobleman's glass, he allowed two, three, four droplets of blood to fall into the wine. The nobleman bared his teeth, clearly displeased by the small amount of blood the Fae male had spared him, but the Fae male just closed the cuff of his shirt, already speckled with blood, picked up his pitcher, and moved on to the next high blood with an empty glass.

They partake all night at these things, I said to Saeris. *By the end of the night, they'll all be sideways from the wine and feral from the blood.*

You've been to one of these balls before?

No. But we've all heard the stories.

The black diamond earrings at Saeris's ears winked in the dim light as she turned to face Tal, who came striding up the steps toward us with purpose. He wore a dove-gray suit this evening, made from fine cloth. The color would have been a foolish choice for a normal male with skin the color of alabaster and hair as silver as moonlight, but Tal was not your normal male. Where the pale gray might have washed another out, it seemed to lend the Keeper of Secrets an ethereal, distinctly Fae air that most high bloods lost when they transitioned.

Tal's loose white shirt was unbuttoned all the way to his solar plexus; when he dropped into a deep bow in front of Saeris, his hand, hovering in front of his chest, did nothing to hide the expanse of skin that suddenly became visible for all to see.

I'd seen Tal without a shirt plenty of times before. We had swum in the waters at the foot of the white cliffs of Inishtar together, back when his heart still beat in his chest and he had grand aspirations of embarrassing his parents by becoming a cartographer and disappearing off on a boat to map uncharted lands. He had given me the shirt off his back numerous times in the maze, too. Reviving after a run-in with Morthil more often than not meant that I woke up freezing cold and naked on a slab of wet stone, just beyond the demon's reach. Most of the time, Tal knew when Morthil had caught me and was already waiting for me when I came to, a fresh set of clothing in hand. Sometimes, my sprawled-out, naked ass took him unawares, though. He didn't once flinch at stripping out of his own attire and giving it to me. He had no reason to; *his* magic answered him in that poisoned pit. He was a creature of the Blood Court, and as such it was no problem at all for him to summon *himself* some new clothes.

Regardless of the scenario, I had seen his chest many times, and recently, too, which meant that the extensive ink I glimpsed now, staining his skin, was new.

I crooked a questioning eyebrow at the male, who registered it immediately but only gave me a small, private smile by way of explanation. "We're almost ready for the petitions, Saeris," he said. "There are five applicants, with five proposed avenues through which they consider themselves useful to you. We'll begin in about thirty minutes. Better to get it done before dinner."

Saeris nodded.

"And, well, the other matter?" Tal said.

"Yes?"

"If it's all the same to you, I'd like to take care of it now, before they're all too drunk to remember that it happened."

The disavowment.

Saeris had told me Tal wanted to sever the bond between them, but she hadn't mentioned the fact that he was so anxious about the matter. Maybe she hadn't noticed the tells: the way the skin between his brows pinched when he spoke of it. The way he stretched out his hand, closed it into a fist, shook it out, as if he were readying for a fight. In fairness, there was nothing overtly anxious about the male…but I *knew* him. Had known him all my life. And these small tics made something inside me prick its ears and sit up, curious.

My mate shifted uncomfortably on the throne, but she nodded. "All right. Yes, let's just get it over with, then."

Tal beamed. "Excellent."

I leaned in close to her and whispered. "Do you know how this works?"

"No. I assumed he just…told everyone he doesn't want to be my maker anymore."

"Not quite."

I was prevented from explaining when Tal jogged down the steps to the dais, snagged a silver bucket from a passing Fae thrall, tossed the ice from inside it onto the floor, and came jogging back up the steps. He thrust the bucket into Saeris's lap and then spun around, holding his arms theatrically in the air.

"Noble high bloods of Sanasroth, your attention, please!"

The soft music that had been playing—some kind of plucked instrument—halted on a discordant note. It took a moment for the hubbub of conversation being conducted throughout the hall to subside, but eventually an expectant silence fell over the gathered vampires.

"Welcome all. This evening we come together to celebrate our evenlight—a gift from the gods that lights our court where nothing else can. As there is every year, there will be singing, and dancing, and feasting, but first, there will be a slight deviation from our usual annual festivities. A new Lord must be appointed to the fifth point of our star, which means that one of you must rise to serve your court. There must always be five."

"There must always be five! There must always be five!"

The cheer went up among the high bloods, resounding throughout the hall.

Taladaius nodded.

As he spoke, going over the order of proceedings, a waif of a low blood approached the dais, creeping forward hesitantly, carrying a platter of sweetmeats in his hands. He could barely have seen his seventeenth birthday before he'd undergone his transition; he would never know what it would have been like to reach his maturity and step into his magic. Flinching, he offered the tray up toward Saeris, too nervous to even climb the steps of the dais.

Saeris beckoned him forward.

The low blood was weak, in a place where being weak doomed your odds of survival. That was why he served with the thralls. He cowered as he ascended the stairs, hands shaking, sweetmeats wobbling...

"I'm not hungry," she whispered. "Come here. I need you to do something for me." No *please*. No *thank you*. The queen of Sanasroth didn't beg favors, and low bloods were not afforded niceties.

What are you up to, Osha? I asked her.

Outwardly, she didn't react to the fact that I'd spoken into her mind. She cupped her hand around the low blood's ear and whispered to him, answering me at the same time with a remarkable show of concentration, *I'll tell you soon. For now, I have to keep it to myself. I'm sorry, I wish I could explain, but I can't.*

Ahh. So this was related to the journal, then.

I relaxed back into my seat, refocusing on Tal's performance down on the five-pointed mosaic below the dais. *It's okay, Osha. That's all you need to say. I won't ask again.*

The low blood scuttled back from Saeris, staring at her as if she had lost her mind. She raised her brows at the male questioningly. "Well? Go. Do as I've asked you, and I'll see to it that you're rewarded."

"*Rewarded?*" Skepticism shone in the male's eyes.

"Yes. Payment. In blood," Saeris said. "Now go."

The low blood didn't need telling twice. At the mention of blood, he bolted from the dais and disappeared into the crowd, who were all still listening to Tal. I followed him, watching his head bob through the knotted mass of bodies, until he ducked through a curtained alcove and was gone.

"But before all of that, there is something else that I, personally, would like to address. When we came together here last to welcome our new queen, accusations were made that I hoped to *control* her. Slanderous accusations that I wished to puppet her for my own purpose and gain. There was no time to refute those claims at the coronation, in light of what transpired..."

Hundreds of angry eyes turned on me.

I shot the crowd a beatific grin.

"...but now that we have reached a *calmer* place, I stand before you all, making that proclamation. I do not have designs on the Sanasrothian throne. I do not wish to control Saeris Fane, regent of this court."

Unrest stirred by the head of the table to my right. I didn't even need to look to know Zovena would be at the center of the angry muttering, but yes, there she was, glowering at Taladaius. I could almost see the steam piping from her ears.

Tal, ever the practiced orator, ignored the disturbance and continued his address. "I do not want, nor have I ever wanted, power over the other Lords of Midnight, and I will happily prove that to you all, right here and right now. I, Taladaius Helyer, once eldest son of the Helyer household, Keeper of Secrets and Lord of Midnight, do hereby rescind the gift of my blood!" He lifted his arms in the air again and turned away from the crowd to face us, his features stormy, eyes as steely as thunderheads. He *winked* at Saeris, raising his voice even louder so that it boomed throughout the hall. "Without rancor and with the deepest respect and humility, I call back my blood, Saeris Fane, queen of Sanasroth. I revoke my lineage and my patronage, so that you may stand alone in your task, and I may do the same. I call upon the gods and the demons of this realm. It is my will!"

I braced for the clap of Tal's hands, knowing what would come with it. The shock wave tore through the hall, causing the ground to buck beneath the palace. The disruption was gone as quickly as it had come, but the smell of sulfur lingered in the air, burning the back of my nose. Next to me, Saeris grimaced. She looked at me, confusion written all over her face.

"What the hell?" she whispered.

And then she pitched forward and vomited a jet of blood into the empty ice bucket Tal had given her before his grand speech.

It's okay. It'll be over quickly. You didn't drink much of his blood, I told her.

It was a rare and messy business, the rescinding of the blood. I'd never seen it performed. I'd heard tales of it happening, though. Over the centuries, Malcolm had sired every single high blood in this court. Occasionally, one of them had displeased him, and he'd had reason to call back his blood.

He had gathered his court around him and made an event out of it, using the spectacle to publicly shame his offspring, but also to demonstrate to his other children what would happen to *them* if they stepped out of line. A high blood would live after a rescinding. On paper, very little changed. They were still alive, inasmuch as *any* vampire was actually *alive*...but they were outcasts. Cut off from the royal blood. Malcolm had often gone a step further and officially shunned a high blood once he had recalled his blood, and that? Well, that *was* a death sentence for most.

Tal couldn't shun Saeris. He'd said plenty of pretty things about no rancor and respect, but what he did here tonight *did* shame her, according to the precedent that Malcolm had set. It was selfish—something so utterly unlike Tal that when Saeris had mentioned it before, I had assumed the suggestion of it would never come to anything. And yet here we were. I would be pinning the bastard up against a wall later and demanding to know what the hell he was playing at, him being *so* concerned about Saeris not appearing weak in front of the court.

Saeris bore the display with considerable dignity, given that she was vomiting blood in front of an entire court who loathed her. It was over quickly, as I'd assured her it would be. A few mouthfuls of blood were all that was owed.

When she was done spitting into the silver bucket, Tal took it from her, bowing low. "Thank you. I'm sorry." Quick as a flash, he faced the crowd again, garish green light washing over his skin as he addressed the court. "Behold! Saeris Fane, first of her name. Scion of no one. Rise for your queen!" he bellowed.

It couldn't be denied: He put on a damn good show when he felt like it. To what end, I couldn't fathom, but still. He had the entire Blood Court on their feet, reluctantly holding their glasses in the air.

"May she be the last monarch this court sees!" Tal shouted, snatching a glass up from a passing thrall's tray. "May she overcome all, for the glory of this holy court. May she usher in a new era and a new beginning for the people of Sanasroth! To Queen Saeris!"

The toast was a confusing one. Had any of the vampires present been faintly sober, they might have questioned Tal's unusual tribute, but half the court was already in its cups, and the other half were catching up. A sea of glasses went up in the air, the light glancing off their gold-edged rims in a dazzling display as all of Ammontraíeth called out my mate's name.

"Queen Saeris!"

Silence followed quick on the heels of the shouting, as the high bloods drained their glasses. It didn't matter that they were probably cursing her name to themselves as they downed their wine—they still drank.

Blood and wine, after all.

Blood and wine.

Seemingly pleased, Taladaius descended the dais steps and set his glass on the table to the right. "And now, there are five loyal members of this court who would ascend to the position of Lord, to safeguard a tithing of its power and become a court protector. I call forth Kavan Dahlish to present his case!"

Kavan Dahlish was a brute. At well over seven and a half feet tall, he towered over everyone as he bulled his way through the crowd and came to stand at the center of the five-pointed star.

The moment he turned and bowed toward the dais, I knew him.

His thick dark hair hung all the way down his back; in life, he had been a fine warrior. Courageous and brave. Funny, too. His nose was flat, pressed to his wide face having been broken many times. *I* had been responsible for one or two of those breaks, courtesy of some rowdy sparring sessions that had ended in blood on both sides.

His eyes were flat and dark now, where once they had been blue. They narrowed imperceptibly as he nodded first not to Saeris, but to me. "Commander." There was no warmth in the greeting. Even less warmth to the greeting he paid Saeris. "Your Highness."

My skin prickled all over; my tattoos were rioting beneath my clothes. How *foolish* of me. I'd made a grave error. Malcolm had stalked the killing fields of so many of our battles. The crows fed from the fallen, plucking out their eyes. Malcolm had done the fucking same. Only, he had taken their *souls* instead of letting them pass peacefully into the beyond.

The tallest. The strongest. The ones who had still been putting up a fight. Because Kavan wouldn't have gone quietly. Malcolm would have *forced* him to take his blood...

How many of my warriors had he taken that way, plucked trembling from the verge of death and made to swallow from his foul veins before they were ended and turned to his will?

Rage painted my vision red. A futile, impotent emotion. What was I supposed to do with the hate that roiled in my gut, for a male who was ash on the wind? There was no one to scream at. No one to blame. There was only the warrior whom I had called friend, who had died on my watch and been condemned to an eternity of debasement and depravity as a result.

"I've served this court for two hundred and seven years, Highness. During that time, I have trained many captains in the art of siege warfare. I have piloted several battalions of the horde in successful campaigns. I have cast the armies of our foe at the gates of hell and pitched their bodies in."

A low droning sound drowned Kavan out.

He stared at me as he rolled off a litany of atrocities that had earned him praise and commendations from Malcolm, and my blood ran cold as ice in my veins.

The training he had received from *me*. The skills *I* had taught him. All of it, turned around and used against us.

Kavan had known how to wield his weapon. He had stood in the shadows and watched as the monsters who had killed him tore apart the friends he had once sworn to protect.

As he spoke, the acrimony in his eyes, the *accusation*, was clear. *You left me here to this. What did you expect?*

"I may not be one of the longest-serving members of this court, but I have brought glory to Sanasroth and upheld my master's will. I propose that *I* be selected as Ammontraíeth's newest Lord of Midnight, specifically as Keeper of Warfare."

Are you okay?

Saeris's eyes were on Kavan. She showed no signs of having noticed my discomfort, but we were sensitive to each other these days. I could sense when she was tense. Worried. Apparently, she could sense when I was so deeply on edge.

I'm fine. I'm okay. He was just... he was one of mine.

Oh, gods, Fisher. I'm so sorry.

To the warrior, she said, "Thank you for your service to this court, Kavan. I will consider your petition thoroughly before I make my decision."

The warrior bowed deeply. His gaze lingered on Saeris for a second before it slipped to me, dark and tense. Once, his eyes would have been full of laughter and fire. Now they were cold and full of hate.

It broke me.

How could I have been so fucking *blind*?

When my fighters had fallen in battle, I had consoled myself with the knowledge that they had gone on to rest, gone into the arms of the loved ones and ancestors who had passed before them. Not for one second had I imagined that they would be *here*, suffering and tormented, and coming to hate me for abandoning them to their fate. How could I not have considered *this*?

Saeris's voice sounded as though it were coming from underwater. "...you, Ibanwae. Tell me, how do *you* see yourself being of service to this court?"

Kavan was gone.

A female high blood had replaced him and was bowing, her eyes glued on the floor. Her hair was a frizzy black mass, so voluminous and wild that it almost hid her whole head. She wore a high-collared black dress, long-sleeved, its skirts brushing the ground, hiding her feet. Aside from her head and her hands, every part of her body was covered.

Her voice swept through the hall in a hoarse whisper. "Your Highness. I am known to every member of this court. I was here at the beginning, when our kind first spilled righteous blood in service of our king. My hands designed and oversaw the construction of the fine palace that you now call your own. My lord father charged me with the engineering and construction of siege machines, sewer systems, and all the infrastructure and planning required when the Cogs were built. He was particularly pleased with the weapons of war I created on his behalf. Weapons of iron, designed to inflict unimaginable pain upon the vile Fae scum who beset our home and attempt to divert us from our glorious purpose."

Vile Fae scum.

I could see only the crown of her head, but I could picture her expression as she spat those words at the ground.

"I put myself forth as the next Lord of Midnight, and request that I be made Keeper of Pain, so that I might renew my efforts in the design of equipment that will bring the Fae dogs to heel once and—"

Saeris spoke over the female. "What is our glorious purpose, Ibanwae?" Unruffled. Calm, even. But my mate was *livid*.

The name Ibanwae was so old and out of style that it probably hadn't been spoken outside of this court in centuries. The woman it belonged to looked up, revealing a face full of tattoos. Runes, to be precise. They were dead runes, though. Long inactive. Barren of magic and turned ash-gray by time. It was a shield. Once upon a time, this female had been an Alchemist.

Her eyes were black, pupil bleeding into iris, bleeding into white. Open scorn met Saeris's question as the female slowly drew up to stand straight. "The same glorious purpose that Sanasroth has *always* striven toward, Your Majesty. Domination over the other courts. Total supremacy over the Fae. Mandatory blood tithes. Livestock breeding farms. Feeding farms—"

Saeris held up a hand. "Yes, thank you. That's enough."

Ibanwae huffed, her dead runes shifting as she pulled a disgruntled face. "Does the reality of your court displease you, Your Majesty?" she asked. "Perhaps you haven't the stomach to rule over a people such as these." She spread her arms wide, gesturing to her fellow high bloods.

A thick silence fell over the crowd. To the right, Tal leaned against the wall by the foot of the dais, arms folded over his chest. His face was blank, his eyes fixed on Saeris, waiting, as everyone else was, to see what she would say.

Saeris regarded Ibanwae, exuding a proud, cool confidence that made me want to cheer on her behalf. She looked every bit the regal, unshakable queen she needed to be in this moment—as unreachable and cold as the distant mountains. She didn't say anything in response to the jibe. Just stared at the female. The high blood took Saeris's silence as a sign that she had caught her on the back foot; she smirked coquettishly, sending sidelong looks at the other vampires gathered at the foot of the dais, who had clearly come to hear her speak and show their support. After a long, long moment, the vampire's smile began to fade, though.

Saeris didn't blink.

Someone cleared their throat.

On the table to the left, someone shifted, causing a chair to complain under their weight.

And still Saeris stared at the female.

Ibanwae lowered her eyes to the ground. "You understand, I do not mean to offend the throne—"

"I understand violence," Saeris said. She spoke softly, with no inflection or emotion. The entire hall heard her words. "I understand...that it is a *tool*." She waited. Looking beyond Ibanwae, she took in the high bloods in their laces and satins, and the gold-rimmed, etched wineglasses spiked with Fae blood, and she addressed them all. "I understand that the high bloods of Sanasroth have run amok these past one thousand years. I understand that Malcolm let chaos reign here, while he was off waging a war he could not win. A war that cost Sanasroth its resources and depleted its wealth at every turn. There will be no livestock breeding farms. There will be no *feeding* farms. Over the coming years, we will focus on rebuilding this court—"

"And while we're rebuilding," a sharp voice called, "what do you propose that we *eat*?"

Fucking Zovena.

I was going to ash her one of these days and wear her fangs as fucking *earrings*.

The Lord was on her feet, slinking around the table toward the dais. Her tittering, imbecilic friends moved aside for her as she passed them. She was dressed in a blood-red velvet gown that cut a savage silhouette, her blond hair braided and wound artfully around her head. Rubies flashed in the hollow of her throat and at her ears. Each of her fingers was clad in gold and precious stones. Atop her head, she wore a golden-leafed laurel that looked suspiciously like a crown.

Saeris ignored the viper, her attention still fixed upon Ibanwae. "These aspirations you speak of. They are not end goals. It sounds to me that the goals for all at Sanasroth are safety, security, legitimacy, and food."

"Hah!" Zovena snorted. She prowled before the dais, acid burning in her eyes as she faced the high bloods. "Isn't that what I just said? *Food*, your highness. We need to know what, or rather *who*, we will be eating!"

Saeris didn't rise from her seat. Didn't even frown as she flicked her hand at the table to the right, and a candelabra—which *had* been crowned with eight shivering points of evenlight—flew from the snow-white tablecloth and twisted in midair. It formed a length of metal two feet long and struck Zovena from behind, curving around the back of her neck. The Lord of Revels let out a shriek as the malformed candelabra dove downward, pulling her off her feet; it slammed into the obsidian floor with a loud, metallic clang, biting into stone, pinning Zovena to the ground by her neck.

I'm pretty sure you just shattered her jaw, I said into Saeris's head.

She'll recover, was my mate's acerbic reply.

I ducked my chin into the collar of my shirt, hiding my smile until I managed to banish it from my face.

"Ahh! You... *bitch!*" Zovena yanked and pulled, but try as she might, strong as she was, she couldn't tug the mangled candelabra from the obsidian floor. The metal was servant to no one but Saeris. "Let me *up!*" the Lord seethed.

Ibanwae, who had started her petition with much the same energy as Zovena's outburst, gawked at the other female, pinned by her neck to the ground, and swallowed thickly. "I would like..." She stopped speaking when Saeris slowly rose from her throne and began to descend the steps.

The hairs on the back of my neck rose, every instinct I owned telling me to get up and put myself between my mate and the danger that stood before her.

I couldn't do that, though. I wouldn't undermine her in front of these leeches. I stayed where I was, and the inaction damned near killed me. What was she doing, though? And why was it making me so fucking hot under the collar?

With shoulders relaxed, spine straight, and head held high, Saeris made her way down the steps and skirted around Zovena. She collected a chair from one of the tables and dragged it, back legs scraping loudly on the floor, over to Zovena, where she set it next to the prone woman, sat down, kicked her feet up, and rested her heels on the female's back.

"Be still," she commanded before the outraged Lord could buck her off.

Zovena screeched. "Get off me, you stupid f—"

"Be quiet."

Calm as the center of a storm, she was. Brutal. Cruel. Lethal. Even I wouldn't have fucked with her in this moment, resting her feet on the back of a female whom most of this court was afraid of. I *would* have fucked her, though. I desperately, *desperately* wanted to do that. There was something deeply arousing about my mate owning her power. Turning to Ibanwae, Saeris plucked a piece of lint from her skirts. "You were saying?"

"Keeper of Pain," the female said, eyes glittering, voice a little shaky. "*I* would like to be the Keeper of Pain."

———+———

Three more petitions.

A would-be Keeper of Monies. A prospective Keeper of Truths. A hopeful Keeper of Antiquities.

The minutes ticked by as Saeris heard the applicants speak, and she did not move from her position, feet resting on Zovena's back. Halfway through the proceedings, she fished out a dagger from the scabbard at her thigh and began cleaning her fingernails with the blade. Zovena didn't move. She didn't say a word.

Only once all the petitions had been heard did she very slowly rise from her chair. She was in no hurry at all as she hooked her little finger underneath the metal band that was cutting into Zovena's neck and gave it the gentlest of pulls, and then the candelabra came free.

"You may move. You may speak," she said in a bored tone as she walked away from the female's shuddering frame and climbed back up the steps.

Zovena was as mad as a spitting snake when she leaped to her feet, but her hostile stance was of no interest to me. The haunted expression Tal wore as he looked away from the female, frowning at a spot on the far wall hanging, though? No wall hanging deserved *that* level of scrutiny.

"You think this is a game?" Zovena shouted.

Saeris still had three steps to go before she reached her throne. She stopped, eyes finding mine briefly before she turned, her skirts rustling around her, and at last gave Zovena her full attention.

"You seem to confuse the dynamic between us, Zovena. I am your master. I could command you to sit at my feet, and you would bow, knowing death chased the edge of my blade. You mistake my patience for weakness. For tolerance. But test me further, and you will discover the *limit* of that patience."

From the moment Saeris had set foot into the Hall of Tears for her coronation, she had been playing a part. She'd played it well, too. But she wasn't acting now. She was as sick of Zovena as I was— impressive, since she'd known the female such a short time. I had no doubt that she *would* put the female down with a smile on her face if she got the opportunity. Zovena shook with the effort it took to cage her retort. For uncounted years, she had bathed in the warm glow of Malcolm's approval. Unchecked. Unchallenged. Beloved of her king. It must have been raw indeed to find herself out in the cold, standing in the shadow of the female who had killed him.

Taladaius sauntered across the five-pointed star, a casual smile playing across his face, but there was a tightness around his eyes that could not be mistaken for anything other than worry. "Come now, high bloods of Sanasroth!" he called. "The petitions have been heard!" He raised his hand high, holding Ereth's ring aloft for all to see. The large amber-orange jewel at the ring's center caught the evenlight, refracting rainbows up the walls. "It is time to discover who will become our next Lord and don the fifth Ring of Midnight—"

"Actually, Taladaius, I believe there's one more petition we've still yet to hear," Saeris said coolly. She took her seat on her throne, calmly smoothing her skirts.

Tal's composure wavered as he looked up the dais, the muscles in his throat working. The fleeting expression that passed over his face seemed to say, *What the fuck are you doing, Saeris Fane?* He knew nothing of a sixth candidate for the ring in his hand. I knew nothing of it, either, which meant that this surprise announcement from Saeris must have had something to do with the journal.

"Our queen surprises us," Taladaius said in a tense voice. "How lucky we are." He swallowed thickly, then closed his hand around the ring he was still holding in the air and lowered his hand to his side. With a flourish of a bow, he said, "As it pleases you, Your Highness. To whom shall we open the floor?"

The tension in the Hall of Tears had already been thick enough to cut with a knife, but it grew suffocating as discord broke out among the high bloods. Saeris had already sighted the figure who emerged from the sea of vampires, but shouts of outrage erupted from the tables as the Blood Court's nobles finally saw who their queen had brought before them.

This was how I remembered him: kitted out in fighting leathers, with a sword strapped to his back and his head held high.

Gold flashed in his mouth as he came and knelt before the throne, offering a chagrined half smile. In a voice that rang loud and clear across the hall, he said, "My name is Foley Briarstone, and I have come to be of service to my queen."

But his dubious expression said something else entirely.

I hope you know what you're doing, half-breed.

39

KEEPER OF SECRETS

SAERIS

Consider a sixth. Only the golden-toothed wolf can be
trusted.

—Entry from the journal of Edina of
the Seven Spires

"SHUNNED! SHUNNED!"

The screams were deafening.

Taladaius spun around, too confounded to speak. Beside me, Fisher
covered his mouth with his hand and laughed softly under his breath.
You certainly know how to light a match, he said, amused. *Are you having
fun yet?*

No! This is not fun, Fisher. This is fucking stressful!

It seemed as though Foley mirrored my sentiments. On his knees,
he winced every time something hit him in the back; the high bloods
were lobbing things at him. Pieces of food. Cutlery. A shoe. A plate
sailed through the air, and that was where I had to draw the line.
"Enough! Sit *down*," I growled. "I name Foley Briarstone friend to this
throne!"

That was all that had to be said. The edict I had made at my coronation took care of everything else. No member of the Blood Court could harm anyone I named a friend. With eight short words, I had ensured that no one in Ammontraíeth would *ever* harm Foley again.

"What farce is this?" Algat had been notably missing from the hall until now. She bullied her way through the knot of high bloods and pushed Taladaius out of the way in her hurry to get to Foley. She circled the male, her small black shadow cat prowling around her feet as she did so. Guru yowled when he saw Foley and stretched out into a bow, rubbing his head against the male's thighs. Algat witnessed this and snarled. She bared yellowed, rat-like teeth and *kicked* the cat. The blow would certainly have done some damage had Guru not dematerialized into a swath of shadows a second before her foot made contact with his side; obviously the creature had practice avoiding her boots.

"He cannot be here," she seethed, stabbing a finger at Foley.

"It is my will."

Foley's cheeks burned bright red. The tips of his ears, too. Guru had rematerialized and had leaped up into his lap and was begging for affection from him. The male didn't seem to know what to do or where to look. He stroked the cat's head, not meeting anyone's gaze.

The witch sputtered, furious. She reminded me of one of the crones who used to stand outside Kala's, spitting on people who emerged from the building and telling them their souls were damned to hell for fornication and drinking. "He can't serve this court. How can he, when he refused to swear fealty to Sanasroth?"

Algat realized her argument was flawed even as she made it. Her rheumy eyes drifted to the Hazrax, which stood at the head of its point on the star mosaic below the dais, unmoving, unspeaking, its long hands tucked inside the belled sleeves of its robe. She already knew what I was about to say.

"The Hazrax is not a member of this court. It has not sworn fealty to Sanasroth or a single vampire here, and yet it has been a Lord of Midnight for many centuries."

"Yes, but that's—"

"Different? I fail to see how." I felt it then: the bullying push at the wall that shielded my mind. It was Algat, scrambling to get in, even though I had forbidden her from rifling around inside my head. Despite the command, she was still trying...and my fury rose like a wave of vengeance summoned by the gods themselves. I imagined knives, scores of them, hovering in the air, pointed tip-first at the wall. I lowered the wall, only long enough to send the blades hurtling forward, then brought it back up as quickly as I could.

Algat swayed, eyelids fluttering, eyes rolling back into her head, as a river of blood gushed from her nose, pouring down her chin.

There would be no more tiptoeing around this one. If she wouldn't toe the line, I would make her. If she wanted violence, it would be hers.

"What have you done?" The shriek came from Zovena. The female bore no love for Algat, but here was an opportunity to create a scene. She was hardly likely to let it pass. And she was afraid. I could scent it on her, the smell like soiled bedsheets and fever. She was afraid that *she* might be next.

"Today is a day of lessons," I said. "Algat will be fine. But she should be careful where she trespasses."

The Keeper of Records wobbled unsteadily, but within a moment or two she had regained her balance and was scowling at me again. Algat cuffed her chin, smearing her blood up her face even as she tried to wipe it away. "My apologies," she rasped. "I only tried to make you see *reason*. The Hazrax does not count in this instance. It does not weigh in on politics. Nor does it ever opt to cast its vote. This male would do both, and to the detriment of this court. If he will not swear fealty—"

"It was *Malcolm* I wouldn't swear fealty to," Foley said softly. "I'll swear it to *her*."

Well, damn.

I hadn't been expecting that.

We'd come a long way from him trying to kill me in the library, it would seem. I would never have dreamed I'd hear those words coming out of Foley's mouth. He was earnest and clear-eyed as he gestured to the steps, asking wordlessly if he could approach the throne.

I nodded my consent.

The male dropped to one knee at my feet, pulling a dagger from the sheath on his belt. He held it up to show me.

Strange, sad eyes, with vertical, slit pupils met mine. "I was reminded recently that I was a wolf," he said, smiling softly. "And wolves do not cower in dusty libraries, afraid of their own shadows. I swear myself to *you*, Saeris Fane. I will carry out your bidding so long as there is breath left in me. And when I pass from this place and move on to the next, I will carry your banners there and storm the gates of heaven in your name if you wish it."

He closed his hand around his blade and drew it free, staining it deepest, darkest crimson with his blood. I accepted the weapon from him and used its point to draw forth a bead of my own blood, which was still somehow the same bright red as that of the living.

"I accept you as my sworn male," I told him. "I accept your loyalty and your service. In return, I offer you the protection of my house. I name you Lord of Midnight."

Leaning forward, I gave him back his dagger. Foley accepted it, and as he did so I took the opportunity to deaden the air around us so that when I whispered to him, no other would hear. "What made you change your mind?" I asked teasingly.

He huffed out an unsteady bark of laughter under his breath. "Well, I figured if *he's* prepared to follow you," he said, nodding in Fisher's direction, "then *I'd* be a fucking idiot not to, wouldn't I?"

Kingfisher snorted under his breath, but I could tell he was pleased. I was about to tell Foley he was wrong, that Fisher didn't *follow* me at all, but the thought never made it to my lips. A shout cut through the air, and then another.

"What *now?*" Just a moment's peace. Was that too much to ask for?

When I searched for the source of the shouting, I found that every-one in the hall was suddenly looking *up*. It had been impossible to tell before, but the sections of the vaulted ceiling were actually panels, and they were peeling back.

"It's here!" someone cried. "It's here!"

"*What's* here?" I twisted around on my chair—my *throne*—trying to figure out what was causing the commotion, but Kingfisher took my hand and gave it a squeeze.

"The evenlight, Osha. Spirit of the gods." He pointed toward the night sky, to the west, where a brilliant green, glittering wave of light was rolling across the heavens at tremendous speed.

"They are with us," Foley muttered, pressing his index finger and middle finger to his forehead, between his brows. Many of the high bloods mirrored the motion, too. Surprising, that. Whether they had chosen this life for themselves, or it had been thrust upon them— undying, a perversion of nature, never to know the rest and peace of the afterlife—it stood to reason that they were beyond the sight of the gods here, in this unholy place. But there were still some among them who worshipped the gods. They bowed their heads in reverence as a wind ripped through the hall, and the pale green light tore overhead in a shimmering pennant that filled the night sky from horizon to horizon.

It was beautiful. Like nothing I'd ever witnessed before. Not even the aurora that had blazed across the sky after Lorreth had named Avisiéth had been this spectacular.

The evenlight in the torches throughout the hall flared, brightening anew. The fires burning in the grates strengthened, roaring violently up the backs of multiple hearths. It was as if, all throughout the Black Palace, the sources of evenlight that already existed were being powered up by the arrival of the shifting green banner in the night sky.

The high bloods forgot Zovena's attempts to sow discord.

They forgot Algat, and the vampire with the golden teeth on his knees at my feet.

They forgot Tal's showmanship, and the ever-present threat my mate posed, sitting beside me. As one, the Blood Court craned their necks upward, and they marveled.

Music filled the air—a frenzy of a piece, full of soaring peaks and crashing crescendos. High bloods flew around on the dance floor, whipping their dance partners around in the dervish, their coattails and full skirts flaring around them as they spun. Above it all, the firmament glowed, stars winking through the evenlight as if through a veil of thin jade silk.

Thralls topped off the high blood's wineglasses, sacrificing a drop of their blood into each cup, and the vampires drank. The whole scene was a sight to behold—and one I would gladly have sacrificed in exchange for the peace and quiet of Cahlish, and the presence of my friends.

Te Léna and Maynir had remained at the estate, watching over Everlayne. Danya was still at the temporary war camp. Iseabail had stayed to continue in her attempts to scry for Ren. Lorreth insisted he come with us back to Ammontraíeth, but Fisher had refused, telling him to check in with the warriors at the makeshift camp instead. Carrion had balked loudly when I'd told him he couldn't come to the ball, but he was the only person Hayden really knew at the estate, and I wanted someone there to keep an eye on him. It would be just like my brother to flee Cahlish in a pique of temper after the argument we'd had, and I was not about to let that happen. I was furious with him, sure, but not angry enough to let him be eaten by some hole-dwelling creature with razors for teeth.

We always did *seem to have more water and food than anyone else.*

Was he really so blind? Didn't he know me *at all*?

I had fought tooth and nail to rescue him from Zilvaren, and all the while he'd suspected that I was a *traitor*?

"Dance with me."

I sucked in a sharp breath, facing Fisher. His eyes were even greener tonight with the sky full of evenlight. He hadn't gotten to his feet yet, but he *was* offering his hand, and he didn't look like he would be deterred from his request.

"Is this the part where you tell me you don't dance, Osha?" he murmured. "The part where you say that you don't know the steps, or that you have two left feet?"

Hah. And he thought he had me all figured out. There were still things about me that Kingfisher of the Ajun Gate was yet to learn. And while I didn't know the steps to any of the graceful dances popular here in Yvelia, I was a quick study and light on my feet. And I was *not* one to be underestimated. I smiled as I considered Fisher's hand and then took it.

"I'll muddle through," I told him.

The next thing I knew, we were among the high bloods, and Fisher was spinning me along with him as he slipped onto the dance floor and into the dance itself. He moved easily, his movements sure as he fell into step with the vampires that surrounded us.

I tried not to smile as he swept me around, lifting me so that my feet barely touched the ground.

"Does this entertain you, Your Majesty?" he murmured, suppressing a smile of his own.

"Oh no. I'm just surprised that *you're* so confident on a dance floor."

He leaned into me and spoke, voice low, his breath fanning warmth over my neck. "Dancing is like fighting, Osha. It's also like fucking. And I pride myself on my skills in both of those arenas."

I laughed. "Oh? Is that so?"

"Mm. Yes. It is." The dimple in his cheek made a brief but satisfying appearance.

"I suppose you've had a lot of practice in those arenas then, have you?" I was toying with him, and he knew it. He puffed out his cheeks, pretending to think about the question.

"Well. I've impaled quite a few people on the end of my sword," he said conspiratorially. "And I've lost count of how many *battles* I've fought in."

"Hey!" I thought about digging him in his ribs, but at that moment his hands found my waist and he lifted me into the air, doing a one-eighty before setting me gently down again—a part of the dance that the other high bloods on the dance floor carried out at the same time. Fisher's eyes were bright, the thread of quicksilver resting dormant in his iris as he took my hand and set off again, careening around the hall in the opposite direction.

"I don't think I want to know about all of this *impaling*," I said, feigning disapproval. "Though, maybe you're not as good at it as you think you are. Maybe you need a little more practice."

The left side of his mouth lifted, his eyebrow following suit. "Oh? You have notes?"

"Yes. *Extensive* notes."

Now it was Fisher's turn to fake injury. His lips brushed my temple as he spoke. "And here I was, thinking I was doing a good job every time I made you beg for my cock."

Gods and sinners, he was trying to kill me. In *public*. "How many of these high bloods can hear your boasting right now, I wonder."

"All of them, I hope. They can already *smell* you on me."

"Fisher—"

"They're lucky I'm not tearing you out of this dress and bending you over that fucking throne right now, Saeris," he growled.

Gods. My blood pounded in my ears. "You wouldn't *dare*."

He looked at me, smile turning into something far more serious. His eyelids lowered, a lazy hunger suddenly lurking in his eyes. "You're right," he agreed. "I wouldn't want to ruin the dress."

I'd thought now that we were sleeping together, that the roar of need I experienced whenever I was around him would dull a little. That had *not* happened. If anything, my appetite for him was growing worse by the day. I looked up at him and remembered what he looked like when he thrust inside me. How his sweat marked his brow. How he tasted of salt, and mint, and *so* godscursed sweet whenever he plunged his tongue into my mouth—

I looked away, unable to bear the eye contact anymore.

I loved him so fucking much.

No other emotion came close to this. Not the hatred I felt for Madra.

Not the hurt I felt over Everlayne, suffering alone in some unknown hell. Not the worry I felt over Ren's disappearance. None of it. The world could be ending and my love for this male would outstrip my fear. Sometimes, I felt like I would burst open from how overwhelming that feeling was.

Fisher's eyes burned when I dared look back at him again. He knew all that I had just been thinking. I was almost certain that he had been feeling it, too.

"You seem overly preoccupied with dresses," I said in a small voice.

"Do I?" His voice was rough.

I nodded. "Every time I enter my chambers here or your rooms at Cahlish—"

"*Our* rooms," he corrected.

I ducked my head. "Every time I enter our rooms at Cahlish, there's a new dress, laid out on the bed and waiting for me."

He took a second before he replied, but then said very carefully, "Don't you like them?"

"Yes. I do. I just..." Gods, why was this so hard to put into words? It shouldn't have been. "It makes me feel like... you're trying to *domesticate* me."

He stumbled to a halt, right there in the middle of the dance floor. Miraculously, no one careened into us; the other dancers course-corrected with grace, flowing around us as Fisher frowned at me, looking rather mystified. "And how in all five hells would I do that, Osha? I'd have better luck trying to domesticate one of your hellcats."

"I don't know. I just..." Still, the words didn't want to come.

Fisher stepped toward me, cupping my face in his hands. "I don't want you to be anything other than what you already are, Saeris. The dresses are just..." His brow furrowed. "They're an *invitation*. The life you lived in Zilvaren was hard. You had to do everything for yourself. I'm here now, and—no, wait. No, let me finish. I'm here now, and just because I am your mate and you are mine doesn't mean that I expect you to sit around looking pretty, or... or put down your weapons and adopt a different way of life. I would *never* want that for you. But you don't have to be *one* thing here, Saeris. You can be many things. You can wear your leathers and fight every day of the year. I would never ask you not to. But sometimes, if you *wanted* to...you're allowed to soften, Saeris. You're allowed to stop baring your teeth at the world and take a breath. Because I've *got* you."

The dancers whirled on by, streaming velvet, silk, and damask out behind them, and I let those words settle into my soul.

Because I've got you.

He *did* have me, didn't he? He was the anchor that kept me from drifting away. Even here, in this horrible place, he hadn't left my side.

"Come on." Fisher nodded, as if he'd just made his mind up about something. "Come over here. I want to show you something. It won't take a second, and then I'll get you out of here."

I followed him. I would have gone *anywhere* with him in that moment, but we didn't travel far—out of the flow of the dancers, away from the long tables, where many sour-faced high bloods still sat, muttering darkly into their wine. Fisher came to a stop in front of a small round table that stood before a particularly graphic wall hanging.

I looked up at the hanging, squinting at the bacchanalia it depicted. "What's the male doing to that goat?" I asked.

"Ignore the goat," Fisher said in a chiding tone. "Look here."

A huge flower arrangement dominated the small table. A variety of blooms, likely selected for their complementary purple hues, had been organized quite expertly in a shining golden vase. They were stunning. At the center of the arrangement, Fisher pointed out the most beautiful bloom of all. It wasn't the largest of the flowers, but its color was the most vibrant. Iridescent, almost. Its petals were ruffled at the edges and pinched in the middle, swelling out at their ends to form the shape of love hearts. On each heart, a tiny droplet of water glittered like a diamond—

"Don't." Fisher's hand closed around my wrist, preventing me from touching the flower. "It won't kill you, but it'll make you really misera-ble, believe me."

"It's poisonous?"

"To most people, it's deadly." Shooting me a crooked smile, he said, "But you're stronger than most. Here, they call it Veridius. Saint's Steeple. In the Fae courts, we call it Widow's Bane. You've heard of it before."

I had. "Lorreth gave me and Carrion some to chew at Gillethrye. Our ribs were broken after we hit the surface of the lake. It took our pain away for a while."

Fisher nodded. "Allow that little dewdrop to come into contact with your skin, and it'll take your pain away forever," he said. "Widow's Bane is safe to chew once that poison has been cleaned from its petals and its leaves have been steeped and dried for a couple of days. So long as you don't swallow the leaves and only chew them, you'll be fine. But I didn't bring you over here to give you a lesson in plant medi-cine. I came to show you that sometimes, it's the most beautiful things that are deadliest. A dress can't make you weak. It won't make you vulnera—"

"Help!" The tremulous scream cut above the music.

In a heartbeat, Fisher had drawn Nimerelle and was scanning the crowd, trying to locate the source of the cry.

"Gods! What's—what's *happening?*" At the table close by, a male high blood was bowed over his place setting and was shuddering, a thick stream of rank black blood pouring from his mouth. It flooded from his eyes, too. Ran from his nose and his ears.

"Help!" The plea went up again, on the other side of the hall this time.

And again, behind us. "Mercy! Please!"

A red-haired female in a royal blue dress slumped to her knees, blood gushing from her mouth as she went down and sprawled out, convulsing on the obsidian floor.

Wide-eyed, Fisher took in the scene in disbelief. "What in all the gods' names is this?" he whispered. "Was this...was this what was in the journal?"

"No! No, it told me to name Foley as Lord! There was nothing in there about *this*!"

Left and right, high bloods started vomiting blood, staining their fine clothes red. Male and female alike, they went down, trembling, fingers grasping, bloody eyes rolling back into their heads.

Soon, most of the vampires in the hall were writhing on the ground. And in the midst of them all stood Taladaius, towering over them like some silver-haired harbinger of death. "Brothers and sisters!" he cried. "Your judgment has come for you at last!"

"What the *fuck*?" Fisher hissed.

"Your gluttony is your undoing! Welcome to your final death. But who am *I* to deny you one last chance at redemption? The thralls you have sipped so greedily upon this evening are passing through the hall with glass vials. Take a vial and swallow its contents, and you will undergo a painful transformation. No, not a transformation. You will be *reborn*, back into life, back into your Fae bodies, where you will face the horrors of what you allowed yourselves to become! Refuse the vials, and you join the other demons in hell with me posthaste!"

"What the fuck has he done?" Fisher stalked toward the Lord, stepping over the bodies of the toppled high bloods as he went. I was right behind him, my mind spiraling at the scene unfolding before us.

"Tal! Tal, are you out of your mind?" Fisher grabbed the Lord and shook him. "What *is* this?"

"This is what should have been done a long time ago. They were never going to *change*, Fisher," he said. "They're incapable of it. Evil through and through. And I wasn't about to put this on your shoulders. I wasn't going to do it to you, either, Saeris." His eyes searched for mine. "*I* made the hard choice so that neither of you would have to. This was my final act as a Lord of Midnight. Now I'll go pay for the sins *I* have committed."

We should have noticed the wineglass in his hand. We should have stopped him from throwing back the viscous red blood inside. We watched in horror as Tal swallowed—whatever was in the glass was a far greater dose than had been delivered to the other high bloods. There was no delay for him. Blood welled in his eyes and trickled from his nose as it immediately took effect.

"Tell Everlayne...I'm...sorry," he said.

He fell to the ground and started to shake.

40

JUDGMENT

SAERIS

BLACK.

Stinking.

Foul.

The blood on the ground was an inch deep and slippery as hell. I barely kept my feet beneath me as I raced for a thrall who was stooping down and pressing something to a female high blood's lips. The female's eyes flashed with silent recrimination as she batted his hand away, rejecting the salvation he offered her, even as she drowned in the putrid blood she had stolen.

"Here, give it to me!" I held out my hand, waiting for the thrall to pass me a vial from the leather bag it was carrying, but the thrall shook his head. "Not for him," he said. "He told us not to."

"I don't give a *fuck* what he told you." I snatched the bag and turned back to where Tal was on the ground, kicking and shaking . . . but Foley was already there, jamming his fingers between Taladaius's teeth.

"Fair . . . turn around," he gritted out. "I told him I didn't want to come back as a vampire. Well, now *he* doesn't get a choice. He's coming back Fae whether . . . he likes it . . . or *not!*"

Taladaius did *not* like it. He raged and he spat, but in the end, Foley forced the clear contents of one of the vials down his neck and massaged his throat until he swallowed.

The vampire stopped vomiting, then...but the blood was replaced by an awful white foam that frothed up from his mouth, forming a bubbling pool on the ground. I couldn't decide what was worse.

There were others lying on the bloody floor, foaming at the mouth. Not as many as I might have thought. One in eight high bloods? No, less. One in *ten* had made the choice to live and face the consequences of their years in Ammontraíeth.

Foley stood, panting as he watched Tal shiver on the ground.

"How are *you* all right?" I asked him.

"He told me not to drink the wine. I thought he was warning me about the blood in it. I could already smell it. I—I wasn't going to drink, anyway."

"He made sure none of the thralls gave us wine with blood in it," I added, rubbing my forehead. "He—fuck, *this* is why he wanted to disavow me!" I closed my eyes, shaking my head. "It's *all* linked. The blood, I mean. *Malcolm's* blood turned these high bloods. It must be some kind of magic."

"Not magic. A spell," Fisher said. "Something to affect Malcolm's line. He severed you from his blood so that it wouldn't affect you. He'd already done the same with you a long time ago, Foley."

"And...what about *me?*"

I rounded on the voice, my mind fighting to make sense of what my eyes were seeing: Zovena, not as she had been earlier, when I had used her as a footstool. There was color in her cheeks. Her eyes were blue. I could hear her heart beating from where I stood, ten feet from her. Tears streamed down her cheeks as she flared her nostrils, staring down at Tal. "He dragged me into an alcove while you were dancing. I wasn't feeling well. I was dizzy. I..." She blinked. "He took me by surprise. I tasted it, whatever he tipped into my mouth, sour and...sweet, and then my eyes were full of stars. I woke up and...and..." She looked at *me*, as if I might be able to provide an explanation for what had happened to her.

I had none to give her.

Tal hadn't mentioned a word of this to me. Not a peep.

"He's having some kind of seizure," Foley said.

"Give him something to bite down on," Fisher fired back. "Make sure he doesn't hurt himself." He was busy scanning the floor of the Hall of Mirrors, looking for something; whatever it was, he couldn't seem to find it. Turning to me, he said, "You're okay? You're feeling okay?"

"Yes, I'm fine."

"Good. Can you wait here for me? Please? Help Foley with Tal?"

I nodded. "Yes. I—"

He whipped around, grabbing Zovena by the arm, and charged up the length of the hall, picking through the bodies as he went.

Everything was happening so quickly. Hundreds of vampires lay dead or dying on the ground. The air was thick with cloying copper, the scent so pungent that I wanted to throw up. Lying on his side, Tal's body trembled violently; his eyes were rolled back into his head. His pale skin was spattered with blood, his beautiful dove-gray suit ruined.

"Is he going to be okay?" A stupid question. Absolutely idiotic. No, *of course* he wasn't going to be okay. Tal had *not* wanted to drink the contents of that vial. He'd orchestrated this literal bloodbath, and he hadn't wanted to stick around to see how it played out.

Foley's dark expression said all of this and more. But there was a grim determination in his eyes, too. One that said he wasn't about to let the Lord of Midnight go without a fight. "He's calming now," he said through gritted teeth. "He's coming through the other side of it."

Was this what it had been like in the maze, after Malcolm had attacked me? My blood, staining the ground. Tal, undertaking dire actions to save me? Yes, it must have been like this, in a way. But...

Fisher had acted as my proxy. He had given consent on my behalf. Here we were, forcing an outcome onto the silver-haired male at my feet explicitly against his will.

I didn't care.

I wasn't about to let him go, and neither were any of his friends.

Tal let out a wheezing gasp, back arching. His eyes snapped open, and Foley fell backward onto his ass, covering his face in his hands. The confidence he had spoken with just now must have been for show, because the strangled sound he made was all relief.

"What...did you do?" Tal croaked. His eyes rolled wildly up at us, though his body was at last still. He pressed a hand against the ground, ringed fingers sticky with blood, as if the room was spinning and he was worried he might not be able to hold on much longer.

"You can't just do—do *this*...and then *leave!*" My emotions were all over the place. Any moment now, I was about to start sobbing. A part of me saw the carnage that surrounded me and was glad. The vast majority of Sanasroth's high bloods were gone. They had accepted their true death, rather than return to what they once were. But we'd had a *plan*, damn it, and Tal had gone and made his *own* plan without telling any of us.

"Why?" I crouched down beside the male and brushed his silver-spun hair out of his face. "Why do *this?*"

But Taladaius only closed his eyes, as if I already had the answer to that question and he could not bear repeating it. A tear formed in the corner of his eye, crystal clear as water, welling before it rolled over the bridge of his nose and fell into the blood. "You have to let me go. I can't stay," he whispered.

"*Hypocrite.*"

Tal's eyelids opened again, his eyes the same thunderhead gray they had always been. He looked at Foley, despair carved into the lines of his face. "You don't understand—"

"I understand perfectly," Foley spat. An anger had come upon him, swift and unforgiving. He shunted himself forward so he could take Tal's jaw in his hand and force the male to look at him. "You told me time and time again that becoming a vampire doesn't alter the foundations of who you are, only highlights them. Look around you. These bastards are crumbling to ash right now because they're evil down to the festering marrow. They choose death over life because they don't want to lose their power. There was no oath forcing them to carry out the atrocities they committed. It was in their *nature*. You—" Foley broke off, shaking Tal's head, forcing him to focus when he tried to turn away. "You are blameless. Whatever horrors *you* committed were forced upon you. Malcolm *knew* how much it would tear you up inside."

Tal closed his eyes, more tears cutting tracks down his cheeks, his features crumpling. "You have to let me..." he whispered.

"You'll forgive yourself," Foley insisted. "You *will*. And in the meantime, you can take that misplaced sense of guilt and use it to make amends. Help fix what Malcolm used you to break, Tal. There is still *hope*."

Taladaius's head kicked back. Another seizure gripped him, twice as bad as before. He shook, face contorted into a rictus of pain.

This was worse than watching my friends in Zilvaren die. There was a tangible enemy there, but it seemed as though Tal's own body was his enemy, and there was nothing I could do to fight that. "Why isn't he getting better? The others..."

There were other high bloods, *former* high bloods, picking their way through all the death. They bore the stunned look of sleepers woken from a bad dream. They stepped over the bodies of their lovers and their friends, frowning in confusion at the scene before them. They seemed fine, aside from the fact that most of them were sobbing. But Tal had started foaming at the mouth again. He flinched, clutching at his chest as if he were in agony.

"Come on. We need to get out of here." Fisher had returned, Zovena with him. He pushed the blond forward, and she staggered, nearly losing her balance. She'd lost her shoes at some point, and her beautiful red dress was torn and filthy. "I can't find Algat anywhere," Fisher said. I've searched high and low. I saw her in the hall not long before I pulled you off the dance floor, though, Osha. She didn't have time to leave before Tal's little stunt came to fruition."

"Which means...?"

"Which means she probably drank from a vial and isn't a high blood anymore," Fisher said. "And trust me, if you thought she was bad as a vampire, you *definitely* do not want to run into her as a witch."

Tal's ring; Zovena's ring; a golden chain bearing the Briarstone family sigil: three new relics, made in the blink of an eye.

No jokes. No secrets. No memories.

The quicksilver had bound to the jewelry as if doing so was the most natural thing in the world. Tal was unconscious when we entered the pool, so Fisher carried him. Foley clamped a hand around Zovena's wrist and held on to her tight as they disappeared into the silver. I followed, casting a look over my shoulder, allowing myself a moment to second-guess all of this. The residents of Ammontraíeth were Fae now. They were confused. Even down in the Cogs, the high bloods were all dead, and disoriented Fae wandered the streets, not knowing what to do or where to go. Was I still their queen? Was this still their home? I couldn't wrap my head around any of it. Leaving right now did *not* seem like a good idea, but what else was there to do?

Cahlish's armory was deserted save for a handful of chickens, which scattered, squawking in surprise, when we emerged from the quicksilver. My head was spinning, and Zovena's relentless sobbing made it impossible to think.

The night air bit at my face as we crossed the yard toward the house. The manor stood proud as a sentinel, blaring light out into the dark, and my pulse picked up when the front door came into view. A part of me felt—foolishly—that everything would be okay as soon as we were inside. That wasn't the case, of course, but I let myself believe it. If only for the next twenty-four hours, I *had* to let myself believe it, or I was going to crumple under the weight of everything that was happening right now.

Taladaius was still convulsing. He would wake for a minute or two and struggle to speak. He kept gasping at the air, as if he'd forgotten what it was like to breathe. But then, I supposed he *had* forgotten. It had been over a thousand years...

Zovena sniffled behind Fisher, occasionally letting out a mournful sob, but she otherwise hadn't said much. She was wobbly on her feet, exhaustion making her unsteady.

Fisher opened the door and gestured for me to enter first, which was probably for the best—the moment I stepped foot into Cahlish, I came face-to-face with my brother, who was brandishing a heavy poker from one of the fireplaces.

His eyes widened as he took me in. "What the fuck happened to you?" He frowned. "What are you *wearing?*"

We'd fled Ammontraíeth as quickly as possible. I sure as shit hadn't bothered to get changed before leaving, although I had taken a moment to grab Edina's book. "It's a *dress,* Hayden," I said tiredly. "Where's Carrion?"

"He's upstairs. He sent me down here to fetch something for him. I heard the noise at the door and thought someone was trying to break in. Why are you *wet,* Saeris? Is that *blood?*" My brother looked more and more dumbfounded as everyone piled into the house—Fisher first, whom he obviously recognized. But then Tal, shaking in his arms, and Foley, and finally Zovena. We all looked like we'd had the tar beaten out of us. "Well, this doesn't look good. I thought you were going to a *party.*" Hayden closed his grip around the poker, as if he wasn't quite sure whether he needed it now or not.

"Where's Te Léna?" I asked. "Have you seen her?"

"I think she's still in the dining room. We just got done with dinner. I was on my way to bed," he answered.

"Bed? Yes, that's probably a good idea." Gods, it wasn't even midnight yet. The hands of the tall grandfather clock in the hallway showed just past eleven thirty, but Hayden probably didn't even know that. It had taken me a while to get used to Yvelian clocks. The sun dials we had in Zilvaren were far less complicated than a Fae timepiece, but also far less accurate. "Why don't you go on up and...we can chat about all of this in the morning?" Why did I sound so strange? So *stiff?* I hardly recognized my own voice.

Hayden made a scoffing sound, at last lowering the poker. "You're sending me away again, then? Hiding the truth from me some more? Because that worked out so well last time?"

I loved him, I did. I had to. But gods have mercy, did he make it difficult sometimes. "All right. Y'know what, Hayden?" I threw up my hands. "Have it your way. You want to know everything? Fine. Come and learn everything. You'll be wishing you could go back to living in ignorance very soon, I promise you."

KINGFISHER

I was barely awake. Saeris sat pale as a ghost next to me at the table. There hadn't been time for baths, and so I'd used my shadows to clean us all up. Tal was still unconscious and had been laid out to rest in one of the rooms upstairs. Zovena, who hadn't stopped wailing, was verging on hysteria, and hadn't even seemed to notice when I'd used my magic to remove the blood from her dress.

Once I'd kitted everyone out in clean clothing, Archer had shown everyone where they could sleep, and then Te Léna had spent an hour assessing everyone's injuries. When she was done, the rest of us had sat down at the table, and I'd explained to Te Léna and Maynir what had happened at Ammontraíeth. I was about halfway through the story when Carrion hurried into the dining room, carrying a small blue pot full of dirt and a sharp dagger clamped between his teeth. He stopped in his tracks when he saw the group of us gathered around the table. "I missed something," he said carefully around the blade. "I *definitely* missed something."

"Sit down and listen," I demanded. Up until very recently, I would have told the smuggler to leave and close the fucking door behind him. But certain thoughts had started to form in the back of my head— thoughts that couldn't be ignored forever. One day very soon, we were going to have to think about the Yvelian throne, and Swift wouldn't be any *less* of a buffoon if I kept treating him like one. I didn't like it, but his comment back in Zilvaren *had* struck a chord.

Carrion's eyebrows shot up. "I was actually just going to take some clippings of the plants out—"

"*Sit down, Carrion.*"

A smile slowly began to spread across his face. "You *want* me to stay. You *missed* me."

"If you don't take that knife out of your mouth and sit down, I'm going to personally smash that plant pot over your head," Saeris muttered in a flat tone.

"Okaaaay. All right. I am sitting." He winked at Saeris as he set his things down and took a seat. The table still felt woefully empty, too many chairs unoccupied. Lorreth and Danya were with the warriors at the temporary camp. The gods only knew where Renfis was. And we were missing one other person, too. Someone I *distinctly* wanted to have a conversation with.

She showed up just as I was detailing to Te Léna and Maynir how few of the high bloods had chosen to accept the chance to become Fae again. A thick silence fell as Iseabail entered the room.

There was no pretense to her. No denial or contrition.

I met her gaze and held it.

"Iseabail, come and join us." Te Léna was always warm, even when the tension in the room was cold as ice. "Fisher was just explaining what happened at Ammontraíeth."

"She knows all about what happened at Ammontraíeth, don't you, Iseabail?" I said.

The witch pressed her hands to her skirts, wiping her palms against the material—they were probably slick with sweat, as they damn well should have been. "I do," she answered in a clear voice. "And I'm sure you want me to be sorry for it, Kingfisher, but I'm not. I can't be."

"You put my mate in danger," I growled.

On my left, Saeris shifted, her attention moving from the red-haired witch to me. She was quicker than most, had already put two and two together, but still she wasn't angry at the female standing at the foot of the table. Placing her hand on top of mine, she let out an exhausted sigh. "I wasn't hurt. That was clearly never their intention."

Carrion propped his elbow on the table, rested his chin in hand, and said, "What in the actual *fuck* are you all talking about?"

"They're angry at me for what happened tonight," Iseabail said, in a calm, even tone.

Te Léna had figured it out. Maynir, too. Both the healer and her husband traded uncomfortable looks. "You didn't want to come back here and help us, did you?" Te Léna said. No one would have blamed Te Léna if she'd been furious over the witch's deception, but it was worse than that. She was hurt. She had thought she'd made a friend.

Iseabail's defiant expression collapsed in the face of the healer's accusation, but she maintained her stiff-backed posture, chin held high regardless. "I'm sorry, Te Léna. I enjoyed spending time with you and learning from you, truly I did. I wanted to help you find Ren as well, but I needed a reason to stay here at Cahlish. I had to be close for the spell to work."

"Ahh. I get it now," Carrion said. "*You're* the one who cast the spell that killed the high bloods. You gave Tal those vials to cure the Blood Court!"

"I did what I had to do. Do you have any idea how long we've waited for an opportunity to get inside Ammontraíeth? Do you know how long—"

"You put my mate in *danger*," I repeated.

She bit her bottom lip, looking down at her hands. There were long gashes at her wrists, angry, still dripping blood onto the dining room floor.

I closed my eyes, laughing humorlessly. "As soon as those high bloods were affected by the blood in that wine, they were freed from the Blood Court's control, weren't they?"

"Yes," she said.

"Any of them could have attacked us."

"Yes."

"And it was *your* blood the thralls dripped into their glasses, wasn't it?"

"Yes. Tal brought them to the river, and I marked them with sigils. When they cut themselves, I bled through their veins. A simple transference spell, really. My blood—"

"Your blood is a curse to all vampires. It kills them unless they take the antidote that *your* clan created."

"Yes."

Yes, she answered, again and again, without shame or regret. Shadows began to spill from me, flowing like smoke down the arms of my chair, rolling across the table toward the witch.

"Fisher," Saeris said. "I wasn't hurt. It's all right. We can deal with this—"

"You lied to Tal," I said.

Iseabail watched the shroud of shadows approaching with growing trepidation. The air hummed with her fear, but she nodded, acknowledging the truth. "I had to. If he'd known that the high bloods might be able to hurt you or Saeris, he would never have agreed to the plan. And I feel bad for lying to him. I do. I would accept whatever punishment he saw fit for my crimes if he'd chosen to be reborn, but—"

"Tal's alive," I snapped. "*You* might be okay with letting people you consider your friends die, but we are not the same."

At this, Iseabail's mouth fell open. She took a step toward the table, her hands forming warding signs to push back my smoke. "He's *alive?*"

"You can't hold my magic back for long, Iseabail. This is *my* house—"

"I don't care, Fisher! Kill me if you like! I knew there would be a price for all of this. It's a price I was *born* to pay!" She spoke quickly, her hands shaking as my shadows shoved against her wards. It wouldn't take long. One firm push from me and I would break through. I'd fucking *kill* her for what she'd done. "Listen to me. Wait!" she cried. "Is he here?"

"He's resting upstairs," Foley snarled. He had kept his peace throughout the entire exchange, but it seemed he could hold his tongue no longer. "He's still convulsing every five minutes. He may never recover from that *shit* we had to pour down his throat."

"No! You need to take me to him. Right *now!*"

"Like hell we do—"

"*Why?*" I demanded. Plainly, the witch was spooked.

Iseabail drew in a ragged breath, her hands shaking even harder as my shadows nearly broke through her ward. She met my eyes and held them, speaking urgently. "The sigils I marked the thralls with, they weren't big enough. Weren't strong enough. I couldn't risk the high bloods sensing the magic on them or seeing large marks. I needed a much bigger conduit to channel the spell, one that would then redirect the energy to the thralls and complete the spell."

"What are you talking about, Iseabail?" Saeris was already getting to her feet; she was following my lead. A grim realization had fallen on me while the witch was speaking—I was already heading toward the door.

The fucking tattoo.

The one I'd seen covering Tal's chest back in the Hall of Tears, beneath his loose shirt. It hadn't been a tattoo after all. It was a *witch mark*.

Fuck.

I tore past the witch, pulling back my shadows. "Will it kill him?" I demanded.

She dropped her ward and followed at a dead sprint. "If I don't get to him immediately, it'll kill *all* of us."

The curtains were already on fire when we reached the bedroom. The bedsheets, too. The paint on the oil landscape hanging above the bed was blistered and melting, running over the gilt frame and down the wall. Taladaius lay still on the bed where we'd left him, hoping he'd feel better after some rest. His body was engulfed in flames, though his skin wasn't burning. Not yet. His shirt was gone, burned away, revealing his bare chest and the monstrous witch mark that spread from shoulder to shoulder, spanning his torso from collarbone to hips.

"Zareth save us," Te Léna hissed, as she barreled into the room behind us and saw the mark. "What the hell were you thinking? The knots on that kind of spellwork can't be undone!"

The lines of it were woven tight, hundreds and hundreds of spells bound together consecutively, forming a tapestry of sigils that would have taken an entire clan of witches a full month to untangle. Te Léna was right: We were fucked.

"I have to *try*," Iseabail cried. "I knotted them. I can undo them!"

"Why would you *do* this to him?" Maynir flinched back from the bed, from the heat of the flames, from the cruelty of the spellwork, as if he couldn't bear to witness any of it.

Iseabail's hands were flying. The mark lit up in her presence, the spell responding to its creator. She plucked and pulled at the threads of the spell, unraveling them as fast as she could. "He was supposed to take it *with* him," she spat through clenched teeth. "He said he was going to die! The spell would have died *with* him!"

It was too late.

We'd survived the fall of the Blood Court and so many other impossible situations, only to fall afoul of the witch mark to end all witch marks. What a fucking joke.

Foley stood outside the bedroom, the flames raging in his eyes. Next to him, Carrion held the knife he'd been carrying in his teeth earlier as if he were ready to use it, but there was no one to use it *against*. "What the fuck is happening?" He winced away from the wall of heat radiating from the bed Tal was lying on. "Why's Tal *on fire?*"

"The mark on his chest. It's borrowed magic. *Dark* magic. It lends power to the one who binds it. But left unchecked, *steals* power. Eventually, it will open a gateway that cannot be closed." Te Léna had to shout over the roar of the fire and Iseabail's frantic chanting.

"What kind of gateway?" Saeris asked. I had shielded her from the heat with my body, but she had stepped around me now and was moving toward the bed. Her right hand was lit up and blazing like an angry star. "A gateway to where?" Her voice was quiet, but all heard it.

"To the realm from where all dark magic hails," Te Léna answered. "The *demon* realm. I will not say its name!"

Iseabail's fingers plucked, untying, blurring in their speed. But she wasn't moving fast enough. This kind of mark wasn't designed to *ever* be undone. It was a death sentence and the reason Tal had begged us to let him die. He'd known about the destruction he was wearing in his skin, and he'd tried to stop it. He'd tried to prevent this from happening, but none of us had listened.

"I can feel them," Saeris muttered. "They want to get through. They're... *hungry.*" Her hair had pulled loose from the elaborate style she had worn for the ball and was floating eerily around her as she stepped toward the bed.

Careful, Osha. The fire's real. It will *take you.* I reached for her and regretted it instantly. The second my hand touched hers, the runes that marked my skin, mirroring hers, exploded with light. A pain like no other tore up my arm and detonated inside my head, bringing me to my knees. I couldn't think around it. Couldn't breathe. Someone was shouting something somewhere—Hayden, screaming for his sister to get back. Foley was holding him, stopping him from rushing into the blazing room.

I had to get to Saeris. I needed to.

The fire blanketed the ceiling, rolling over the depiction of the night sky painted there, defying gravity and swallowing the stars.

Hell was coming.

Hell was *here.*

But then Saeris was leaning over Tal's flaming body, and she was pressing her hands to his chest. Her whole right arm was illuminated brilliant white-blue.

In the space between heartbeats, where my seized lungs tried and failed to take a breath, the glowing filaments of Iseabail's spell fell apart, and the fires of hell went out.

41

PROCESSING

SAERIS

"SHE DIDN'T EVEN *try* to find Ren."

Sunlight dappled the grass, spearing through the canopy of the trees. Through the small window created by the branches overhead, a bird circled, little more than a black speck against the cerulean sky. The thick, warm air hummed with the drone of some winged insect. Fisher stalked barefoot through the grass, viciously stripping the leaves from a stick he'd found on the ground and spitting out a litany of curse words in Old Fae that I could tell were *highly* offensive, even though I had no idea what he was saying.

I hugged my knees to my chest, relishing the feel of the sun on my bare arms. We had both been so tired when we'd passed out earlier that I'd assumed neither of us would dream, but here we were in Ballard. Fisher had explained that this was one of his favorite places to come when he was little. The clearing was small, skirted by forest on three sides and bounded by a rushing stream on the other. Silver fish glimmered like knives in the water, battling against the current.

I wound the blade of grass I'd been fiddling with around my index finger, trying to find some order in my thoughts. It was difficult to concentrate in the dreams sometimes. It was as though I was missing information, and I *knew* I was missing it, and no matter how hard I tried, I couldn't figure out what I didn't know.

Most people's hair lightened a little in the sunlight, throwing a little red or chocolate, but not Kingfisher's. His hair looked blacker than ever as the light beat down on him. His shoulder-length waves flicked up around his ears, making way for their pointed tips. What a strange thing he was. He was a winter creature. He'd said so himself. All pale skin, wintergreen eyes, and shadows. He seemed the most himself when there were snowflakes dusting his shoulders and his cheeks were flushed from the cold. But he was a different version of himself here, too. He belonged here just as much as at Cahlish or on the banks of the Darn. Ballard suited him. There was something about seeing him with bare feet and his shirt open to his stomach, displaying his roving ink ...

His eyes glowed with rage as he turned and pointed his stick at me. "It would have taken her five minutes. Five *minutes*!" He stabbed the stick in the air, using it to punctuate his words. "And yet look at where we are. Ammontraíeth is a fucking graveyard, Tal is half dead, I have a witch *and* Zovena locked in separate bedrooms at the estate, and we *still* don't know where Renfis is!"

"You're cutting a new trail in the grass over there," I told him.

"And! *And!*" He spun and hurled the stick into the river. "You have another rune, and we have no idea what this one is!"

The third rune had shown up when I'd touched Tal's chest. I hadn't meant to walk into that burning bedroom. Hadn't *meant* to touch the male's marked chest. Something had pulled me forward, unbidden, with a sense of urgency I had been powerless to ignore. My body hadn't been my own. That had been a terrifying experience, and I certainly didn't want it repeated, but I had helped Tal as a result of it. More than helped him. According to the others, I'd *saved* him and prevented a portal to hell from consuming Cahlish. I couldn't be mad about that, even if none of us understood how it had happened.

I held out my hand to Fisher, wriggling my fingers. "Can you come here, please?"

He clenched his jaw, eyeing me suspiciously. "If I come over there, I can't pace," he said.

"Really?" I pretended to look shocked. "Oh, *no.*"

"If I come over there, I'll stop being mad at Iseabail."

I waggled my fingers even harder. "Will being mad at her get you anywhere right now?" He gave me a deadpan look that would have made me laugh had the past day not been one of the shittiest I'd ever lived through. "Can you please just come here and hold me?"

That did it. His hands fell limp to his sides, his eyes burning into me for a second before he finally padded toward me across the grass. A second later, he was sitting cross-legged in front of me, reaching for me; he pulled me into his lap so that I was facing him, guiding my legs so that they were wrapped around his waist. His hands rested against the underside of my thighs, his thumbs working out the knots below my hips as he looked up at me.

"You just asked me to *hold* you," he said softly.

"I did."

"Have you ever asked anyone else to do that?"

I shook my head, throwing my arms over his shoulders, then burying my face in the crook of his neck. "No. And if you tell anyone I asked *you* to, I will vehemently deny it."

He laughed, deep and low. "Out of the two of us, only one of us can't lie, Osha. I think people will know who to believe."

"Godscursed Firinn Stone."

His laughter reverberated through his chest and into me. Such a comforting feeling. He stroked his hand over my hair, smoothing it down my back. He'd never said so, but he liked stroking my hair. I didn't know why. I'd never felt like asking him, either. It was a reassuring touch. It calmed me more than anything else could. "So," he whispered. "Do you want to talk about the fact that there's a cure for the blood curse again?"

And just like that, my calm went up in smoke.

"Not really, no," I mumbled into his chest.

He had to lean back and duck down before he could find my eyes. "Why not? Why are you hiding from me?"

"I'm not hiding. I'm *processing*." I groaned, pushing away from his chest and flopping back into the grass, throwing my hands up over my head. I was still technically sitting in Fisher's lap. *Kind* of. My legs were definitely still wrapped around his waist.

Fisher raised both eyebrows, looking down at me, amusement playing over his features. My shirt had ridden up. His gaze trailed over my lower stomach, over the patch of bare skin I was now showing, a tiny smile lifting the corners of his mouth. He moved casually, resting his hands there, right where he was looking, his calloused palms rough against my skin, and I couldn't resist.

"What's that *look* on your face, Kingfisher?"

His eyebrows inched higher. "Look? There's a *look*?"

I nodded, the grass rustling around my ears. "There's a look."

"Oh, I don't know." He shrugged, looking off toward the river. "My mate's ass is rubbing up against my cock, and she's stretched out in front of me, her hip bones showing—"

"You like my hip bones?"

He trailed his fingers over them without looking, then moved quickly, wrapping his hands around my waist and digging his fingers firmly into my skin. "I *love* your hip bones," he corrected. "I love the way your breasts look right now, straining against your shirt like that. If there's a *look*, it's because I'm horribly distracted by you, and I'm trying to talk about very serious things."

Horribly distracted? I liked the sound of that. Slowly, I wriggled my ass, shimmying so that my shirt rode up a little higher. "I don't want to talk about *very serious things*." I emphasized the words.

His eyes snagged on my stomach again, moving as slow as a glacier as they traveled higher, toward my chest. "I would have thought you'd be excited about the possibility of becoming Fae," he said.

"I would be. I *am*. But..." I hooked my thumbs into my pockets and pulled, tugging my pants down a little lower over my hips. They were scandalously low now, bordering on inappropriate.

Fisher gave me an open-mouthed smile, canines on full display, as he slowly shook his head. "You think I don't know what you're doing?"

"I'm not doing anything," I lied.

He scoffed at that. "Do you think..." He ran his fingers lightly up my side. "That this is the first time..." He caught his bottom lip between his teeth and bit down when I shivered. "A beautiful female..." His hand slipped up, inside my shirt and trailed it up my rib cage. "Has tried to *seduce* me?" He pinched my nipple, rolling it savagely as he leaned into the word *seduce*.

I hissed through my teeth, bucking against him at the bright stab of pain that fired down my body and settled between my legs.

Fisher's eyes flared, the tattoos at his throat swirling as they came to life beneath his skin. "Are you trying to lead me astray?" he asked.

"Only a little."

"Only a little?"

"Mm." I arched my hips again, angling my ass down, rolling my hips a little, and Fisher's eyelids shuttered.

"Okay. Only a little. I'll let you lead me astray *only a little* if you answer the question properly."

"There was a question?" I teased.

"Tell me," he rumbled. "Why isn't this good news? Regardless of how much I disapprove of Iseabail's methods, there are no high bloods in Ammontraíeth anymore. *You* don't have to be a high blood anymore."

Gods alive. I wasn't going to get my way if I didn't give him what he wanted first, was I? But this topic felt fragile, too delicate to navigate just yet. I breathed deep and gave him the truth, even though it felt like bad luck to do so. "Because what if it doesn't work on me? I'm not a full vampire, am I? What if it *kills* me?"

"It isn't going to kill you," Fisher said, squeezing my breast. His other hand worked to unfasten my pants.

I closed my eyes, processing what he was about to do. "What if..."

"What if?" he whispered.

"What if I *don't* die? What if it makes me *human* again? Whatever is in those vials made Tal and the high bloods revert to their original state. What's to say it wouldn't revert me back to mine?"

Fisher's expression remained steady, as if what I'd said wasn't terrifying at all. "Then you go back to being human," he said.

"And what would happen when I get old and die?"

He shrugged. "Then you get old, and you die."

"And you'd just—just—" I couldn't even say it. He would do what he'd always done. He would help the people of Yvelia, and fight against the likes of Belikon and whoever else might pose a threat to those he loved, and I would want him to. I wouldn't want him to just give up because I was gone, but—

"I would go *with* you, Osha." He spoke as if I were insane to think he would do anything else.

My heart squeezed tight as a fist in my chest. He was serious—I saw it in his eyes—and he wasn't slightly fazed about the prospect. "I'm young in the eyes of this place," he said. "And yes, there are plenty of things I still want to see and experience in this realm. But I wouldn't want to see any of it without *you*."

"Fisher, it isn't that *simple*."

He crooked his head to one side. "Isn't it?" he asked softly. "It seems very simple to me. Wouldn't you want to come and spend the afterlife with me if *I* died?"

"Of course I would!"

"Then let my love be equal to yours." He spoke with a tenderness that made tears prick my eyes.

"But what if there *is* no afterlife?"

He smiled sadly, letting his head hang for a second. When he looked back at me, his expression was all affectionate frustration. "Then there isn't," he answered. "There is only nothing. And that will *still* be better than being here without you."

"Stop. Stop talking." I cuffed my eyes with the back of my hands. "You're going to make me cry."

"You're already crying," he whispered. "Come on. Come back up here. I need you."

I need you.

Words I had never thought I'd hear from him. Fisher had been nothing short of vile to me when he'd brought me through the quick-silver into this realm. He had been cold and aggressive, and I had hated him with ninety-nine percent of my heart.

But the one percent? That had already been his. And now *all* of it was his, and he was holding on to me like I was the only thing that mattered in his entire fucking universe.

Need still pulsed in the pit of my stomach, but it had shifted into something more now. Something deeper. I didn't just want his body. I needed his mind and his soul. I needed for time to stand still so we could stay here, where nothing could disturb our peace, and we could just *live*.

And in that moment, I would have been selfish. If we'd been able to stay in Ballard and lie in the grass and hold each other forever, I would have done it.

But all dreams had to come to an end.

I flinched, stomach rolling, as I made my way to the forge. The sun wasn't fully up yet, but it was already wreaking havoc on my body. I shouldn't have been awake. By all rights, I should have passed out about an hour ago, but I'd only just woken up. My body clock was upside down, and I didn't even know where I was anymore.

"Hey. Where are *you* headed in such a hurry?" Carrion was coming the other way down the hallway. His hair was sticking up all over the place, and there was a stack of books in his hands. His shirt was unbe-lievably rumpled.

"You haven't been to bed yet, have you?" I kept walking, which meant that, obviously, Carrion performed an about-face and started walking with me, back the way he'd come.

"I have not," he confirmed.

"Aren't you tired? How the hell are you running on so little sleep?"

Carrion waved off my concern. "Oh, y'know. Centuries of debauchery and general delinquency. Hey, seriously, where are you going? I could use your help with something."

The last time Carrion had said this to me, he'd coerced me into helping break into one of Madra's food stores. At least, that's what he'd *told* me we were breaking into. The building in the Hub had turned out to be a haberdashery; Carrion had only wanted me to act as a distraction so he could steal a bolt of fabric that the owner had refused to sell him. I'd been chased through the city by two guardians and had spent nine hours hiding in a sweltering attic space as a result, and...anyway, the point was that nothing good ever happened when Carrion said he needed my help.

"Whatever it is, the answer's no," I told him.

"What? Oh, come on! There's no need to be like *that*, Fane."

"I'm going to speak to Iseabail about what happened yesterday. I need to know more about what she did and how the cure affects people—"

"That sounds more like a *Fisher* thing."

Gods, he was exasperating. "It's a *me* thing, Carrion." I pointed at myself. "*I'm* the half vampire. It was *my* court that was affected."

"Whoa! When did your *veins* turn silver?" He tried to grab my wrist to get a better look, nearly dropping his books in the process. "For that matter, we haven't spoken about the new tricks you can do now. That Alchimeran shield you lit up when you were fighting those guards was pretty fucking cool. What were all those icons around the outside of it?"

"I don't know, Carrion. I'm still trying to figure that out. They're probably other elements of threads of magic I might be able to control one day."

"*Sinners.*" He whistled. "That's a whole lot of potential power. Do you think you'll be able to turn invisible at some point? If I could have access to magic, *I* would definitely opt for invisibility."

"I'd love to pretend I didn't know why you'd pick that, Carrion, but sadly I know you too well. Look, Fisher's checking in with Tal and Foley. I have a bunch of things to take care of before heading back to

Ammontraíeth, and I have no idea where my brother is. What do you need, exactly?"

Carrion hoisted books in his hands, adjusting the stack so that he had a better grip on them. "Well, if you're busy..."

I stopped walking and faced him. "Can you please just spit it out?"

"You're going to help me, then?"

"No, I'm going to find out what it is you're up to so I can gauge whether I need to put a stop to it. And *then* I'm going to decide whether I'll help you."

"You are *so* untrusting," he muttered. "Whatever. I need you to come with me."

"And then?"

"And then I need you to tell me if I'm going crazy."

"Are you planning on setting fire to anything?" I demanded.

"No."

"Blowing anything up?"

Carrion made a face. "I haven't blown up a *single* thing since I've been here."

I folded my arms across my chest.

The smuggler rolled his eyes. "All right. No, I am not going to blow anything up."

Letting out a deep sigh, I threw up my hands in defeat. "Fine. You've got me for ten minutes."

"Careful, sunshine," he said, grinning. "The things I could do to you in ten minutes. Whoa, wai—wait! Ow! That hurt! I'm joking, I'm *joking*! I'm gonna drop my books!"

I didn't elbow him a second time. Instead, I took the top three books from the stack he was carrying and gave him a half-amused look. "You just love flirting with danger, don't you?"

"Ahh, you know me." He winked at me suggestively. "I'll flirt with *most* things, given half a chance."

When we'd first arrived in Cahlish, Carrion and I had woken in the same room—a huge room, granted, with four large beds in it. There was only one bed in that room now, and Carrion had well and truly made the space his own. There were shelves with a multitude of books. A chaise by one of the windows. There had already been a wardrobe here. Now there were *two*, though given the wrinkled clothes discarded in piles across the room, Carrion didn't appear to be using either of them. The windows were fogged up with condensation, probably due to the extraordinary number of potted plants he'd managed to cram inside the room. The place resembled...well, I didn't know what it resembled, actually. I'd never seen anything like it before.

"What the hell have you been up to in here, Swift? Have you stolen all this stuff?"

"What? No! How can I have stolen it if it's all under the same roof? I've only *relocated* it. Totally different."

"Uh-huh." I spun around, taking it all in. There were drawings tacked to the walls, and numerous half-full bottles of whiskey sitting on the windowsill. He'd definitely stolen *those*. A muddy trowel on the floor by the foot of his bed. A trail of dirty paw prints led from the bed, across the floor, toward one of the wardrobes.

I heard the plaintive whine before I pieced what I was seeing together...but then it hit me.

I stormed across the room and ripped open the wardrobe door, and there was Onyx, curled up into a ball in a thick green blanket at the bottom of the wardrobe.

"Carrion! You shut him in the *wardrobe*?"

"No. He goes in there to sleep sometimes! The wind must have blown the door shut on him."

The wind. A likely story. Still, I knew when Carrion was lying most of the time and he didn't appear to be doing so now. Onyx stretched, his pink tongue curling as he yawned, then he hopped sleepily out of the nest he'd made for himself and looked up at me expectantly, as if to say, *Okay, what are we doing?*

I scratched the back of the fox's neck, giving the very same look to Carrion. "You wanted my opinion?" I reminded him. "I came here to tell you if you're going crazy, remember?"

"I remember," he said in a high-pitched, defensive tone. "Come look at this." He went to the closest window and pointed at the sill.

With Onyx on my heels, closer than my shadow, I went to see what the fuss was about. "Why do you have all of these books here, anyway?" I muttered. "You *can* read in the library."

"Not naked, I can't."

"You shouldn't be reading these *naked*. It's not *sanitary*—"

"Relax. I'm joking. I'm reading them here because I don't want to get in anyone's way. And besides. It's private. I'm researching."

"Researching what?"

"Ahh, stuff. Y'know, Yvelian stuff. *Court* stuff." He shrugged awkwardly.

"As in, Winter Court histories? And the roles and responsibilities of, say...a *king*?"

Carrion's cheeks flamed. "Maybe. Don't make a big deal out of it. And don't tell anyone. I haven't changed my mind or anything yet. I'm just... researching."

"Carrion, this *is* a big deal. Imagine what would have happened if there had been someone of royal blood to stand against Madra. The people would have...they'd..." My train of thought abandoned me. I was staring at the plant in the little blue pot sitting on the windowsill. Its leaves were glossy and rich, deep green. White flowers bloomed all over it, tiny and shaped like little flutes, their petals curling up at the ends. I watched as more of them seemed to grow, their petals forming and turning from green to white right before my eyes.

"See, this is why I didn't tell you. You're getting way ahead of yourself. I'm *just* researching. I don't even know how I'd try to reclaim my throne. I don't—" He shook his head violently. "It doesn't even feel right calling it my throne. I'm just thinking that..."

"Carrion," I whispered.

The more he spoke, the more the plant next to him on the sill flowered. New shoots formed as he rambled, and those shoots became branches.

"...and even if I did want to take back the Winter Court, how would that even work? Would I have to challenge Belikon to a duel or something? Because *that's* not happening. And there are five million other things to consider—"

"Carrion?"

"—I'm not a fucking *duelist*, Saeris. That evil bastard would kill me in a heartbeat—"

"Carrion!"

He ceased his tirade and threw his hands in the air. "What?"

"Are you *seeing* this?" I pointed at the plant. It was twice the size it had been a minute ago and it was covered in those tiny white blooms. "The plant...it's growing like crazy."

"Oh. Yeah. That's what I was trying to show you. They all keep doing that. I started collecting these plants yesterday. They were just little cuttings, or seeds I planted, and now, well..." He gestured to the veritable garden in his bedroom. He hurried to the bed and picked up an open book from his bedside table, quickly bringing it back to show me. "Look here," he said tapping the page. These leaves are the same, right?" The illustration in the book was identical to the leaves on the plant in the blue pot. I studied both closely before nodding.

"Looks like it."

He snapped the book closed. "This plant isn't even supposed to *flower*," he said. "It releases spores once every ten years instead. But those...those are flowers, right? And they keep blooming every time I speak, don't they? I'm not losing my mind?"

Even as he said it, another cluster of the little white flowers grew and bloomed, turning green to white. "No, Carrion. You are not losing your mind. That's *exactly* what's happening."

"Do you suppose that's normal?"

I was about to answer him, to ask him what exactly *was* normal anymore, but before I could open my mouth, the foundations of the estate began to shake. "What in all five hells?" I gasped.

Carrion's look of confusion matched my own, as he looked out of the window and pointed. "There. In the distance. Coming from the trees," he said.

And indeed there they were. My heart surged like a piston at sight of the small, dark shapes of figures emerging from the forest. Not just tens of them. Not even hundreds, but *thousands*.

"Holy fucking shit." Swift whistled under his breath. "Is that...?"

The horde? That's what he was thinking. What I was too afraid to ask out loud, too. But no. As the figures gathered at the tree line, forming into ranks, I saw that it wasn't an army of feeders.

It was the warriors from Irrín.

They had abandoned their temporary camp and marched on Cahlish, ten thousand strong, and Lorreth of the Broken Spire rode at their head.

42

BLACK DAWN

SAERIS

"I FUCKING KNEW it! I *knew* that witch was up to no good. What did I say?" Lorreth's hair was wet. It had started to rain as the warriors made their final approach to the estate, and both Lorreth and Danya were soaked down to their skin. Both left puddles of water on the floorboards as they prowled around Cahlish's formal reception room.

All the furniture was draped in white sheets. Dust motes eddied on the air, captured in the beams of cold light that lanced in through the windows and outlined Fisher where he stood, leaning against a table. He groaned, pressing his fingertips into the space between his brows. "I don't think anyone really wants to hear 'I told you so' right now, brother," he rumbled.

Lorreth's nostrils flared, his hands in fists at his sides, knuckles white...but he inclined his head. "You're right. That's an asshole move. Sorry, I just...they're *witches*," he said, as if that explained everything.

"I know. I know." Fisher sounded so tired. "We'll deal with Iseabail later. Right now, I'm far more concerned with what you just told me. Run through what you saw again, would you?"

"Danya's the one who saw it," Lorreth answered. "You're better off hearing it from her."

The female warrior shivered a little as she stepped forward and began recounting what Lorreth had just told us in greater detail. "Some of the fighters noticed it two days ago. The northwestern slope of Omnamerrin is streaked with black veins. The rot has formed channels, cutting through the snow. It made it down the mountain in a day and reached the camp shortly after. We tried to scorch the ground ahead of time to pen it in, but that didn't work. When Lorreth showed up yesterday, we tried to come back through the shadow gate to tell you what was happening, but we were too late. It had already closed. We set off immediately to warn everyone here, but we lost another twenty-three warriors to the rot along the way. It's moving fast now. Way faster than before."

"And it'll reach Cahlish in how long?" Fisher asked.

Danya shook her head. "Twelve hours? Sixteen max."

"Gods a-fucking-live." Fisher hissed between his teeth.

Lorreth stepped forward, tucking his thumbs into his belt. He seemed reluctant to speak but summoned the courage to do so. "We know about the book, Saeris. Perhaps now would be a good time to see if Lady Edina had any sage advice for us, given how dire the situation is."

The book. Of course. I'd brought it downstairs with me for this exact reason, but the tension in the room had made me forget about it momentarily. I drew it out from inside my leathers—

"By all means, check it, Osha," Fisher said. "But make sure that it's your decision to do so. I have a feeling that my mother's guidance was designed specifically for you and you alone." My mate looked to Lorreth. "I know you don't mean any harm by the suggestion, but she shouldn't be compelled."

The warrior ducked his head. "Of course."

"It's fine. If there was any time we could use a little advice, I think it's now." I held my breath as I opened the book, flipping through the pages until I reached where I had left off.

Consider a sixth. Only the golden-toothed wolf can be trusted.

I turned the page, and the words written there swam as I tried to focus.

Read on after Evenlight.

Damn it! I hadn't even thought to check the next page after the ball. I hadn't considered how Edina might have communicated when I was supposed to receive guidance from her in the past. It turned out there were direct cues, and I'd already missed an entry. My palms broke out in a cold sweat as I turned the page.

Do not undo Zareth's work. You are as you are for a reason. Do not drink from the vial. Do not let your new Lord drink.
The time will come, but not yet.

Gods. A shock wave of adrenaline traveled from the crown of my head to my feet. I'd thought about it just hours ago. Being Fae and *only* Fae was an appealing prospect, but I needed my half-vampiric blood, at least for the time being. Foley needed his, too. To what end, I could only guess, but Edina had foreseen a reason to tell us not to take Iseabail's cure. I'd nearly missed her warning. This was a lot to take in. Too much, maybe, but I couldn't afford the time to process. Again, the paper rustled as I quickly turned the page.

Read on at the white cliffs.

I stared at Edina's handwriting, desperately trying to make the elegant, slanted script say something else. Something that would be useful to us *right now.*

"What is it?" Lorreth asked. "What does it say?"

Frustrated, I snapped the book closed. "It says that I can only read on at the white cliffs, wherever that is. There's nothing in there about how to deal with the rot."

Lorreth's attention immediately swung back to Fisher. "There we have it then," he said.

"There we have *what?*"

"The white cliffs, Osha," Kingfisher said. "That tells us what to do all by itself. We need to evacuate Cahlish and rally at Inishtar. We should move quickly. I need to open the biggest fucking shadow gate I've ever made, and we need to start shifting the troops. We have to get everyone to safety."

"That's the plan?" Danya said, voice stony. "*Retreat?* Based on a single line of scribble in a book? I know your mother was a powerful oracle, but this is ridiculous."

"What else are we supposed to do, Danya? This isn't an army we can face and fight. Our weapons can't kill it. Our magic *feeds* it, for fuck's sake. Every person it infects becomes our enemy in the space of moments. We need to regroup and figure out how to—"

"We need *brimstone.*" The room went deathly silent for a moment. Danya's chest heaved when she continued. "Lorreth told me about what happened with Archer. He said that infected feeder was killed instantly when the brimstone came into contact with it. With enough brimstone, we could stop the rot in its tracks here, before it infects the rest of the fucking realm—"

"All right." Fisher shoved away from the covered table and stormed across the room. He reached for a dagger from the scabbard at his waist and slammed it against Danya's chest. "Go on, then. Go down into the pyre and start killing our friends. Or wait. No." He took the knife back. "I'll do it, shall I? I'll go down there, and I'll drain the creatures who swore to serve and protect my fam—"

"You're being dramatic—"

They shouted over one another, their words lost to their anger. Lorreth cut them both off. "STOP YELLING, BOTH OF YOU!"

The pair fell silent...but only for a second. "You've forgotten how to lead," Danya accused. "If you find yourself unequal to the task, then step aside. Sometimes *sacrifices* need to be made."

The laughter that bubbled out of my mate was scathing and short-lived. "I know," he said slowly, "that anyone willing to forfeit the lives of their people and tally their loss as collateral damage is no leader. Certainly not the kind of leader that I will *ever* be—"

"Then maybe you're just not cut for the role," Danya snapped.

Helpless: That's how it felt, watching them fight like this. But if Danya spoke to Fisher one more time like that, I was going to fucking spear her to the fucking wall.

Lorreth held up his hands in a placating gesture, again attempting to be the voice of reason. "You're both right. We should absolutely evacuate Cahlish. And yes, the brimstone is our best chance of destroying this infection. But we *don't* need to cull the sprites to gather enough brimstone to accomplish that, do we? There *is* another way."

Fisher was already shaking his head. I'd never seen him look more vehement. "No. Absolutely not."

There was a note of hysteria in Danya's laughter. "You're out of your fucking *mind*, bard."

"What do you mean?" I asked. "What's the other way?"

"*No,*" Fisher repeated. "Lorreth's wrong. There is no other way." His tone brooked no argument.

"So that's that, then? You want to leave the place you fought so hard to get back to, with no plan and no idea of how we're going to get through any of this?" Danya demanded.

"We will figure it out." Fisher's voice was firm, but Danya did not look impressed. Even Lorreth looked a little uncertain.

"Come on. We're not doing anyone any good standing here fighting among ourselves," the warrior said.

"All mad as dogs," Danya hissed under her breath as she stalked out of the room.

Fisher pointed the business end of his blade at her as she went. "So help me, Danya, I will kill you my fucking self if you touch a single *one* of those sprites."

"Fisher—"

He faced me quickly, his pallor ghostly and haunted. He placed a kiss against my forehead and then pulled away. "I know what you're going to ask. I know you want to understand. And I *will* explain," he said. "I promise I will. Just…right now, I need a moment. And your *brother* needs you, Osha." He nodded his head toward the window. The rain sheeted against the glass, but I could still make out the single figure, standing out there alone on the snowy lawn. How long had he been out there, standing in the downpour? How had I not noticed him? "Go to him," Fisher said. "I'll come find you soon, I swear it."

───────┼───────

He wasn't wearing any shoes.

His hair was soaked and flat against his scalp, his curls driven straight by the downpour. Hayden stared up at the sky, a deep frown carving into his forehead. He didn't look at me when I arrived beside him, but he knew I was there. I held the jacket over my head, mostly to protect myself from the deluge, but also to ward off the bleak sunlight eking through the thick cloud cover overhead.

"What's going on, Hay?" Our mother had called him that. After her death, I'd refused to use the name for fear of invoking her memory. It destroyed me when that happened, and I couldn't keep him afloat if we were *both* drowning. Weak of me, that. I should have let him keep the name she'd called him. Should have let him keep that piece of her.

"I—I don't know who I'm supposed to be here, Saeris. Everything's just so…*different*," he said.

"I know. It *is* different. There's a lot to get used to. But different doesn't have to be *bad*, does it?"

He blinked, the rain running into his eyes. He looked bewildered. "I don't know. I really don't. I mean…this?" He wiped the rain from his face, shaking his head. Droplets of water ran over his palm, dripping down into the snow. "I had no idea a place like this could exist." He swallowed. Looked at me at last. "Who am I supposed to *be* here, Saeris?"

"Who were you in Zilvaren?" I countered.

"I don't know. I just...I always thought you would tell me what I needed to do. Who I needed to be. You were always there, so strong. You always had a plan."

Oh, gods. I wanted to laugh at that. If only he knew. Sadly, I took his hand in mine and squeezed it. "I never had a plan, Hay. And you were always going to have to figure out who you wanted to be on your own. That was never my decision to make. I know this is so overwhelming. I know it probably feels like I'm giving you a worse hand than the one you were dealt in Zilvaren. With the rot and the feeders, and everything else going on here, I get it. Yvelia might not seem like such a safe place to be. I will understand if you want to go back."

Hayden's jaw tightened, the muscles in his throat working as he thought about that. But he shook his head. "No. No matter what, you're the only family I have. If you're staying, then so am I. I'm sorry I doubted you. And I'm sorry I never appreciated everything you did for me back in the Third. I am going to figure this out. I'm gonna do better. I want to be useful here, Saeris. I don't want to be a burden."

"There'll be time for all of that. Don't worry about it now. We should get you inside. You're going to catch your death out here in the rain, Hayden. It's freezing."

My brother sniffed, wiping his nose with the back of his hand as he nodded, turning back toward the house. I hadn't been able to tell because of the rain, but he was crying.

We'd almost reached the warmth of the house when the same strangeness that had pulled me into Tal's burning bedroom cinched tight in my stomach again. I wanted to go in with him, but something was stopping me. Like a hand clenched around my insides, an overwhelming force pulled me back out into the rain.

"You go on ahead. I'll be right behind you," I said to Hayden.

"Are you all right? You look worried."

"I'm fine, I promise. I—I'm just going to grab something from the forge. It's quicker to cut through the courtyard this way."

Hayden didn't have a clue where the forge was. Nor did he have a true understanding of Cahlish's layout. If he did, he would have known for a fact I was lying. As it was, he only suspected...so he gave me a nod and went inside.

It was good that he was gone.

It was only moments later that I rounded the corner and discovered the cause of the unpleasant tugging in my gut...and Hayden probably would have passed out if *he'd* come face-to-face with the Hazrax.

"You'll forgive the rain," it said. "But I'm not overly fond of the cold. Rain is at least a little warmer than snow."

"Why are you here?"

The strange creature's head rocked to one side, its lips peeling back to reveal rows of needlelike teeth—a show of displeasure if ever I saw one. "You're a mannerless thing, aren't you? Quite feral. I believe the last time we spoke, we observed the ritual of small talk, did we not?"

"I don't have time for small talk. There are fifteen thousand warriors waiting on the other side of the estate. The rot infecting this land is almost on top of us. There are sick people here. My friends need to be moved to safety, and you have just literally dragged me away from ten things that I urgently need to attend to, so forgive me if I'm not inclined to observe social etiquette."

The rain drove down harder, pelting the side of the house and drumming loud as thunder on top of the tin roof we stood under. The Hazrax hissed, its slitted nostrils flaring. "You'd be wise to reconsider."

"Why are you here?"

"I admit, I wasn't expecting the display that took place at Ammontraíeth yesterday. That was quite the scene." It spoke in an accusatory tone.

"It had nothing to do with me," I rasped.

"I am aware of *that*," the Hazrax replied. "I know of the deal with the witch now. A risky play on the Balquhidder clan's part, employing such dark and fetid magic for an opportunity to wipe out the vampires.

Perhaps the play will work out in their favor. Perhaps not. Time will tell. But I am forced to admit their little gambit has rather ruined things for me."

The Hazrax made a bizarre clicking sound—no human or Fae could ever have replicated it—and slowly shook its hairless head. "You know, you're only the third person I have broken my silence for in over a millennium? I have to say, you're not a very stimulating conversation partner."

I glowered at it, refusing to rise to the bait.

The creature's eyes shuttered again, narrowing slightly in what I assumed was annoyance. "As you wish. I have come to provide aid to you, child queen."

"What *aid*?"

The Hazrax made a rattling, wheezing sound. Was it *laughing*? "A two-part gift," it said. "I gave you the first part last night."

"What are you talking about?"

Its eyes, unnervingly black and bottomless, drifted down my body and settled on my hand.

Oh, for fuck's *sake*. "This?" I held up my hand, showing my runes. "*This* was from you?"

"Indeed. You will have to work for most of your runes, but some of them may come as gifts. And this one was gifted just in the nick of time, wouldn't you agree?"

"What does it do? What does it mean? I can't find a translation for it anywhere."

"And you won't. It is blasphemy to record such things on paper, King Killer. The rune is my name. It does not grant you magic, the same way other runes do. The *ability* my rune grants you is complicated. It allows you to...*undo*. Or maybe..." It pulled a strange face that I could not decipher. "*Break?*" it offered.

I had ice water for blood. I was going to throw up. "And if I don't want this rune? If I don't want your *name* inked into my skin? What then?"

The Hazrax plucked at its robes then slid its absurdly long hands into sleeves. "You would return a gift? And such a powerful one, too? You'll be grateful for it soon enough, believe me. You should *already* be grateful for it. It saved your friend's life last night."

What did it want, a fucking thank-you card? "I don't want to owe *you* anything," I told it.

"The ability was freely given," the Hazrax said. "No debt has been incurred. It is a silent rune, already sealed to your soul. It will act as a grounding rod for the runes you already have, and the ones that are yet to come, too. For a while, anyway. It will buy you some time while you work on sealing that brimstone mark."

"Why? Why would you give it?" If the rune was everything the creature claimed it to be, then it was a valuable boon indeed. But I'd learned the hard way that nothing was free in Yvelia. There was always a price, and usually a hefty one at that. It made no sense that this thing, whatever it was, would just give me access to powerful magic. It made no sense that it could gift it to me in the first place.

"Think of it as an apology," it said. "For what is to come. I have seen through the eyes of your oracle, and your future is not an easy one. There are those who would consider me partially to blame for that."

"What have you seen? For the love of the gods, what *else* is coming?" The Hazrax seemed to blur for a second, its outline smudging black and gray against the overcast world behind it. I blinked, and the creature was solid again.

"No more questions," it said. "I must give you the second part of my gift and then depart."

The Hazrax drifted forward, extending its hand to me. Gold glinted in its waxy palm. When it flipped its hand over, a ring dropped at my feet: the ring of office that marked it as a Lord of Midnight. A large polished ruby flashed at the ring's center, winking in the fading light.

"Give it to the apostate with the golden smile," the Hazrax ordered. "He will need it."

I stared at the ring first, then up at the ungodly-looking thing that loomed over me, my mind racing too fast for a proper thought to take shape. "People call you the Hazrax. But that's not the name inked into my skin now, is it?"

"Clever child. It is not."

"You're never going to tell me what you are, are you?"

The Hazrax smiled its needle smile. "Why would I when you're so close to piecing it all together, King Killer? You've *almost* figured it out."

43

DARK SPOTS

KINGFISHER

"I'M SORRY. I'VE done my best, but I don't see him anywhere. I've scoured the entire realm, and he's nowhere to be found. But you know as well as I do, Fisher, this realm is full of dark spots. Just because I can't find him doesn't mean he's not there. It just means that his blood is being shielded from me somehow."

"You're saying this is intentional, then? That someone has taken him and is hiding him?"

Iseabail was out of her room.

I hadn't wanted to let her out, but what other choice did I have?

She'd refused to be questioned while under lock and key like some sort of prisoner...even though that was *precisely* what she was. I couldn't have kept her in there forever, anyway, since half of the estate had already disappeared through the monstrous shadow gate I'd opened on the slope leading down to the forest. The other half were patiently waiting their turn to pass through and evacuate Cahlish. Soon enough, I would have to send *her* through, along with all the others...apart from Ren, *because Ren was still fucking missing.*

For now, we were in the drawing room. My father had used it as a study once upon a time, though I had no recollection of that.

"Quicksilver pools. Sprite colonies. The black markets in Dow and on Tarran Ross. There are so many locations that are either warded from external magic or contain so much powerful magic that they drown out all other energy. Scrying isn't—"

"Yes, I *know* scrying isn't fucking perfect." The floorboards creaked as I paced in front of the window, dragging my hands through my hair. "Try again," I demanded. Then, out of sheer force of habit, coupled with a pinch of desperation, I added, *"Please."*

Lorreth, who had been standing by the door glowering sullenly at the witch for the past half an hour, shot me a filthy look that implied I had just personally betrayed him. "We should just throw her in the jail down in the basement and let the rot take her," he said.

Iseabail had endangered Saeris. She'd also used Tal in the most horrific way, and we'd *all* nearly died as a result. She was probably my least favorite person in a two-hundred-mile radius right now, but I still wasn't going to lock her up in a cell and let the rot infect her. That was a fate worse than death, and I just didn't have it in me.

Iseabail bridled at Lorreth's comment but didn't say anything to him directly. Wouldn't even look at the warrior. To me, she said, "Fine. I'll try again for you, but you shouldn't expect a different result. I've been staring at this map for so long that my eyes feel like they're about to shrivel up and fall out of my head. If this was going to work, it would have done so five hours ago."

What did she think I was going to do? Just say, *Okay, then, I guess that's it. We won't look for him anymore, then?* I gave her a reproving look. "Just... try again, Iseabail."

I'd noted when she'd returned from Nevercross that she had been promoted to prioress. Only the ascended elders of the Balquhidder clan were permitted to wear their hair braided and pinned up the way Iseabail did now. Normally, a witch was hundreds of years old before she was even considered for the priory. Iseabail hadn't even seen the end of her first century yet. The leaders of her clan had rewarded her prematurely for the spellwork she'd wrought at Ammontraíeth. It

made perfect sense that they had. Iseabail had single-handedly erad-
icated thousands of high bloods in one night—something the Balquhidder clan hadn't been able to achieve in all the years that had passed
since they'd discovered the cure to the blood curse that was placed on
the Fae.

But the witches were sticklers for honor and tradition. They were
rule *makers*, not rule breakers. And they did *not* hold with dark magic.
"I'm sending you back to Nevercross once you're done here," I told her,
leaning back against the wall. Iseabail's head snapped up. Lorreth's
shoulders tensed at the same time, utter disbelief in his dark eyes. "I'll
come and pay the high priestess a visit, too. I'm thinking about bringing Tal with me," I continued.

The scrying pendulum Iseabail held swung wildly—not because she
had located Ren at last, but because her hands were shaking. She straightened slowly, looking up from the detailed map of the courts she had been
poring over.

"Why would you do that?" she asked stiffly. "I'd have thought you
had far too much going on, what with your sister, and Ren, and the
evacuation."

I considered her for a while. Let her stew a moment before I decided
she had sweat enough. "Well, the witches have done us all a great service, cleansing the Blood Court. I need to *thank* them. It'd be remiss of
me to let their sacrifice go unacknowledged."

"That's really unnecessary. We didn't act on behalf of the Fae, Kingfisher. This was done for the betterment of our clan. No sacrifice was
made."

"Of course there was," I said airily. "The High Council outlawed
dark magic millennia ago. That's how Algat found herself cast out of
the Kinross clan, wasn't it? If they authorized forceful cleansing and
the use of black *hell gate* spellwork to rid Sanasroth of the vampire
nobles, then they made a grave sacrifice indeed. They sacrificed their
ethics. Their morals. Their—"

"Stop." The word echoed around the drawing room.

I had her.

It had only been a suspicion, but now I knew it to be fact: The matriarchs of Iseabail's house had no idea what she had done. A lethal smile began to spread across my face, slow as honey. "What did you tell them?" I asked, narrowing my eyes at her. "Did you say you'd *convince* the high bloods that it was in their best interests to return to their natural-born states?"

Iseabail locked eyes with me, defiance radiating from every pore of her as her face went carefully blank. "Yes," she said. "That's what I told them."

Lorreth made a scathing sound at the back of his throat, his leathers creaking as he looked away, out of the window, shaking his head, as if such a thing could ever have been done. More than once, the witches had tried to convince the high bloods who had rejected the cure to reconsider their decisions. The Fae kings had tried, too. Rurik Daianthus from Yvelia. Royan from Gilaria. Shara from Lissia. No one had succeeded in persuading the high bloods that they would be better off as members of the Fae courts again. How they'd believed Iseabail would persuade them now was a mystery.

I tutted, shaking my head from side to side in faux disapproval. "Oh dear. They're going to be very disappointed when they find out about the fucking *bloodbath* you orchestrated then, aren't they?"

"You can't tell them." Iseabail skirted around my father's old desk, raising her hands. My shadows were at the ready, but Lorreth got there first. He rarely used his own innate magic. Once, he had told me that his people swore an oath not to use the magic they were born with. From the North, his people lived in the wilds and carved a pitiful life for themselves out of the tundra. They were strange folk, with even stranger beliefs. They considered their magic sacred, accidentally stolen from nature during the process of being born. To use their gifts was to flout that theft in front of the gods. For Lorreth's family, it was a sin worse than murder to use magic—inherited, small, or otherwise.

Though he was nothing like his family and didn't share their beliefs, he had still been raised under their roof, and some things stuck with you, whether you believed in them or not. I'd seen my friend wield his power only twice before, and both times had been to save someone else. Later, if I asked him why he did it, he'd probably say he unleashed his power because he had thought Iseabail was going to attack me, and he'd be able to say it because he *believed* it. But I saw the look on his face as he threw out his hands; he also did it because he was angry.

Iseabail was lifted from her feet. In a flash, she flew backward, slamming into the dusty old bookcase behind the desk. Books toppled to the floor. A vase full of dried flowers fell and shattered on the ground. White light snapped around Iseabail's wrists and ankles, lashing her to the bookcase. The band of energy that whipped around the witch's throat dug into her skin and cinched tight.

"I . . . was . . ." Iseabail gasped. "Wasn't . . ."

"*Shut* your mouth," Lorreth snapped.

Iseabail's eyes found mine, beseeching. "You're . . . just going to . . . stand there? You're not the . . . ethical, high and . . . mighty hero you pr . . . pretend to be around . . . your *mate*."

Hero? I wanted to laugh. Gods, how I wanted to. I'd never heard anything more ridiculous in all my life. "*I* don't pretend to be anything," I told her. "Saeris makes me kinder than I should be. Do not misjudge me. I would do all manner of unconscionable things in the pursuit of her safety. I'd take my friends and my mate to another realm and let this one burn if I thought for one second that it was what she wanted. I've given everything I have to protect the people of Yvelia, and they spit on me and bay for my head because of it. I'm about to lose my home to this godscursed rot. I have no love left for this place, and I have very little good left in *me*. I'm afraid if you're hoping for a hero, you'll have to look somewhere else."

Iseabail blinked at that, the accusation in her watering eyes cutting into me. "You don't . . . mean that. I see you . . ." She rasped. "Your *soul*. You'd fight and bleed . . . for this . . . realm—"

"Lorreth!" The door to the drawing room was open. There Saeris stood, hair and clothes dripping wet, her mouth hanging open in dismay. "What are you *doing*?"

Lorreth reacted as though he'd been scalded. His power crackled out of existence, leaving the reek of ozone in its wake. Iseabail slid down the bookcase, coughing as she crumpled into a heap amid the fallen books. The warrior's cheeks and ears burned bright red as he turned away from the witch and set his gaze on the casement above the window, unable to meet Saeris's eyes.

"What the hell is going on?" Saeris brought the scent of rain with her as she entered the room. She looked from Iseabail to Lorreth and then to me. "Are we torturing people now?" she asked quietly.

"It's all right," Iseabail croaked. "Lorreth wasn't going to hurt me."

"I fucking *was*," the warrior argued.

There were witches among the clans who *could* look into a person's soul. It was said that they could get the measure of a male just by taking one look at him. Good. Bad. Kind. Cold. It was all there, apparently: the blueprints to our souls, laid bare for certain witches to read as easily as the lines of a book. Iseabail had never mentioned that she was such a witch, but the certainty she spoke with gave the impression that she might have been.

Regardless of her abilities, she was right about Lorreth. He wouldn't have hurt her. The damned witch had him acting the fool—to say his people had history with the Balquhidder clan would have been an understatement—but he wouldn't have caused her any harm, even if *he* didn't believe that right now.

Saeris shot the warrior a baleful glance as she crossed the room and offered her hand to the witch, helping her to her feet. "Have you found Ren?" She posed the question to all three of us as one.

"No," Iseabail answered. "I've tried every which way I can think of, but he's nowhere that *my* spellwork can detect."

"All right, then. If you're certain he's not on his way here, then we'll have to regroup and pick this up later. I just ran into Danya as I was coming back into the house. She says the rot is here."

Black vines snaked over the blanket of snow that covered the lawns. Wherever the rot touched, the snow melted, already softened by the rain, and the ground was momentarily exposed—blades of grass, still green thanks to my father's wards, saw the light for the first time in centuries, only to wilt, turn brittle, and break seconds later. The necrotic spread crept forward before my eyes, its progress startlingly efficient as it made for the house.

The last remaining unit of warriors moved quickly through the shadow gate. Only two hundred fighters waited in rank and file to be transported. The warriors who had already gone through had carried large trunks with them, full of the family rings and other items of jewelry and that I'd once tasked Saeris to turn into relics. The last of the warriors carried the silver that we'd brought back from Zilvaren. Their breath clouded the air, their laughter nervous as they watched the hellish tide come in. Swords, daggers, staffs, bows, and arrows: They were armed to the teeth, and magic danced at their fingertips, but still, they were not equipped to face this foe.

"As fast as you can!" I called. "When you're through, wait at the campsite! Do not go down into the village. The satyrs aren't expecting us. The last time this many fighting Fae showed up on their doorstep, a bloody battle ensued. Let's not give them the wrong impression!"

I was met with curiosity and uncertainty as the troops stepped single file through the lucent smoke and shadow. Down to the last one of them, they knew me. I had led them once. Been their commander. I had charged with them up the steep slope of victory and fallen back with them in retreat. Every horror I had ever asked them to face, I'd made damned sure *I* had faced it first...and then I'd *left* them. None of them had known why. None had known where I'd gone. Thanks to Tal, Renfis had known. Everlayne, too. But they'd been Oath Bound not to tell anyone where I was. They hadn't been able to explain to these fighters that I had *not* abandoned them willingly. They knew the truth now—the details of Gillethrye and what had taken place there had spread through Irrín quickly enough after we'd faced Malcolm in the maze. But a hundred years was a long time, and trust was lost far quicker than that.

Renfis was their leader now. *Ren* should have been the one urging them through the shadow gate toward safety, but he was missing, and I was an unreliable substitute.

The rain had stopped a little while ago. It was almost dusk, and the clouds were low and dense enough that Saeris could stand to be outside. She wore a heavy woolen cloak with the hood drawn up to shield her from the last of the day's light. As she crossed the snowy slope toward me, Onyx trotting close on her heels, I was once again struck by how strange but *normal* it was to have her here, to have her as my mate. She wasn't what I'd expected. She was so much more. She really had come blazing into my life like a comet, and now she was changing every-thing.

She was different, too. The past few weeks had changed her. There was a lithe confidence to her as she approached, her boots crunching in the snow. She'd always looked good in her fighting leathers, but now they *belonged* on her. My chest tightened with unspeakable pride when I saw her black tresses now hung in war braids beneath her hood. *Fae* war braids. She had become a part of this world—a part of *me*—and I wouldn't have had it any other way.

Her eyes flashed daggers at me when she pitched up at my side, and I braced for the shit-kicking I was about to receive. "We *don't* torture people," she said, her tone full of ice.

"Carrion tortures me daily," I muttered.

"If we torture people, then we're like *them*," she said, ignoring me.

"And if we capture an enemy warrior and they have information we need?" I asked.

She gave me a dry, displeased, sidelong look from the depths of her hood.

I held up my hands. "All right. Okay. We don't torture people."

"I think we should send Iseabail back to Nevercross. We might need to call on the witches again. We won't be able to do that if we're holding one of them hostage."

Decisive. Strategic. I knew Saeris could be both, but I liked seeing this side of her right now. She was making plans, working to stay one step ahead, and that cheered me no end. I nodded, setting my eyes on the fading horizon, trying not to look at the black infection that was slithering ever closer toward my family home. "You're right. As soon as everyone's through the gate, I'll make sure she finds her way back to clan lands."

"And in the morning, I'd like to go back to Ammontraíeth. All those people—"

"Aren't your responsibility," I told her gently. "Not if you don't want them to be. There is no Blood Court anymore, Saeris."

"But there's still Ammontraíeth. There's still *Sanasroth*. And we have no idea if the horde is where I commanded them to stay. What if they've broken free and are tearing through the palace right now, draining all the people who chose to come back?"

I worked my jaw, not wanting to answer. That scenario had crossed my mind, too, and my initial response had not been very generous.

Did their renewed Fae status undo all the terrible crimes they'd committed over the centuries? Thank fuck it wasn't up to me to make that call.

"Most of those people didn't *choose* to become high bloods," Saeris said. She had no way of knowing what I was thinking. Not even with the connection we shared as mates. I supposed it made sense that she was also contemplating the question of their guilt. "Malcolm murdered most of them. They might have been kind people before. Good. And despite your frown, I don't think you'd leave them there to be eaten by feeders. Just on the off chance that they're not assholes."

"On the off chance that they're not assholes. *Gods.*" I laughed mirthlessly at that, and the laughter turned into a sigh. An uncomfortable realization had struck while she'd been talking. What if these were the people from Gillethrye? The ones I hadn't been able to save. The ones I had ordered to be burned when Malcolm's feeders had scaled the walls of the city and torn through its streets, leaving death and decay in their wake.

What if I *had* been able to save them? Saeris wanted the same opportunity, and I wasn't about to deny her that. I wouldn't sentence her to endure the same kind of regret that gnawed on my soul every day. "We won't take Tal with us," I said abruptly. "I doubt he's up to it. And anyway, after everything he went through there, I think it's best if he never has to step foot in Ammontraíeth again."

Saeris's eyes went wide. "Wait. So you agree, then? We can go back?" Her surprise was endearing. I wrapped my arm around her and pressed a kiss to her temple through her hood.

"I shouldn't tell you this, since you seem blissfully unaware of the power you hold over me, but...I will give you whatever you want, Saeris Fane. Always. No matter *what* it costs me."

It wasn't a promise, but it was the truth, and I would honor it. Somehow, even though the rot was on the verge of eating Cahlish and my last lingering connection to my family, I managed to smile. I suspected the smile was lopsided, but still. "I'm yours to command, Queen Saeris," I whispered into her hair.

There was no eye roll at the title this time. Before, she'd ruled over a court of monsters. There was a slim chance that the remnants of her court might be redeemable after the events of the Evenlight Ball, and Saeris's attitude toward her people had done a drastic one-eighty as a result. Not because she craved power or wealth but because she saw *hope* in a situation and wanted to help.

The odds had never been in her favor back in Zilvaren. Madra was a monster. Her officials were corrupt. The people of Saeris's ward were dirt poor and barely making it from one day to the next, but Saeris had never abandoned *them*. Perhaps the way she clung to hope made her a fool in some people's eyes, but it was just one of the things that made her extraordinary in mine.

The way she looked at me made me want to do better. To *be* better. Every day of my life, I was going to have to work my absolute fucking hardest to deserve her love and respect. I wasn't afraid of the challenge.

Saeris's smile made something profound inside me *thrum*. The echoes of fate and all the universe vibrated behind my breastbone, promising... *what?* I wasn't like my mother. I hadn't been blessed with visions of the future. I was just going to have to live my life and find out.

Saeris's eyes drifted over my shoulder, focusing on the estate, and the moment was lost. "They're coming," she said.

The last of us.

They came down the slope from the house together: Te Léna and her mate, Maynir, who carried a bundled-up Everlayne in his arms; Iseabail, walking ahead of the group, her skirts pinned up with one hand, her crimson hair stark and bright against the white of the snow; Lorreth, helping a weary-looking Tal, who was up, dressed, and walking (though rather shakily) on his own two feet. Carrion, Foley, and Hayden brought up the rear, each carrying a towering stack of books.

Relief stabbed through me at the sight. In an estate full of valuables and riches, it was the *books* they were saving. The information inside some of those tomes couldn't be found anywhere else in Yvelia. It had been Belikon's first priority when he'd assumed the throne of the Winter Palace to seek out and destroy anything that might threaten his reign. For as evil as he was, he was also smart.

He knew that, to control his people, he had to control the information they had access to. Hide the truth from people, and you kept them in the dark. Burn the books, and you got to rewrite history *and* the future.

Those books would be replicated. They'd be shared among the masses. If I had to copy every single fucking one of them out by hand myself, I would see it done.

The last of the warriors were gone now. Our small group was all that remained, standing on the brink of something that none of us understood or knew how to fix.

Everlayne looked so tiny in Maynir's arms. She'd always been small. But *strong*, too. Full of fire and passion. I'd always wondered how such a small vessel could contain so much energy. She was diminished like this—an echo of her true self. Purple shadows rimmed her eyes, her skin wan and pasty. Her hair had lost its luster, the normally bright blond strands dull and stringy in her thick, single braid. Her eyes shuttled quickly left, right, left, right beneath eyelids that looked so paper thin they were almost translucent.

"She's burning up," Te Léna said. "We need to get her back indoors as quickly as possible. I have a friend in Inishtar. Someone I trust. I'll take her to them and make her comfortable, Fisher. I'll send Maynir to let you know if there are any updates."

"Thank you." Everlayne had only ever had Belikon as a parent, and yet she had still turned out to be as kind and sweet as her mother. The blood we shared had bound us, even when the king had determined to keep us apart. She was my sister, and I *knew* she was in there somewhere, fighting to get back to us. I could *feel* her.

Te Léna and Maynir disappeared through the shadow gate, taking her with them. Iseabail was next to go. The witch hugged Saeris briefly, offered me a stiff nod, then was gone.

"If these satyrs don't have anything stronger than ale, I'm holding you personally accountable," Lorreth said as he passed us. "Just 'cause they can't hold their liquor doesn't mean the rest of us can't."

"I'll find you in a tavern, then?" I asked, arching an eyebrow at him.

"I think we could all use a drink after this. I have the headache from hell, thanks to those sprites."

He was referring to the *fire* sprites in particular. The other household creatures had already gone through the shadow gate, but the fire sprites were still below ground. Lorreth had gone into the bowels of Cahlish, as deep into the pyre as he could tolerate, and he'd tried to convince Archer and his friends to leave with us, but they had refused. They couldn't survive very long without the heat of the pyre to sustain them—a day or two, at most—and anyway, they believed their brimstone would protect them from the rot.

They were likely right, but it still didn't feel good leaving friends behind.

Tal was even paler than normal as he dipped his head to me. "I won't be a burden on the camp," he said in a raspy voice. "As soon as you're through, I want you to send me back to Bayland's End."

Bayland's End. I hadn't heard that name spoken out loud in centuries. Hearing it now brought a wave of nostalgia crashing down on me. Taladaius's ancestral seat had been a well-loved, if a little run-down, haunt of mine in my youth. We had gotten up to all kinds of mischief there together—two young Faelings discovering their magic and learning the lessons their realm had to teach them the hard way. Taladaius wanted to go back. Whether his mother would *have* him back was another matter.

"Bayland's End is less than a hundred leagues from Cahlish," I said. "The rot won't stop once it's finished with Cahlish. It will keep spreading in all directions and be on your doorstep again in a matter of days."

Tal shrugged half-heartedly. "Only if you don't stop it first." He wore an amused smile. "I get the feeling that the two of you will have found a way to put a stop to all of this by tomorrow night, anyway. You're each as stubborn as the other when it comes to getting your way."

He wasn't wrong there. The outlines of a plan *were* forming in my mind. It was a long shot, and by all the gods was it dangerous, but if it worked...

Saeris would be *safe*.

The realm would be safe, at least for a little while.

The mess I would have to create would be catastrophic. Sometimes, the cure was more dangerous than the affliction, but at least it would buy us some time...

"Do you guys mind if I skip ahead in line? These books are really heavy." Carrion grimaced awkwardly as he leaned around Tal's shoulder. The smuggler was wearing three coats layered one on top of the other. His hands were encased in mittens.

"Why are you dressed like that?" Saeris asked.

"Because I always end up sitting in a snowbank, waiting around for hours while everyone else disappears off to do something dangerous. I don't *love* being cold, Saeris."

"Why are you saying that like the weather is *my* fault?" she asked.

"It *is* your fault. You could have fallen in love with an outcast warrior from Gilaria or, better yet, from Lissia, but no. You fell for the one from the frozen wasteland that is Yvelia."

"You do realize that that's *your* land you're talking about," I reminded him.

But Carrion was already trudging toward the shadow gate. A moment later he had vanished, books and all.

"The Randy Swine," Lorreth said.

"*Excuse* me?" Saeris's eyebrows shot up.

"That's the name of the tavern we'll be at."

"Oh. Right."

Lorreth gave us a wink and went, supporting Tal under his arm. That left only the four us: Hayden, Foley, Saeris, and myself.

Saeris's brother squinted worriedly over the top of his stack of books at the shadow gate, apparently not sure what to make of it. "I'll go through with you," Saeris said. "You'll feel like shit on the other side, but that only happens the first time. After that, traveling through the gates won't affect you anymore."

"Great." He sounded breathless. If he hadn't been able to see the rot blackening the hillside and corrupting the ground with his own two eyes, he probably would have insisted on staying at Cahlish. As it stood, the rot was growing closer by the second, and we were running out of time. "Will you bring Onyx for me?" Saeris asked. "I can't carry him, carry some of these books, *and* catch Hayden on the other side."

"I'm not going to *pass out* again," Hayden objected.

"Yes, you are," Saeris fired back.

"You probably will," Foley said at the same time.

"Of course. I've got the fox. Don't worry about him," I told her. "Go on. I'm right behind you." I gave her another kiss on her forehead. "Go." And then, so that only she could hear: *I love you, Little Osha.*

I love you, too.

I felt the moment that she passed through the shadows and moved beyond my reach. It was as though I had been cut off from life itself, and only the cold, empty void of death remained. I shivered at the sensation, something unpleasant twisting in my gut, but the feeling was instantly forgotten when I had to dart forward and grab Onyx, who was about to leap through the shadow gate after Saeris all by himself.

"Gods alive," Foley said. "You told me up on the roof, and I believed you, I did. But seeing you pine over a female *in the flesh*?" He shook his head, his golden fangs glinting in the muted light as he laughed at me. "I mean, it's just something I never thought I'd see with my own two eyes."

I pulled a *very* dour face at him as I herded him toward the gate. "Shut up, Foley. I can't fucking help it, okay?"

He grunted but then elbowed me playfully in the side. "Are you okay with this? Leaving Cahlish? I know how much this place means to you."

Before I could stop myself, I'd turned back to look at the estate. There were other houses that were larger. Finer. More impressive to look upon. But Cahlish was my parents' home. And for a very long time, it had been the only thing that was mine. Leaving it felt like abandoning a dying family member, but we had run out of options. "I have to let it go," I murmured. "If there's a way to save the place, then I'll find it. And if there isn't…" I shrugged. "Then there's no point in looking back. There'll be time to build new homes for ourselves once this is said and done."

"Mm. Very pragmatic," Foley said teasingly. "You think we'll succeed, then? Find a way through all of this?"

I faced the shadow gate again, steeling myself. "I do. I have to believe it."

"For *her*?" he finished.

I gave him yet another dry look. I didn't deny it, though.

"By the gods, you've got it bad." Foley slapped me on the shoulder, grinning. The sound of his laughter rang in my ears as my friend disappeared through the shadow gate. I could still hear it as I stepped in after him, Onyx pressed tight against my chest plate. Wind howled past my ears as the world went black...and then the laughter morphed into something else.

A voice, calling out from the space between worlds.

"Hello, Dog."

44

INISHTAR

SAERIS

FIRST CAME THE smoke.

Then came the scream.

The bloodcurdling cry painted the air with terror.

"Cut off its fucking head!"

This was the moment—*this* was the split second in time around which reality pivoted, where everything that preceded it was *before* and all that followed became *after*.

I was still smiling from teasing Hayden. I felt the strange shift in the pit of my stomach that came with exiting a shadow gate... and then we were in hell.

The sky was thick with black smoke, the air rank with it. We were on top of a hill that overlooked a small township—small, neat little buildings with terracotta roofs below us, stretching out toward lumi-nescent cliffs of chalk that dove into vast blackness beyond. Fae war-riors sprinted across my field of vision, swords in their hands, blood staining their skin. The glow from campfires, kicked over and burning out of control amid the long, dry grass, washed over their faces and made them appear ghoulish.

At the bottom of the hill, one of the buildings exploded, sending a pillar of light and flame up seventy feet in the air. The ground rocked beneath my feet. I covered my head with my arms, trying to understand what the fuck was happening. And then my senses kicked in.

Hayden.

Where the *fuck* was Hayden?

My palms found the hilts of my short swords. The weight of the twin god swords was reassuring as I spun them around, power flaring up my arms.

The shield on my right hand lit up the chaos like a signal flare.

There he was, on his knees in the grass, choking. Books scattered the ground around him. *"Hayden!"*

Ten feet. Only ten feet. I could get to him. My lungs burned as I bolted for him. He was fine. No injuries. No blood. He tried to look at me as I crouched down in front of him, but his eyes rolled back into his head. I slapped him as hard as I could. "No! Stay awake, Hay! There's no time for that now." He regained a little control, an alertness coming back to him, pupils focusing.

"What the fuck's happening?" he gasped.

"I don't know. I—" Another tower of flames jetted toward the sky, briefly illuminating the hillside. I heard the snarl before I heard the feeder. It was a woman. *Had* been one once. It was naked, its breasts flat and droopping, its long hair snarled into mats. Its ribs were visible, as if they might tear through the monster's skin any second.

Its teeth glistened black ichor, red with blood.

It had fed.

The smoke cleared, and then there was another one, huge, clad in golden armor, the rays of a sun embellished into the blood-spattered chest plate. It pinned a Fae warrior to the ground, its head bent to the warrior's throat. Its body undulated as it drank, draining the warrior dry. The warrior's hands groped, yanking handfuls of grass from the ground as he tried to *do* something... and then he fell still.

"Saeris! Gods, Saeris! To the left!"

Hayden's cry shocked me from my stupor.

The naked feeder was coming. I got my blades up just in time to run her through with the points of both before she fell on me. Light blossomed in my right hand, flowing down Erromar's blade, and pouring into the feeder. It lit up from the inside, its ribs stark and black as charcoal beneath the unnatural waxen white of the monster's skin. It trembled, vibrating, letting out an ungodly scream, and then burst into flames.

Move, Saeris. Fucking move.

My boots pounded the ground as I sprinted. My hand closed around the top of Hayden's arm. I dragged him to his feet. "You need to run," I yelled.

He spun around, eyes wild. *"Where?"* Ren had carried me to a bed my first time through a shadow gate, and I was telling Hayden he had to run? Fuck. I didn't know which direction to point him in anyway. The hillside was all smoke and killing. There was no shelter here. Nowhere for him to go. I cast around, searching for Fisher, but no...he wasn't here. He—

Something slammed into me from behind. I went down, rolling, sticks and debris poking me through my clothes. A mindless groan filled my ears, and then there were fingers clawing at me, trying to open my leathers and find skin.

I slammed the hilt of a blade into the feeder's face. It was fresh, its skin still flushed pink. A male, maybe twenty or so. Human. It let out a high-pitched keening wail. "Pleeeeeease. *Please!*"

More than fresh. It hadn't fed yet. It wanted me to be its first. I threw my leg over its shoulder and flipped it, groaning with the effort. It was heavy. *So* fucking heavy. It was wearing armor—

Teeth snapped too close for comfort. I watched, horrified, as those teeth fell out of the feeder's mouth and new, razor-sharp, needlelike fangs speared from its gums to replace them. It lunged for me again, snapping its jaws together like a rabid dog, and I scissored my short swords and separated its head from its body.

I was on my feet and running back up the slope to where I'd left Hayden.

"Banking right! Right, right, right!" a shout came. I recognized the voice. Had no time to process who it was. Suddenly, there were feeders everywhere. The warriors who had been evacuated from Cahlish fought them all around me, but there were more of them than there were of us. A flicker of blistering white-hot light forked across the hillside, landing multiple strikes, and the smell of char and ash hit the back of my nose.

I blocked and I parried, throwing off each feeder as it came for me. I took arms and opened their stomachs. I claimed their heads as quickly as I could in my haste to get back up the fucking hill.

Carnage and screaming, everywhere I looked.

No Hayden to be found.

I barely paid attention as more feeders came for me and fell afoul of my blades.

Angel's Breath crackled through the air to my right. At least I knew Lorreth was somewhere amid the fray. But where the fuck was Fisher? Why couldn't I sense him anywhere?

Where are you? Come on, Fisher, tell me where you are!

Deafening silence rang in my ears.

Had he stepped through the shadow gate and run straight into a feeder? Was he already among the fallen, bloodless and dead? No, there was no way. I'd know. I *would*.

"Hayden!" I spun, slicing a gangly feeder open, nearly slipping in its rotting entrails as they spilled like wet, glistening snakes from a tear in its stomach. It lunged for me, trying to rake me with its claws, but I slashed with both swords, carving the monster in two and sending its head rolling back down the slope.

"Saeris!" I nearly eviscerated the blood-soaked figure who came running out of the smoke; I saw the flash of gold in his mouth and stayed my hand. "Thank the gods," Foley panted. "You're all right. Where's Fisher? We need a blanket approach to this, and we need it now."

"He was with you! Didn't you come through together?" My heart couldn't beat any faster, so I stopped it altogether. The thunder in my ears wasn't helping.

Foley swore in Old Fae, spinning around and peering into the melee. "I thought he might have been with you. He was *right* behind me. I came through just now and was met with this. Took me a second to get my head on straight. He—"

I didn't hear what he said next. A feeder barged past him, nearly sending him to the ground in its haste to get to me. It didn't spare Foley a second glance. Foley was a vampire, after all—he had nothing that a feeder might crave. Me, on the other hand? I was half Fae, and apparently the scent of half-Fae blood was still enough to drive a feeder into a frenzy.

I threw up my hands instinctively, projecting my shield, the white-blue light flaring bright. The quicksilver icon had *almost* taken shape in the air when the feeder barreled straight through it.

The creature hit me square in the chest, knocking the breath out of me. I didn't need it anymore, but the impact still shocked me.

My ass hit the ground hard. My feet were up in an instant, preventing it from sinking its teeth into me, forcing it back. "Stop!" The authority that had fallen to me when I'd been crowned queen of the Blood Court rose up inside me—I felt it there, a tangible thing that I might have been able to take hold of. *"STOP!"* I repeated, imbuing the words with as much command as I could...but the feeder didn't even flinch. My command held no power over it at all.

Fuck!

I was about to drive the sword in my left hand up through its jaw and into its skull, but suddenly the feeder's head was gone. Red mist rained down on me, spattering the front of my leathers as Foley came into view over the feeder's headless shoulders. He held a weapon the likes of which I had never seen before: a length of thick chain with a wooden handle on one end and a heavy metal ball studded with vicious spikes at the other.

The spikes dripped red.

"I only swore fealty to you yesterday, and I'm already saving your life?" he said. If it weren't for the horror show taking place around us and the fact that neither of us knew where my mate was, I would have thought he was trying to be funny. The decapitated feeder slumped sideways into the grass. Foley went to help me up but then caught sight of the god swords I still held in both hands and thought better of it. Back on my feet, I wiped my face and faced him. *"Tell* me he came through with you."

"I thought he had. But when I turned around, he wasn't there. The shadow gate closed, and..."

I knew it before he'd confirmed it. No matter what the circumstances were, Fisher would have answered via our bond if I'd called out to him. He hadn't come through the gate.

My blood turned to ice in my veins. Foley was still saying something. I shook my head, cutting him off as I walked around him. *"Hayden!"*

Renfis.

Now *Fisher* was gone?

I wasn't losing my brother, too.

"Hayden! Where the fuck *are* you?"

He didn't answer. Didn't call out.

And then I saw him, lying on the ground, shielded by the tall grass. His face was pale, his eyes closed.

No. No, no, no, this wasn't happening. He was *not* dead. I didn't drag him all the way here for him to be savaged by a fucking feeder on a hillside in the middle of nowhere. He was alive. He was—

He *was* alive. Gods and martyrs, I could hear his heart beating—his pulse was shallow, but it was there. I dropped to my knees, patting him down, grateful when my hands didn't come away bloody.

"He's okay," Foley said. "He's just unconscious. He passed out. We knew he would. Here, take this a second." He handed me his unusual weapon. It was even heavier than it looked. Unwieldy, too.

"What *is* this?"

"A flail." Foley picked Hayden up and slung him over his shoulder. "It was the first thing I found when I came through the shadow gate. Very effective at caving in the heads of your attackers." Now that my brother was secured over his shoulder, he held out his hand requesting it back. "Maybe not as effective as a god sword, but still handy to have. Come on. The fighting's dying down. There are fewer feeders now. We should find the others."

Lorreth was the easiest to find thanks to the Angel's Breath that rippled from Avisiéth as he fought. Carrion was with him, Simon held aloft, his copper hair sticking up in three different directions. I watched, half impressed, as he fended off a feeder, twisting the god sword I'd forged for him with a reasonable level of expertise that he *hadn't* possessed when he'd arrived in Yvelia.

The feeder sagged to the floor, lifeless, head cleaved from its body, and Carrion looked up and saw us.

It was a strange thing, to make eye contact with Zilvaren's cockiest smuggler and find no smile on his face. *Relief* flashed over his features when he registered who we were. Then the smile came, but it didn't reach his eyes. "Ahh, *here* she is," he said, his chest heaving. "Too used to queenly perks these days, are you? Leaving us to do all the heavy lifting?"

I looked down at myself. I was drenched in blood. I could *smell* it, drying on my face. I had clearly carved my way through hell itself in order to stand in front of him, and he knew it.

Suddenly, I was in Lorreth's arms. "Fucking merciful gods. Thank you. Thank you," he chanted. He hugged me so hard, I couldn't breathe. When he pulled back, I saw the state of him and nearly wept. His hair plastered to his cheeks with sweat. There were two huge rents in his leathers. His arm was bleeding profusely. It was rare for anyone other than Fisher to wear a gorget, but Lorreth was wearing one now, and it looked like it had saved his life. Deep grooves were gouged into the metal protecting his neck, giving the impression that something had tried—and mercifully failed—to rip his throat out.

"I sent Te Léna and Maynir down into Inishtar with Everlayne, Zovena, and Iseabail," he said. "Hopefully they made it."

"And Tal?" Foley asked.

Lorreth let out a deep breath. Avisiéth rested point-first in the ground at his feet; he must have speared the god sword there when he'd swept me into that bone crushing hug. He collected the sword now, handling it reverently, sliding it back into the scabbard over his shoulder. "I told him to go with the others, but he refused. He started burning the blood out of feeders left, right, and center. The last I saw of him, he had a sword in his hand, and he was cutting the bastards down like a farmer scything wheat. I couldn't keep up with him. He threw himself into a pack of feeders back there somewhere. I haven't seen him since. We'll find him, though. Come on. We need to get down into the town. The place is starting to burn."

Foley and Lorreth started making plans. It was only when they started walking down the hill at a fast clip that they realized I wasn't following. My hands shook as I opened the book. Not one of the ones we'd brought from the library. This was the one I'd been carrying in the front of my leathers. My most prized possession, alongside my short swords: Edina's book.

"What are you doing, Saeris? We need to go!" Foley called.

Carrion hadn't left my side. "What does it say?"

It took a moment to flip through the front half of the book. *Come on, come on, come on.* It was here. It had to be. There was no way the book didn't have the information I needed. An eternity passed while I scanned through lines of text relating to Alchemy and my power. My breath stalled when I found the page I'd read back with the others at Cahlish.

Read on at the white cliffs.

Edina was going to tell me where to go, where to find him, and everything was going to be okay. Hope soared in my chest when I turned the page for the third time, and...

I blinked, trying to understand what I was reading.

Read on after the trade.

What? The *trade*? What the fuck did *that* mean? Where was the message? This was another cue to proceed onto the *next* message. But the one I was looking for wasn't there. I flipped back to the previous page and saw only "Read on at the white cliffs."

The pages were stuck together. They had to be. My fingers plucked at the paper, trying to will there to be two sheets fused together where there was only one. No page had been torn out. The message just wasn't there.

"Saeris?"

I looked up and found Lorreth looking down on me with worry-filled eyes. "There's a lot to figure out, but we can't do it here," he said. "I'm sure there's a perfectly good reason why Fisher didn't come through the gate. I'd bet good money he'll be with us by morning. In the meantime, I have to get you inside. He'll murder me if I let anything happen to you out here."

I let him guide me away. I tucked the book back inside my leathers, trying to believe Lorreth's reassurances, but it was impossible to make myself believe. Deep down, I felt it. Something was *very* wrong.

On a clear day, you could see the archipelago that defended the island court of Lissia from the chalk cliffs of Inishtar. The islands were known as the Shield. I'd read that in a book recently. There had been an illustration of the small town, built into the cliffside by the proud satyr population that called Inishtar home. The satyrs were architects. Engineers. Mathematicians. They loved music and art, and taught their children to conquer their fear by challenging them to scale the vertical cliffs of their home and dive into the sea.

That was not the Inishtar we were met with as we made our way into the township. This was an Inishtar on fire. An Inishtar dressed in blood. Wives shed tears in the cobbled streets, cradling their husbands. Children wailed, wandering through the confusion, trying to find their parents. Nearly every window was smashed. A thick carpet of glass crunched underfoot as we passed countless homes with their doors hanging off their hinges. The homes still stood, at least. They had been constructed out of granite and limestone to withstand the rigors of the salt-laden coastal air. Doors could be replaced. The windows, too. But the lives that had been taken . . .

Lorreth and Foley led the way. They knew how to move through the smoking ruins of a city without letting the horrors of it crush them. This was new to me. Carrion wore a dark look on his face as he walked beside me. Hayden had woken and insisted on walking, but he had completely shut down. He was somewhere far, far away, pretending that none of this was happening, and for a brief moment, I was jealous. How nice it would be to retreat inside my own head and block out the world, knowing that someone else was making the decisions and dealing with the repercussions.

The nearness of the ocean flooded my senses. The tang of it cut above the smoke. The rushing *shushhhhh* of its waves crashed against the rocks at the bottom of the cliffs. I knew it was out there, vast beyond imagining—a body of water so immense that it swallowed the horizon. I'd been excited to come and witness it for myself, but not under these circumstances. Not like this.

We followed a paved walkway all the way to the edge of the cliffs, at which point we veered *off* the walkway and Lorreth forged a path for us among the scrubby vegetation and loose rocks. He was following a scent, that much was clear. It must have been strong for him to be able to pick it out over smoke and salt. I couldn't smell a thing around the two.

Eventually, we came to a small two-story house, perched on a ledge that overhung the cliff. The glass in the window frames had been smashed here, too. On the ground floor, double sets of thick curtains had all been sucked outward, through the open windows, and snapped angrily on the breeze.

"They're inside," Lorreth said in a tired voice, gesturing to the front door.

Carrion and Foley carried what remained of the books we'd brought from Cahlish. More than half of the titles had been destroyed or lost in the fight. I knocked on the front door, hissing when I discovered the hard way that my knuckles were raw and bleeding. There was a scuffling and then came the sound of something heavy scraping against the floor. A moment later, the door opened, and a tall female satyr with skin the color of warm mahogany stood before us. Her eyes were silver-flecked gold. Her tightly curled hair looked to have been tied back quickly into a messy bun atop her head, from which loose strands corkscrewed down, framing her face. She wore a black sleeveless shirt that displayed the extensive tattoos on her arms, and loose-fitting black pants that cinched tight three quarters of the way down her legs, revealing shaggy dappled gray and black fur and cloven black hooves.

She put her hands on her hips, regarding us in a very displeased manner. "Forget it. You can bunk back in the town center with the other troops. There's no more room here." Her voice was warm. Her tone was not.

"Orellis, it's okay! They're friends." Te Léna appeared behind the female. Soot stained the healer's left cheek. Her bottom lip was split open, though the blood had congealed and dried. She was alive. I pushed past the satyr and threw my arms around the female, hugging her just as tightly as Lorreth had hugged me. She returned the embrace, her heartbeat pounding in my ears, her body trembling. "We were so worried about you," she whispered. "All of you."

"Likewise. The others?"

Te Léna retreated, sniffing, her emotions getting the better of her as she gestured behind her. Iseabail was there, back pressed against the granite hearth that dominated the cozy kitchen beyond. The witch smiled at me briefly, the slight upward tilt of her mouth faltering when she saw Lorreth. Maynir sat at a table in the center of the kitchen, elbows on the table, interlaced fingers propping his chin up as if he wouldn't be able to hold his head up otherwise.

"Layne's upstairs," Te Léna said. "Still unconscious."

I scanned the room, searching for the one person I didn't see. "Zovena?"

Maynir shook his head. "She darted off into the crowd as soon as we realized we were leaving the battlefield. She couldn't be reasoned with, and I wasn't leaving my mate to go chasing after her."

Zovena was gone, then. And Tal had bolted into the fray as well. Half of me had hoped he'd be here, with the others. The other half of me had known he wouldn't be. Maybe later there would be time to pick apart what that meant. For now, I could only focus on what was right in front of me.

"Fisher didn't make it through the shadow gate."

Maynir sat up very straight. Te Léna held a hand nervously to the base of her throat. "What do you mean, *he didn't make it through?*"

"I'm aware that my house isn't exactly weatherproof right now, but I'd rather not stand here with the front door wide open if it's all the same to you people," the satyr, Orellis, said. She was less angry and more resigned to the fact that she had more guests than she wanted, it seemed. Stepping aside, she gestured for us all to come in.

Bang! Bang! Bang!

Foley hammered nails into the planks of driftwood he and Carrion had scavenged from outside, blocking off the windows. The night rested heavy over Inishtar, a mournful weight pressing down on all of us.

A cup of earthy tea sat on the table in front of me, long cold. Orellis's faun, Lanny—only two years old—squirmed in my lap, her tiny hooves leaving bruises on my thighs as she pulled on my braids and sucked on her plump fists.

"The forge was destroyed by the blast. Our blacksmith, Jaymes, was killed, too. There's the old forge, though, on the outskirts of town. It isn't much, but you could set up there?" Orellis said.

"I'm sure it'll be fine," I told her, "but without access to a large amount of quicksilver, I can't make the relics anyway. I was supposed to make them at Cahlish. That way I could have used some of the pool there to imbue the rings with, but now..."

Now we were *very* far away from Cahlish, and the one person who could have transported me back there was missing. As if that point had been made out loud, all eyes turned to Iseabail. She was bent over the map spread out over the other side of the table, frowning deeply at the scrying pendulum that hung, stubbornly still, from her hand. "I'm sorry. I really am. There's no sign of Ren *or* Kingfisher now. It's not as if they're just very far away, either. I'd still get some kind of reading if that were the case, but there's nothing."

By the fire, Lorreth scrubbed his face with his hands. "We have to find them. And we *have* to get those relics made. We need them now more than ever. The infected are spreading like wildfire. Something tells me the attack last night was just the first of many. If more infected hit the smaller towns between here and the Gilarian foothills, they'll be wiped out. With relics, we could evacuate the smallholdings, at least. The warrior had been honing Avisiéth's edge for well over an hour before Orellis had begged him to quit the incessant metallic grinding sound. She didn't want him waking the baby. Lanny had woken up shortly after anyway, but Lorreth had refrained from resuming his sharpening. His jaw worked as he looked at Iseabail. "Are you sure you're not *purposefully* struggling to locate them?" he asked, the question measured and flat.

The witch carefully set the brass pendulum down on top of the map and faced the warrior. "How many leagues is it between Inishtar and Nevercross, Lorreth of the Broken Spire?"

Lorreth shrugged. "I don't know. Two, three thousand?"

"And how long would it take to cover that distance?"

"A week or two on horseback if the beast was sound."

Iseabail's words might have clouded the air with frost had so many warm bodies not crowded the kitchen. "I don't *have* a horse, Lorreth," she snapped. "Nor do I have two weeks to get back to Nevercross. I need to get back to my coven *now*, and Kingfisher is the only person I know who can make that happen. It behooves me to find him as quickly as possible, and—"

"It *behooves* you, does it?" The warrior glowered at her.

The witch reddened. She turned and speared Carrion to the armchair he sat in with eyes full of glittering rage. She pointed at Lorreth.

"Were any of those books you carted here from Cahlish dictionaries? This *male* doesn't seem to understand the meaning of simple words."

"Hey, don't drag me into this. I don't know what *behooves* means, either."

"I know what it *means*," Lorreth snapped. "I just don't *believe* you. There's a difference."

"Enough!" These fucking two. It had taken Iseabail a while to start sniping back at the warrior, but she had finally reached the end of her rope with him. I didn't blame her for it. They just both needed to fuck-ing *stop*. "Put the map away, Iseabail. If scrying won't work, then that's the end of it. We'll find another way to track Fisher down." I *had* to believe that. There was no other option available. "Fisher would want us to help the injured and make Inishtar safe before we went off on a mission to track him down. We need to provide aid where possible. While we're doing that, *all* of us can brainstorm ways to track him. In the meantime, we should discuss what we just walked into."

"The horde must have broken loose," Te Léna said.

Around the kitchen, Foley, Lorreth, and I all shook our heads.

"Those feeders were human before they turned," Lorreth said.

Foley cracked his thumb, staring into the fire. "They didn't respond to Saeris's commands."

"They were *Zilvarens*," I added.

Orellis looked around the room, her confusion plain. "An army of feeders just attacked my home. They killed scores of my people. It doesn't matter where they came from."

"It does." I grinned down at Lanny. The little faun was wide-eyed, soft little curls backlit by the fire, staring at me intently as she tried to grab hold of my bottom lip. "It matters a lot. Does Inishtar have a quicksilver pool?"

"*Psshhh!*" Orellis rolled her eyes. "Of course not. We're just a little backwater town by the sea. Why would *we* have a realm portal?"

Realm portal. I hadn't heard it called that before, but the name *was* appropriate. Orellis's answer was unsurprising. I was hypersensitive to the quicksilver now. I could feel it from miles and miles away, and I'd already reached out, activating the quicksilver rune on the back of my hand to see if I could sense any close by. I hadn't heard even the faintest whispering in response, but I'd had to ask. "Where *is* the closest pool, then?" I put the question to the room as a whole.

Lorreth answered. "Lissia has one. Gilaria, too. They're both probably equidistant from Inishtar, but the Shallow Mountains stand between here and the Gilarians. The shield and an ocean stand between here and the water Fae."

"It'll take *way* too long to travel either of those places without a shadow gate," Iseabail said.

"I don't want to use their pools for travel. Not yet, at least," I explained. "I'm trying to work out how those feeders *got* here. Most of them were freshly dead. Some of them hadn't even fed yet. We can rule out the Lissian pool. Most of the feeders back at the Darn were terrified of running water. There's no way the feeders that attacked today crossed a whole channel to reach land. They *could* have come from Gilaria, but it would have taken them days to make it down through the mountains. They would have been in much worse shape by the time they reached Inishtar."

"Which means Madra has found another way to travel between this realm and Zilvaren," Carrion said.

The occupants of the kitchen all turned to look at him. He arched an eyebrow at us in return. "What, *I'm* not allowed to theorize? It makes sense, doesn't it? The infected feeders that attacked Irrín were Zilvarens too, and they didn't come through the pool at Cahlish or Ammontraíeth. They had to have found themselves on the banks of the river somehow. And Madra has been controlling magic for centuries in Zilvaren. Who's to say she hasn't accumulated enough power to find a way to travel from there to here?"

It *did* make sense. It was, in fact, that *only* likely explanation for what had happened. "Is it possible?" I asked Foley. He'd spent the last thousand years reading books and researching in the library at

Ammontraíeth. If any of us were going to know the answer to that question, it would be him.

The vampire shifted uncomfortably, casting his eyes up at the soot-marked ceiling. "I never came across any texts that spoke of interrealm travel that didn't rely on quicksilver. I certainly read about individuals absorbing the powers of others to bolster their own magic, but...the kind of magic it would take to open a portal between realms? Well, that would require an inordinate amount of power."

"The kind of power that would take a thousand years to steal?" I asked. "The kind of power that would require a whole *city* to fuel?"

Carrion stared at me, eyes widening. I saw it happen: We were piecing this whole thing together at the same time. Foley hadn't quite come to the conclusion that I had yet, though. "I suppose so. That would probably be enough power. Yes. What are you getting at, Saeris?"

"You said it yourself, didn't you? Back in the library, the second time we met. You said..." I tried to remember his exact words. They came back to me, ringing in my ears like a struck bell. "'You cannot eradicate magic from a city. Once it takes root within a community, it never leaves. It will find a way to thrive, one way or another. You just didn't care to look for it.'" Something *else* had come back to me, too. My heart started to race. "And what you said about the sigils in that book! 'The strongest magic is circular. Like a wheel. It is the symbol of forever, the beginning and the end of everything. It carries magic on a loop, amplifying it, giving it strength.'"

Foley nodded, though he looked somewhat confused. "I remember."

"Zilvaren," I said breathlessly. "The city, fashioned after the shape of a wheel. The walls form the wards, but they aren't spokes. The whole thing..." My head was spinning. "It's a *sigil*. This entire time, Madra has been using the city itself to siphon the magic of its inhabitants. *Zilvaren* is the biggest piece of spellwork ever created."

The revelation sat there like a stone. It might never have mattered to the people of Yvelia that my home was ruled over by a maniacal despot—they had their own to contend with, after all—but the news that Madra might now be in possession of *this* kind of power had stunned everyone to silence. If it was true, then nowhere was safe. She could open a portal and deliver more feeders whenever she liked, wherever she liked. And *that* made her even more dangerous than Belikon to the people of this realm.

"If we wanted to create a ward against her magic, could it be done?" Te Léna asked at last.

Iseabail seemed startled that all eyes had turned to her. "No. That kind of magic…" She hesitated, then looked anxiously around the kitchen, as if she wasn't sure of what to say next. "You're talking about warding a *realm*. That kind of spellwork would require Fae *and* witch magic, working side by side. You'd need an entire coven of powerful witches and at least ten strong Fae wielders to build something that monumental. You'd also need something that belonged to Madra. And not just something she touched once. You'd need something far more personal if we were going to block her magic."

I was already handing Lanny back to Orellis and getting to my feet. "Well, apparently, you're a member of one of the most powerful witch clans to ever exist," I said to the witch. "I'm sure if your sisters understood what was at stake here, they'd agree to work with us on something that might just save the realm. And I don't know ten of the most powerful members of the Fae, but I know *one* of them, and I'm personally going to figure out where the fuck he is and bring him back to us. As for something personal that belongs to Madra? I think I've got you covered there, too."

45

REDEMPTION

SAERIS

Total known dead: 4,769
Total infected: Unknown
Estimated infected landmass: 289 leagues and growing

THE SUN BLED red across the horizon.

Scores of votive lanterns rose to meet the dawn, released by sleep-starved residents of Inishtar hoping to buoy their dead loved ones' souls toward the heavens.

By the cliffs, gulls squawked, dive-bombing the satyrs who'd gathered there to work, angry that the commotion was disturbing their nests. We nearly didn't make it in time.

"Wait! Wait, *stop*!" I cried. Two of the satyrs—males with thick, shaggy brown fur covering their legs and proud horns curving away from their brows—both wobbled precariously, nearly toppling over the edge of the cliff themselves as they clung to the body they had been about to toss over the edge.

"What the hell are you *doing*?" the one on the right snarled.

"We need that body," I panted.

"It's one of the unclean. It doesn't even have a head. What could you possibly want with it?"

"The ones...with the armor," Carrion said breathlessly. "Are there any more...like that?"

"Yes," the satyr on the left answered, no friendlier than his companion. "They're all down there, though." He jerked his head over the side of the cliff. "You'll have to climb down the bairn's track if you want them."

I peered over the side of the cliff, my stomach rolling at the drop that stretched away from me...and then again at the sight of all the bodies that lay contorted into unnatural shapes on the black rocks below. The dawn light glinted off burnished golden armor—the very same golden armor that had started all of this. White foam rolled in, submerging the bodies from sight from a moment, then rolled back out again, revealing the macabre scene once more.

Carrion peered over the ledge, too. "You actually *go* down that path?" he said, eyeing the cliff face nervously.

"*We* do," the satyr on the left said. "*You* don't. This place wasn't built for clumsy Fae feet."

An oxymoron if ever I'd heard one. The Fae were far from clumsy. They were preternaturally light-footed in my experience, but it seemed the satyrs were nimbler still. I couldn't even see a clear line that led down to the rocks below. The cliffs were fucking *vertical*.

"Don't even *think* about asking us to go down there for you," the satyr with the curlier horns said. "We don't hold with looting corpses. The fallen should keep their possessions. They're death-touched."

"We don't want to loot them," Carrion said, disgusted. "We *need* something from one of them. In your shoes, I can see how, well, no, wait, satyrs don't wear shoes, do you. Let us check that body, and we'll be out of your hair. I mean fur. I mean—"

"Carrion, stop talking."

Carrion stopped talking.

I stepped forward, careful to keep my hood drawn up over my head. Thankfully there were few external signs that I wasn't wholly Fae, but my skin did tend to smoke a little in direct daylight. The high bloods had rarely left the Blood Court—the people of Inishtar probably hadn't seen one in centuries—but I didn't want to risk someone spotting me and making assumptions about my intentions. "We're not crows. We don't want to take anything valuable. Not... *traditionally* valuable anyway. Can we please just see that body for a moment, and then we'll leave you in peace."

"Fucking Fae," the satyr on the left hissed. Both males eyed us malevolently as they dropped the body they were holding; it hit the ground with a *clang*.

"Do as you like," Curled Horns said. "But be sure to roll it over the edge when you're done. We don't want it haunting us because of something *you* took."

The satyrs had strange beliefs. Turned out, they also weren't very fond of the Fae. I bowed my head, agreeing to their terms, and the two of them darted away, expertly clambering up the rock face to the left.

"So mean," Carrion mused. "How can you be so angry when you have a view like *that* to look at all day?" He nodded toward the staggering sight of the ocean, but I trained my eyes on the guardian's corpse at my feet, refusing to look at the vista. I couldn't. Not with Fisher missing. Nothing was allowed to be beautiful in the world without him.

Carrion's smile faded as we flipped over the body. As if he knew precisely what I was thinking, he said, "We *will* find him, Saeris." And then he let out an excited whoop that startled the gulls.

"Gods, Carrion, you nearly gave me a heart attack!"

"Don't be ridiculous. Your heart doesn't even need to beat. And anyway, aren't you happy? Look!"

We'd gotten lucky. *Very* lucky. The object we'd sprinted down here hoping to find was right there, still strapped to the guardian's belt. The pious fucker had been stupid enough to carry around one of Madra's ridiculous plague bags on his hip. But *she* was the one arrogant enough to believe herself a god. The plague bags were full of ashes from the sacrifices who were burned in Madra's honor... but they also contained *her hair*.

We rolled the guardian's headless body over the edge of the cliff as we had agreed to. We watched the golden clad corpse tumble through the air and land on the rocks without saying a word. There were those who might have deserved a prayer to the gods as their body was laid to rest, but not him. Whoever he was, whoever he had been, he had served a monster, which made him a monster, too.

We were walking back up the steps, away from the cliff face, when I noticed the figure sitting alone by a large chalk boulder that jutted out over the drop to our right. I knew him straight away.

It was *Tal*.

I pressed the plague bag into Carrion's hand. "You go on without me," I told him. "Get this to Iseabail and Te Léna as quickly as you can. Let them know I'll be back soon. There's something I need to take care of."

———+———

I was wrong.

He wasn't alone.

A body lay next to him on the chalk, red dress torn and dirty, blond hair pooling around her head. Zovena looked like she was sleeping, but I had seen enough death by now to recognize its subtle hue creeping into the female's pale cheeks. Tal sat on the very edge of the cliff with his legs dangling over the side. He wasn't touching Zovena, though he must have carried her here and laid her down. The wind blew his silver hair about his face, the strands glowing orange and red, reflecting the bloody sunrise.

A sword rested on the ground beside him. His hands were covered in cuts and scrapes; he absently twisted the chunky ring he wore on his thumb around, around, around as tears streamed down his face.

He didn't look at me as I took a seat beside him, letting my legs dangle over the edge, too. "The fates scorn me," he whispered airily. "Every time I try to die, they rob me of my peace."

"What are we doing, Tal?"

The muscles in his neck worked as he swallowed. I had only ever witnessed the male in shadow, his features carved in monochrome or maybe washed green from the evenlight. The morning had painted him in peaches, purples, and pinks as soft as silk. He had been remade. His heart pumped warm blood around his body for the first time in centuries. For a second, he looked so *young*. But then he turned to look at me, and there was that ancient sorrow in his eyes.

"I was having Fisher send me home so I could die there instead. At Bayland's End. The inconvenience of *that* unpleasantness would have served my mother right. But then we were in the middle of a battle, surrounded by feeders, and for once..." He choked on the word, biting back a strangled sob. "For *once*, I got to fight on the right side." He shook his head, batting away fresh tears before they could fall. "I found this sword in the grass and picked it up. I ran straight at Death, then. I *knew* that he'd take me. But every feeder I faced, I killed. And then there were no more, and...I found *her* in the dirt."

His gaze went back to the rising sun, smudging light across the rippling surface of the ocean. He did *not* look at Zovena. "She was a horrible person," he said, letting out a cracked bark of laughter. "I found myself laughing at the insanity of it all the time. I do *know* it was insane," he said, nodding. "All of it. Imagine..." He squinted, for a moment seeing something I couldn't see. "Imagine loving Kingfisher. Imagine not being able to stop yourself. And then imagine that he couldn't give a fuck about you, and he took pleasure in hurting you every opportunity that he got. And *then* imagine selling your soul to the devil so that you could follow him into hell." I couldn't tell if he was laughing or crying now. "Willingly! *Hah!*"

"Tal—"

"She was already dead when I found her. Drained dry." He sniffed loudly. "And when I looked at her, I stood there, waiting for the grief to land, to absolutely *destroy* me, and do you know what?" He threw back his head, closing his eyes and sighing loudly. "I didn't feel... fucking...*anything*. It was always a game to her. I don't know how she did it. If it was magic, or...or..." He shrugged helplessly. "It wasn't real.

It was a game, and now I feel as though I've woken up, and all the sacrifices I made were for nothing. How fucking *stupid* I was."

"You're *not* stupid, Tal."

"A thousand years..." He stared blindly off into the distance, lips parted, as if the gravity of it all had struck him dumb. "So I came here to give her to the sea. I came here to die...and once again the fates have snatched back my peace."

"What do you mean?"

Taladaius held up a hand, turned palm up, and pointed at the dawn. He closed his eyes again, and the sunlight bathed the angular planes of his face. "One thousand...and sixty-three years, five months...three days..." His voice tapered to a whisper. "That's how long it's been since I felt the sun on my face, Saeris. If I'd gotten here an hour earlier, I would have done it. I would have jumped." He blinked his eyelids open, a stillness falling over him as he looked out at the water. "But now?" A crooked, heartbroken smile hovered at the corners of his mouth. "How can I consign myself to another endless dark when I've been given back the light?"

I didn't speak. What was I supposed to say? The only thing I could do was take my friend's hand. We sat in silence for a long time. Eventually, I picked up the sword that he'd found and carried here, turning it over in my hands. It was a pretty thing, narrow-bladed and elegant as a rapier. Its razor-sharp edge was lethal. Something about it reminded me of Tal.

I knew what I had to do—knew that it would be right. With steady hands, I drew Erromar from its scabbard and held the god sword over the narrow sword.

There was no need for silver now. No need for jokes, or games, or bargains. The quicksilver rune on the back of my hand blazed brilliant blue-white for a second, and then a bead of shining metal formed on the end of my short sword. It rolled until it welled and dripped down onto the other blade and immediately sank into the metal.

Tal watched, his expression a little stunned. "What are you doing?"

Out of nowhere, pain zipped up my arm, sinking its teeth into my shoulder. I dropped the sword between us, shaking out my hand.

"What was *that*?"

"That," I said, a little disgruntled, "was a warning. I held it too long. And you know as well as I do that a god sword may only be held by the warrior it chooses to wield it."

I tried not to laugh at the surprise that flashed over Tal's face. He pointed at the sword. "You're not...serious? That's a *god sword* now? That's all it took?"

I shrugged. "A bit of borrowed quicksilver from my blade. A little bit of magic. An abundance of good intentions."

The former vampire looked lost for words. "And it's for me?"

"Yes, it's for you."

"What am I supposed to *do* with it?"

"I'd recommend you start by *picking it up*."

"But what...if it doesn't choose me? What if it doesn't think I'm worthy?"

"You are, Tal."

"But—"

"You *are*."

He stared at me long and hard, the muscles in his jaw twitching. And then he picked up the sword. Breathing fast, he ran his finger along its edge, donating a token amount of his own blood so that the sword might judge him. I saw the moment that the quicksilver began whispering to him: He started a little, his shoulders tensed, and his eyes darted to me as he listened.

Whatever it said to him, it wasn't for me to hear.

Tal's fingers closed around the sword's hilt, holding it tight. A claiming, then. He and the god sword were one.

"What's its name?" I asked. This was becoming something of a ritual—one I enjoyed more than I could explain.

Tal let out a long, shaky breath, considering the sword. "Tarsarinn," he said. "It means...redemption."

I grinned at that. Couldn't help myself, despite everything. "Fitting. I like it."

Tal then asked the same question Carrion had after he'd bonded with Simon. "And...will it have magic? Like Avisiéth and your short swords?"

I bumped him with my shoulder. "I can't tell you that, I'm afraid. *That* is between you and the gods. As for everything else, I'm not arrogant enough to declare that we're fighting on the side of right. I *hope* we are, but your precious fates are going to have to be the judges of that. Either way, right or wrong, from now on, Tal, you'll *always* be fighting with *us*."

The former Keeper of Secrets to the Blood Court of Sanasroth smiled.

"Tell me what you meant." It wasn't a request. I gouged my fingernails into my palms, knuckles blanching white behind my back as I fought to look relaxed.

We'd left Orellis's home. She had other friends who needed the shelter far more than we did. Neighbors who'd lost their homes. Caustic though she was, Danya was an excellent leader. The warriors respected her. She had spearheaded the logistics required to set up camp on the outskirts of Inishtar and had already put everyone to work, finding supplies to help repair or rebuild the damaged township as best they could. Everlayne was safe there, bundled up in a tent with Te Léna watching over her. The rest of us had been about various tasks throughout the town, helping where we could.

The explosions that had rocked the hillside during the battle had caused untold damage. Inishtar's healing center and its town hall had been targeted. The cause of the explosions was still a mystery, but the locations where they took place? Well, the reasoning behind why *those* buildings had been chosen was obvious. Without a town hall, it was harder for Inishtar's people to gather and regroup. Without its healing center, the injured populace had nowhere to go to receive help that might save their lives.

Along with the town's officials, Foley and Maynir were sifting through the debris at the town hall, helping to recover whatever important documentation they could lay their hands on. Lorreth, Carrion, Iseabail, Hayden, and I had been doing the same at the healing center, hoping to salvage supplies, but the structure of the building had been drastically compromised. We'd fled the center in the nick of time, only seconds before the roof had come crashing down.

Since then, Carrion, Hayden, and Iseabail had been playing some sort of game with a crew of adolescent fauns in the town square, kicking a ball around and trying to score points against each other. By the sounds of things, the fauns were roundly beating them. Lorreth and I stood together on the sagging stone steps that had once led up to the town hall, watching the game, though neither of us were actually seeing it.

Lorreth threw the piece of stone he'd been fiddling with, deep lines of concern carved between his brows. "I spoke out of turn, Saeris. I shouldn't have. Fisher was right. The suggestion I was going to make back in the drawing room was mad. It wouldn't have worked. You should pretend I never said anything."

I was going to fucking scream. Any second now, my fury and frustration would explode out of me, and I wouldn't be able to stop it. A cyclone of panic, fear, and desperation whipped around me, invisible to everyone else. I stood at the eye of a storm, fighting to stay calm, but I was losing my grip. Maybe I could hold on for another hour. I was damn well going to try, but the way things were going, I only had minutes before my panic knocked my feet out from underneath me and I became *unreasonable*.

"Fisher was going to explain it to me. He promised he would. You *heard* him make that promise. So now I need you to keep that promise for him, Lorreth."

"He's not gone off on some harebrained suicide mission without you, if that's what you're thinking."

"That's *exactly* what I'm thinking. That's what he did at Gillethrye. He left me in Ballard and went off alone to save Everlayne by himself. Remember that?"

Lorreth's frown deepened. "You're making this very difficult, y'know?"

"Good. That's what I'm aiming for."

The warrior sat down heavily on the steps, collecting another handful of rubble. He began tossing them one at a time down the steps. "He can't have gone off to enact that plan, Saeris. He would have needed you. There's no way he could have done it *without* you."

"Perfect. Then, if he definitely hasn't gone off to carry out this impossible plan, you should have no problem telling me what it was."

Down in the square, Carrion let out a shout, performing a victory lap with his hands in the air after scoring a point against the fauns.

I could hear Lorreth's teeth grinding from ten feet away. "The problem, Saeris, is that *you* could carry out the impossible plan without *him*, and I'm very concerned that you might get it into your head that it's a good idea—"

"I promise you I won't."

The warrior shot me a complicated look. "You'll forgive me, sister, but you aren't exactly Oath Bound."

Selanir was in my hand before he'd finished the sentence—the sword named Honor. I went to the warrior and held it out for him to see as I dropped down and closed my hand around the blade. My blood ran down Selanir's edges and dripped the sword's point onto the stone next to Lorreth. "I *promise*," I said. "I swear I will not act upon whatever you tell me now, unless it's with Fisher's explicit knowledge and help."

Lorreth stared down at the blood I had shed.

"Are you satisfied?" I asked.

He took a deep breath and began to speak.

When he was done, I understood. It *was* an impossible plan. A terrifying one. I'd needed to hear it, though. Without knowing what I knew now, I would never have been able to put it out of my mind. I would have assumed that my mate had gone off without me again with the intention of saving me and the rest of the realm by himself. The thought would have eaten me alive. Now that I knew that wasn't the case...I didn't feel any better. If Fisher had gone off on some ridiculous mission, I could have gone after him. Now I had no idea where he was or what he was doing, which made my insides fucking *boil*.

Overhead, the gulls screamed. Hundreds of them circled in a great column over the cliffs. Occasionally, one dropped from the wheeling mass and dove, plummeting from the air like a stone. Lorreth had told me that's how they caught the fish they ate.

"Are they always like this?" I asked. "So loud. So *many* of them?"

Lorreth nodded. "Yes. Always. Birds don't care about war, Saeris. It doesn't matter to them that half of Inishtar was wiped out last night. This is their home. They only care about protecting their nests and their young."

I chewed on the inside of my cheek, thinking about that. I couldn't stop staring at all those flapping wings. There were hundreds of them. Maybe thousands. The sight of them stirred something inside me, though I couldn't name the sensation. It was like a memory, floating below the surface of a frozen river, trying to find a crack in the thick ice so that it could rise to the surface and find open air. If I pushed a little harder, I might—

Lorreth cursed, dropping his handful of rocks. "*Sheascar.* What's *this* now?" He was looking off to the left, to the street fed into the town square...and the droves of satyrs marching down it brandishing all kinds of weapons in their hands. Swords. Daggers. More flails like the one Foley had found in the grass last night. They were even carrying pitchforks and brooms with them. Their voices drowned out the screeching gulls as they poured into the square.

The game taking place in the square came to a stop. As more and more satyrs piled into the square instead of passing through and heading on down to the cliffs, it became apparent that they'd come here for *us*.

A stout female with raven-black hair, nubby velvet-covered horns, and matching shaggy black fur covering her legs approached the bottom step of the stairs. Her hand rested on the hilt of the sword that hung from a belt at her waist—the blade was so long that its tip almost scraped the ground as she walked. "Where is he?" she demanded.

"I'm sorry, Galwynnian. Kingfisher isn't with us. And even if he were, he's not responsible for any of this," Lorreth said, holding up his hands and gesturing to the destruction that surrounded us.

"Not Kingfisher," the female said. "The Forgotten King."

"The Forgotten *who*?" My gaze skipped over the crowd, trying to discern their mood. It was difficult to get a proper read on the satyrs. They were proud, serious creatures. Their tempers seemed to skew on the angry side. Lorreth swore under his breath again, shifting uncomfortably in his armor as he got to his feet and straightened himself out.

"Now isn't the time for strife, Gal. We have no crowned kings among our party—"

"Achht. Away with your Fae sidestepping, Lorreth of the Broken Spire. I won't be fooled by careful wording. I know you have no crowned kings with you. The lad hasn't been coronated yet. But he *is* with you, I know. The whole of the South Lands is ringing with the news. Rurik's boy has returned, and he travels with the Bane."

Ahhh, right.

Shit.

I knew who she meant *perfectly* well now. On the other side of the square, Carrion stood with his hands resting atop the shoulders of one of the male fauns he'd been playing with, a stricken look on his face. For the first time, I noticed that there were no auburn-haired satyrs. Save for Iseabail, Carrion was the only redhead in the square, and he stuck out like a sore thumb because of it. Even from so far away, I could see his cheeks coloring. He drew his hands from the faun's shoulders and slowly began backing toward the corner of the square, where a small side street offered the promise of escape.

Lorreth would have made an excellent poker player. Not once did his gaze flit toward Carrion. I, on the other hand, was openly staring at him. Kicking myself, I looked away, focusing on my boots, but it was too late. The damage was done. Slowly, the crowd started to turn and face the back of the square.

"Gods and martyrs," I muttered. This was going to be bad. There were hundreds of satyrs in the square now. They were strong, they were angry, and they were *armed*. If they planned on hurting Carrion, there was literally nothing we could do about it. I moved forward, boot hovering over the stone step in front of me, but Lorreth grabbed my wrist and pulled me back, shaking his head.

"It's done," he rumbled. "No taking it back now. Some things he's just going to have to face on his own, Saeris. Let him work it out for himself."

Carrion sent a pleading look at us over the top of the crowd. Horns—twisted, straight, curved—bristled in the air, all pointed and deadly. I knew what he was thinking. He was imagining a set of those horns plunging into his stomach and disemboweling him. It would be a horrific way to die. Bloody, painful, slow. But when the satyrs present lowered their heads, they didn't charge Carrion. They dropped to their knees at the same time and laid their weapons down in offering, bowing to the Daianthus heir. All was silent, save for the scraping of hooves and the clatter of metal against stone.

"Ahhh, gods. He's going to be *insufferable* after this," I groaned.

The satyrs started to sing. The low ululation was so deep that it made the smaller pieces of rubble at our feet jump and dance. I'd never heard such a resonant sound. As far as I knew, no human or member of the Fae could have replicated the bass in the somber melody. It was so powerful it made the air inside my lungs vibrate.

"What is that?" I asked Lorreth. "What are they singing?"

"A welcome dirge," he answered. "A traditional song of the satyrs. Nuanced. It's the song you would sing to a family member of a dear friend you've lost. It's...like a promise. That you will show the love and respect you can no longer give to your friend to the living who still share their blood. It's complicated. The satyrs have a song for everything. They're too dramatic and flowery for my tastes."

The satyrs' voices were thunderous, the tone so droning, that I couldn't separate one word from another. Despite Lorreth's less-than-favorable critique, the music still made the hair on my arms stand to attention. The song was moving.

"What should I *do?*" Carrion mouthed over the tops of the satyrs' heads.

I performed a one shoulder shrug, unable to answer that question for him.

Carrion scowled and then set out toward us, gingerly picking a path around the kneeling satyrs, who didn't seem to notice he was on the move at first. When they did notice, they hurriedly spun around on their knees so as not to give him their backs.

Carrion looked a little unhinged when he pitched up at the top of the steps. "I bet you're loving this, Fane."

"I was actually just thinking how inconvenient this is. Not to mention how disappointed they're all going to be when you tell them you won't be challenging Belikon for the throne."

Carrion went to speak, about to volley back a tart response, no doubt, but then the satyrs' singing cut off. The female who'd addressed Lorreth lifted her head, fixing a potent gaze on Carrion. "We welcome you to Inishtar, sire," she said. "We would usually have arranged a festival to celebrate your arrival, but given the current circumstances, we hope you'll understand..."

Lorreth angled his body slightly, so that he could speak without the female, Galwynnian, seeing. "Be careful," he cautioned. "If you say anything to acknowledge you *are* the heir to the Yvelian throne, it'll be public record. You won't be able to take it back. It'll be tantamount to declaring war against Belikon."

A tight, unhappy smile contorted Carrion's features. "Well, fuck *me,*" he whispered through clenched teeth.

"Will you address us?" Galwynnian requested. "It would be an honor to hear the son and heir of Rurik Daianthus speak."

Carrion bounced on the balls of his feet, his eyes traveling over the crowd. Above us, the birds' cries cut through the air, haunting and lonely. There were even more of them now, dancing gracefully on the thermals above the cliffs.

Thirty seconds passed.

A minute.

"Well, you'd better say *something*," Lorreth muttered.

"All right, all right. Give me a moment. I'm trying to come up with something pithy."

Gods alive. "Forget *pithy*," I hissed through my teeth. He was going to cause some sort of political incident at this rate. "Aim for short and sweet."

"Great idea. Yes. Short and sweet," Lorreth concurred.

The satyrs held their breath when Carrion opened his mouth. He swung left, then right, eyebrows creeping higher and higher toward his hairline. "My name is Carrion," he said. "Nice to meet you all. I really like your horns."

There were historians among the crowd. *Someone* would record this moment—the day the satyr community received the Daianthus heir—and when they documented the first thing their Forgotten King had said to them, it would be this:

I really like your horns.

Lorreth groaned. I managed to hold my own groan back, but it was a close thing. I sent my gaze upward, unable to look upon the confused frowns the satyrs were exchanging while keeping a straight face. My eyes caught on a bird, pinwheeling down toward the ocean . . . and the second I saw it, it struck me: the memory that had eluded me earlier.

It had been right there, a millimeter from my fingertips. It was so *obvious*! Gods and martyrs, how stupid I'd been.

I'd missed something.

And now I knew what it was.

I retreated from Carrion's side, pulse like lightning in my veins. Lorreth's head snapped around, his nostrils flaring, his pupils contracting to pinpoints as he sensed the sudden change in me. "What is it? What's wrong?"

"It's—it's *something*." A horrible answer, but I didn't know how—or have time—to explain what had just occurred to me. "I *might* know how to find Fisher."

"Wait! Let me come with you, then!"

"No, I'm sorry, Lorreth!" I called, running down the steps. "Please, I need you to watch Hayden. Where I'm going, you can't follow, anyway! I have to go alone! I'll come back and make those relics, I swear!"

46

BREAK

SAERIS

THE WAR CAMP was bustling. Fae warriors milled around fires, eating from tin pots. They wrestled in the mud. Satyrs wove through the mud-spattered tents, hawking grilled meat on skewers and roasted corn. The smell of the food—and all the blood—was maddening, but I didn't have any time for that. I'd searched half the camp by the time I'd found what, or rather *who*, I was looking for. She stood in the middle of a group of males, poring over a rumpled piece of paper. When she looked up from whatever it was that busied her, she did *not* look happy.

"Saeris," she said, folding the piece of paper and handing it off to one of her friends. "To what do we owe the pleasure?"

"I need your help, Danya."

The hair she'd lost during the attack on Irrín would grow back, but it would take time. The shorn side of her scalp was marked with stubble now, a darker blond than the rest of her hair. The warrior crooked an eyebrow at me, her surprise at war with her annoyance. "Help? From *me*?" She snorted. "Impossible. Not our precious Alchemist, admitting that something's beyond her. My ears must be deceiving me."

I did not have time for this. "Danya, ever since I got here, I've done nothing but tell anyone who will listen that I am *not* equipped to deal with the tasks that have been sent my way. I've never pretended otherwise."

She spat on the ground, her face impassive.

"I need a word with you." I eyed her friends. *"Alone."*

"If this is about Carrion Swift, you can relax, *Little Osha*. I don't have designs on your friend. Not long-term ones, anyway." She used Fisher's name for me in a cold way. Made it sound small and pathetic. Her friends bit their lips, snickering under their breath.

So this was how she wanted to play it?

Fine.

She was fucking with the wrong person if she thought I wouldn't humiliate her in front of her friends. I drew Erromar and Selanir and spun the blades in my hand, rushing her. She reached for her blade. And she was a seasoned warrior. She'd slain more feeders than I could count, but *I* wasn't a feeder. I wasn't a Fae warrior, either. I had been *human* first, and now there was a good dose of vampire blood in my veins. I was faster than I had any right to be, and I was stronger than Danya to boot. With the edges of my short swords grazing her jaw, Danya had no other option but to surrender—

But she was stupid.

So fucking *arrogant*.

She raised her hands, but the action was a ruse. She tried to grab my right wrist, to punch my own sword back into my face, but trains of thought kindled and died in my head in the time it took her to curl her fingers around my wrist.

My right foot slipped behind her left. My leg hooked inside her leg, and I slammed my left palm into her chest, right between her breasts. She left the ground and sailed through the air, and a part of me crowed with satisfaction when she landed on her ass in the mud ten feet away. I kept that part of me hidden. A good leader never demonstrated pleasure at the embarrassment of an ally. Not that I was Danya's leader...and not that I was one hundred percent sure I could call her an *ally*, but it was still poor form to gloat.

Her friends weren't laughing anymore. They averted their eyes, looking anywhere and everywhere but at Danya, as I trudged through the mud and held out my hand to the female. I kept my expression blank and my voice even as I repeated, "I need your help."

She glowered at me, all venom and suspicion. "And why would I *help* you, Alchemist? You've been nothing but a thorn in my side since you arrived in this realm." She sneered at my hand as if it were a dune asp, reared back and ready to strike.

"You'll help me because we're on the same team," I told her. "Because, despite how many fights you pick with him and how angry you are with him, Fisher is still your commander, and you still love him."

Her objection was instantaneous. "I don't love hi—"

I cut her off. "Yes. You *do*. I don't mean romantically, and you know it. You love Fisher because of all that he's done for this realm. Because he's always been there for you—"

"Until he *wasn't*," she snapped. I knew the anger that burned in her eyes too well. She was furious with Fisher, but not for the reasons that she pretended.

"Yes, until he wasn't," I said, agreeing. "But you're not angry with *him* for leaving you, are you, Danya? You're angry with yourself for not believing in him enough to start with. You knew he'd never abandon his warriors, and yet you chose to hide behind the lie Belikon told. That was easier than losing your friend, wasn't it? Easier than not knowing where he was and not being able to find him, not being able to help him. He doesn't *blame* you, Danya."

"Shut the fuck up," she hissed.

"He knows you would have come for him if you could have."

"You don't know what you're fucking talking about!"

"I know Kingfisher," I said slowly. "But I haven't known him any-where near as long as you. He was your brother—your *blood*—for centuries before I was born. And I know there's no way you fought alongside him all those years without forming an unshakable bond with him. This rage inside of you is a shield. It protects you from the emotions you can't face. From the guilt and the knowledge that you left him in Gillethrye. You were with him on the battlements, weren't you? You helped him defend that city. When it fell, you helped him burn it. And then you listened to the vicious lies of a male you knew to be evil, and you left your friend there, to suffer in that eternal maze—"

"Stop."

Her tone lacked its previous acid. The word was small, a hiccup of a thing, jarring the air between us. Danya stared at me, propping herself up on her elbows in the mud, her eyes reflective as drowning pools. She was as stubborn as they came. She wouldn't admit that I was right. But she *couldn't* deny that I was wrong, either. "What do you *want* from me, Alchemist?" she muttered.

"Want? *Hah!*" Laughter boiled up the back of my throat. I clamped my lips shut and caught it before it could burst out of my mouth and make me look crazy. *Feeling* crazy was enough, thank you very much. "It's very simple, Danya. You'll probably even enjoy it. I want you to punch me in the face as hard as you can."

Danya's eyes widened. "What?"

"I need you to knock me out."

She recoiled, sinking deeper into the mud. "You're insane," she said.

"Probably. But it'll help save Fisher. Now, do you want to abandon him to his fate for a second time, or do you want to help him, Danya? Because there are at least three other people I can ask—"

"I'll do it," she rushed out. "I mean, I've been wanting to knock you out cold ever since I met you. I'd be a fool to turn down the opportunity, wouldn't I?"

"That's the spirit. You should hit me right here, under the—"

The female leaped to her feet. She swung, and I saw it coming. I did nothing to stop her. I'd asked for it anyway. What would have been the poi—

———✝———

Dust motes hung in the frigid air. They caught the eerie light that prowled in through the windows but didn't move, as if they had been frozen in place. The dining table was set for eight. In the center of the table, a copper tureen shuddered, its lid rattling. The plates were piled high with delicacies: roasted fowl, buttered vegetables, miniature pies, and trenchers full of gravy. All of it was rotten. Maggots crawled among the meat. Flies crawled over the silverware and feasted on the decay. At each place setting, crystal goblets overflowed with viscous black liquid, moving...gods, there was something *moving* inside the glasses.

My surroundings drew in tight as I realized where I was. This wasn't the huntsman's cottage. I'd focused very hard, right before Danya's fist had found my jaw, to make sure I *wouldn't* wake up there. I was right where I needed to be—in *Cahlish*.

The windows were all smashed out in the dining room, just as they had been the first time I'd encountered the feeders. A fire spat in the hearth, but the flames were not yellow. They weren't even the strange green of evenlight. They were gray and black, the color of smoke and shadow, though there was nothing brilliant or magical about it. It was just a lifeless fire, all the vibrancy drained from it and gone.

The rot covered the walls and crept along the baseboards. Black tendrils of malignant power, searching for something biological to feast upon. It had already drained the house. The paint peeled from the cracked walls. The rugs were worn to ash, the floorboards beneath brittle and dry as ancient old bones.

Even here, in my dream, Cahlish had been claimed. It was a hollow shell of what it had been just yesterday, and seeing it like this, so faded and dead, tore something at the root of my soul. The faces of the males and females in the paintings on the walls, Fisher's ancestors all, looked down on me with consternation, as if they blamed me for the state of their home and hoped that I would *do* something about it. But there was nothing to be done. Cahlish was gone.

"*Fisher!*"

My shout echoed through the infected estate. I held my breath and waited.

Waited...

"Kingfisher! Where are you?"

Only my own panicked shout came back to me.

Where are you?

…are you?

Gods. This was *not* good. I'd had so many questions back in the huntsman's cottage. Pertinent questions that I should have asked, like, "Hey, how does any of this work? How did we end up here? How do we control where we go or what we do in this place?" And, most importantly, "Will you always be here if *I'm* here?" But I hadn't asked any of those questions, because Fisher had seemed as bemused by the whole thing as me. He hadn't had the first fucking clue why we'd ended up in that cottage, even though we were in entirely different realms. And now, here I was, unconscious in the dreamscape version of Cahlish, and I had no idea if Fisher was here.

I'd tried to go to sleep, but my thoughts had been spinning so fast I knew there was no way I was going to fall asleep naturally. Ergo, finding Danya at the camp. Ergo the black eye I was bound to have whenever I woke up…

"Fisher!"

No cry came back to me. Nothing. Only the sad, desolate echo of a house that had been full of life only yesterday. Was this what it was like in reality? Was the rot choking the stonework and rooting into the foundations of the building?

It was heartbreaking to see the estate like this, under attack and dying, but I didn't have time to lament the loss. I'd hoped Fisher would be here, so I could talk to him and find out where the hell he was in reality, but if he wasn't here in this dreamscape, then I couldn't afford to linger. I had another task to tend to, and I was praying I wasn't too late.

The door fell off its hinges when I tugged it open. It crumpled to the floor, dry as a husk. The rot snaked a path across the floor, filaments of glossy black corruption rearing into the air, searching for… *me?* Was I real here? Could the rot sense me as I hurried down the hallway? Could it infect me here? It wouldn't pay to find out.

My footfalls echoed loudly as I hurried along the hallway, passing drawing rooms, the library, and a dozen other closed doors as I made my way to the stairs. The sole of my right boot had just hit the first step when there was a prodigious groan overhead; I looked up just in time to see the crystal chandelier above fall from the cracked ceiling.

"Fuck!"

I leaped back with no time to spare, and the crystal prisms and festoons shattered against the steps. My pulse beat out an erratic tattoo as I looked at the spot on the stairs where I'd just stood, and the giant hole that now yawned open like a snarling mouth in the ceiling. The rot dripped from the ruined plasterwork, *pat, pat, patt*ing onto the ground beside me.

Gods alive, this place was *not* safe.

I needed to get out of here and fast.

The foundations of the house shuddered as I skirted around the chandelier and bolted up the stairs, taking them two at a time. The rot hadn't succeeded in smashing the windows up here yet. The glossy black vines spiderwebbed up the walls and almost covered the glass in the windowpanes completely, though, shutting out the fading light.

At the end of the long hallway, Fisher's bedroom door was closed. I went to open it and wrenched my hand back, cursing through my teeth. The handle was cold as ice. Colder. The metal felt as though it had been forged in the fifth circle of hell itself. A red welt marked my palm, as angry and painful as if I'd just closed my hand around a poker that had been left in a fire too long. It hurt to make a fist. It fucking hurt to keep my hand open, too.

Another fit of cursing under my breath.

"You don't want me to go in there, do you?" The accusation was for the rot. For the house itself. Clearly, neither wanted me here. I took a moment to study the door—why wasn't it splintering and dry like all of the other woodwork in the house?—and quickly assessed where best to show it to the sole of my boot. Decision made, I kicked the door right by the handle as hard as I could...

...and nothing happened.

The door held strong.

I tried again.

And again.

And *again*.

The wood didn't even scuff, and I put everything I had behind my kicks. My Fae and vampire strength combined should easily have brought the damned thing off its hinges, and yet it didn't budge. A scream built in my throat, gaining momentum, but I clamped my jaw shut and focused.

I didn't need brute strength for this. I had something better. I'd blown a twenty-foot-wide hole in the side of Ammontraíeth's library with my power, hadn't I? I could take out a fucking *door*.

Hand outstretched, I summoned my power, trying to remember what it felt like back in the library, right before I'd blasted that hole in the stonework. The prickling, the tingling, the powerful rush, and then the wave of adrenaline that had cascaded through me as the magic fired out of me.

It rose inside me. I closed my mind around the surging sensation, attempting to stem the flow a little, to control how much of it would jettison out of me...and it worked. Kind of. The bolt of white-blue energy that burst from my hand wasn't quite as astronomical as it had been back at the Black Palace, but it was pretty damned close. Surprise rocked me as the magic slammed into the wall. I hadn't even really believed my magic would work; this *was* a dream, after all.

The very *instant* the magic came into contact with the door—and its frame and three feet of wall on either side—I knew I'd made a mistake. The tendrils of rot that covered the wood pulsed, flaring white, then doubled in size right before my eyes.

The threads of dark power expanded, working itself into knots, forming a hard shell over the door—

"Oh, come on! You've gotta be fucking *kidding* me!" The rot had *absorbed* my power. Tiny white-blue orbs glowed inside its vines, traveling through the crosshatched network of threads that now barred the door. I'd made it worse, infinitely so, and it was my own fucking fault.

Fisher and Ren had used their power on the infected feeders, and it had only made them more powerful. I should have known my magic would do the same thing here.

Idiot.

Okay. So I couldn't use my power. I couldn't force the door open. So what *could* I do? What was missing? There had to be some way to get inside that bedroom. This was a dream. It shouldn't have been this hard. This was—

I stilled, chewing on my bottom lip as I stared at the cursed door.

This was *my* dream.

I was here right now because *I'd* willed it. Back in Zilvaren, I'd made a game out of changing the face of my dreams as a child. I'd willed the sky pink. I'd willed it so that the desert became an ocean. Later, when I was older, I'd willed it so that my mother wasn't dead.

I *would* will this godscursed door open.

I closed my eyes and focused. I pictured the door. I imagined it free of the rot. In my mind, it opened easily, swinging open. I opened my eyes again...

...and the door was *still* closed.

The gods and all four winds take this fucking place. I gnawed on the end of my thumbnail, thinking furiously. How was I going to do it? I could run back down to the forge and get a crowbar. No, that wouldn't work. I'd used enough force to kick the thing down just now and it hadn't even cracked. A crowbar wouldn't work, and I couldn't risk touching the rot. The door was obviously warded. Magic was keeping me out, which meant that I'd need magic to get in. A different kind of magic, then. Something...

I stopped chewing my thumbnail, staring down at the back of my hand.

Wow. I wasn't thinking clearly *at all*.

The quicksilver rune was sealed there in metallic blue-black. The brimstone rune was outlined, requesting to be sealed. I had work to do before I accomplished *that*. There was research to be done, and challenges to be faced. Edina had said that sealing the rune—and being able to access its magic as a result—would cost me dearly. I hadn't even felt a glimmer of power coming from the brimstone rune yet, so that was no help. But then there was the third rune. Gods, the *third* rune, which the Hazrax had given me! It was right there. And what had he called it? A rune for undoing? For breaking? He'd said it didn't give me magic. It gave me an ability. If I used it on the door...

I closed my mind and sought it out. There *was* an energy there. I'd felt it the other night, quiet but powerful, when I'd gone to Tal's bedside and severed the spellwork he'd let Iseabail ink into his chest. I'd been afraid of it, then. I hadn't been in control, hadn't had a clue what was happening. But now...

I reached for the Hazrax's rune and held it as tightly as I could. It woke and answered inside the same breath. The ink didn't light up on the back of my hand. No energy surged through me. I knew it was listening thanks to the faint, barely there vibration that buzzed at the ends of my fingertips.

"Break," the Hazrax had said.

I probed for the warding spell that guarded the door. I found it there, wispy and intangible, the vaporous strands of magic slipping through my fingers as if it were sentient and determined to elude me. I lunged for it in my mind, grasping with all my focus, and before it could slip away again, I *broke* it.

The Hazrax's rune tingled briefly, and the rot that encased the door crumbled. It had been thrumming with power a second ago— admittedly, an awful lot of that power *mine*—and now its vines were desiccated husks. They withered and broke apart as the door opened at last...and revealed Kingfisher sitting in the high-backed chair in front of the fire.

———+———

"What the hell are you *doing*? Didn't you hear me trying to kick the door down?"

Fisher stared into the fire. His hair was wet, the ends made spiky, curling in every direction. Water dripped onto his leathers and onto the wooden floorboards, where it formed a large puddle. He had been sitting here for some time.

The room was cold.

The fire in the grate was colorless, all shadow-black, blizzard-gray.

"Fisher? Fisher, look at me!"

He didn't move.

I stepped into the room and something crunched, gritty, beneath my feet. *Sand.* The sand from Yvelia that Fisher had poured from his boots only days ago. There were still two piles of it, sitting there, in the middle of the floor. The sight brought tears to my eyes. He'd held me that day. Laughed with me. Shown me what it meant to be loved and worshipped by someone body, mind, and soul. He had told me here, in the bed on the other side of the room, that he would sacrifice the sun and surrender the stars if it meant that he could keep me safe.

And now he was missing and lost to me...because I could already tell he *wasn't* here with me now.

I didn't want to cross the room and stand in front of his chair. I didn't want to turn around and face him...but I had to.

I covered my mouth with my hands, stifling a sob when I saw him. His eyes were clouded over, the vivid green turned to murk and shadow. His pallor was deathly, his skin cadaverous. His bottom lip was split wide open, and a steady, thin trickle of blood ran down his chin and dripped down onto the silver wolf-head gorget he still wore around his neck.

"Fisher?"

He didn't answer. Worse, he showed no sign of having heard me at all. Whatever his eyes were seeing, it wasn't the fireplace or his room at Cahlish. Or me. Wherever he had gone, it was somewhere I could not follow.

"Fisher, please." His hand was freezing, his fingers stiff. He could take on the entire realm with these hands normally, but when I lifted his left hand and took it in mine, it was so limp and lifeless that for a terrible moment I thought that he was dead.

His rasping breaths refuted this, but it was hard to trust the shallow rise and fall of his chest when his lips were so blue.

I squeezed his hand, begging him to respond both out loud and into his head.

"Fisher. Fisher, you *promised*."

Had he promised? I couldn't remember. The Fae were loath to make promises they weren't one hundred percent sure they could keep. He wouldn't have been able to promise that he would never leave me. Death would have claimed one of us eventually...

"Wake up," I whispered. "Wake...the fuck...up. Are you seriously going to do this to me? Are you going to leave me here alone, to fix this without you? This—" I huffed, my desperation rising. "This is your *fucking* realm, Fisher. Your friends. Your people. And you're just going to disappear and leave it to everyone else to defend them?"

His right eye twitched—the tiniest flicker of movement—but then he was still again. Could he hear me? Did he know, wherever he was, that I was here? There was no way of telling.

"Fisher, if you love me...If you care about me, or...or any of us, you will figure this out and wake up right now. We need you. *I* need you—"

"Save your breath, King Killer."

The voice took me by surprise. I'd been so fixated on Fisher that I hadn't heard it enter the room. The Hazrax hovered by the bed, its hands tucked formally inside the belled sleeves of its robes. Its pale skin was shot through with black veins—the same kind of black veins that marked the infected feeders. The former Keeper of Silence drifted across the floorboards, making that eerie ticking sound in the back of its throat.

"Wait. Stay over there. This isn't your dream, okay? You're not *welcome* here."

The Hazrax snorted. "I am welcome everywhere, Saeris. Do you forget so quickly that you and I have a deal?"

"The deal was for you to observe the Blood Court. I hate to break it to you, but the Blood Court doesn't exist anymore, so you're going to have to find someone else to observe."

The Hazrax grimaced, showing its needle teeth. I'd been around it long enough to know that it was smiling. "You're really hopeless at this, aren't you, child? I almost feel bad for you."

"What's that supposed to mean?"

"That means that when you asked me in the forge if I wanted to strike the same bargain with you that I struck with Malcolm and I said yes, the details of my deal with the old vampire king became the details of our arrangement, too. The fine print of the deal I made with Malcolm stated that I could observe him, not his court. *Him.* It is irrelevant whether the Blood Court exists, Saeris. It is *you* who I observe. Wherever you go, whatever you do, you have given me permission to follow and witness alongside you."

Gods fucking damn it.

Again! I'd walked into another terrible bargain *again*! If I made it out of this nightmare and life somehow found some level of normalcy, I was going to make sure I had someone on hand at all times to vet the agreements I made. The sneaky, underhanded, vile piece of shit! "Why? Why do you care about what I'm doing? This has *nothing* to do with you!"

The Hazrax's slitted nostrils flared. "Naive child," he said in a piteous tone. "Of course it does. I have a hand in everything, but you will learn that soon enough, I suspect."

"Wait! The—the favor! You said I could call it in at any time."

The Hazrax made a hiccupping sound, but it nodded. "Yes. That is true."

"Then I want to use my favor now. Can you bring Fisher back to me?"

The Hazrax shook its head. "That is not within my power, I'm afraid. There are accords that prevent it."

"Then tell me where he is!"

"I'm sorry. I cannot do that, either." The Hazrax didn't sound apologetic. It sounded amused by the situation I found myself in and pleased that it couldn't help. I'd had enough of it. "Fine," I snarled. "I'll use my favor for this, then. I want you to go away and *not* observe me for the rest of the term of our one-year agreement. And when you come back to renegotiate the deal for another year like *I* stipulated, you should know ahead of time that I will not be interested in renewing."

"Be *careful*, Saeris," the Hazrax warned.

"What, don't lie to me and say that you can't do that. I'm literally asking you to leave me the fuck alone. That is *definitely* in your power."

"It is," the Hazrax said, laughing its strange, stilted laugh.

"Then don't bother threatening me—"

"I'm not *threatening* you, silly child," it snapped, its humor suddenly gone. "I'm suggesting you err on the side of caution because, per our agreement, you only get to ask me for *one* favor. And you desperately need that favor right now, Saeris Fane."

"Of course you'd say that! Just honor the request!"

The Hazrax shivered, as though the magic that bound our agreement were trying to force it to comply. I'd never seen anything like it: a being capable of denying a bargain, even for a moment. "First, answer me this. Why did you come here, child?" the Hazrax demanded.

"I came here for *him!*"

It shook its head. "No."

"I came..." I remembered, then. The realization I'd had on the steps in Inishtar. The piece of information that had come back to me as Carrion had addressed the satyrs.

"I will allow you to change your mind," the Hazrax said. "You have one minute to fulfill the task you came here to complete and request a *different* favor. I suggest you *move*."

One minute. In exactly sixty seconds, the Hazrax would disappear, and I wouldn't see it again for a year. And that would be bliss. But... what if it was right? What if I needed my favor for something else?

Another shudder rippled through the Hazrax's body. "You're wasting time!" it hissed.

I let go of Fisher's hand and sprinted across the room. The nightstand by the bed was cluttered with books. So many books. There were pencils, and an empty water glass that I knocked over. It shattered on the ground, but I ignored the broken glass. String. A length of leather cord...

Where the fuck is it?

I put it here, I know *I did.*

"Forty seconds..."

"Shut *up*! That's not helping!" I vaulted over the bed and picked through the sparse items on Fisher's nightstand. I hadn't put it there, but maybe it had been moved? Fisher was tidier than me. A single book. An ivory-toothed comb...no, no, it wasn't here.

Shit! Where else could it be? Where else? Where *else*! Fisher's desk was bare. The windowsill, choked with black veins of rot, was empty. The shelves...

"Twenty-five seconds."

I didn't waste my breath admonishing the asshole this time. There was nowhere else to look! There was...

No. Wait. There! On the bookshelf.

I'd seen it before. When I'd found Archer in here, drawing me a bath. His friends had been helping. One of them had been looking at the items sitting on the shelf in front of the books. Lady Edina's favorite thing in the world...

I ran across the room and picked up the tiny ceramic figurine of the kingfisher bird.

Its left wing was chipped. Its blue and orange glaze was a little faded, thanks to the many years it had sat on this shelf, but otherwise it was perfect. I saw what had been placed underneath the figurine immediately: a small, crumpled piece of paper.

The same crumpled piece of paper I'd dumped on my nightstand a week ago, along with all the other bits and pieces I'd been carrying in my pockets.

But it wasn't a crumpled piece of paper.

It was a *folded* piece of paper...artfully crafted into the shape of a stargazer.

It was the *first* little bird. The one that had lost its magic and fallen to the ground when it had left the library.

The missing page from Edina's journal, not torn out, because it had never been bound *in*. I'd had it here all along!

"Ten seconds, Saeris!" the Hazrax warned.

My hands trembled as I unfolded the bird and frantically began to read.

The words ran together, Edina's neat handwriting swimming on the paper as I tried to process the information she had written there.

"Five seconds!" There was genuine concern in the Hazrax's voice.

I looked up from the paper, suddenly covered in a nervous sweat, and spoke as quickly as I could. "I've changed my mind, watcher! I beg you for my favor. I need you to transport me to the Wicker Wood!"

47

UNLESS...

SAERIS

I DIDN'T HAVE a choice.

Edina's message had told me exactly where I could find my mate and had given me the tools to save, him, too. What it *hadn't* given me was the means to reach him in time. That part, she had said, was up to me. So I'd done what I'd had to. A full year with the Hazrax looking over my shoulder, in exchange for a one-way ticket to the Wicker Wood.

I'd held the page bearing Edina's instructions as tightly as I could in my hands when the Hazrax had told me to brace myself, but three seconds later, when I awoke on my back in the snow, it was no longer there. It didn't matter. The information I needed was seared into my memory now. The chances of forgetting what I'd read were absolute zero.

Fog billowed on my breath. Overhead, the bare branches of the trees scraped at the night sky like twisted fingers. The sky was clear for once, and the stars stippled the heavens in a breathtaking display. The Hazrax's robed form appeared suddenly in my field of vision, making me jump. Its eyes shone reflectively in the dark, as if they were brushed with silver.

I waited for it to make some kind of cryptic remark, or at least tell me to hurry, but it said nothing. I got to my feet. "Well, since you seem to know so much about all of this, which way do I need to go?"

The Hazrax didn't make a peep.

I shivered against the cold as I got to my feet and brushed myself off. "Seriously? *Now?* After all the interfering, you're going back to *watching?*"

The creature just looked at me. I took its silence as a very annoying yes. "All right. Fine. I don't need you anyway."

I didn't. I could feel Fisher now. In a roundabout way. What I could actually feel was the *tiny* thread of quicksilver that was still trapped in his eye. It was a negligible amount—barely enough to be worth mentioning. Before I'd sealed my quicksilver rune, I probably wouldn't have been able to sense it. Now, that tiny sliver of metal stood out like a flickering flame in a sea of darkness.

He was here, and I *was* going to find him.

The Hazrax floated an inch above the ground, gliding along behind me as I set off into the woods. It cut a ghostly figure as we hurried through the trees...but no more ghostly than the shades themselves. Fisher had told me about them the last time I'd found myself in this wretched wood: the souls of the damned, condemned to haunt these woods, constantly reliving their gruesome deaths as punishment for their crimes. Fisher had offered to give me the Sight, so I could see the shades for myself. I had not-so-politely declined. But I was Fae now. I had the Sight whether I wanted it or not, and the visions that stalked me as I ran through the trees were downright horrific.

A female in a tattered gown, dragging a dead infant behind her through the snow.

A mutilated male, screaming and on fire as he sprinted across the pathway up ahead.

Another male with chains wrapped around his body and attached to a large, transparent boulder, who thrashed and writhed, head tipped back as he seemingly drowned, and drowned, and drowned...

Everywhere I looked, the souls of the dead endured their torment on a loop. They howled and cried, the sound sending convulsions of dread up and down my spine.

Fisher was *here*. From his appearance back in the dreamscape of Cahlish, he was suffering along with the dead. Alive for now, at least, but *why*? And how?

I'd only been running through the forest for five minutes before I stumbled into a campsite. No fire. No smoke. There had been *nothing* to warn me of the group of warriors, lurking in the dark up ahead. I didn't see them until it was too late.

Five? Eight? I scrambled to count, but they were already moving, drawing bows and reaching for blades.

Ten warriors at least.

No words were exchanged.

The carnage commenced.

I'd had my short swords back in the camp with Danya. I hadn't had them in the dreamscape. Mercifully, they *were* at my hips now. I didn't know how the Hazrax had done it, but it had transported my physical body from Inishtar, weapons and all.

Thanking the gods and all four winds, I drew my weapons and prepared to fight like hell.

The first male to my left came for me. His blade cut through the air, whistling close to my ear, but didn't find its target. I ducked, shoving the metal in the blade away with my mind, and was met with immediate resistance.

Fucking *null* blade.

They all had them. The unnatural weapons felt like blind spots in my vision—black holes, sucking at my energy and the magic of the woods itself. I couldn't manipulate them. Couldn't shove them away like I might have been able to with a normal sword or dagger. Just as I had back in Ammontraíeth's sepulcher, I was going to have to fight these fuckers the normal way, without using my magic to disarm them ... but I was ready for it.

These motherfuckers had taken my mate. They had him trapped here, I knew it. They had officially fucked up, and *boy*, were they about to pay.

One of the warriors with a bow loosed an arrow. They'd learned from their mistakes back in the tomb: the tips of their arrows weren't made of iron this time. They were crafted from the same material as the null blades. The arrow maintained its course, coming straight for me...

I ducked, seizing the opportunity to bat aside another attacker's null blade as he came in to slash at my side. Parrying the attack, I flicked Erromar around, ripping the null blade from the guard's hand. The null blade sailed off into the dark. I flipped Erromar over in my hand and plunged the god sword in between the fucker's ribs, lighting him up from the inside.

Holy fire blazed out of the male's eyes and mouth as he died.

The arrow had thudded into a tree now on my right. I ripped it free from the trunk and ran at another guard, plunging the appropriated weapon into his neck. As I spun away, I caught another warrior across the back of her legs with Selanir, and the female went down with a blunted cry. She'd be back up on her feet in a second, but I only needed a second to step over her and inside the guard of yet another attacker. This one was huge. A mean scar twisted his skin from his temple, down his left cheek, through both lips, and down under his chin. He snarled, baring his teeth as he grabbed me by the throat and squeezed.

Fuck. Oh, fuck. Oh, fuck...

My vision danced.

Lorreth's voice screamed at me from the past, urging me into action. *"Move, Saeris! Fucking move! Do you want to die?"*

I wasn't dying here. Not tonight. No fucking way.

None of these assholes was going to stop me from finding my mate.

The male jerked, his eyes going wide. Disbelief rendered his features slack as he looked down and saw the two glowing short swords sticking out of his chest. As he dropped me, I pulled back Erromar and Selanir, then drove them into his massive torso again, again, again—

"For the love of the gods, *contain* her!" a rumbling bellow demanded. "She's one single female! Take her to the ground!"

That voice haunted my nightmares. In Gillethrye, the owner of that voice had mocked my mate. He had crowed with satisfaction as he'd encouraged Fisher to explain the bargain he'd used to trick him into one hundred and ten years of misery. I couldn't see him, but he *was* here: Belikon De Barra, king of a stolen throne, oppressor of an entire court.

A hail of arrows streamed through the air. I dropped to the ground and rolled, gritting my teeth against the pain that exploded in my mouth. I'd bitten my tongue. *Fuck*, that hurt. I pushed the throb of it away, freeing myself from it.

"Now! She's done the hard work for you! *Pin her!*" Belikon raged. One of the archers threw himself on top of me, obeying his king's command. I drove Erromar up into his armpit, and the point of the burning white god sword burst out of the side of his neck. Smoke puffed out of the guard's mouth, and then he was dead.

Another came, and then another, and another. I let them pile on top of me. A nauseating jolt of pain fired up my leg—impossible to push away this time—but I forced myself to bear it, waiting for the right moment.

A fourth set of hands tried to grab me, fingers digging into my throat again, and I let go.

My quicksilver rune wasn't just useful for manipulating metals and making relics. It was also great at expelling *very* large amounts of power in *very* short blasts.

None of the guards had noticed the rune on the back of my right hand glowing brighter and brighter, lighting up the thick, oddly shaped tree trunks that surrounded us. Belikon apparently noticed, though, but far too late to save his men. "Back! Pull back! She's going to—"

My shield blazed to life, and the interlocking Alchimeran runes projected in the air shone like a falling star. The quicksilver icon burned brightest, pulsing. When I flicked my wrist, the shield rotated, the icon growing larger...

Magic roared inside me, swelling, mounting, growing...

Belikon's mouth fell open as he watched my shield detonate, and the force of the resulting pulse of energy launched the guards into the air and obliterated them. A fine mist of blood and pulverized meat rained down, speckling the snow red.

Six of them were dead now? Seven? I'd lost count. I got up again, ready for the next attack... but no one came.

Belikon De Barra stared in wonder at the shield still hovering in the air in a way that made panic chase along my nerves. "Spectacular," he breathed. "Never before have I seen such layered power. It cannot be allowed to exist in this world, unless it is bound to *me*."

"Well, I guess you should have thought about that before you killed all of the other Alchemists then, shouldn't you?" I slammed my hands closed, and the shield snapped out of existence. I shouldn't have let him see it. The madness in his eyes declared that he'd never stop until he'd found a way to chain me to him now, and that prospect was terrifying.

"Is that what they told you? That *I* killed off your kind? You should do more research before—"

"I don't want to hear it. Before you start spinning lies—"

"Insolent female! You are too fond of interrupting your betters! Hold your tongue. You won't make it out this wood without my say-so," he barked.

Chest heaving, I lowered Erromar and Selanir to my sides and spat on the ground, running him through with the most contemptuous look I could muster. "*Won't* I?"

"No. You won't. And you know *why* you won't, too. You will stand right there, and you will behave yourself, because you want your mate to live. Orious, why don't you show the little Alchemist where her precious dog has been spending his time the past few days?"

Orious.

That sniveling, greasy piece of shit.

He was here, too?

Yes. The rail-thin male stepped out from behind a tree, chin held high as he met my gaze. "I warned you, girl. You had your chance. This could have all been much easier. Much less... *painful* for you."

"*Fuck* you, Orious. Tell me where Fisher is."

Off to Orious's left, the Hazrax hovered in the dark, eerily lumines-cent in the moonlight, *watching*...

"Oh, but he's right in front of you, girl," Orious purred. "Don't you see?"

Belikon's seneschal casually stepped to one side, moving out of the way, and suddenly I *did* see. The woods pitched, the trees seesawing, and a brutal cry cut through the night air. At first, I thought the blood-curdling scream had come from one of the Wicker Wood's tortured shades, but then I tasted blood, and I realized it had come from me. I'd screamed so loud that I'd torn my fucking throat open.

A monstrous tree stood before me, fifty feet tall, its bark black as sin. A huge rent ran down the center of its trunk—a split in its wood so rotten and foul that it actually looked like a *wound*. That's where Fisher was, at the center of that wound. The lower part of the tree looked like it had healed around his body. All the way up to his shoul-ders, in fact, the wood had grown around my mate, caging his body inside it. It had almost swallowed him whole.

Fisher's eyes were closed, his eyelashes a stark black ink against his cheeks. His hair was plastered to his head. He looked far worse than back in the dream—seconds away from death. At the base of the tree, Nimerelle rested on top of a flat piece of stone, spewing clouds of thick shadow from her blade. Fisher's god sword was not happy in the slight-est. "What are you *doing* to him?" I whispered.

Belikon grinned a wolfish grin then turned his back on me, con-fident now that he had my attention. "You may recall, when we met first, Saeris, that I said this male, this... *dog*, was to face trial for his part in the death and destruction that took place in my beloved city of Gillethrye. He fled my palace without my knowledge and then sought harbor in an illegally warded refuge. Since he refused to stand before the court that he serves and give his account of what happened at Gillethrye—"

"You fucking monster. He didn't have anything to do with those people's deaths," I spat.

"—the trial was conducted without him and judgment rendered in his absence." Belikon's grin widened to terrifying, unnatural degrees. "As you might have guessed, he was found guilty of mass genocide. Why he would have killed so many of his own people remains a mystery," he said, a false airiness in his voice. "But as a just and fair king who cares about the welfare of his subjects, there was only one thing for me to do." He fixed me in his gaze then, his expression going blank, and I saw the cold, evil thing inside him, peering out from behind his rheumy eyes. "I sentenced him to life imprisonment, of course. Here, in an oubliette."

"What is it doing to him? Why is it trapping him like that?" I *hated* the panic in my voice. I *hated* the way it shook.

"Tell her, Orious," Belikon said in a bored voice. "The Alchemist will learn eventually. And it's better for us if she understands her predicament sooner rather than later."

Orious, bootlicker that he was, bowed until he was bent double at the waist. "Certainly, Your Majesty." He rose and set about explaining. "You might assume that you are surrounded by trees right now, but you would be wrong. These are no ordinary trees. They were once a clan of dryads. Self-righteous and arrogant as they were, they took it upon themselves to stand up to one of the northern witch clans. No one really remembers why. That doesn't matter. What matters is that they lost their feud and suffered the consequences forthwith. The witches cursed the dryads and turned them into these prisons. They were damned to find no solace or comfort in the daylight that they worshipped and instead were doomed to feed only on the suffering and misery of others. The witches transformed the dryads into everything they abhorred...and here they still stand today, fueled by the fear and the never-ending pain of those they house inside of them. They keep their prisoners alive, you know. Their relationship becomes symbiotic. It's fascinating really. I have—"

"Enough, Orious. I think she understands now," Belikon intoned.

His seneschal stopped speaking, falling into an even deeper bow than the first.

To me, the king said, "These dryads are on *my* land. They exist at my discretion. They obey me in everything, and in return I keep them fed. Try to cut this one down or hack your mate free, and it will kill him in an instant. They've turned into spiteful things over the years." He laughed. "I have to admit, I admire their ability to inspire such fear into their captives. Sometimes, if you place your hand against their trunks, they'll show the symphony of terror they are conducting inside the minds of those they harbor within."

"Let him *go*," I seethed. "You know Malcolm's horde killed the people of Gillethrye. Fisher had nothing to do with it!"

"Fisher has been nothing but trouble since the moment he was born, and the only way I will suffer him to live is like *this*, where he can't stir up my people and cause any more trouble. He will remain here until I am satisfied he no longer poses a threat to my crown. He will stay here," he repeated, "until I have seen you bow before the Firinn Stone and you have rendered yourself Oath Bound into my service. You will accept this without complaint, and after you have proven yourself to me...become my tool to wield, eventually, in a couple thousand years, I may set him free. This is the only way he lives, girl," Belikon sneered. "Make your peace with it."

I would not make my peace with it. Never in a million years. But Belikon didn't know that. He thought he had me cornered with nowhere to go. I nodded to the god sword still churning out black smoke on the stone at the foot of Fisher's prison. "And Nimerelle?" I asked. "What happens to Fisher's god sword while he's trapped inside this prison for thousands of years?"

Belikon's gaze was feverish as it fell upon the sword in question.

CALLIE HART

"Since Kingfisher stole what was rightfully mine and took Solace when he fled the palace, it's only right that I take *his* god sword from *him*. Soon, the oubliette will consume your mate. When the dryad encapsulates him fully, it will not kill him, but he will enter a state very much like death. The bond between god sword and male will be broken, and Nimerelle will be mine. A gratifying justice, I think. With such a legendary god sword in my hand, I will bring those who refuse to bow before me to their knees by force. For the good of Yvelia—" His words died on his lips. "Wait. What are you doing?"

I had used the time while he was speaking to press Erromar and Selanir together. The short swords had become one again, reforming Solace. The singular sword *was* far bigger than was comfortable for me, but I could wield it just fine. And I was going to need *two* hands for what was coming next.

"He isn't staying in that thing." It was a statement. A simple fact.

Orious barked out harsh laughter, though he shuffled his feet. "Stubborn until the end, Your Majesty. What did I tell you? She can't be reasoned with."

But Belikon wasn't listening to his seneschal. He was staring, eyes narrowed into slits, at me. "What are you hiding, girl? What do you know?"

I took a step forward. "I know the history of that god sword over there. Do *you*?"

The bastard's frown deepened. He drew his cloak about him, arranging the fabric so that it hung correctly at his feet. "It is a sword, half-breed. Swing and it cuts. What else do I need to know?"

"It was given to Fisher by the gods themselves. Did you know that it's made of iron?"

The king laughed dismissively. "Don't be stupid. No member of the Fae can wield iron. One second holding that in his bare hands, and the dog would have been dead. He's carried it since Ajun—"

"Since Ajun. Yes. Ajun, where he closed the iron gate that protects the city, again with his bare hands. He knew *that* would kill him.

And it should have. But Bal and Mithin chose to take pity on their favorite, didn't they? They saved him. They gave him a sword of iron, because he had shown strength enough to wield it. And there on the killing fields, his friend was slain by the dragon they fought. The very same whose skull you display behind your throne as if it were *you* who slayed him.

"You chastise me for claiming what's rightfully mine? The spoils of war *always* belong to the crown, you fool."

Another step. I was nearly close enough. Almost, now...

"Her name was Merelle, twin sister to Renfis, the male who later became general of your army."

Wrinkling his nose, Belikon shook his head. "Am I supposed to feel something? How am I supposed to remember everyone who falls in service of their king? I didn't even know the male *had* a sister."

I swallowed down the bile that rose up the back of my throat. "She died screaming. Fisher and the other members of the Lupo Proelia brought down that hateful beast, and Fisher found himself trapped inside its jaws. Merelle came to him there. Her spirit, that is. She bound her soul to that blade, so she would always be with her friends. That's why he named the sword that. Ni' Merelle. For Merelle, in Old Fae."

Orious sneered, his top lip curling in disdain. "Do not lecture us on the etymology of words formed in a language *you* do not speak."

Another step closer. Only one more, and I'd be close enough.

I made a point of ignoring Orious's jab. "The blade, then, as you can discern from the tale, is no simple god sword. It's made of iron. It houses the echo of a soul that died because of *you*. It doesn't matter if Kingfisher lives or dies. You'll *never* be able to wield Nimerelle. If the metal doesn't kill you, then the warrior who lives inside it will."

He clearly hadn't known about the iron. God swords always made the people they weren't bonded to uncomfortable. That was just the way of them. He'd put his unease around the sword down to that. He hadn't touched the sword without gloves yet. That would have been a death sentence, given who he was and the fact that the blade was still bonded to Fisher. The realization came crashing down on the king now—a hole in his plan. A disruption, souring the taste of victory in his mouth.

He tried to wave the matter off. "So be it. Fine. If no other member of the Fae can touch the damned iron, then it'll be disposed of. Buried in an unmarked site. Thrown into a chasm. It will be forgotten, and you will make me a *new* god sword—"

"There *is* one," I interrupted.

Orious's mouth flapped, his anger over the fact that I'd spoken over his precious king evident. Belikon just sighed. "One *what?*"

"One other who isn't affected by iron."

"Pray enlighten me. Who—"

"*Me.*"

I called the sword, and the sword came.

I sent up a fervent prayer as Nimerelle shot up from the stone at the foot of the tree and flew through the air...

Please don't kill me. Please don't kill me. Please *don't fucking kill*—

The sword slammed into my bare palm, and the Wicker Wood stood still as I closed my hand around the hilt of the mighty Nimerelle. A brief, unpleasant shock wave traveled up my arm, but then it was... *gone.*

There was no voice in my head. No chiding from the small thread of quicksilver it contained, nor from the gods who had made it, nor the warrior who possessed it. The faintest smell of juniper tickled the back of my nose. I heard distant, playful laughter on a breeze that wasn't there. And then, simultaneously, the god sword in my left hand formed a pillar of blazing white... and the god sword in my right erupted with a wall of shadow and smoke.

For the first time in Yvelian history, a god sword had entrusted itself into the hands of someone it wasn't bonded to. Because Kingfisher loved me. I had come here to *save* him... and that was good enough for his sword.

"Impossible," Belikon whispered. But of course it *would* seem impossible to him. A heart ruled by hatred and fear could not experience miracles. You had to know love, joy, and trust for that, and those concepts were as foreign to him as the idea of Yvelia had been to *me* not too long ago.

"He's dead. The second you touch the dryad with either of those swords, he's *dead!*" Belikon shouted.

"The swords aren't for the dryad, Belikon." I spun them end over end, trailing light and shadow. "They're for *you.*"

I'd experienced the male's power back in the throne room of the Winter Palace. I'd felt like crawling out of my own skin. Again, I'd witnessed it in Gillethrye, when Fisher had run him through with Nimerelle and the male had *not* died. His power snapped against my skin again now, as I prowled toward him. It tried to stop me in my tracks, but I wasn't the same girl who'd stood there and watched him torment her mate. I had power of my own now, and it was just as formidable as this pretender king's.

With every step I took toward him, overcoming the shield he'd thrown up around himself, Belikon's eyes widened. "What do you hope to accomplish? You cannot *kill* me, girl."

Killing him would be a win for Yvelia, but I *did* know that I wouldn't accomplish that goal tonight. That was for another day, another time, and another hand to plunge the knife. All I had to do was keep him busy long enough to say the words...

"Orious, I'm done with this nonsense," Belikon spat. "Tell the dryad to take him."

Shit. Once that tree closed around Fisher, this was over. I had to act. *Now.*

Belikon's seneschal darted toward the tree. He placed a hand on its trunk, and the whole thing shook at the contact.

I hurled Solace, throwing the sword like a spear. It struck Orious clean through the side, cleaving him straight through the chest. But the damage was already done. A groaning, cracking, creaking sound filled the air, and the open, festering trunk around Fisher's shoulders and head began to close.

Belikon was in front of me.

He'd moved so fast. *Too* fast. I'd let my focus drift for a split second, and now I was going to pay.

The air rushed out of me as he punched me in the solar plexus. I should have flown back and slammed into the tree—the *dryad*—behind me, but I didn't. I was anchored in place. Belikon had hold of me *from the inside*. He hadn't just punched me. He'd punched through my breastbone, into my chest cavity... and now he had me by the heart. "This seems to be the source of our issues here. Such a problematic piece of meat. Could you survive without it, I wonder? Halfling that you are, I still think you need your *heart*, Saeris. Are you going to make me rip it out? Or will you start behaving so that I'll let you keep it?"

I couldn't answer. I could stop my heart from beating, but I definitely still needed it to stay inside my chest. Panic cinched tight around my chest, taking hold...

"Bend the knee, Saeris," Belikon rumbled. His breath fanned over my face, foul and reeking of death.

Monster.

Murderer.

Villain.

I would rather die than chain myself to a demon like him. Blood spewed up and out of my mouth. It ran down my chin in a river and coated my tongue in metal. "I have... a message... for you," I wheezed. "From... your dead... wife."

It happened so quickly that anyone could have missed it, but not me. *I* saw the bastard flinch. I choked on another mouthful of blood. "She told me... to tell you... *never.*" Quick as lightning, I called Solace back. At the same time, I drove Nimerelle into Belikon's stomach and up, out of his back, mirroring the blow Fisher had dealt him back in Gillethrye.

The king dropped me, tottering back, eyes locked on the sword buried in his stomach and the glowing point of the other protruding from his chest. Funnels of shadow whipped around the male, spinning faster and faster, cocooning him in a lethal shroud. Cuts began to form all over his skin, crosshatched and bleeding, but they healed before they could fully form. Impaled upon the huge god swords and wreathed in smoke, he fell to his knees, but still he threw back his head and laughed. "Not enough," he bellowed. "It'll *never* be enough!"

There was a fucking hole in my chest—a *big* one—but even as I took a staggering step toward the dryad, the wound was knitting closed. It should probably have killed me. If I had been *only* Fae, or *only* vampire, that might have been the case, but it seemed my Fae powers coupled with high blood powers had increased my healing capabilities exponentially. I didn't understand it, but I'd take it. I would live long enough to finish what I'd started here, at least, and for now, that was all that mattered.

"An Oath Bound Fae male cannot walk away from the promises he makes," I said. "On pain of death, they must obey."

"Have you *just* learned this lesson, half-breed? Kingfisher is already mine to command. You may as well join him." The king moved to pull Nimerelle from his stomach, but he had nothing to hold her hilt with.

I left him where he knelt and made for the dryad. Only Fisher's face was visible now. Soon, it would be gone. "Unless..." I said under my breath. The wording was important. I had to get it right.

"What do you mean, *unless?*"

"Names hold meaning in this place. There is no power in this realm or any other that can supersede an order given using someone's true name. A true name can undo oaths. It can open doors." I pressed my hand against the dryad's trunk, and I felt him for the first time. Fisher *was* in there. And he could hear me.

Saeris...

The sound of his voice inside my head, weak though it was, filled me with courage. I steeled myself and spoke in a loud, steady voice, for all the realm to hear. This was a tricky maneuver. One that *had* to pay off. I crossed my fingers and prayed. "Kingfisher of the Ajun Gate, I hereby call you by your true name. I declare all oaths you have sworn null and void. Rise, *Khydan Graystar Finvarra*, in honor of the name you were given at birth! Rise up and *fight!*"

48

FOLLY

KINGFISHER
(Khydan Graystar Finvarra)

THE ENDLESS DARK shattered.

As it did, the lump of ice in my chest thawed and exploded like a newly formed star taking its place among the celestial sphere. Time contracted, and as I opened my eyes, the wood surrounding me came into brilliant focus.

Many new pieces of information took root in my mind at once.

I had been *inside* the shadow gate.

I'd heard Belikon's voice. I'd registered his command to come to him... and I'd been powerless to refuse. Things were blurry after that.

I knew precisely where I was now, though, and my mate's cry was still ringing in my ears like a desperate call to arms.

Rise, Khydan Graystar Finvarra, in honor of the name you were given at birth! Rise up and fight!

The name resonated in my chest, triggering something fundamental, deep within the foundations of my soul. I *knew* the name. Knew it like I knew the sky was blue and which way was up. It was a part of me—had *always* been a part of me—and now it had settled on me like a perfectly tailored cloak.

The command that came along with my name set my soul alight, but it was darkness and vengeance that poured out of me as I obeyed it. My magic thrummed, soaring up from the well of power faster than it ever had before. Glittering and furious, it slammed out of me in every direction, obliterating the cage that held me.

Not a cage. An *oubliette*.

Shards of decaying wood fired through the air like shrapnel. The air filled with smoke...

...and when it cleared, the first thing to emerge from the destruction was my mate. Was I really seeing this? She'd come for me? *By herself?*

Her hair was wild, her blue eyes wide as saucers, full of defiance and shock. Her mouth and jaw were painted red with blood. The front of her fighting leathers, too. When she saw my growing panic, she shook her head, running to close the last few feet between us. "It's okay. It's nothing. I'm fine. Belikon—"

Oh, I'd already seen *him*.

The bastard was kneeling in the churned-up snow with not one but two god swords spearing him through the chest. They weren't enough to kill him, but the iron in Nimerelle was leaching his power. That alone was keeping him on his knees. He was dressed as if for a great celebration. His thick, chocolate-brown ermine cloak was of the highest quality, though obviously ruined now thanks to the god swords. Atop his head, he wore an elaborate crown I hadn't seen before, far more ostentatious than the humble winter laurel he had stolen from Rurik Daianthus. Blood trickled from his mouth and down his narrow chin. He laughed when he saw me stalking toward him through the snow.

"If you want your sword back, you're going to have to pull it out of me. And trust me when I say you don't want to do that."

I kicked him square in the face as hard as I could, and the king sprawled on his ass in the snow. The obnoxious jeweled crown fell from his brow and went rolling off into the wood.

"I've been waiting a long time to do *that*." My voice was raw. I had screamed plenty in the hellish landscape the dryad had created for me, and it felt like I'd done all that screaming out loud.

The king lay on his side, unable to roll onto his back thanks to the swords impaling him. I had questions about how Nimerelle had become wedged between the asshole's ribs, but I was a patient male. They could wait.

"My guards are posted throughout this wood. You'll never get past them all," Belikon said.

I cocked my head, considering him. "Won't we?"

Another burst of laughter spluttered out of the king. He sighed, lying back in the snow. "You know," he said, squinting up at the sky, "you have done your mate a woeful disservice. She knows nothing of how this realm works. Nothing of our ways. Nothing of the rules that govern our existence here."

I prowled toward him, wondering where I should hurt him first. "Is that so?"

A deep, rattling cough seized the king. For a moment, he couldn't breathe. When he'd recovered again, he spoke. "She came here and used your true name to free you. And it worked. But it's a *hollow victory*," he said, emphasizing the words as if I were stupid. "She used your true name... in front of *me*. She armed me with the most powerful tool I could have hoped for. You're *fucked*, Kingfisher. Or should I say *Khydan*? Let us see if I recall it correctly, shall I? Khydan Graystar Finvarra, I command you to draw this sword from my chest and use it to kill your pretty little mate!"

The air around me shivered. His will crashed down on me, bringing me forward, urging my hand to reach for Nimerelle. I grabbed the blade. I drew it out of him. I carried it over to where Saeris stood, bloodied and swaying on her feet, and I lifted it, aiming the point of the smoking black blade at my mate's throat.

Now that he was free of Nimerelle, Belikon was slowly getting back to his feet. "Do it! I've had enough of this charade!" he barked.

Looking at my mate, I fixed her with a sorrowful smile. "I'm so sorry, Osha."

She didn't blink. Didn't move. She returned my sad smile with one of her own. "It's okay. None of this is your fault."

I swung the blade, spinning at the same time, and plunged it *back* into Belikon's chest. I drove the sword through him with both hands, slamming Nimerelle down so hard that she went straight through the sorry excuse for a male, pushing him back down to his knees and pinning him to the frozen ground.

"But—what—I—command—*commanded*—" Belikon insisted, panting out his words.

It was Saeris who stepped forward to break the news. "You see this?" she said, holding out her right hand so that he could see the back of it. The simple interlocking rune she traced with her left index finger didn't glow, but Belikon's face turned the color of ash when he saw it. "A rune for undoing. For breaking." She cut him with a bloodletting smile. "Did you really think I would be stupid enough to speak my mate's true name in front of *you* without protecting him first? You're out of your addled fucking mind. I couldn't *command* the oath he spoke to you and render it moot. But with this, I could *undo* it. And after I'd spoken his name and told him to be free, what do you think I did *then*, Belikon?"

"His name. You—you—"

She nodded. "Yes. I undid the magic that binds it. No one can use it against him now. No one will *ever* control him again."

"You poor...deluded thing." The king bared bloodstained teeth. "You are simple if you believe that. So long as...you or your friends exist, there will always be leverage to control *him*."

Pay him no heed, Osha. He'll say whatever he can to get under your skin. Let's get out of here before those other guards show up.

I knew better than to hang around. We'd gotten lucky. I hadn't been permanently trapped inside the dryad, and that was something to be *seriously* grateful for. Once you went in, you normally didn't come out again. Saeris flared her nostrils, her hatred pouring out of every pore as she slowly shoved away from the prone king. She grabbed Solace's hilt and began to draw her sword from the king's back—and a flurry of motion to our right came out of nowhere. Black, swirling robes. A rough-edged dagger slicing downward toward Saeris's neck. And then white fur and snarling teeth, and eyes the color of polished jet.

Orious had been a second away from slitting Saeris's throat...but then there was *Onyx*. The little fox raced out of the shadows and launched himself at the seneschal's face. He snarled and scratched, sinking his teeth into the thin male's jaw and cheek.

"Demon dog!" the seneschal growled. He clawed at Onyx's fur, trying to get a hold of it. "I thought you were *dead*!"

"Onyx, *no!*" Saeris was gone before I could stop her. She left Solace buried in Belikon's chest. She had the dagger I'd given her weeks ago—it was in her hand by the time she reached the male, who was cursing fitfully as he tried to shake off the fox. Canines sharp as needles sank into Orious's wrist. The male let out a howl of pain...

The fox had saved Saeris. He had already done enough. Saeris sank the dagger I'd gifted her into Orious's side, burying the Fae steel deep. I sent out tendrils of smoke at the same time, lashing the piece of shit around his ankles. My magic swirled around his torso, about to draw tight and crush his ribs, when the seneschal pivoted, snarling like a rabid beast, and slashed out at Saeris again. The weapon—a null blade, carved an arc through the air, its wicked edge seeking flesh.

And it found it. It just didn't belong to Saeris.

Onyx let out an agonized yelp, dropping to the ground, and Orious let out a victorious whoop. The fox had darted in front of the blade, ruining his opportunity to end Saeris, but from the gleeful grin on his face, the seneschal didn't care. He wobbled, staggering sideways, mad laughter boiling out of him. "At last!" he hissed. "I got you*uulllcchh*—" Saeris's response was instant and ruthless. She buried her face in the seneschal's neck, and she ripped out his fucking throat. Blood and viscera sprayed the snow. My magic struck the male a second later.

In, I ordered. *Destroy.*

My shadows went hunting. I'd never commanded my magic with a mind to cause pain, but I sure as hell did now. Smoke and shadow tore down the male's mangled throat, eviscerating him from the inside out. He died in agony, robbed of the ability to scream.

"No, no, no." Saeris went to the small bundle that lay on top of the snow. Onyx's side was torn open, his eyes rolling and tongue lolling as he panted, trying to catch his breath. His fur was stained the brightest red.

My mate turned and grabbed me by the arm, dragging me to the fox's side. "Help him!" She was sobbing. "Like you did back at Ammontraíeth. Do the thing where you, you know, where you held him, you touched him, and you—you healed him. Please. *Please!*"

I gently took her hand from my arm—she was digging her fingers *desperately* into my bracer—and forced her to release her grip, pulling her into my chest. "I can't, Osha. I'm sorry," I whispered.

"But—you must have some healing magic left. Your small magic. Just a little bit. *He's* small, you said so yourself. Just—just *try!*"

I stroked her hair, holding her tight to me as I slowly shook my head. "I'm sorry." My voice broke. "I *would* try, I promise I would. But it's too late, Osha. He's already gone."

Onyx had taken one last stuttering breath while she'd been crying. He'd shivered and let out a trembling sigh, and then he'd gone.

Saeris shoved me in the chest, hard, pushing away from me. She shook her head as if denying the truth made it false. "No. No, he's not gone. He's *not!*" But then she saw him, saw how still he was and how peaceful he looked, and the truth closed around her like a vise. She dropped to her knees and sobbed. "I wasn't holding him. I wasn't...he went and I...wasn't..."

Gods. I needed to comfort her, but what comfort could I be, with my own tears streaming down my face? I went to her anyway, crouching down behind her and folding her into my arms.

Cold laughter echoed through the Wicker Wood as we grieved.

"That cursed fox. It plagued us day and night while we waited for you,

Alchemist," Belikon croaked. "We thought it nothing more...than a feral beast, trying to steal food. It bit three of my men. It took...Orious's finger...last night. It harried the camp at all hours, yelping...and... scratching at...the tree."

The tree.

The *dryad* that had imprisoned me. I'd been carrying Onyx in my arms when I'd entered the shadow gate to leave Cahlish. I had inadvertently brought him here with me...and he'd never left me.

Saeris lifted Onyx into her arms, cradling him gently.

Velvet ears tipped with black.

Tiny white eyelashes.

Toe pads, cracked and bleeding, again...

He looked so small, curled in on himself like that.

But he was *not* small.

In all my years alive and traveling this realm, I had *never* encountered anything so mighty and brave as this little fox with the heart of a wolf.

My mate was breaking right now, but she couldn't break here. The sun would be coming up soon, and the woods weren't safe. *Osha, we have to go.* I spoke for Saeris and Saeris alone; the bastard pinned to the ground back there didn't deserve to hear another word out of either of us. *Bring him. We will honor him.*

"There's *always* a price for this kind of folly," Belikon called. "Allow weakness into your heart, and it *will* break you."

My anger crystallized at those words. I needed to keep myself together for Saeris, but gods alive, was this bastard making it hard. I took my mate's hand and got her to her feet. I would carry her if she couldn't walk. But first...

I stood before the male who caused my father's death.

Who had tormented me even from my youth.

Who had murdered my mother.

Who had stolen an entire court and sacrificed its people for sport.

A male I was no longer Oath Bound to.

He regarded me with impassive eyes, as if bored by my presence now. "You know the moment you pull out this iron, you're doomed, don't you? Once I have access to my magic again, I'll call my guards. You can only get so far. I will follow you wherever you go, and I *will* end you both."

"I guess I'd better do something to improve our chances of escape then, hadn't I?" I called on a shadow gate, forming it behind me without looking. The portal pulsed as it snapped open, and my shadows began to spin.

Come on, Osha. Take Solace. I should have worded it differently. There would be no solace for her, given what she carried in her arms, but she needed her god sword. She wept as she pulled it from the king, not even bothering to look at him as he grinned at her loss.

"I hope you're ready," Belikon snarled.

"Are *you?*"

I'd been afraid of him as a Faeling. I had hidden from him in the palace whenever I could. But over the years, especially after I came out of the quicksilver with silver-rimmed eyes, I began to understand the truth. That even though I was just a child and he was a male who had claimed an entire kingdom, Belikon was actually afraid of *me*. And I was about to prove to him that he should be. There was still one place that he couldn't follow me, and it just so happened that we had to go there anyway. It was the only way, if we were going to stop this rot. I'd refused the plan out of hand at first, but we didn't have that luxury anymore.

I took hold of Nimerelle and counted down from three.

Two...

One...

The blade's edge juddered along bone as I wrenched it free. Belikon moved, instantly free of the iron that deadened his magic, but *I* hadn't stopped moving, either. I brought Nimerelle up, sweeping the sword around my head, and then flattened the blade, swinging it around with all my might. She cut clean through Belikon De Barra's neck and severed his head from his body in one fell swoop. The sheer force of the blow sent his head spinning off into the trees, where it hit the ground and bounced away into the dark.

He wasn't dead. Whatever dark magic ran through his veins would save him from this end. I knew that, but being beheaded would sure as hell make it harder for him to call on his men and come chasing after us.

49

WHEN WE NEED THEM MOST

SAERIS

ONE SHADOW GATE turned into another, and then another, and another. My head swam as we leaped between them, barely taking three steps after exiting one swirling portal before Fisher called another into existence and pulled me through it.

Five hundred leagues. That's how far we could travel without Belikon sensing Fisher's magic and following us. But by the twelfth shadow gate, I'd had enough. I needed a moment. I needed to breathe. I needed to sit down and fucking *cry*. When my feet found solid ground, the soles of my boots sinking into powdery white snow, I tugged against Fisher's hand and shook my head. "Enough," I pleaded. "Please. I . . ."

He drew me to him and hugged me fiercely, his heart thundering behind his chest plate. "It's okay, Osha. We're here," he said.

I didn't give a fuck where *here* was. I sank down into the snow, and I ran my fingers through Onyx's thick fur, hating the way that he was growing cold. "I should have listened to you," I whispered. "Back at the Winter Palace, when you said he'd make a terrible pet. He wasn't supposed to be around any of this. He was supposed to be *free*." I sniffed, wiping my nose with the back of my hand.

Fisher sat down heavily in the snow beside me. Gently, he put his hand on Onyx's head and left it there. "We believe," he started. But then he stopped. He looked up at the stars—more stars than I had *ever* seen—drawing in deep, slow breaths. The night was so cold that you couldn't even feel it. Twin plumes of fog formed as he exhaled down his nose. "We believe that animals are too pure for this life. They are all ascended beings who live in the after. Everything is perfect there. No pain or misfortune or heartbreak. But sometimes, they peer beyond the veil between this life and the next, and they see us here in the depths of our suffering, and they choose someone. One soul they want to help over any other. They come to us as...dear friends"—he cleared his throat—"when we need them most. You *needed* Onyx when you first got here, Saeris. He saw that perhaps, and he came. But now—"

I shook my head, blind with tears, refusing to hear him. "No. I *still* need him. I still—" I tried to continue speaking. I failed. The loss was too great.

Fisher leaned against me and shared in my grief. His hand, so much bigger than mine, remained on top of Onyx's head as shooting stars traced banners of light overhead. The sight would have been spectacular if it had been any other night, but it was *this* night, and all was terrible in the world.

I held Onyx's paw until ice crept along my bones and hoarfrost formed in my blood-drenched hair. "I thought he was in Ballard," I whispered. "I hoped..."

"I'm so sorry, Saeris."

I brushed away his apology, fighting to swallow the lump in my throat so I could talk again. "It wasn't your fault. It was him. *Belikon*. It was..."

Bad luck?

A cruel twist of fate?

Horrible timing?

None of it made me feel any better.

I stroked the broken little form in my lap, wishing harder than I'd wished for anything since my mother had died. I was sinking deeper into the depths of despair, hoping I would reach the bottom soon, when I stilled, staring down at the hand that I had buried in Onyx's fur.

One of the runes on the back of my hand was shimmering. It hadn't flared before. Not when I'd used it on Taladaius. Not when I'd used it to undo the magic that gave Fisher's name power, either. But... was I imagining it? Was there a faint blue glowing line, slowly tracing the outline of the Hazrax's rune? I held my hand up, heart stalling behind my ribs.

"You see that?" I gasped.

"See what?"

Of course the light would fucking go out when I tried to show it to Fisher. I bit on my bottom lip, staring at my hand, willing it to reappear. Nothing happened. I knew what I'd seen, though. It *had* been there. My mind wouldn't play tricks on me just because I wanted something badly. *It just wouldn't.* "Here. Take him a moment." I handed Onyx over to Fisher as carefully as I could, trying to calm my breathing as I got to my feet and spun around.

"I—*oh.*" Fuck. We were on the side of a mountain. A steep one, at that. At the top of the slope we sat on, an entire city lit up the night, its two white towers so tall that I had to crane my neck back to find the top of them. It was beautiful. It was...

"Ajun," Fisher said quietly, twisting to look back over his shoulder. "We should head up to the gate. This far north the sun rises later, but it'll be here soon."

Ajun.

Ajun *Sky.*

I knew why they called it that now: This luminescent city had been built among the clouds. I'd wanted to see it for myself, but now that I was on its doorstep, I wasn't ready to go inside. I spun around, feeling utterly helpless as I scanned the dark that surrounded us. "Where *are* you?" I shouted.

Where are you?

...Are you?

Where are you?

The question echoed back to me, far away, then near, then far again.

"Come on! I know you're here. You got your way, didn't you? I said that you could watch!"

Watch.

Watch...

WATCH!

"Osha, what are you doing?"

"Come on!" I screamed. *"Show yourself!"*

Every bit of hope I had left in me flared and died as I waited for the figure to come floating out of the dark. I had almost given up completely when it suddenly appeared on the snowy mountainside in front of us.

The Hazrax.

Fisher reached for Nimerelle, but I stepped in front of him, shaking my head. "No. Don't. It's okay."

"What is it doing here?" he hissed.

I hadn't kept the deal I'd made with the Hazrax a secret from him on purpose. Fisher was gone when it visited me in the forge, and there hadn't been time to explain what had just happened with it in the dreamscape I conjured in Cahlish.

I'll explain everything, I promise, I said into his mind. To the Hazrax, I said, "I need to ask you a question."

The creature looked even more sickly and unnatural under the canopy of stars. As always, its coal-black eyes were bottomless voids. With its slitted nose, the gills at its neck, and its hairless, waxen skin, it looked like the kind of creature that lived in deep, inky waters at the bottom of an ocean. I had seen something very similar to it in one of Foley's books. It was impossible to read its mood normally, but right now I could feel the anger radiating from it like heat. "Our agreement gives me leave to watch you at my leisure, Saeris Fane. It does not give you leave to *summon* me and ask questions."

"Then why are you here?" I demanded. "Why did you even come?"

"I will not come again. I am here now to make this very clear to you. I am not your subject. You do not command me—"

"Please. Just one question! I'll never call upon you again, I swear it."

I would drop down on my knees and beg. I wasn't above it. I'd make another deal. I'd let it watch me for the next *ten* years in return. I just needed to know one thing.

"Why would I help you, child? I have no interest in assisting you with your questions."

I needed to hold my tongue. I just couldn't. "You're lying."

Easy, Saeris, Fisher warned. *It's more powerful than the two of us put together. Can't you feel it?*

Oh, I felt it. The Hazrax's power flooded the air with electricity and the distinct scent of ozone. The creature was only just taller than your average Fae male, it was true, but the reek of strange magic that rolled off it was so strong that it turned my stomach. But what else could I do? I had to try. "If you didn't care, you wouldn't have invaded my dream of Cahlish. You wouldn't have told me that I needed to change my favor."

The Hazrax pondered this silently.

"Just tell me. *Please.* Can you see the spirits of the dead?"

The moonlight threw wild shadows over the Hazrax's face. It grimaced, displaying row upon row of curved, sharp teeth. "It would be blasphemy to admit such a thing," it hissed.

"I don't care about blasphemy. I care about my fox. Is he still here? Right now. I need to know if he's already..." Sometimes, words were steep hills, so fucking hard to summit. "If he's already gone, then I'll leave him in peace. But if he's still here..."

The Hazrax clacked its teeth together in a strange gesture that felt disdainful. "What does it matter either way, child? The fox is dead. It will move on eventually."

The tenuous hope I had lost soared from the ashes of my grief and rekindled at once. "So you *can* see him then? He *is* still here?"

"I will not speak on it—"

"Please." The request was quiet. It hadn't come from me. Fisher was up on his feet now and still holding Onyx's lifeless form in his arms. He took a step forward, tucking his chin to his chest and bowing respectfully as he approached the Hazrax. "You do not know me," he said. "You owe me nothing. I won't make you promises or strike bargains with

you, but if it's within your power to give my mate the information she seeks, I would be forever grateful. I'm sure that means little to you, but—"

"Fine." The former Lord of Midnight didn't look at Fisher. It continued staring at me. "If it means *so* much to you, then I will answer your question. But in return for a question of my own."

"Anything. Ask!"

The Hazrax made that perturbing clicking sound at the back of its throat. "What does it *feel* like . . . to lose something that you love so dearly?"

The strangest question. Had it never known loss before? Had it been so sheltered its entire existence that it had *never* lost anyone that it cared about? The odds seemed impossible, especially when you considered how old the creature was. *I* was well equipped to answer it, though. I'd experienced more than my fair share of loss in my lifetime. My mother. My father. The few friends I'd been stupid enough to make when I was younger, back in the Third. There were bodies piled high in the mausoleum of *my* memory. "It feels like trying to make sand flow backward in an hourglass. It feels like being surrounded by people and being the only one who can't find the air in the room. It's drowning on dry land. It's the hollow ache of something that you know, from that moment on, will always be missing. It is a pain so acute and incurable that poets, pirates, and politicians alike die from it. And it never ends."

The Hazrax's robes blew about it on the gentle, icy breeze. It was silent. For a long time, it remained that way. And then: "The fox's soul is still with you. It is currently sitting at your feet. It seems that the beast hasn't realized that it's dead yet. It follows you like a little lost shadow. Does that make you feel better?"

Onyx hadn't gone. He was still here with me. I glanced down at my boots, knowing what he would look like if I could see him—glassy eyes black as little chips of jet, looking up at me so trustingly, so full of love—and I shook my head. "No. It doesn't make me feel better. But I am hoping it'll make what I'm about to do easier."

Give him to me, Fisher. Please. I need him.

What are you going to do? Fisher asked, sounding cautious, but he did as I asked. I took Onyx from him and dropped down on my knees in the snow.

"Belikon and Madra were afraid of the Alchemists. They were afraid, because the people who came before me were capable of things they would never be able to do. The Alchemists sought perfect knowledge, and they possessed remarkable control over elemental magic. But they also chased immortality. I don't want to make anyone immortal. But if I'm capable of healing myself from awful burns and a hole in my chest, then I can heal a tiny fox."

The Hazrax had already been fairly still, but now it froze, its entire being locked in place as if cast in marble.

Fisher laid a hand on my shoulder, dropping down beside me in the snow. "Saeris, that's not..." The second his eyes met mine, he abandoned whatever he had been about to say, though. "Never mind. If you think you can do it, then I believe you," he said.

"Such a thing is impossible," the Hazrax said. "The Alchemists tried and failed for centuries to bring their Fae loved ones back from the dead."

"And I'm sure they tried very hard," I bit out, already pulling my magic into me. "But they were trying to bring back people. Onyx is tiny. I *know* I can do it." The reserve of energy inside me flooded and brimmed over. I kept on drawing my magic to me, regardless, the words Taladaius had spoken to me once in his office at the Fool's Paradise playing on a loop inside my head. *The fact that your hands are healed now, after the damage I just witnessed, implies that you also have regenerative magic. Physical magic. Power over the body. At some point, you might be able to heal others with your abilities...*

"No amount of magic can cheat death," the Hazrax said, in a pitying tone.

"That's true." I held up my hand for the Hazrax to see—the faint glimmers of light that had returned and were trailing around the outline of the rune it had given to me. "But with the gift you gave to me, I'm betting I can *undo* it for a moment."

"You want to *undo* death?" it said disbelievingly.

"I do." My magic was making me dizzy now. Such a tide of it poured into me, gaining momentum, saturating my entire being. I let it come, welcoming it in, allowing it to fill me until the rush of it felt almost unstoppable.

"All this for a *fox*?" the Hazrax scoffed. "Speak to her, Child of Shadow. Make her see sense. She'll kill herself before she revives the animal."

I wanted to tell Fisher not to stop me, but the power relaying around my body was too great now. I couldn't find the clarity to speak, not even into his mind. Fisher's hand pressed into the small of my back—strong, warm, comforting. I waited for the words of common sense to come…

Fisher spoke with resolve. "He isn't just a fox. He's family. And if Saeris says she's going to save him, then she's going to."

"Such blind faith?"

"In *her*? Yes," Fisher answered.

"And if she dies while trying to accomplish this fool's errand?"

I felt my mate's shrug. "It is her life to spend. *Her* decision. I will respect it."

The sheer volume of power was starting to hurt now. It clawed at my insides as if my body were a cage and it wanted to get out. I wouldn't be able to hold it for much longer. I concentrated on splitting it down the middle. I called on a part of myself that I'd never reached for before—on a rune I didn't even have yet—and I fucking hoped with every last part of me that this would work.

"Look at me, child," the Hazrax ordered. "All magic has its limits. If you proceed any further, you will shatter the rune I gave you. You will not be able to use it to save anyone else. You will not be able to use it to free your other friends from *their* oaths, as you freed your mate."

I didn't care.

There would be another way to free the others. I would find one. *Make* one if I had to. Right now, I was saving Onyx. I could sense the flicker of his spirit there, sitting next to me in the snow, watching me as I held my hands over his cold body.

"Do it, Osha," Fisher whispered.

The Hazrax's rune blazed, lighting up the night. The creature had called it a silent rune, had said that it didn't possess magic the way my others did, but it sure as hell responded when I forced the flow of my magic *into* it.

And it hurt.

It kept on hurting as my palms swelled with light and poured into Onyx's broken and bloody body.

So much magic. A monumental tide rolled through me and kept on going...and I was met with darkness. A nothingness so vast that trying to fill it felt like a ridiculous task.

Cold seeped into my fingertips and into my hands. It climbed up my arms, creeping slowly, slowly up toward my elbows. The agony of it fractured me—my body, my mind, my hope—leaving only my will intact. I would not give up here. Even if I wanted to, I suspected that I couldn't.

I'd opened a door, and death stood on the other side of it. If I didn't push it back and succeed in my goal, he would step through and claim *me* instead.

Higher.

Higher.

The cold of the eternal dark crawled up to my armpits.

Come on, Osha. You can do this.

Wind whipped at my hair. My eyes were closed or unseeing—I couldn't differentiate. I was locked in a tug-of-war, funneling my magic into a bottomless vessel that did not want to be filled—

Keep going! Fisher urged inside my head.

The cold clamped around my throat, closing off my airways. It beckoned to me, promising such restful sleep...

I pushed harder, hurling my magic into the Hazrax's rune. Blisters ballooned on the backs of both of my hands, filling and bursting in seconds, the flesh beneath raw and singed.

Yes. That's it, Saeris. Go! Go!

One last push. One huge shove...and the door between this life and the next slammed closed.

The cold in my chest disappeared.

I—I—

Onyx's eyes were closed. He was so still. He—

He moved. His paw. There! I saw it! It moved!

But his body was still broken. His side was torn wide open and bleeding afresh. He didn't have long. I'd brought him back into his body, and it could not sustain him. He had a minute, maybe. Seconds. I reached for the magic I had bet everything on and found . . . *nothing*.

I'd used it all. There was nothing left. I'd drawn so much power to me, and it was all gone.

I reached for it again, again found nothing. I was falling through the air, stomach churning, weightless, trying to find a handhold, *something* to stop the fall, but there was nothing.

Panic—

No. There was no time for that.

I reached beyond my magic. Beyond my runes. Beyond the bond there, connecting me to my mate. I reached, fighting millimeter by millimeter, until I finally found what I was looking for.

I didn't know the words.

Was I even supposed to *say* anything?

Was there some kind of covenant, or . . . ahh, fuck it, my intentions would have to be good enough. Death rattled the door handle. I could feel it. He was coming for Onyx a second time. I acted quickly, plucking up a small kernel of the energy I had discovered, and I pushed it up, past my bond with Fisher, past the empty reserve where my magic should have been, into my body, into the raw Alchimeran shield that was smoking on the back of my hand . . . and then into the little white fox.

The world trembled in response, a shock wave rocking the snowy slope, and out of nowhere a grim white dawn broke over the saw-toothed mountain range of Ajun, casting back the dark.

50

KNIGHT

SAERIS

Stargazers, also known as kingfishers, can be found in abundance from the Gilarian Mountains all the way down to the coastal cities of Marinth, Bodish, and Inishtar. Many individuals among the Fae, selkies, elemental sprites, and satyr populations consider the stargazer a symbol of hope.

—Excerpt from *Fae Creatures of the Gilarian Mountains*,
a missing tome from the royal libraries
of the Winter Palace

"PLEASE! *PLEASE!*"

The scream burned as it rose up my throat. My skin, too.

Everything hurt.

I was being jostled.

Carried.

Kingfisher was running.

"Hang on, Little Osha. Almost there," he rumbled. The sky was wrung out, streaked pink, as if someone had taken a paintbrush and slashed over a warped canvas. I craned my head back, trying to remember where the hell we were—what the hell we were *doing*—and the details of the last twenty-four hours suddenly came rushing back in with stunning clarity. A solemn, dark figure stood motionless, a hundred feet down the slope of the mountainside. The Hazrax watched us flee, the shape of it smudged around the edges, as if it were only half there.

My head was killing me.

I looked down at the snow as it whipped by beneath me. Fisher's boots left deep indentations in the brilliant white carpet, and...and there were other impressions in the snow, too. Not quite as deep. Much smaller, and certainly not Fae.

They were *paw prints*.

Lightning swept through me, clearing the haze in my head. "Put me down, Fisher!"

"No. You were unconscious," he snarled.

"Please! I'm fine now, I swear!"

He wasn't happy about it, but he slowed his run. He hadn't managed to set me down before I heard a chittering squeal and a small white fox was leaping into my arms.

He was alive.

Alive!

Onyx squirmed so hard I nearly dropped him. He *screamed* with excitement, his whole body wagging as he licked my chin and my cheeks. His tiny heart battered against his newly healed ribs, pure joy radiating from him as he turned and rained kisses down on Fisher, too.

"I know, little one. I know. We're happy to see you, too," he said, his voice rough.

I stared up at my mate in wonder. "It worked?" Could I trust this? Was it real?

Fisher nodded. "It worked. You did it." His expression was breathtaking—pride and a dash of wonder thrown in for good measure. "You accomplished something that's never been done before."

"And will never be done again," I added, glancing down at my shield. The Hazrax's rune hadn't just faded. It was *gone*. My other runes were raw, blood oozing from my mangled skin. Even the God Bindings spiraling around my wrist and up my arm were pulsing with pain, but the hurt could have been a thousand times worse and it would still have been worth it.

Onyx was alive. He whimpered, frantically rubbing his muzzle against my cheeks and butting my chin with the top of his head. I'd saved him. I'd done it. But the cost...

"You must think I'm crazy." I didn't even want to look at my mate...but when I did, I found no consternation or anger within the endless green of his striking eyes.

He laughed a little breathlessly. "Yes," he agreed. "You *are* crazy. You came looking for me. You took on Belikon by yourself *and* you outsmarted him. And you made a costly sacrifice to save a friend," he added. "Only a crazy person would have done all of that. But *I* would have made the same choices, Saeris. So I suppose we're well suited."

"Lo, visitors on the mountain!"

The cry boomed through the air. It echoed off the faces of the other mountains that crowded around the one on which we stood. Fisher and I turned as one, looking up the slope—

I hadn't noticed it before: the monstrous palace of bones protruding from the snow and ice to the right of us on the slope.

Arched ribs, soaring up to meet the brightening sky.

Notched vertebrae, the size of small houses.

It made sense that the remains of the dragon were still here. Fisher and his friends had slain it and ended its tyranny. Belikon had troubled himself to claim its head as a trophy. But the rest of it was too big to clear from the mountainside. The Ajun Fae had let the beast's bones rest where they had fallen, and now they formed a megalithic structure almost as impressive as the city of Ajun Sky itself.

People were gathering along the parapets of the city. Someone shouted down to us again, waving frantically. *"Lo! Hurry!"* they cried. *"A black tide comes!"*

Fisher twisted automatically, peering down the mountain, and cursed. It took me a second to see what he was seeing. The Hazrax was gone. But farther down the hillside, the dark outline of guards with bows and swords in hand could be seen, scrambling toward us with startling speed.

"Shit," Fisher hissed. "*Belikon.* He shouldn't have found us. Not *this* quickly, anyway. Come on. We have to go."

I didn't need telling twice. I had enough energy to sprint toward the towering black metal gate that encompassed the city. I did *not* have enough energy to face Belikon a second time in one day. I sure as hell wasn't losing Onyx again, either. I ran like the wind. If the fox knew we were in danger, he didn't seem to care; he chittered and relentlessly licked my face, and he was *still* doing so when we pitched up in front of the ominous black gates that barred our way into Ajun.

They were closed.

"Hey!" Fisher hollered. "Let us in!" His shout rebounded around the abandoned courtyard on the other side of the high metal bars.

Belikon's guards were gaining ground, still more than two hundred feet below, but they were coming. They'd catch up to us eventually. "*Hello?*" Fisher bellowed.

Hello...

Hello?

Hello!

Suddenly, the black gate jerked. It let out an almighty, metallic groan...and very slowly, it began to slide. The sound of thick chain feeding through a winch system rattled my bones for a moment, and then the ancient gate began to open.

How many souls called Ajun Sky home? From the outside, with its huge recess pushing deep into the mountainside and its glittering towers of quartz and calcite, it looked like it could house thousands. Tens of thousands.

But only *one* person calmly descended the stairs that led down into the courtyard and crossed the cobbled stones to greet us. He wore a shit-eating grin that would have put Carrion's to shame when he came to a stop before us.

"You should have told us you were coming," he said, with that warm, lilting accent of his. "It's a point of pride for the people of Ajun that these gates should *always* open to *you*, brother."

Renfis.

By the time Belikon's soldiers reached Ajun, we were already moving.

Furious shouts boomed beyond the walls, bouncing off stone. The sound traveled strangely through the bitter air. Salvos of magic, blue and green, burst harmlessly against invisible wards that protected the city from attack. Even the arrows and hurled spears crashed into the boundary magic and were deflected, shooting off in other directions or splintering to shards upon impact.

The mountain shook as they attacked the battlements. The tall struts of iron remained unmolested, though. Belikon's guards were still Fae, after all. They wouldn't touch the *gate*.

"How sure are we that they won't get through?" The wind caught my words and carried them away. I wasn't even sure my mate had heard me until he replied.

"Very sure," he answered. "This city has never been breached. And there are only a thousand or so guards out there. Far greater forces have tried and failed to bully their way into Ajun Sky. There's only one way in or out, and Belikon has no friends here. No one in their right minds will just *let him in*."

"Nevertheless, we should hurry," Renfis said. "Time is of the essence."

Lorreth had explained more of what had happened at Ajun, particularly with Merelle, Ren's twin sister, but there had still been more...

The city of Ajun was made of stone. Its foundations were robust and deep. The tall, terraced houses that lined its streets were pretty, their ice-adorned fascias glowing a soft pink in the early morning light. Ren hurried ahead of us, though still took time to tousle the hair of Faelings with rosy cheeks who ran up to him and tugged playfully at the pristine white cloak draped around his shoulders, marking him as a knight of the Orrithian.

I'd heard him referred to by that name plenty of times: Renfis of the Orrithian. Foolishly, I'd never questioned what the title meant. Now, as he guided us through the mountainous keep, he explained everything that had happened to him after he'd left Cahlish, and it all began to make sense.

"The Gilarians listened, thank the gods. They were already making preparations when I left them. I was almost at the border of the forest. I would have reached Ballard inside a day at the rate I was traveling, but the second I hit the foothills of the Shallow Mountains, I felt a searing, burning sensation in my chest. It knocked the air right out of me, and I fell from my horse. Thought I was being attacked. I figured I'd triggered some kind of ward, but..." He shook his head. "I ripped off my chest plate and tore my shirt open, and there it was."

Kingfisher had been making frustrated, grumbling noises ever since Ren had stopped hugging him and clapping him on the back—there had been a *lot* of hugging and back clapping once we were inside the walls of the city and the gate had closed behind us. Now, my mate was audibly berating himself for not solving the mystery of the general's disappearance sooner.

"Your oath mark," he sighed, shaking his head.

Renfis nodded. "My oath mark. I was being called to serve. I didn't have any choice but to go."

I followed Renfis up a narrow set of stone steps cut into the face of the mountain, doing my damnedest not to look down or slip and fall on the treacherous ice. Onyx bounded up the stairs ahead of the brown-haired general, tongue lolling out of his head and full of energy, as if he *hadn't* been dead less than an hour ago.

I grinned at the fox, overcome with relief... but I still managed to fake annoyance when I said, "Don't leave me out, you two. What oath mark? What did you swear, Ren?"

The general ducked his head, seemingly embarrassed. His cloak swirled around him as he continued on up the stone steps. "You explain, brother," he said, handing the task off to Fisher. "I've never liked telling this one."

Kingfisher had insisted on coming up the steps behind me. He'd whispered something obscene into my head—something about staring at my ass and planning all the scandalous things he was going to do to it—but I knew he was only bringing up the rear so he could make sure I didn't topple from the narrow steps and fall to my death. I was exhausted and genuinely worried I actually might do that, and so I hadn't put up a fight.

He grunted under his breath. The wind whistled past my ears, but he didn't raise his voice above its normal level; my hearing was just as sharp as his these days. "After we killed Old 'Shacry, the horde left Ajun, descending back down the mountain, and the people inside the city came out to bury their dead. Renfis's sister was among their number. Merelle had always loved Ajun, so Ren asked the city elders if she could be buried here. They gave her a burial site at the very top of the mountain—a high honor, in thanks for the sacrifice she made to protect the Ajun Fae.

"As soon as we were done laying Merelle to rest, Renfis felt a burning pain in his chest, much like the one he described just now. We were on our way back down into the city when he dropped down to his knees and let out a terrible roar."

"It wasn't that bad," Renfis cut in.

"So loud it caused an *avalanche*," Fisher said, attitude coloring his voice. "The other mourners who'd been burying their loved ones at the top of the mountain knelt with Ren and began to pray. None of us had any clue what was happening. But the Ajun Fae told us that, as soon as your blood was one with the mountain, you belonged to it in a way. That, because Ren had buried his blood relative here, and she was his twin, no less, he was now a member of the Ajun Fae."

"And only the Ajun can be called to join the knighthood who guard its gate," Ren said quietly.

"So . . . you were called back here to watch the gate?"

"Not the gate that protects the city, Osha. The *other* gate."

A thrill of panic and adrenaline chased up my spine at that. Lorreth had told me of the other gate in the square at Inishtar. I'd promised that I wouldn't go off on some harebrained mission to secure the brimstone we needed to stop the rot without Fisher, and in return Lorreth had told me where brimstone *came* from.

"There's always been a city here," Fisher said. "Because there's always been a gate. A portal between this world and another."

"Like quicksilver but not," I breathed. I could sense Fisher's annoyance at that, that Lorreth had obviously told me what he had, but he refrained from voicing those feelings out loud.

"Yes. In many ways, the same. But in others not. The original Alchemists could never control it. Not even the strongest of them. It sent most of them mad. The gate would open by itself, and it wouldn't close. Foul creatures used it as a doorway into this realm. They caused chaos and terror throughout Yvelia. Since no one could close the portal, the Knights of Orrithian were created. They were imbued with an old line of magic. Powerful. Six of them stand watch over the gate at all times, channeling their magic into wards that prevent all manner of evil from spilling into this world. They take it in shifts to protect not just Ajun but *all* of Yvelia."

"When the quicksilver was stilled here, cutting us off from the other realms," Renfis said, joining in the explanation despite himself, "the gate at Ajun remained open. Belikon declared it was a sign. He said that because it was the only gate left open, it would lead us to riches and glory. He brought a Faeling here to Ajun, to visit the gate. He was barely more than a boy. Belikon put a sword in his hand and declared that he should be the first to go through the gate and behold the paradise that waited for us on the other side."

"Since this pool was different from all the other pools, he said I wouldn't need the relic my mother gave me," Fisher whispered.

Wait.

Lorreth hadn't said anything about *this*.

The stairs were steep, and the air was cold as ice, but those things had nothing to do with my sudden shortness of breath. "What are you talking about, Fisher?"

He carried on, speaking slowly, carefully, stripping all emotion from his words. "I was Oath Bound to him. Eleven years old. He said that I was already a fully grown male in his eyes, that I was ready to become a vaunted warrior of Yvelia, held in high esteem in his court. My mother had been dead a week, and he planted me on my knees in front of that stone and made me promise. It was easy for him after that. He ordered me to give him the relic, and then he ordered me into the pool."

The wind howled as we climbed higher. It grew colder, too, sinking vicious teeth into the sensitive tips of my ears. I was trying to keep up, to understand what I was being told, but the cruelty of it all made it almost impossible. *This* was where Kingfisher had entered the quicksilver. *This* was where it had infected him from the inside out and almost driven him mad.

"I did as my king commanded. I stepped into the pool. As soon as my bare feet touched the tainted ore, I knew I was going to die. I was transported to another realm. A place..." Fisher trailed off, as if he'd reached the midpoint of his sentence and found the rest of the words suddenly missing.

"The king and his men waited for two hours for the Faeling to return," Ren said. "And when he didn't come back, the king feigned the loss of his stepson, the only remaining link to his precious Edina. He'd already bequeathed Cahlish along with the title that accompanied the land to his seneschal when the pool erupted and spat the Faeling out. His eyes were rimmed silver like the stars."

"I didn't know myself," Fisher whispered. "It took me a long time to come back... *mentally*. Belikon was disappointed. He'd thought it a good way to dispose of me. One of the Orrithian Knights returned my relic to me, and Belikon sent me off to learn the trade of killing in his war camps."

Ren had reached the top of the stairs and was waiting for us, grim-faced. "Inexplicably, the Ajun pool closed that day," he said. "It's opened and closed three times since, without warning. The knights always remained to guard it, just in case. No one's been called to replace any of them in centuries. Until now."

Those words. Where had I heard them before? It came back to me quickly. Back in Cahlish, in Everlayne's room. Fisher's sister had thrashed and shook on the bed, and that awful, dead voice had risen and come forth from her mouth. *The gate is open. It cannot be closed. The gate is open. The gate is open...*

"It opened again, didn't it?" I whispered.

Ren nodded, resting a hand on the hilt of the sword that hung at his hip. "It did. And the beast that crawled through it killed all six knights on watch and dragged their bodies back through with it when it left. I was summoned as a result. Since then, it's opened every day, for a period of three hours each time. We've been recording the timings. We've been waiting."

"Waiting?" I already wished I hadn't asked.

"For the wards to break once and for all," Ren said, looking down at his boots. "For the monsters of old to return and wreak havoc anew on Yvelia. It's only a matter of time."

I hadn't asked where Ren was taking us as he led us through Ajun and up the steps into the clouds. But I knew now. I could feel it, seething, close by. Too close. It was behind the ornate carved wooden door Renfis stood before.

It was a cold thing—bitter and detached.

A black gate.

It had been corrupted a long, long time ago. It wanted Yvelia to *burn*, and that was precisely what would happen if the malevolent forces that gathered on the other side of that gate got their way.

Onyx whined, jumping up at me, begging to be picked up. I held him tight, shivering when Ren put his palm on the door handle and slowly began to turn it.

"Wait. We're going *now*? Fisher, what are we doing?"

"The gate will close soon," Ren explained. "You could wait until it opens tomorrow. But..." He grimaced awkwardly.

"Waiting a day might be catastrophic," Fisher said. "We're losing ground to the rot too quickly. People are dying, and the gods only know when more infected feeders might show up. We need you to seal that brimstone rune. And brimstone only has *one* source."

I'd known it. Even when Lorreth had told me in the square what we'd have to do if we wanted to secure *any* amount of brimstone that wouldn't kill our sprite friends, I'd *known* we'd wind up here eventually. The fates were at play yet. Renfis had been drawn to Ajun for a reason, and so had we.

Fear lashed tight around my chest and squeezed. Fisher's eyes softened a little, as if he could feel it crystallizing like ice in my veins. He placed a reassuring hand in the small of my back. "But if you're not ready—"

"I *have* to be." I didn't say any more. Didn't need to. Ren hadn't had a choice. Neither had Fisher. They had duty. They had honor. They did what they needed to, because it was the right thing to do. I would do the same.

"And you?" Ren asked, turning to his friend. "Are you sure about this? There'll be consequences. More sacrifices to be made."

Solemnly, Kingfisher bowed his head. But...no. Even as I watched him, something shifted in my mind. He wasn't Kingfisher anymore. He *was* Khydan. Undeniably, the name fit him. It was like discovering the long-lost, missing piece of a puzzle. Like snapping it into place to complete an image, and finally seeing and understanding it in its entirety.

He could *only* ever be Khydan to me now. And he *was* ready to face whatever awaited us on the other side of this door.

"All right, then. Hold your breath." Ren turned the handle and opened the door. "The *smell* can be a little overpowering."

Inside, it took a moment for my eyes to adjust to the dark. Another moment for me to comprehend what I was seeing and wish I could turn back around. Onyx let out a panicked yip and hid his face in my armpit. The pool wasn't like any of the others. There was no stone lintel surrounding it. No stone basin to contain it, either. It was organic, like... some sort of festering sore. And the roiling liquid inside it was *black*.

"Where does it go?" I asked. "What's the realm called?"

Only Fisher knew the answer to that question. He had gone there as a boy. The troubled look on my mate's face didn't inspire confidence as he admitted, "It's never been given an official name here. The pantheon of undergods and the dragons they breed there call it Diaxis. But personally... I've always called it *hell*."

51

THE OBVIOUS...

KHYDAN GRAYSTAR FINVARRA

I FUCKING *HATE* dragons.

52

PROMISES AND HOPE

SAERIS

THICK. CLOYING. PUTRID.

Usually, the quicksilver rolled away, beading from clothes, hair, and skin alike whenever we exited one of its pools. Not so this time. Whatever the foul substance was that filled the pool at Ajun, it was nothing like quicksilver. It probed up my nose and coated my tongue, filling my mouth with the taste of rot. Passing through it felt like drowning. Unbridled panic ratcheted in my chest as my lungs pulled, desperate for air, urging me to *Breathe! Breathe! Breathe!*

My head breached the pool, and I immediately sucked down a lungful of—

PAIN.

I'd inhaled razor blades.

I—

I couldn't—

Easy, Osha. Don't panic. Khydan was close.

I didn't so much rise from the pool as find myself being spat out by it. On my hands and knees, I crawled forward, gasping and choking as I tried to make sense of the sensations assaulting my body.

The reek of sulfur and a wall of tremendous heat slapped me in the face. Until very recently, I'd spent my life in a desert. I'd never imagined anything could be hotter than the Third during reckoning...but this? This was unimaginable.

I was in shock. Panic spiraling up and down my spine as waves of adrenaline warned me to move, to step *out* of the fire, to retreat to safety. But there was no retreat. There was no safety. There was only a crushing dark, and air so superheated that it felt like it was tearing my lungs to ribbons.

My eyes stung—either from the sulfur or from the heat, I couldn't tell. It seemed as though they should be watering. Perhaps they were, and the moisture wicking from the surface of my eyes was the source of the unbearable stinging.

"Osha? Can you stand?" Khydan's voice was low and quiet, but the worry in his words made them loud as a shout. I felt his hand on my back, then on my arm. He helped me to my feet as I tried to hack the tar-like, disgusting filth up and out of my throat. "That's it. Spit it out. Whatever you do, don't swallow it."

Oh, gods. "What *is* it?" I rasped.

Khy took longer than I would have liked to answer. "It's probably best if you don't ask," he said. His voice was too quiet, as if it were being carried away by an invisible wind. "Are you okay?"

His hand found mine in the dark again; the squeeze he gave me calmed my nerves enough that my voice only shook a little when I spoke. "I'm fine. At least I *think* I am. I can't see anything. And I feel like I'm being cooked."

Pale green light flared next to me, almost white but not quite. Khydan held a thin tube in his other hand, the top half of which glowed with evenlight. He held it out to me. Once I'd accepted it, he produced another of the strange tubes from his pocket and shook it hard, activating it so that he held one, too.

My mate's eyes were dark as drowning pools, the brilliant green muted almost to black. His hair dripped with foul liquid that still churned in the pool behind us. It mottled his skin, viscous and thick, his fighting leathers sticky with it. My own hair was plastered to my skull, the liquid soaking all the way through my leathers.

I would have taken that fall into the lake outside Gillethrye all over again, broken ribs and everything, if it meant that I could wash this filth from my body. It wasn't *right*.

Shooting me a lopsided smile that was probably supposed to be reassuring, Khydan said, "Two hours. That's all the time we can spend here, otherwise you *will* wind up cooked. Your body wasn't made for this place."

"Then we'd better get moving. But... where do we need to go?" Had I really been so foolish? *"You'll need to pass through the gate at Ajun,"* Lorreth had said. *"You'll need to bargain with the creatures there for access to their brimstone."* I had accepted that doing so would be gravely dangerous—but I hadn't thought to ask how to find these creatures. Didn't know where they would be... or where *we* would be when we stepped out of the pool, for that matter. Our evenlight torches were far from enough to fully illuminate our surroundings. A six-foot-wide sphere of light embraced us, but on the other side of it waited the unwavering darkness.

Roiling beyond the bounds of evenlight, it felt sentient. Cold and cruel. Khydan swept a hand over his face, smearing the black muck in a futile attempt to wipe it away. His eyes roved, sharp, staring out into the dark. The moment he opened his mouth to speak again, a thunderous rumble split the fetid air, and two glowing orange-red points blazed to life in the near distance, piercing the veil of dark.

They were balls of living flame, those twin points of orange and red. Only they weren't, because they were *eyes*, and they burned with hate. The ground shook beneath our feet as a booming voice spoke: *"Bolddddd."*

The darkness retreated, unveiling a cavernous stone hall draped in shadows and littered with bones. When the beast ahead opened its maw, its giant jaws parting to reveal the glowing glands at the back of its raw, bleeding throat, the air buzzed with sulfur so badly that the stench nearly upended my stomach.

I knew what it was.

The name of the monster bounced around inside my head.

I didn't dare speak it out loud.

It was seventy feet tall from its huge, taloned feet to its withers. Its long, articulated neck was stooped thanks to the rough rock ceiling. The gods only knew—possibly *feared*—how tall it might have been if it was able to rise to its full height. My breath stoppered in my lungs as I took it in.

Flashing scales of gold? No—black. It was hard to tell, given that the beast itself was the only source of light. A horned ridge protruded from its wide, bony head like a crown. Enormous bulky wings were tucked tightly into its sides. And its *teeth*. They were three feet long and jagged, like the edge of one of Elroy's saws.

I had been filled with awe at the sight of the massive skull that had loomed behind Belikon's throne at the Winter Palace, but it hadn't translated, not truly: just how big the rest of the creature would have to be to warrant a head that monstrous. I understood now…and I was afraid.

The temperature climbed, fresh waves of sweat breaking across my brow and evaporating as the dragon slowly propped itself up on taloned elbows and then pushed itself up from the ground. "Boldddd *indeed*," it rumbled.

Don't…run. Khydan's warning was fortuitously timed. I'd been considering it. The noxious pool was right behind us, still open. How many seconds would it take to turn and dive back below the choppy surface? Two? Three at most? From the edge in my mate's voice, *any* amount of time wouldn't be long enough. Out of the corner of my eye, I watched as Khy slowly reached over his shoulder and drew his blade.

Should I—

He gave a single, firm shake of his head. *Don't touch your swords. If it takes umbrage with anyone, let it be me. Don't move, Osha. Just…stay* exactly *where you are.*

Smoke rolled off Nimerelle, thick and angry. If the dragon cared, it was impossible to tell. Like a dog waking from a long nap, it shook its giant head, sparks flying from its flared nostrils. The horns atop its head smashed awkwardly into the rough-hewn rock, and a large section of the ceiling sloughed away and came crashing down around the beast, rock turning to shrapnel where it struck the ground.

Run, my heart urged. *What in all five hells are you doing, Fane? Fucking* run.

I stood my ground, boots firmly planted, heeding Khydan's command.

"Two thousand yearrrrssss have I lived. Never has a meal walked straight into my mouth," the dragon snarled. Its mouth didn't move. The words *were* spoken out loud—the walls wouldn't have quaked so terribly otherwise—but it must have formed its words differently to Fae and humankind. Its tongue, forked and blackened, darted between its teeth, as if it was tasting the air. I'd seen plenty of dune asps do this back in Zilvaren. I'd never seen a snake lick a mouthful of yard-long yellowed teeth, though.

"You are not *of* this place."

"We are not." The hall rang with Khydan's voice. Clear and steady, he didn't sound afraid. I sensed his fear, though. He didn't try to shield *me* from it. "We're from—"

"I know the name of your home," the dragon interrupted. "Do not speak it out loud." It seemed to gather, pulling back, its neck arching and tucking into its broad, gleaming chest. The temperature in the ancient hall rose a degree or two. "Why have you come?" it demanded.

"We—"

"The *other* must speak!"

Me. *I* was the other. For some reason, it wanted me to answer. But I wasn't as practiced an actor as my mate. Khydan's hand tightened around Nimerelle's hilt. The blade was kicking out so much smoke that it almost drowned out the light cast by our torches. Was it Khydan's worry, bleeding into his god sword? Or was it the spark of Ren's sister that still resided in the blade concerned for me? *Don't give it much,* Khydan warned. *Tell it we need to speak to—*

"I hear you, boy," the dragon snarled. "There is no dark corner where you may hide your whisperings from *me.*"

Boy? How old was this thing that it would consider Khydan a *boy?*

And, disturbingly, it could hear us speaking directly into each other's minds? Could it hear our *thoughts*, too? Our—

"I hear the grindings of the gears that drive the universe toward destruction. I hear all. I know..." Its tongue probed between shattered teeth, flickering back and forth in the air. "... *all.*"

The stone floor was formed of hexagonal tiles covered in husks and dried leaves and all kinds of debris. When the dragon spoke, the ground rocked so hard that the tile in front of me cracked into three pieces.

The beast breathed rancid smoke as it slowly advanced. "*You* know nothing, name breaker. Your mind is too young to even know *itself.*"

"You're right." I felt my pulse everywhere. In my fingertips. The roof of my mouth. At my temples. I was going to throw up, for fuck's sake. My very first confrontation with a mythical beast, and I was going to lose the contents of my stomach like a fucking coward. I would *not* piss myself. Just... *no.* "I am young. But at least I'm not hiding in the dark, waiting to do my master's bidding."

"*Saeris.*" This time, the warning was immediate. Out loud. Khydan's tone suggested he thought I had lost my fucking mind. And maybe I had. Maybe a little madness was what it would take to make it through this situation alive. Who knew. But trying to approach this from a sane person's perspective was beyond me. A sane person would never have stepped into that pool.

"What master do you claim rules *me*, girl child?" the dragon hissed.

Lorreth hadn't told me who ruled Diaxis when we had spoken of this place. Ren hadn't, either, as he'd led us up the winding stairs toward our death. Maybe they didn't know the name of the god who ruled these dark, dead halls. Or maybe they didn't speak his name because, as I knew all too well, to speak a name gave it power. But Khydan spoke it now, his voice flat and cold.

"Styx. Lord of the charred aerie. King of dragons. *He* is your master. *He* is the one you must obey."

The dragon had been creeping forward, lithe and sinuous. It was too big to conceal its approach, though. It stopped dead now, snarling at Khydan's declaration.

"Who are you to speak *his* name?"

"I am Kingf—" Khydan stopped himself. Old habits died hard. It was true—I had made the shift and referred to him by his true name easily enough, but something inside of me knew it was right. His whole life, Khydan had only known himself as Kingfisher. How much of a person's identity resided in their name? How much of their soul? A strange thought. Khydan's soul was the same as it had ever been. His personality, too. But... something fundamental *had* changed inside him. It was subtle. It was because he was *free*.

"I am Khydan Graystar Finvarra. I walked these halls before, many years ago—"

"Little more than a Faeling, you were then. You were tortured here, I remember. You have come to exact revenge upon this place, then? To destroy my kind, and all who call this place home?"

"No. I come as an ambassador of my realm, as does my mate. We request an audience with Styx, per the rules of engagement between our realms. Etiquette—"

A jet of stinking, superheated air suddenly spewed from the dragon's mouth, a plume of fire and molten rock chasing after it. There was no time to react. No time for anything. There was only the fire, and the heat, and our imminent deaths. Too late, I drew my shield, bigger and brighter than it had ever been before. It flickered and guttered as the brimstone tore through it.

We were dead.

We were fucking dead!

We were...

...hunched over, clinging to each other, panting breathlessly, but somehow still alive. The flames ripped over our heads, slamming into the wall behind us, flashing blue and green as they struck the stone. The beast had missed us. On purpose, it seemed. It could have easily engulfed us if it had wanted to; the fact that it wasn't roasting us to char and bone must have been intentional.

Khydan's heart sang in my ears. He cradled the back of my head, pressing my face into the front of his leathers, his blood spiked with adrenaline and panic. I could smell it roaring through his veins in the hollow of his throat; even now, with death sharing the same air as us, the scent of his blood was enough to drive me toward insanity.

I should have drunk from him. At least that way we'd both go out on a high. But that was a ridiculous thought. Selfish. We weren't *allowed* to die. There was too much riding on us. Khydan and I held the future of Yvelia in our hands. More than that. If Zareth was to be believed, we held the futures of millions of realms in our hands. Billions of *lives*.

We stood at a nexus in the threads of fate. If we died, so did everything else. For a moment, I believed the dragon had seen *that* in our minds, and that was why it had redirected its fire. After all, if it killed us, chances were it would die soon, too.

I clung to Khydan so tightly that my hands went numb. Then they started to tingle. No…huh. Strange. Only my right hand was tingling. The sensation was neither pleasant nor painful. It built until the unnerving feeling had traveled all the way up my arm and settled in my shoulder, blooming up my neck and prickling along my jaw.

The air was alive, as if a thousand flies were buzzing around a corpse. The brimstone kept coming. It spattered as it hit the wall, throwing burning gobs of glowing molten rock and metal in every direction.

Khydan stiffened, his fingers digging into my back, but he didn't let me go.

A hollow thrum pounded inside of me. A hammering at a door. A second pulse that served no purpose. Magic. Unfamiliar. Unrealized.

The brimstone. My body was reacting to it. It drew me to it, but I didn't know what to do. I couldn't *reach* it. And even if I'd been able to, I wouldn't have known what to do with it once I had.

We would die soon. What else was there to do? My power over the quicksilver wouldn't help me here. Khydan was more powerful than most of the Fae, but his shadows wouldn't be enough to bring down this beast. The air burned, scorching my airways, but all we could do was endure.

Eventually, the torrent of fire stopped.

Mercy. The reprieve from the heat alone was a mercy…

"I am Arissan, keeper of this gate," the dragon boomed. "And I have *not* spared you out of mercy. That word does not exist in this place. Your lives are temporary. I have spared you for one reason, and one reason alone."

"Why?" My voice echoed around the dragon's lair.

Khydan reached out and gripped my hand. The muscles in his jaw ticked as he glowered up at the megalithic monster. Flames and smoke wreathed her teeth as it ducked its head and snarled. "Your mate knows the answer to this question. Don't you, Khydan Finvarra?"

Slowly, Khydan nodded. "You've spared us so that *I* can be brought before your master for judgment."

"And your criiiiime?" Arissan's tongue dripped blue-tinged flames as it flicked back and forth through the air like a switch.

"I've committed no crime. I have done nothing more than defend my people and my lands. But you've seen my thoughts... and my past. You have seen me on the mountainside at Ajun. The undergods of Diaxis will charge me with murder—"

"The murder of my offspring!" The dragon roared. There was fury in the deafening sound, but also anguish. A pillar of flame erupted from Arissan's throat again—though totally different from the thick, molten brimstone it had spewed at us just now. This was white hot hellfire. It bloomed against the ceiling of the cavern and fanned outward, rolling over the soot-stained rock as if defying gravity.

The heat swelled beyond imagining. Too much. Too hot. I was physically far stronger than I had ever been, but there were still limits to what my new body could endure.

As my vision tunneled, Khydan's voice echoed inside my head.

Don't speak. When you wake, for the love of all the gods, do not *say a single word.*

———————+———————

Metal.

Hot metal.

I knew the smell well. So well, in fact, that I could identify it in my sleep. I was back in the forge. Elroy was chiding me for spilling metal shavings all over the floor. I was—

Fuck!

I was upside down! I was hanging over a hall ten times the size of the one at Ammontraíeth. I was fucking *swinging*...

Blood rushed in my ears. A thunderous swelling of sound, so loud my head spun. But it wasn't my blood. It was the *crowd*.

Below, a thrumming mass jostled and shouted. Thousands of people were gathered beneath my head, and from their raised voices and the way they were throwing their fists in the air, they were celebrating something monumental.

Khydan.

Where the fuck was my mate?

I couldn't spin. Couldn't turn. Open space stretched out around me, eventually giving way to darkness. My arms hung loosely over my head. Pain sang along every nerve I possessed as I tried to reach down to my hips. My short swords. My knives. Were they still there?

Relief exploded in my chest as my hand found hot metal. The hilts of my god swords were almost too hot to touch, but they *were* there. And so was Khydan. When I'd moved my arms, I'd turned a fraction—just enough to see him hanging upside down in the air next to me. His chest plate was still strapped tight, Nimerelle still in her scabbard. Khy's face was pale and running with sweat. His eyes were closed, eyelashes stark, midnight-black against his skin. Even passed out, he looked troubled, a small frown drawing his brows together as if he were hammering at the door of his consciousness, demanding to be let back into his body.

A thick chain, pitted orange with flaking rust, looped around his ankles, suspending him. The same kind of chain cinched around my own feet, cutting off my circulation. Above, a huge statue of a robed figure clasped the ends of the lengths of chain in its huge stone hand. There were other lengths of chain dangling from the statue's grasp, some longer than the ones we were suspended from. Some shorter. All were vacant bar one.

A corpse hung from a chain dangling from the statue's other hand. The body—or what was left of it—was rotting, its skin swollen and purple, its tongue fat and protruding through its teeth. The remains of a shredded white cape hung from its shoulders, partially shrouding its head from view. A huge black spear with a vicious, serrated razor head lanced through the body's torso—a very clear cause of death.

The cheering below surged, reaching a fever pitch of excitement.

Khydan? Why the hell was I whispering? I wasn't speaking out loud. *Khy!*

Nothing. He couldn't hear me. Couldn't answer.

A maelstrom of energy whipped and whirled behind my breast-plate, begging to be unleashed. The magic tied to my quicksilver rune was awake here. Alert. It would answer if I called, there was no doubt about that. But who the fuck was I supposed to attack? There were thousands of people—

"*Silence.*"

The noise stopped. My uneven breath was all I could hear.

Below, the mass of bodies was so quiet it felt as though they'd suddenly disappeared. They hadn't. They stood stock-still, their arms by their sides, staring straight ahead, none of them looking up at their new captives.

The voice that had ordered silence spoke again, the sound reverberating and inhumane. No creature—human, Fae, or otherwise—had a voice *that* low. "Bring them down," it intoned.

No one on the hall floor stirred. There must have been others lurking in the shadows, because a moment passed and then the thick chains clanked, jerked, and dropped us. We only fell a foot before the tension returned to the chain, but terror still turned my blood to ice. I didn't scream. It was damned near impossible to trap the cry behind my teeth, but somehow, I managed it.

With more clanking and jerking, the chains slowly began to descend toward the hall floor.

Cursed Fae eyesight. I'd already been able to see what was going on below perfectly, but with every inch we lowered, more details came into view.

The sickly pale cast of the people's faces.

Their cold, oddly flashing eyes.

Their threadbare clothes and worn leathers, and the weapons strapped to their chests, hips, and backs.

The crowd was an even split of males and females, from what I could tell. Some had pointed ears, some rounded—both human and Fae.

"Khydan?" I spoke loud now. "*Khy!*" Speaking into his mind hadn't worked. Maybe the sound of my voice would help wake him. "Shit's getting weird out here. I could *really* use you right now."

He didn't stir. Damp waves of hair hung in his face. He might have been unconscious, but the ink on the backs of his hands was not; it swirled wildly, forming shapes and geometric patterns that I didn't recognize.

We were almost two thirds of the way to the ground now.

"*Khydan!*" I let my fear slip in this time. I could not navigate whatever was about to happen alone. I *needed* him. "Please, Khy. *Wake. Up.*"

In an instant, eyes the color of the tall grasses that grew around Ballard met mine. Silver rimmed the pupil of his right eye, constricting the pool of black with a band of solid quicksilver. It didn't move. Didn't shift. I could feel it bristling, attention sharp, reading the situation. "Saeris," Khy whispered. We were hanging upside down in a strange new place. Danger waited for us below, but my mate's gaze didn't waver from mine. "Breathe," he said. "It's gonna be okay. I won't let anything happen to you."

Only once he'd said this did he glance away to assess our surroundings. His mouth flattened into a taut line as he took it all in.

There was no dais here. A circle had formed in the middle of the crowd, at the center of which stood two figures. As the ground approached, I braced, tucking my shoulders up as best I could to protect my head and neck. It didn't do much good. The top of my head cracked against the stone as I struck the ground, and then I toppled, landing hard on my side.

Boots and filthy bare feet: That was all I could see for a split second. I tried to sit up, to kick my feet free of the chains, but no sooner had I touched down than there were hands under my arms, dragging me... dragging me upright.

A trail of black smoke slashed through the air to my left. A male had been standing there. Now he was three wet pieces of meat, smoking on the floor. The female standing on my right stepped forward, gritting her teeth, her hand still gripping my shoulder, but a second later her whole arm was thumping to the floor. Khydan swept Nimerelle through the air, both male and sword flowing like liquid smoke. He moved too fast to see, but I knew what was coming next. The female who had lost her arm was about to find herself headless. But...

"Enough." A different voice this time. Slightly higher in pitch, but no less commanding.

My knees buckled.

I dropped, agony exploding in my kneecaps as they struck stone. Khydan hissed as he, too, fell to his knees next to me. I couldn't move. Invisible pressure encapsulated my body, rendering me immobile. My hands wouldn't respond. My arms hung pinned to my sides. My chest was so tight I could only expand my ribs an inch, barely allowing me to breathe.

I didn't *need* to move to speak to Khy. *What the fuck is going on?*

It's okay. Don't panic. Just try to stay calm.

Are you calm? You just killed someone and disarmed someone else!

Despite everything, Khydan's mouth twitched. *Disarmed? You've been spending too much time with Swift, Osha. You're cracking jokes now?*

I'm being serious! You just attacked two people.

Slowly, his hint of a smile faded, leaving behind cold, hard fury as he scowled up at the strangers who surrounded us. *Well. They shouldn't have touched you if they'd wanted to live, should they?*

The male hadn't made a peep when he'd died. The female, who was still on her feet next to me, hadn't made a sound when Khydan had taken her arm, either. Out of the corner of my eye, I could see that she was suffering. As she held her bleeding stump, she shook violently, tears tracking down her cheeks, but her jaw was clenched shut as if she didn't *dare* cry out.

Legs came into view. A torso. A tall, thin male with sunken black pits for eyes. A moment later, he was followed by another tall male, almost identical in features and stature, except that his eyes were glowing red coals. Long black hair hung down their backs, knotted into the most elaborate war braids I had ever seen. They were dressed for battle.

On the right, the male with the black eyes spoke first, revealing himself as the owner of the deeper voice. "Look, Githrand. The old one has brought us some new toys to play with. Warm bloods. *Yvelians.*"

The red-eyed male sniffed, his upper lip curling in disgust. "That one isn't Yvelian."

"Oh? Really?" The male regarded me with a curiosity at war with Githrand's distaste. Gods, but their features were strikingly similar. Surely they *had* to be brothers. "And what might she be, then?" he pondered.

"I know not, Crave. But there's a scent on her that I dislike."

"It's called soap. Maybe you ought to try it." Khydan had warned me not to say anything, and then he came out with *that*? He wasn't that stupid. This was something else. A tactic designed to...what?

The males didn't look at either of us, didn't even acknowledge that Khydan had spoken, but the look they shared implied that he had just made our situation significantly worse. A laughable thought, really, considering how bad our situation already was.

Next to me, Khydan tensed, his back stiffening as he straightened. Nimerelle was still in his hand, the end of the blade resting on the ground. The god sword rattled, as if the piece of Mirelle's soul that lived inside it was doing her best to shatter the magic holding us in place and get back to the business of killing.

Red, burning eyes drifted slowly down to look at the sword. "Where did you get *that*, pet?" Crave might have asked in a disinterested way, but *damn*, was he interested. He cocked his head to one side, narrowing his gaze as he studied the sword, even going so far as to take a step toward the god sword. As he came forward, the female with the bleeding stump let out a tiny whimper. She took a step back, away from Crave, and scores of eyes widened as the crowd realized what she'd done. Some of the strangers gathered around us even looked down at the ground, as if they didn't have the stomach to watch what would happen next.

Crave just smirked coldly at the female, then ever so slowly crouched down and turned his head so that he was eye-to-eye with Khydan. "I repeat," he said icily. *"Where did you get the sword, pet?"*

Anger roiled in my mate's eyes, plain as day. A muscle ticked in his jaw as he spoke through gritted teeth. "It was a gift from the gods." He still couldn't lie, even here. He had no choice but to tell the truth.

"Hmm." Crave arched an eyebrow down at Nimerelle, for a second revealing the hunger that he was trying so carefully to hide. "You see this, brother?" He spoke loudly for show, so all could hear. "A weapon from one of the dead houses. Older than the halls of this kingdom and theirs combined, and he expects us to believe that the traitor gods *gave* it to him."

"It's just a sword," Khydan growled.

Crave huffed down his nose, looking at Khydan, a sour smile twisting his mouth. "That sword could end worlds in the right hands. If it's what I think it is, it is one of the forgotten blades of our ancestors . . . and *you* do not have the right to wield it."

"Is that so?" Khydan answered Crave's smirk with one of his own. "You should probably go ahead and take it, then."

"Mm. Yes." Crave nodded enthusiastically. "You'd like that, wouldn't you?"

"I really *would.*"

Crave made a sucking sound, rocketing to his feet. There were golden clasps on the straps of his leathers. They gleamed like someone had spent hours polishing them. Crave let out a bark of laughter, drawing his own sword that hung at his waist. It looked very similar to Nimerelle from where I was kneeling. A little smaller, perhaps. Less beautifully made. In short, the sword in Crave's hand was a very poor imitation of Nimerelle. The male held the weapon aloft and pointed it at Khydan's god sword. "I can scent the magic on that thing," he said. "It smells like death."

"You're afraid to take it from me, then?" Khy suggested. As soon as he'd uttered the accusation, Githrand launched into action. He let out a raw shout, tearing around his brother to get at Khydan, but Crave calmly grabbed Githrand by the arm and held him tight.

"It's all right. He does not know how he insults me. He does not know his place. Not yet."

"Oh, I know my place here," Khydan said. "And I *know* what's about to happen."

Githrand let out a stiff, disbelieving laugh. "I doubt you can imagine the kind of torment you're about to suffer. If you wanted to survive this place, you should have guarded your mind a little better. Arissan saw what you did to her child. 'Shacry was her only surviving offspring. You desecrated his body and let your king carry off his head. For that alone, your penance will be death. But you killed our father's emissary, too. You severed his only thread of power in Yvelia. You *weakened* him—"

What emissary? What was he talking about? Khydan didn't kill an emissary. He—

Oh.

Oh, no.

He couldn't mean—

"Ereth was a traitor to his people," Khy said. "His own actions against Yvelia signed his death warrant. But he tried to attack my mate. Of course I killed him. No one will *ever* harm her while I still draw breath."

Ereth. The Lord of Midnight who had attacked me at the coronation. He'd been a religious leader of sorts. He had told Khydan that he worshipped different gods. *Undergods...*

"Petulant fool," Githrand scolded. "You spill blood in the defense of your precious mate, but then you bring her *here*? You've condemned her to hell, Khydan Finvarra. You will be dismembered piece by piece. She will watch, and when we're done with you, we will make her one of our concubines. We will breed from her until it kills her or we grow tired of her. She will know nothing but humiliation and shame in this place. She will never see the sky again—"

Shadows and smoke tore out of Khydan—a blast of magic so powerful that, for a moment, glittering darkness stole the light from the flickering torches. It happened fast. When the shadows drew back, a tall, semitranslucent wall stood between us and the crowd of Diaxians who had gathered to watch. Even if Githrand or Crave commanded them to attack, they wouldn't be able to. At least for a short while.

Khydan rolled his shoulders and shook his arms out, casually shrugging off the magic that still pinned me to the floor. How? *How* was he doing that?

Sorry, Osha. Arissan has always guarded Diaxis. I've spent centuries practicing at hiding information behind locked doors in my head. She saw what I wanted her to see. But you? I knew she'd look into your *mind. You wouldn't have been able to hide it from her. There just wasn't time to prepare you.* Khydan's words were laced with regret.

My heart had already been laboring, but now I couldn't hear myself think over the sound of my blood thrumming in my ears. I stopped it from beating altogether, then said, *Prepare me for what?*

Khydan's jaw worked. *I'll tell you everything. I promise. As soon as we're safe, I'll explain.* He wasn't looking at me. He was focused on Githrand and Crave.

"Impossible," Crave whispered. "You can't—You aren't—" The male shook his head, clearly struggling to understand what he was seeing. "Shadow magic doesn't belong in your realm. Where did you get this power?"

"The same place I got the sword," Khydan snarled. Tendrils of shadow whipped from his hands. At the same time, shadows spilled from Crave and Githrand, but their magic was nothing compared to Khydan's. Paler. Weaker, somehow. Less...corporeal. Khydan's shadows cut through the magic they hurled at him like a blade slicing through water.

The two males flew back through the air and landed on the ground

CALLIE HART

with a bone-shattering thud. Still holding Nimerelle loosely at his side, Khydan stalked forward toward the males. He held the point of the sword over Githrand's throat. "Release her," he commanded. *"Now."*

The pressure pinning me to the floor vanished in an instant. I toppled forward but caught myself, preventing myself from falling onto my face. Khydan was there immediately, helping me to my feet. His hands were in my hair, then, cradling my face, his beautiful eyes full of concern, skipping over my features and searching for injury.

"I'm okay," I said. "Don't worry about me. Just...tell me what's *happening.*"

My heart squeezed as he took my right hand in his and pressed my palm against the center of his chest, holding it there for a second. "Do you trust me?" he asked.

"Yes. *Always.* Yes."

And for a split second, he smiled the most heartbreakingly beautiful smile. "I *love* you, Saeris Fane." He kissed me hard, and so many unspoken things passed between us as he did. Promises and hope. Oaths and regrets.

He tore away from me and was gone.

In four long strides, he was towering over the one called Crave, grabbing him by the front of his armor and pulling him up from the ground.

"Who...*are* you?" Crave choked. "Only...half-gods may wield shadows."

Khydan drew in a deep breath, ignoring the male's question. "I've come for a dragon, as is my right. Summon our father. *Tell him I've come to make a trade.*"

HODDERSCAPE

WANT MORE HODDERSCAPE? JOIN US!

Sign up to our mailing list to get exclusive
early sneak peeks and offers:

Follow us on our social channels:
○ ♪ @hodderscape

Buy our books, find out more, and discover exclusive content:
www.hodderscape.co.uk